Initiation
Stories and Short Novels on Three Themes

SECOND EDITION

Initiation

Stories and Short Novels on Three Themes

SECOND EDITION

Edited by David Thorburn

Yale University

HARCOURT BRACE JOVANOVICH, INC.

New York   Chicago   San Francisco   Atlanta

ISBN: 0-15-541512-3

Library of Congress Catalog Card Number: 75-32644

Printed in the United States of America

For Daniel, for Adam, and for Rachel

Preface

All serious literature is grounded in the paradox that variety, fullness, and resonance are achieved by strategies of constraint and exclusion. Hemingway's remarks that good stories are written by those who have learned the art of leaving things out, and Robert Frost's more playful observation that writing poetry without rhyme is like playing tennis without a net, are writerly versions of this paradox. The twenty-one stories and three short novels in this revised and enlarged edition of *Initiation* all demonstrate in their own ways that the materials of art are liberated, discovered in their full subtlety and possibility, only when artists embrace limitation. The most obvious, and in some ways the most significant, limit observed by all the selections in this book is that of length. Different as they may be in other respects, the stories and short novels collected here rely for their intensity on their relative compactness, exert their power over us in part because of their conscious, artful willingness to do their work within a brief, containing space.

This assumption about literature—the assumption that limitation, containment, can be liberating—is the justification for the arrangement of this anthology. Each of the three parts of this book groups together seven stories and one short novel, all dealing with the same basic subject. The subjects, of course, are large, encompassing ones. They are subjects that have fascinated, even obsessed, writers in all cultures and at all times. Still, such an organization contains, gives special shape to, the fiction I have chosen. And if this arrangement excludes the range of subject matter inherent in a random collection of fiction, it also suggests some special advantages that are a consequence precisely of the limitations imposed by thematic organization.

These advantages seem to me crucial, particularly for readers who are beginning the serious study of fiction. There is, first, the advantage of being able to examine a given theme in the depth and variety afforded by eight different treatments. Wallace Stevens has a poem called "Thirteen Ways of Looking at a Blackbird," and although it does not, finally, tell us much about blackbirds, it does say some valuable things about seeing and defining and understanding, one of these being that thirteen ways are better than one. Good fiction has the seductive power to persuade even experienced readers that its handling of its subject is somehow definitive, and it is always useful to be reminded that even the most compelling works of art give us but a part of the truth.

A second, more important advantage of thematic organization is that it seems likely to encourage readers to respond more fully and precisely to individual stories. It is undeniable, for example, that one's understanding of Conrad's *The Shadow-Line* will be measurably enhanced if it is read with the knowledge that initiation stories constitute a particular, definable category and if it is read with some minimal acquaintance with the ways in which other excellent writers have handled the same subject.

This is not to suggest that the stories under each heading are mere restatements of one another. In fact, my own guess is that most readers will find the selections in each part so fiercely individual and private that they will question the propriety of grouping them together in the first place. And within limits this is a response I am counting on. For one measure of good fiction is its ability to resist categories, or to press beyond them, even categories as encompassing as those in this book. Isolation, the defining theme in the part titled "Outsiders," is a recurring problem as well in a number of the stories in the first two parts, and a good many of the stories listed under the last two headings might be described as initiation stories, since they are concerned with characters who are forced, often at great cost and pain, to discover some hard truths about themselves and their circumstances.

Other ways of grouping the stories included here will surely occur to attentive readers. There are a number of stories that respond with special fullness to ethnic or regional pressures. There are several stories that are deeply committed to psychological realism, and others—a particularly interesting group, it seems to me—that eschew individual psychology entirely and aspire to the austere directness of fable or parable. Comedy, light and not so light, is the key to at least five of the stories. There is a wide and contrasting range of narrative strategies and styles. And, of course, one might choose to group the selections according to genre, using the three short novels to help measure and define the special attributes of the short story and also to begin a study of the particular character of longer fiction.

This new version of *Initiation* contains seven stories in each section in place of the original six and differs from its predecessor also in offering a richer sampling of contemporary writing. Of the seven writers who are new to this edition, two—Henry James and Ernest Hemingway—are classic figures whose omission from the first edition had always troubled me, and five—John

Barth, John Updike, Doris Lessing, Gabriel García Márquez, and Philip Roth—are lively, influential contemporaries who are represented here by powerful and innovative stories that can reasonably suggest something of the range as well as the singularity of the best recent fiction. In their urgent self-reflexiveness and in their blurring of conventional distinctions between fiction and autobiography or between fiction and literary criticism, several of these stories offer especially instructive contrasts to many of the pieces retained from the first edition.

The questions at the back of the book are somewhat more elaborate than those usually found in anthologies of this sort. They have been placed at the back in order to avoid distracting readers who might find them intrusive if they were located after each selection. The questions offer brief definitions of a few basic critical terms and occasionally make analytic comments designed to draw attention to matters of particular complexity or importance. In many of the questions my own sense of the central problems raised in the stories is undisguised, and I hope this openness will encourage alternative interpretations.

Because the questions try in a modest way to supply a minimal critical vocabulary and because instructors will have their own preferences concerning these matters, the introduction does not attempt a systematic discussion of the elements of fiction but restricts itself to a consideration of the broad assumptions that I believe must guide us when we read fiction, and when we teach and write about it.

For helpful advice concerning this second edition I wish to thank Professors Irving Howe, John Paul Riquelme, and Roberta S. Matthews. Christina Norum copyedited with a rare sharp eye, and my editor Sidney Zimmerman was a nourishing source of sympathy and valuable counsel all through the work of revision. William Pullin first suggested that I prepare a book of this sort and has helped me ever since. My wife, Barbara, contributed directly to all aspects of my work and especially to the task of unearthing appropriate stories.

David Thorburn

Contents

part one   Initiation

part two   Love

part three   Outsiders

Introduction

The spirit in which we approach literature, the assumptions that govern our reading of individual literary works, have a decisive importance. Immense learning, wide experience with literature, critical ingenuity—these and other virtues will ultimately count for little, and may in fact lead us into extraordinary foolishness, if we have not begun in the proper spirit: if we have not, that is to say, tried to identify some first principles for the whole enterprise of reading and studying literature. Ideally, our response to single works, passages, even single lines, ought to proceed from a firm general conviction about the task of reading and about the nature of literature. But in practice it is sometimes difficult to keep our ground assumptions in clear view. Especially in dealing with literary works that are particularly taxing and absorbing, we may be led to forget or to ignore the principles that ought to guide us, and so begin to lose sight of what we are doing, and why.

We are encouraged in this loss of direction and purpose by the profound respect our technological age accords to the idea of specialization, of expertise and inside knowledge. This respect for the expert finds peculiar, even bizarre, expression in what can be called the puzzle-solving school of literature. According to this school, the language of literature is an alien one, a matter of dark, inscrutable "symbols" and learned allusions whose secrets can be unlocked, not by ordinary men, but only by specially tutored decoders, experts in the hieroglyph, masters of the labyrinth. Although their premises are rarely set forth in such hostile form, the critic who is guilty of an overingenious interpretation and the student who distrusts the obvious, surface interests of a literary work are both tacit, working members of the puzzle-solving school. Ironically, this attitude toward literature is usually rooted in a misguided re-

1

spect for imaginative writing, a respect that sees difficulty and obscurity as marks of excellence and that embraces the conviction that good literature must resist the ordinary, untrained intelligence precisely because it is good. But it is surely a curious respect that assumes one must guard against accepting what literary works seem most directly and most clearly to be saying, and that assumes their "true" meanings, their "hidden" meanings, lie concealed beneath an ocean of details whose prime function is to mislead uncautious or inexperienced readers. This view of literature transforms the act of reading into a kind of game in which the reader-players, like mice in a scientist's maze, are rewarded for their cleverness in not allowing themselves to be tricked; and it transforms writers into mere conjurers whose art is that of riddle-making and trivial deception.

Critics and students who, consciously or not, take such a view of literature are implicitly insisting that only experts and specialists can understand literature. Apparently a tribute to the seriousness of imaginative writing in our age of the expert, such an insistence is ultimately destructive, for it denies the inspiriting fact that literature is one of the very few activities left to us which refuses to participate in an otherwise almost universal process of fragmentation and narrow specialization. There are, of course, some writers and some texts that are reluctant to yield themselves to the common reader. But these are rare exceptions and need not affect our working assumptions, which may be put, most simply, as follows: Literature is accessible to the alert intelligence; literature is not written for teachers and scholars but for a much larger community of literate people.

If these statements were not broadly true—if, that is, the stories and short novels collected here, and most other literary works, could be read with profit only by a coterie of specialists—then literature itself would have but a small claim on our lives. But literature is crucial to us, precious and rare to us, precisely because it belongs to everyone, precisely because it wants and expects to be understood by physicists and mechanics as well as by literary scholars. In practical terms, this constitutes an incitement to simple common sense. Remembering this, we can remind ourselves that writers intend to communicate with us; and we can remind ourselves that those things which *seem* most important in literary works usually *are* most important. A fine teacher once distilled these matters for me in a wise epigram: Never ignore the fascinating surface in favor of the mere depths.

It is perhaps easier to speak abstractly about the virtues of common sense in the reading of literature than it is to demonstrate how such virtues apply in practice. What follows is intended to be such a demonstration, a kind of model —not by any means a complete critical analysis—designed to clarify the general assumptions sketched above as they apply particularly to fiction. James Joyce's "An Encounter," the second selection in this anthology, will serve with special aptness as a demonstration piece because Joyce is widely regarded as a difficult, esoteric writer and also because, predictably, this story has elicited some strange criticism of the puzzle-solving variety.

We need not linger over this strange criticism, but it is perhaps helpful to begin by remarking that "An Encounter" has been variously interpreted by readers who appear to be bored or impatient with its unpretentious directness. Perhaps feeling that what is clear is of necessity superficial, these puzzle solvers have been driven to perverse extremes of interpretation. One such interpretation sees the story in theological terms, claiming that the boys' aborted journey to the Pigeon House is really a search for a father and, by extension, for the Father in the Christian Trinity.

The existence of such criticism is a disquieting reminder that in literary analysis, as in other things, to fail to take account of the obvious is to run very grave risks. But beyond this, such interpretations also raise some theoretical questions which are crucial to all literary study: How does one generalize from a story's particular evidence? What are the reasonable limits of critical interpretation? What checks or controls do writers impose on their fictions so as to make us understand their stories' larger significance and so as to keep us from reading our own intentions and concerns into their texts?

The answer to all these questions is uncomplicated and decisive. To be persuasive any general interpretation must grow out of the particular details in the story and must remain anchored to those details. In virtually all fiction the larger, abstracted meaning—what one might call the "symbolic meaning"—works (as one distinguished critic has written) "characteristically, by a natural extension of the implications of the narrative content, and retains a consistent closeness to it."*

Thus, the root error of the theological interpretation of Joyce's story is the simple fact that the very surface of "An Encounter"—its plot, the circumstances of its characters, their professed motives, the nature of their adventures: everything, in short, that is *manifest,* explicit, central in the story—gives no hint that the boys are searching for a father. In fact, the narrator tells us explicitly that he and Mahony go off on their travels in search of adventure:

> . . . I wanted real adventures to happen to myself. But real adventures, I reflected, do not happen to people who remain at home: they must be sought abroad.

In order for a reader to ignore these remarks he or she must find evidence in the text that will justify this refusal to accept the narrator's explanation for his actions. If such a reader wishes to argue that the narrator is really in search of a father, he or she must supply us with orphans or discussions among the characters concerning parents or with some other event or suggestion or persuasive implication that will cause us to question whether the narrator knows his own mind when he says he wanted to seek adventure. Since there is nothing of this sort in the story, simple common sense requires that we believe the narrator.

* Ian Watt, "Conrad Criticism and *The Nigger of the 'Narcisscus',*" *Nineteenth-Century Fiction* 12 (1958): 274.

To put the matter more broadly: No general interpretation of a piece of fiction will be valid if it fails to account for the story's essential parts—for its plot, for its people, for its style and tone. What the characters in a story say and what they do, what the author or narrator says and the tone in which he or she says it—these are the "facts" that must be accounted for in any convincing interpretation. *The surface of fiction controls meaning.*

How, given these premises, might we come at a convincing general reading of "An Encounter"? We would begin, as all effective criticism must begin, with the simple act of *description;* we would try as accurately and as fully as possible *to describe* the story's central elements. And the more complete we are able to make our description, the closer we will be to the story's larger significance, to what I called a moment ago its "symbolic meaning."

There is no rigid order in which the separate parts of a piece of fiction must be taken up in this process of description, for fiction is the freest, the least rule-bound of all literary modes. But most stories are about people, most have some sort of narrative thrust or direction, and all are written in language. So unless we are in the presence of a really eccentric story, it is usually fruitful to examine the characters, the plot, and the style. It is most important to remember that we must first account for the obvious things. In our description of "An Encounter," therefore, we might first notice that the story concerns young boys, probably not yet teen-agers, if we can judge from the opening sentences:

> It was Joe Dillon who introduced the Wild West to us. He had a little library made up of old numbers of *The Union Jack, Pluck* and *The Half-penny Marvel.* Every evening after school we met in his back garden and arranged Indian battles.

This simple beginning ought to alert us to the dangers of overinterpretation. For although it is not impossible, surely it is unlikely that these wild Indians should be oppressed by theological agonies.

Like most stories, "An Encounter" supplies us with a good deal of information in its opening passages, and even minimal attention to what is explicitly indicated there will reveal the essential interests and direction of the whole story.

> He [Joe Dillon] and his fat young brother Leo, the idler, held the loft of the stable while we tried to carry it by storm; or we fought a pitched battle on the grass. But however well we fought, we never won siege or battle and all our bouts ended with Joe Dillon's war dance of victory. His parents went to eight-o'clock mass every morning in Gardiner Street and the peaceful odour of Mrs. Dillon was prevalent in the hall of the house. But he played too fiercely for us who were younger and more timid. He looked like some kind of an Indian when he capered round the garden, an old tea-cosy on his head, beating a tin with his fist and yelling:
> "Ya! yaka, yaka, yaka!"

Everyone was incredulous when it was reported that he had a vocation for the priesthood. Nevertheless it was true.

A spirit of unruliness diffused itself among us and, under its influence, differences of culture and constitution were waived. We banded ourselves together, some boldly, some in jest and some almost in fear: and of the number of these latter, the reluctant Indians who were afraid to seem studious or lacking in robustness, I was one. The adventures related in the literature of the Wild West were remote from my nature but, at least, they opened doors of escape.

This quiet opening passage establishes the character of the protagonist with unambiguous economy, tells us a good deal about the kind of world he lives in, and even enacts in small compass the essential motion, the defining pattern, of the story's action. And what is most important for our present purposes, it does all this quite clearly: it *wants us* to perceive these things; Joyce is not out to trick or mislead us but to communicate with us.

From these opening paragraphs we learn, for example, that the central character is both like and unlike his fellows. He is like them because he too engages in mock battles, because the western pulp fiction that appeals to his companions with its visions of adventure and excitement appeals also to him. But he is unlike them, we are explicitly told, in being more timid than most. He is a "reluctant Indian," drawn into their mock warfare as much by his own fear of being thought too studious as by his boy's impulse to play at games of escape. He is, we can infer, less active than most of his fellows, more intelligent, more self-conscious.

These defining characteristics of his nature are validated for us as the story continues: The hero's later actions and responses are explicable because of this opening portrait of him and they are consistent with that portrait. And if we have read the beginning of the story with attention—not with symbol-mongering ingenuity but with simple alertness—we will not be surprised to discover that the narrator takes the lead in planning the day's "miching"—"I brought the first stage of the plot to an end by collecting sixpence from the other two, at the same time showing them my own sixpence"—but that Mahony, the activist, is the one who proceeds decisively when their plans go awry:

> We waited on for a quarter of an hour more but still there was no sign of Leo Dillon. Mahony, at last, jumped down and said:
> "Come along. I knew Fatty'd funk it."
> "And his sixpence . . . ?" I said.
> "That's forfeit," said Mahony. "And so much the better for us. . . ."

This difference between the narrator and Mahony—the one reflective, intellectual and timid; the other quick to act, physically more vigorous, unrestrained—is quietly dramatized again and again throughout the story. And because their characters are so precisely and consistently delineated, virtually all of their actions become for us expressions of their individual natures.

> Mahony began to play the Indian as soon as we were out of public sight. He chased a crowd of ragged girls, . . . and, when two ragged boys began, out of chivalry, to fling stones at us, he proposed that we should charge them. I objected that the boys were too small, and so we walked on. . . .

The narrator's objection that the boys are too small to attack quickens with significance once we have noticed his timid nature. For we must recognize that his reluctance to defend himself is grounded more in his own shyness and fear than in his sense of fair play. In its unpretentious way, this moment is typical of the whole story: it *is* complex, it *is* rich in suggestiveness, but these virtues are a consequence not of the story's obscure ingenuity but of its essential clarity; they are a consequence of Joyce's attention to a crucial matter of surface, of his having established early and explicitly the character of his protagonist.

Let me turn to another example of the way the story depends on and exploits our early perception of the difference between the boy and his companion. When Mahony joins the protagonist at their meeting place he displays a slingshot that he has brought along, as he says, "to have some gas with the birds." The hero's response to this remark reveals their separateness and constitutes also a subtle judgment on his own bookish restraint. "Mahony," we are informed, "used slang freely and spoke of Father Butler [their parochial school teacher] as Old Bunser." The negative judgment against the protagonist that is so deftly implicit here—he is so fastidious, after all; boys ought not to be so stuffy—becomes chillingly explicit in the climactic encounter with the old pervert:

> "Ah, I can see you are a bookworm like myself. Now," he added, pointing to Mahony who was regarding us with open eyes, "he is different; he goes in for games."

And in that final encounter, also, the earlier contrasts between the hero's physical passivity and Mahony's spontaneous and easy activeness are dramatized once more. Being more intelligent and more sensitive than Mahony, the narrator comes to understand quite clearly the corrupt unnaturalness which is revealed in the pervert's "strangely liberal" talk of young boys and their sweethearts. But by the time he has perceived this, he has also acknowledged a kinship with the pervert, for he had been tacitly pleased by the old man's ominous suggestion that as bookworms they shared interests from which Mahony was excluded and he had at one point in their conversation become "agitated" at the possibility that the old man "would think I was as stupid as Mahony." And so, when the old pervert gets up suddenly and walks a short distance away, the narrator rehearses in his mind some strategies of escape, afflicted now by fear of the old man and also by his sense of complicity in what he has come to recognize as corruption. But his meditations on escape are interrupted by the old man's return:

> I was still considering whether I would go away or not when the man came back and sat down beside us again. Hardly had he sat down when Mahony, catching sight of the cat which had escaped him [earlier in the day], sprang up and pursued her across the field. The man and I watched the chase.

This is surely one of the story's most terrible moments: the young boy, his separateness defined and enacted many times earlier, sits half-unwilling beside this corrupt old man and watches his companion racing in unsullied freedom across the field. The separation of the protagonist from the innocent pursuits of his boyhood, a separation prefigured a moment before when Mahony had stared wide-eyed at the boy and the old man together—"Mahony . . . was regarding *us* . . ." (my italics)—is now a literal as well as a figurative one: *The man and I watched the chase.*

But if we have been reading attentively—and this is the crucial issue for me—this dramatic moment, however terrible, is not unexpected. We have been prepared for the protagonist's frozen immobility, for this small but quite real instance of moral paralysis; and we have been prepared, equally, for Mahony's easy, thoughtless escape; by all those earlier times during the day in which Mahony's decisiveness has been juxtaposed against the hero's timid hesitations: by all those moments in which each boy had, as we say, acted "in character."

If the opening paragraphs of "An Encounter" carefully establish the particular identity of the central figure and thus make it possible for us to understand the motives and impulses which control his behavior later in the story, something of the same thing is true of the way in which the early pages act out in miniature the basic pattern of the larger plot. We can most easily see how this is so by considering the story in its largest outlines first. A one-sentence description, a simple, bare précis of the action of "An Encounter" might be formulated as follows: Two boys, in search of adventure, encounter a pervert. Partly because it is stripped of details and all nuance, this description helps us to see with particular clarity that "An Encounter" acts out a psychological as well as literal movement from expectation to frustration or, as it is more fashionable to say, from illusion to disillusion. Joyce's basic subject, as our discussion of the hero's character has already indicated, is the loss of innocence, the cost of growth. And the plot, in its largest contours and in its smallest details, dramatizes this meaning. We have only to describe what happens in the story as a whole or in any of its individual episodes in order to see how this is true; wherever we look this meaning is validated.

From the longest perspectives: the boys set out for the Pigeon House but they are deflected from their goal and never get there. The narrator begins his adventure full of high expectation and under a bright sun, but falls into weariness and "jaded" disappointment in the sunless afternoon, and ends in fear and self-accusation.

Or again, consider the opening pages where we are given a smaller version of this pattern of expectation and subsequent frustration. The first paragraph tells of the Indian battles between the hero's comrades and Joe Dillon and his brother, battles in which the narrator's side is never victorious. The discussion now shifts to Joe Dillon's parents, who attend mass each morning and whose pious example and peaceful home contrast comically with their son's wild, noisy caperings. Then we are told: "Everyone was incredulous when it was reported that he had a vocation for the priesthood. Nevertheless, it was true." The amused reportorial tone here calls our attention unmistakably to the fact that Joe Dillon's career is a kind of parable of life's unexpectedness, and this parable, of course, is enacted also, though in darker and more ominous terms, in the story of the narrator's day of adventure.

What Joyce's plot in its largest and smallest aspects is repeatedly telling us is also set forth in an explicit symbolism. At one point during their travels, the boys stop at the waterfront to watch some foreign sailors unloading their ship:

> Some bystanders said that she was a Norwegian vessel. I went to the stern and tried to decipher the legend upon it but, failing to do so, I came back and examined the foreign sailors to see had any of them green eyes for I had some confused notion. . . . The sailors' eyes were blue and grey and even black.

The boy's confused notion is clearly a private association of green eyes with the strange and the exciting. Naturally these sailors do not conform to his dream vision of what an exotic face should be like; they have ordinary-colored eyes.

Later, in a terrible but far from sly irony, the boy will find his green eyes, his symbol of the exotic and the attractive. He finds them, of course, in the pervert:

> I . . . glanced up at his face. As I did so I met the gaze of a pair of bottle-green eyes peering at me from under a twitching forehead. I turned my eyes away.

The thundering explicitness of Joyce's symbolism here is especially helpful for our purposes because it reinforces the proposition that the meanings and fundamental techniques of most fiction are wholly accessible. Although it is true that not all symbolic references will be so insistently obtrusive, the green eyes work in this story as virtually all true symbols work: They are items in the physical universe that are invested with a significance not usually attached to them. But what they signify is made clear by the context, and it requires only good sense and careful attention to perceive this.

Still, the almost brutal assertiveness of this particular symbol is unusual, and I think it can be said that the excessive bluntness of Joyce's irony serves his theme in a crucial and brilliant way. For when the boy discovers his private symbol of exotic glamor in the very face of corruption, we are made to feel both the shock and the cruelty of the lesson he is getting. We surrender our illusions reluctantly and slowly, as the day's adventures peter out in ennui and weariness. But, also, we may undergo the experience of their final loss as a single moment, an instant of intolerable harshness and trauma: The green eyes belong to the pervert and neither the boy in the story nor the reader can fail to grasp their meaning.

There remain to be said a few words about the way in which Joyce's style contributes to the meaning of his story. Perhaps the two most prominent features of the language in "An Encounter" are the first-person point of view and the understated irony embedded in the narrator's diction and syntax. These central and in some respects contrasting elements of style work together to create a balance of sympathy and judgment in our attitude toward the hero— a balance that is essential in a story that depends on the idea that the protagonist's painful journey toward disillusionment and self-knowledge is worthy of respect, but that depends also on a recognition of the hero's childish self-deceptions and follies. Our sympathies are engaged and held by the first-person telling, which imparts an immediacy, a personal urgency, to the material as no other point of view could. At the same time, our distance from the hero, our continuous sense of his youthfulness and immaturity, is maintained by a steady current of detached, amused irony. Sometimes this detachment is suggested merely by the unexcited simplicity of Joyce's choice of words and of the structure of his sentences. But at other times the irony becomes more explicit, as, for example, when the hero is described as a "reluctant Indian" or as in this fine sentence:

> But when the restraining influence of the school was at a distance I began to hunger again for wild sensations, for the escape which those chronicles of disorder alone seemed to offer me.

To describe a ten-year-old boy's dream of adventure as a hungering for wild sensations and to call his favorite books chronicles of disorder is to expose the boy to gentle mockery. Such mockery, although it is tolerant, amused, even affectionate, nonetheless judges the boy's innocent foolishness.

That the boy himself would be wholly incapable of such a judgment is obvious, and to perceive this is to realize that in this story the narrator and the boy are not precisely identical: the narrator is the boy grown older, he is the boy after his encounter with the pervert, and, we must assume, after many other disillusionments. By separating the young boy from the older self who narrates the story, Joyce not only achieves a particularly delicate mingling of sympathy and judgment, of dramatic immediacy and ironic distance, he also causes his story to acknowledge its own limits.

The story concerns but a minor incident, after all, and part of its deep wisdom is to recognize that one encounter with the world's frustrations will not transform a child into a sage. If the boy had told his own story, we may be sure that in his inexperience he would have endowed his meeting with the pervert with apocalyptic decisiveness. But the narrator's austere vocabulary and syntax, his whole quiet, gently ironic tone—these insist on a more restrained assessment, reminding us that it takes many lessons to make a man, that what we are reading is not *Paradise Lost* but a single short story: reminding us, finally, that the narrator's good sense and tact and humanity are essential qualities also for readers of literature, and far more valuable than a gift for puzzle-solving or a specialist's trained eye.

part one

Initiation

Nathaniel Hawthorne

My Kinsman, Major Molineux

After the kings of Great Britain had assumed the right of appointing the colonial governors, the measures of the latter seldom met with the ready and general approbation which had been paid to those of their predecessors, under the original charters. The people looked with most jealous scrutiny to the exercise of power which did not emanate from themselves, and they usually rewarded their rulers with slender gratitude for the compliances by which, in softening their instructions from beyond the sea, they had incurred the reprehension of those who gave them. The annals of Massachusetts Bay will inform us, that of six governors in the space of about forty years from the surrender of the old charter, under James II., two were imprisoned by a popular insurrection; a third, as Hutchinson inclines to believe, was driven from the province by the whizzing of a musket-ball; a fourth, in the opinion of the same historian, was hastened to his grave by continual bickering with the House of Representatives; and the remaining two, as well as their successors, till the Revolution, were favored with few and brief intervals of peaceful sway. The inferior members of the court party, in times of high political excitement, led scarcely a more desirable life. These remarks may serve as a preface to the following adventures, which chanced upon a summer night, not far from a hundred years ago. The reader, in order to avoid a long and dry detail of colonial affairs, is requested to dispense with an account of the train of circumstances that had caused much temporary inflammation of the popular mind.

MY KINSMAN, MAJOR MOLINEUX by Nathaniel Hawthorne was first published in 1832 in the *Boston Token*. Hawthorne drew his information from Thomas Hutchinson's *The History of the Colony of Massachusetts-Bay,* first published in two volumes in 1764 and 1767.

13

It was near nine o'clock of a moonlight evening, when a boat crossed the ferry with a single passenger, who had obtained his conveyance at that unusual hour by the promise of an extra fare. While he stood on the landing-place, searching in either pocket for the means of fulfilling his agreement, the ferry-man lifted a lantern, by the aid of which, and the newly risen moon, he took a very accurate survey of the stranger's figure. He was a youth of barely eighteen years, evidently country-bred, and now, as it should seem, upon his first visit to town. He was clad in a coarse gray coat, well worn, but in excellent repair; his under garments were durably constructed of leather, and fitted tight to a pair of serviceable and well-shaped limbs; his stockings of blue yarn were the incontrovertible work of a mother or a sister; and on his head was a three-cornered hat, which in its better days had perhaps sheltered the graver brow of the lad's father. Under his left arm was a heavy cudgel formed of an oak sapling, and retaining a part of the hardened root; and his equipment was completed by a wallet, not so abundantly stocked as to incommode the vigorous shoulders on which it hung. Brown, curly hair, well-shaped features, and bright, cheerful eyes were nature's gifts, and worth all that art could have done for his adornment.

The youth, one of whose names was Robin, finally drew from his pocket the half of a little province bill of five shillings, which, in the depreciation in that sort of currency, did but satisfy the ferryman's demand, with the surplus of a sexangular piece of parchment, valued at three pence. He then walked forward into the town, with as light a step as if his day's journey had not already exceeded thirty miles, and with as eager an eye as if he were entering London city, instead of the little metropolis of a New England colony. Before Robin had proceeded far, however, it occurred to him that he knew not whither to direct his steps; so he paused, and looked up and down the narrow street, scrutinizing the small and mean wooden buildings that were scattered on either side.

"This low hovel cannot be my kinsman's dwelling," thought he, "nor yonder old house, where the moonlight enters at the broken casement; and truly I see none hereabouts that might be worthy of him. It would have been wise to inquire my way of the ferryman, and doubtless he would have gone with me, and earned a shilling from the Major for his pains. But the next man I meet will do as well."

He resumed his walk, and was glad to perceive that the street now became wider, and the houses more respectable in their appearance. He soon discerned a figure moving on moderately in advance, and hastened his steps to overtake it. As Robin drew nigh, he saw that the passenger was a man in years, with a full periwig of gray hair, a wide-skirted coat of dark cloth, and silk stockings rolled above his knees. He carried a long and polished cane, which he struck down perpendicularly before him at every step; and at regular intervals he uttered two successive hems, of a peculiarly solemn and sepulchral intonation. Having made these observations, Robin laid hold of the skirt of the old man's coat, just when the light from the open door and windows of a barber's shop fell upon both their figures.

"Good evening to you, honored sir," said he, making a low bow, and still retaining his hold of the skirt. "I pray you tell me whereabouts is the dwelling of my kinsman, Major Molineux."

The youth's question was uttered very loudly; and one of the barbers, whose razor was descending on a well-soaped chin, and another who was dressing a Ramillies wig, left their occupations, and came to the door. The citizen, in the mean time, turned a long-favored countenance upon Robin, and answered him in a tone of excessive anger and annoyance. His two sepulchral hems, however, broke into the very centre of his rebuke, with most singular effect, like a thought of the cold grave obtruding among wrathful passions.

"Let go my garment, fellow! I tell you, I know not the man you speak of. What! I have authority, I have—hem, hem—authority; and if this be the respect you show for your betters, your feet shall be brought acquainted with the stocks by daylight, tomorrow morning!"

Robin released the old man's skirt, and hastened away, pursued by an ill-mannered roar of laughter from the barber's shop. He was at first considerably surprised by the result of his question, but, being a shrewd youth, soon thought himself able to account for the mystery.

"This is some country representative," was his conclusion, "who has never seen the inside of my kinsman's door, and lacks the breeding to answer a stranger civilly. The man is old, or verily—I might be tempted to turn back and smite him on the nose. Ah, Robin, Robin! even the barber's boys laugh at you for choosing such guide! You will be wiser in time, friend Robin."

He now became entangled in a succession of crooked and narrow streets, which crossed each other, and meandered at no great distance from the water-side. The smell of tar was obvious to his nostrils, the masts of vessels pierced the moonlight above the tops of the buildings, and the numerous signs, which Robin paused to read, informed him that he was near the center of business. But the streets were empty, the shops were closed, and lights were visible only in the second stories of a few dwelling-houses. At length, on the corner of a narrow lane, through which he was passing, he beheld the broad countenance of a British hero swinging before the door of an inn, whence proceeded the voices of many guests. The casement of one of the lower windows was thrown back, and a very thin curtain permitted Robin to distinguish a party at supper, round a well-furnished table. The fragrance of the good cheer steamed forth into the outer air, and the youth could not fail to recollect that the last remnant of his travelling stock of provision had yielded to his morning appetite, and that noon had found and left him dinnerless.

"Oh, that a parchment three-penny might give me a right to sit down at yonder table!" said Robin, with a sigh. "But the Major will make me welcome to the best of his victuals; so I will even step boldly in, and inquire my way to his dwelling."

He entered the tavern, and was guided by the murmur of voices and the fumes of tobacco to the public-room. It was a long and low apartment, with oaken walls, grown dark in the continual smoke, and a floor which was thickly sanded, but of no immaculate purity. A number of persons—the larger part of whom appeared to be mariners, or in some way connected with the sea—occupied the wooden benches, or leather-bottomed chairs, conversing on various matters, and occasionally lending their attention to some topic of general interest. Three or four little groups were draining as many bowls of punch, which the West India trade had long since made a familiar drink in the colony. Others, who had the appearance of men who lived by regular and laborious handicraft, preferred the insulated bliss of an unshared potation, and became more taciturn under its influence. Nearly all, in short, evinced a predilection for the Good Creature in some of its various shapes, for this is a vice to which, as Fast Day sermons of a hundred years ago will testify, we have a long hereditary claim. The only guests to whom Robin's sympathies inclined him were two or three sheepish countrymen, who were using the inn somewhat after the fashion of a Turkish caravansary; they had gotten themselves into the darkest corner of the room, and heedless of the Nicotian atmosphere, were supping on the bread of their own ovens, and the bacon cured in their own chimney-smoke. But though Robin felt a sort of brotherhood with these strangers, his eyes were attracted from them to a person who stood near the door, holding whispered conversation with a group of ill-dressed associates. His features were separately striking almost to grotesqueness, and the whole face left a deep impression on the memory. The forehead bulged out into a double prominence, with a vale between; the nose came boldly forth in an irregular curve, and its bridge was of more than a finger's breadth; the eyebrows were deep and shaggy, and the eyes glowed beneath them like fire in a cave.

While Robin deliberated of whom to inquire respecting his kinsman's dwelling, he was accosted by the innkeeper, a little man in a stained white apron, who had come to pay his professional welcome to the stranger. Being in the second generation from a French Protestant, he seemed to have inherited the courtesy of his parent nation; but no variety of circumstances was ever known to change his voice from the one shrill note in which he now addressed Robin.

"From the country, I presume, sir?" said he, with a profound bow. "Beg leave to congratulate you on your arrival, and trust you intend a long stay with us. Fine town here, sir, beautiful buildings, and much that may interest a stranger. May I hope for the honor of your commands in respect to supper?"

"The man sees a family likeness! the rogue has guessed that I am related to the Major!" thought Robin, who had hitherto experienced little superfluous civility.

All eyes were now turned on the country lad, standing at the door, in his worn three-cornered hat, gray coat, leather breeches, and blue yarn stockings, leaning on an oaken cudgel, and bearing a wallet on his back.

Robin replied to the courteous innkeeper, with such an assumption of confidence as befitted the Major's relative. "My honest friend," he said, "I shall make it a point to patronize your house on some occasions, when"—here he could not help lowering his voice—"when I may have more than a parchment three-pence in my pocket. My present business," continued he, speaking with lofty confidence, "is merely to inquire my way to the dwelling of my kinsman, Major Molineux."

There was a sudden and general movement in the room, which Robin interpreted as expressing the eagerness of each individual to become his guide. But the innkeeper turned his eyes to a written paper on the wall, which he read, or seemed to read, with occasional recurrences to the young man's figure.

"What have we here?" said he, breaking his speech into little dry fragments. " 'Left the house of the subscriber, bounden servant, Hezekiah Mudge, —had on, when he went away, gray coat, leather breeches, master's third-best hat. One pound currency reward to whosoever shall lodge him in any jail of the province.' Better trudge, boy; better trudge!"

Robin had begun to draw his hand towards the lighter end of the oak cudgel, but a strange hostility in every countenance induced him to relinquish his purpose of breaking the courteous innkeeper's head. As he turned to leave the room, he encountered a sneering glance from the bold-featured personage whom he had before noticed; and no sooner was he beyond the door, than he heard a general laugh, in which the innkeeper's voice might be distinguished, like the dropping of small stones into a kettle.

"Now, is it not strange," thought Robin, with his usual shrewdness,—"is it not strange that the confession of an empty pocket should outweigh the name of my kinsman, Major Molineux? Oh, if I had one of those grinning rascals in the woods, where I and my oak sapling grew up together, I would teach him that my arm is heavy though my purse be light!"

On turning the corner of the narrow lane, Robin found himself in a spacious street, with an unbroken line of lofty houses on each side, and a steepled building at the upper end, whence the ringing of a bell announced the hour of nine. The light of the moon, and the lamps from the numerous shop-windows, discovered people promenading on the pavement, and amongst them Robin hoped to recognize his hitherto inscrutable relative. The result of his former inquiries made him unwilling to hazard another, in a scene of such publicity, and he determined to walk slowly and silently up the street, thrusting his face close to that of every elderly gentleman, in search of the Major's lineaments. In his progress, Robin encountered many gay and gallant figures. Embroidered garments of showy colors, enormous periwigs, gold-laced hats, and silver-hilted swords glided past him and dazzled his optics. Travelled youths, imitators of the European fine gentlemen of the period, trod jauntily along, half dancing to the fashionable tunes which they hummed, and making poor Robin ashamed of his quiet and natural gait. At length, after many pauses to examine the gorgeous display of goods in the shop-windows, and after suffering some rebukes for the impertinence of his scrutiny into people's faces, the Major's kinsman found himself near the steepled building, still unsuccessful in his search. As yet, however, he had seen only one side of the thronged street; so Robin crossed, and continued the same sort of inquisition down the opposite pavement, with stronger hopes than the philosopher seeking an honest man, but with no better fortune. He had arrived about midway towards the lower end, from which his course began, when he overheard the approach of some one who struck down a cane on the flag-stones at every step, uttering, at regular intervals, two sepulchral hems.

"Mercy on us!" quoth Robin, recognizing the sound.

Turning the corner, which chanced to be close at his right hand, he hastened to pursue his researches in some other part of the town. His patience now was wearing low, and he seemed to feel more fatigue from his rambles since he crossed the ferry, than from his journey of several days on the other side. Hunger also pleaded loudly within him, and Robin began to balance the propriety of demanding, violently, and with lifted cudgel, the necessary guidance from the first solitary passenger whom he should meet. While a resolution to this effect was gaining strength, he entered a street of mean appearance, on either side of which a row of ill-built houses was straggling towards the harbor. The moonlight fell upon no passenger along the whole extent, but in the third domicile which Robin passed there was a half-opened door, and his keen glance detected a woman's garment within.

"My luck may be better here," said he to himself.

Accordingly, he approached the door, and beheld it shut closer as he did so; yet an open space remained, sufficing for the fair occupant to observe the stranger, without a corresponding display on her part. All that Robin could discern was a strip of scarlet petticoat, and the occasional sparkle of an eye, as if the moonbeams were trembling on some bright thing.

"Pretty mistress," for I may call her so with a good conscience, thought the shrewd youth, since I know nothing to the contrary—"my sweet pretty mistress, will you be kind enough to tell me whereabouts I must seek the dwelling of my kinsman, Major Molineux?"

Robin's voice was plaintive and winning, and the female, seeing nothing to be shunned in the handsome country youth, thrust open the door, and came forth into the moonlight. She was a dainty little figure, with a white neck, round arms, and a slender waist, at the extremity of which her scarlet petticoat jutted out over a hoop, as if she were standing in a balloon. Moreover, her face was oval and pretty, her hair dark beneath the little cap, and her bright eyes possessed a sly freedom, which triumphed over those of Robin.

"Major Molineux dwells here," said this fair woman.

Now, her voice was the sweetest Robin had heard that night, the airy counterpart of a stream of melted silver; yet he could not help doubting whether that sweet voice spoke Gospel truth. He looked up and down the mean street, and then surveyed the house before which they stood. It was a small, dark edifice of two stories, the second of which projected over the lower floor, and the front apartment had the aspect of a shop for petty commodities.

"Now, truly, I am in luck," replied Robin, cunningly, "and so indeed is my kinsman, the Major, in having so pretty a housekeeper. But I prithee trouble him to step to the door; I will deliver him a message from his friends in the country, and then go back to my lodgings at the inn."

"Nay, the Major has been abed this hour or more," said the lady of the scarlet petticoat; "and it would be to little purpose to disturb him to-night, seeing his evening draught was of the strongest. But he is a kind-hearted man, and it would be as much as my life's worth to let a kinsman of his turn away from the door. You are the good old gentleman's very picture, and I could swear that was his rainy-weather hat. Also he has garments very much resembling those leather small-clothes. But come in, I pray, for I bid you hearty welcome in his name."

So saying, the fair and hospitable dame took our hero by the hand; and the touch was light, and the force was gentleness, and though Robin read in her eyes what he did not hear in her words, yet the slender-waisted woman in the scarlet petticoat proved stronger than the athletic country youth. She had drawn his half-willing footsteps nearly to the threshold, when the opening of a door in the neighborhood startled the Major's housekeeper, and leaving the Major's kinsman, she vanished speedily into her own domicile. A heavy yawn preceded the appearance of a man, who, like the Moonshine of Pyramus and Thisbe, carried a lantern, needlessly aiding his sister luminary in the heavens. As he walked sleepily up the street, he turned his broad, full face on Robin, and displayed a long staff, spiked at the end.

"Home, vagabond, home!" said the watchman, in accents that seemed to fall asleep as they were uttered. "Home, or we'll set you in the stocks by peep of day!"

"This is the second hint of the kind," thought Robin. "I wish they would end my difficulties, by setting me there to-night."

Nevertheless, the youth felt an instinctive antipathy towards the guardian of midnight order, which at first prevented him from asking his usual question. But just when the man was about to vanish behind the corner, Robin resolved not to lose the opportunity, and shouted lustily after him,—

"I say, friend! will you guide me to the house of my kinsman, Major Molineux?"

The watchman made no reply, but turned the corner and was gone; yet Robin seemed to hear the sound of drowsy laughter stealing along the solitary street. At that moment, also, a pleasant titter saluted him from the open window above his head; he looked up, and caught the sparkle of a saucy eye; a round arm beckoned to him, and next he heard light footsteps descending the staircase within. But Robin, being of the household of a New England clergyman, was a good youth, as well as a shrewd one; so he resisted temptation, and fled away.

He now roamed desperately, and at random, through the town, almost ready to believe that a spell was on him, like that by which a wizard of his country had once kept three pursuers wandering, a whole winter night, within twenty paces of the cottage which they sought. The streets lay before him, strange and desolate, and the lights were extinguished in almost every house. Twice, however, little parties of men, among whom Robin distinguished individuals in outlandish attire, came hurrying along; but, though on both occasions they paused to address him, such intercourse did not at all enlighten his perplexity. They did but utter a few words in some language of which Robin knew nothing, and perceiving his inability to answer, bestowed a curse upon him in plain English and hastened away. Finally, the lad determined to knock at the door of every mansion that might appear worthy to be occupied by his kinsman, trusting that perseverance would overcome the fatality that had hitherto thwarted him. Firm in this resolve, he was passing beneath the walls of a church, which formed the corner of two streets, when, as he turned into the shade of its steeple, he encountered a bulky stranger, muffled in a cloak. The man was proceeding with the speed of earnest business, but Robin planted himself full before him, holding the oak cudgel with both hands across his body as a bar to further passage.

"Halt, honest man, and answer me a question," said he, very resolutely. "Tell me, this instant, whereabouts is the dwelling of my kinsman, Major Molineux!"

"Keep your tongue between your teeth, fool, and let me pass!" said a deep, gruff voice, which Robin partly remembered. "Let me pass, I say, or I'll strike you to the earth!"

"No, no, neighbor!" cried Robin, flourishing his cudgel, and then thrusting its larger end close to the man's muffled face. "No, no, I'm not the fool you take me for, nor do you pass till I have an answer to my question. Whereabouts is the dwelling of my kinsman, Major Molineux?"

The stranger, instead of attempting to force his passage, stepped back into the moonlight, unmuffled his face, and stared full into that of Robin.

"Watch here an hour, and Major Molineux will pass by," said he.

Robin gazed with dismay and astonishment on the unprecedented physiognomy of the speaker. The forehead with its double prominence, the broad hooked nose, the shaggy eyebrows, and fiery eyes were those which he had noticed at the inn, but the man's complexion had undergone a singular, or, more properly, a twofold change. One side of the face blazed an intense red, while the other was black as midnight, the division line being in the broad bridge of the nose; and a mouth which seemed to extend from ear to ear was black or red, in contrast to the color of the cheek. The effect was as if two individual devils, a fiend of fire and a fiend of darkness, had united themselves to form this infernal visage. The stranger grinned in Robin's face, muffled his party-colored features, and was out of sight in a moment.

"Strange things we travellers see!" ejaculated Robin.

He seated himself, however, upon the steps of the church-door, resolving to wait the appointed time for his kinsman. A few moments were consumed in philosophical speculations upon the species of man who had just left him; but having settled this point shrewdly, rationally, and satisfactorily, he was compelled to look elsewhere for his amusement. And first he threw his eyes along the street. It was of more respectable appearance than most of those into which he had wandered; and the moon, creating, like the imaginative power, a beautiful strangeness in familiar objects, gave something of romance to a scene that might not have possessed it in the light of day. The irregular and often quaint architecture of the houses, some of whose roofs were broken into numerous little peaks, while others ascended, steep and narrow, into a single point, and others again were square; the pure snow-white of some of their complexions, the aged darkness of others, and the thousand sparklings, reflected from bright substances in the walls of many; these matters engaged Robin's attention for a while, and then began to grow wearisome. Next he endeavored to define the forms of distant objects, starting away, with almost ghostly indistinctness, just as his eye appeared to grasp them; and finally he took a minute survey of an edifice which stood on the opposite side of the street, directly in front of the church-door, where he was stationed. It was a large, square mansion, distinguished from its neighbors by a balcony, which rested on tall pillars, and by an elaborate Gothic window, communicating therewith.

"Perhaps this is the very house I have been seeking," thought Robin.

Then he strove to speed away the time, by listening to a murmur which swept continually along the street, yet was scarcely audible, except to an unaccustomed ear like his; it was a low, dull, dreamy sound, compounded of many noises, each of which was at too great a distance to be separately heard. Robin marvelled at this snore of a sleeping town, and marvelled more whenever its continuity was broken by now and then a distant shout, apparently loud where it originated. But altogether it was a sleep-inspiring sound, and, to shake off its drowsy influence, Robin arose, and climbed a window-frame, that he might view the interior of the church. There the moonbeams came trembling in, and fell down upon the deserted pews, and extended along the quiet aisles. A fainter yet more awful radiance was hovering around the pulpit, and one solitary ray had dared to rest upon the open page of the great Bible. Had nature, in that deep hour, become a worshipper in the house which man had builded? Or was that heavenly light the visible sanctity of the place,—visible because no earthly and impure feet were within the walls? The scene made Robin's heart shiver with a sensation of loneliness stronger than he had ever felt in the remotest depths of his native woods; so he turned away and sat down again before the door. There were graves around the church, and now an uneasy thought obtruded into Robin's breast. What if the object of his search, which had been so often and so strangely thwarted, were all the time mouldering in his shroud? What if his kinsman should glide through yonder gate, and nod and smile to him in dimly passing by?

"Oh that any breathing thing were here with me!" said Robin.

Recalling his thoughts from this uncomfortable track, he sent them over forest, hill, and stream, and attempted to imagine how that evening of ambiguity and weariness had been spent by his father's household. He pictured them assembled at the door, beneath the tree, the great old tree, which had been spared for its huge twisted trunk and venerable shade, when a thousand leafy brethren fell. There, at the going down of the summer sun, it was his father's custom to perform domestic worship, that the neighbors might come and join with him like brothers of the family, and that the wayfaring man might pause to drink at that fountain, and keep his heart pure by freshening the memory of home. Robin distinguished the seat of every individual of the little audience; he saw the good man in the midst, holding the Scriptures in the golden light that fell from the western clouds; he beheld him close the book and all rise up to pray. He heard the old thanksgiving for daily mercies, the old supplications for their continuance, to which he had so often listened in weariness, but which were now among his dear remembrances. He perceived the slight inequality of his father's voice when he came to speak of the absent one; he noted how his mother turned her face to the broad and knotted trunk; how his elder brother scorned, because the beard was rough upon his upper lip, to permit his features to be moved; how the younger sister drew down a low hanging branch before her eyes; and how the little one of all, whose sports had hitherto broken the decorum of the scene, understood the prayer for her playmate, and burst into clamorous grief. Then he saw them go in at the door; and when Robin would have entered also, the latch tinkled into its place, and he was excluded from his home.

"Am I here, or there?" cried Robin, starting; for all at once, when his thoughts had become visible and audible in a dream, the long, wide, solitary street shone out before him.

He aroused himself, and endeavored to fix his attention steadily upon the large edifice which he had surveyed before. But still his mind kept vibrating between fancy and reality; by turns, the pillars of the balcony lengthened into the tall, bare stems of pines, dwindled down to human figures, settled again into their true shape and size, and then commenced a new succession of changes. For a single moment, when he deemed himself awake, he could have sworn that a visage—one which he seemed to remember, yet could not absolutely name as his kinsman's—was looking towards him from the Gothic window. A deeper sleep wrestled with and nearly overcame him, but fled at the sound of footsteps along the opposite pavement. Robin rubbed his eyes, discerned a man passing at the foot of the balcony, and addressed him in a loud, peevish, and lamentable cry.

"Hallo, friend! must I wait here all night for my kinsman, Major Molineux?"

The sleeping echoes awoke, and answered the voice; and the passenger, barely able to discern a figure sitting in the oblique shade of the steeple, traversed the street to obtain a nearer view. He was himself a gentleman in his prime, of open, intelligent, cheerful, and altogether prepossessing countenance. Perceiving a country youth, apparently homeless and without friends, he accosted him in a tone of real kindness, which had become strange to Robin's ears.

"Well, my good lad, why are you sitting here?" inquired he. "Can I be of service to you in any way?"

"I am afraid not, sir," replied Robin, despondingly; "yet I shall take it kindly, if you'll answer me a single question. I've been searching, half the night, for one Major Molineux; now, sir, is there really such a person in these parts, or am I dreaming?"

"Major Molineux! The name is not altogether strange to me," said the gentleman, smiling. "Have you any objection to telling me the nature of your business with him?"

Then Robin briefly related that his father was a clergyman, settled on a small salary, at a long distance back in the country, and that he and Major Molineux were brothers' children. The Major, having inherited riches, and acquired civil and military rank, had visited his cousin, in great pomp, a year or two before; had manifested much interest in Robin and an elder brother, and, being childless himself, had thrown out hints respecting the future establishment of one of them in life. The elder brother was destined to succeed to the farm which his father cultivated in the interval of sacred duties; it was therefore determined that Robin should profit by his kinsman's generous intentions, especially as he seemed to be rather the favorite, and was thought to possess other necessary endowment.

"For I have the name of being a shrewd youth," observed Robin, in this part of his story.

"I doubt not you deserve it," replied his new friend, good-naturedly; "but pray proceed."

"Well, sir, being nearly eighteen years old, and well grown, as you see," continued Robin, drawing himself up to his full height, "I thought it high time to begin the world. So my mother and sister put me in handsome trim, and my father gave me half the remnant of his last year's salary, and five days ago I started for this place, to pay the Major a visit. But, would you believe it, sir! I crossed the ferry a little after dark, and have yet found nobody that would show me the way to his dwelling; only, an hour or two since, I was told to wait here, and Major Molineux would pass by."

"Can you describe the man who told you this?" inquired the gentleman.

"Oh, he was a very ill-favored fellow, sir," replied Robin, "with two great bumps on his forehead, a hook nose, fiery eyes; and, what struck me as the strangest, his face was of two different colors. Do you happen to know such a man, sir?"

"Not intimately," answered the stranger, "but I chanced to meet him a little time previous to your stopping me. I believe you may trust his word, and that the Major will very shortly pass through this street. In the mean time, as I have a singular curiosity to witness your meeting, I will sit down here upon the steps and bear you company."

He seated himself accordingly, and soon engaged his companion in animated discourse. It was but of brief continuance, however, for a noise of shouting, which had long been remotely audible, drew so much nearer that Robin inquired its cause.

"What may be the meaning of this uproar?" asked he. "Truly, if your town be always as noisy, I shall find little sleep while I am an inhabitant."

"Why, indeed, friend Robin, there do appear to be three or four riotous fellows abroad to-night," replied the gentleman. "You must not expect all the stillness of your native woods here in our streets. But the watch will shortly be at the heels of these lads and—"

"Ay, and set them in the stocks by peep of day," interrupted Robin, recollecting his own encounter with the drowsy lantern-bearer. "But, dear sir, if I may trust my ears, an army of watchmen would never make head against such a multitude of rioters. There were at least a thousand voices went up to make that one shout."

"May not a man have several voices, Robin, as well as two complexions?" said his friend.

"Perhaps a man may; but Heaven forbid that a woman should!" responded the shrewd youth, thinking of the seductive tones of the Major's housekeeper.

The sounds of a trumpet in some neighboring street now became so evident and continual, that Robin's curiosity was strongly excited. In addition to the shouts, he heard frequent bursts from many instruments of discord, and a wild and confused laughter filled up the intervals. Robin rose from the steps, and looked wistfully towards a point whither people seemed to be hastening.

"Surely some prodigious merry-making is going on," exclaimed he. "I have laughed very little since I left home, sir, and should be sorry to lose an opportunity. Shall we step round the corner by that darkish house, and take our share of the fun?"

"Sit down again, sit down, good Robin," replied the gentleman, laying his hand on the skirt of the gray coat. "You forget that we must wait here for your kinsman; and there is reason to believe that he will pass by, in the course of a very few moments."

The near approach of the uproar had now disturbed the neighborhood; windows flew open on all sides; and many heads, in the attire of the pillow, and confused by sleep suddenly broken, were protruded to the gaze of whoever had leisure to observe them. Eager voices hailed each other from house to house, all demanding the explanation, which not a soul could give. Half-dressed men hurried towards the unknown commotion, stumbling as they went over the stone steps that thrust themselves into the narrow foot-walk. The shouts, the laughter, and the tuneless bray, the antipodes of music, came onwards with increasing din, till scattered individuals, and then denser bodies, began to appear round a corner at the distance of a hundred yards.

"Will you recognize your kinsman, if he passes in this crowd?" inquired the gentleman.

"Indeed, I can't warrant it, sir; but I'll take my stand here, and keep a bright lookout," answered Robin, descending to the outer edge of the pavement.

A mighty stream of people now emptied into the street, and came rolling slowly towards the church. A single horseman wheeled the corner in the midst of them, and close behind him came a band of fearful wind-instruments, sending forth a fresher discord now that no intervening buildings kept it from the ear. Then a redder light disturbed the moonbeams, and a dense multitude of torches shone along the street, concealing, by their glare, whatever object they illuminated. The single horseman, clad in a military dress, and bearing a drawn sword, rode onward as the leader, and, by his fierce and variegated countenance, appeared like war personified; the red of one cheek was an emblem of fire and sword; the blackness of the other betokened the mourning that attends them. In his train were wild figures in the Indian dress, and many fantastic shapes without a model, giving the whole march a visionary air, as if a dream had broken forth from some feverish brain, and were sweeping visibly through the midnight streets. A mass of people, inactive, except as applauding spectators, hemmed the procession in; and several women ran along the sidewalk, piercing the confusion of heavier sounds with their shrill voices of mirth or terror.

"The double-faced fellow has his eye upon me," muttered Robin, with an indefinite but an uncomfortable idea that he was himself to bear a part in the pageantry.

The leader turned himself in the saddle, and fixed his glance full upon the country youth, as the steed went slowly by. When Robin had freed his eyes from those fiery ones, the musicians were passing before him, and the torches were close at hand; but the unsteady brightness of the latter formed a veil which he could not penetrate. The rattling of wheels over the stones sometimes found its way to his ear, and confused traces of a human form appeared at intervals, and then melted into the vivid light. A moment more, and the leader thundered a command to halt: the trumpets vomited a horrid breath, and then held their peace; the shouts and laughter of the people died away, and there remained only a universal hum, allied to silence. Right before Robin's eyes was an uncovered cart. There the torches blazed the brightest, there the moon shone out like day, and there, in tar-and-feathery dignity, sat his kinsman, Major Molineux!

He was an elderly man, of large and majestic person, and strong, square features, betokening a steady soul; but steady as it was, his enemies had found means to shake it. His face was pale as death, and far more ghastly; the broad forehead was contracted in his agony, so that his eyebrows formed one grizzled line; his eyes were red and wild, and the foam hung white upon his quivering lip. His whole frame was agitated by a quick and continual tremor, which his pride strove to quell, even in those circumstances of overwhelming humiliation. But perhaps the bitterest pang of all was when his eyes met those of Robin; for he evidently knew him on the instant, as the youth stood witnessing the foul disgrace of a head grown gray in honor. They stared at each other in silence, and Robin's knees shook, and his hair bristled, with a mixture of pity and terror. Soon, however, a bewildering excitement began to seize upon his mind; the preceding adventures of the night, the unexpected appearance of the crowd, the torches, the confused din and the hush that followed, the spectre of his kinsman reviled by that great multitude,—all this, and, more than all, a perception of tremendous ridicule in the whole scene, affected him with a sort of mental inebriety. At that moment a voice of sluggish merriment saluted Robin's ears; he turned instinctively, and just behind the corner of the church stood the lantern-bearer, rubbing his eyes, and drowsily enjoying the lad's amazement. Then he heard a peal of laughter like the ringing of silvery bells; a woman twitched his arm, a saucy eye met his, and he saw the lady of the scarlet petticoat. A sharp, dry cachinnation appealed to his memory, and, standing on tiptoe in the crowd, with his white apron over his head, he beheld the courteous little innkeeper. And lastly, there sailed over the heads of the multitude a great, broad laugh, broken in the midst by two sepulchral hems; thus, "Haw, haw, haw,—hem, hem,—haw, haw, haw, haw!"

The sound proceeded from the balcony of the opposite edifice, and thither Robin turned his eyes. In front of the Gothic window stood the old citizen, wrapped in a wide gown, his gray periwig exchanged for a nightcap, which was thrust back from his forehead, and his silk stockings hanging about his legs. He supported himself on his polished cane in a fit of convulsive merriment, which manifested itself on his solemn old features like a funny inscription on a tombstone. Then Robin seemed to hear the voices of the barbers, of the guests of the inn, and of all who had made sport of him that night. The contagion was spreading among the multitude, when all at once, it seized upon Robin, and he sent forth a shout of laughter that echoed through the street,—every man shook his sides, every man emptied his lungs, but Robin's shout was the loudest there. The cloud-spirits peeped from their silvery islands, as the congregated mirth went roaring up the sky! The Man in the Moon heard the far bellow. "Oho," quoth he, "the old earth is frolicsome to-night!"

When there was a momentary calm in that tempestuous sea of sound, the leader gave the sign, the procession resumed its march. On they went, like fiends that throng in mockery around some dead potentate, mighty no more, but majestic still in his agony. On they went, in counterfeited pomp, in senseless uproar, in frenzied merriment, trampling all on an old man's heart. On swept the tumult, and left a silent street behind.

.   .   .

"Well, Robin, are you dreaming?" inquired the gentleman, laying his hand on the youth's shoulder.

Robin started, and withdrew his arm from the stone post to which he had instinctively clung, as the living stream rolled by him. His cheek was somewhat pale, and his eye not quite as lively as in the earlier part of the evening.

"Will you be kind enough to show me the way to the ferry?" said he, after a moment's pause.

"You have, then, adopted a new subject of inquiry?" observed his companion, with a smile.

"Why, yes, sir," replied Robin, rather dryly. "Thanks to you, and to my other friends, I have at last met my kinsman, and he will scarce desire to see my face again. I begin to grow weary of a town life, sir. Will you show me the way to the ferry?"

"No, my good friend Robin,—not to-night, at least," said the gentleman. "Some few days hence, if you wish it, I will speed you on your journey. Or, if you prefer to remain with us, perhaps, as you are a shrewd youth, you may rise in the world without the help of your kinsman, Major Molineux."

An Encounter

It was Joe Dillon who introduced the Wild West to us. He had a little library made up of old numbers of *The Union Jack, Pluck* and *The Halfpenny Marvel*. Every evening after school we met in his back garden and arranged Indian battles. He and his fat young brother Leo, the idler, held the loft of the stable while we tried to carry it by storm; or we fought a pitched battle on the grass. But, however well we fought, we never won siege or battle and all our bouts ended with Joe Dillon's war dance of victory. His parents went to eight-o'clock mass every morning in Gardiner Street and the peaceful odour of Mrs. Dillon was prevalent in the hall of the house. But he played too fiercely for us who were younger and more timid. He looked like some kind of an Indian when he capered round the garden, an old tea-cosy on his head, beating a tin with his fist and yelling:

"Ya! yaka, yaka, yaka!"

Everyone was incredulous when it was reported that he had a vocation for the priesthood. Nevertheless it was true.

A spirit of unruliness diffused itself among us and, under its influence, differences of culture and constitution were waived. We banded ourselves together, some boldly, some in jest and some almost in fear: and of the number of these latter, the reluctant Indians who were afraid to seem studious or lacking in robustness, I was one. The adventures related in the literature of the Wild West were remote from my nature but, at least, they opened doors of escape. I liked better some American detective stories which were traversed

AN ENCOUNTER From *Dubliners* by James Joyce. Originally published by B. W. Huebsch, Inc. in 1916. Copyright © 1967 by the Estate of James Joyce. All rights reserved. Reprinted by permission of The Viking Press, Inc.

from time to time by unkempt fierce and beautiful girls. Though there was nothing wrong in these stories and though their intention was sometimes literary they circulated secretly at school. One day when Father Butler was hearing the four pages of Roman History clumsy Leo Dillon was discovered with a copy of *The Halfpenny Marvel.*

"This page or this page? This page? Now, Dillon, up! *'Hardly had the day'* . . . Go on! What day? *'Hardly had the day dawned'* . . . Have you studied it? What have you there in your pocket?"

Everyone's heart palpitated as Leo Dillon handed up the paper and everyone assumed an innocent face. Father Butler turned over the pages, frowning.

"What is this rubbish?" he said. *"The Apache Chief!* Is this what you read instead of studying your Roman History? Let me not find any more of this wretched stuff in this college. The man who wrote it, I suppose, was some wretched fellow who writes these things for a drink. I'm surprised at boys like you, educated, reading such stuff. I could understand it if you were . . . National School boys. Now, Dillon, I advise you strongly, get at your work or . . ."

This rebuke during the sober hours of school paled much of the glory of the Wild West for me and the confused puffy face of Leo Dillon awakened one of my consciences. But when the restraining influence of the school was at a distance I began to hunger again for wild sensations, for the escape which those chronicles of disorder alone seemed to offer me. The mimic warfare of the evening became at last as wearisome to me as the routine of school in the morning because I wanted real adventures to happen to myself. But real adventures, I reflected, do not happen to people who remain at home: they must be sought abroad.

The summer holidays were near at hand when I made up my mind to break out of the weariness of schoollife for one day at least. With Leo Dillon and a boy named Mahony I planned a day's miching. Each of us saved up sixpence. We were to meet at ten in the morning on the Canal Bridge. Mahony's big sister was to write an excuse for him and Leo Dillon was to tell his brother to say he was sick. We arranged to go along the Wharf Road until we came to the ships, then to cross in the ferryboat and walk out to see the Pigeon House. Leo Dillon was afraid we might meet Father Butler or someone out of the college; but Mahony asked, very sensibly, what would Father Butler be doing out at the Pigeon House. We were reassured: and I brought the first stage of the plot to an end by collecting sixpence from the other two, at the same time showing them my own sixpence. When we were making the last arrangements on the eve we were all vaguely excited. We shook hands, laughing, and Mahony said:

"Till to-morrow, mates!"

That night I slept badly. In the morning I was firstcomer to the bridge as I lived nearest. I hid my books in the long grass near the ashpit at the end of the garden where nobody ever came and hurried along the canal bank. It was a mild sunny morning in the first week of June. I sat up on the coping of the bridge admiring my frail canvas shoes which I had diligently pipeclayed overnight and watching the docile horses pulling a tramload of business people up the hill. All the branches of the tall trees which lined the mall were gay with little light green leaves and the sunlight slanted through them on to the water. The granite stone of the bridge was beginning to be warm and I began to pat it with my hands in time to an air in my head. I was very happy.

When I had been sitting there for five or ten minutes I saw Mahony's grey suit approaching. He came up the hill, smiling, and clambered up beside me on the bridge. While we were waiting he brought out the catapult which bulged from his inner pocket and explained some improvements which he had made in it. I asked him why he had brought it and he told me he had brought it to have some gas with the birds. Mahony used slang freely, and spoke of Father Butler as Old Bunser. We waited on for a quarter of an hour more but still there was no sign of Leo Dillon. Mahony, at last, jumped down and said:

"Come along. I knew Fatty'd funk it."

"And his sixpence . . . ?" I said.

"That's forfeit," said Mahony. "And so much the better for us—a bob and a tanner instead of a bob."

We walked along the North Strand Road till we came to the Vitriol Works and then turned to the right along the Wharf Road. Mahony began to play the Indian as soon as we were out of public sight. He chased a crowd of ragged girls, brandishing his unloaded catapult and, when two ragged boys began, out of chivalry, to fling stones at us, he proposed that we should charge them. I objected that the boys were too small, and so we walked on, the ragged troop screaming after us: *"Swaddlers! Swaddlers!"* thinking that we were Protestants because Mahony, who was dark-complexioned, wore the silver badge of a cricket club in his cap. When we came to the Smoothing Iron we arranged a siege; but it was a failure because you must have at least three. We revenged ourselves on Leo Dillon by saying what a funk he was and guessing how many he would get at three o'clock from Mr. Ryan.

We came then near the river. We spent a long time walking about the noisy streets flanked by high stone walls, watching the working of cranes and engines and often being shouted at for our immobility by the drivers of groaning carts. It was noon when we reached the quays and, as all the labourers seemed to be eating their lunches, we bought two big currant buns and sat down to eat them on some metal piping beside the river. We pleased ourselves with the spectacle of Dublin's commerce—the barges signalled from far away by their curls of woolly smoke, the brown fishing fleet beyond Ringsend, the big white sailingvessel which was being discharged on the opposite quay. Mahony said it would be right skit to run away to sea on one of those big ships and even I, looking at the high masts, saw, or imagined, the geography which had been scantily dosed to me at school gradually taking substance under my eyes. School and home seemed to recede from us and their influences upon us seemed to wane.

We crossed the Liffey in the ferryboat, paying our toll to be transported in the company of two labourers and a little Jew with a bag. We were serious to the point of solemnity, but once during the short voyage our eyes met and we laughed. When we landed we watched the discharging of the graceful three-master which we had observed from the other quay. Some bystander said that she was a Norwegian vessel. I went to the stern and tried to decipher the legend upon it but, failing to do so, I came back and examined the foreign sailors to see had any of them green eyes for I had some confused notion. . . . The sailors' eyes were blue and grey and even black. The only sailor whose eyes could have been called green was a tall man who amused the crowd on the quay by calling out cheerfully every time the planks fell:

"All right! All right!"

When we were tired of this sight we wandered slowly into Ringsend. The day had grown sultry, and in the windows of the grocers' shops musty biscuits lay bleaching. We bought some biscuits and chocolate which we ate sedulously as we wandered through the squalid streets where the families of the fishermen live. We could find no dairy and so we went into a huckster's shop and bought a bottle of raspberry lemonade each. Refreshed by this, Mahony chased a cat down a lane, but the cat escaped into a wide field. We both felt rather tired and when we reached the field we made at once for a sloping bank over the ridge of which we could see the Dodder.

It was too late and we were too tired to carry out our project of visiting the Pigeon House. We had to be home before four o'clock lest our adventure should be discovered. Mahony looked regretfully at his catapult and I had to suggest going home by train before he regained any cheerfulness. The sun went in behind some clouds and left us to our jaded thoughts and the crumbs of our provisions.

There was nobody but ourselves in the field. When we had lain on the bank for some time without speaking I saw a man approaching from the far end of the field. I watched him lazily as I chewed one of those green stems on which girls tell fortunes. He came along by the bank slowly. He walked with one hand upon his hip and in the other hand he held a stick with which he tapped the turf lightly. He was shabbily dressed in a suit of greenish-black and wore what we used to call a jerry hat with a high crown. He seemed to be fairly old for his moustache was ashen-grey. When he passed at our feet he glanced up at us quickly and then continued his way. We followed him with our eyes and saw that when he had gone on for perhaps fifty paces he turned about and began to retrace his steps. He walked towards us very slowly, always tapping the ground with his stick, so slowly that I thought he was looking for something in the grass.

He stopped when he came level with us and bade us good-day. We answered him and he sat down beside us on the slope slowly and with great care. He began to talk of the weather, saying that it would be a very hot summer and adding that the seasons had changed greatly since he was a boy—a long time ago. He said that the happiest time of one's life was undoubtedly one's school-boy days and that he would give anything to be young again. While he expressed these sentiments which bored us a little we kept silent. Then he began to talk of school and of books. He asked us whether we had read the poetry of Thomas Moore or the works of Sir Walter Scott and Lord Lytton. I pretended that I had read every book he mentioned so that in the end he said:

"Ah, I can see you are a bookworm like myself. Now," he added, pointing to Mahony who was regarding us with open eyes, "he is different; he goes in for games."

He said he had all Sir Walter Scott's works and all Lord Lytton's works at home and never tired of reading them. "Of course," he said, "there were some of Lord Lytton's works which boys couldn't read." Mahony asked why couldn't boys read them—a question which agitated and pained me because I was afraid the man would think I was as stupid as Mahony. The man, however, only smiled. I saw that he had great gaps in his mouth between his yellow teeth. Then he asked us which of us had the most sweethearts. Mahony mentioned lightly that he had three totties. The man asked me how many I had. I answered that I had none. He did not believe me and said he was sure I must have one. I was silent.

"Tell us," said Mahony pertly to the man, "how many have you yourself?"

The man smiled as before and said that when he was our age he had lots of sweethearts.

"Every boy," he said, "has a little sweetheart."

His attitude on this point struck me as strangely liberal in a man of his age. In my heart I thought that what he said about boys and sweethearts was reasonable. But I disliked the words in his mouth and I wondered why he shivered once or twice as if he feared something or felt a sudden chill. As he proceeded I noticed that his accent was good. He began to speak to us about girls, saying what nice soft hair they had and how soft their hands were and how all girls were not so good as they seemed to be if one only knew. There was nothing he liked, he said, so much as looking at a nice young girl, at her nice white hands and her beautiful soft hair. He gave me the impression that he was repeating something which he had learned by heart or that, magnetised by some words of his own speech, his mind was slowly circling round and round in the same orbit. At times he spoke as if he were simply alluding to some fact that everybody knew, and at times he lowered his voice and spoke mysteriously as if he were telling us something secret which he did not wish others to overhear. He repeated his phrases over and over again, varying them and surrounding them with his monotonous voice. I continued to gaze towards the foot of the slope, listening to him.

After a long while his monologue paused. He stood up slowly, saying that he had to leave us for a minute or so, a few minutes, and, without changing the direction of my gaze, I saw him walking slowly away from us towards the near end of the field. We remained silent when he had gone. After a silence of a few minutes I heard Mahony exclaim:

"I say! Look what he's doing!"

As I neither answered nor raised my eyes Mahony exclaimed again:

"I say . . . He's a queer old josser!"

"In case he asks us for our names," I said, "let you be Murphy and I'll be Smith."

We said nothing further to each other. I was still considering whether I would go away or not when the man came back and sat down beside us again. Hardly had he sat down when Mahony, catching sight of the cat which had escaped him, sprang up and pursued her across the field. The man and I watched the chase. The cat escaped once more and Mahony began to throw stones at the wall she had escaladed. Desisting from this, he began to wander about the far end of the field, aimlessly.

After an interval the man spoke to me. He said that my friend was a very rough boy and asked did he get whipped often at school. I was going to reply indignantly that we were not National School boys to be whipped, as he called it; but I remained silent. He began to speak on the subject of chastising boys. His mind, as if magnetised again by his speech, seemed to circle slowly round and round its new centre. He said that when boys were that kind they ought to be whipped and well whipped. When a boy was rough and unruly there was nothing would do him any good but a good sound whipping. A slap on the hand or a box on the ear was no good: what he wanted was to get a nice warm whipping. I was surprised at this sentiment and involuntarily glanced up at his face. As I did so I met the gaze of a pair of bottle-green eyes peering at me from under a twitching forehead. I turned my eyes away again.

The man continued his monologue. He seemed to have forgotten his recent liberalism. He said that if ever he found a boy talking to girls or having a girl for a sweetheart he would whip him and whip him; and that would teach him not to be talking to girls. And if a boy had a girl for a sweetheart and told lies about it then he would give him such a whipping as no boy ever got in this world. He said that there was nothing in this world he would like so well as that. He described to me how he would whip such a boy as if he were unfolding some elaborate mystery. He would love that, he said, better than anything in this world; and his voice, as he led me monotonously through the mystery, grew almost affectionate and seemed to plead with me that I should understand him.

I waited till his monologue paused again. Then I stood up abruptly. Lest I should betray my agitation I delayed a few moments pretending to fix my shoe properly and then, saying that I was obliged to go, I bade him good-day. I went up the slope calmly but my heart was beating quickly with fear that he would seize me by the ankles. When I reached the top of the slope I turned round and, without looking at him, called loudly across the field:

"Murphy!"

My voice had an accent of forced bravery in it and I was ashamed of my paltry stratagem. I had to call the name again before Mahony saw me and hallooed in answer. How my heart beat as he came running across the field to me! He ran as if to bring me aid. And I was pentitent; for in my heart I had always despised him a little.

The Story of My Dovecot

To Maxim Gorky

When I was a kid I longed for a dovecot. Never in all my life have I wanted a thing more. But not till I was nine did father promise the wherewithal to to buy the wood to make one and three pairs of pigeons to stock it with. It was then 1904, and I was studying for the entrance exam to the preparatory class of the secondary school at Nikolayev in the Province of Kherson, where my people were at that time living. This province of course no longer exists, and our town has been incorporated in the Odessa region.

I was only nine, and I was scared stiff of the exams. In both subjects, Russian language and arithmetic, I couldn't afford to get less than top marks. At our secondary school the *numerus clausus* was stiff: a mere five percent. So that out of forty boys only two that were Jews could get in the preparatory class. The teachers used to put cunning questions to Jewish boys; no one else was asked such devilish questions. So when father promised to buy the pigeons he demanded top marks with distinction in both subjects. He absolutely tortured me to death. I fell into a state of permanent daydream, into an endless, despairing, childish reverie. I went to the exam deep in this dream, and nevertheless did better than everybody else.

I had a knack for book-learning. Even though they asked cunning questions, the teachers could not rob me of my intelligence and my avid memory. I was good at learning, and got top marks in both subjects. But then everything went wrong. Khariton Efrussi, the corn-dealer who exported wheat to Marseille, slipped someone a 500-rouble bribe. My mark was changed from A to A—, and Efrussi Junior went to the secondary school instead of me. Father took it very badly. From the time I was six he had been cramming me with every scrap of learning he could, and that A— drove him to despair. He wanted to beat Efrussi up, or at least bribe two longshoremen to beat Efrussi up, but mother talked him out of the idea, and I started studying for the second exam the following year, the one for the lowest class. Behind my back my people got the teacher to take me in one year through the preparatory and first-year courses simultaneously, and conscious of the family's despair, I got three whole books by heart. These were Smirnovsky's *Russian Grammar,* Yevtushevsky's *Problems,* and Putsykovich's *Manual of Early Russian History.* Children no longer cram from these books, but I learned them by heart line upon line, and the following year in the Russian exam Karavayev gave me an unrivaled A+.

This Karavayev was a red-faced, irritable fellow, a graduate of Moscow University. He was hardly more than thirty. Crimson glowed in his manly cheeks as it does in the cheeks of peasant children. A wart sat perched on one cheek, and from it there sprouted a tuft of ash-colored cat's whiskers. At the exam, besides Karavayev, there was the Assistant Curator Pyatnitsky, who was reckoned a big noise in the school and throughout the province. When the Assistant Curator asked me about Peter the Great a feeling of complete oblivion came over me, an awareness that the end was near: an abyss seemed to yawn before me, an arid abyss lined with exultation and despair.

About Peter the Great I knew things by heart from Putsykovich's book and Pushkin's verses. Sobbing, I recited these verses, while the faces before me suddenly turned upside down, were shuffled as a pack of cards is shuffled. This card-shuffling went on, and meanwhile, shivering, jerking my back straight, galloping headlong, I was shouting Pushkin's stanzas at the top of my voice. On and on I yelled them, and no one broke into my crazy mouthings. Through a crimson blindness, through the sense of absolute freedom that had filled me, I was aware of nothing but Pyatnitsky's old face with its silver-touched beard bent toward me. He didn't interrupt me, and merely said to Karavayev, who was rejoicing for my sake and Pushkin's:

"What a people," the old man whispered, "those little Jews of yours! There's a devil in them!"

And when at last I could shout no more, he said:

"Very well, run along, my little friend."

I went out from the classroom into the corridor, and there, leaning against a wall that needed a coat of whitewash, I began to awake from my trance. About me Russian boys were playing, the school bell hung not far away above the stairs, the caretaker was snoozing on a chair with a broken seat. I looked at the caretaker, and gradually woke up. Boys were creeping toward me from all sides. They wanted to give me a jab, or perhaps just have a game, but Pyatnitsky suddenly loomed up in the corridor. As he passed me he halted for a moment, the frock coat flowing down his back in a slow heavy wave. I discerned embarrassment in that large, fleshy, upper-class back, and got closer to the old man.

"Children," he said to the boys, "don't touch this lad." And he laid a fat hand tenderly on my shoulder.

"My little friend," he went on, turning me towards him, "tell your father that you are admitted to the first class."

On his chest a great star flashed, and decorations jingled in his lapel. His great black uniformed body started to move away on its stiff legs. Hemmed in by the shadowy walls, moving between them as a barge moves through a deep canal, it disappeared in the doorway of the headmaster's study. The little serving-man took in a tray of tea, clinking solemnly, and I ran home to the shop.

In the shop a peasant customer, tortured by doubt, sat scratching himself. When he saw me my father stopped trying to help the peasant make up his mind, and without a moment's hesitation believed everything I had to say. Calling to the assistant to start shutting up shop, he dashed out into Cathedral Street to buy me a school cap with a badge on it. My poor mother had her work cut out getting me away from the crazy fellow. She was pale at that moment, she was experiencing destiny. She kept smoothing me, and pushing me away as though she hated me. She said there was always a notice in the paper about those who had been admitted to the school, and that God would punish us, and that folk would laugh at us if we bought a school cap too soon. My mother was pale; she was experiencing destiny through my eyes. She looked at me with bitter compassion as one might look at a little cripple boy, because she alone knew what a family ours was for misfortunes.

All the men in our family were trusting by nature, and quick to ill-considered actions. We were unlucky in everything we undertook. My grandfather had been a rabbi somewhere in the Belaya Tserkov region. He had been thrown out for blasphemy, and for another forty years he lived noisily and sparsely, teaching foreign languages. In his eightieth year he started going off his head. My Uncle Leo, my father's brother, had studied at the Talmudic Academy in Volozhin. In 1892 he ran away to avoid doing military service, eloping with the daughter of someone serving in the commissariat in the Kiev military district. Uncle Leo took this woman to California, to Los Angeles, and there he abandoned her, and died in a house of ill fame among Negroes and Malays. After his death the American police sent us a heritage from Los Angeles, a large trunk bound with brown iron hoops. In this trunk there were dumbbells, locks of women's hair, uncle's talith, horsewhips with gilt handles, scented tea in boxes trimmed with imitation pearls. Of all the family there remained only crazy Uncle Simon-Wolf, who lived in Odessa, my father, and I. But my father had faith in people, and he used to put them off with the transports of first love. People could not forgive him for this, and used to play him false. So my father believed that his life was guided by an evil fate, an inexplicable being that pursued him, a being in every respect unlike him. And so I alone of all our family was left to my mother. Like all Jews I was short, weakly, and had headaches from studying. My mother saw all this. She had never been dazzled by her husband's pauper pride, by his incomprehensible belief that our family would one day be richer and more powerful than all others on earth. She desired no success for us, was scared of buying a school jacket too soon, and all she would consent to was that I should have my photo taken.

On September 20, 1905, a list of those admitted to the first class was hung up at the school. In the list my name figured too. All our kith and kin kept going to look at this paper, and even Shoyl, my granduncle, went along. I loved that boastful old man, for he sold fish at the market. His fat hands were moist, covered with fish-scales, and smelt of worlds chill and beautiful. Shoyl also differed from ordinary folk in the lying stories he used to tell about the Polish Rising of 1861. Years ago Shoyl had been a tavern-keeper at Skvira. He had seen Nicholas I's soldiers shooting Count Godlevski and other Polish insurgents. But perhaps he hadn't. *Now* I know that Shoyl was just an old ignoramus and a simple-minded liar, but his cock-and-bull stories I have never forgotten: they were good stories. Well now, even silly old Shoyl went along to the school to read the list with my name on it, and that evening he danced and pranced at our pauper ball.

My father got up the ball to celebrate my success, and asked all his pals— grain-dealers, real-estate brokers, and the traveling salesmen who sold agricultural machinery in our parts. These salesmen would sell a machine to anyone. Peasants and landowners went in fear of them: you couldn't break loose without buying something or other. Of all Jews, salesmen are the widest-awake and the jolliest. At our party they sang Hasidic songs consisting of three words only but which took an awful long time to sing, songs performed with endless comical intonations. The beauty of these intonations may only be recognized by those who have had the good fortune to spend Passover with the Hasidim or who have visited their noisy Volhynian synagogues. Besides the salesmen, old Lieberman who had taught me the Torah and ancient Hebrew honored us with his presence. In our circle he was known as Monsieur Lieberman. He drank more Bessarabian wine than he should have. The ends of the traditional silk tassels poked out from beneath his waistcoat, and in ancient Hebrew he proposed my health. In this toast the old man congratulated my parents and said that I had vanquished all my foes in single combat: I had vanquished the Russian boys with their fat cheeks, and I had vanquished the sons of our own vulgar parvenus. So too in ancient times David King of Judah had overcome Goliath, and just as I had triumphed over Goliath, so too would our people by the strength of their intellect conquer the foes who had encircled us and were thirsting for our blood. Monsieur Lieberman started to weep as he said this, drank more wine as he wept, and shouted *"Vivat!"* The guests formed a circle and danced an old-fashioned quadrille with him in the middle, just as at a wedding in a little Jewish town. Everyone was happy at our ball. Even mother took a sip of vodka, though she neither liked the stuff nor understood how anyone else could—because of this she considered all Russians cracked, and just couldn't imagine how women managed with Russian husbands.

But our happy days came later. For mother they came when of a morning, before I set off for school, she would start making me sandwiches; when we went shopping to buy my school things—pencil box, money box, satchel, new books in cardboard bindings, and exercise books in shiny covers. No one in the world has a keener feeling for new things than children have. Children shudder at the smell of newness as a dog does when it scents a hare, experiencing the madness which later, when we grow up, is called inspiration. And mother acquired this pure and childish sense of the ownership of new things. It took us a whole month to get used to the pencil box, to the morning twilight as I drank my tea on the corner of the large, brightly-lit table and packed my books in my satchel. It took us a month to grow accustomed to our happiness, and it was only after the first half-term that I remembered about the pigeons.

I had everything ready for them: one rouble fifty and a dovecot made from a box by Grandfather Shoyl, as we called him. The dovecot was painted brown. It had nests for twelve pairs of pigeons, carved strips on the roof, and a special grating that I had devised to facilitate the capture of strange birds. All was in readiness. On Sunday, October 20, I set out for the bird market, but unexpected obstacles arose in my path.

The events I am relating, that is to say my admission to the first class at the secondary school, occurred in the autumn of 1905. The Emperor Nicholas was then bestowing a constitution on the Russian people. Orators in shabby overcoats were clambering onto tall curbstones and haranguing the people. At night shots had been heard in the streets, and so mother didn't want me to go to the bird market. From early morning on October 20 the boys next door were flying a kite right by the police station, and our water carrier, abandoning all his buckets, was walking about the streets with a red face and brilliantined hair. Then we saw baker Kalistov's sons drag a leather vaulting-horse out into the street and start doing gym in the middle of the roadway. No one tried to stop them: Semernikov the policeman even kept inciting them to jump higher. Semernikov was girt with a silk belt his wife had made him, and his boots had been polished that day as they had never been polished before. Out of his customary uniform, the policeman frightened my mother more than anything else. Because of him she didn't want me to go out, but I sneaked out by the back way and ran to the bird market, which in our town was behind the station.

At the bird market Ivan Nikodimych, the pigeon-fancier, sat in his customary place. Apart from pigeons, he had rabbits for sale too, and a peacock. The peacock, spreading its tail, sat on a perch moving a passionless head from side to side. To its paw was tied a twisted cord, and the other end of the cord was caught beneath one leg of Ivan Nikodimych's wicker chair. The moment I got there I bought from the old man a pair of cherry-colored pigeons with luscious tousled tails, and a pair of crowned pigeons, and put them away in a bag on my chest under my shirt. After these purchases I had only forty copecks left, and for this price the old man was not prepared to let me have a male and female pigeon of the Kryukov breed. What I liked about Kryukov pigeons was their short, knobbly, good-natured beaks. Forty copecks was the proper price, but the fancier insisted on haggling, averting from me a yellow face scorched by the unsociable passions of bird-snarers. At the end of our bargaining, seeing that there were no other customers, Ivan Nikodimych beckoned me closer. All went as I wished, and all went badly.

Toward twelve o'clock, or perhaps a bit later, a man in felt boots passed across the square. He was stepping lightly on swollen feet, and in his worn-out face lively eyes glittered.

"Ivan Nikodimych," he said as he walked past the bird-fancier, "pack up your gear. In town the Jerusalem aristocrats are being granted a constitution. On Fish Street Grandfather Babel has been constitutioned to death."

He said this and walked lightly on between the cages like a barefoot plough-man walking along the edge of a field.

"They shouldn't," murmured Ivan Nikodimych in his wake. "They shouldn't!" he cried more sternly. He started collecting his rabbits and his peacock, and shoved the Kryukov pigeons at me for forty copecks. I hid them in my bosom and watched the people running away from the bird market. The peacock on Ivan Nikodimych's shoulder was last of all to depart. It sat there like the sun in a raw autumnal sky; it sat as July sits on a pink riverbank, a white-hot July in the long cool grass. No one was left in the market, and not far off shots were rattling. Then I ran to the station, cut across a square that had gone topsy-turvy, and fled down an empty lane of trampled yellow earth. At the end of the lane, in a little wheeled armchair, sat the legless Makarenko, who rode about town in his wheel-chair selling cigarettes from a tray. The boys in our street used to buy smokes from him, children loved him, I dashed toward him down the lane.

"Makarenko," I gasped, panting from my run, and I stroked the legless one's shoulder, "have you seen Shoyl?"

The cripple did not reply. A light seemed to be shining through his coarse face built up of red fat, clenched fists, chunks of iron. He was fidgeting on his chair in his excitement, while his wife Kate, presenting a wadded behind, was sorting out some things scattered on the ground.

"How far have you counted?" asked the legless man, and moved his whole bulk away from the woman, as though aware in advance that her answer would be unbearable.

"Fourteen pair of leggings," said Kate, still bending over, "six undersheets. Now I'm a-counting the bonnets."

"Bonnets!" cried Makarenko, with a choking sound like a sob, "it's clear, Catherine, that God has picked on me, that I must answer for all. People are carting off whole rolls of cloth, people have everything they should, and we're stuck with bonnets."

And indeed a woman with a beautiful burning face ran past us down the lane. She was clutching an armful of fezzes in one arm and a piece of cloth in the other, and in a voice of joyful despair she was yelling for her children, who had strayed. A silk dress and a blue blouse fluttered after her as she flew, and she paid no attention to Makarenko who was rolling his chair in pursuit of her. The legless man couldn't catch up. His wheels clattered as he turned the handles for all he was worth.

"Little lady," he cried in a deafening voice, "where did you get that striped stuff?"

But the woman with the fluttering dress was gone. Round the corner to meet her leaped a rickety cart in which a peasant lad stood upright.

"Where've they all run to?" asked the lad, raising a red rein above the nags jerking in their collars.

"Everybody's on Cathedral Street," said Makarenko pleadingly, "everybody's there, sonny. Anything you happen to pick up, bring it along to me. I'll give you a good price."

The lad bent down over the front of the cart and whipped up his piebald nags. Tossing their filthy croups like calves, the horses shot off at a gallop. The yellow lane was once more yellow and empty. Then the legless man turned his quenched eyes upon me.

"God's picked on me, I reckon," he said lifelessly, "I'm a son of man, I reckon."

And he stretched a hand spotted with leprosy toward me.

"What's that you've got in your sack?" he demanded, and took the bag that had been warming my heart.

With his fat hand the cripple fumbled among the tumbler pigeons and dragged to light a cherry-colored she-bird. Jerking back its feet, the bird lay still on his palm.

"Pigeons," said Makarenko, and squeaking his wheels he rode right up to me. "Damned pigeons," he repeated, and struck me on the cheek.

He dealt me a flying blow with the hand that was clutching the bird. Kate's wadded back seemed to turn upside down, and I fell to the ground in my new overcoat.

"Their spawn must be wiped out," said Kate, straightening up over the bonnets. "I can't a-bear their spawn, nor their stinking menfolk."

She said more things about our spawn, but I heard nothing of it. I lay on the ground, and the guts of the crushed bird trickled down from my temple. They flowed down my cheek, winding this way and that, splashing, blinding me. The tender pigeon-guts slid down over my forehead, and I closed my solitary unstopped-up eye so as not to see the world that spread out before me. This world was tiny, and it was awful. A stone lay just before my eyes, a little stone so chipped as to resemble the face of an old woman with a large jaw. A piece of string lay not far away, and a bunch of feathers that still breathed. My world was tiny, and it was awful. I closed my eyes so as not to see it, and pressed myself tight into the ground that lay beneath me in soothing dumbness. This trampled earth in no way resembled real life, waiting for exams in real life. Somewhere far away Woe rode across it on a great steed, but the noise of the hoofbeats grew weaker and died away, and silence, the bitter silence that sometimes overwhelms children in their sorrow, suddenly deleted the boundary between my body and the earth that was moving nowhither. The earth smelled of raw depths, of the tomb, of flowers. I smelled its smell and started crying, unafraid. I was walking along an unknown street set on either side with white boxes, walking in a getup of bloodstained feathers, alone between the pavements swept clean as on Sunday, weeping bitterly, fully and happily as I never wept again in all my life. Wires that had grown white hummed above my head, a watchdog trotted on in front, in the lane on one side a young peasant in a waistcoat was smashing a window frame in the house of Khariton Efrussi. He was smashing it with a wooden mallet, striking out with his whole body. Sighing, he smiled all around with the amiable grin of drunkenness, sweat and spiritual power. The whole street was filled with a splitting, a snapping, the song of flying wood. The peasant's whole existence consisted in bending over, sweating, shouting queer words in some unknown, non-Russian language. He shouted the words and sang, shot out his blue eyes; till in the street there appeared a procession bearing the Cross and moving from the Municipal Building. Old men bore aloft the portrait of the neatly-combed Tsar, banners with graveyard saints swayed above their heads, inflamed old women flew on in front. Seeing the procession, the peasant pressed his mallet to his chest and dashed off in pursuit of the banners, while I, waiting till the tail-end of the procession had passed, made my furtive way home. The house was empty. Its white doors were open, the grass by the dovecot had been trampled down. Only Kuzma was still in the yard. Kuzma the yardman was sitting in the shed laying out the dead Shoyl.

"The wind bears you about like an evil wood-chip," said the old man when he saw me. "You've been away ages. And now look what they've done to granddad."

Kuzma wheezed, turned away from me, and started pulling a fish out of a rent in grandfather's trousers. Two pike perch had been stuck into grandfather: one into the rent in his trousers, the other into his mouth. And while grandfather was dead, one of the fish was still alive, and struggling.

"They've done grandfather in, but nobody else," said Kuzma, tossing the fish to the cat. "He cursed them all good and proper, a wonderful damning and blasting it was. You might fetch a couple of pennies to put on his eyes."

But then, at ten years of age, I didn't know what need the dead had of pennies.

"Kuzma," I whispered, "save us."

And I went over to the yardman, hugged his crooked old back with its one shoulder higher than the other, and over this back I saw grandfather. Shoyl lay in the sawdust, his chest squashed in, his beard twisted upwards, battered shoes on his bare feet. His feet, thrown wide apart, were dirty, lilac-colored, dead. Kuzma was fussing over him. He tied the dead man's jaws and kept glancing over the body to see what else he could do. He fussed as though over a newly-purchased garment, and only cooled down when he had given the dead man's beard a good combing.

"He cursed the lot of 'em right and left," he said, smiling, and cast a loving look over the corpse. "If Tartars had crossed his path he'd have sent them packing, but Russians came, and their women with them, Rooski women. Russians just can't bring themselves to forgive, I know what Rooskis are."

The yardman spread some more sawdust beneath the body, threw off his carpenter's apron, and took me by the hand.

"Let's go to father," he mumbled, squeezing my hand tighter and tighter. "Your father has been searching for you since morning, sure as fate you was dead."

And so with Kuzma I went to the house of the tax-inspector, where my parents, escaping the pogrom, had sought refuge.

Translated from the Russian
by Walter Morison

Ernest Hemingway

The Killers

The door of Henry's lunch-room opened and two men came in. They sat down at the counter.

"What's yours?" George asked them.

"I don't know," one of the men said. "What do you want to eat, Al?"

"I don't know," said Al. "I don't know what I want to eat."

Outside it was getting dark. The street-light came on outside the window. The two men at the counter read the menu. From the other end of the counter Nick Adams watched them. He had been talking to George when they came in.

"I'll have a roast pork tenderloin with apple sauce and mashed potatoes," the first man said.

"It isn't ready yet."

"What the hell do you put it on the card for?"

"That's the dinner," George explained. "You can get that at six o'clock."

George looked at the clock on the wall behind the counter.

"It's five o'clock."

"The clock says twenty minutes past five," the second man said.

"It's twenty minutes fast."

"Oh, to hell with the clock," the first man said. "What have you got to eat?"

"I can give you any kind of sandwiches," George said. "You can have ham and eggs, bacon and eggs, liver and bacon, or a steak."

"Give me chicken croquettes with green peas and cream sauce and mashed potatoes."

"That's the dinner."

"Everything we want's the dinner, eh? That's the way you work it."

"I can give you ham and eggs, bacon and eggs, liver—"

"I'll take ham and eggs," the man called Al said. He wore a derby hat and a black overcoat buttoned across the chest. His face was small and white and he had tight lips. He wore a silk muffler and gloves.

"Give me bacon and eggs," said the other man. He was about the same size as Al. Their faces were different, but they were dressed like twins. Both wore overcoats too tight for them. They sat leaning forward, their elbows on the counter.

"Got anything to drink?" Al asked.

"Silver beer, bevo, ginger-ale," George said.

"I mean you got anything to *drink?*"

"Just those I said."

"This is a hot town," said the other. "What do they call it?"

"Summit."

"Ever hear of it?" Al asked his friend.

"No," said the friend.

"What do you do here nights?" Al asked.

"They eat the dinner," his friend said. "They all come here and eat the big dinner."

"That's right," George said.

"So you think that's right?" Al asked George.

"Sure."

"You're a pretty bright boy, aren't you?"

"Sure," said George.

"Well, you're not," said the other little man. "Is he, Al?"

"He's dumb," said Al. He turned to Nick. "What's your name?"

"Adams."

"Another bright boy," Al said. "Ain't he a bright boy, Max?"

"The town's full of bright boys," Max said.

George put the two platters, one of ham and eggs, the other of bacon and eggs, on the counter. He set down two side-dishes of fried potatoes and closed the wicket into the kitchen.

"Which is yours?" he asked Al.

"Don't you remember?"

"Ham and eggs."

"Just a bright boy," Max said. He leaned forward and took the ham and eggs. Both men ate with their gloves on. George watched them eat.

"What are *you* looking at?" Max looked at George.

"Nothing."

"The hell you were. You were looking at me."

"Maybe the boy meant it for a joke, Max," Al said.

George laughed.

"*You* don't have to laugh," Max said to him. "*You* don't have to laugh at all, see?"

"All right," said George.

"So he thinks it's all right." Max turned to Al. "He thinks it's all right. That's a good one."

"Oh, he's a thinker," Al said. They went on eating.

"What's the bright boy's name down the counter?" Al asked Max.

"Hey, bright boy," Max said to Nick. "You go around on the other side of the counter with your boy friend."

"What's the idea?" Nick asked.

"There isn't any idea."

"You better go around, bright boy," Al said. Nick went around behind the counter.

"What's the idea?" George asked.

"None of your damn business," Al said. "Who's out in the kitchen?"

"The nigger."

"What do you mean the nigger?"

"The nigger that cooks."

"Tell him to come in."

"What's the idea?"

"Tell him to come in."

"Where do you think you are?"

"We know damn well where we are," the man called Max said. "Do we look silly?"

"You talk silly," Al said to him. "What the hell do you argue with this kid for? Listen," he said to George, "tell the nigger to come out here."

"What are you going to do to him?"

"Nothing. Use your head, bright boy. What would we do to a nigger?"

George opened the slit that opened back into the kitchen. "Sam," he called. "Come in here a minute."

The door to the kitchen opened and the nigger came in. "What was it?" he asked. The two men at the counter took a look at him.

"All right, nigger. You stand right there," Al said.

Sam, the nigger, standing in his apron, looked at the two men sitting at the counter. "Yes, sir," he said. Al got down from his stool.

"I'm going back to the kitchen with the nigger and bright boy," he said. "Go on back to the kitchen, nigger. You go with him, bright boy." The little man walked after Nick and Sam, the cook, back into the kitchen. The door shut after them. The man called Max sat at the counter opposite George. He didn't look at George but looked in the mirror that ran along back of the counter. Henry's had been made over from a saloon into a lunch-counter.

"Well, bright boy," Max said, looking into the mirror, "why don't you say something?"

"What's it all about?"

"Hey, Al," Max called, "bright boy wants to know what it's all about."

"Why don't you tell him?" Al's voice came from the kitchen.

"What do you think it's all about?"

"I don't know."

"What do you think?"

Max looked into the mirror all the time he was talking.

"I wouldn't say."

"Hey, Al, bright boy says he wouldn't say what he thinks it's all about."

"I can hear you, all right," Al said from the kitchen. He had propped open the slit that dishes passed through into the kitchen with a catsup bottle. "Listen, bright boy," he said from the kitchen to George. "Stand a little further along the bar. You move a little to the left, Max." He was like a photographer arranging for a group picture.

"Talk to me, bright boy," Max said. "What do you think's going to happen?"

George did not say anything.

"I'll tell you," Max said. "We're going to kill a Swede. Do you know a big Swede named Ole Andreson?"

"Yes."

"He comes here to eat every night, don't he?"

"Sometimes he comes here."

"He comes here at six o'clock, don't he?"

"If he comes."

"We know all that, bright boy," Max said. "Talk about something else. Ever go to the movies?"

"Once in a while."

"You ought to go to the movies more. The movies are fine for a bright boy like you."

"What are you going to kill Ole Andreson for? What did he ever do to you?"

"He never had a chance to do anything to us. He never even seen us."

"And he's only going to see us once," Al said from the kitchen.

"What are you going to kill him for, then?" George asked.

"We're killing him for a friend. Just to oblige a friend, bright boy."

"Shut up," said Al from the kitchen. "You talk too goddam much."

"Well, I got to keep bright boy amused. Don't I, bright boy?"

"You talk too damn much," Al said. "The nigger and my bright boy are amused by themselves. I got them tied up like a couple of girl friends in the convent."

"I suppose you were in a convent?"

"You never know."

"You were in a kosher convent. That's where you were."

George looked up at the clock.

"If anybody comes in you tell them the cook is off, and if they keep after it, you tell them you'll go back and cook yourself. Do you get that bright boy?"

"All right," George said. "What you going to do with us afterward?"

"That'll depend," Max said. "That's one of those things you never know at the time."

George looked up at the clock. It was a quarter past six. The door from the street opened. A street-car motorman came in.

"Hello, George," he said. "Can I get supper?"

"Sam's gone out," George said. "He'll be back in about half an hour."

"I'd better go up the street," the motorman said. George looked at the clock. It was twenty minutes past six.

"That was nice, bright boy," Max said. "You're a regular little gentleman."

"He knew I'd blow his head off," Al said from the kitchen.

"No," said Max. "It ain't that. Bright boy is nice. He's a nice boy. I like him."

At six-fifty-five George said: "He's not coming."

Two other people had been in the lunch-room. Once George had gone out to the kitchen and made a ham-and-egg sandwich "to go" that a man wanted to take with him. Inside the kitchen he saw Al, his derby hat tipped back, sitting on a stool beside the wicket with the muzzle of a sawed-off shotgun resting on the ledge. Nick and the cook were back to back in the corner, a towel tied in each of their mouths. George had cooked the sandwich, wrapped it up in oiled paper, put it in a bag, brought it in, and the man had paid for it and gone out.

"Bright boy can do everything," Max said. "He can cook and everything. You'd make some girl a nice wife, bright boy."

"Yes?" George said. "Your friend, Ole Andreson, isn't going to come."

"We'll give him ten minutes," Max said.

Max watched the mirror and the clock. The hands of the clock marked seven o'clock, and then five minutes past seven.

"Come on, Al," said Max. "We better go. He's not coming."

"Better give him five minutes," Al said from the kitchen.

In the five minutes a man came in, and George explained that the cook was sick.

"Why the hell don't you get another cook?" the man asked. "Aren't you running a lunch-counter?" He went out.

"Come on, Al," Max said.

"What about the two bright boys and the nigger?"

"They're all right."

"You think so?"

"Sure. We're through with it."

"I don't like it," said Al. "It's sloppy. You talk too much."

"Oh, what the hell," said Max. "We got to keep amused, haven't we?"

"You talk too much, all the same," Al said. He came out from the kitchen. The cut-off barrels of the shotgun made a slight bulge under the waist of his too tight-fitting overcoat. He straightened his coat with his gloved hands.

"So long, bright boy," he said to George. "You got a lot of luck."

"That's the truth," Max said. "You ought to play the races, bright boy."

The two of them went out the door. George watched them, through the window, pass under the arc-light and cross the street. In their tight overcoats and derby hats they looked like a vaudeville team. George went back through the swinging-door into the kitchen and untied Nick and the cook.

"I don't want any more of that," said Sam, the cook. "I don't want any more of that."

Nick stood up. He had never had a towel in his mouth before.

"Say," he said. "What the hell?" He was trying to swagger it off.

"They were going to kill Ole Andreson," George said. "They were going to shoot him when he came in to eat."

"Ole Andreson?"

"Sure."

The cook felt the corners of his mouth with his thumbs.

"They all gone?" he asked.

"Yeah," said George. "They're gone now."

"I don't like it," said the cook. "I don't like any of it at all."

"Listen," George said to Nick. "You better go see Ole Andreson."

"All right."

"You better not have anything to do with it at all," Sam, the cook, said. "You better stay way out of it."

"Don't go if you don't want to," George said.

"Mixing up in this ain't going to get you anywhere," the cook said. "You stay out of it."

"I'll go see him," Nick said to George. "Where does he live?"

The cook turned away.

"Little boys always know what they want to do," he said.

"He lives up at Hirsch's rooming-house," George said to Nick.

"I'll go up there."

Outside the arc-light shone through the bare branches of a tree. Nick walked up the street beside the car-tracks and turned at the next arc-light down a side-street. Three houses up the street was Hirsch's rooming-house. Nick walked up the two steps and pushed the bell. A woman came to the door.

"Is Ole Andreson here?"

"Do you want to see him?"

"Yes, if he's in."

Nick followed the woman up a flight of stairs and back to the end of a corridor. She knocked on the door.

"Who is it?"

"It's somebody to see you, Mr. Andreson," the woman said.

"It's Nick Adams."

"Come in."

Nick opened the door and went into the room. Ole Andreson was lying on the bed with all his clothes on. He had been a heavyweight prizefighter and he was too long for the bed. He lay with his head on two pillows. He did not look at Nick.

"What was it?" he asked.

"I was up at Henry's," Nick said, "and two fellows came in and tied up me and the cook, and they said they were going to kill you."

It sounded silly when he said it. Ole Andreson said nothing.

"They put us out in the kitchen," Nick went on. "They were going to shoot you when you came in to supper."

Ole Andreson looked at the wall and did not say anything.

"George thought I better come and tell you about it."

"There isn't anything I can do about it," Ole Andreson said.

"I'll tell you what they were like."

"I don't want to know what they were like," Ole Andreson said. He looked at the wall. "Thanks for coming to tell me about it."

"That's all right."

Nick looked at the big man lying on the bed.

"Don't you want me to go and see the police?"

"No," Ole Andreson said. "That wouldn't do any good."

"Isn't there something I could do?"

"No. There ain't anything to do."

"Maybe it was just a bluff."

"No. It ain't just a bluff."

Ole Andreson rolled over toward the wall.

"The only thing is," he said, talking toward the wall, "I just can't make up my mind to go out. I been in here all day."

"Couldn't you get out of town?"

"No," Ole Andreson said. "I'm through with all that running around."

He looked at the wall.

"There ain't anything to do now."

"Couldn't you fix it up some way?"

"No. I got in wrong." He talked in the same flat voice. "There ain't anything to do. After a while I'll make up my mind to go out."

"I better go back and see George," Nick said.

"So long," said Ole Andreson. He did not look toward Nick. "Thanks for coming around."

Nick went out. As he shut the door he saw Ole Andreson with all his clothes on, lying on the bed looking at the wall.

"He's been in his room all day," the landlady said down-stairs. "I guess he don't feel well. I said to him: 'Mr. Andreson, you ought to go out and take a walk on a nice fall day like this,' but he didn't feel like it."

"He doesn't want to go out."

"I'm sorry he don't feel well," the woman said. "He's an awfully nice man. He was in the ring, you know."

"I know it."

"You'd never know it except from the way his face is," the woman said. They stood talking just inside the street door. "He's just as gentle."

"Well, good-night, Mrs. Hirsch," Nick said.

"I'm not Mrs. Hirsch," the woman said. "She owns the place. I just look after it for her. I'm Mrs. Bell."

"Well, good-night, Mrs. Bell," Nick said.

"Good-night," the woman said.

Nick walked up the dark street to the corner under the arc-light, and then along the car-tracks to Henry's eating-house. George was inside, back of the counter.

"Did you see Ole?"

"Yes," said Nick. "He's in his room and he won't go out."

The cook opened the door from the kitchen when he heard Nick's voice. "I don't even listen to it," he said and shut the door.

"Did you tell him about it?" George asked.

"Sure. I told him but he knows what it's all about."

"What's he going to do?"

"Nothing."

"They'll kill him."

"I guess they will."

"He must have got mixed up in something in Chicago."

"I guess so," said Nick.

"It's a hell of a thing."

"It's an awful thing," Nick said.

They did not say anything. George reached down for a towel and wiped the counter.

"I wonder what he did?" Nick said.

"Double-crossed somebody. That's what they kill them for."

"I'm going to get out of this town," Nick said.

"Yes," said George. "That's a good thing to do."

"I can't stand to think about him waiting in the room and knowing he's going to get it. It's too damned awful."

"Well," said George, "you better not think about it."

Ralph Ellison

Battle Royal

It goes a long way back, some twenty years. All my life I had been looking for something, and everywhere I turned someone tried to tell me what it was. I accepted their answers too, though they were often in contradiction and even self-contradictory. I was naïve. I was looking for myself and asking everyone except myself questions which I, and only I, could answer. It took me a long time and much painful boomeranging of my expectations to achieve a realization everyone else appears to have been born with: That I am nobody but myself. But first I had to discover that I am an invisible man!

And yet I am no freak of nature, nor of history. I was in the cards, other things having been equal (or unequal) eighty-five years ago. I am not ashamed of my grandparents for having been slaves. I am only ashamed of myself for having at one time been ashamed. About eighty-five years ago they were told they were free, united with others of our country in everything pertaining to the common good, and, in everything social, separate like the fingers of the hand. And they believed it. They exulted in it. They stayed in their place, worked hard, and brought up my father to do the same. But my grandfather is the one. He was an odd old guy, my grandfather, and I am told I take after him. It was he who caused the trouble. On his deathbed he called my father to him and said, "Son, after I'm gone I want you to keep up the good fight. I never told you, but our life is a war and I have been a traitor all my born days, a spy in the enemy's country ever since I give up my gun back in the Reconstruction. Live with your head in the lion's mouth. I want you to overcome 'em with yeses, undermine 'em with grins, agree 'em to death and destruction, let 'em swoller you till they vomit or bust wide open." They thought the old man had gone out of his mind. He had been the meekest of men. The younger children were rushed from the room, the shades drawn and the flame of the lamp turned so low that it sputtered on the wick like the old man's breathing: "Learn it to the younguns," he whispered fiercely; then he died.

But my folks were more alarmed over his last words than over his dying. It was as though he had not died at all, his words caused so much anxiety. I was warned emphatically to forget what he had said and, indeed, this is the first time it has been mentioned outside the family circle. It had a tremendous effect upon me, however. I could never be sure of what he meant. Grandfather had been a quiet old man who never made any trouble, yet on his deathbed he had called himself a traitor and a spy, and he had spoken of his meekness as a dangerous activity. It became a constant puzzle which lay unanswered in the back of my mind. And whenever things went well for me I remembered my grandfather and felt guilty and uncomfortable. It was as though I was carrying out his advice in spite of myself. And to make it worse, everyone loved me for it. I was praised by the most lily-white men of the town. I was considered an example of desirable conduct—just as my grandfather had been. And what puzzled me was that the old man had defined it as *treachery*. When I was praised for my conduct I felt a guilt that in some way I was doing something that was really against the wishes of the white folks, that if they had understood they would have desired me to act just the opposite, that I should have been sulky and mean, and that that really would have been what they wanted, even though they were fooled and thought they wanted me to act as I did. It made me afraid that some day they would look upon me as a traitor and I would be lost. Still I was more afraid to act any other way because they didn't like that at all. The old man's words were like a curse. On my graduation day I delivered an oration in which I showed that humility was the secret, indeed, the very essence of progress. (Not that I believed this—how could I, remembering my grandfather?—I only believed that it worked.) It was a great success. Everyone praised me and I was invited to give the speech at a gathering of the town's leading white citizens. It was a triumph for our whole community.

It was in the main ballroom of the leading hotel. When I got there I discovered that it was on the occasion of a smoker, and I was told that since I was to be there anyway I might as well take part in the battle royal to be fought by some of my schoolmates as part of the entertainment. The battle royal came first.

All of the town's big shots were there in their tuxedoes, wolfing down the buffet foods, drinking beer and whiskey and smoking black cigars. It was a large room with a high ceiling. Chairs were arranged in neat rows around three sides of a portable boxing ring. The fourth side was clear, revealing a gleaming space of polished floor. I had some misgivings over the battle royal, by the way. Not from a distaste for fighting but because I didn't care too much for the other fellows who were to take part. They were tough guys who seemed to have no grandfather's curse worrying their minds. No one could mistake their toughness. And besides, I suspected that fighting a battle royal might detract from the dignity of my speech. In those pre-invisible days I visualized myself as a potential Booker T. Washington. But the other fellows didn't care too much for me either, and there were nine of them. I felt superior to them in my way, and I didn't like the manner in which we were all crowded together into the servants' elevator. Nor did they like my being there. In fact, as the warmly lighted floors flashed past the elevator we had words over the fact that I, by taking part in the fight, had knocked one of their friends out of a night's work.

We were led out of the elevator through a rococo hall into an anteroom and told to get into our fighting togs. Each of us was issued a pair of boxing gloves and ushered out into the big mirrored hall, which we entered looking cautiously about us and whispering, lest we might accidentally be heard above the noise of the room. It was foggy with cigar smoke. And already the whiskey was taking effect. I was shocked to see some of the most important men of the town quite tipsy. They were all there—bankers, lawyers, judges, doctors, fire chiefs, teachers, merchants. Even one of the more fashionable pastors. Something we could not see was going on up front. A clarinet was vibrating sensuously and the men were standing up and moving eagerly forward. We were a small tight group, clustered together, our bare upper bodies touching and shining with anticipatory sweat; while up front the big shots were becoming increasingly excited over something we still could not see. Suddenly I heard the school superintendent, who had told me to come, yell, "Bring up the shines, gentlemen! Bring up the little shines!"

We were rushed up to the front of the ballroom, where it smelled even more strongly of tobacco and whiskey. Then we were pushed into place. I almost wet my pants. A sea of faces, some hostile, some amused, ringed around us, and in the center, facing us, stood a magnificent blonde—stark naked. There was dead silence. I felt a blast of cold air chill me. I tried to back away, but they were behind me and around me. Some of the boys stood with lowered heads, trembling. I felt a wave of irrational guilt and fear. My teeth chattered, my skin turned to goose flesh, my knees knocked. Yet I was strongly attracted and looked in spite of myself. Had the price of looking been blindness, I would have looked. The hair was yellow like that of a circus kewpie doll, the face heavily powdered and rouged, as though to form an abstract mask, the eyes hollow and smeared a cool blue, the color of a baboon's butt. I felt a desire to spit upon her as my eyes brushed slowly over her body. Her breasts were firm and round as the domes of East Indian temples, and I stood so close as to see the fine skin texture and beads of pearly perspiration glistening like dew around the pink and erected buds of her nipples. I wanted at one and the same time to run from the room, to sink through the floor, or go to her and cover her from my eyes and the eyes of the others with my body; to feel the soft thighs, to caress her and destroy her, to love her and murder her, to hide from her, and yet to stroke where below the small American flag tattooed upon her belly her thighs formed a capital V. I had a notion that of all in the room she saw only me with her impersonal eyes.

And then she began to dance, a slow sensuous movement; the smoke of a hundred cigars clinging to her like the thinnest of veils. She seemed like a fair bird-girl girdled in veils calling to me from the angry surface of some gray and threatening sea. I was transported. Then I became aware of the clarinet playing and the big shots yelling at us. Some threatened us if we looked and others if we did not. On my right I saw one boy faint. And now a man grabbed a silver pitcher from a table and stepped close as he dashed ice water upon him and stood him up and forced two of us to support him as his head hung and moans issued from his thick bluish lips. Another boy began to plead to go home. He was the largest of the group, wearing dark red fighting trunks much too small to conceal the erection which projected from him as though in answer to the insinuating low-registered moaning of the clarinet. He tried to hide himself with his boxing gloves.

And all the while the blonde continued dancing, smiling faintly at the big shots who watched her with fascination, and faintly smiling at our fear. I noticed a certain merchant who followed her hungrily, his lips loose and drooling. He was a large man who wore diamond studs in a shirtfront which swelled with the ample paunch underneath, and each time the blonde swayed her undulating hips he ran his hand through the thin hair of his bald head and, with his arms upheld, his posture clumsy like that of an intoxicated panda, wound his belly in a slow and obscene grind. This creature was completely hypnotized. The music had quickened. As the dancer flung herself about with a detached expression on her face, the men began reaching out to touch her. I could see their beefy fingers sink into the soft flesh. Some of the others tried to stop them and she began to move around the floor in graceful circles, as they gave chase, slipping and sliding over the polished floor. It was mad. Chairs went crashing, drinks were spilt, as they ran laughing and howling after her. They caught her just as she reached a door, raised her from the floor, and tossed her as college boys are tossed at a hazing, and above her red, fixed-smiling lips I saw the terror and disgust in her eyes, almost like my own terror and that which I saw in some of the other boys. As I watched, they tossed her twice and her soft breasts seemed to flatten against the air and her legs flung wildly as she spun. Some of the more sober ones helped her to escape. And I started off the floor, heading for the anteroom with the rest of the boys.

Some were still crying and in hysteria. But as we tried to leave we were stopped and ordered to get into the ring. There was nothing to do but what we were told. All ten of us climbed under the ropes and allowed ourselves to be blindfolded with broad bands of white cloth. One of the men seemed to feel a bit sympathetic and tried to cheer us up as we stood with our backs against the ropes. Some of us tried to grin. "See that boy over there?" one of the men said. "I want you to run across at the bell and give it to him right in

the belly. If you don't get him, I'm going to get you. I don't like his looks."
Each of us was told the same. The blindfolds were put on. Yet even then I
had been going over my speech. In my mind each word was as bright as flame.
I felt the cloth pressed into place, and frowned so that it would be loosened
when I relaxed.

But now I felt a sudden fit of blind terror. I was unused to darkness. It was
as though I had suddenly found myself in a dark room filled with poisonous
cottonmouths. I could hear the bleary voices yelling insistently for the battle
royal to begin.

"Get going in there!"

"Let me at that big nigger!"

I strained to pick up the school superintendent's voice, as though to squeeze
some security out of that slightly more familiar sound.

"Let me at those black sonsabitches!" someone yelled.

"No, Jackson no!" another voice yelled. "Here, somebody, help me hold
Jack."

"I want to get at that ginger-colored nigger. Tear him limb from limb," the
first voice yelled.

I stood against the ropes trembling. For in those days I was what they called
ginger-colored, and he sounded as though he might crunch me between his
teeth like a crisp ginger cookie.

Quite a struggle was going on. Chairs were being kicked about and I could
hear voices grunting as with a terrific effort. I wanted to see, to see more
desperately than ever before. But the blindfold was as tight as a thick skin-
puckering scab and when I raised my gloved hands to push the layers of white
aside a voice yelled, "Oh, no you don't, black bastard! Leave that alone!"

"Ring the bell before Jackson kills him a coon!" someone boomed in the
sudden silence. And I heard the bell clang and the sound of the feet scuffling
forward.

A glove smacked against my head. I pivoted, striking out stiffly as someone
went past, and felt the jar ripple along the length of my arm to my shoulder.
Then it seemed as though all nine of the boys had turned upon me at once.
Blows pounded me from all sides while I struck out as best I could. So many
blows landed upon me that I wondered if I were not the only blindfolded
fighter in the ring, or if the man called Jackson hadn't succeeded in getting me
after all.

Blindfolded, I could no longer control my motions. I had no dignity. I
stumbled about like a baby or a drunken man. The smoke had become thicker
and with each new blow it seemed to sear and further restrict my lungs. My
saliva became like hot bitter glue. A glove connected with my head, filling my
mouth with warm blood. It was everywhere. I could not tell if the moisture
I felt upon my body was sweat or blood. A blow landed hard against the nape
of my neck. I felt myself going over, my head hitting the floor. Streaks of
blue light filled the black world behind the blindfold. I lay prone, pretending
that I was knocked out, but felt myself seized by hands and yanked to my feet.

"Get going, black boy! Mix it up!" My arms were like lead, my head smarting from blows. I managed to feel my way to the ropes and held on, trying to catch my breath. A glove landed in my mid-section and I went over again, feeling as though the smoke had become a knife jabbed into my guts. Pushed this way and that by the legs milling around me, I finally pulled erect and discovered that I could see the black, sweat-washed forms weaving in the smoky-blue atmosphere like drunken dancers weaving to the rapid drumlike thuds of blows.

Everyone fought hysterically. It was complete anarchy. Everybody fought everybody else. No group fought together for long. Two, three, four, fought one, then turned to fight each other, were themselves attacked. Blows landed below the belt and in the kidney, with the gloves open as well as closed, and with my eye partly opened now there was not so much terror. I moved carefully, avoiding blows, although not too many to attract attention, fighting from group to group. The boys groped about like blind, cautious crabs crouching to protect their mid-sections, their heads pulled in short against their shoulders, their arms stretched nervously before them, with their fists testing the smoke-filled air like the knobbed feelers of hypersensitive snails. In one corner I glimpsed a boy violently punching the air and heard him scream in pain as he smashed his hand against a ring post. For a second I saw him bent over holding his hand, then going down as a blow caught his unprotected head. I played one group against the other, slipping in and throwing a punch then stepping out of range while pushing the others into the melee to take the blows blindly aimed at me. The smoke was agonizing and there were no rounds, no bells at three minute intervals to relieve our exhaustion. The room spun round me, a swirl of lights, smoke, sweating bodies surrounded by tense white faces. I bled from both nose and mouth, the blood spattering upon my chest.

The men kept yelling, "Slug him, black boy! Knock his guts out!"

"Uppercut him! Kill him! Kill that big boy!"

Taking a fake fall, I saw a boy going down heavily beside me as though we were felled by a single blow, saw a sneaker-clad foot shoot into his groin as the two who had knocked him down stumbled upon him. I rolled out of range, feeling a twingle of nausea.

The harder we fought the more threatening the men became. And yet, I had begun to worry about my speech again. How would it go? Would they recognize my ability? What would they give me?

I was fighting automatically when suddenly I noticed that one after another of the boys was leaving the ring. I was surprised, filled with panic, as though I had been left alone with an unknown danger. Then I understood. The boys had arranged it among themselves. It was the custom for the two men left in the ring to slug it out for the winner's prize. I discovered this too late. When the bell sounded two men in tuxedoes leaped into the ring and removed the blindfold. I found myself facing Tatlock, the biggest of the gang. I felt sick at my stomach. Hardly had the bell stopped ringing in my ears than it clanged again and I saw him moving swiftly toward me. Thinking of nothing else to do I hit him smash on the nose. He kept coming, bringing the rank sharp violence of stale sweat. His face was a black blank of a face, only his eyes alive—with hate of me and aglow with a feverish terror from what had happened to us all. I became anxious. I wanted to deliver my speech and he came at me as though he meant to beat it out of me. I smashed him again and again, taking his blows as they came. Then on a sudden impulse I struck him lightly as we clinched, I whispered, "Fake like I knocked you out, you can have the prize."

"I'll break your behind," he whispered hoarsely.

"For *them*?"

"For *me*, sonofabitch!"

They were yelling for us to break it up and Tatlock spun me half around with a blow, and as a joggled camera sweeps in a reeling scene, I saw the howling red faces crouching tense beneath the cloud of blue-gray smoke. For a moment the world wavered, unraveled, flowed, then my head cleared and Tatlock bounced before me. That fluttering shadow before my eyes was his jabbing left hand. Then falling forward, my head against his damp shoulder, I whispered,

"I'll make it five dollars more."

"Go to hell!"

But his muscles relaxed a trifle beneath my pressure and I breathed, "Seven?"

"Give it to your ma," he said, ripping me beneath the heart.

And while I still held him I butted him and moved away. I felt myself bombarded with punches. I fought back with hopeless desperation. I wanted to deliver my speech more than anything else in the world, because I felt that only these men could judge my ability, and now this stupid clown was ruining my chances. I began fighting carefully now, moving in to punch him and out again with my greater speed. A lucky blow to his chin and I had him going too—until I heard a loud voice yell, "I got my money on the big boy."

Hearing this, I almost dropped my guard. I was confused: Should I try to win against the voice out there? Would not this go against my speech, and was not this a moment for humility, for nonresistance? A blow to my head as I danced about sent my right eye popping like a jack-in-the-box and settled my dilemma. The room went red as I fell. It was a dream fall, my body languid and fastidious as to where to land, until the floor became impatient and smashed up to meet me. A moment later I came to. An hypnotic voice said FIVE emphatically. And I lay there, hazily watching a dark red spot of my own blood shaping itself into a butterfly, glistening and soaking into the soiled gray world of the canvas.

When the voice drawled TEN I was lifted up and dragged to a chair. I sat dazed. My eye pained and swelled with each throb of my pounding heart and I wondered if now I would be allowed to speak. I was wringing wet, my mouth still bleeding. We were grouped along the wall now. The other boys ignored me as they congratulated Tatlock and speculated as to how much they would be paid. One boy whimpered over his smashed hand. Looking up front, I saw attendants in white jackets rolling the portable ring away and placing a small square rug in the vacant space surrounded by chairs. Perhaps, I thought, I will stand on the rug to deliver my speech.

Then the M.C. called to us, "Come on up here boys and get your money."

We ran forward to where the men laughed and talked in their chairs, waiting. Everyone seemed friendly now.

"There it is on the rug," the man said. I saw the rug covered with coins of all dimensions and a few crumpled bills. But what excited me, scattered here and there, were the gold pieces.

"Boys, it's all yours," the man said. "You get all you grab."

"That's right, Sambo," a blond man said, winking at me confidentially.

I trembled with excitement, forgetting my pain. I would get the gold and the bills, I thought. I would use both hands. I would throw my body against the boys nearest to me to block them from the gold.

"Get down around the rug now," the man commanded, "and don't anyone touch it until I give the signal."

"This ought to be good," I heard.

As told, we got around the square rug on our knees. Slowly the man raised his freckled hand as we followed it upward with our eyes.

I heard, "These niggers look like they're about to pray!"

Then, "Ready," the man said. "Go!"

I lunged for a yellow coin lying on the blue design of the carpet, touching it and sending a surprised shriek to join those rising around me. I tried frantically to remove my hand but could not let go. A hot, violent force tore through my body, shaking me like a wet rat. The rug was electrified. The hair bristled up on my head as I shook myself free. My muscles jumped, my nerves jangled, writhed. But I saw this was not stopping the other boys. Laughing in fear and embarrassment, some were holding back and scooping up the coins knocked off by the painful contortions of the others. The men roared above us as we struggled.

"Pick it up, goddamnit, pick it up!" someone called like a bass-voiced parrot. "Go on, get it!"

I crawled rapidly around the floor, picking up the coins, trying to avoid the coppers and to get greenbacks and the gold. Ignoring the shock by laughing, as I brushed the coins off quickly, I discovered that I could contain the electricity—a contradiction, but it works. Then the men began to push us onto the rug. Laughing embarrassedly, we struggled out of their hands and kept after the coins. We were all wet and slippery and hard to hold. Suddenly I saw a boy lifted into the air, glistening with sweat like a circus seal, and dropped, his wet back landing flush upon the charged rug, heard him yell and saw him literally dance upon his back, his elbows beating a frenzied tattoo upon the floor, his muscles twitching like the flesh of a horse stung by many flies. When he finally rolled off, his face was gray and no one stopped him when he ran from the floor amid booming laughter.

"Get the money," the M.C. called. "That's good hard American cash!"

And we snatched and grabbed, snatched and grabbed. I was careful not to come too close to the rug now, and when I felt the hot whiskey breath descend upon me like a cloud of foul air I reached out and grabbed the leg of a chair. It was occupied and I held on desperately.

"Leggo, nigger! Leggo!"

The huge face wavered down to mine as he tried to push me free. But my body was slippery and he was too drunk. It was Mr. Colcord, who owned a chain of movie houses and "entertainment palaces." Each time he grabbed me I slipped out of his hands. It became a real struggle. I feared the rug more than I did the drunk, so I held on, surprising myself for a moment by trying to topple *him* upon the rug. It was such an enormous idea that I found myself actually carrying it out. I tried not to be obvious, yet when I grabbed his leg, trying to tumble him out of the chair, he raised up roaring with laughter, and, looking at me with soberness dead in the eye, kicked me viciously in the chest. The chair leg flew out of my hand and I felt myself going and rolled. It was as though I had rolled through a bed of hot coals. It seemed a whole century would pass before I rolled free, a century in which I was seared through the deepest levels of my body to the fearful breath within me and the breath seared and heated to the point of explosion. It'll all be over in a flash, I thought as I rolled clear. It'll all be over in a flash.

But not yet, the men on the other side were waiting, red faces swollen as though from apoplexy as they bent forward in their chairs. Seeing their fingers coming toward me I rolled away as a fumbled football rolls off the receiver's fingertips, back into the coals. That time I luckily sent the rug sliding out of place and heard the coins ringing against the floor and the boys scuffling to pick them up and the M.C. calling, "All right, boys, that's all. Go get dressed and get your money."

I was limp as a dish rag. My back felt as thought it had been beaten with wires.

When we had dressed the M.C. came in and gave us each five dollars, except Tatlock, who got ten for being last in the ring. Then he told us to leave. I was not to get a chance to deliver my speech, I thought. I was going out into the dim alley in despair when I was stopped and told to go back. I returned to the ballroom, where the men were pushing back their chairs and gathering in groups to talk.

The M.C. knocked on a table for quiet. "Gentlemen," he said, "we almost forgot an important part of the program. A most serious part, gentlemen. This boy was brought here to deliver a speech which he made at his graduation yesterday . . ."

"Bravo!"

"I'm told that he is the smartest boy we've got out there in Greenwood. I'm told that he knows more big words than a pocket-sized dictionary."

Much applause and laughter.

"So now, gentlemen, I want you to give him your attention."

There was still laughter as I faced them, my mouth dry, my eye throbbing. I began slowly, but evidently my throat was tense, because they began shouting, "Louder! Louder!"

"We of the younger generation extol the wisdom of that great leader and educator," I shouted, "who first spoke these flaming words of wisdom: 'A ship lost at sea for many days suddenly sighted a friendly vessel. From the mast of the unfortunate vessel was seen a signal: "Water, water; we die of thirst!" The answer from the friendly vessel came back: "Cast down your bucket where you are." The captain of the distressed vessel, at last heeding the injunction, cast down his bucket, and it came up full of fresh sparkling water from the mouth of the Amazon River.' And like him I say, and in his words, 'To those of my race who depend upon bettering their condition in a foreign land, or who underestimate the importance of cultivating friendly relations with the Southern white man, who is his next-door neighbor, I would say: "Cast down your bucket where you are"—cast it down in making friends in every manly way of the people of all races by whom we are surrounded . . .' "

I spoke automatically and with such fervor that I did not realize that the men were still talking and laughing until my dry mouth, filling up with blood from the cut, almost strangled me. I coughed, wanting to stop and go to one of the tall brass, sand-filled spittoons to relieve myself, but a few of the men, especially the superintendent, were listening and I was afraid. So I gulped it down, blood, saliva and all, and continued. (What powers of endurance I had during those days! What enthusiasm! What a belief in the rightness of things!) I spoke even louder in spite of the pain. But still they talked and still they laughed, as though deaf with cotton in dirty ears. So I spoke with greater emotional emphasis. I closed my ears and swallowed blood until I was nauseated. The speech seemed a hundred times as long as before, but I could not leave out a single word. All had to be said, each memorized nuance considered, rendered. Nor was that all. Whenever I uttered a word of three or more syllables a group of voices would yell for me to repeat it. I used the phrase "social responsibility" and they yelled:

"What's that word you say, boy?"

"Social responsibility," I said.

"What?"

"Social . . ."

"Louder."

". . . responsibility."

"More!"

"Respon—"

"Repeat!"

"—sibility."

The room filled with the uproar of laughter until, no doubt, distracted by having to gulp down my blood, I made a mistake and yelled a phrase I had often seen denounced in newspaper editorials, heard debated in private.

"Social . . ."

"What?" they yelled.

". . . equality—"

The laughter hung smokelike in the sudden stillness. I opened my eyes, puzzled. Sounds of displeasure filled the róom. The M.C. rushed forward. They shouted hostile phrases at me. But I did not understand.

A small dry mustached man in the front row blared out, "Say that slowly, son!"

"What sir?"

"What you just said!"

"Social responsibility, sir," I said.

"You weren't being smart, were you, boy?" he said, not unkindly.

"No, sir!"

"You sure that about 'equality' was a mistake?"

"Oh, yes, sir," I said. "I was swallowing blood."

"Well, you had better speak more slowly so we can understand. We mean to do right by you, but you've got to know your place at all times. All right, now, go on with your speech."

I was afraid. I wanted to leave but I wanted also to speak and I was afraid they'd snatch me down.

"Thank you, sir," I said, beginning where I had left off, and having them ignore me as before.

Yet when I finished there was a thunderous applause. I was surprised to see the superintendent come forth with a package wrapped in white tissue paper, and, gesturing for quiet, address the men.

"Gentlemen, you see that I did not overpraise this boy. He makes a good speech and some day he'll lead his people in the proper paths. And I don't have to tell you that that is important in these days and times. This is a good, smart boy, and so to encourage him in the right direction, in the name of the Board of Education I wish to present him a prize in the form of this . . ."

He paused, removing the tissue paper and revealing a gleaming calfskin brief case.

". . . in the form of this first-class article from Shad Whitmore's shop."

"Boy," he said, addressing me, "take this prize and keep it well. Consider it a badge of office. Prize it. Keep developing as you are and some day it will be filled with important papers that will help shape the destiny of your people."

I was so moved that I could hardly express my thanks. A rope of bloody saliva forming a shape like an undiscovered continent drooled upon the the leather and I wiped it quickly away. I felt an importance that I had never dreamed.

"Open it and see what's inside," I was told.

My fingers a-tremble, I complied, smelling the fresh leather and finding an official-looking document inside. It was a scholarship to the state college for Negroes. My eyes filled with tears and I ran awkwardly off the floor.

I was overjoyed; I did not even mind when I discovered that the gold pieces I had scrambled for were brass pocket tokens advertising a certain make of automobile.

When I reached home everyone was excited. Next day the neighbors came to congratulate me. I even felt safe from grandfather, whose deathbed curse usually spoiled my triumphs. I stood beneath his photograph with my brief case in hand and smiled triumphantly into his stolid black peasant's face. It was a face that fascinated me. The eyes seemed to follow everywhere I went.

That night I dreamed I was at a circus with him and that he refused to laugh at the clowns no matter what they did. Then later he told me to open my brief case and read what was inside and I did, finding an official envelope stamped with the state seal; and inside the envelope I found another and another, endlessly, and I thought I would fall of weariness. "Them's years," he said. "Now open that one." And I did and in it I found an engraved document containing a short message in letters of gold. "Read it," my grandfather said. "Out loud."

"To Whom It May Concern," I intoned. "Keep This Nigger-Boy Running."

I awoke with the old man's laughter ringing in my ears.

Good Country People

Besides the neutral expression that she wore when she was alone, Mrs. Freeman had two others, forward and reverse, that she used for all her human dealings. Her forward expression was steady and driving like the advance of a heavy truck. Her eyes never swerved to left or right but turned as the story turned as if they followed a yellow line down the center of it. She seldom used the other expression because it was not often necessary for her to retract a statement, but when she did, her face came to a complete stop, there was an almost imperceptible movement of her black eyes, during which they seemed to be receding, and then the observer would see that Mrs. Freeman, though she might stand there as real as several grain sacks thrown on top of each other, was no longer there in spirit. As for getting anything across to her when this was the case, Mrs. Hopewell had given it up. She might talk her head off. Mrs. Freeman could never be brought to admit herself wrong on any point. She would stand there and if she could be brought to say anything, it was something like, "Well, I wouldn't of said it was and I wouldn't of said it wasn't," or letting her gaze range over the top kitchen shelf where there was an assortment of dusty bottles, she might remark, "I see you ain't ate many of them figs you put up last summer."

They carried on their most important business in the kitchen at breakfast. Every morning Mrs. Hopewell got up at seven o'clock and lit her gas heater and Joy's. Joy was her daughter, a large blonde girl who had an artificial leg. Mrs. Hopewell thought of her as a child though she was thirty-two years old and highly educated. Joy would get up while her mother was eating and lumber into the bathroom and slam the door, and before long, Mrs. Freeman would arrive at the back door. Joy would hear her mother call, "Come on in," and then they would talk for a while in low voices that were indistinguishable in the bathroom. By the time Joy came in, they had usually finished the weather report and were on one or the other of Mrs. Freeman's daughters, Glynese or Carramae. Joy called them Glycerin and Caramel. Glynese, a redhead, was eighteen and had many admirers; Carramae, a blonde, was only fifteen but already married and pregnant. She could not keep anything on her stomach. Every morning Mrs. Freeman told Mrs. Hopewell how many times she had vomited since the last report.

Mrs. Hopewell liked to tell people that Glynese and Carramae were two of the finest girls she knew and that Mrs. Freeman was a *lady* and that she was never ashamed to take her anywhere or introduce her to anybody they might meet. Then she would tell how she had happened to hire the Freemans in the first place and how they were a godsend to her and how she had had them four years. The reason for her keeping them so long was that they were not trash. They were good country people. She had telephoned the man whose name they had given as a reference and he had told her that Mr. Freeman was a good farmer but that his wife was the nosiest woman ever to walk the earth. "She's got to be into everything," the man said. "If she don't get there before the dust settles, you can bet she's dead, that's all. She'll want to know all your business. I can stand him real good," he had said, "but me nor my wife neither could have stood that woman one more minute on this place." That had put Mrs. Hopewell off for a few days.

She had hired them in the end because there were no other applicants but she had made up her mind beforehand exactly how she would handle the woman. Since she was the type who had to be into everything, then, Mrs. Hopewell had decided, she would not only let her be into everything, she would *see to it* that she was into everything—she would give her the responsibility of everything, she would put her in charge. Mrs. Hopewell had no bad qualities of her own but she was able to use other people's in such a constructive way that she never felt the lack. She had hired the Freemans and she had kept them four years.

Nothing is perfect. This was one of Mrs. Hopewell's favorite sayings. Another was: that is life! And still another, the most important, was: well, other people have their opinions too. She would make these statements, usually at the table, in a tone of gentle insistence as if no one held them but her, and the large hulking Joy, whose constant outrage had obliterated every expression from her face, would stare just a little to the side of her, her eyes icy blue, with the look of someone who had achieved blindness by an act of will and means to keep it.

When Mrs. Hopewell said to Mrs. Freeman that life was like that, Mrs. Freeman would say, "I always said so myself." Nothing had been arrived at by anyone that had not first been arrived at by her. She was quicker than

Mr. Freeman. When Mrs. Hopewell said to her after they had been on the place a while. "You know, you're the wheel behind the wheel," and winked, Mrs. Freeman had said, "I know it. I've always been quick. It's some that are quicker than others."

"Everybody is different," Mrs. Hopewell said.

"Yes, most people is," Mrs. Freeman said.

"It takes all kinds to make the world."

"I always said it did myself."

The girl was used to this kind of dialogue for breakfast and more of it for dinner; sometimes they had it for supper too. When they had no guest they ate in the kitchen because that was easier. Mrs. Freeman always managed to arrive at some point during the meal and to watch them finish it. She would stand in the doorway if it were summer but in the winter she would stand with one elbow on top of the refrigerator and look down on them, or she would stand by the gas heater, lifting the back of her skirt slightly. Occasionally she would stand against the wall and roll her head from side to side. At no time was she in any hurry to leave. All this was very trying on Mrs. Hopewell but she was a woman of great patience. She realized that nothing is perfect and that in the Freemans she had good country people and that if, in this day and age, you get good country people, you had better hang onto them.

She had had plenty of experience with trash. Before the Freemans she had averaged one tenant family a year. The wives of these farmers were not the kind you would want to be around you for very long. Mrs. Hopewell, who had divorced her husband long ago, needed someone to walk over the fields with her; and when Joy had to be impressed for these services, her remarks were usually so ugly and her face so glum that Mrs. Hopewell would say, "If you can't come pleasantly, I don't want you at all," to which the girl, standing square and rigid-shouldered with her neck thrust slightly forward, would reply, "If you want me, here I am—LIKE I AM."

Mrs. Hopewell excused this attitude because of the leg (which had been shot off in a hunting accident when Joy was ten). It was hard for Mrs. Hopewell to realize that her child was thirty-two now and that for more than twenty years she had had only one leg. She thought of her still as a child because it tore her heart to think instead of the poor stout girl in her thirties who had never danced a step or had any *normal* good times. Her name was really Joy but as soon as she was twenty-one and away from home, she had had it legally changed. Mrs. Hopewell was certain that she had thought and thought until she had hit upon the ugliest name in any language. Then she had gone and had the beautiful name, Joy, changed without telling her mother until after she had done it. Her legal name was Hulga.

When Mrs. Hopewell thought the name, Hulga, she thought of the broad blank hull of a battleship. She would not use it. She continued to call her Joy to which the girl responded but in a purely mechanical way.

Hulga had learned to tolerate Mrs. Freeman who saved her from taking walks with her mother. Even Glynese and Carramae were useful when they occupied attention that might otherwise have been directed at her. At first she had thought she could not stand Mrs. Freeman for she had found that it was not possible to be rude to her. Mrs. Freeman would take on strange resentments and for days together she would be sullen but the source of her displeasure was always obscure; a direct attack, a positive leer, blatant ugliness to her face—these never touched her. And without warning one day, she began calling her Hulga.

She did not call her that in front of Mrs. Hopewell who would have been incensed but when she and the girl happened to be out of the house together, she would say something and add the name Hulga to the end of it, and the big spectacled Joy-Hulga would scowl and redden as if her privacy had been intruded upon. She considered the name her personal affair. She had arrived at it first purely on the basis of its ugly sound and then the full genius of its fitness had struck her. She had a vision of the name working like the ugly sweating Vulcan who stayed in the furnace and to whom, presumably, the goddess had to come when called. She saw it as the name of her highest creative act. One of her major triumphs was that her mother had not been able to turn her dust into Joy, but the greater one was that she had been able to turn it herself into Hulga. However, Mrs. Freeman's relish for using the name only irritated her. It was as if Mrs. Freeman's beady steel-pointed eyes had penetrated far enough behind her face to reach some secret fact. Something about her seemed to fascinate Mrs. Freeman and then one day Hulga realized that it was the artificial leg. Mrs. Freeman had a special fondness for the details of secret infections, hidden deformities, assaults upon children. Of diseases, she preferred the lingering or incurable. Hulga had heard Mrs. Hopewell give her the details of the hunting accident, how the leg had been literally blasted off, how she had never lost consciousness. Mrs. Freeman could listen to it any time as if it had happened an hour ago.

When Hulga stumped into the kitchen in the morning (she could walk without making the awful noise but she made it—Mrs. Hopewell was certain —because it was ugly-sounding), she glanced at them and did not speak. Mrs. Hopewell would be in her red kimono with her hair tied around her head in rags. She would be sitting at the table, finishing her breakfast and Mrs. Freeman would be hanging by her elbow outward from the refrigerator, looking down at the table. Hulga always put her eggs on the stove to boil and then stood over them with her arms folded, and Mrs. Hopewell would look at her—a kind of indirect gaze divided between her and Mrs. Freeman—and would think that if she would only keep herself up a little, she wouldn't be so bad looking. There was nothing wrong with her face that a pleasant expression wouldn't help. Mrs. Hopewell said that people who looked on the bright side of things would be beautiful even if they were not.

Whenever she looked at Joy this way, she could not help but feel that it would have been better if the child had not taken the Ph.D. It had certainly not brought her out any and now that she had it, there was no more excuse for her to go to school again. Mrs. Hopewell thought it was nice for girls to go to school to have a good time but Joy had "gone through." Anyhow, she would not have been strong enough to go again. The doctors had told Mrs.

Hopewell that with the best of care, Joy might see forty-five. She had a weak heart. Joy had made it plain that if it had not been for this condition, she would be far from these red hills and good country people. She would be in a university lecturing to people who knew what she was talking about. And Mrs. Hopewell could very well picture her there, looking like a scarecrow and lecturing to more of the same. Here she went about all day in a six-year-old skirt and a yellow sweat shirt with a faded cowboy on a horse embossed on it. She thought this was funny; Mrs. Hopewell thought it was idiotic and showed simply that she was still a child. She was brilliant but she didn't have a grain of sense. It seemed to Mrs. Hopewell that every year she grew less like other people and more like herself—bloated, rude, and squint-eyed. And she said such strange things! To her own mother she had said—without warning, without excuse, standing up in the middle of a meal with her face purple and her mouth half full—"Woman! do you ever look inside? Do you ever look inside and see what you are *not?* God!" she had cried sinking down again and staring at her plate. "Malebranche was right: we are not our own light: We are not our own light!" Mrs. Hopewell had no idea to this day what brought that on. She had only made the remark, hoping Joy would take it in, that a smile never hurt anyone.

The girl had taken the Ph.D. in philosophy and this left Mrs. Hopewell at at complete loss. You could say, "My daughter is a nurse," or "My daughter is a school teacher," or even, "My daughter is a chemical engineer." You could not say, "My daughter is a philosopher." That was something that had ended with the Greeks and Romans. All day Joy sat on her neck in a deep chair, reading. Sometimes she went for walks but she didn't like dogs or cats or birds or flowers or nature or nice young men. She looked at nice young men as if she could smell their stupidity.

One day Mrs. Hopewell had picked up one of the books the girl had just put down and opening it at random, she read, "Science, on the other hand, has to assert its soberness and seriousness afresh and declare that it is concerned solely with what-is. Nothing—how can it be for science anything but a horror and a phantasm? If science is right, then one thing stands firm: science wishes to know nothing of nothing. Such is after all the strictly scientific approach to Nothing. We know it by wishing to know nothing of Nothing." These words had been underlined with a blue pencil and they worked on Mrs. Hopewell like some evil incantation in gibberish. She shut the book quickly and went out of the room as if she were having a chill.

This morning when the girl came in, Mrs. Freeman was on Carramae. "She thrown up four times after supper," she said, "and was up twict in the night after three o'clock. Yesterday she didn't do nothing but ramble in the bureau drawer. All she did. Stand up there and see what she could run up on."

"She's got to eat," Mrs. Hopewell muttered, sipping her coffee, while she watched Joy's back at the stove. She was wondering what the child had said to the Bible salesman. She could not imagine what kind of a conversation she could possibly have had with him.

He was a tall gaunt hatless youth who had called yesterday to sell them a Bible. He had appeared at the door, carrying a large black suitcase that weighted him so heavily on one side that he had to brace himself against the door facing. He seemed on the point of collapse but he said in a cheerful voice, "Good morning, Mrs. Cedars!" and set the suitcase down on the mat. He was not a bad-looking young man though he had on a bright blue suit and yellow socks that were not pulled up far enough. He had prominent face bones and a streak of sticky-looking brown hair falling across his forehead.

"I'm Mrs. Hopewell," she said.

"Oh!" he said, pretending to look puzzled but with his eyes sparkling, "I saw it said 'The Cedars,' on the mailbox so I thought you was Mrs. Cedars!" and he burst out in a pleasant laugh. He picked up the satchel and under cover of a pant, he fell forward into her hall. It was rather as if the suitcase had moved first, jerking him after it. "Mrs. Hopewell!" he said and grabbed her hand. "I hope you are well!" and he laughed again and then all at once his face sobered completely. He paused and gave her a straight earnest look and said, "Lady, I've come to speak of serious things."

"Well, come in," she muttered, none too pleased because her dinner was almost ready. He came into the parlor and sat down on the edge of a straight chair and put the suitcase between his feet and glanced around the room as if he were sizing her up by it. Her silver gleamed on the two sideboards; she decided he had never been in a room as elegant as this.

"Mrs. Hopewell," he began, using her name in a way that sounded almost intimate, "I know you believe in Chrustian service."

"Well yes," she murmured.

"I know," he said and paused, looking very wise with his head cocked on one side, "that you're a good woman. Friends have told me."

Mrs. Hopewell never like to be taken for a fool. "What are you selling?" she asked.

"Bibles," the young man said and his eyes raced around the room before he added, "I see you have no family Bible in your parlor, I see that is the one lack you got!"

Mrs. Hopewell could not say, "My daughter is an atheist and won't let me keep the Bible in the parlor." She said, stiffening slightly, "I keep my Bible by my bedside." This was not the truth. It was in the attic somewhere.

"Lady," he said, "the word of God ought to be in the parlor."

"Well, I think that's a matter of taste," she began. "I think . . ."

"Lady," he said, "for a Chrustian, the word of God ought to be in every room in the house besides in his heart. I know you're a Chrustian because I can see it in every line of your face."

She stood up and said, "Well, young man, I don't want to buy a Bible and I smell my dinner burning."

He didn't get up. He began to twist his hands and looking down at them, he said softly, "Well lady, I'll tell you the truth—not many people want to buy one nowadays and besides, I know I'm real simple. I don't know how to say a thing but to say it. I'm just a country boy." He glanced up into her unfriendly face. "People like you don't like to fool with country people like me!"

"Why!" she cried, "good country people are the salt of the earth! Besides, we all have different ways of doing, it takes all kinds to make the world go 'round. That's life!"

"You said a mouthful," he said.

"Why, I think there aren't enough good country people in the world!" she said, stirred. "I think that's what's wrong with it!"

His face had brightened. "I didn't inraduce myself," he said. "I'm Manley Pointer from out in the country around Willohobie, not even from a place, just from near a place."

"You wait a minute," she said, "I have to see about my dinner." She went out to the kitchen and found Joy standing near the door where she had been listening.

"Get rid of the salt of the earth," she said, "and let's eat."

Mrs. Hopewell gave her a pained look and turned the heat down under the vegetables. "*I* can't be rude to anybody," she murmured and went back into the parlor.

He had opened the suitcase and was sitting with a Bible on each knee.

"You might as well put those up," she told him. "I don't want one."

"I appreciate your honesty," he said. "You don't see any more real honest people unless you go way out in the country."

"I know," she said, "real genuine folks!" Through the crack in the door she heard a groan.

"I guess a lot of boys come tell you they're working their way through college," he said, "but I'm not going to tell you that. Somehow," he said, "I don't want to go to college. I want to devote my life to Christian service. See," he said, lowering his voice, "I got this heart condition. I may not live long. When you know it's something wrong with you and you may not live long, well then, lady . . ." He paused, with his mouth open, and stared at her.

He and Joy had the same condition! She knew that her eyes were filling with tears but she collected herself quickly and murmured, "Won't you stay for dinner? We'd love to have you!" and was sorry the instant she heard herself say it.

"Yes mam," he said in an abashed voice, "I would sher love to do that!"

Joy had given him one look on being introduced to him and then throughout the meal had not glanced at him again. He had addressed several remarks to her, which she had pretended not to hear. Mrs. Hopewell could not understand deliberate rudeness, although she lived with it, and she felt she had always to overflow with hospitality to make up for Joy's lack of courtesy. She urged him to talk about himself and he did. He said he was the seventh child of twelve and that his father had been crushed under a tree when he himself was eight year old. He had been crushed very badly, in fact, almost cut in two and was practically not recognizable. His mother had got along the best she could by hard working and she had always seen that her children went to Sunday School and that they read the Bible every evening. He was now nineteen year old and he had been selling Bibles for four months. In that time he had sold seventy-seven Bibles and had the promise of two more sales. He wanted to become a missionary because he thought that was the way you could do most for people. "He who losest his life shall find it," he said simply and he was so sincere, so genuine and earnest that Mrs. Hopewell would not for the world have smiled. He prevented his peas from sliding onto the table by blocking them with a piece of bread which he later cleaned his plate with. She could see Joy observing sidewise how he handled his knife and fork and she saw too that every few minutes, the boy would dart a keen appraising glance at the girl as if he were trying to attract her attention.

After dinner Joy cleared the dishes off the table and disappeared and Mrs. Hopewell was left to talk with him. He told her again about his childhood and his father's accident and about various things that had happened to him. Every five minutes or so she would stifle a yawn. He sat for two hours until finally she told him she must go because she had an appointment in town. He packed his Bibles and thanked her and prepared to leave, but in the doorway he stopped and wrung her hand and said that not on any of his trips had he met a lady as nice as her and he asked if he could come again. She had said she would always be happy to see him.

Joy had been standing in the road, apparently looking at something in the distance, when he came down the steps toward her, bent to the side with his heavy valise. He stopped where she was standing and confronted her directly. Mrs. Hopewell could not hear what he said but she trembled to think what Joy would say to him. She could see that after a minute Joy said something and that then the boy began to speak again, making an excited gesture with his free hand. After a minute Joy said something else at which the boy began to speak once more. Then to her amazement, Mrs. Hopewell saw the two of them walk off together, toward the gate. Joy had walked all the way to the gate with him and Mrs. Hopewell could not imagine what they had said to each other, and she had not yet dared to ask.

Mrs. Freeman was insisting upon her attention. She had moved from the refrigerator to the heater so that Mrs. Hopewell had to turn and face her in order to seem to be listening. "Glynese gone out with Harvey Hill again last night," she said. "She had this sty."

"Hill," Mrs. Hopewell said absently, "is that the one who works in the garage?"

"Nome, he's the one that goes to chiropracter school," Mrs. Freeman said. "She had this sty. Been had it two days. So she says when he brought her in the other night he says, 'Lemme get rid of that sty for you,' and she says 'How?' and he says, 'You just lay yourself down acrost the seat of that car and I'll show you.' So she done it and he popped her neck. Kept on a-popping it several times until she made him quit. This morning," Mrs. Freeman said, "she ain't got no sty. She ain't got no traces of a sty."

"I never heard of that before," Mrs. Hopewell said.

"He ast her to marry him before the Ordinary," Mrs. Freeman went on, "and she told him she wasn't going to be married in no *office*."

"Well, Glynese is a fine girl," Mrs. Hopewell said. "Glynese and Carramae are both fine girls."

"Carramae said when her and Lyman was married Lyman said it sure felt sacred to him. She said he said he wouldn't take five hundred dollars for being married by a preacher."

"How much would he take?" the girl asked from the stove.

"He said he wouldn't take five hundred dollars," Mrs. Freeman repeated.

"Well, we all have work to do," Mrs. Hopewell said.

"Lyman said it just felt more sacred to him," Mrs. Freeman said. "The doctor wants Carramae to eat prunes. Says instead of medicine. Says them cramps is coming from pressure. You know where I think it is?"

"She'll be better in a few weeks," Mrs. Hopewell said.

"In the tube," Mrs. Freeman said. "Else she wouldn't be as sick as she is."

Hulga had cracked her two eggs into a saucer and was bringing them to the table along with a cup of coffee that she had filled too full. She sat down carefully and began to eat, meaning to keep Mrs. Freeman there by questions if for any reason she showed an inclination to leave. She could perceive her mother's eye on her. The first roundabout question would be about the Bible salesman and she did not wish to bring it on. "How did he pop her neck?" she asked.

Mrs. Freeman went into a description of how he had popped her neck. She said he owned a '55 Mercury but that Glynese said she would rather marry a man with only a '36 Plymouth who would be married by a preacher. The girl asked what if he had a '32 Plymouth and Mrs. Freeman said what Glynese had said was a '36 Plymouth.

Mrs. Hopewell said there were not many girls with Glynese's common sense. She said what she admired in those girls was their common sense. She said that reminded her that they had had a nice visitor yesterday, a young man selling Bibles. "Lord," she said, "he bored me to death but he was so sincere and genuine I couldn't be rude to him. He was just good country people, you know," she said, "—just the salt of the earth."

"I seen him walk up," Mrs. Freeman said, "and then later—I seen him walk off," and Hulga could feel the slight shift in her voice, the slight insinuation, that he had not walked off alone, had he? Her face remained expressionless but the color rose into her neck and she seemed to swallow it down with the next spoonful of egg. Mrs. Freeman was looking at her as if they had a secret together.

"Well, it takes all kinds of people to make the world go 'round," Mrs. Hopewell said. "It's very good we aren't all alike."

"Some people are more alike than others," Mrs. Freeman said.

Hulga got up and stumped, with about twice the noise that was necessary, into her room and locked the door. She was to meet the Bible salesman at ten o'clock at the gate.

She had thought about it half the night. She had started thinking of it as a great joke and then she had begun to see profound implications in it. She had lain in bed imagining dialogues for them that were insane on the surface but that reached below to depths that no Bible salesman would be aware of. Their conversation yesterday had been of this kind.

He had stopped· in front of her and had simply stood there. His face was bony and sweaty and bright, with a little pointed nose in the center of it, and his look was different from what it had been at the dinner table. He was gazing at her with open curiosity, with fascination, like a child watching a new fantastic animal at the zoo, and he was breathing as if he had run a great distance to reach her. His gaze seemed somehow familiar but she could not think where she had been regarded with it before. For almost a minute he didn't say anything. Then on what seemed an insuck of breath, he whispered, "You ever ate a chicken that was two days old?"

The girl looked at him stonily. He might have just put this question up for consideration at the meeting of a philosophical association. "Yes," she presently replied as if she had considered it from all angles.

"It must have been mighty small!" he said triumphantly and shook all over with little nervous giggles, getting very red in the face, and subsiding finally into his gaze of complete admiration, while the girl's expression remained exactly the same.

"How old are you?" he asked softly.

She waited some time before she answered. Then in a flat voice she said, "Seventeen."

His smiles came in succession like waves breaking on the surface of a little lake. "I see you got a wooden leg," he said. "I think you're real brave. I think you're real sweet."

The girl stood blank and solid and silent.

"Walk to the gate with me," he said. "You're a brave sweet little thing and I liked you the minute I seen you walk in the door."

Hulga began to move forward.

"What's your name?" he asked, smiling down on the top of her head.

"Hulga," she said.

"Hulga," he murmured, "Hulga. Hulga. I never heard of anybody name Hulga before. You're shy, aren't you, Hulga?" he asked.

She nodded, watching his large red hand on the handle of the giant valise.

"I like girls that wear glasses," he said. "I think a lot. I'm not like these people that a serious thought don't ever enter their heads. It's because I may die."

"I may die too," she said suddenly and looked up at him. His eyes were very small and brown, glittering feverishly.

"Listen," he said, "don't you think some people was meant to meet on account of what all they got in common and all? Like they both think serious thoughts and all?" He shifted the valise to his other hand so that the hand nearest her was free. He caught hold of her elbow and shook it a little. "I don't work on Saturday," he said. "I like to walk in the woods and see what

Mother Nature is wearing. O'er the hills and far away. Pic-nics and things. Couldn't we go on a pic-nic tomorrow? Say yes, Hulga," he said and gave her a dying look as if he felt his insides about to drop out of him. He had even seemed to sway slightly toward her.

During the night she had imagined that she seduced him. She imagined that the two of them walked on the place until they came to the storage barn beyond the two back fields and there, she imagined, that things came to such a pass that she very easily seduced him and that then, of course, she had to reckon with his remorse. True genius can get an idea across even to an inferior mind. She imagined that she took his remorse in hand and changed it into a deeper understanding of life. She took all his shame away and turned it into something useful.

She set off for the gate at exactly ten o'clock, escaping without drawing Mrs. Hopewell's attention. She didn't take anything to eat, forgetting that food is usually taken on a pic-nic. She wore a pair of slacks and a dirty white shirt, and as an afterthought, she had put some Vapex on the collar of it since she did not own any perfume. When she reached the gate no one was there.

She looked up and down the empty highway and had the furious feeling that she had been tricked, that he had only meant to make her walk to the gate after the idea of him. Then suddenly he stood up, very tall, from behind a bush on the opposite embankment. Smiling, he lifted his hat which was new and wide-brimmed. He had not worn it yesterday and she wondered if he had bought it for the occasion. It was toast-colored with a red and white band around it and was slightly too large for him. He stepped from behind the bush still carrying the black valise. He had on the same suit and the same yellow socks sucked down in his shoes from walking. He crossed the highway and said, "I knew you'd come!"

The girl wondered acidly how he had known this. She pointed to the valise and asked, "Why did you bring your Bibles?"

He took her elbow, smiling down on her as if he could not stop. "You can never tell when you'll need the word of God, Hulga," he said. She had a moment in which she doubted that this was actually happening and then they began to climb the embankment. They went down into the pasture toward the woods. The boy walked lightly by her side, bouncing on his toes. The valise did not seem to be heavy today; he even swung it. They crossed half the pasture without saying anything and then, putting his hand easily on the small of her neck, he asked softly, "Where does your wooden leg join on?"

She turned an ugly red and glared at him and for an instant the boy looked abashed. "I didn't mean you no harm," he said. "I only meant you're so brave and all. I guess God takes care of you."

"No," she said, looking forward and walking fast, "I don't even believe in God."

At this he stopped and whistled. "No!" he exclaimed as if he were too astonished to say anything else.

She walked on and in a second he was bouncing at her side, fanning with his hat. "That's very unusual for a girl," he remarked, watching her out of the corner of his eye. When they reached the edge of the wood, he put his hand on her back again and drew her against him without a word and kissed her heavily.

The kiss, which had more pressure than feeling behind it, produced that extra surge of adrenalin in the girl that enables one to carry a packed trunk out of a burning house, but in her, the power went at once to the brain. Even before he released her, her mind, clear and detached and ironic anyway, was regarding him from a great distance, with amusement but with pity. She had never been kissed before and she was pleased to discover that it was an unexceptional experience and all a matter of the mind's control. Some people might enjoy drain water if they were told it was vodka. When the boy, looking expectant but uncertain, pushed her gently away, she turned and walked on, saying nothing as if such business, for her, were common enough.

He came along panting at her side, trying to help her when he saw a root that she might trip over. He caught and held back the long swaying blades of thorn vine until she had passed beyond them. She led the way and he came breathing heavily behind her. Then they came out on a sunlit hillside, sloping softly into another one a little smaller. Beyond, they could see the rusted top of the old barn where the extra hay was stored.

The hill was sprinkled with small pink weeds. "Then you ain't saved?" he asked suddenly, stopping.

The girl smiled. It was the first time she had smiled at him at all. "In my economy," she said, "I'm saved and you are damned but I told you I didn't believe in God."

Nothing seemed to destroy the boy's look of admiration. He gazed at her now as if the fantastic animal at the zoo had put its paw through the bars and given him a loving poke. She thought he looked as if he wanted to kiss her again and she walked on before he had the chance.

"Ain't there somewheres we can sit down sometime?" he murmured, his voice softening toward the end of the sentence.

"In that barn," she said.

They made for it rapidly as if it might slide away like a train. It was a large two-story barn, cool and dark inside. The boy pointed up the ladder that led into the loft and said, "It's too bad we can't go up there."

"Why can't we?" she asked.

"Yer leg," he said reverently.

The girl gave him a contemptuous look and putting both hands on the ladder, she climbed it while he stood below, apparently awestruck. She pulled herself expertly through the opening and then looked down at him and said, "Well, come on if you're coming," and he began to climb the ladder, awkwardly bringing the suitcase with him.

"We won't need the Bible," she observed.

"You never can tell," he said, panting. After he had got into the loft, he was a few seconds catching his breath. She had sat down in a pile of straw. A wide sheath of sunlight, filled with dust particles, slanted over him. She lay back against a bale, her face turned away, looking out the front opening of the barn where hay was thrown from a wagon into the loft. The two pink-speckled hillsides lay back against a dark ridge of woods. The sky was cloud-less and cold blue. The boy dropped down by her side and put one arm under her and the other over her and began methodically kissing her face, making little noises like a fish. He did not remove his hat but it was pushed far enough back not to interfere. When her glasses got in his way, he took them off of her and slipped them into his pocket.

The girl at first did not return any of the kisses but presently she began to and after she had put several on his cheek, she reached his lips and remained there, kissing him again and again as if she were trying to draw all the breath out of him. His breath was clear and sweet like a child's and the kisses were sticky like a child's. He mumbled about loving her and about knowing when he first seen her that he loved her, but the mumbling was like the sleepy fret-ting of a child being put to sleep by his mother. Her mind, throughout this, never stopped or lost itself for a second to her feelings. "You ain't said you loved me none," he whispered finally, pulling back from her. "You got to say that."

She looked away from him off into the hollow sky and then down at a black ridge and then down farther into what appeared to be two green swelling lakes. She didn't realize he had taken her glasses but this landscape could not seem exceptional to her for she seldom paid any close attention to her sur-roundings.

"You got to say it," he repeated. "You got to say you love me."

She was always careful how she committed herself. "In a sense," she began, "if you use the word loosely, you might say that. But it's not a word I use. I don't have illusions. I'm one of those people who see *through* to nothing."

The boy was frowning. "You got to say it. I said it and you got to say it," he said.

The girl looked at him almost tenderly. "You poor baby," she murmured. "It's just as well you don't understand," and she pulled him by the neck, face-down, against her. "We are all damned," she said, "but some of us have taken off our blindfolds and see that there's nothing to see. It's a kind of salvation."

The boy's astonished eyes looked blankly through the ends of her hair. "Okay," he almost whined, "but do you love me or don'tcher?"

"Yes," she said and added, "in a sense. But I must tell you something. There mustn't be anything dishonest between us." She lifted his head and looked him in the eye. "I am thirty years old," she said. "I have a number of degrees."

The boy's look was irritated but dogged. "I don't care," he said. "I don't care a thing about what all you done. I just want to know if you love me or don'tcher?" and he caught her to him and wildly planted her face with kisses until she said, "Yes, yes."

"Okay then," he said, letting her go. "Prove it."

She smiled, looking dreamily out on the shifty landscape. She had seduced him without even making up her mind to try. "How?" she asked, feeling that he should be delayed a little.

He leaned over and put his lips to the ear. "Show me where your wooden leg joins on," he whispered.

The girl uttered a sharp little cry and her face instantly drained of color. The obscenity of the suggestion was not what shocked her. As a child she had sometimes been subject to feelings of shame but education had removed the last traces of that as a good surgeon scrapes for cancer; she would no more have felt it over what he was asking than she would have believed in his Bible. But she was as sensitive about the artificial leg as a peacock about his tail. No one ever touched it but her. She took care of it as someone else would his soul, in private and almost with her own eyes turned away. "No," she said.

"I known it," he muttered, sitting up. "You're just playing me for a sucker."

"Oh no no!" she cried. "It joins on at the knee. Only at the knee. Why do you want to see it?"

The boy gave her a long penetrating look. "Because," he said, "it's what makes you different. You ain't like anybody else."

She sat staring at him. There was nothing about her face or her round freezing-blue eyes to indicate that this had moved her; but she felt as if her heart had stopped and left her mind to pump her blood. She decided that for the first time in her life she was face to face with real innocence. This boy, with an instinct that came from beyond wisdom, had touched the truth about her. When after a minute, she said in a hoarse high voice, "All right," it was like surrendering to him completely. It was like losing her own life and finding it again, miraculously, in his.

Very gently he began to roll the slack leg up. The artificial limb, in a white sock and brown flat shoe, was bound in a heavy material like canvas and ended in an ugly jointure where it was attached to the stump. The boy's face and his voice were entirely reverent as he uncovered it and said, "Now show me how to take it off and on."

She took it off for him and put it back on again and then he took it off himself, handling it as tenderly as if it were a real one. "See!" he said with a delighted child's face. "Now I can do it myself!"

"Put it back on," she said. She was thinking that she would run away with him and that every night he would take the leg off and every morning put it back on again. "Put it back on," she said.

"Not yet," he murmured, setting it on its foot out of her reach. "Leave it off for a while. You got me instead."

She gave a little cry of alarm but he pushed her down and began to kiss her again. Without the leg she felt entirely dependent on him. Her brain seemed to have stopped thinking altogether and to be about some other function that it was not very good at. Different expressions raced back and forth over her face. Every now and then the boy, his eyes like two steel spikes, would glance behind him where the leg stood. Finally she pushed him off and said, "Put it back on me now."

"Wait," he said. He leaned the other way and pulled the valise toward him and opened it. It had a pale blue spotted lining and there were only two Bibles in it. He took one of these out and opened the cover of it. It was hollow and contained a pocket flask of whiskey, a pack of cards, and a small blue box with printing on it. He laid these out in front of her one at a time in an evenly-spaced row, like one presenting offerings at the shrine of a goddess. He put the blue box in her hand. THIS PRODUCT TO BE USED ONLY FOR THE PRE-VENTION OF DISEASE, she read, and dropped it. The boy was unscrewing the top of the flask. He stopped and pointed, with a smile, to the deck of cards. It was not an ordinary deck but one with an obscene picture on the back of each card. "Take a swig," he said, offering the bottle first. He held it in front of her, but like one mesmerized, she did not move.

Her voice when she spoke had an almost pleading sound. "Aren't you," she murmured, "aren't you just good country people?"

The boy cocked his head. He looked as if he were just beginning to under-stand that she might be trying to insult him. "Yeah," he said, curling his lip slightly, "but it ain't held me back none. I'm as good as you any day in the week."

"Give me my leg," she said.

He pushed it farther away with his foot. "Come on now, let's begin to have us a good time," he said coaxingly. "We ain't got to know one another good yet."

"Give me my leg!" she screamed and tried to lunge for it but he pushed her down easily.

"What's the matter with you all of a sudden?" he asked, frowning as he screwed the top on the flask and put it quickly back inside the Bible. "You just a while ago said you didn't believe in nothing. I thought you was some girl!"

Her face was almost purple. "You're a Christian!" she hissed. "You're a fine Christian! You're just like them all—say one thing and do another. You're a perfect Christian, you're . . ."

The boy's mouth was set angrily. "I hope you don't think," he said in a lofty indignant tone, "that I believe in that crap! I may sell Bibles but I know which end is up and I wasn't born yesterday and I know where I'm going!"

"Give me my leg!" she screeched. He jumped up so quickly that she barely saw him sweep the cards and the blue box back into the Bible and throw the Bible into the valise. She saw him grab the leg and then she saw it for an instant slanted forlornly against the inside of the suitcase with a Bible at either side of its opposite ends. He slammed the lid shut and snatched up the valise and swung it down the hole and then stepped through himself.

When all of him had passed but his head, he turned and regarded her with a look that no longer had any admiration in it. "I've gotten a lot of interesting things," he said. "One time I got a woman's glass eye this way. And you needn't to think you'll catch me because Pointer ain't really my name. I use a different name at every house I call at and don't stay nowhere long. And I'll tell you another thing, Hulga," he said, using the name as if he didn't think much of it, "you ain't so smart. I been believing in nothing ever since I was born!" and then the toast-colored hat disappeared down the hole and the girl was left, sitting on the straw in the dusty sunlight. When she turned her churning face toward the opening, she saw his blue figure struggling successfully over the green speckled lake.

Mrs. Hopewell and Mrs. Freeman, who were in the back pasture, digging up onions, saw him emerge a little later from the woods and head across the meadow toward the highway. "Why, that looks like that nice dull young man that tried to sell me a Bible yesterday," Mrs. Hopewell said, squinting. "He must have been selling them to the Negroes back in there. He was so simple," she said, "but I guess the world would be better off if we were all that simple."

Mrs. Freeman's gaze drove forward and just touched him before he disappeared under the hill. Then she returned her attention to the evil-smelling onion shoot she was lifting from the ground. "Some can't be that simple," she said. "I know I never could."

John Barth

Lost in the Funhouse

For whom is the funhouse fun? Perhaps for lovers. For Ambrose it is *a place of fear and confusion.* He has come to the seashore with his family for the holiday, *the occasion of their visit is Independence Day, the most important secular holiday of the United States of America.* A single straight underline is the manuscript mark for italic type, *which in turn* is the printed equivalent to oral emphasis of words and phrases as well as the customary type for titles of complete works, not to mention. Italics are also employed, in fiction stories especially, for "outside," intrusive, or artificial voices, such as radio announcements, the texts of telegrams and newspaper articles, et cetera. They should be used *sparingly.* If passages originally in roman type are italicized by someone repeating them, it's customary to acknowledge the fact. *Italics mine.*

Ambrose was "at that awkward age." His voice came out high-pitched as a child's if he let himself get carried away; to be on the safe side, therefore, he moved and spoke with *deliberate calm* and *adult gravity.* Talking soberly of unimportant or irrelevant matters and listening consciously to the sound of your own voice are useful habits for maintaining control in this difficult interval. *En route* to Ocean City he sat in the back seat of the family car with his brother Peter, age fifteen, and Magda G——, age fourteen, a pretty girl an exquisite young lady, who lived not far from them on B—— Street in the town of D——, Maryland. Initials, blanks, or both were often substituted for proper names in nineteenth-century fiction to enhance the illusion of reality. It is as if the author felt it necessary to delete the names for reasons of tact or legal liability. Interestingly, as with other aspects of realism, it is an *illusion* that is being enhanced, by purely artificial means. Is it likely, does it violate the principle of verisimilitude, that a thirteen-year-old boy could make such a sophisticated observation? A girl of fourteen is *the psychological coeval* of a boy of fifteen or sixteen; a thirteen-year-old boy, therefore, even one precocious in some other respects, might be three years *her emotional junior.*

Thrice a year—on Memorial, Independence, and Labor Days—the family visits Ocean City for the afternoon and evening. When Ambrose and Peter's father was their age, the excursion was made by train, as mentioned in the novel *The 42nd Parallel* by John Dos Passos. Many families from the same neighborhood used to travel together, with dependent relatives and often with Negro servants; schoolfuls of children swarmed through the railway cars; everyone shared everyone else's Maryland fried chicken, Virginia ham, deviled eggs, potato salad, beaten biscuits, iced tea. Nowadays (that is, in 19—, the year of our story) the journey is made by automobile—more comfortably and quickly though without the extra fun though without the *camaraderie* of a general excursion. It's all part of the deterioration of American life, their father declares, Uncle Karl supposes that when the boys take *their* families to Ocean City for the holidays they'll fly in Autogiros. Their mother, sitting in the middle of the front seat like Magda in the second, only with her arms on the seat-back behind the men's shoulders, wouldn't want the good old days back again, the steaming trains and stuffy long dresses; on the other hand she can do without Autogiros, too, if she has to become a grandmother to fly in them.

Description of physical appearance and mannerisms is one of several standard methods of characterization used by writers of fiction. It is also important to "keep the senses operating"; when a detail from one of the five senses, say visual, is "crossed" with a detail from another, say auditory, the reader's imagination is oriented to the scene, perhaps unconsciously. This procedure may be compared to the way surveyors and navigators determine their positions by two or more compass bearings, a process known as triangulation. The brown hair on Ambrose's mother's forearms gleamed in the sun like. Though right-handed, she took her left arm from the seat-back to press the dashboard cigar lighter for Uncle Karl. When the glass bead in its handle glowed red, the lighter was ready for use. The smell of Uncle Karl's cigar smoke reminded one of. The fragrance of the ocean came strong to the picnic ground where they always stopped for lunch, two miles inland from Ocean City. Having to pause for a full hour almost within sound of the breakers was difficult for Peter and Ambrose when they were younger; even at their present age it was not easy to keep their anticipation, *stimulated by the briny spume,* from turning into short temper. The Irish author James Joyce, in his unusual novel entitled *Ulysses,* now available in this country, uses the adjectives *snot-green* and *scrotum-tightening* to describe the sea. Visual, auditory, tactile, olfactory, gustatory. Peter and Ambrose's father, while steering their black 1936 LaSalle sedan with one hand, could with the other remove the first cigarette from a white pack of Lucky Strikes and, more remarkably, light it with a match forefingered from its book and thumbed against the flint paper without being detached. The matchbook cover merely advertised U. S. War Bonds and Stamps. A fine metaphor, simile, or other figure of speech, in addition to its obvious "first-order" relevance to the thing it describes, will be seen upon reflection to have a second order of significance: it may be drawn from the *milieu* of the action, for example, or be particularly appropriate to the sensibility of the narrator, even hinting to the reader things of which the narrator is unaware; or it may cast further and subtler lights upon the thing it describes, sometimes ironically qualifying the more evident sense of the comparison.

To say that Ambrose's and Peter's mother was *pretty* is to accomplish nothing; the reader may acknowledge the proposition, but his imagination is not engaged. Besides, Magda was also pretty, yet in an altogether different way. Although she lived on B—— Street she had very good manners and did better than average in school. Her figure was very well developed for her age. Her right hand lay casually on the plush upholstery of the seat, very near Ambrose's left leg, on which his own hand rested. The space between their legs, between her right and his left leg, was out of the line of sight of anyone sitting on the other side of Magda, as well as anyone glancing into the rear-view mirror. Uncle Karl's face resembled Peter's—rather, vice versa. Both had dark hair and eyes, short husky statures, deep voices. Magda's left hand was probably in a similar position on her left side. The boy's father is difficult to describe; no particular feature of his appearance or manner stood out. He wore glasses and was principal of a T—— County grade school. Uncle Karl was a masonry contractor.

Although Peter must have known as well as Ambrose that the latter, because of his position in the car, would be the first to see the electrical towers of the power plant at V——, the halfway point of their trip, he leaned forward and slightly toward the center of the car and pretended to be looking for them through the flat pinewoods and tuckahoe creeks along the highway. For as long as the boys could remember, "looking for the Towers" had been a feature of the first half of their excursions to Ocean City, "looking for the standpipe" of the second. Though the game was childish, their mother preserved the tradition of rewarding the first to see the Towers with a candy-bar or piece of fruit. She insisted now that Magda play the game; the prize, she said, was "something hard to get nowadays." Ambrose decided not to join in; he sat far back in his seat. Magda, like Peter, leaned forward. Two sets of straps were discernible through the shoulders of her sun dress; the inside right one, a brassiere-strap, was fastened or shortened with a small safety pin. The right armpit of her dress, presumably the left as well, was damp with perspiration. The simple strategy for being first to espy the Towers, which Ambrose had understood by the age of four, was to sit on the right-hand side of the car. Whoever sat there, however, had also to put up with the worst of the sun, and so Ambrose, without mentioning the matter, chose sometimes the one and sometimes the other. Not impossibly Peter had never caught on to the trick, or thought that his brother hadn't simply because Ambrose on occasion preferred shade to a Baby Ruth or tangerine.

The shade-sun situation didn't apply to the front seat, owing to the windshield; if anything the driver got more sun, since the person on the passenger side not only was shaded below by the door and dashboard but might swing down his sunvisor all the way too.

"Is that them?" Magda asked. Ambrose's mother teased the boys for letting Magda win, insinuating that "somebody [had] a girlfriend." Peter and Ambrose's father reached a long thin arm across their mother to butt his cigarette in the dashboard ashtray, under the lighter. The prize this time for seeing the Towers first was a banana. Their mother bestowed it after chiding their father for wasting a half-smoked cigarette when everything was so scarce. Magda, to take the prize, moved her hand from so near Ambrose's that he could have touched it as though accidentally. She offered to share the prize, things like that were so hard to find; but everyone insisted it was hers alone. Ambrose's mother sang an iambic trimeter couplet from a popular song, femininely rhymed:

> *"What's good is in the Army;*
> *What's left will never harm me."*

Uncle Karl tapped his cigar ash out the ventilator window; some particles were sucked by the slipstream back into the car through the rear window on the passenger side. Magda demonstrated her ability to hold a banana in one hand and peel it with her teeth. She still sat forward; Ambrose pushed his glasses back onto the bridge of his nose with his left hand, which he then negligently let fall to the seat cushion immediately behind her. He even permitted the single hair, gold, on the second joint of his thumb to brush the fabric of her skirt. Should she have sat back at that instant, his hand would have been caught under her.

Plush upholstery prickles uncomfortably through gabardine slacks in the July sun. The function of the *beginning* of a story is to introduce the principal characters, establish their initial relationships, set the scene for the main action, expose the background of the situation if necessary, plant motifs and foreshadowings where appropriate, and initiate the first complication or whatever of the "rising action." Actually, if one imagines a story called "The Funhouse," or "Lost in the Funhouse," the details of the drive to Ocean City don't seem especially relevant. The *beginning* should recount the events between Ambrose's first sight of the funhouse early in the afternoon and his entering it with Magda and Peter in the evening. The *middle* would narrate all relevant events from the time he goes in to the time he loses his way; middles have the double and contradictory function of delaying the climax while at the same time preparing the reader for it and fetching him to it. Then the *ending* would tell what Ambrose does while he's lost, how he finally finds his way out, and what everybody makes of the experience. So far there's been no real dialogue, very little sensory detail, and nothing in the way of a *theme*. And a long time has gone by already without anything happening; it makes a person wonder. We haven't even reached Ocean City yet: we will never get out of the funhouse.

The more closely an author identifies with the narrator, literally or metaphorically, the less advisable it is, as a rule, to use the first-person narrative viewpoint. Once three years previously the young people *aforementioned* played Niggers and Masters in the backyard; when it was Ambrose's turn to be Master and theirs to be Niggers Peter had to go serve his evening papers; Ambrose was afraid to punish Magda alone, but she led him to the white-washed Torture Chamber between the woodshed and the privy in the Slaves Quarters; there she knelt sweating among bamboo rakes and dusty Mason jars, pleadingly embraced his knees, and while bees droned in the lattice as if on an ordinary summer afternoon, purchased clemency at a surprising price set by herself. Doubtless she remembered nothing of this event; Ambrose on the other hand seemed unable to forget the least detail of his life. He even recalled how, standing beside himself with awed impersonality in the reeky heat, he'd stared the while at an empty cigar box in which Uncle Karl kept stone-cutting chisels: beneath the words *El Producto,* a laureled, loose-toga'd lady regarded the sea from a marble bench; beside her, forgotten or not yet turned to, was a five-stringed lyre. Her chin reposed on the back of her right hand; her left depended negligently from the bench-arm. The lower half of scene and lady was peeled away; the words EXAMINED BY —— were inked there into the wood. Nowadays cigar boxes are made of pasteboard. Ambrose wondered what Magda would have done, Ambrose wondered what Magda would do when she sat back on his hand as he resolved she should. Be angry. Make a teasing joke of it. Give no sign at all. For a long time she leaned forward, playing cow-poker with Peter against Uncle Karl and Mother and watching for the first sign of Ocean City. At nearly the same instant, picnic ground and Ocean City standpipe hove into view; an Amoco filling station on their side of the road cost Mother and Uncle Karl fifty cows and the game; Magda bounced back, clapping her right hand on Mother's right arm; Ambrose moved clear "in the nick of time."

At this rate our hero, at this rate our protagonist will remain in the fun-house forever. Narrative ordinarily consists of alternating dramatization and summarization. One symptom of nervous tension, paradoxically, is repeated and violent yawning; neither Peter nor Magda nor Uncle Karl nor Mother reacted in this manner. Although they were no longer small children, Peter and Ambrose were each given a dollar to spend on boardwalk amusements in addition to what money of their own they'd brought along. Magda too, though she protested she had ample spending money. The boys' mother made a little scene out of distributing the bills: she pretended that her sons and Magda were small children and cautioned them not to spend the sum too quickly or in one place. Magda promised with a merry laugh and, having both hands free, took the bill with her left. Peter laughed also and pledged in a falsetto to be a good boy. His imitation of a child was not clever. The boys' father was tall and thin, balding, fair-complexioned. Assertions of that sort are not effective; the reader may acknowledge the proposition, but. We should be much farther along than we are; something has gone wrong; not much of this preliminary rambling seems relevant. Yet everyone begins in the same place; how is it that most go along without difficulty but a few lose their way?

"Stay out from under the boardwalk," Uncle Karl growled from the side of his mouth. The boys' mother pushed his shoulder *in mock annoyance*. They were all standing before Fat May the Laughing Lady who advertised the fun-house. Larger than life, Fat May mechanically shook, rocked on her heels, slapped her thighs while recorded laughter—uproarious, female—came amplified from a hidden loudspeaker. It chuckled, wheezed, wept; tried in vain to catch its breath; tittered, groaned, exploded raucous and anew. You couldn't hear it without laughing yourself, no matter how you felt. Father came back from talking to a Coast-Guardsman on duty and reported that the surf was spoiled with crude oil from tankers recently torpedoed offshore. Lumps of it, difficult to remove, made tarry tidelines on the beach and stuck on swimmers. Many bathed in the surf nevertheless and came out speckled; others paid to use a municipal pool and only sunbathed on the beach. We would do the latter. We would do the latter. We would do the latter.

Under the boardwalk, matchbook covers, grainy other things. What is the story's theme? Ambrose is ill. He perspires in the dark passages; candied apples-on-a-stick, delicious-looking, disappointing to eat. Funhouses need men's and ladies' rooms at intervals. Others perhaps have also vomited in corners and corridors; may even have had bowel movements liable to be stepped in in the dark. The word *fuck* suggests suction and/or and/or flatu-lence. Mother and Father; grandmothers and grandfathers on both sides; great-grandmothers and great-grandfathers on four sides, et cetera. Count a generation as thirty years: in approximately the year when Lord Baltimore was granted charter to the province of Maryland by Charles I, five hundred twelve women—English, Welsh, Bavarian, Swiss—of every class and char-acter, received into themselves the penises the intromittent organs of five hun-dred twelve men, ditto, in every circumstance and posture, to conceive the five hundred twelve ancestors of the two hundred fifty-six ancestors of the et cetera et cetera et cetera et cetera et cetera et cetera et cetera et cetera of the author, of the narrator, of this story, *Lost in the Funhouse*. In alleyways, ditches, canopy beds, pinewoods, bridal suites, ship's cabins, coach-and-fours, coaches-and-four, sultry toolsheds; on the cold sand under boardwalks, littered with *El Producto* cigar butts, treasured with Lucky Strike cigarette stubs, Coca-Cola caps, gritty turds, cardboard lollipop sticks, matchbook covers warn-ing that A Slip of the Lip Can Sink a Ship. The shluppish whisper, continu-ous as seawash round the globe, tidelike falls and rises with the circuit of dawn and dusk.

Magda's teeth. She *was* left-handed. Perspiration. They've gone all the way, through, Magda and Peter, they've been waiting for hours with Mother and Uncle Karl while Father searches for his lost son; they draw french-fried potatoes from a paper cup and shake their head. They've named the children they'll one day have and bring to Ocean City on holidays. Can spermatozoa properly be thought of as male animalcules when there are no female spermatozoa? They grope through hot, dark windings, past Love's Tunnel fearsome obstacles. Some perhaps lose their way.

Peter suggested then and there that they do the funhouse; he had been through it before, so had Magda. Ambrose hadn't and suggested, his voice cracking on account of Fat May's laughter, that they swim first. All were chuckling, couldn't help it; Ambrose's father, Ambrose's and Peter's father came up grinning like a lunatic with two boxes of syrup-coated popcorn, one for Mother, one for Magda; the men were to help themselves. Ambrose walked on Magda's right; being by nature left-handed, she carried the box in her left hand. Up front the situation was reversed.

"What are you limping for?" Magda inquired of Ambrose. He supposed in a husky tone that his foot had gone to sleep in the car. Her teeth flashed. "Pins and needles?" It was the honeysuckle on the lattice of the former privy that drew the bees. Imagine being stung there. How long is this going to take?

The adults decided to forgo the pool; but Uncle Karl insisted they change into swimsuits and do the beach. "He wants to watch the pretty girls," Peter teased, and ducked behind Magda from Uncle Karl's pretended wrath. "You've got all the pretty girls you need right here," Magda declared, and Mother said: "Now that's the gospel truth." Magda scolded Peter, who reached over her shoulder to sneak some popcorn. "Your brother and father aren't getting any." Uncle Karl wondered if they were going to have fireworks that night, what with the shortages. It wasn't the shortages, Mr. M—— replied; Ocean City had fireworks from pre-war. But it was too risky on account of the enemy submarines, some people thought.

"Don't seem like Fourth of July without fireworks," said Uncle Karl. The inverted tag in dialogue writing is still considered permissible with proper names or epithets, but sounds old-fashioned with personal pronouns. "We'll have 'em again soon enough," predicted the boys' father. Their mother declared she could do without fireworks: they reminded her too much of the real thing. Their father said all the more reason to shoot off a few now and again. Uncle Karl asked *rhetorically* who needed reminding, just look at people's hair and skin.

"The oil, yes," said Mrs. M——.

Ambrose had a pain in his stomach and so didn't swim but enjoyed watching the others. He and his father burned red easily. Magda's figure was exceedingly well developed for her age. She too declined to swim, and got mad, and became angry when Peter attempted to drag her into the pool. She always swam, he insisted; what did she mean not swim? Why did a person come to Ocean City?

"Maybe I want to lay here with Ambrose," Magda teased.

Nobody likes a pedant.

"Aha," said Mother. Peter grabbed Magda by one ankle and ordered Ambrose to grab the other. She squealed and rolled over on the beach blanket. Ambrose pretended to help hold her back. Her tan was darker than even Mother's and Peter's. "Help out, Uncle Karl!" Peter cried. Uncle Karl went to seize the other ankle. Inside the top of her swimsuit, however, you could see the line where the sunburn ended and, when she hunched her shoulders and squealed again, one nipple's auburn edge. Mother made them behave themselves. *"You* should certainly know," she said to Uncle Karl. Archly. "That when a lady says she doesn't feel like swimming, a gentleman doesn't ask questions." Uncle Karl said excuse *him;* Mother winked at Magda; Ambrose blushed, stupid Peter kept saying "Phooey on *feel like!"* and tugging at Magda's ankle; then even he got the point, and cannonballed with a holler into the pool.

"I swear," Magda said, in mock *in feigned* exasperation.

The diving would make a suitable literary symbol. To go off the high board you had to wait in a line along the poolside and up the ladder. Fellows tickled girls and goosed one another and shouted to the ones at the top to hurry up, or razzed them for bellyfloppers. Once on the springboard some took a great while posing or clowning or deciding on a dive or getting up their nerve; others ran right off. Especially among the younger fellows the idea was to strike the funniest pose or do the craziest stunt as you fell, a thing that got harder to do as you kept on and kept on. But whether you hollered *Geronimo!* or *Sieg heil!,* held your nose or "rode a bicycle," pretended to be shot or did a perfect jackknife or changed your mind halfway down and ended up with nothing, it was over in two seconds, after all that wait. Spring, pose, splash. Spring, neat-o, splash. Spring, aw fooey, splash.

The grown-ups had gone on; Ambrose wanted to converse with Magda; she was remarkably well developed for her age; it was said that that came from rubbing with a turkish towel, and there were other theories. Ambrose could think of nothing to say except how good a diver Peter was, who was showing off for her benefit. You could pretty well tell by looking at their bathing suits and arm muscles how far along the different fellows were. Ambrose was glad he hadn't gone in swimming, the cold water shrank you up so. Magda pretended to be uninterested in the diving; she probably weighed as much as he did. If you knew your way around in the funhouse like your own bedroom, you could wait until a girl came along and then slip away without ever getting caught, even if her boyfriend was right with her. She'd think *he* did it! It would be better to be the boyfriend, and act outraged, and tear the funhouse apart.

Not act; *be.*

"He's a master diver," Ambrose said. In feigned admiration. "You really have to slave away at it to get that good." What would it matter anyhow if he asked her right out whether she remembered, even teased her with it as Peter would have?

There's no point in going farther; this isn't getting anybody anywhere;

they haven't even come to the funhouse yet. Ambrose is off the track, in some new or old part of the place that's not supposed to be used; he strayed into it by some one-in-a-million chance, like the time the roller-coaster car left the tracks in the nineteen-teens against all the laws of physics and sailed over the boardwalk in the dark. And they can't locate him because they don't know where to look. Even the designer and operator have forgotten this other part, that winds around on itself like a whelk shell. That winds around the right part like the snakes on Mercury's caduceus. Some people perhaps, don't "hit their stride" until their twenties, when the growing-up business is over and women appreciate other things besides wisecracks and teasing and strutting. Peter didn't have one-tenth the imagination *he* had, not one-tenth. Peter did the naming-their-children thing as a joke, making up names like Aloysius and Murgatroyd, but Ambrose knew *exactly* how it would feel to be married and have children of your own, and be a loving husband and father, and go comfortably to work in the morning and to bed with your wife at night, and wake up with her there. With a breeze coming through the sash and birds and mockingbirds singing in the Chinese-cigar trees. His eyes watered, there aren't enough ways to say that. He would be quite famous in his line of work. Whether Magda was his wife or not, one evening when he was wise-lined and gray at the temples he'd smile gravely, at a fashionable dinner party, and remind her of his youthful passion. The time they went with his family to Ocean City; the *erotic fantasies* he used to have about her. How long ago it seemed, and childish! Yet tender, too, *n'est-ce pas?* Would she have imagined that the world-famous whatever remembered how many strings were on the lyre on the bench beside the girl on the label of the cigar box he'd stared at in the toolshed at age ten while she, age eleven. Even then he had felt *wise beyond his years;* he'd stroked her hair and said in his deepest voice and correctest English, as to a dear child: "I shall never forget this moment."

But though he had breathed heavily, groaned as if ecstatic, what he'd really felt throughout was an odd detachment, as though someone else were Master. Strive as he might to be transported, he heard his mind take notes upon the scene: *This is what they call* passion. *I am experiencing it.* Many of the digger machines were out of order in the penny arcades and could not be repaired or replaced for the duration. Moreover the prizes, made now in USA, were less interesting than formerly, pasteboard items for the most part, and some of the machines wouldn't work on white pennies. The gypsy fortune-teller machine might have provided a foreshadowing of the climax of this story if Ambrose had operated it. It was even dilapidateder than most: the silver coating was worn off the brown metal handles, the glass windows around the dummy were cracked and taped, her kerchiefs and silks long-faded. If a man lived by himself, he could take a department-store manne-quin with flexible joints and modify her in certain ways. *However:* by the time he was that old he'd have a real woman. There was a machine that stamped your name around a white-metal coin with a star in the middle: *A ——*. His son would be the second, and when the lad reached thirteen or so he would put a strong arm around his shoulder and tell him calmly: "It is perfectly normal. We have all been through it. It will not last forever." Nobody knew how to be what they were right. He'd smoke a pipe, teach his son how to fish and softcrab, assure him he needn't worry about himself. Magda would certainly give, Magda would certainly yield a great deal of milk, although guilty of occasional solecisms. It don't taste so bad. Suppose the lights came on now!

The day wore on. You think you're yourself, but there are other persons in you. Ambrose gets hard when Ambrose doesn't want to, *and obversely.* Ambrose watches them disagree; Ambrose watches him watch. In the funhouse mirror-room you can't see yourself go on forever, because no matter how you stand, your head gets in the way. Even if you had a glass periscope, the image of your eye would cover up the thing you really wanted to see. The police will come; there'll be a story in the papers. That must be where it happened. Unless he can find a surprise exit, an unofficial backdoor or escape hatch opening on an alley, say, and then stroll up to the family in front of the funhouse and ask where everybody's been, *he's* been out of the place for ages. That's just where it happened, in that last lighted room: Peter and Magda found the right exit; he found one that you weren't supposed to find and strayed off into the works somewhere. In a perfect funhouse you'd be able to go only one way, like the divers off the high-board; getting lost would be impossible; the doors and halls would work like minnow traps or the valves in veins.

On account of German U-boats, Ocean City was "browned out": streetlights were shaded on the seaward side; shop-windows and boardwalk amusement places were kept dim, not to silhouette tankers and Liberty-ships for torpedoing. In a short story about Ocean City, Maryland, during World War II, the author could make use of the image of sailors on leave in the penny arcades and shooting galleries, sighting through the crosshairs of toy machine guns at swastika'd subs, while out in the black Atlantic a U-boat skipper squints through his periscope at real ships outlined by the glow of penny arcades. After dinner the family strolled back to the amusement end of the boardwalk. The boys' father had burnt red as always and was masked with Noxzema, a minstrel in reverse. The grown-ups stood at the end of the boardwalk where the Hurricane of '33 had cut an inlet from the ocean to Assawoman Bay.

"Pronounced with a long *o*," Uncle Karl reminded Magda with a wink. His shirt sleeves were rolled up; Mother punched his brown biceps with the arrowed heart on it and said his mind was naughty. Fat May's laugh came suddenly from the funhouse, as if she'd just got the joke; the family laughed too at the coincidence. Ambrose went under the boardwalk to search for out-of-town matchbook covers with the aid of his pocket flashlight; he looked out from the edge of the North American continent and wondered how far their laughter carried over the water. Spies in rubber rafts, survivors in lifeboats. If the joke had been beyond his understanding, he would have said: *"The laughter was over his head."* And let the reader see the serious wordplay on second reading.

He turned the flashlight on and then off at once even before the woman whooped. He sprang away, heart athud, dropping the light. What had the man grunted? Perspiration drenched and chilled him by the time he scrambled up to the family. "See anything?" his father asked. His voice wouldn't come; he shrugged and violently brushed sand from his pants legs.

"Let's ride the old flying horses!" Magda cried. I'll never be an author. It's been forever already, everybody's gone home, Ocean City's deserted, the ghost-crabs are tickling across the beach and down the littered cold streets. And the empty halls of clapboard hotels and abandoned funhouses. A tidal wave; an enemy air raid; a monster-crab swelling like an island from the sea. *The inhabitants fled in terror.* Magda clung to his trouser leg; he alone knew the maze's secret. "He gave his life that we might live," said Uncle Karl with a scowl of pain, as he. The fellow's hands had been tattooed; the woman's legs, the woman's fat white legs had. *An astonishing coincidence.* He yearned to tell Peter. He wanted to throw up for excitement. They hadn't even chased him. He wished he were dead.

One possible ending would be to have Ambrose come across another lost person in the dark. They'd match their wits together against the funhouse, struggle like Ulysses past obstacle after obstacle, help and encourage each other. Or a girl. By the time they found the exit they'd be closest friends, sweethearts if it were a girl; they'd know each other's inmost souls, be bound together *by the cement of shared adventure;* then they'd emerge into the light and it would turn out that his friend was a Negro. A blind girl. President Roosevelt's son. Ambrose's former archenemy.

Shortly after the mirror room he'd groped along a musty corridor, his heart already misgiving him at the absence of phosphorescent arrows and other signs. He'd found a crack of light—not a door, it turned out, but a seam between the plyboard wall panels—and squinting up to it, espied a small old man, *in appearance not unlike* the photographs at home of Ambrose's late grandfather, nodding upon a stool beneath a bare, speckled bulb. A crude panel of toggle- and knife-switches hung beside the open fuse box near his head; elsewhere in the little room were wooden levers and ropes belayed to boat cleats. At the time, Ambrose wasn't lost enough to rap or call; later he couldn't find that crack. Now it seemed to him that he'd possibly dozed off for a few minutes somewhere along the way; certainly he was exhausted from the afternoon's sunshine and the evening's problems; he couldn't be sure he hadn't dreamed part or all of the sight. Had an old black wall fan droned like bees and shimmied two flypaper streamers? Had the funhouse operator— gentle, somewhat sad and tired-appearing, in expression not unlike the photographs at home of Ambrose's late Uncle Konrad—murmured in his sleep? Is there really such a person as Ambrose, or is he a figment of the author's imagination? Was it Assawoman Bay or Sinepuxent? Are there other errors of fact in this fiction? Was there another sound besides the little slap slap of thigh on ham, like water sucking at the chine-boards of a skiff?

When you're lost, the smartest thing to do is stay put till you're found, hollering if necessary. But to holler guarantees humiliation as well as rescue; keeping silent permits some saving of face—you can act surprised at the fuss when your rescuers find you and swear you weren't lost, if they do. What's more you might find your own way yet, *however belatedly.*

"Don't tell me your foot's still asleep!" Magda exclaimed as the three young people walked from the inlet to the area set aside for ferris wheels, carrousels, and other carnival rides, they having decided in favor of the vast and ancient merry-go-round instead of the funhouse. What a sentence, everything was wrong from the outset. People don't know what to make of him, he doesn't know what to make of himself, he's only thirteen, *athletically and socially inept,* not astonishingly bright, but there are antennae; he has . . . some sort of receivers in his head; things speak to him, he understands more than he should, the world winks at him through its objects, grabs grinning at his coat. Everybody else is in on some secret he doesn't know; they've forgotten to tell him. Through simple *procrastination* his mother put off his baptism until this year. Everyone else had it done as a baby; he'd assumed the same of himself, as had his mother, so she claimed, until it was time for him to join Grace Methodist-Protestant and the oversight came out. He was mortified, but pitched sleepless through his private catechizing, intimidated by the ancient mysteries, a thirteen year old would never say that, resolved to experience conversion like St. Augustine. When the water touched his brow and Adam's sin left him, he contrived by a strain like defecation to bring tears into his eyes—but felt nothing. There was some simple, radical difference about him; he hoped it was genius, feared it was madness, devoted himself to amiability and inconspicuousness. Alone on the seawall near his house he was seized by the terrifying transports he'd thought to find in toolshed, in Communion-cup. The grass was alive! The town, the river, himself, were not imaginary; time roared in his ears like wind; the world was *going on!* This part ought to be dramatized. The Irish author James Joyce once wrote. Ambrose M—— is going to scream.

There is no *texture of rendered sensory detail,* for one thing. The faded distorting mirrors beside Fat May; the impossibility of choosing a mount when one had but a single ride on the great carrousel; the *vertigo attendant on his recognition* that Ocean City was worn out, the place of fathers and grandfathers, straw-boatered men and parasoled ladies survived by their amusements. Money spent, the three paused at Peter's insistence beside Fat May to watch the girls get their skirts blown up. The object was to tease Magda, who said: "I swear, Peter M——, you've got a one-track mind! Amby and me aren't *interested* in such things." In the tumbling-barrel, too, just inside the Devil's-mouth entrance to the funhouse, the girls were upended and their boyfriends and others could see up their dresses if they cared to. Which was the whole point, Ambrose realized. Of the entire funhouse! If you looked around, you noticed that almost all the people on the boardwalk were paired off into couples except the small children; in a way, that was the whole point of Ocean City! If you had X-ray eyes and could see everything going on at that instant under the boardwalk and in all the hotel rooms and cars and alleyways, you'd realized that all that normally *showed,* like restaurants and dance halls and clothing and test-your-strength machines, was merely preparation and intermission. Fat May screamed.

Because he watched the goings-on from the corner of his eye, it was Ambrose who spied the half-dollar on the boardwalk near the tumbling-barrel. Losers weepers. The first time he'd heard some people moving through a corridor not far away, just after he lost sight of the crack of light, he'd decided not to call to them, for fear they'd guess he was scared and poke fun; it sounded like roughnecks; he'd hoped they'd come by and he could follow in the dark without their knowing. Another time he'd heard just one person, unless he imagined it, bumping along as if on the other side of the plywood; perhaps Peter coming back for him, or Father, or Magda lost too. Or the owner and operator of the funhouse. He'd called out once, as though merrily: "Anybody know where the heck we are?" But the query was too stiff, his voice cracked, when the sounds stopped he was terrified: maybe it was a queer who waited for fellows to get lost, or a longhaired filthy monster that lived in some cranny of the funhouse. He stood rigid for hours it seemed like, scarcely respiring. His future was shockingly clear, in outline. He tried holding his breath to the point of unconsciousness. There ought to be a button you could push to end your life absolutely without pain; disappear in a flick, like turning out a light. He would push it instantly! He despised Uncle Karl. But he despised his father too, for not being what he was supposed to be. Perhaps his father hated *his* father, and so on, and his son would hate him, and so on. Instantly!

Naturally he didn't have nerve enough to ask Magda to go through the funhouse with him. With incredible nerve and to everyone's surprise he invited Magda, quietly and politely, to go through the funhouse with him. "I warn you, I've never been through it before," he added, *laughing easily;* "but I reckon we can manage somehow. The important thing to remember, after all, is that it's meant to be a *fun*house; that is, a place of amusement. If people really got lost or injured or too badly frightened in it, the owner'd go out of business. There'd even be lawsuits. No character in a work of fiction can make a speech this long without interruption or acknowledgment from the other characters."

Mother teased Uncle Karl: "Three's a crowd, I always heard." But actually Ambrose was relieved that Peter now had a quarter too. Nothing was what it looked like. Every instant, under the surface of the Atlantic Ocean, millions of living animals devoured one another. Pilots were falling in flames over Europe; women were being forcibly raped in the South Pacific. His father should have taken him aside and said: "There is a simple secret to getting through the funhouse, as simple as being first to see the Towers. Here it is. Peter does not know it; neither does your Uncle Karl. You and I are different. Not surprisingly, you've often wished you weren't. Don't think I haven't noticed how unhappy your childhood has been! But you'll understand, when

I tell you, why it had to be kept secret until now. And you won't regret not being like your brother and your uncle. *On the contrary!*" If you knew all the stories behind all the people on the boardwalk, you'd see that *nothing* was what it looked like. Husbands and wives often hated each other; parents didn't necessarily love their children; et cetera. A child took things for granted because he had nothing to compare his life to and everybody acted as if things were as they should be. Therefore each saw himself as the hero of the story, when the truth might turn out to be that he's the villain, or the coward. And there wasn't one thing you could do about it!

Hunchbacks, fat ladies, fools—that no one chose what he was was unbearable. In the movies he'd meet a beautiful young girl in the funhouse; they'd have hairs-breadth escapes from real dangers; he'd do and say the right things; she also; in the end they'd be lovers; their dialogue lines would match up; he'd be perfectly at ease; she'd not only like him well enough, she'd think he was *marvelous;* she'd lie awake thinking about *him,* instead of vice versa— the way *his* face looked in different lights and how he stood and exactly what he'd said—and yet that would be only one small episode in his wonderful life, among many many others. Not a *turning point* at all. What had happened in the toolshed was nothing. He hated, he loathed his parents! One reason for not writing a lost-in-the-funhouse story is that either everybody's felt what Ambrose feels, in which case it goes without saying, or else no normal person feels such things, in which case Ambrose is a freak. "Is anything more tiresome, in fiction, than the problems of sensitive adolescents?" And it's all too long and rambling, as if the author. For all a person knows the first time through, the end could be just around any corner; perhaps, *not impossibly* it's been within reach any number of times. On the other hand he may be scarcely past the start, with everything yet to get through, an intolerable idea.

Fill in: His father's raised eyebrows when he announced his decision to do the funhouse with Magda. Ambrose understands now, but didn't then, that his father was wondering whether he knew what the funhouse was *for*— especially since he didn't object, as he should have, when Peter decided to come along too. The ticket-woman, witchlike, mortifying him when inadvertently he gave her his name-coin instead of the half-dollar, then unkindly calling Magda's attention to the birthmark on his temple: "Watch out for him, girlie, he's a marked man!" She wasn't even cruel, he understood, only vulgar and insensitive. Somewhere in the world there was a young woman with such splendid understanding that she'd see him entire, like a poem or story, and find his words so valuable after all that when he confessed his apprehensions she would explain why they were in fact the very things that made him precious to her . . . and to Western Civilization! There was no such girl, the simple truth being. Violent yawns as they approached the mouth. Whispered advice from an old-timer on a bench near the barrel: "Go crabwise and ye'll get an eyeful without upsetting!" Composure vanished at the first pitch: Peter hollered joyously, Magda tumbled, shrieked, clutched her skirt; Ambrose scrambled crabwise, tight-lipped with terror, was soon out, watched his dropped name-coin slide among the couples. Shamefaced he saw that to get through expeditiously was not the point; Peter feigned assistance in order to trip Magda up, shouted "I see Christmas!" when her legs went flying. The old man, his latest betrayer, cackled approval. A dim hall then of black-thread cobwebs and recorded gibber: he took Magda's elbow to steady her against revolving discs set in the slanted floor to throw your feet out from under, and explained to her a calm, deep voice his theory that each phase of the funhouse was triggered either automatically, by a series of photoelectric devices, or else manually by operators stationed at peepholes. But he lost his voice thrice as the discs unbalanced him; Magda was anyhow squealing; but at one point she clutched him about the waist to keep from falling, and her right cheek pressed for a moment against his belt-buckle. Heroically he drew her up, it was his chance to clutch her close as if for support and say. "I love you." He even put an arm lightly about the small of her back before a sailor-and-girl pitched into them from behind, sorely treading his left big toe and knocking Magda asprawl with them. The sailor's girl was a string-haired hussy with a loud laugh and light blue drawers; Ambrose realized that he wouldn't have said "I love you" anyhow, and was smitten with self-contempt. How much better it would be to be that common sailor! A wiry little Seaman 3rd, the fellow squeezed a girl to each side and stumbled hilarious into the mirror room, closer to Magda in thirty seconds than Ambrose had got in thirteen years. She giggled at something the fellow said to Peter; she drew her hair from her eyes with a movement so womanly it struck Ambrose's heart; Peter smacking her backside then seemed particularly coarse. But Magda made a pleased indignant face and cried, "All right for *you,* mister!" and pursued Peter into the maze without a backward glance. The sailor followed after, leisurely, drawing his girl against his hip; Ambrose understood not only that they were all so relieved to be rid of his burdensome company that they didn't even notice his absence, but that he himself shared their relief. Stepping from the treacherous passage at last into the mirror-maze, he saw once again, more clearly than ever, how readily he deceived himself into supposing he was a person. He even foresaw, wincing at his dreadful self-knowledge, that he would repeat the deception, at ever-rarer intervals, all his wretched life, so fearful were the alternatives. Fame, madness, suicide; perhaps all three. It's not believable that so young a boy could articulate that reflection, and in fiction the merely true must always yield to the plausible. Moreover, the symbolism is in places heavy-footed. Yet Ambrose M—— understood, as few adults do, that the famous loneliness of the great was no popular myth but a general truth—furthermore, that it was as much cause as effect.

All the preceding except the last few sentences is exposition that should've been done earlier or interspersed with the present action instead of lumped together. No reader would put up with so much with such *prolixity.* It's interesting that Ambrose's father, though presumably an intelligent man (as indicated by his role as grade-school principal), neither encouraged nor discouraged his sons at all in any way—as if he either didn't care about them or cared all right but didn't know how to act. If this fact should contribute to one of them´s becoming a celebrated but wretchedly unhappy scientist, was it a good thing or not? He too might someday face the question; it would be useful to know whether it had tortured his father for years, for example, or never once crossed his mind.

In the maze two important things happened. First, our hero found a name-coin someone else had lost or discarded: *AMBROSE,* suggestive of the famous lightship and of his late grandfather's favorite dessert, which his mother used to prepare on special occasions out of coconut, oranges, grapes, and what else. Second, as he wondered at the endless replication of his image in the mirrors, second, as he *lost himself in the reflection* that the necessity for an observer makes perfect observation impossible, better make him eighteen at least, yet that would render other things unlikely, he heard Peter and Magda chuckling somewhere together in the maze. "Here!" "No, here!" they shouted to each other; Peter said, "Where's Amby?" Magda murmured. "Amb?" Peter called. In a pleased, friendly voice. He didn't reply. The truth was, his brother was a *happy-go-lucky youngster* who'd've been better off with a regular brother of his own, but who seldom complained of his lot and was generally cordial. Ambrose's throat ached; there aren't enough different ways to say that. He stood quietly while the two young people giggled and thumped through the glittering maze, hurrah'd their discovery of its exit, cried out in joyful alarm at what next beset them. Then he set his mouth and followed after, as he supposed, took a wrong turn, strayed into the pass *wherein he lingers yet.*

The action of conventional dramatic narrative may be represented by a diagram called Freitag's Triangle:

or more accurately by a variant of that diagram:

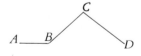

in which *AB* represents the exposition, *B* the introduction of conflict, *BC* the "rising action," complication, or development of the conflict, *C* the climax, or turn of the action, *CD* the dénouement, or resolution of the conflict. While there is no reason to regard this pattern as an absolute necessity, like many other conventions it became conventional because great numbers of people over many years learned by trial and error that it was effective; one ought not to forsake it, therefore, unless one wishes to forsake as well the effect of drama or has clear cause to feel that deliberate violation of the "normal" pattern can better can better effect that effect. This can't go on much longer; it can go on forever. He died telling stories to himself in the dark; years later, when that vast unsuspected area of the funhouse came to light, the first expedition found his skeleton in one of its labyrinthine corridors and mistook it for part of the entertainment. He died of starvation telling himself stories in the dark; but unbeknownst unbeknownst to him, an assistant operator of the funhouse, happening to overhear him, crouched just behind the plyboard partition and wrote down his every word. The operator's daughter, an exquisite young woman with a figure unusually well developed for her age, crouched just behind the partition and transcribed his every word. Though she had never laid eyes on him, she recognized that here was one of Western Culture's truly great imaginations, the eloquence of whose suffering would be an inspiration to unnumbered. And her heart was torn between her love for the misfortunate young man (yes, she loved him, though she had never laid though she knew him only—but how well!—through his words, and the deep, calm voice in which he spoke them) between her love et cetera and her womanly intuition that only in suffering and isolation could he give voice et cetera. Lone dark dying. Quietly she kissed the rough plyboard, and a tear fell upon the page. Where she had written in shorthand *Where she had written in shorthand* Where she had written in shorthand *Where she* et cetera. A long time ago we should have passed the apex of Freitag's Triangle and made brief work of the *dénouement;* the plot doesn't rise by meaningful steps but winds upon itself, digresses, retreats, hesitates, sighs, collapses, expires. The climax of the story must be its protagonist's discovery of a way to get through the funhouse. But he has found none, may have ceased to search.

What relevance does the war have to the story? Should there be fireworks outside or not?

Ambrose wandered, languished, dozed. Now and then he fell into his habit of rehearsing to himself the unadventurous story of his life, narrated from the third-person point of view, from his earliest memory parenthesis of maple leaves stirring in the summer breath of tidewater Maryland end of parenthesis to the present moment. Its principal events, on this telling, would appear to have been *A, B, C,* and *D.*

He imagined himself years hence, successful, married, at ease in the world, the trials of his adolescence far behind him. He has come to the seashore with his family for the holiday: how Ocean City has changed! But at one seldom at one ill-frequented end of the boardwalk a few derelict amusements survive from times gone by: the great carrousel from the turn of the century, with its monstrous griffins, and mechanical concert band; the roller coaster rumored since 1916 to have been condemned; the mechanical shooting gallery in which only the image of our enemies changed. His own son laughs with Fat May and wants to know what a funhouse is; Ambrose hugs the sturdy lad close and smiles around his pipestem at his wife.

The family's going home. Mother sits between Father and Uncle Karl, who teases him good-naturedly who chuckles over the fact that the comrade with whom he'd fought his way shoulder to shoulder through the funhouse had turned out to be a blind Negro girl—to their mutual discomfort, as they'd opened their souls. But such are the walls of custom, which even. Whose arm is where? How must it feel. He dreams of a funhouse vaster by far than any yet constructed; but by then they may be out of fashion, like steamboats and excursion trains. Already quaint and seedy: the draperied ladies on the frieze of the carrousel are his father's father's mooncheeked dreams; if he thinks of it more he will vomit his apple-on-a-stick.

He wonders: will he become a regular person? Something has gone wrong; his vaccination didn't take; at the Boy-Scout initiation campfire he only pretended to be deeply moved, as he pretends to this hour that it is not so bad after all in the funhouse, and that he has a little limp. How long will it last? He envisions a truly astonishing funhouse, incredibly complex yet utterly controlled from a great central switchboard like the console of a pipe organ. Nobody had enough imagination. He could design such a place himself, wiring and all, and he's only thirteen years old. He would be its operator: panel lights would show what was up in every cranny of its cunning of its multifarious vastness; a switch-flick would ease this fellow's way, complicate that's, to balance things out; if anyone seemed lost or frightened, all the operator had to do was.

He wishes he had never entered the funhouse. But he has. Then he wishes he were dead. But he's not. Therefore he will construct funhouses for others and be their secret operator—though he would rather be among the lovers for whom funhouses are designed.

The Shadow-Line

. . . D'autres fois, calme plat, grand miroir
De mon désespoir.

BAUDELAIRE

I

Only the young have such moments. I don't mean the very young. No. The very young have, properly speaking, no moments. It is the privilege of early youth to live in advance of its days in all the beautiful continuity of hope which knows no pauses and no introspection.

One closes behind one the little gate of mere boyishness—and enters an enchanted garden. Its very shades glow with promise. Every turn of the path has its seduction. And it isn't because it is an undiscovered country. One knows well enough that all mankind had streamed that way. It is the charm of universal experience from which one expects an uncommon or personal sensation —a bit of one's own.

One goes on recognising the landmarks of the predecessors, excited, amused, taking the hard luck and the good luck together—the kicks and the halfpence, as the saying is—the picturesque common lot that holds so many possibilities for the deserving or perhaps for the lucky. Yes. One goes on. And the time, too, goes on—till one perceives ahead a shadow-line warning one that the region of early youth, too, must be left behind.

This is the period of life in which such moments of which I have spoken are likely to come. What moments? Why, the moments of boredom, of weariness, of dissatisfaction. Rash moments. I mean moments when the still young are inclined to commit rash actions, such as getting married suddenly or else throwing up a job for no reason.

THE SHADOW-LINE by Joseph Conrad. Reprinted by permission of J. M. Dent & Sons Ltd. and the Trustees of the Joseph Conrad Estate. First published in book form in 1917.

This is not a marriage story. It wasn't so bad as that with me. My action, rash as it was, had more the character of divorce—almost of desertion. For no reason on which a sensible person could put a finger I threw up my job—chucked my berth—left the ship of which the worst that could be said was that she was a steamship and therefore, perhaps, not entitled to that blind loyalty which . . . However, it's no use trying to put a gloss on what even at the time I myself half suspected to be a caprice.

It was in an Eastern port. She was an Eastern ship, inasmuch as then she belonged to that port. She traded among dark islands on a blue reef-scarred sea, with the Red Ensign over the taffrail and at her masthead a house-flag, also red, but with a green border and with a white crescent in it. For an Arab owned her, and a Syed at that. Hence the green border on the flag. He was the head of a great House of Straits Arabs, but as loyal a subject of the complex British Empire as you could find east of the Suez Canal. World politics did not trouble him at all, but he had a great occult power amongst his own people.

It was all one to us who owned the ship. He had to employ white men in the shipping part of his business, and many of those he so employed had never set eyes on him from the first to the last day. I myself saw him but once, quite accidentally on a wharf—an old, dark little man blind in one eye, in a snowy robe and yellow slippers. He was having his hand severely kissed by a crowd of Malay pilgrims to whom he had done some favour, in the way of food and money. His almsgiving, I have heard, was most extensive, covering almost the whole Archipelago. For isn't it said that "The charitable man is the friend of Allah"?

Excellent (and picturesque) Arab owner, about whom one needed not to trouble one's head, a most excellent Scottish ship—for she was that from the keel up—excellent sea-boat, easy to keep clean, most handy in every way, and if it had not been for her internal propulsion, worthy of any man's love, I cherish to this day a profound respect for her memory. As to the kind of trade she was engaged in and the character of my shipmates, I could not have been happier if I had had the life and the men made to my order by a benevolent Enchanter.

And suddenly I left all this. I left it in that, to us, inconsequential manner in which a bird flies away from a comfortable branch. It was as though all un-knowing I had heard a whisper or seen something. Well—perhaps! One day I was perfectly right and the next everything was gone—glamour, flavour, interest, contentment—everything. It was one of those moments, you know. The green sickness of late youth descended on me and carried me off. Carried me off that ship, I mean.

We were only four white men on board, with a large crew of Kalashes and two Malay petty officers. The Captain stared hard as if wondering what ailed me. But he was a sailor, and he, too, had been young at one time. Presently a smile came to lurk under his thick iron-grey moustache, and he observed that, of course, if I felt I must go he couldn't keep me by main force. And it was arranged that I should be paid off the next morning. As I was going out of the chart-room he added suddenly, in a peculiar, wistful tone, that he hoped I would find what I was so anxious to go and look for. A soft, cryptic utterance which seemed to reach deeper than any diamond-hard tool could have done. I do believe he understood my case.

But the second engineer attacked me differently. He was a sturdy young Scot, with a smooth face and light eyes. His honest red countenance emerged out of the engine-room companion and then the whole robust man, with shirt sleeves turned out, wiping slowly the massive fore-arms with a lump of cotton-waste. And his light eyes expressed bitter distaste, as though our friendship had turned to ashes. He said weightily: "Oh! Aye! I've been thinking it was about time for you to run away home and get married to some silly girl."

It was tacitly understood in the port that John Nieven was a fierce misogynist; and the absurd character of the sally convinced me that he meant to be nasty—very nasty—had meant to say the most crushing thing he could think of. My laugh sounded deprecatory. Nobody but a friend could be so angry as that. I became a little crestfallen. Our chief engineer also took a characteristic view of my action, but in a kindlier spirit.

He was young, too, but very thin, and with a mist of fluffy brown beard all round his haggard face. All day long, at sea or in harbour, he could be seen walking hastily up and down the after-deck, wearing an intense, spiritually rapt expression, which was caused by a perpetual consciousness of unpleasant physical sensations in his internal economy. For he was a confirmed dyspeptic. His view of my case was very simple. He said it was nothing but deranged liver. Of course! He suggested I should stay for another trip and meantime dose myself with a certain patent medicine in which his own belief was absolute. "I'll tell you what I'll do. I'll buy you two bottles, out of my own pocket. There. I can't say fairer than that, can I?"

I believe he would have perpetrated the atrocity (or generosity) at the merest sign of weakening on my part. By that time, however, I was more discontented, disgusted, and dogged than ever. The past eighteen months, so full of new and varied experience, appeared a dreary, prosaic waste of days. I felt—how shall I express it?—that there was no truth to be got out of them.

What truth? I should have been hard put to it to explain. Probably, if pressed, I would have burst into tears simply. I was young enough for that.

Next day the Captain and I transacted our business in the Harbour Office. It was a lofty, big, cool, white room, where the screened light of day glowed serenely. Everybody in it—the officials, the public—was in white. Only the heavy polished desks gleamed darkly in a central avenue, and some papers lying on them were blue. Enormous punkahs sent from on high a gentle draught through that immaculate interior and upon our perspiring heads.

The official behind the desk we approached grinned amiably and kept it up till, in answer to his perfunctory question, "Sign off and on again?" my Captain answered, "No! Signing off for good." And then his grin vanished in sudden solemnity. He did not look at me again till he handed me my papers with a sorrowful expression, as if they had been my passports for Hades.

While I was putting them away he murmured some question to the Captain, and I heard the latter answer good-humouredly:

"No. He leaves us to go home."

"Oh!" the other exclaimed, nodding mournfully over my sad condition. I didn't know him outside the official building, but he leaned forward over the desk to shake hands with me, compassionately, as one would with some poor devil going out to be hanged; and I am afraid I performed my part ungraciously, in the hardened manner of an impenitent criminal.

No homeward-bound mail-boat was due for three or four days. Being now a man without a ship, and having for a time broken my connection with the sea—become, in fact, a mere potential passenger—it would have been more appropriate perhaps if I had gone to stay at an hotel. There it was, too, within a stone's throw of the Harbour Office, low, but somehow palatial, displaying its white, pillared pavilions surrounded by trim grass plots. I would have felt a passenger indeed in there! I gave it a hostile glance and directed my steps towards the Officers' Sailors' Home.

I walked in the sunshine, disregarding it, and in the shade of the big trees on the Esplanade without enjoying it. The heat of the tropical East descended through the leafy boughs, enveloping my thinly clad body, clinging to my rebellious discontent, as if to rob it of its freedom.

The Officers' Home was a large bungalow with a wide verandah and a curiously suburban-looking little garden of bushes and a few trees between it and the street. That institution partook somewhat of the character of a residential club, but with a slightly Governmental flavour about it, because it was administered by the Harbour Office. Its manager was officially styled Chief Steward. He was an unhappy, wizened little man, who if put into a jockey's rig would have looked the part to perfection. But it was obvious that at some time or other in his life, in some capacity or other, he had been connected with the sea. Possibly in the comprehensive capacity of a failure.

I should have thought his employment a very easy one, but he used to affirm for some reason or other that his job would be the death of him some day. It was rather mysterious. Perhaps everything naturally was too much trouble for him. He certainly seemed to hate having people in the house.

On entering it I thought he must be feeling pleased. It was as still as a tomb. I could see no one in the living rooms; and the verandah, too, was empty, except for a man at the far end dozing prone in a long chair. At the noise of my footsteps he opened one horribly-fish-like eye. He was a stranger to me. I retreated from there, and, crossing the dining-room—a very bare apartment with a motionless punkah hanging over the centre table—I knocked at a door labelled in black letters: "Chief Steward."

The answer to my knock being a vexed and doleful plaint: "Oh, dear! Oh, dear! What is it now?" I went in at once.

It was a strange room to find in the tropics. Twilight and stuffiness reigned in there. The fellow had hung enormously ample, dusty, cheap lace curtains over his windows, which were shut. Piles of cardboard boxes, such as milliners and dressmakers use in Europe, cumbered the corners; and by some means he had procured for himself the sort of furniture that might have come out of a respectable parlour in the East End of London—a horsehair sofa, arm-chairs of the same. I glimpsed grimy antimacassars, scattered over that horrid upholstery, which was awe-inspiring, insomuch that one could not guess what mysterious accident, need, or fancy had collected it there. Its owner had taken off his tunic, and in white trousers and a thin short-sleeved singlet prowled behind the chair-backs nursing his meagre elbows.

An exclamation of dismay escaped him when he heard that I had come for a stay; but he could not deny that there were plenty of vacant rooms.

"Very well. Can you give me the one I had before?"

He emitted a faint moan from behind a pile of cardboard boxes on the table, which might have contained gloves or handkerchiefs or neckties. I wonder what the fellow did keep in them? There was a smell of decaying coral, or Oriental dust, of zoological specimens in that den of his. I could only see the top of his head and his unhappy eyes levelled at me over the barrier.

"It's only for a couple of days," I said, intending to cheer him up.

"Perhaps you would like to pay in advance?" he suggested eagerly.

"Certainly not!" I burst out directly I could speak. "Never heard of such a thing! This is the most infernal cheek. . . ."

He had seized his head in both hands—a gesture of despair which checked my indignation.

"Oh, dear! Oh, dear! Don't fly out like this. I am asking everybody."

"I don't believe it," I said bluntly.

"Well, I am going to. And if you gentlemen all agreed to pay in advance I could make Hamilton pay up too. He's always turning up ashore dead broke, and even when he has some money he won't settle his bills. I don't know what to do with him. He swears at me and tells me I can't chuck a white man out into the street here. So if you only would . . ."

I was amazed. Incredulous too. I suspected the fellow of gratuitous impertinence. I told him with marked emphasis that I would see him and Hamilton hanged first, and requested him to conduct me to my room with no more of his nonsense. He produced then a key from somewhere and led the way out of his lair, giving me a vicious sidelong look in passing.

"Any one I know staying here?" I asked him before he left my room.

He had recovered his usual pained impatient tone, and said that Captain Giles was there, back from a Solo Sea trip. Two other guests were staying also. He paused. And, of course, Hamilton, he added.

"Oh, yes! Hamilton," I said, and the miserable creature took himself off with a final groan.

His impudence still rankled when I came into the dining-room at tiffin time. He was there on duty overlooking the Chinamen servants. The tiffin was laid on one end only of the long table, and the punkah was stirring the hot air lazily—mostly above a barren waste of polished wood.

We were four around the cloth. The dozing stranger from the chair was one. Both his eyes were partly opened now, but they did not seem to see anything. He was supine. The dignified person next him, with short side whiskers and a carefully scraped chin, was, of course, Hamilton. I have never seen any one so full of dignity for the station in life Providence had been pleased to place him in. I had been told that he regarded me as a rank outsider. He raised not only his eyes, but his eyebrows as well, at the sound I made pulling back my chair.

Captain Giles was at the head of the table. I exchanged a few words of greeting with him and sat down on his left. Stout and pale, with a great shiny dome of a bald forehead and prominent brown eyes, he might have been anything but a seaman. You would not have been surprised to learn that he was an architect. To me (I know how absurd it is) he looked like a church-warden. He had the appearance of a man from whom you would expect sound advice, moral sentiments, with perhaps a platitude or two thrown in on occasion, not from a desire to dazzle, but from honest conviction.

Though very well known and appreciated in the shipping world, he had no regular employment. He did not want it. He had his own peculiar position. He was an expert. An expert in—how shall I say it?—in intricate navigation. He was supposed to know more about remote and imperfectly charted parts of the Archipelago than any man living. His brain must have been a perfect warehouse of reefs, positions, bearings, images of headlands, shapes of obscure coasts, aspects of innumerable islands, desert and otherwise. Any ship, for instance, bound on a trip to Palawan or somewhere that way would have Captain Giles on board, either in temporary command or "to assist the master." It was said that he had a retaining fee from a wealthy firm of Chinese steamship owners, in view of such services. Besides, he was always ready to relieve any man who wished to take a spell ashore for a time. No owner was ever known to object to an arrangement of that sort. For it seemed to be the established opinion at the port that Captain Giles was as good as the best, if not a little better. But in Hamilton's view he was an "outsider." I believe that for Hamilton the generalisation "outsider" covered the whole lot of us; though I suppose that he made some distinctions in his mind.

I didn't try to make conversation with Captain Giles, whom I had not seen more than twice in my life. But, of course, he knew who I was. After a while, inclining his big shiny head my way, he addressed me first in his friendly fashion. He presumed from seeing me there, he said, that I had come ashore for a couple of days' leave.

He was a low-voiced man. I spoke a little louder, saying that: No—I had left the ship for good.

"A free man for a bit," was his comment.

"I suppose I may call myself that—since eleven o'clock," I said.

Hamilton had stopped eating at the sound of our voices. He laid down his knife and fork gently, got up, and muttering something about "this infernal heat cutting one's appetite," went out of the room. Almost immediately we heard him leave the house down the verandah steps.

On this Captain Giles remarked easily that the fellow had no doubt gone off to look after my old job. The Chief Steward, who had been leaning against the wall, brought his face of an unhappy goat nearer to the table and addressed us dolefully. His object was to unburden himself of his eternal grievance against Hamilton. The man kept him in hot water with the Harbour Office as to the state of his accounts. He wished to goodness he would get my job, though in truth what would it be? Temporary relief at best.

I said: "You needn't worry. He won't get my job. My successor is on board already."

He was surprised, and I believe his face fell a little at the news. Captain Giles gave a soft laugh. We got up and went out on the verandah, leaving the supine stranger to be dealt with by the Chinamen. The last thing I saw they had put a plate with a slice of pineapple on it before him and stood back to watch what would happen. But the experiment seemed a failure. He sat insensible.

It was imparted to me in a low voice by Captain Giles that this was an officer of some Rajah's yacht which had come to our port to be dry-docked. Must have been "seeing life" last night, he added, wrinkling his nose in an intimate, confidential way which pleased me vastly. For Captain Giles had prestige. He was credited with wonderful adventures and with some mysterious tragedy in his life. And no man had a word to say against him. He continued:

"I remember him first coming ashore here some years ago. Seems only the other day. He was a nice boy. On! these nice boys!"

I could not help laughing aloud. He looked startled, then joined in the laugh. "No! No! I didn't mean that," he cried. "What I meant is that some of them do go soft mighty quick out here."

Jocularly I suggested the beastly heat as the first cause. But Captain Giles disclosed himself possessed of a deeper philosophy. Things out East were made easy for white men. That was all right. The difficulty was to go on keeping white, and some of these nice boys did not know how. He gave me a searching look, and in a benevolent, heavy-uncle manner asked point blank:

"Why did you throw up your berth?"

I became angry all of a sudden; for you can understand how exasperating such a question was to a man who didn't know. I said to myself that I ought to shut up that moralist; and to him aloud I said with challenging politeness:

"Why? . . . Do you disapprove?"

He was too disconcerted to do more than mutter confusedly: "I! . . . In a general way . . ." and then gave me up. But he retired in good order, under the cover of an heavily humorous remark that he, too, was getting soft, and that this was his time for taking his little siesta—when he was on shore. "Very bad habit. Very bad habit."

The simplicity of the man would have disarmed a touchiness even more youthful than mine. So when next day at tiffin he bent his head towards me and said that he had met my late Captain last evening, adding in an undertone: "He's very sorry you left. He had never had a mate that suited him so well," I answered him earnestly, without any affectation, that I certainly hadn't been so comfortable in any ship or with any commander in all my sea-going days.

"Well—then," he murmured.

"Haven't you heard, Captain Giles, that I intend to go home?"

"Yes," he said benevolently. "I have heard that sort of thing so often before."

"What of that?" I cried. I thought he was the most dull, unimaginative man I had ever met. I don't know what more I would have said, but the much-belated Hamilton came in just then and took his usual seat. So I dropped into a mumble.

"Anyhow, you shall see it done this time."

Hamilton, beautifully shaved, gave Captain Giles a curt nod, but didn't even condescend to raise his eyebrows at me; and when he spoke it was only to tell the Chief Steward that the food on his plate wasn't fit to be set before a gentleman. The individual addressed seemed much too unhappy to groan. He only cast his eyes up to the punkah and that was all.

Captain Giles and I got up from the table, and the stranger next to Hamilton followed our example, manoeuvring himself to his feet with difficulty. He, poor fellow, not because he was hungry but I verily believe only to recover his self-respect, had tried to put some of that unworthy food into his mouth. But after dropping his fork twice and generally making a failure of it, he had sat still with an air of intense mortification combined with a ghastly glazed stare. Both Giles and I had avoided looking his way at table.

On the verandah he stopped short on purpose to address to us anxiously a long remark which I failed to understand completely. It sounded like some horrible unknown language. But when Captain Giles, after only an instant for reflection, answered him with homely friendliness, "Aye, to be sure. You are right there," he appeared very much gratified indeed, and went away (pretty straight too) to seek a distant long chair.

"What was he trying to say?" I asked with disgust.

"I don't know. Mustn't be down too much on a fellow. He's feeling pretty wretched, you may be sure; and to-morrow he'll feel worse yet."

Judging by the man's appearance it seemed impossible. I wondered what sort of complicated debauch had reduced him to that unspeakable condition. Captain Giles' benevolence was spoiled by a curious air of complacency which I disliked. I said with a little laugh:

"Well, he will have you to look after him."

He made a deprecatory gesture, sat down, and took up a paper. I did the same. The papers were old and uninteresting, filled up mostly with dreary stereotyped descriptions of Queen Victoria's first jubilee celebrations. Probably we should have quickly fallen into a tropical afternoon doze if it had not been for Hamilton's voice raised in the dining-room. He was finishing his tiffin there. The big double doors stood wide open permanently, and he could not have had any idea how near the doorway our chairs were placed. He was heard in a loud, supercilious tone answering some statement ventured by the Chief Steward.

"I am not going to be rushed into anything. They will be glad enough to get a gentleman I imagine. There is no hurry."

A loud whispering from the steward succeeded and then again Hamilton was heard with even intenser scorn.

"What? That young ass who fancies himself for having been chief mate with Kent so long? . . . Preposterous."

Giles and I looked at each other. Kent being the name of my late commander, Captain Giles' whisper, "He's talking of you," seemed to me sheer waste of breath. The Chief Steward must have stuck to his point whatever it was, because Hamilton was heard again more supercilious, if possible, and also very emphatic:

"Rubbish, my good man! One doesn't *compete* with a rank outsider like that. There's plenty of time."

Then there was pushing of chairs, footsteps in the next room, and plaintive expostulations from the Steward, who was pursuing Hamilton, even out of doors through the main entrance.

"That's a very insulting sort of man," remarked Captain Giles—superfluously, I thought. "Very insulting. You haven't offended him in some way, have you?"

"Never spoke to him in my life," I said grumpily. "Can't imagine what he means by competing. He has been trying for my job after I left—and didn't get it. But that isn't exactly competition."

Captain Giles balanced his big benevolent head thoughtfully. "He didn't get it," he repeated very slowly. "No, not likely either, with Kent. Kent is no end sorry you left him. He gives you the name of a good seaman too."

I flung away the paper I was still holding. I sat up, I slapped the table with my open palm. I wanted to know why he would keep harping on that, my absolutely private affair. It was exasperating, really.

Captain Giles silenced me by the perfect equanimity of his gaze. "Nothing to be annoyed about," he murmured reasonably, with an evident desire to soothe the childish irritation he had aroused. And he was really a man of an appearance so inoffensive that I tried to explain myself as much as I could. I told him that I did not want to hear any more about what was past and gone. It had been very nice while it lasted, but now it was done with I preferred not to talk about it or even think about it. I had made up my mind to go home.

He listened to the whole tirade in a particular, lending-the-ear attitude, as if trying to detect a false note in it somewhere; then straightened himself up and appeared to ponder sagaciously over the matter.

"Yes. You told me you meant to go home. Anything in view there?"

Instead of telling him that it was none of his business I said sullenly:

"Nothing that I know of."

I had indeed considered that rather blank side of the situation I had created for myself by leaving suddenly my very satisfactory employment. And I was not very pleased with it. I had it on the tip of my tongue to say that common sense had nothing to do with my action, and that therefore it didn't deserve the interest Captain Giles seemed to be taking in it. But he was puffing at a short wooden pipe now, and looked so guileless, dense, and commonplace, that it seemed hardly worth while to puzzle him either with truth or sarcasm.

He blew a cloud of smoke, then surprised me by a very abrupt: "Paid your passage money yet?"

Overcome by the shameless pertinacity of a man to whom it was rather difficult to be rude, I replied with exaggerated meekness that I had not done so yet. I thought there would be plenty of time to do that to-morrow.

And I was about to turn away, withdrawing my privacy from his fatuous, objectless attempts to test what sort of stuff it was made of, when he laid down his pipe in an extremely significant manner, you know, as if a critical moment had come, and leaned sideways over the table between us.

"Oh! You haven't yet!" He dropped his voice mysteriously. "Well, then I think you ought to know that there's something going on here."

I had never in my life felt more detached from all earthly goings on. Freed from the sea for a time, I preserved the sailor's consciousness of complete independence from all land affairs. How could they concern me? I gazed at Captain Giles' animation with scorn rather than with curiosity.

To his obviously preparatory question whether our Steward had spoken to me that day I said he hadn't. And what's more he would have had precious little encouragement if he had tried to. I didn't want the fellow to speak to me at all.

Unrebuked by my petulance, Captain Giles, with an air of immense sagacity, began to tell me a minute tale about a Harbour Office peon. It was absolutely pointless. A peon was seen walking that morning on the verandah with a letter in his hand. It was in an official envelope. As the habit of these fellows is, he had shown it to the first white man he came across. That man was our friend in the arm-chair. He, as I knew, was not in a state to interest himself in any sublunary matters. He could only wave the peon away. The peon then wandered on along the verandah and came upon Captain Giles, who was there by an extraordinary chance. . . .

At this point he stopped with a profound look. The letter, he continued, was addressed to the Chief Steward. Now what would Captain Ellis, the Master Attendant, want to write to the Steward for? The fellow went every morning, anyhow, to the Harbour Office with his report, for orders or what not. He hadn't been back more than an hour before there was an office peon chasing him with a note. Now what was that for?

And he began to speculate. It was not for this—and it could not be for that. As to that other thing it was unthinkable.

The fatuousness of all this made me stare. If the man had not been some-how a sympathetic personality I would have resented it like an insult. As it was, I felt only sorry for him. Something remarkably earnest in his gaze prevented me from laughing in his face. Neither did I yawn at him. I just stared.

His tone became a shade more mysterious. Directly the fellow (meaning the Steward) got that note he rushed for his hat and bolted out of the house. But it wasn't because the note called him to the Harbour Office. He didn't go there. He was not absent long enough for that. He came darting back in no time, flung his hat away, and raced about the dining-room moaning and slapping his forehead. All these exciting facts and manifestations had been observed by Captain Giles. He had, it seems, been meditating upon them ever since.

I began to pity him profoundly. And in a tone which I tried to make as little sarcastic as possible I said that I was glad he had found something to occupy his morning hours.

With his disarming simplicity he made me observe, as if it were a matter of some consequence, how strange it was that he should have spent the morning indoors at all. He generally was out before tiffin, visiting various offices, seeing his friends in the harbour, and so on. He had felt out of sorts somewhat on rising. Nothing much. Just enough to make him feel lazy.

All this with a sustained, holding stare which, in conjunction with the general inanity of the discourse, conveyed the impression of mild, dreary lunacy. And when he hitched his chair a little and dropped his voice to the low note of mystery, it flashed upon me that high professional reputation was not necessarily a guarantee of sound mind.

It never occurred to me then that I didn't know in what soundness of mind exactly consisted and what a delicate and, upon the whole, unimportant matter it was. With some idea of not hurting his feelings I blinked at him in an interested manner. But when he proceeded to ask me mysteriously whether I remembered what had passed just now between that Steward of ours and "that man Hamilton," I only grunted sour assent and turned away my head.

"Aye. But do you remember every word?" he insisted tactfully.

"I don't know. It's none of my business," I snapped out, consigning, moreover, the Steward and Hamilton aloud to eternal perdition.

I meant to be very energetic and final, but Captain Giles continued to gaze at me thoughtfully. Nothing could stop him. He went on to point out that my personality was involved in that conversation. When I tried to preserve the semblance of unconcern he became positively cruel. I heard what the man had said? Yes? What did I think of it then?—he wanted to know.

Captain Giles' appearance excluding the suspicion of mere sly malice, I came to the conclusion that he was simply the most tactless idiot on earth. I almost despised myself for the weakness of attempting to enlighten his common understanding. I started to explain that I did not think anything whatever. Hamilton was not worth a thought. What such an offensive loafer . . . —

"Aye! that he is," interjected Captain Giles— . . . thought or said was below any decent man's contempt, and I did not propose to take the slightest notice of it.

This attitude seemed to me so simple and obvious that I was really aston-ished at Giles giving no sign of assent. Such perfect stupidity was almost interesting.

"What would you like me to do?" I asked laughing. "I can't start a row with him because of the opinion he has formed of me. Of course, I've heard of the contemptuous way he alludes to me. But he doesn't intrude his con-tempt on my notice. He has never expressed it in my hearing. For even just now he didn't know we could hear him. I should only make myself ridiculous."

That hopeless Giles went on puffing at his pipe moodily. All at once his face cleared, and he spoke.

"You missed my point."

"Have I? I am very glad to hear it," I said.

With increasing animation he stated again that I had missed his point. Entirely. And in a tone of growing self-conscious complacency he told me that few things escaped his attention, and he was rather used to thinking them out, and generally from his experience of life and men arrived at the right conclusion.

This bit of self-praise, of course, fitted excellently the laborious inanity of the whole conversation. The whole thing strengthened in me that obscure feeling of life being but a waste of days, which, half-unconsciously, had driven me out of a comfortable berth, away from men I liked, to flee from the menace of emptiness . . . and to find inanity at the first turn. Here was a men of recognised character and achievement disclosed as an absurd and dreary chatterer. And it was probably like this everywhere—from east to west, from the bottom to the top of the social scale.

A great discouragement fell on me. A spiritual drowsiness. Giles' voice was going on complacently; the very voice of the universal hollow conceit. And I was no longer angry with it. There was nothing original, nothing new, startling, informing to expect from the world: no opportunities to find out something about oneself, no wisdom to acquire, no fun to enjoy. Everything was stupid and overrated, even as Captain Giles was. So be it.

The name of Hamilton suddenly caught my ear and roused me up.

"I thought we had done with him," I said, with the greatest possible distaste.

"Yes. But considering what we happened to hear just now I think you ought to do it."

"Ought to do it?" I sat up bewildered. "Do what?"

Captain Giles confronted me very much surprised.

"Why! Do what I have been advising you to try. You go and ask the Steward what was there in that letter from the Harbour Office. Ask him straight out."

I remained speechless for a time. Here was something unexpected and original enough to be altogether incomprehensible. I murmured, astounded:

"But I thought it was Hamilton that you . . ."

"Exactly. Don't you let him. You do what I tell you. You tackle that

Steward. You'll make him jump, I bet," insisted Captain Giles, waving his smouldering pipe impressively at me. Then he took three rapid puffs at it.

His aspect of triumphant acuteness was indescribable. Yet the man remained a strangely sympathetic creature. Benevolence radiated from him ridiculously, mildly, impressively. It was irritating, too. But I pointed out coldly, as one who deals with the incomprehensible, that I didn't see any reason to expose myself to a snub from the fellow. He was a very unsatisfactory steward and a miserable wretch besides, but I would just as soon think of tweaking his nose.

"Tweaking his nose," said Captain Giles in a scandalised tone. "Much use it would be to you."

That remark was so irrelevant that one could make no answer to it. But the sense of the absurdity was beginning at last to exercise its well-known fascination. I felt I must not let the man talk to me any more. I got up, observing curtly that he was too much for me—that I couldn't make him out.

Before I had time to move away he spoke again in a changed tone of obstinacy and puffing nervously at his pipe.

"Well—he's a—no account cuss—anyhow. You just—ask him. That's all."

That new manner impressed me—or rather made me pause. But sanity asserting its sway, at once I left the verandah after giving him a mirthless smile. In a few strides I found myself in the dining-room, now cleared and empty. But during that short time various thoughts occurred to me, such as: that Giles had been making fun of me, expecting some amusement at my expense; that I probably looked silly and gullible; that I knew very little of life. . . .

The door facing me across the dining-room flew open to my extreme surprise. It was the door inscribed with the word "Steward" and the man himself ran out of his stuffy Philistinish lair in his absurd hunted animal manner, making for the garden door.

To this day I don't know what made me call after him: "I say! Wait a minute." Perhaps it was the sidelong glance he gave me; or possibly I was yet under the influence of Captain Giles' mysterious earnestness. Well, it was an impulse of some sort; an effect of that force somewhere within our lives which shapes them this way or that. For if these words had not escaped from my lips (my will had nothing to do with that) my existence would, to be sure, have been still a seaman's existence, but directed on now to me utterly inconceivable lines.

No. My will had nothing to do with it. Indeed, no sooner had I made that fateful noise than I became extremely sorry for it. Had the man stopped and faced me I would have had to retire in disorder. For I had no notion to carry out Captain Giles' idiotic joke, either at my own expense or at the expense of the Steward.

But here the old human instinct of the chase came into play. He pretended to be deaf, and I, without thinking a second about it, dashed along my own side of the dining table and cut him off at the very door.

"Why can't you answer when you are spoken to?" I asked roughly.

He leaned against the side of the door. He looked extremely wretched. Human nature is, I fear, not very nice right through. There are ugly spots in it. I found myself growing angry, and that, I believe, only because my quarry looked so woe-begone. Miserable beggar!

I went for him without more ado. "I understand there was an official communication to the Home from the Harbour Office this morning. Is that so?"

Instead of telling me to mind my own business, as he might have done, he began to whine with an undertone of impudence. He couldn't see me anywhere this morning. He couldn't be expected to run all over the town after me.

"Who wants you to?" I cried. And then my eyes became opened to the inwardness of things and speeches the triviality of which had been so baffling and tiresome.

I told him I wanted to know what was in that letter. My sternness of tone and behaviour was only half assumed. Curiosity can be a very fierce sentiment —at times.

He took refuge in a silly, muttering sulkiness. It was nothing to me, he mumbled. I had told him I was going home. And since I was going home he didn't see why he should . . .

That was the line of his argument, and it was irrelevant enough to be almost insulting. Insulting to one's intelligence, I mean.

In that twilight region between youth and maturity, in which I had my being then, one is peculiarly sensitive to that kind of insult. I am afraid my behaviour to the Steward became very rough indeed. But it wasn't in him to face out anything or anybody. Drug habit or solitary tippling, perhaps. And when I forgot myself so far as to swear at him he broke down and began to shriek.

I don't mean to say that he made a great outcry. It was a cynical shrieking confession, only faint—piteously faint. It wasn't very coherent either, but sufficiently so to strike me dumb at first. I turned my eyes from him in righteous indignation, and perceived Captain Giles in the verandah doorway surveying quietly the scene, his own handiwork, if I may express it in that way. His smouldering black pipe was very noticeable in his big, paternal fist. So, too, was the glitter of his heavy gold watch-chain across the breast of his white tunic. He exhaled an atmosphere of virtuous sagacity thick enough for any innocent soul to fly to confidently. I flew to him.

"You would never believe it," I cried. "It was a notification that a master is wanted for some ship. There's a command apparently going about and this fellow puts the thing in his pocket."

The Steward screamed out in accents of loud despair, "You will be the death of me!"

The mighty slap he gave his wretched forehead was very loud, too. But when I turned to look at him he was no longer there. He had rushed away somewhere out of sight. This sudden disappearance made me laugh.

This was the end of the incident—for me. Captain Giles, however, staring at the place where the Steward had been, began to haul at his gorgeous gold chain till at last the watch came up from the deep pocket like solid truth from a well. Solemnly he lowered it down again and only then said:

"Just three o'clock. You will be in time—if you don't lose any, that is."

"In time for what?" I asked.

"Good Lord! For the Harbour Office. This must be looked into."

Strictly speaking, he was right. But I've never had much taste for investigation, for showing people up and all that, no doubt, ethically meritorious kind of work. And my view of the episode was purely ethical. If any one had to be the death of the Steward I didn't see why it shouldn't be Captain Giles himself, a man of age and standing, and a permanent resident. Whereas I, in comparison, felt myself a mere bird of passage in that port. In fact, it might have been said that I had already broken off my connection. I muttered that I didn't think—it was nothing to me. . . .

"Nothing!" repeated Captain Giles, giving some signs of quiet, deliberate indignation. "Kent warned me you were a peculiar young fellow. You will tell me next that a command is nothing to you—and after all the trouble I've taken, too!"

"The trouble!" I murmured, uncomprehending. What trouble? All I could remember was being mystified and bored by his conversation for a solid hour after tiffin. And he called that taking a lot of trouble.

He was looking at me with a self-complacency which would have been odious in any other man. All at once, as if a page of a book had been turned over disclosing a word which made plain all that had gone before, I perceived that this matter had also another than an ethical aspect.

And still I did not move. Captain Giles lost his patience a little. With an angry puff at his pipe he turned his back on my hesitation.

But it was not hesitation on my part. I had been, if I may express myself so, put out of gear mentally. But as soon as I had convinced myself that this stale, unprofitable world of my discontent contained such a thing as a command to be seized, I recovered my powers of locomotion.

It's a good step from the Officers' Home to the Harbour Office, but with the magic word "Command" in my head I found myself suddenly on the quay as if transported there in the twinkling of an eye, before a portal of dressed white stone above a flight of shallow white steps.

All this seemed to glide towards me swiftly. The whole great roadstead to the right was just a mere flicker of blue, and the dim cool hall swallowed me up out of the heat and glare of which I had not been aware till the very moment I passed in from it.

The broad inner staircase insinuated itself under my feet somehow. Command is a strong magic. The first human beings I perceived distinctly since I had parted with the indignant back of Captain Giles was the crew of the harbour steam-launch lounging on the spacious landing about the curtained archway of the shipping office.

It was there that my buoyancy abandoned me. The atmosphere of official-dom would kill anything that breathes the air of human endeavour, would extinguish hope and fear alike in the supremacy of paper and ink. I passed heavily under the curtain which the Malay coxswain of the harbour launch raised for me. There was nobody in the office except the clerks, writing in two industrious rows. But the head shipping-master hopped down from his elevation and hurried along on the thick mats to meet me in the broad central passage.

He had a Scottish name, but his complexion was of a rich olive hue, his short beard was jet black, and his eyes, also black, had a languishing expres-sion. He asked confidentially:

"You want to see Him?"

All lightness of spirit and body having departed from me at the touch of officialdom, I looked at the scribe without animation and asked in my turn wearily:

"What do you think? Is it any use?"

"My goodness! He has asked for you twice to-day."

This emphatic He was the supreme authority, the Marine Superintendent, the Harbour-Master—a very great person in the eyes of every single quill-driver in the room. But that was nothing to the opinion he had of his own greatness.

Captain Ellis looked upon himself as a sort of divine (pagan) emanation, the deputy-Neptune for the circumambient seas. If he did not actually rule the waves, he pretended to rule the fate of the mortals whose lives were cast upon the waters.

This uplifting illusion made him inquisitorial and peremptory. And as his temperament was choleric there were fellows who were actually afraid of him. He was redoubtable, not in virtue of his office, but because of his unwar-rantable assumptions. I had never had anything to do with him before.

I said: "Oh! He has asked for me twice. Then perhaps I had better go in."

"You must! You must!"

The shipping-master led the way with a mincing gait round the whole system of desks to a tall and important-looking door, which he opened with a deferential action of the arm.

He stepped right in (but without letting go of the handle) and, after gazing reverently down the room for a while, beckoned me in by a silent jerk of the head. Then he slipped out at once and shut the door after me most delicately.

Three lofty windows gave on the harbour. There was nothing in them but the dark-blue sparkling sea and the paler luminous blue of the sky. My eye caught in the depths and distances of these blue tones the white speck of some big ship just arrived and about to anchor in the outer roadstead. A ship from home—after perhaps ninety days at sea. There is something touching about a ship coming in from sea and folding her white wings for a rest.

The next thing I saw was the top-knot of silver hair surmounting Captain

Ellis' smooth red face, which would have been apoplectic if it hadn't had such a fresh appearance.

Our deputy-Neptune had no beard on his chin, and there was no trident to be seen standing in a corner anywhere, like an umbrella. But his hand was holding a pen—the official pen, far mightier than the sword in making or marring the fortune of simple toiling men. He was looking over his shoulder at my advance.

When I had come well within range he saluted me by a nerve-shattering: "Where have you been all this time?"

As it was no concern of his I did not take the slightest notice of the shot. I said simply that I had heard there was a master needed for some vessel, and being a sailing-ship man I thought I would apply. . . ,

He interrupted me. "Why! Hang it! *You* are the right man for that job—if there had been twenty others after it. But no fear of that. They are all afraid to catch hold. That's what's the matter."

He was very irritated. I said innocently: "Are they, sir? I wonder why?"

"Why!" he fumed. "Afraid of the sails. Afraid of a white crew. Too much trouble. Too much work. Too long out here. Easy life and deck-chairs more their mark. Here I sit with the Consul-General's cable before me, and the only man fit for the job not to be found anywhere. I began to think you were funking it too. . . ."

"I haven't been long getting to the office," I remarked calmly.

"You have a good name out here, though," he growled savagely without looking at me.

"I am very glad to hear it from you, sir," I said.

"Yes. But you are not on the spot when you are wanted. You know you weren't. That steward of yours wouldn't dare to neglect a message from this office. Where the devil did you hide yourself for the best part of the day?"

I only smiled kindly down on him, and he seemed to recollect himself, and asked me to take a seat. He explained that the master of a British ship having died in Bankok the Consul-General had cabled to him a request for a competent man to be sent out to take command.

Apparently, in his mind, I was the man from the first, though for the looks of the thing the notification addressed to the Sailors' Home was general. An agreement had already been prepared. He gave it to me to read, and when I handed it back to him with the remark that I accepted its terms, the deputy-Neptune signed it, stamped it with his own exalted hand, folded it in four (it was a sheet of blue foolscap), and presented it to me—a gift of extraordinary potency, for, as I put it in my pocket, my head swam a little.

"This is your appointment to the command," he said with a certain gravity. "An official appointment binding the owners to conditions which you have accepted. Now—when will you be ready to go?"

I said I would be ready that very day if necessary. He caught me at my word with great readiness. The steamer *Melita* was leaving for Bankok that evening about seven. He would request her captain officially to give me a passage and wait for me till ten o'clock.

Then he rose from his office chair, and I got up too. My head swam, there was no doubt about it, and I felt a heaviness of limbs as if they had grown bigger since I had sat down on that chair. I made my bow.

A subtle change in Captain Ellis' manner became perceptible as though he had laid aside the trident of deputy-Neptune. In reality, it was only his official pen that he had dropped on getting up.

II

He shook hands with me: "Well, there you are, on your own, appointed officially under my responsibility."

He was actually walking with me to the door. What a distance off it seemed! I moved like a man in bonds. But we reached it at last. I opened it with the sensation of dealing with mere dream-stuff, and then at the last moment the fellowship of seamen asserted itself, stronger than the difference of age and station. It asserted itself in Captain Ellis' voice.

"Good-bye—and good luck to you," he said so heartily that I could only give him a grateful glance. Then I turned and went out, never to see him again in my life. I had not made three steps into the outer office when I heard behind my back a gruff, loud, authoritative voice, the voice of our deputy-Neptune.

It was addressing the head shipping-master, who, having let me in, had, apparently, remained hovering in the middle distance ever since.

"Mr. R., let the harbour launch have steam up to take the captain here on board the *Melita* at half-past nine to-night."

I was amazed at the startled assent of R.'s "Yes, sir." He ran before me out on the landing. My new dignity sat yet so lightly on me that I was not aware that it was I, the Captain, the object of this last graciousness. It seemed as if all of a sudden a pair of wings had grown on my shoulders. I merely skimmed along the polished floor.

But R. was impressed.

"I say!" he exclaimed on the landing, while the Malay crew of the steam-launch standing by looked stonily at the man for whom they were going to be kept on duty so late, away from their gambling, from their girls, or their pure domestic joys. "I say! His own launch. What have you done to him?"

His stare was full of respectful curiosity. I was quite confounded.

"Was it for me? I hadn't the slightest notion," I stammered out.

He nodded many times. "Yes. And the last person who had it before you was a Duke. So, there!"

I think he expected me to faint on the spot. But I was in too much of a hurry for emotional displays. My feelings were already in such a whirl that this staggering information did not seem to make the slightest difference. It fell into the seething cauldron of my brain, and I carried it off with me after a short but effusive passage of leave-taking with R.

The favour of the great throws an aureole round the fortunate object of its selection. That excellent man inquired whether he could do anything for me. He had known me only by sight, and he was well aware he would never see me again; I was, in common with the other seamen of the port, merely a subject for official writing, filling up of forms with all the artificial superiority of a man of pen and ink to the men who grapple with realities outside the consecrated walls of official buildings. What ghosts we must have been to him! Mere symbols to juggle with in books and heavy registers, without brains and muscles and perplexities; something hardly useful and decidedly inferior.

And he—the office hours being over—wanted to know if he could be of any use to me!

I ought, properly speaking—I ought to have been moved to tears. But I did not even think of it. It was only another miraculous manifestation of that day of miracles. I parted from him as if he had been a mere symbol. I floated down the staircase. I floated out of the official and imposing portal. I went on floating along.

I use that word rather than the word "flew," because I have a distinct impression that, though uplifted by my aroused youth, my movements were deliberate enough. To that mixed white, brown, and yellow portion of mankind, out abroad on their own affairs, I presented the appearance of a man walking rather sedately. And nothing in the way of abstraction could have equalled my deep detachment from the forms and colours of this world. It was, as it were, absolute.

And yet, suddenly, I recognised Hamilton. I recognised him without effort, without a shock, without a start. There he was, strolling towards the Harbour Office with his stiff, arrogant dignity. His red face made him noticeable at a distance. It flamed, over there, on the shady side of the street.

He had perceived me too. Something (unconscious exuberance of spirits perhaps) moved me to wave my hand to him elaborately. This lapse from good taste happened before I was aware that I was capable of it.

The impact of my impudence stopped him short, much as a bullet might have done. I verily believe he staggered, though as far as I could see he didn't actually fall. I had gone past in a moment and did not turn my head. I had forgotten his existence.

The next ten minutes might have been ten seconds or ten centuries for all my consciousness had to do with it. People might have been falling dead around me, houses crumbling, guns firing, I wouldn't have known. I was thinking: "By Jove! I have got it." *It* being the command. It had come about in a way utterly unforeseen in my modest day-dreams.

I perceived that my imagination had been running in conventional channels and that my hopes had always been drab stuff. I had envisaged a command as a result of a slow course of promotion in the employ of some highly respectable firm. The reward of faithful service. Well, faithful service was all right. One would naturally give that for one's own sake, for the sake of the ship, for the love of the life of one's choice; not for the sake of the reward.

There is something distasteful in the notion of a reward.

And now here I had my command, absolutely in my pocket, in a way undeniable indeed, but most unexpected; beyond my imaginings, outside all reasonable expectations, and even notwithstanding the existence of some sort of obscure intrigue to keep it away from me. It is true that the intrigue was feeble, but it helped the feeling of wonder—as if I had been specially destined for that ship I did not know, by some power higher than the prosaic agencies of the commercial world.

A strange sense of exultation began to creep into me. If I had worked for that command ten years or more there would have been nothing of the kind. I was a little frightened.

"Let us be calm," I said to myself.

Outside the door of the Officers' Home the wretched Steward seemed to be waiting for me. There was a broad flight of a few steps, and he ran to and fro on the top of it as if chained there. A distressed cur. He looked as though his throat were too dry for him to bark.

I regret to say I stopped before going in. There had been a revolution in my moral nature. He waited open-mouthed, breathless, while I looked at him for half a minute.

"And you thought you could keep me out of it," I said scathingly.

"You said you were going home," he squeaked miserably. "You said so. You said so."

"I wonder what Captain Ellis will have to say to that excuse," I uttered slowly with a sinister meaning.

His lower jaw had been trembling all the time and his voice was like the bleating of a sick goat. "You have given me away? You have done for me?"

Neither his distress nor yet the sheer absurdity of it was able to disarm me. It was the first instance of harm being attempted to be done to me— at any rate, the first I had ever found out. And I was still young enough, still too much on this side of the shadow-line, not to be surprised and indignant at such things.

I gazed at him inflexibly. Let the beggar suffer. He slapped his forehead and I passed in, pursued, into the dining-room, by his screech: "I always said you'd be the death of me."

This clamour not only overtook me, but went ahead, as it were, on to the verandah and brought out Captain Giles.

He stood before me in the doorway in all the commonplace solidity of his wisdom. The gold chain glittered on his breast. He clutched a smouldering pipe.

I extended my hand to him warmly and he seemed surprised, but did respond heartily enough in the end, with a faint smile of superior knowledge which cut my thanks short as if with a knife. I don't think that more than one word came out. And even for that one, judging by the temperature of my face, I had blushed as if for a bad action. Assuming a detached tone, I wondered how on earth he had managed to spot the little underhand game that had been going on.

He murmured complacently that there were but few things done in the town that he could not see the inside of. And as to this house, he had been using it off and on for nearly ten years. Nothing that went on in it could escape his great experience. It had been no trouble to him. No trouble at all.

Then in his quiet thick tone he wanted to know if I had complained formally of the Steward's action.

I said that I hadn't—though, indeed, it was not for want of opportunity. Captain Ellis had gone for me bald-headed in a most ridiculous fashion for being out of the way when wanted.

"Funny old gentleman," interjected Captain Giles. "What did you say to that?"

"I said simply that I came along the very moment I heard of his message. Nothing more. I didn't want to hurt the Steward. I would scorn to harm such an object. No. I made no complaint, but I believe he thinks I've done so. Let him think. He's got a fright that he won't forget in a hurry, for Captain Ellis would kick him out into the middle of Asia. . . ."

"Wait a moment," said Captain Giles, leaving me suddenly. I sat down feeling very tired, mostly in my head. Before I could start a train of thought he stood again before me, murmuring the excuse that he had to go and put the fellow's mind at ease.

I looked up with surprise. But in reality I was indifferent. He explained that he had found the Steward lying face downwards on the horsehair sofa. He was all right now.

"He would not have died of fright," I said contemptuously.

"No. But he might have taken an overdose out of one of those little bottles he keeps in his room," Captain Giles argued seriously. "The confounded fool has tried to poison himself once—a couple of years ago."

"Really," I said without emotion. "He doesn't seem very fit to live, anyhow."

"As to that, it may be said of a good many."

"Don't exaggerate like this!" I protested, laughing irritably. "But I wonder what this part of the world would do if you were to leave off looking after it, Captain Giles? Here you have got me a command and saved the Steward's life in one afternoon. Though why you should have taken all that interest in either of us is more than I can understand."

Captain Giles remained silent for a minute.

Then gravely:

"He's not a bad steward really. He can find a good cook, at any rate.

And, what's more, he can keep him when found. I remember the cooks we had here before his time. . . ."

I must have made a movement of impatience, because he interrupted himself with an apology for keeping me yarning there, while no doubt I needed all my time to get ready.

What I really needed was to be alone for a bit. I seized this opening hastily. My bedroom was a quiet refuge in an apparently uninhabited wing of the building. Having absolutely nothing to do (for I had not unpacked my things), I sat down on the bed and abandoned myself to the influences of the hour. To the unexpected influences. . . .

And first I wondered at my state of mind. Why was I not more surprised? Why? Here I was, invested with a command in the twinkling of an eye, not in the common course of human affairs, but more as if by enchantment. I ought to have been lost in astonishment. But I wasn't. I was very much like people in fairy tales. Nothing ever astonishes them. When a fully appointed gala coach is produced out of a pumpkin to take her to a ball Cinderella does not exclaim. She gets in quietly and drives away to her high fortune.

Captain Ellis (a fierce sort of fairy) had produced a command out of a drawer almost unexpectedly as in a fairy tale. But a command is an abstract idea, and it seemed a sort of "lesser marvel" till it flashed upon me that it involved the concrete existence of a ship.

A ship! My ship! She was mine, more absolutely mine for possession and care than anything in the world; an object of responsibility and devotion. She was there waiting for me, spellbound, unable to move, to live, to get out into the world (till I came), like an enchanted princess. Her call had come to me as if from the clouds. I had never suspected her existence. I didn't know how she looked, I had barely heard her name, and yet we were indissolubly united for a certain portion of our future, to sink or swim together!

A sudden passion of anxious impatience rushed through my veins and gave me such a sense of the intensity of existence as I have never felt before or since. I discovered how much of a seaman I was, in heart, in mind, and, as it were, physically—a man exclusively of sea and ships; the sea the only world that counted, and the ships the test of manliness, of temperament, of courage and fidelity—and of love.

I had an exquisite moment. It was unique also. Jumping up from my seat, I paced up and down my room for a long time. But when I came into the dining-room I behaved with sufficient composure. Only I couldn't eat anything at dinner.

Having declared my intention not to drive but to walk down to the quay, I must render the wretched Steward justice that he bestirred himself to find me some coolies for the luggage. They departed, carrying all my worldly possessions (except a little money I had in my pocket) slung from a long pole. Captain Giles volunteered to walk down with me.

We followed the sombre, shaded alley across the Esplanade. It was moderately cool there under the trees. Captain Giles remarked, with a sudden laugh: "I know who's jolly thankful at having seen the last of you."

I guessed that he meant the Steward. The fellow had borne himself to me in a sulkily frightened manner at the last. I expressed my wonder that he should have tried to do me a bad turn for no reason at all.

"Don't you see that what he wanted was to get rid of our friend Hamilton by dodging him in front of you for that job? That would have removed him for good, see?"

"Heavens!" I exclaimed, feeling humiliated somehow. "Can it be possible? What a fool he must be! That overbearing, impudent loafer! Why! He couldn't. . . . And yet he's nearly done it, I believe; for the Harbour Office was bound to send somebody."

"Aye. A fool like our Steward can be dangerous sometimes," declared Captain Giles sententiously. "Just because he is a fool," he added, imparting further instruction in his complacent low tones. "For," he continued in the manner of a set demonstration, "no sensible person would risk being kicked out of the only berth between himself and starvation just to get rid of a simple annoyance—a small worry. Would he now?"

"Well, no," I conceded, restraining a desire to laugh at that something mysteriously earnest in delivering the conclusions of his wisdom as though they were the product of prohibited operations. "But that fellow looks as if he were rather crazy. He must be."

"As to that, I believe everybody in the world is a little mad," he announced quietly.

"You make no exceptions?" I inquired, just to hear his answer.

He kept silent for a little while, then got home in an effective manner.

"Why! Kent says that even of you."

"Does he?" I retorted, extremely embittered all at once against my former captain. "There's nothing of that in the written character from him which I've got in my pocket. Has he given you any instances of my lunacy?"

Captain Giles explained in a conciliating tone that it had been only a friendly remark in reference to my abrupt leaving the ship for no apparent reason.

I muttered grumpily: "Oh! leaving his ship," and mended my pace. He kept up by my side in the deep gloom of the avenue as if it were his conscientious duty to see me out of the colony as an undesirable character. He panted a little, which was rather pathetic in a way. But I was not moved. On the contrary. His discomfort gave me a sort of malicious pleasure.

Presently I relented, slowed down, and said:

"What I really wanted was to get a fresh grip. I felt it was time. Is that so very mad?"

He made no answer. We were issuing from the avenue. On the bridge over the canal a dark, irresolute figure seemed to be awaiting something or somebody.

It was a Malay policeman, barefooted, in his blue uniform. The silver band on his little round cap shone dimly in the light of the street lamp. He peered in our direction timidly.

Before we could come up to him he turned about and walked in front of us in the direction of the jetty. The distance was some hundred yards; and then I found my coolies squatting on their heels. They had kept the pole on their shoulders, and all my worldly goods, still tied to the pole, were resting on the ground between them. As far as the eye could reach along the quay there was not another soul abroad except the police peon, who saluted us.

It seems he had detained the coolies as suspicious characters, and had forbidden them the jetty. But at a sign from me he took off the embargo with alacrity. The two patient fellows, rising together with a faint grunt, trotted off along the planks, and I prepared to take my leave of Captain Giles, who stood there with an air as though his mission were drawing to a close. It could not be denied that he had done it all. And while I hesitated about an appropriate sentence he made himself heard:

"I expect you'll have your hands pretty full of tangled up business."

I asked him what made him think so; and he answered that it was his general experience of the world. Ship a long time away from her port, owners inaccessible by cable, and the only man who could explain matters dead and buried.

"And you yourself new to the business in a way," he concluded in a sort of unanswerable tone.

"Don't insist," I said. "I know it only too well. I only wish you could impart to me some small portion of your experience before I go. As it can't be done in ten minutes I had better not begin to ask you. There's that harbour launch waiting for me too. But I won't feel really at peace till I have that ship of mine out in the Indian Ocean."

He remarked casually that from Bankok to the Indian Ocean was a pretty long step. And this murmur, like a dim flash from a dark lantern, showed me for a moment the broad belt of islands and reefs between that unknown ship, which was mine, and the freedom of the great waters of the globe.

But I felt no apprehension. I was familiar enough with the Archipelago by that time. Extreme patience and extreme care would see me through the region of broken land, of faint airs and of dead water to where I would feel at last my command swing on the great swell and list over to the great breath of regular winds, that would give her the feeling of a large, more intense life. The road would be long. All roads are long that lead towards one's heart's desire. But this road my mind's eye could see on a chart, professionally, with all its complications and difficulties, yet simple enough in a way. One is a seaman or one is not. And I had no doubt of being one.

The only part I was a stranger to was the Gulf of Siam. And I mentioned this to Captain Giles. Not that I was concerned very much. It belonged to the same region the nature of which I knew, into whose very soul I seemed to have looked during the last months of that existence with which I had broken now, suddenly, as one parts with some enchanting company.

"The Gulf . . . Ay! A funny piece of water—that," said Captain Giles.

Funny, in this connection, was a vague word. The whole thing sounded like an opinion uttered by a cautious person mindful of actions for slander.

I didn't inquire as to the nature of that funniness. There was really no time. But at the very last he volunteered a warning.

"Whatever you do, keep to the east side of it. The west side is dangerous at this time of the year. Don't let anything tempt you over. You'll find nothing but trouble there."

Though I could hardly imagine what could tempt me to involve my ship amongst the currents and reefs of the Malay shore, I thanked him for the advice.

He gripped my extended arm warmly, and the end of our acquaintance came suddenly with the words: "Good-night."

That was all he said: "Good-night." Nothing more. I don't know what I intended to say, but surprise made me swallow it, whatever it was. I choked slightly, and then exclaimed with a sort of nervous haste: "Oh! Good-night, Captain Giles, good-night."

His movements were always deliberate, but his back had receded some distance along the deserted quay before I collected myself enough to follow his example and made a half turn in the direction of the jetty.

Only my movements were not deliberate. I hurried down to the steps and leaped into the launch. Before I had fairly landed in her stern-sheets the slim little craft darted away from the jetty with a sudden swirl of her propeller and the hard, rapid puffing of the exhaust in her vaguely gleaming brass funnel amidships.

The misty churning at her stern was the only sound in the world. The shore lay plunged in the silence of the deepest slumber. I watched the town recede still and soundless in the hot night, till the abrupt hail, "Steam-launch, ahoy!" made me spin round face forward. We were close to a white, ghostly steamer. Lights shone on her decks, in her port-holes. And the same voice shouted from her: "Is that our passenger?"

"It is," I yelled.

Her crew had been obviously on the jump. I could hear them running about. The modern spirit of haste was loudly vocal in the orders to "Heave away on the cable"—to "Lower the side-ladder," and in urgent requests to me to "Come along, sir! We have been delayed three hours for you. . . . Our time is seven o'clock, you know!"

I stepped on the deck. I said, "No! I don't know." The spirit of modern hurry was embodied in a thin, long-armed, long-legged man, with a closely clipped grey beard. His meagre hand was hot and dry. He declared feverishly: "I am hanged if I would have waited another five minutes—harbour-master or no harbour-master."

"That's your own business," I said. "I didn't ask you to wait for me."

"I hope you don't expect any supper," he burst out. "This isn't a boarding-house afloat. You are the first passenger I ever had in my life and I hope to goodness you will be the last."

I made no answer to this hospitable communication; and, indeed, he didn't wait for any, bolting away on to his bridge to get his ship under way.

For the four days he had me on board he did not depart from that half-hostile attitude. His ship having been delayed three hours on my account, he couldn't forgive me for not being a more distinguished person. He was not exactly outspoken about it, but that feeling of annoyed wonder was peeping out perpetually in his talk.

He was absurd.

He was also a man of much experience, which he liked to trot out; but no greater contrast with Captain Giles could have been imagined. He would have amused me if I had wanted to be amused. But I did not want to be amused. I was like a lover looking forward to a meeting. Human hostility was nothing to me. I thought of my unknown ship. It was amusement enough, torment enough, occupation enough.

He perceived my state, for his wits were sufficiently sharp for that, and he poked sly fun at my preoccupation in the manner some nasty, cynical old men assume towards the dreams and illusions of youth. I, on my side, refrained from questioning him as to the appearance of my ship, though I knew that being in Bankok every month or so he must have known her by sight. I was not going to expose the ship, my ship! to some slighting reference.

He was the first really unsympathetic man I had ever come in contact with. My education was far from being finished, though I didn't know it. No! I didn't know it.

All I knew was that he disliked me and had some contempt for my person. Why? Apparently because his ship had been delayed three hours on my account. Who was I to have such a thing done for me? Such a thing had never been done for him. It was a sort of jealous indignation.

My expectation, mingled with fear, was wrought to its highest pitch. How slow had been the days of the passage and how soon they were over. One morning early, we crossed the bar, and while the sun was rising splendidly over the flat spaces of the land we steamed up the innumerable bends, passed under the shadow of the great gilt pagoda, and reached the outskirts of the town.

There it was, spread largely on both banks, the Oriental capital which had as yet suffered no white conqueror; an expanse of brown houses of bamboo, of mats, of leaves, of a vegetable-matter style of architecture, sprung out of the brown soil on the banks of the muddy river. It was amazing to think that in those miles of human habitations there was not probably half a dozen pounds of nails. Some of those houses of sticks and grass, like the nests of an aquatic race, clung to the low shores. Others seemed to grow out of the water; others again floated in long anchored rows in the very middle of the stream. Here and there in the distance, above the crowded mob of low, brown roof ridges, towered great piles of masonry, King's Palace, temples, gorgeous and dilapidated, crumbling under the vertical sunlight, tremendous, overpowering, almost palpable, which seemed to enter one's breast with the breath of one's nostrils and soak into one's limbs through every pore of one's skin.

The ridiculous victim of jealousy had for some reason or other to stop his engines just then. The steamer drifted slowly up with the tide. Oblivious of my new surroundings I walked the deck, in anxious, deadened abstraction, a commingling of romantic reverie with a very practical survey of my qualifications. For the time was approaching for me to behold my command and to prove my worth in the ultimate test of my profession.

Suddenly I heard myself called by that imbecile. He was beckoning me to come up on his bridge.

I didn't care very much for that, but as it seemed that he had something particular to say I went up the ladder.

He laid his hand on my shoulder and gave me a slight turn, pointing with his other arm at the same time.

"There! That's your ship, Captain," he said. I felt a thump in my breast— only one, as if my heart had then ceased to beat. There were ten or more ships moored along the bank, and the one he meant was partly hidden from my sight by her next astern. He said: "We'll drift abreast her in a moment."

What was his tone? Mocking? Threatening? Or only indifferent? I could not tell. I suspected some malice in this unexpected manifestation of interest.

He left me, and I leaned over the rail of the bridge looking over the side. I dared not raise my eyes. Yet it had to be done—and, indeed, I could not have helped myself. I believe I trembled.

But directly my eyes had rested on my ship all my fear vanished. It went off swiftly, like a bad dream. Only that a dream leaves no shame behind it, and that I felt a momentary shame at my unworthy suspicions.

Yes, there she was. Her hull, her rigging filled my eye with a great content. That feeling of life-emptiness which had made me so restless for the last few months lost its bitter plausibility, its evil influence, dissolved in a flow of joyous emotion.

At the first glance I saw that she was a high-class vessel, a harmonious creature in the lines of her fine body, in the proportioned tallness of her spars. Whatever her age and her history, she had preserved the stamp of her origin. She was one of those craft that in virtue of their design and complete finish will never look old. Amongst her companions moored to the bank, and all bigger than herself, she looked like a creature of high breed—an Arab steed in a string of cart-horses.

A voice behind me said in a nasty equivocal tone: "I hope you are satisfied with her, Captain." I did not even turn my head. It was the master of the steamer, and whatever he meant, whatever he thought of her, I knew that, like some rare women, she was one of those creatures whose mere existence is enough to awaken an unselfish delight. One feels that it is good to be in the world in which she has her being.

That illusion of life and character which charms one in men's finest handiwork radiated from her. An enormous baulk of teak-wood timber swung over her hatchway; lifeless matter, looking heavier and bigger than anything aboard of her. When they started lowering it the surge of the tackle sent a quiver through her from water-line to the trucks up the fine nerves of her rigging, as though she had shuddered at the weight. It seemed cruel to load her so. . . .

Half-an-hour later, putting my foot on her deck for the first time, I received the feeling of deep physical satisfaction. Nothing could equal the fullness of that moment, the ideal completeness of that emotional experience which had come to me without the preliminary toil and disenchantments of an obscure career.

My rapid glance ran over her, enveloped, appropriated the form concreting the abstract sentiment of my command. A lot of details perceptible to a seaman struck my eye vividly in that instant. For the rest, I saw her disengaged from the material conditions of her being. The shore to which she was moored was as if it did not exist. What were to me all the countries of the globe? In all the parts of the world washed by navigable waters our relation to each other would be the same—and more intimate than there are words to express in the language. Apart from that, every scene and episode would be a mere passing show. The very gang of yellow coolies busy about the main hatch was less substantial than the stuff dreams are made of. For who on earth would dream of Chinamen? . . .

I went aft, ascended the poop, where, under the awning, gleamed the brasses of the yacht-like fittings, the polished surfaces of the rails, the glass of the skylights. Right aft two seamen, busy cleaning the steering-gear, with the reflected ripples of light running playfully up their bent backs, went on with their work, unaware of me and of the almost affectionate glance I threw at them in passing towards the companion-way of the cabin.

The doors stood wide open, the slide was pushed right back. The half-turn of the staircase cut off the view of the lobby. A low humming ascended from below, but it stopped abruptly at the sound of my descending footsteps.

III

The first thing I saw down there was the upper part of a man's body projecting backwards, as it were, from one of the doors at the foot of the stairs. His eyes looked at me very wide and still. In one hand he held a dinner plate, in the other a cloth.

"I am your new captain," I said quietly.

In a moment, in the twinkling of an eye, he had got rid of the plate and the cloth and jumped to open the cabin door. As soon as I passed into the saloon he vanished, but only to reappear instantly, buttoning up a jacket he had put on with the swiftness of a "quick-change" artist.

"Where's the chief mate?" I asked.

"In the hold, I think, sir. I saw him go down the after-hatch ten minutes ago."

"Tell him I am on board."

The mahogany table under the skylight shone in the twilight like a dark pool of water. The sideboard, surmounted by a wide looking-glass in an ormolu frame, had a marble top. It bore a pair of silver-plated lamps and some other pieces—obviously a harbour display. The saloon itself was panelled in two kinds of wood in the excellent, simple taste prevailing when the ship was built.

I sat down in the arm-chair at the head of the table—the captain's chair, with a small tell-tale compass swung above it—a mute reminder of unremitting vigilance.

A succession of men had sat in that chair. I became aware of that thought suddenly, vividly, as though each had left a little of himself between the four walls of these ornate bulkheads; as if a sort of composite soul, the soul of command, had whispered suddenly to mine of long days at sea and of anxious moments.

"You, too!" it seemed to say, "you, too, shall taste of that peace and that unrest in a searching intimacy with your own self—obscure as we were and as supreme in the face of all the winds and all the seas, in an immensity that receives no impress, preserves no memories, and keeps no reckoning of lives."

Deep within the tarnished ormolu frame, in the hot half-light sifted through the awning, I saw my own face propped between my hands. And I stared back at myself with the perfect detachment of distance, rather with curiosity than with any other feeling, except of some sympathy for this latest representative of what for all intents and purposes was a dynasty; continuous not in blood, indeed, but in its experience, in its training, in its conception of duty, and in the blessed simplicity of its traditional point of view on life.

It struck me that this quietly staring man whom I was watching, both as if he were myself and somebody else, was not exactly a lonely figure. He had his place in a line of men whom he did not know, of whom he had never heard; but who were fashioned by the same influences, whose souls in relation to their humble life's work had no secrets for him.

Suddenly I perceived that there was another man in the saloon, standing a little on one side and looking intently at me. The chief mate. His long, red moustache determined the character of his physiognomy, which struck me as pugnacious in (strange to say) a ghastly sort of way.

How long had he been there looking at me, appraising me in my unguarded day-dreaming state? I would have been more disconcerted if, having the clock set in the top of the mirror-frame right in front of me, I had not noticed that its long hand had hardly moved at all.

I could not have been in that cabin more than two minutes altogether. Say three. . . . So he could not have been watching me more than a mere fraction of a minute, luckily. Still, I regretted the occurrence.

But I showed nothing of it as I rose leisurely (it had to be leisurely) and greeted him with perfect friendliness.

There was something reluctant and at the same time attentive in his bearing. His name was Burns. We left the cabin and went round the ship together. His face in the full light of day appeared very worn, meagre, even haggard. Somehow I had a delicacy as to looking too often at him; his eyes, on the contrary, remained fairly glued on my face. They were greenish and had an expectant expression.

He answered all my questions readily enough, but my ear seemed to catch a tone of unwillingness. The second officer, with three or four hands, was busy forward. The mate mentioned his name and I nodded to him in passing. He was very young. He struck me as rather a cub.

When we returned below I sat down on one end of a deep, semi-circular, or, rather, semi-oval settee, upholstered in red plush. It extended right across the whole after-end of the cabin. Mr. Burns, motioned to sit down, dropped into one of the swivel-chairs round the table, and kept his eyes on me as persistently as ever, and with that strange air as if all this were make-believe and he expected me to get up, burst into a laugh, slap him on the back, and vanish from the cabin.

There was an odd stress in the situation which began to make me uncomfortable. I tried to react against this vague feeling.

"It's only my inexperience," I thought.

In the face of that man, several years, I judged, older than myself, I became aware of what I had left already behind me—my youth. And that was indeed poor comfort. Youth is a fine thing, a mighty power—as long as one does not think of it. I felt I was becoming self-conscious. Almost against my will I assumed a moody gravity. I said: "I see you have kept her in very good order, Mr. Burns."

Directly I had uttered these words I asked myself angrily why the deuce did I want to say that? Mr. Burns in answer had only blinked at me. What on earth did he mean?

I fell back on a question which had been in my thoughts for a long time—the most natural question on the lips of any seaman whatever joining a ship. I voiced it (confound this self-consciousness) in a *dégagé* cheerful tone: "I suppose she can travel—what?"

Now a question like this might have been answered normally, either in accents of apologetic sorrow or with a visibly suppressed pride, in a "I don't want to boast, but you shall see" sort of tone. There are sailors, too, who would have been roughly outspoken: "Lazy brute," or openly delighted: "She's a flyer." Two ways, if four manners.

But Mr. Burns found another way, a way of his own which had, at all events, the merit of saving his breath, if no other.

Again he did not say anything. He only frowned. And it was an angry frown. I waited. Nothing more came.

"What's the matter? . . . Can't you tell after being nearly two years in the ship?" I addressed him sharply.

He looked as startled for a moment as though he had discovered my presence only that very moment. But this passed off almost at once. He put on an air of indifference. But I suppose he thought it better to say something. He said that a ship needed, just like a man, the chance to show the best she could do, and that this ship had never had a chance since he had been on board of her. Not that he could remember. The last captain . . . He paused.

"Has he been so very unlucky?" I asked him with frank incredulity. Mr. Burns turned his eyes away from me. No, the late captain was not an unlucky man. One couldn't say that. But he had not seemed to want to make use of his luck.

Mr. Burns—man of enigmatic moods—made this statement with an inanimate face and staring wilfully at the rudder-casing. The statement itself was obscurely suggestive. I asked quietly:

"Where did he die?"

"In this saloon. Just where you are sitting now," answered Mr. Burns.

I repressed a silly impulse to jump up; but upon the whole I was relieved to hear that he had not died in the bed which was now to be mine. I pointed out to the chief mate that what I really wanted to know was where he had buried his late captain.

Mr. Burns said that it was at the entrance to the Gulf. A roomy grave; a sufficient answer. But the mate, overcoming visibly something within him— something like a curious reluctance to believe in my advent (as an irrevocable fact, at any rate), did not stop at that—though, indeed, he may have wished to do so.

As a compromise with his feelings, I believe, he addressed himself persistently to the rudder-casing, so that to me he had the appearance of a man talking in solitude, a little unconsciously, however.

His tale was that at seven bells in the forenoon watch he had all hands mustered on the quarter-deck and told them that they had better go down to say good-bye to the captain.

Those words, as if grudged to an intruding personage, were enough for me to evoke vividly that strange ceremony: The bare-footed, bare-headed seamen crowding shyly into that cabin, a small mob pressed against that sideboard, uncomfortable rather than moved, shirts open on sunburnt chests, weather-beaten faces, and all staring at the dying man with the same grave and expectant expression.

"Was he conscious?" I asked.

"He didn't speak, but he moved his eyes to look at them," said the mate.

After waiting a moment Mr. Burns motioned the crew to leave the cabin, but he detained the two eldest men to stay with the captain while he went on deck with his sextant to "take the sun." It was getting towards noon and he was anxious to obtain a good observation for latitude. When he returned below to put his sextant away he found that the two men had retreated out into the lobby. Through the open door he had a view of the captain lying easy against the pillows. He had "passed away" while Mr. Burns was taking his observation. As near noon as possible. He had hardly changed his position.

Mr. Burns sighed, glanced at me inquisitively, as much as to say, "Aren't you going yet?" and then turned his thoughts from his new captain back to the old, who, being dead, had no authority, was not in anybody's way, and was much easier to deal with.

Mr. Burns dealt with him at some length. He was a peculiar man—of about sixty-five—iron grey, hard-faced, obstinate, and uncommunicative. He used to keep the ship loafing at sea for inscrutable reasons. Would come on deck at night sometimes, take some sail off her, God only knows why or wherefore, then go below, shut himself up in his cabin, and play on the violin for hours —till daybreak perhaps. In fact, he spent most of his time day or night playing the violin. That was when the fit took him. Very loud, too.

It came to this, that Mr. Burns mustered his courage one day and remonstrated earnestly with the captain. Neither he nor the second mate could get a wink of sleep in their watches below for the noise. . . . And how could they be expected to keep awake while on duty? he pleaded. The answer of that stern man was that if he and the second mate didn't like the noise, they were welcome to pack up their traps and walk over the side. When this alternative was offered the ship happened to be 600 miles from the nearest land.

Mr. Burns at this point looked at me with an air of curiosity. I began to think that my predecessor was a remarkably peculiar old man.

But I had to hear stranger things yet. It came out that this stern, grim, wind-tanned, rough, sea-salted, tactiturn sailor of sixty-five was not only an artist, but a lover as well. In Haiphong, when they got there after a course of most unprofitable peregrinations (during which the ship was nearly lost twice), he got himself, in Mr. Burns' own words, "mixed up" with some woman. Mr. Burns had had no personal knowledge of that affair, but positive evidence of it existed in the shape of a photograph taken in Haiphong. Mr. Burns found it in one of the drawers in the captain's room.

In due course I, too, saw that amazing human document (I even threw it overboard later). There he sat with his hands reposing on his knees, bald, squat, bristly, recalling a wild boar somehow; and by his side towered an awful, mature, white female with rapacious nostrils and a cheaply ill-omened stare in her enormous eyes. She was disguised in some semi-oriental, vulgar, fancy costume. She resembled a low-class medium or one of those women who tell fortunes by cards for half-a-crown. And yet she was striking. A professional sorceress from the slums. It was incomprehensible. There was something awful in the thought that she was the last reflection of the world of passion for the fierce soul which seemed to look at one out of the sardonically savage face of that old seaman. However, I noticed that she was holding some musical instrument—guitar or mandoline—in her hand. Perhaps that was the secret of her sortilege.

For Mr. Burns that photograph explained why the unloaded ship was kept sweltering at anchor for three weeks in a pestilential hot harbour without air. They lay there and gasped. The captain, appearing now and then on short visits, mumbled to Mr. Burns unlikely tales about some letters he was waiting for.

Suddenly, after vanishing for a week, he came on board in the middle of the night and took the ship out to sea with the first break of dawn. Daylight showed him looking wild and ill. The mere getting clear of the land took two days, and somehow or other they bumped slightly on a reef. However, no leak developed, and the captain, growling "no matter," informed Mr. Burns that he had made up his mind to take the ship to Hong-Kong and dry-dock her there.

At this Mr. Burns was plunged into despair. For indeed, to beat up to Hong-Kong against a fierce monsoon, with a ship not sufficiently ballasted and with her supply of water not completed, was an insane project.

But the captain growled peremptorily, "Stick her at it," and Mr. Burns, dismayed and enraged, stuck her at it, and kept her at it, blowing away sails, straining the spars, exhausting the crew—nearly maddened by the absolute conviction that the attempt was impossible and was bound to end in some catastrophe.

Meantime the captain, shut up in his cabin and wedged in a corner of his settee against the crazy bounding of the ship, played the violin—or, at any rate, made continuous noise on it.

When he appeared on deck he would not speak and not always answer when spoken to. It was obvious that he was ill in some mysterious manner, and beginning to break up.

As the days went by the sounds of the violin became less and less loud, till at last only a feeble scratching would meet Mr. Burns' ear as he stood in the saloon listening outside the door of the captain's state-room.

One afternoon in perfect desperation he burst into that room and made such a scene, tearing his hair and shouting such horrid imprecations that he cowed the contemptuous spirit of the sick man. The water-tanks were low, they had not gained 50 miles in a fortnight. She would never reach Hong-Kong.

It was like fighting desperately towards destruction for the ship and the men. This was evident without argument. Mr. Burns, losing all restraint, put his face close to his captain's and fairly yelled: "You, sir, are going out of the world. But I can't wait till you are dead before I put the helm up. You must do it yourself. You must do it now!"

The man on the couch snarled in contempt: "So I am going out of the world—am I?"

"Yes, sir—you haven't many days left in it," said Mr. Burns calming down. "One can see it by your face."

"My face, eh? . . . Well, put the helm up and be damned to you."

Burns flew on deck, got the ship before the wind, then came down again, composed but resolute.

"I've shaped a course for Pulo Condor, sir," he said. "When we make it, if you are still with us, you'll tell me into what port you wish me to take the ship and I'll do it."

The old man gave him a look of savage spite, and said these atrocious words in deadly, slow tones:

"If I had my wish, neither the ship nor any of you would ever reach a port. And I hope you won't."

Mr. Burns was profoundly shocked. I believe he was positively frightened at the time. It seems, however, that he managed to produce such an effective laugh that it was the old man's turn to be frightened. He shrank within himself and turned his back on him.

"And his head was not gone then," Mr. Burns assured me excitedly. "He meant every word of it."

Such was practically the late captain's last speech. No connected sentence passed his lips afterwards. That night he used the last of his strength to throw his fiddle over the side. No one had actually seen him in the act, but after his death Mr. Burns couldn't find the thing anywhere. The empty case was very much in evidence, but the fiddle was clearly not in the ship. And where else could it have gone to but overboard?

"Threw his violin overboard!" I exclaimed.

"He did," cried Mr. Burns excitedly. "And it's my belief he would have tried to take the ship down with him if it had been in human power. He never meant her to see home again. He wouldn't write to his owners, he never wrote to his old wife either—he wasn't going to. He had made up his mind to cut adrift from everything. That's what it was. He didn't care for business, or freights, or for making a passage—or anything. He meant to have gone wandering about the world till he lost her with all hands."

Mr. Burns looked like a man who had escaped great danger. For a little he would have exclaimed: "If it hadn't been for me!" And the transparent innocence of his indignant eyes was underlined quaintly by the arrogant pair of moustaches which he proceeded to twist, and as if extend, horizontally.

I might have smiled if I had not been busy with my own sensations, which were not those of Mr. Burns. I was already the man in command. My sensations could not be like those of any other man on board. In that community I stood, like a king in his country, in a class all by myself. I mean an hereditary king, not a mere elected head of a state. I was brought there to rule by an agency as remote from the people and as inscrutable almost to them as the Grace of God.

And like a member of a dynasty, feeling a semi-mystical bond with the dead, I was profoundly shocked by my immediate predecessor.

That man had been in all essentials but his age just such another man as myself. Yet the end of his life was a complete act of treason, the betrayal of a tradition which seemed to me as imperative as any guide on earth could be. It appeared that even at sea a man could become the victim of evil spirits. I felt on my face the breath of unknown powers that shape our destinies.

Not to let the silence last too long I asked Mr. Burns if he had written to his captain's wife. He shook his head. He had written to nobody.

In a moment he became sombre. He never thought of writing. It took him all his time to watch incessantly the loading of the ship by a rascally Chinese stevedore. In this Mr. Burns gave me the first glimpse of the real chief mate's soul which dwelt uneasily in his body.

He mused, then hastened on with gloomy force.

"Yes! The captain died as near noon as possible. I looked through his papers in the afternoon. I read the service over him at sunset and then I stuck the ship's head north and brought her in here. I—brought—her—in."

He struck the table with his fist.

"She would hardly have come in by herself," I observed. "But why didn't you make for Singapore instead?"

His eyes wavered. "The nearest port," he muttered sullenly.

I had framed the question in perfect innocence, but this answer (the difference in distance was insignificant) and his manner offered me a clue to the simple truth. He took the ship to a port where he expected to be confirmed in his temporary command from lack of a qualified master to put over his head. Whereas Singapore, he surmised justly, would be full of qualified men.

But his naïve reasoning forgot to take into account the telegraph cable reposing on the bottom of the very Gulf up which he had turned that ship which he imagined himself to have saved from destruction. Hence the bitter flavour of our interview. I tasted it more and more distinctly—and it was less and less to my taste.

"Look here, Mr. Burns," I began, very firmly. "You may as well understand that I did not run after this command. It was pushed in my way. I've accepted it. I am here to take the ship home first of all, and you may be sure that I shall see to it that every one of you on board here does his duty to that end. This is all I have to say—for the present."

He was on his feet by this time, but instead of taking his dismissal he remained with trembling, indignant lips, and looking at me hard as though, really, after this, there was nothing for me to do in common decency but to vanish from his outraged sight. Like all very simple emotional states this was moving. I felt sorry for him—almost sympathetic, till (seeing that I did not vanish) he spoke in a tone of forced restraint.

"If I hadn't a wife and child at home you may be sure, sir, I would have asked you to let me go the very minute you came on board."

I answered him with matter-of-course calmness as though some remote third person were in question.

"And I, Mr. Burns, would not have let you go. You have signed the ship's articles as chief officer, and till they are terminated at the final port of discharge I shall expect you to attend to your duty and give me the benefit of your experience to the best of your ability."

Stony incredulity lingered in his eyes; but it broke down before my friendly attitude. With a slight upward toss of his arms (I got to know that gesture well afterwards) he bolted out of the cabin.

We might have saved ourselves that little passage of harmless sparring. Before many days had elapsed it was Mr. Burns who was pleading with me anxiously not to leave him behind; while I could only return him but doubtful answers. The whole thing took on a somewhat tragic complexion.

And this horrible problem was only an extraneous episode, a mere complication in the general problem of how to get that ship—which was mine with her appurtenances and her men, with her body and her spirit now slumbering in that pestilential river—how to get her out to sea.

Mr. Burns, while still acting captain, had hastened to sign a charter-party which in an ideal world without guile would have been an excellent document. Directly I ran my eye over it I foresaw trouble ahead unless the people of the other part were quite exceptionally fair-minded and open to argument.

Mr. Burns, to whom I imparted my fears, chose to take great umbrage at them. He looked at me with that usual incredulous stare, and said bitterly:

"I suppose, sir, you want to make out I've acted like a fool?"

I told him, with my systematic kindliness which always seemed to augment his surprise, that I did not want to make out anything. I would leave that to the future.

And, sure enough, the future brought in a lot of trouble. There were days when I used to remember Captain Giles with nothing short of abhorrence. His confounded acuteness had let me in for his job; while his prophecy that I "would have my hands full" coming true, made it appear as if done on purpose to play an evil joke on my young innocence.

Yes. I had my hands full of complications which were most valuable as "experience." People have a great opinion of the advantages of experience. But in that connection experience means always something disagreeable as opposed to the charm and innocence of illusions.

I must say I was losing mine rapidly. But on these instructive complications I must not enlarge more than to say that they could all be résuméd in the one word: Delay.

A mankind which has invented the proverb, "Time is money," will understand my vexation. The word "Delay" entered the secret chamber of my brain, resounded there like a tolling bell which maddens the ear, affected all my senses, took on a black colouring, a bitter taste, a deadly meaning.

"I am really sorry to see you worried like this. Indeed, I am . . ."

It was the only humane speech I used to hear at that time. And it came from a doctor, appropriately enough.

A doctor is humane by definition. But that man was so in reality. His speech was not professional. I was not ill. But other people were, and that was the reason of his visiting the ship.

He was the doctor of our Legation and, of course, of the Consulate too. He looked after the ship's health, which generally was poor, and trembling, as it were, on the verge of a break-up. Yes. The men ailed. And thus time was not only money, but life as well.

I had never seen such a steady ship's company. As the doctor remarked to me: "You seem to have a most respectable lot of seamen." Not only were they consistently sober, but they did not even want to go ashore. Care was taken to expose them as little as possible to the sun. They were employed on light work under the awnings. And the humane doctor commended me.

"Your arrangements appear to me to be very judicious, my dear Captain."

It is difficult to express how much that pronouncement comforted me. The doctor's round full face framed in a light-coloured whisker was the perfection of a dignified amenity. He was the only human being in the world who seemed to take the slightest interest in me. He would generally sit in the cabin for half-an-hour or so at every visit.

I said to him one day:

"I suppose the only thing now is to take care of them as you are doing, till I can get the ship to sea?"

He inclined his head, shutting his eyes under the large spectacles, and murmured:

"The sea . . . undoubtedly."

The first member of the crew fairly knocked over was the steward—the first man to whom I had spoken on board. He was taken ashore (with choleraic symptoms) and died there at the end of a week. Then, while I was still under the startling impression of this first home-thrust of the climate, Mr. Burns gave up and went to bed in a raging fever without saying a word to anybody.

I believe he had partly fretted himself into that illness; the climate did the rest with the swiftness of an invisible monster ambushed in the air, in the water, in the mud of the river bank. Mr. Burns was a predestined victim.

I discovered him lying on his back, glaring sullenly and radiating heat on one like a small furnace. He would hardly answer my questions, and only grumbled: Couldn't a man take an afternoon off duty with a bad headache—for once?

That evening, as I sat in the saloon after dinner, I could hear him muttering continuously in his room. Ransome, who was clearing the table, said to me:

"I am afraid, sir, I won't be able to give the mate all the attention he's likely to need. I will have to be forward in the galley a great part of my time."

Ransome was the cook. The mate had pointed him out to me the first day, standing on the deck, his arms crossed on his broad chest, gazing on the river.

Even at a distance his well-proportioned figure, something thoroughly sailor-like in his poise, made him noticeable. On nearer view the intelligent, quiet eyes, a well-bred face, the disciplined independence of his manner made up an attractive personality. When, in addition, Mr. Burns told me that he was the best seaman in the ship, I expressed my surprise that in his earliest prime and of such appearance he should sign on as cook on board a ship.

"It's his heart," Mr. Burns had said. "There's something wrong with it. He mustn't exert himself too much or he may drop dead suddenly."

And he was the only one the climate had not touched—perhaps because, carrying a deadly enemy in his breast, he had schooled himself into a systematic control of feelings and movements. When one was in the secret this was apparent in his manner. After the poor steward died, and as he could not be replaced by a white man in this Oriental port, Ransome had volunteered to do the double work.

"I can do it all right, sir, as long as I go about it quietly," he had assured me.

But obviously he couldn't be expected to take up sick-nursing in addition. Moreover, the doctor peremptorily ordered Mr. Burns ashore.

With a seaman on each side holding him up under the arms, the mate went over the gangway more sullen than ever. We built him up with pillows in the gharry, and he made an effort to say brokenly:

"Now—you've got—what you wanted—got me out of—the ship."

"You were never more mistaken in your life, Mr. Burns," I said quietly, duly smiling at him; and the trap drove off to a sort of sanatorium, a pavilion of bricks which the doctor had in the grounds of his residence.

I visited Mr. Burns regularly. After the first few days, when he didn't know anybody, he received me as if I had come either to gloat over a crushed enemy or else to curry favour with a deeply-wronged person. It was either one or the other, just as it happened according to his fantastic sick-room moods. Whichever it was, he managed to convey it to me even during the period when he appeared almost too weak to talk. I treated him to my invariable kindliness.

Then one day, suddenly, a surge of downright panic burst through all this craziness.

If I left him behind in this deadly place he would die. He felt it, he was certain of it. But I wouldn't have the heart to leave him ashore. He had a wife and child in Sydney.

He produced his wasted fore-arms from under the sheet which covered him and clasped his fleshless claws. He would die! He would die here. . . .

He absolutely managed to sit up, but only for a moment, and when he fell back I really thought that he would die there and then. I called to the Bengali dispenser, and hastened away from the room.

Next day he upset me thoroughly by renewing his entreaties. I returned an evasive answer, and left him the picture of ghastly despair. The day after I went in with reluctance, and he attacked me at once in a much stronger voice and with an abundance of argument which was quite startling. He presented his case with a sort of crazy vigour, and asked me finally how would I like to have a man's death on my conscience? He wanted me to promise that I would not sail without him.

I said that I really must consult the doctor first. He cried out at that. The doctor! Never! That would be a death sentence.

The effort had exhausted him. He closed his eyes, but went on rambling in a low voice. I had hated him from the start. The late captain had hated him too. Had wished him dead. Had wished all hands dead. . . .

"What do you want to stand in with that wicked corpse for, sir? He'll have you too," he ended, blinking his glazed eyes vacantly.

"Mr. Burns," I cried, very much discomposed, "what on earth are you talking about?"

He seemed to come to himself, though he was too weak to start.

"I don't know," he said languidly. "But don't ask that doctor, sir. You and I are sailors. Don't ask him, sir. Some day perhaps you will have a wife and child yourself."

And again he pleaded for the promise that I would not leave him behind. I had the firmness of mind not to give it to him. Afterwards this sternness seemed criminal; for my mind was made up. That prostrated man, with hardly strength enough to breathe and ravaged by a passion of fear, was irresistible. And, besides, he had happened to hit on the right words. He and I were sailors. That was a claim, for I had no other family. As to the wife-and-child (some day) argument it had no force. It sounded merely bizarre.

I could imagine no claim that would be stronger and more absorbing than the claim of that ship, of these men snared in the river by silly commercial complications, as if in some poisonous trap.

However, I had nearly fought my way out. Out to sea. The sea—which was pure, safe, and friendly. Three days more.

That thought sustained and carried me on my way back to the ship. In the saloon the doctor's voice greeted me, and his large form followed his voice, issuing out of the starboard spare cabin where the ship's medicine chest was kept securely lashed in the bed-place.

Finding that I was not on board he had gone in there, he said, to inspect the supply of drugs, bandages, and so on. Everything was completed and in order.

I thanked him; I had just been thinking of asking him to do that very thing, as in a couple of days, as he knew, we were going to sea, where all our troubles of every sort would be over at last.

He listened gravely and made no answer. But when I opened to him my mind as to Mr. Burns he sat down by my side, and, laying his hand on my knee amicably, begged me to think what it was I was exposing myself to.

The man was just strong enough to bear being moved and no more. But he couldn't stand a return of the fever. I had before me a passage of sixty days perhaps, beginning with intricate navigation and ending probably with a lot of bad weather. Could I run the risk of having to go through it single-handed, with no chief officer and with a second quite a youth? . . .

He might have added that it was my first command too. He did probably think of that fact, for he checked himself. It was very present to my mind.

He advised me earnestly to cable to Singapore for a chief officer, even if I had to delay my sailing for a week.

"Not a day," I said. The very thought gave me the shivers. The hands seemed fairly fit, all of them, and this was the time to get them away. Once at sea I was not afraid of facing anything. The sea was now the only remedy for all my troubles.

The doctor's glasses were directed at me like two lamps searching the genuineness of my resolution. He opened his lips as if to argue further, but shut them again without saying anything. I had a vision of poor Burns so vivid in his exhaustion, helplessness, and anguish, that it moved me more than the reality I had come away from only an hour before. It was purged from the drawbacks of his personality, and I could not resist it.

"Look here," I said. "Unless you tell me officially that the man must not be moved I'll make arrangements to have him brought on board to-morrow, and shall take the ship out of the river next morning, even if I have to anchor outside the bar for a couple of days to get her ready for sea."

"Oh! I'll make all the arrangements myself," said the doctor at once. "I spoke as I did only as a friend—as a well-wisher, and that sort of thing."

He rose in his dignified simplicity and gave me a warm handshake, rather solemnly, I thought. But he was as good as his word. When Mr. Burns appeared at the gangway carried on a stretcher, the doctor himself walked by its side. The programme had been altered in so far that this transportation had been left to the last moment, on the very morning of our departure.

It was barely an hour after sunrise. The doctor waved his big arm to me from the shore and walked back at once to his trap, which had followed him empty to the riverside. Mr. Burns, carried across the quarter-deck, had the appearance of being absolutely lifeless. Ransome went down to settle him in his cabin. I had to remain on deck to look after the ship, for the tug had got hold of our tow-rope already.

The splash of our shore-fasts falling in the water produced a complete change of feeling in me. It was like the imperfect relief of awakening from a nightmare. But when the ship's head swung down the river away from that town, Oriental and squalid, I missed the expected elation of that striven-for moment. What there was, undoubtedly, was a relaxation of tension which translated itself into a sense of weariness after an inglorious fight.

About mid-day we anchored a mile outside the bar. The afternoon was busy for all hands. Watching the work from the poop, where I remained all the time, I detected in it some of the languor of the six weeks spent in the steaming heat of the river. The first breeze would blow that away. Now the calm was complete. I judged that the second officer—a callow youth with an unpromising face—was not, to put it mildly, of that invaluable stuff from which a commander's right hand is made. But I was glad to catch along the main deck a few smiles on those seamen's faces at which I had hardly had time to have a good look as yet. Having thrown off the mortal coil of shore affairs, I felt myself familiar with them and yet a little strange, like a long-lost wanderer among his kin.

Ransome flitted continually to and fro between the galley and the cabin. It was a pleasure to look at him. The man positively had grace. He alone of all the crew had not had a day's illness in port. But with the knowledge of that uneasy heart within his breast I could detect the restraint he put on the natural sailor-like agility of his movements. It was as though he had something very fragile or very explosive to carry about his person and was all the time aware of it.

I had occasion to address him once or twice. He answered me in his pleasant quiet voice and with a faint, slightly wistful smile. Mr. Burns appeared to be resting. He seemed fairly comfortable.

After sunset I came out on deck again to meet only a still void. The thin, featureless crust of the coast could not be distinguished. The darkness had risen around the ship like a mysterious emanation from the dumb and lonely waters. I leaned on the rail and turned my ear to the shadows of the night. Not a sound. My command might have been a planet flying vertiginously on its appointed path in a space of infinite silence. I clung to the rail as if my sense of balance were leaving me for good. How absurd. I hailed nervously.

"On deck there!"

The immediate answer, "Yes, sir," broke the spell. The anchor-watch man ran up the poop ladder smartly. I told him to report at once the slightest sign of a breeze coming.

Going below I looked in on Mr. Burns. In fact, I could not avoid seeing him, for his door stood open. The man was so wasted that, in that white cabin, under a white sheet, and with his diminished head sunk in the white pillow, his red moustaches captured one's eyes exclusively, like something artificial—a pair of moustaches from a shop exhibited there in the harsh light of the bulkhead-lamp without a shade.

While I stared with a sort of wonder he asserted himself by opening his eyes and even moving them in my direction. A minute stir.

"Dead calm, Mr. Burns," I said resignedly.

In an unexpectedly distinct voice Mr. Burns began a rambling speech. Its tone was very strange, not as if affected by his illness, but as if of a different nature. It sounded unearthly. As to the matter, I seemed to make out that it was the fault of the "old man"—the late captain—ambushed down there under the sea with some evil intention. It was a weird story.

I listened to the end; then stepping into the cabin I laid my hand on the mate's forehead. It was cool. He was light-headed only from extreme weakness. Suddenly he seemed to become aware of me, and in his own voice—of course, very feeble—he asked regretfully:

"Is there no chance at all to get under way, sir?"

"What's the good of letting go our hold of the ground only to drift, Mr. Burns?" I answered.

He sighed, and I left him to his immobility. His hold on life was as slender as his hold on sanity. I was oppressed by my lonely responsibilities. I went into my cabin to seek relief in a few hours' sleep, but almost before I closed my eyes the man on deck came down reporting a light breeze. Enough to get under way with, he said.

And it was no more than just enough. I ordered the windlass manned, the sails loosed, and the topsails set. But by the time I had cast the ship I could hardly feel any breath of wind. Nevertheless, I trimmed the yards and put everything on her. I was not going to give up the attempt.

IV

With her anchor at the bow and clothed in canvas to her very trucks, my command seemed to stand as motionless as a model ship set on the gleams and shadows of polished marble. It was impossible to distinguish land from water in the enigmatical tranquillity of the immense forces of the world. A sudden impatience possessed me.

"Won't she answer the helm at all?" I said irritably to the man whose strong brown hands grasping the spokes of the wheel stood out lighted on the darkness, like a symbol of mankind's claim to the direction of its own fate.

He answered me:

"Yes, sir. She's coming-to slowly."

"Let her head come up to south."

"Aye, aye, sir."

I paced the poop. There was not a sound but that of my footsteps, till the man spoke again.

"She is at south now, sir."

I felt a slight tightness of the chest before I gave out the first course of my first command to the silent night, heavy with dew and sparkling with stars. There was a finality in the act committing me to the endless vigilance of my lonely task.

"Steady her head at that," I said at last. "The course is south."

"South, sir," echoed the man.

I sent below the second mate and his watch and remained in charge, walking the deck through the chill, somnolent hours that precede the dawn.

Slight puffs came and went, and whenever they were strong enough to wake up the black water the murmur alongside ran through my very heart in a delicate crescendo of delight and died away swiftly. I was bitterly tired. The very stars seemed weary of waiting for daybreak. It came at last with a mother-of-pearl sheen at the zenith, such as I had never seen before in the tropics, unglowing, almost grey, with a strange reminder of high latitudes.

The voice of the look-out man hailed from forward:

"Land on the port bow, sir."

"All right."

Leaning on the rail I never even raised my eyes. The motion of the ship was imperceptible. Presently Ransome brought me the cup of morning coffee. After I had drunk it I looked ahead, and in the still streak of very bright pale orange light I saw the land profiled flatly as if cut out of black paper and seeming to float on the water as light as cork. But the rising sun turned it into mere dark vapour, a doubtful, massive shadow trembling in the hot glare.

The watch finished washing decks. I went below and stopped at Mr. Burns' door (he could not bear to have it shut), but hesitated to speak to him till he moved his eyes. I gave him the news.

"Sighted Cape Liant at daylight. About fifteen miles."

He moved his lips then, but I heard no sound till I put my ear down, and caught the peevish comment: "This is crawling. . . . No luck."

"Better luck than standing still, anyhow," I pointed out resignedly, and left him to whatever thoughts or fancies haunted his hopeless prostration.

Later that morning, when relieved by my second officer, I threw myself on my couch and for some three hours or so I really found oblivion. It was so perfect that on waking up I wondered where I was. Then came the immense relief of the thought: on board my ship! At sea! At sea!

Through the port-holes I beheld an unruffled, sun-smitten horizon. The horizon of a windless day. But its spaciousness alone was enough to give me a sense of a fortunate escape, a momentary exultation of freedom.

I stepped out into the saloon with my heart lighter than it had been for days. Ransome was at the sideboard preparing to lay the table for the first sea dinner of the passage. He turned his head, and something in his eyes checked my modest elation.

Instinctively I asked: "What is it now?" not expecting in the least the answer I got. It was given with that sort of contained serenity which was characteristic of the man.

"I am afraid we haven't left all sickness behind us, sir."

"We haven't! What's the matter?"

He told me then that two of our men had been taken bad with fever in the night. One of them was burning and the other was shivering, but he thought that it was pretty much the same thing. I thought so too. I felt shocked by the news. "One burning, the other shivering, you say? No. We haven't left the sickness behind. Do they look very ill?"

"Middling bad, sir." Ransome's eyes gazed steadily into mine. We exchanged smiles. Ransome's a little wistful, as usual, mine no doubt grim enough, to correspond with my secret exasperation.

I asked:

"Was there any wind at all this morning?"

"Can hardly say that, sir. We've moved all the time though. The land ahead seems a little nearer."

That was it. A little nearer. Whereas if we had only had a little more wind, only a very little more, we might, we should, have been abreast of Liant by this time and increasing our distance from that contaminated shore. And it was not only the distance. It seemed to me that a stronger breeze would have blown away the infection which clung to the ship. It obviously did cling to the ship. Two men. One burning, one shivering. I felt a distinct reluctance to go and look at them. What was the good? Poison is poison. Tropical fever is tropical fever. But that it should have stretched its claw after us over the sea seemed to me an extraordinary and unfair licence. I could hardly believe that it could be anything worse than the last desperate pluck of the evil from which we were escaping into the clean breath of the sea. If only that breath had been a little stronger. However, there was the quinine against the fever. I went into the spare cabin where the medicine chest was kept to prepare two doses. I opened it full of faith as a man opens a miraculous shrine. The upper part was inhabited by a collection of bottles, all square-shouldered and as like each other as peas. Under that orderly array there were two drawers, stuffed as full of things as one could imagine—paper packages, bandages, cardboard boxes officially labelled. The lower of the two, in one of its compartments, contained our provision of quinine.

There were five bottles, all round and all of a size. One was about a third full. The other four remained still wrapped up in paper and sealed. But I did not expect to see an envelope lying on top of them. A square envelope, belonging, in fact, to the ship's stationery.

It lay so that I could see it was not closed down, and on picking it up and turning it over I perceived that it was addressed to myself. It contained a half-sheet of notepaper, which I unfolded with a queer sense of dealing with the uncanny, but without any excitement as people meet and do extraordinary things in a dream.

"My dear Captain," it began, but I ran to the signature. The writer was the doctor. The date was that of the day on which, returning from my visit to Mr. Burns in the hospital, I had found the excellent doctor waiting for me in the cabin; and when he told me that he had been putting in time inspecting the medicine chest for me. How bizarre! While expecting me to come in at any moment he had been amusing himself by writing me a letter, and then as I came in had hastened to stuff it into the medicine chest drawer. A rather incredible proceeding. I turned to the text in wonder.

In a large, hurried, but legible hand the good, sympathetic man for some reason, either of kindness or more likely impelled by the irresistible desire to express his opinion, with which he didn't want to damp my hopes before, was warning me not to put my trust in the beneficial effects of a change from land to sea. "I didn't want to add to your worries by discouraging your hopes," he wrote. "I am afraid that, medically speaking, the end of your troubles is not yet." In short, he expected me to have to fight a probable return of tropical illness. Fortunately I had a good provision of quinine. I should put my trust in that, and administer it steadily, when the ship's health would certainly improve.

I crumpled up the letter and rammed it into my pocket. Ransome carried off two big doses to the men forward. As to myself, I did not go on deck as yet. I went instead to the door of Mr. Burns' room, and gave him that news too.

It was impossible to say the effect it had on him. At first I thought that he was speechless. His head lay sunk in the pillow. He moved his lips enough, however, to assure me that he was getting much stronger; a statement shockingly untrue on the face of it.

That afternoon I took my watch as a matter of course. A great over-heated stillness enveloped the ship and seemed to hold her motionless in a flaming ambience composed in two shades of blue. Faint, hot puffs eddied nervelessly from her sails. And yet she moved. She must have. For, as the sun was setting, we had drawn abreast of Cape Liant and dropped it behind us: an ominous retreating shadow in the last gleams of twilight.

In the evening, under the crude glare of his lamp, Mr. Burns seemed to have come more to the surface of his bedding. It was as if a depressing hand had been lifted off him. He answered my few words by a comparatively long, connected speech. He asserted himself strongly. If he escaped being smothered by this stagnant heat, he said, he was confident that in a very few days he would be able to come up on deck and help me.

While he was speaking I trembled lest this effort of energy should leave him lifeless before my eyes. But I cannot deny that there was something comforting in his willingness. I made a suitable reply, but pointed out to him that the only thing that could really help us was wind—a fair wind.

He rolled his head impatiently on the pillow. And it was not comforting in the least to hear him begin to mutter crazily about the late captain, that old man buried in latitude 8° 20', right in our way—ambushed at the entrance of the Gulf.

"Are you still thinking of your late captain, Mr. Burns?" I said. "I imagine the dead feel no animosity against the living. They care nothing for them."

"You don't know that one," he breathed out feebly.

"No, I didn't know him, and he didn't know me. And so he can't have any grievance against me, anyway."

"Yes. But there's all the rest of us on board," he insisted.

I felt the inexpugnable strength of common sense being insidiously menaced by this gruesome, by this insane delusion. And I said:

"You mustn't talk so much. You will tire yourself."

"And there is the ship herself," he persisted in a whisper.

"Now, not a word more," I said, stepping in and laying my hand on his cool forehead. It proved to me that this atrocious absurdity was rooted in the man himself and not in the disease, which, apparently, had emptied him of every power, mental and physical, except that one fixed idea.

I avoided giving Mr. Burns any opening for conversation for the next few days. I merely used to throw him a hasty, cheery word when passing his door. I believe that if he had had the strength he would have called out after me more than once. But he hadn't the strength. Ransome, however, observed to me one afternoon that the mate "seemed to be picking up wonderfully."

"Did he talk any nonsense to you of late?" I asked casually.

"No, sir." Ransome was startled by the direct question; but, after a pause, he added equably: "He told me this morning, sir, that he was sorry he had to bury our late captain right in the ship's way, as one may say, out of the Gulf."

"Isn't this nonsense enough for you?" I asked, looking confidently at the intelligent, quiet face on which the secret uneasiness in the man's breast had thrown a transparent veil of care.

Ransome didn't know. He had not given a thought to the matter. And with a faint smile he flitted away from me on his never-ending duties, with his usual guarded activity.

Two more days passed. We had advanced a little way—a very little way—into the larger space of the Gulf of Siam. Seizing eagerly upon the elation of the first command thrown into my lap, by the agency of Captain Giles, I had yet an uneasy feeling that such luck as this has got perhaps to be paid for in some way. I had held, professionally, a review of my chances. I was competent enough for that. At least, I thought so. I had a general sense of my preparedness which only a man pursuing a calling he loves can know. That feeling seemed to me the most natural thing in the world. As natural as breathing. I imagined I could not have lived without it.

I don't know what I expected. Perhaps nothing else than that special intensity of existence which is the quintessence of youthful aspirations. Whatever I expected I did not expect to be beset by hurricanes. I knew better than that. In the Gulf of Siam there are no hurricanes. But neither did I expect to find myself bound hand and foot to the hopeless extent which was revealed to me as the days went on.

Not that the evil spell held us always motionless. Mysterious currents drifted us here and there, with a stealthy power made manifest by the changing vistas of the islands fringing the east shore of the Gulf. And there were winds too, fitful and deceitful. They raised hopes only to dash them into the bitterest disappointment, promises of advance ending in lost ground, expiring in sighs, dying into dumb stillness in which the currents had it all their own way—their own inimical way.

The island of Koh-ring, a great, black, upheaved ridge amongst a lot of tiny islets, lying upon the glassy water like a triton amongst minnows, seemed to be the centre of the fatal circle. It seemed impossible to get away from it. Day after day it remained in sight. More than once, in a favourable breeze, I would take its bearing in the fast-ebbing twilight, thinking that it was for the last time. Vain hope. A night of fitful airs would undo the gains of temporary favour, and the rising sun would throw out the black relief of Koh-ring, looking more barren, inhospitable, and grim than ever.

"It's like being bewitched, upon my word," I said once to Mr. Burns, from my usual position in the doorway.

He was sitting up in his bed-place. He was progressing towards the world of living men, if he could hardly have been said to have rejoined it yet. He nodded to me his frail and bony head in a wisely mysterious assent.

"Oh, yes, I know what you mean," I said. "But you cannot expect me to believe that a dead man has the power to put out of joint the meteorology of this part of the world. Though indeed it seems to have gone utterly wrong. The land and sea breezes have got broken up into small pieces. We cannot depend upon them for five minutes together."

"It won't be very long now before I can come up on deck," muttered Mr. Burns, "and then we shall see."

Whether he meant this for a promise to grapple with this supernatural evil I couldn't tell. At any rate, it wasn't the kind of assistance I needed. On the other hand, I had been living on deck practically night and day so as to take advantage of every chance to get my ship a little more to the southward. The mate, I could see, was extremely weak yet, and not quite rid of his delusion, which to me appeared but a symptom of his disease. At all events, the hopefulness of an invalid was not to be discouraged. I said:

"You will be most welcome there, I am sure, Mr. Burns. If you go on improving at this rate you'll be presently one of the healthiest men in the ship."

This pleased him, but his extreme emaciation converted his self-satisfied smile into a ghastly exhibition of long teeth under the red moustache.

"Aren't the fellows improving, sir?" he asked soberly, with an extremely sensible expression of anxiety on his face.

I answered him only with a vague gesture and went away from the door. The fact was that disease played with us capriciously very much as the winds did. It would go from one man to another with a lighter or heavier touch, which always left its mark behind, staggering some, knocking others over for a time, leaving this one, returning to another, so that all of them had now an invalidish aspect and a hunted, apprehensive look in their eyes; while Ransome and I, the only two completely untouched, went amongst them assiduously distributing quinine. It was a double fight. The adverse weather held us in front and the disease pressed on our rear. I must say that the men were very good. The constant toil of trimming the yards they faced willingly. But all spring was out of their limbs, and as I looked at them from the poop I could not keep from my mind the dreadful impression that they were moving in poisoned air.

Down below, in his cabin, Mr. Burns had advanced so far as not only to be able to sit up, but even to draw up his legs. Clasping them with bony arms, like an animated skeleton, he emitted deep, impatient sighs.

"The great thing to do, sir," he would tell me on every occasion, when I gave him the chance, "the great thing is to get the ship past 8° 20' of latitude. Once she's past that we're all right."

At first I used only to smile at him, though, God knows, I had not much heart left for smiles. But at last I lost my patience.

"Oh, yes. The latitude 8° 20'. That's where you buried your late captain, isn't it?" Then with severity: "Don't you think, Mr. Burns, it's about time you dropped all that nonsense?"

He rolled at me his deep-sunken eyes in a glance of invincible obstinacy.

But for the rest, he only muttered, just loud enough for me to hear, something about "Not surprised . . . find . . . play us some beastly trick yet . . ."

Such passages as this were not exactly wholesome for my resolution. The stress of adversity was beginning to tell on me. At the same time I felt a contempt for that obscure weakness of my soul. I said to myself disdainfully that it should take much more than that to affect in the smallest degree my fortitude.

I didn't know then how soon and from what unexpected direction it would be attacked.

It was the very next day. The sun had risen clear of the southern shoulder of Koh-ring, which still hung, like an evil attendant, on our port quarter. It was intensely hateful to my sight. During the night we had been heading all round the compass, trimming the yards again and again, to what I fear must have been for the most part imaginary puffs of air. Then just about sunrise we got for an hour an inexplicable, steady breeze, right in our teeth. There was no sense in it. It fitted neither with the season of the year, nor with the secular experience of seamen as recorded in books, nor with the aspect of the sky. Only purposeful malevolence could account for it. It sent us travelling at a great pace away from our proper course; and if we had been out on pleasure sailing bent it would have been a delightful breeze, with the awakened sparkle of the sea, with the sense of motion and a feeling of unwonted freshness. Then all at once, as if disdaining to carry farther the sorry jest, it dropped and died out completely in less than five minutes. The ship's head swung where it listed; the stilled sea took on the polish of a steel plate in the calm.

I went below, not because I meant to take some rest, but simply because I couldn't bear to look at it just then. The indefatigable Ransome was busy in the saloon. It had become a regular practice with him to give me an informal health report in the morning. He turned away from the sideboard with his usual pleasant, quiet gaze. No shadow rested on his intelligent forehead.

"There are a good many of them middling bad this morning, sir," he said in a calm tone.

"What? All knocked out?"

"Only two actually in their bunks, sir, but . . ."

"It's the last night that has done for them. We have had to pull and haul all the blessed time."

"I heard, sir. I had a mind to come out and help only, you know. . . ."

"Certainly not. You mustn't. . . . The fellows lie at night about the decks, too. It isn't good for them."

Ransome assented. But men couldn't be looked after like children. Moreover, one could hardly blame them for trying for such coolness and such air as there were to be found on deck. He himself, of course, knew better.

He was, indeed, a reasonable man. Yet it would have been hard to say that the others were not. The last few days had been for us like the ordeal of the fiery furnace. One really couldn't quarrel with their common, imprudent humanity making the best of the moments of relief, when the night brought in the illusion of coolness and the starlight twinkled through the heavy, dew-laden air. Moreover, most of them were so weakened that hardly anything could be done without everybody that could totter mustering on the braces. No, it was no use remonstrating with them. But I fully believed that quinine was of very great use indeed.

I believed in it. I pinned my faith to it. It would save the men, the ship, break the spell by its medicinal virtue, make time of no account, the weather but a passing worry, and, like a magic powder working against mysterious malefices, secure the first passage of my first command against the evil powers of calms and pestilence. I looked upon it as more precious than gold, and unlike gold, of which there ever hardly seems to be enough anywhere, the ship had a sufficient store of it. I went in to get it with the purpose of weighing out doses. I stretched my hand with the feeling of a man reaching for an unfailing panacea, took up a fresh bottle and unrolled the wrapper, noticing as I did so that the ends, both top and bottom, had come unsealed. . . .

But why record all the swift steps of the appalling discovery. You have guessed the truth already. There was the wrapper, the bottle, and the white powder inside, some sort of powder! But it wasn't quinine. One look at it was quite enough. I remember that at the very moment of picking up the bottle, before I even dealt with the wrapper, the weight of the object I had in my hand gave me an instant of premonition. Quinine is as light as feathers; and my nerves must have been exasperated into an extraordinary sensibility. I let the bottle smash itself on the floor. The stuff, whatever it was, felt gritty under the sole of my shoe. I snatched up the next bottle and then the next. The weight alone told the tale. One after another they fell, breaking at my feet, not because I threw them down in my dismay, but slipping through my fingers as if this disclosure were too much for my strength.

It is a fact that the very greatness of a mental shock helps one to bear up against it, by producing a sort of temporary insensibility. I came out of the state-room stunned, as if something heavy had dropped on my head. From the other side of the saloon, across the table, Ransome, with a duster in his hand, stared open-mouthed. I don't think that I looked wild. It is quite possible that I appeared to be in a hurry because I was instinctively hastening up on deck. An example of this training become instinct. The difficulties, the dangers, the problems of a ship at sea must be met on deck.

To this fact, as it were of nature, I responded instinctively; which may be taken as a proof that for a moment I must have been robbed of my reason.

I was certainly off my balance, a prey to impulse, for at the bottom of the stairs I turned and flung myself at the doorway of Mr. Burns' cabin. The wildness of his aspect checked my mental disorder. He was sitting up in his bunk, his body looking immensely long, his head drooping a little sideways, with affected complacency. He flourished, in his trembling hand, on the end of a fore-arm no thicker than a stout walking-stick, a shining pair of scissors which he tried before my very eyes to jab at his throat.

I was to a certain extent horrified; but it was rather a secondary sort of effect, not really strong enough to make me yell at him in some such manner as: "Stop!" . . . "Heavens!" . . . "What are you doing?"

In reality he was simply overtaxing his returning strength in a shaky attempt to clip off the thick growth of his red beard. A large towel was spread over his lap, and a shower of stiff hairs, like bits of copper wire, was descending on it at every snip of the scissors.

He turned to me his face grotesque beyond the fantasies of mad dreams, one cheek all bushy as if with a swollen flame, the other denuded and sunken, with the untouched long moustache on that side asserting itself, lonely and fierce. And while he stared thunderstruck, with the gaping scissors on his fingers, I shouted my discovery at him fiendishly, in six words, without comment.

V

I heard the clatter of the scissors escaping from his hand, noted the perilous heave of his whole person over the edge of the bunk after them, and then, returning to my first purpose, pursued my course on to the deck. The sparkle of the sea filled my eyes. It was gorgeous and barren, monotonous and without hope under the empty curve of the sky. The sails hung motionless and slack, the very folds of their sagging surfaces moved no more than carved granite. The impetuosity of my advent made the man at the helm start slightly. A block aloft squeaked incomprehensibly, for what on earth could have made it do so? It was a whistling note like a bird's. For a long, long time I faced an empty world, steeped in an infinity of silence, through which the sunshine poured and flowed for some mysterious purpose. Then I heard Ransome's voice at my elbow.

"I have put Mr. Burns back to bed, sir."

"You have?"

"Well, sir, he got out, all of a sudden, but when he let go of the edge of his bunk he fell down. He isn't light-headed, though, it seems to me."

"No," I said dully, without looking at Ransome. He waited for a moment, then, cautiously as if not to give offence: "I don't think we need lose much of that stuff, sir," he said, "I can sweep it up, every bit of it almost, and then we could sift the glass out. I will go about it at once. It will not make the breakfast late, not ten minutes."

"Oh, yes," I said bitterly. "Let the breakfast wait, sweep up every bit of it, and then throw the damned lot overboard!"

The profound silence returned, and when I looked over my shoulder Ransome—the intelligent, serene Ransome—had vanished from my side. The intense loneliness of the sea acted like poison on my brain. When I turned my eyes to the ship, I had a morbid vision of her as a floating grave. Who hasn't heard of ships found drifting, haphazard, with their crews all dead? I looked at the seaman at the helm, I had an impulse to speak to him, and, indeed, his face took on an expectant cast as if he had guessed my intention. But in the end I went below, thinking I would be alone with the greatness of my trouble for a little while. But through his open door Mr. Burns saw me come down, and addressed me grumpily: "Well, sir?"

I went in. "It isn't well at all," I said.

Mr. Burns, re-established in his bed-place, was concealing his hirsute cheek in the palm of his hand.

"That confounded fellow has taken away the scissors from me," were the next words he said.

The tension I was suffering from was so great that it was perhaps just as well that Mr. Burns had started on this grievance. He seemed very sore about it and grumbled, "Does he think I am mad, or what?"

"I don't think so, Mr. Burns," I said. I looked upon him at that moment as a model of self-possession. I even conceived on that account a sort of admiration for that man, who had (apart from the intense materiality of what was left of his beard) come as near to being a disembodied spirit as any man can do and live. I noticed the preternatural sharpness of the ridge of his nose, the deep cavities of his temples, and I envied him. He was so reduced that he would probably die very soon. Enviable man! So near extinction— while I had to bear within me a tumult of suffering vitality, doubt, confusion, self-reproach, and an indefinite reluctance to meet the horrid logic of the situation. I could not help muttering: "I feel as if I were going mad myself."

Mr. Burns glared spectrally, but otherwise wonderfully composed.

"I always thought he would play us some deadly trick," he said, with a peculiar emphasis on the *he*.

It gave me a mental shock, but I had neither the mind nor the heart nor the spirit to argue with him. My form of sickness was indifference. The creeping paralysis of a hopeless outlook. So I only gazed at him. Mr. Burns broke into further speech.

"Eh? What? No! You won't believe it? Well, how do you account for this? How do you think it could have happened?"

"Happened?" I repeated dully. "Why, yes, how in the name of the infernal powers did this thing happen?"

Indeed, on thinking it out, it seemed incomprehensible that it should just be like this: the bottles emptied, refilled, rewrapped, and replaced. A sort of plot, a sinister attempt to deceive, a thing resembling sly vengeance—but for what?—or else a fiendish joke. But Mr. Burns was in possession of a theory. It was simple, and he uttered it solemnly in a hollow voice.

"I suppose they have given him about fifteen pounds in Haiphong for that little lot."

"Mr. Burns!" I cried.

He nodded grotesquely over his raised legs, like two broomsticks in the pyjamas, with enormous bare feet at the end.

"Why not? The stuff is pretty expensive in this part of the world, and they were very short of it in Tonkin. And what did he care? You have not known him. I have, and I have defied him. He feared neither God, nor devil, nor man, nor wind, nor sea, nor his own conscience. And I believe he hated everybody and everything. But I think he was afraid to die. I believe I am the only man who ever stood up to him. I faced him in that cabin where you live now, when he was sick, and I cowed him then. He thought I was going to twist his neck for him. If he had had his way we would have been beating up against the North-East monsoon, as long as he lived and afterwards too, for ages and ages. Acting the Flying Dutchman in the China Sea! Ha! Ha!"

"But why should he replace the bottles like this?" . . . I began.

"Why shouldn't he? Why should he want to throw the bottles away? They fit the drawer. They belong to the medicine chest."

"And they were wrapped up," I cried.

"Well, the wrappers were there. Did it from habit, I suppose, and as to refilling, there is always a lot of stuff they send in paper parcels that burst after a time. And then, who can tell? I suppose you didn't taste it, sir? But, of coure, you are sure . . ."

"No," I said. "I didn't taste it. It is all overboard now."

Behind me, a soft, cultivated voice said: "I have tasted it. It seemed a mixture of all sorts, sweetish, saltish, very horrible."

Ransome, stepping out of the pantry, had been listening for some time, as it was very excusable in him to do.

"A dirty trick," said Mr. Burns. "I always said he would."

The magnitude of my indignation was unbounded. And the kind, sympathetic doctor too. The only sympathetic man I ever knew . . . instead of writing that warning letter, the very refinement of sympathy, why didn't the man make a proper inspection? But, as a matter of fact, it was hardly fair to blame the doctor. The fittings were in order and the medicine chest is an officially arranged affair. There was nothing really to arouse the slightest suspicion. The person I could never forgive was myself. Nothing should ever be taken for granted. The seed of everlasting remorse was sown in my breast.

"I feel it's all my fault," I exclaimed, "mine, and nobody else's. That's how I feel. I shall never forgive myself."

"That's very foolish, sir," said Mr. Burns fiercely.

And after this effort he fell back exhausted on his bed. He closed his eyes, he panted; this affair, this abominable surprise had shaken him up too. As I turned away I perceived Ransome looking at me blankly. He appreciated what it meant, but he managed to produce his pleasant, wistful smile. Then he stepped back into his pantry, and I rushed up on deck again to see whether there was any wind, any breath under the sky, any stir of the air, any sign of hope. The deadly stillness met me again. Nothing was changed except that there was a different man at the wheel. He looked ill. His whole figure drooped, and he seemed rather to cling to the spokes than hold them with a controlling grip. I said to him:

"You are not fit to be here."

"I can manage, sir," he said feebly.

As a matter of fact, there was nothing for hfm to do. The ship had no steerage way. She lay with her head to the westward, the everlasting Koh-ring visible over the stern, with a few small islets, black spots in the great blaze, swimming before my troubled eyes. And but for those bits of land there was no speck on the sky, no speck on the water, no shape of vapour, no wisp of smoke, no sail, no boat, no stir of humanity, no sign of life, nothing!

The first question was, what to do? What could one do? The first thing to do obviously was to tell the men. I did it that very day. I wasn't going to let the knowledge simply get about. I would face them. They were assembled on the quarter-deck for the purpose. Just before I stepped out to speak to them I discovered that life could hold terrible moments. No confessed criminal had ever been so oppressed by his sense of guilt. This is why, perhaps, my face was set hard and my voice curt and unemotional while I made my declaration that I could do nothing more for the sick, in the way of drugs. As to such care as could be given them they knew they had had it.

I would have held them justified in tearing me limb from limb. The silence which followed upon my words was almost harder to bear than the angriest uproar. I was crushed by the infinite depth of its reproach. But, as a matter of fact, I was mistaken. In a voice which I had great difficulty in keeping firm, I went on: "I suppose, men, you have understood what I said, and you know what it means."

A voice or two were heard: "Yes, sir. . . . We understand."

They had kept silent simply because they thought that they were not called to say anything; and when I told them that I intended to run into Singapore and that the best chance for the ship and the men was in the efforts all of us, sick and well, must make to get her along out of this, I received the encouragement of a low assenting murmur and of a louder voice exclaiming: "Surely there is a way out of this blamed hole."

Here is an extract from the notes I wrote at the time:

> We have lost Koh-ring at last. For many days now I don't think I have been two hours below altogether. I remain on deck, of course, night and day, and the nights and the days wheel over us in succession, whether long or short, who can say? All sense of time is lost in the monotomy of expectation, of hope, and of desire—which is only one: Get the ship to the southward! Get the ship to the southward! The effect is curiously mechanical; the sun climbs and descends, the night swings over our heads as if somebody below the horizon were turning a crank. It is the pettiest, the most aimless! . . . and all through that miserable performance I go on, tramping, tramping the deck. How many miles have I walked on the poop of that ship! A stubborn pilgrimage of sheer restlessness, diversified by short excursions below to look upon Mr. Burns. I don't know whether it is an illusion, but he seems to become more substantial from day to day. He doesn't say much, for, indeed, the situation doesn't lend itself to idle remarks. I notice this even with the men as I watch them moving or sitting

about the decks. They don't talk to each other. It strikes me that if there exist an invisible ear catching the whispers of the earth, it will find this ship the most silent spot on it. . . .

No, Mr. Burns has not much to say to me. He sits in his bunk with his beard gone, his moustaches flaming, and with an air of silent determination on his chalky physiognomy. Ransome tells me he devours all the food that is given him to the last scrap, but that, apparently, he sleeps very little. Even at night, when I go below to fill my pipe, I notice that, though dozing flat on his back, he still looks very determined. From the side glance he gives me when awake it seems as though he were annoyed at being interrupted in some arduous mental operation; and as I emerge on deck the ordered arrangement of the stars meets my eye, unclouded, infinitely wearisome. There they are: stars, sun, sea, light, darkness, space, great waters; the formidable Work of the Seven Days, into which mankind seems to have blundered unbidden. Or else decoyed. Even as I have been decoyed into this awful, this death-haunted command. . . .

The only spot of light in the ship at night was that of the compass-lamps, lighting up the faces of the succeeding helmsmen; for the rest we were lost in the darkness, I walking the poop and the men lying about the decks. They were all so reduced by sickness that no watches could be kept. Those who were able to walk remained all the time on duty, lying about in the shadows of the main deck, till my voice raised for an order would bring them to their enfeebled feet, a tottering little group, moving patiently about the ship, with hardly a murmur, a whisper amongst them all. And every time I had to raise my voice it was with a pang of remorse and pity.

Then about four o'clock in the morning a light would gleam forward in the galley. The unfailing Ransome with the uneasy heart, immune, serene, and active, was getting ready the early coffee for the men. Presently he would bring me a cup up on the poop, and it was then that I allowed myself to drop into my deck chair for a couple of hours of real sleep. No doubt I must have been snatching short dozes when leaning against the rail for a moment in sheer exhaustion; but, honestly, I was not aware of them, except in the painful form of convulsive starts that seemed to come on me even while I walked. From about five, however, until after seven I would sleep openly under the fading stars.

I would say to the helmsman: "Call me at need," and drop into that chair and close my eyes, feeling that there was no more sleep for me on earth. And then I would know nothing till, some time between seven and eight, I would feel a touch on my shoulder and look up at Ransome's face, with its faint, wistful smile and friendly, grey eyes, as though he were tenderly amused at my slumbers. Occasionally the second mate would come up and relieve me at early coffee time. But it didn't really matter. Generally it was a dead calm, or else faint airs so changing and fugitive that it really wasn't worth while to touch a brace for them. If the air steadied at all the seaman at the helm could be trusted for a warning shout: "Ship's all aback, sir!" which like a trumpet-call would make me spring a foot above the deck. Those were the words which it seemed to me would have made me spring up from eternal sleep. But this was not often. I have never met since such breathless sunrises. And if the second mate happened to be there (he had generally one day in three free of fever) I would find him sitting on the skylight half-senseless, as it were, and with an idiotic gaze fastened on some object near by—a rope, a cleat, a belaying pin, a ringbolt.

That young man was rather troublesome. He remained cubbish in his sufferings. He seemed to have become completely imbecile; and when the return of fever drove him to his cabin below the next thing would be that we would miss him from there. The first time it happened Ransome and I were very much alarmed. We started a quiet search and ultimately Ransome discovered him curled up in the sail-locker, which opened into the lobby by a sliding-door. When remonstrated with, he muttered sulkily, "It's cool in there." That wasn't true. It was only dark there.

The fundamental defects of his face were not improved by its uniform livid hue. It was not so with many of the men. The wastage of ill-health seemed to idealize the general character of the features, bringing out the unsuspected nobility of some, the strength of others, and in one case revealing an essentially comic aspect. He was a short, gingery, active man with a nose and chin of the Punch type, and whom his shipmates called "Frenchy." I don't know why. He may have been a Frenchman, but I have never heard him utter a single word in French.

To see him coming aft to the wheel comforted one. The blue dungaree trousers turned up the calf, one leg a little higher than the other, the clean check shirt, the white canvas cap, evidently made by himself, made up a whole of peculiar smartness, and the persistent jauntiness of his gait, even, poor fellow, when he couldn't help tottering, told of his invincible spirit. There was also a man called Gambril. He was the only grizzled person in the ship. His face was of an austere type. But if I remember all their faces, wasting tragically before my eyes, most of their names have vanished from my memory.

The words that passed between us were few and puerile in regard of the situation. I had to force myself to look them in the face. I expected to meet reproachful glances. There were none. The expression of suffering in their eyes was indeed hard enough to bear. But that they couldn't help. For the rest, I ask myself whether it was the temper of their souls or the sympathy of their imagination that made them so wonderful, so worthy of my undying regard.

For myself, neither my soul was highly tempered, nor my imagination properly under control. There were moments when I felt, not only that I would go mad, but that I had gone mad already; so that I dared not open my lips for fear of betraying myself by some insane shriek. Luckily I had only orders to give, and an order has a steadying influence upon him who has to give it. Moreover, the seaman, the officer of the watch, in me was sufficiently sane. I was like a mad carpenter making a box. Were he ever so convinced that he was King of Jerusalem, the box he would make would be a sane box. What I feared was a shrill note escaping me involuntarily and upsetting my balance. Luckily, again, there was no necessity to raise one's voice. The brooding stillness of the world seemed sensitive to the slightest sound like a whispering gallery. The conversational tone would almost carry a word from one end of the ship to the other. The terrible thing was that the only voice that I ever heard was my own. At night especially it reverberated very lonely amongst the planes of the unstirring sails.

Mr. Burns, still keeping to his bed with that air of secret determination, was moved to grumble at many things. Our interviews were short five-minute affairs, but fairly frequent. I was everlastingly diving down below to get a light, though I did not consume much tobacco at that time. The pipe was always going out; for in truth my mind was not composed enough to enable me to get a decent smoke. Likewise, for most of the time during the twenty-four hours I could have struck matches on deck and held them aloft till the flame burnt my fingers. But I always used to run below. It was a change. It was the only break in the incessant strain; and, of course, Mr. Burns through the open door could see me come in and go out every time.

With his knees gathered up under his chin and staring with his greenish eyes over them, he was a weird figure, and with my knowledge of the crazy notion in his head, not a very attractive one for me. Still, I had to speak to him now and then, and one day he complained that the ship was very silent. For hours and hours, he said, he was lying there, not hearing a sound, till he did not know what to do with himself.

"When Ransome happens to be forward in his galley everything's so still that one might think everybody in the ship was dead," he grumbled. "The only voice I do hear sometimes is yours, sir, and that isn't enough to cheer me up. What's the matter with the men? Isn't there one left that can sing out at the ropes?"

"Not one, Mr. Burns," I said. "There is no breath to spare on board this ship for that. Are you aware that there are times when I can't muster more than three hands to do anything?"

He asked swiftly but fearfully:

"Nobody dead yet, sir?"

"No."

"It wouldn't do," Mr. Burns declared forcibly. "Mustn't let him. If he gets hold of one he will get them all."

I cried out angrily at this. I believe I even swore at the disturbing effect of these words. They attacked all the self-possession that was left to me. In my endless vigil in the face of the enemy I had been haunted by gruesome images enough. I had had visions of a ship drifting in calms and swinging in light airs, with all her crew dying slowly about her decks. Such things had been known to happen.

Mr. Burns met my outburst by a mysterious silence.

"Look here," I said. "You don't believe yourself what you say. You can't. It's impossible. It isn't the sort of thing I have a right to expect from you. My position's bad enough without being worried with your silly fancies."

He remained unmoved. On account of the way in which the light fell on his head I could not be sure whether he had smiled faintly or not. I changed my tone.

"Listen," I said. "It's getting so desperate that I had thought for a moment, since we can't make our way south, whether I wouldn't try to steer west and make an attempt to reach the mail-boat track. We could always get some quinine from her, at least. What do you think?"

He cried out: "No, no, no. Don't do that, sir. You mustn't for a moment give up facing that old ruffian. If you do he will get the upper hand of us."

I left him. He was impossible. It was like a case of possession. His protest, however, was essentially quite sound. As a matter of fact, my notion of heading out west on the chance of sighting a problematical steamer could not bear calm examination. On the side where we were we had enough wind, at least from time to time, to struggle on towards the south. Enough, at least, to keep hope alive. But suppose that I had used those capricious gusts of wind to sail away to the westward, into some region where there was not a breath of air for days on end, what then? Perhaps my appalling vision of a ship floating with a dead crew would become a reality for the discovery weeks afterwards by some horror-stricken mariners.

That afternoon Ransome brought me up a cup of tea, and while waiting there, tray in hand, he remarked in the exactly right tone of sympathy:

"You are holding out well, sir."

"Yes." I said. "You and I seem to have been forgotten."

"Forgotten, sir?"

"Yes, by the fever-devil who has got on board this ship," I said.

Ransome gave me one of his attractive, intelligent, quick glances and went away with the tray. It occurred to me that I had been talking somewhat in Mr. Burns' manner. It annoyed me. Yet often in darker moments I forgot myself into an attitude towards our troubles more fit for a contest against a living enemy.

Yes. The fever-devil had not laid his hand yet either on Ransome or on me. But he might at any time. It was one of those thoughts one had to fight down, keep at arm's length at any cost. It was unbearable to contemplate the possibility of Ransome, the housekeeper of the ship, being laid low. And what would happen to my command if I got knocked over, with Mr. Burns too weak to stand without holding on to his bed-place and the second mate reduced to a state of permanent imbecility? It was impossible to imagine, or, rather, it was only too easy to imagine.

I was alone on the poop. The ship having no steerage way, I had sent the helmsman away to sit down or lie down somewhere in the shade. The men's strength was so reduced that all unnecessary calls on it had to be avoided. It was the austere Gambril with the grizzly beard. He went away readily enough, but he was so weakened by repeated bouts of fever, poor fellow, that in order to get down the poop ladder he had to turn sideways and hang on with both hands to the brass rail. It was just simply heart-breaking to watch. Yet he was neither very much worse nor much better than most of the half-dozen miserable victims I could muster up on deck.

It was a terribly lifeless afternoon. For several days in succession low clouds had appeared in the distance, white masses with dark convolutions resting on the water, motionless, almost solid, and yet all the time changing their aspects subtly. Towards evening they vanished as a rule. But this day they awaited the setting sun, which glowed and smouldered sulkily amongst them before it sank down. The punctual and wearisome stars reappeared over our mastheads, but the air remained stagnant and oppressive.

The unfailing Ransome lighted the binnacle lamps and glided, all shadowy, up to me.

"Will you go down and try to eat something, sir?" he suggested.

His low voice startled me. I had been standing looking out over the rail, saying nothing, feeling nothing, not even the weariness of my limbs, overcome by the evil spell.

"Ransome," I asked abruptly, "how long have I been on deck? I am losing the notion of time."

"Fourteen days, sir," he said. "It was a fortnight last Monday since we left the anchorage."

His equable voice sounded mournful somehow. He waited a bit, then added: "It's the first time that it looks as if we were to have some rain."

I noticed then the broad shadow on the horizon extinguishing the low stars completely, while those overhead, when I looked up, seemed to shine down on us through a veil of smoke.

How it got there, how it had crept up so high, I couldn't say. It had an ominous appearance. The air did not stir. At a renewed invitation from Ransome I did go down into the cabin to—in his words—"try and eat something." I don't know that the trial was very successful. I suppose at that period I did exist on food in the usual way; but the memory is now that in those days life was sustained on invincible anguish, as a sort of infernal stimulant exciting and consuming at the same time.

It's the only period of my life in which I attempted to keep a diary. No, not the only one. Years later, in conditions of moral isolation, I did put down on paper the thoughts and events of a score of days. But this was the first time. I don't remember how it came about or how the pocket-book and the pencil came into my hands. It's inconceivable that I should have looked for them on purpose. I suppose they saved me from the crazy trick of talking to myself.

Strangely enough, in both cases I took to that sort of thing in circumstances in which I did not expect, in colloquial phrase, "to come out of it." Neither could I expect the record to outlast me. This shows that it was purely a personal need for intimate relief and not a call of egotism.

Here I must give another sample of it, a few detached lines, now looking very ghostly to my own eyes, out of the part scribbled that very evening:—

> There is something going on in the sky like a decomposition, like a corruption of the air, which remains as still as ever. After all, mere clouds, which may or may not hold wind or rain. Strange that it should trouble me so. I feel as if all my sins had found me out. But I suppose the trouble is that the ship is still lying motionless, not under command; and that I have nothing to do to keep my imagination from running wild amongst the disastrous images of the worst that may befall us. What's going to happen? Probably nothing. Or anything. It may be a furious squall coming, butt-end foremost. And on deck there are five men with the vitality and the strength of, say, two. We may have all our sails blown away. Every stitch of canvas has been on her since we broke ground at the mouth of the Mei-nam, fifteen days ago . . . or fifteen centuries. It seems to me that all my life before that momentous day is infinitely remote, a fading memory of light-hearted youth, something on the other side of a shadow. Yes, sails may very well be blown away. And that would be like a death sentence on the men. We haven't strength enough on board to bend another suit; incredible thought, but it is true. Or we may even get dismasted. Ships have been dismasted in squalls simply because they weren't handled quick enough, and we have no power to whirl the yards around. It's like being bound hand and foot preparatory to having one's throat cut. And what appals me most of all is that I shrink from going on deck to face it. It's due to the ship, it's due to the men who are there on deck—some of them, ready to put out the last remnant of their strength at a word from me. And I am shrinking from it. From the mere vision. My first command. Now I understand that strange sense of insecurity in my past. I always suspected that I might be no good. And here is proof positive, I am shirking it, I am no good.

At that moment, or, perhaps, the moment after, I became aware of Ransome standing in the cabin. Something in his expression startled me. It had a meaning which I could not make out. I exclaimed:

"Somebody's dead."

It was his turn then to look startled.

"Dead? Not that I know of, sir. I have been in the fore-castle only ten minutes ago and there was no dead man there then."

"You did give me a scare," I said.

His voice was extremely pleasant to listen to. He explained that he had come down below to close Mr. Burns' port in case it should come on to rain. He did not know that I was in the cabin, he added.

"How does it look outside?" I asked him.

"Very black indeed, sir. There is something in it for certain."

"In what quarter?"

"All round, sir."

I repeated idly: "All round. For certain," with my elbows on the table.

Ransome lingered in the cabin as if he had something to do there, but hesitated about doing it. I said suddenly:

"You think I ought to be on deck?"

He answered at once but without any particular emphasis or accent: "I do, sir."

I got to my feet briskly, and he made way for me to go out. As I passed through the lobby I heard Mr. Burns' voice saying:

"Shut the door of my room, will you, steward?" And Ransome's rather surprised: "Certainly, sir."

I thought that all my feelings had been dulled into complete indifference. But I found it as trying as ever to be on deck. The impenetrable blackness beset the ship so close that it seemed that by thrusting one's hand over the side one could touch some unearthly substance. There was in it an effect of inconceivable terror and of inexpressible mystery. The few stars overhead shed a dim light upon the ship alone, with no gleams of any kind upon the water, in detached shafts piercing an atmosphere which had turned to soot. It was something I had never seen before, giving no hint of the direction from which any change would come, the closing in of a menace from all sides.

There was still no man at the helm. The immobility of all things was perfect. If the air had turned black, the sea, for all I knew, might have turned solid. It was no good looking in any direction, watching for any sign, speculating upon the nearness of the moment. When the time came the blackness would overwhelm silently the bit of starlight falling upon the ship, and the end of all things would come without a sigh, stir, or murmur of any kind, and all our hearts would cease to beat like run-down clocks.

It was impossible to shake off that sense of finality. The quietness that came over me was like a foretaste of annihilation. It gave me a sort of comfort, as though my soul had become suddenly reconciled to an eternity of blind stillness.

The seaman's instinct alone survived whole in my moral dissolution. I descended the ladder to the quarter-deck. The starlight seemed to die out before reaching that spot, but when I asked quietly: "Are you there, men?" my eyes made out shadowy forms starting up around me, very few, very indistinct; and a voice spoke: "All here, sir." Another amended anxiously:

"All that are any good for anything, sir."

Both voices were very quiet and unringing; without any special character of readiness or discouragement. Very matter-of-fact voices.

"We must try to haul this mainsail close up," I said.

The shadows swayed away from me without a word. Those men were the ghosts of themselves, and their weight on a rope could be no more than the weight of a bunch of ghosts. Indeed, if ever a sail was hauled up by sheer spiritual strength it must have been that sail, for, properly speaking, there was not muscle enough for the task in the whole ship, let alone the miserable lot of us on deck. Of course, I took the lead in the work myself. They wandered feebly after me from rope to rope, stumbling and panting. They toiled like Titans. We were an hour at it at least, and all the time the black universe made no sound. When the last leech-line was made fast, my eyes, accustomed to the darkness, made out the shapes of exhausted men drooping over the rails, collapsed on hatches. One hung over the after-capstan, sobbing for breath; and I stood amongst them like a tower of strength, impervious to disease and feeling only the sickness of my soul. I waited for some time fighting against the weight of my sins, against my sense of unworthiness, and then I said:

"Now, men, we'll go aft and square the mainyard. That's about all we can do for the ship; and for the rest she must take her chance."

VI

As we all went up it occurred to me that there ought to be a man at the helm. I raised my voice not much above a whisper, and, noiselessly, an uncomplaining spirit in a fever-wasted body appeared in the light aft, the head with hollow eyes illuminated against the blackness which had swallowed up our world—and the universe. The bare fore-arm extended over the upper spokes seemed to shine with a light of its own. I murmured to that luminous appearance:

"Keep the helm right amidships."

It answered in a tone of patient suffering:

"Right amidships, sir."

Then I descended to the quarter-deck. It was impossible to tell whence the blow would come. To look round the ship was to look into a bottomless, black pit. The eye lost itself in inconceivable depths. I wanted to ascertain whether the ropes had been picked up off the deck. One could only do that by feeling with one's feet. In my cautious progress I came against a man in whom I recognized Ransome. He possessed an unimpaired physical solidity which was manifest to me at the contact. He was leaning against the quarter-deck capstan and kept silent. It was like a revelation. He was the collapsed figure sobbing for breath I had noticed before we went on the poop.

"You have been helping with the mainsail!" I exclaimed in a low tone.

"Yes, sir," sounded his quiet voice.

"Man! What were you thinking of? You mustn't do that sort of thing."

After a pause he assented. "I suppose I mustn't." Then after another short silence he added: "I am all right now," quickly, between the tell-tale gasps.

I could neither hear nor see anybody else; but when I spoke up, answering sad murmurs filled the quarter-deck, and its shadows seemed to shift here and there. I ordered all the halyards laid down on deck clear for running.

"I'll see to that, sir," volunteered Ransome in his natural, pleasant tone, which comforted one and aroused one's compassion too, somehow.

That man ought to have been in his bed, resting, and my plain duty was to send him there. But perhaps he would not have obeyed me. I had not the strength of mind to try. All I said was:

"Go about it quietly, Ransome."

Returning on the poop I approached Gambril. His face, set with hollow shadows in the light, looked awful, finally silenced. I asked him how he felt, but hardly expected an answer. Therefore I was astonished at his comparative loquacity.

"Them shakes leaves me as weak as a kitten, sir," he said, preserving finely that air of unconsciousness as to anything but his business a helmsman should never lose. "And before I can pick up my strength that there hot fit comes along and knocks me over again."

He sighed. There was no complaint in his tone, but the bare words were enough to give me a horrible pang of self-reproach. It held me dumb for a time. When the tormenting sensation had passed off I asked:

"Do you feel strong enough to prevent the rudder taking charge if she gets sternway on her? It wouldn't do to get something smashed about the steering-gear now. We've enough difficulties to cope with as it is."

He answered with just a shade of weariness that he was strong enough to hang on. He could promise me that she shouldn't take the wheel out of his hands. More he couldn't say.

At that moment Ransome appeared quite close to me, stepping out of the darkness into visibility suddenly, as if just created with his composed face and pleasant voice.

Every rope on deck, he said, was laid down clear for running, as far as one could make certain by feeling. It was impossible to see anything. Frenchy had stationed himself forward. He said he had a jump or two left in him yet.

Here a faint smile altered for an instant the clear, firm design of Ransome's lips. With his serious, clear, grey eyes, his serene temperament, he was a priceless man altogether. Soul as firm as the muscles of his body.

He was the only man on board (except me, but I had to preserve my liberty of movement) who had a sufficiency of muscular strength to trust to. For a moment I thought I had better ask him to take the wheel. But the dreadful knowledge of the enemy he had to carry about him made me hesitate. In my ignorance of physiology it occurred to me that he might die suddenly, from excitement, at a critical moment.

While this gruesome fear restrained the ready words on the tip of my tongue, Ransome stepped back two paces and vanished from my sight.

At once an uneasiness possessed me, as if some support had been withdrawn. I moved forward too, outside the circle of light, into the darkness that stood in front of me like a wall. In one stride I penetrated it. Such must have been the darkness before creation. It had closed behind me. I knew I was invisible to the man at the helm. Neither could I see anything. He was alone, I was alone, every man was alone where he stood. And every form was gone, too, spar, sail, fittings, rails; everything was blotted out in the dreadful smoothness of that absolute night.

A flash of lightning would have been a relief—I mean physically. I would have prayed for it if it hadn't been for my shrinking apprehension of the thunder. In the tension of silence I was suffering from it seemed to me that the first crash must turn me into dust.

And thunder was, most likely, what would happen next. Stiff all over and hardly breathing, I waited with a horribly strained expectation. Nothing happened. It was maddening. But a dull, growing ache in the lower part of my face made me aware that I had been grinding my teeth madly enough, for God knows how long.

It's extraordinary I should not have heard myself doing it; but I hadn't. By an effort which absorbed all my faculties I managed to keep my jaw still. It required much attention, and while thus engaged I became bothered by curious, irregular sounds of faint tapping on the deck. They could be heard single, in pairs, in groups. While I wondered at this mysterious devilry, I received a slight blow under the left eye and felt an enormous tear run down my cheek. Raindrops. Enormous. Forerunners of something. Tap. Tap. Tap. . . .

I turned about, and, addressing Gambril earnestly, entreated him to "hang on to the wheel." But I could hardly speak from emotion. The fatal moment had come. I held my breath. The tapping had stopped as unexpectedly as it had begun, and there was a renewed moment of intolerable suspense; something like an additional turn of the racking screw. I don't suppose I would have ever screamed, but I remember my conviction that there was nothing else for it but to scream.

Suddenly—how am I to convey it? Well, suddenly the darkness turned into water. This is the only suitable figure. A heavy shower, a downpour, comes along, making a noise. You hear its approach on the sea, in the air too, I verily believe. But this was different. With no preliminary whisper or rustle, without a splash, and even without the ghost of impact, I became instantaneously soaked to the skin. Not a very difficult matter, since I was wearing only my sleeping suit. My hair got full of water in an instant, water streamed on my skin, it filled my nose, my ears, my eyes. In a fraction of a second I swallowed quite a lot of it.

As to Gambril, he was fairly choked. He coughed pitifully, the broken cough of a sick man; and I beheld him as one sees a fish in an aquarium by the light of an electric bulb, an elusive, phosphorescent shape. Only he did not glide away. But something else happened. Both binnacle lamps went out. I suppose the water forced itself into them, though I wouldn't have thought that possible, for they fitted into the cowl perfectly.

The last gleam of light in the universe had gone, pursued by a low exclamation of dismay from Gambril. I groped for him and seized his arm. How startlingly wasted it was.

"Never mind," I said. "You don't want the light. All you need to do is to keep the wind, when it comes, at the back of your head. You understand?"

"Aye, aye, sir. . . . But I should like to have a light," he added nervously.

All that time the ship lay as steady as a rock. The noise of the water pouring off the sails and spars, flowing over the break of the poop, had stopped short. The poop scuppers gurgled and sobbed for a little while longer, and then perfect silence, joined to perfect immobility, proclaimed the yet unbroken spell of our helplessness, poised on the edge of some violent issue, lurking in the dark.

I started forward restlessly. I did not need my sight to pace the poop of my ill-starred first command with perfect assurance. Every square foot of her decks was impressed indelibly on my brain, to the very grain and knots of the planks. Yet, all of a sudden, I fell clean over something, landing full length on my hands and face.

It was something big and alive. Not a dog—more like a sheep, rather. But there were no animals in the ship. How could an animal. . . . It was an added and fantastic horror which I could not resist. The hair of my head stirred even as I picked myself up, awfully scared; not as a man is scared while his judgment, his reason still try to resist, but completely, boundlessly, and, as it were, innocently scared—like a little child.

I could see It—that Thing! The darkness, of which so much had just turned into water, had thinned down a little. There It was! But I did not hit upon the notion of Mr. Burns issuing out of the companion on all fours till he attempted to stand up, and even then the idea of a bear crossed my mind first.

He growled like one when I seized him round the body. He had buttoned himself up into an enormous winter overcoat of some woolly material, the weight of which was too much for his reduced state. I could hardly feel the incredibly thin lath of his body, lost within the thick stuff, but his growl had depth and substance: Confounded dumb ship with a craven, tip-toeing crowd. Why couldn't they stamp and go with a brace? Wasn't there one God-forsaken lubber in the lot fit to raise a yell on a rope?

"Skulking's no good, sir," he attacked me directly. "You can't slink past the old murderous ruffian. It isn't the way. You must go for him boldly—as I did. Boldness is what you want. Show him that you don't care for any of his damned tricks. Kick up a jolly old row."

"Good God, Mr. Burns," I said angrily. "What on earth are you up to? What do you mean by coming up on deck in this state?"

"Just that! Boldness. The only way to scare the old bullying rascal."

I pushed him, still growling, against the rail. "Hold on to it," I said roughly. I did not know what to do with him. I left him in a hurry, to go to Gambril, who had called faintly that he believed there was some wind aloft. Indeed, my own ears had caught a feeble flutter of wet canvas, high up overhead, the jingle of a slack chain sheet. . . .

These were eerie, disturbing, alarming sounds in the dead stillness of the air around me. All the instances I had heard of topmasts being whipped out of a ship while there was not wind enough on her deck to blow out a match rushed into my memory.

"I can't see the upper sails, sir," declared Gambril shakily.

"Don't move the helm. You'll be all right," I said confidently.

The poor man's nerve was gone. I was not in much better case. It was the moment of breaking strain and was relieved by the abrupt sensation of the ship moving forward as if of herself under my feet. I heard plainly the soughing of the wind aloft, the low cracks of the upper spars taking the strain, long before I could feel the least draught on my face turned aft, anxious and sightless like the face of a blind man.

Suddenly a louder sounding note filled our ears, the darkness started streaming against our bodies, chilling them exceedingly. Both of us, Gambril and I, shivered violently in our clinging, soaked garments of thin cotton. I said to him:

"You are all right now, my man. All you've got to do is to keep the wind at the back of your head. Surely you are up to that. A child could steer this ship in smooth water."

He muttered: "Aye! A healthy child." And I felt ashamed of having been passed over by the fever which had been preying on every man's strength but mine, in order that my remorse might be the more bitter, the feeling of unworthiness more poignant, and the sense of responsibility heavier to bear.

The ship had gathered great way on her almost at once on the calm water. I felt her slipping through it with no other noise but a mysterious rustle alongside. Otherwise she had no motion at all, neither lift nor roll. It was a disheartening steadiness which had lasted for eighteen days now; for never, never had we had wind enough in that time to raise the slightest run of the sea. The breeze freshened suddenly. I thought it was high time to get Mr. Burns off the deck. He worried me. I looked upon him as a lunatic who would be very likely to start roaming over the ship and break a limb or fall overboard.

I was truly glad to find he had remained holding on where I had left him, sensibly enough. He was, however, muttering to himself ominously.

This was discouraging. I remarked in a matter-of-fact tone:

"We have never had so much wind as this since we left the roads."

"There's some heart in it too," he growled judiciously. It was a remark of a perfectly sane seaman. But he added immediately: "It was about time I should come on deck. I've been nursing my strength for this—just for this. Do you see it, sir?"

I said I did, and proceeded to hint that it would be advisable for him to go below now and take a rest.

His answer was an indignant: "Go below! Not if I know it, sir."

Very cheerful! He was a horrible nuisance. And all at once he started to argue. I could feel his crazy excitement in the dark.

"You don't know how to go about it, sir. How could you? All this whispering and tip-toeing is no good. You can't hope to slink past a cunning, wideawake, evil brute like he was. You never heard him talk. Enough to make your hair stand on end. No! No! He wasn't mad. He was no more mad than I am. He was just downright wicked. Wicked so as to frighten most people. I will tell you what he was. He was nothing less than a thief and a murderer at heart. And do you think he's any different now because he's dead? Not he! His carcass lies a hundred fathom under, but he's just the same . . . in latitude 8° 20′ North."

He snorted defiantly. I noted with weary resignation that the breeze had got lighter while he raved. He was at it again.

"I ought to have thrown the beggar out of the ship over the rail like a dog. It was only on account of the men. . . . Fancy having to read the Burial

Service over a brute like that! . . . 'Our departed brother' . . . I could have laughed. That was what he couldn't bear. I suppose I am the only man that ever stood up to laugh at him. When he got sick it used to scare that . . . brother . . . Brother . . . Departed . . . Sooner call a shark brother."

The breeze had let go so suddenly that the way of the ship brought the wet sails heavily against the mast. The spell of deadly stillness had caught us up again. There seemed to be no escape.

"Hallo!" exclaimed Mr. Burns in a startled voice. "Calm again!"

I addressed him as though he had been sane.

"This is the sort of thing we've been having for seventeen days, Mr. Burns," I said with intense bitterness. "A puff, then a calm, and in a moment, you'll see, she'll be swinging on her heel with her head away from her course to the devil somewhere."

He caught at the word. "The old dodging Devil," he screamed piercingly, and burst into such a loud laugh as I had never heard before. It was a provoking, mocking peal, with a hair-raising, screeching over-note of defiance. I stepped back utterly confounded.

Instantly there was a stir on the quarter-deck, murmurs of dismay. A distressed voice cried out in the dark below us: "Who's that gone crazy, now?"

Perhaps they thought it was their captain! Rush is not the word that could be applied to the utmost speed the poor fellows were up to; but in an amazingly short time every man in the ship able to walk upright had found his way on to that poop.

I shouted to them: "It's the mate. Lay hold of him a couple of you. . . ."

I expected this performance to end in a ghastly sort of fight. But Mr. Burns cut his derisive screeching dead short and turned upon them fiercely, yelling:

"Aha! Dog-gone ye! You've found your tongues—have ye? I thought you were dumb. Well, then—laugh! Laugh—I tell you. Now then—all together. One, two, three—laugh!"

A moment of silence ensued, of silence so profound that you could have heard a pin drop on the deck. Then Ransome's unperturbed voice uttered pleasantly the words:

"I think he has fainted, sir—" The little motionless knot of men stirred, with low murmurs of relief. "I've got him under the arms. Get hold of his legs, someone."

Yes. It was a relief. He was silenced for a time—for a time. I could not have stood another peal of that insane screeching. I was sure of it; and just then Gambril, the austere Gambril, treated us to another vocal performance. He began to sing out for relief. His voice wailed pitifully in the darkness: "Come aft, somebody! I can't stand this. Here she'll be off again directly and I can't. . . ."

I dashed aft myself meeting on my way a hard gust of wind whose approach Gambril's ear had detected from afar and which filled the sails on the main in a series of muffled reports mingled with the low plaint of the spars. I was just in time to seize the wheel while Frenchy, who had followed me, caught up the collapsing Gambril. He hauled him out of the way, admonished him to lie still where he was, and then stepped up to relieve me, asking calmly:

"How am I to steer her, sir?"

"Dead before it, for the present. I'll get you a light in a moment."

But going forward I met Ransome bringing up the spare binnacle lamp. That man noticed everything, attended to everything, shed comfort around him as he moved. As he passed me he remarked in a soothing tone that the stars were coming out. They were. The breeze was sweeping clear the sooty sky, breaking through the indolent silence of the sea.

The barrier of awful stillness which had encompassed us for so many days as though we had been accursed was broken. I felt that. I let myself fall on to the skylight seat. A faint white ridge of foam, thin, very thin, broke alongside. The first for ages—for ages. I could have cheered, if it hadn't been for the sense of guilt which clung to all my thoughts secretly. Ransome stood before me.

"What about the mate," I asked anxiously. "Still unconscious?"

"Well, sir—it's funny." Ransome was evidently puzzled. "He hasn't spoken a word, and his eyes are shut. But it looks to me more like sound sleep than anything else."

I accepted this view as the least troublesome of any, or at any rate, least disturbing. Dead faint or deep slumber, Mr. Burns had to be left to himself for the present. Ransome remarked suddenly:

"I believe you want a coat, sir."

"I believe I do," I sighed out.

But I did not move. What I felt I wanted were new limbs. My arms and legs seemed utterly useless, fairly worn out. They didn't even ache. But I stood up all the same to put on the coat when Ransome brought it up. And when he suggested that he had better now "take Gambril forward," I said:

"All right. I'll help you to get him down on the main deck."

I found that I was quite able to help, too. We raised Gambril up between us. He tried to help himself along like a man, but all the time he was inquiring piteously:

"You won't let me go when we come to the ladder? You won't let me go when we come to the ladder?"

The breeze kept on freshening and blew true, true to a hair. At daylight by careful manipulation of the helm we got the foreyards to run square by themselves (the water keeping smooth) and then went about hauling the ropes tight. Of the four men I had with me at night, I could see now only two. I didn't inquire as to the others. They had given in. For a time only I hoped.

Our various tasks forward occupied us for hours, the two men with me moved so slowly and had to rest so often. One of them remarked that "every blamed thing in the ship felt about a hundred times heavier than its proper weight." This was the only complaint uttered. I don't know what we should have done without Ransome. He worked with us, silent too, with a little smile

frozen on his lips. From time to time I murmured to him: "Go steady"—
"Take it easy, Ransome"—and received a quick glance in reply.

When we had done all we could do to make things safe, he disappeared
into his galley. Some time afterwards, going forward for a look round, I
caught sight of him through the open door. He sat upright on the locker in
front of the stove, with his head leaning back against the bulkhead. His eyes
were closed; his capable hands held open the front of his thin cotton shirt
baring tragically his powerful chest, which heaved in painful and laboured
gasps. He didn't hear me.

I retreated quietly and went straight on to the poop to relieve Frenchy,
who by that time was beginning to look very sick. He gave me the course with
great formality and tried to go off with a jaunty step, but reeled widely twice
before getting out of my sight.

And then I remained all alone aft, steering my ship, which ran before the
wind with a buoyant lift now and then, and even rolling a little. Presently
Ransome appeared before me with a tray. The sight of food made me ravenous
all at once. He took the wheel while I sat down on the after grating to eat my
breakfast.

"This breeze seems to have done for our crowd," he murmured. "It just
laid them low—all hands."

"Yes," I said. "I suppose you and I are the only two fit men in the ship."

"Frenchy says there's still a jump left in him. I don't know. It can't be
much," continued Ransome with his wistful smile. "Good little man that. But
suppose, sir, that this wind flies round when we are close to the land—what
are we going to do with her?"

"If the wind shifts round heavily after we close in with the land she will
either run ashore or get dismasted or both. We won't be able to do anything
with her. She's running away with us now. All we can do is to steer her. She's
a ship without a crew."

"Yes. All laid low," repeated Ransome quietly. "I do give them a look-in
forward every now and then, but it's precious little I can do for them."

"I, and the ship, and everyone on board of her, are very much indebted to
you, Ransome," I said warmly.

He made as though he had not heard me, and steered in silence till I was
ready to relieve him. He surrendered the wheel, picked up the tray, and for a
parting shot informed me that Mr. Burns was awake and seemed to have a
mind to come up on deck.

"I don't know how to prevent him, sir. I can't very well stop down below
all the time."

It was clear that he couldn't. And sure enough Mr. Burns came on deck
dragging himself painfully aft in his enormous overcoat. I beheld him with
a natural dread. To have him around and raving about the wiles of a dead
man while I had to steer a wildly rushing ship full of dying men was a rather
dreadful prospect.

But his first remarks were quite sensible in meaning and tone. Apparently he had no recollection of the night scene. And if he had he didn't betray himself once. Neither did he talk very much. He sat on the skylight looking desperately ill at first, but that strong breeze, before which the last remnant of my crew had wilted down, seemed to blow a fresh stock of vigour into his frame with every gust. One could almost see the process.

By way of sanity test I alluded on purpose to the late captain. I was delighted to find that Mr. Burns did not display undue interest in the subject. He ran over the old tale of that savage ruffian's iniquities with a certain vindictive gusto and then concluded unexpectedly:

"I do believe, sir, that his brain began to go a year or more before he died."

A wonderful recovery. I could hardly spare it as much admiration as it deserved, for I had to give all my mind to the steering.

In comparison with the hopeless languor of the preceding days this was dizzy speed. Two ridges of foam streamed from the ship's bows; the wind sang in a strenuous note which under other circumstances would have expressed to me all the joy of life. Whenever the hauled-up mainsail started trying to slat and bang itself to pieces in its gear, Mr. Burns would look at me apprehensively.

"What would you have me do, Mr. Burns? We can neither furl it nor set it. I only wish the old thing would thrash itself to pieces and be done with it. This beastly racket confuses me."

Mr. Burns wrung his hands, and cried out suddenly:

"How will you get the ship into harbour, sir, without men to handle her?"

And I couldn't tell him.

Well—it did get done about forty hours afterwards. By the exorcising virtue of Mr. Burns' awful laugh, the malicious spectre had been laid, the evil spell broken, the curse removed. We were now in the hands of a kind and energetic Providence. It was rushing us on. . . .

I shall never forget the last night, dark, windy, and starry. I steered. Mr. Burns, after having obtained from me a solemn promise to give him a kick if anything happened, went frankly to sleep on the deck close to the binnacle. Convalescents need sleep. Ransome, his back propped against the mizzenmast and a blanket over his legs, remained perfectly still, but I don't suppose he closed his eyes for a moment. That embodiment of jauntiness, Frenchy, still under the delusion that there was "a jump" left in him, had insisted on joining us; but mindful of discipline, had laid himself down as far on the forepart of the poop as he could get, alongside the bucket-rack.

And I steered, too tired for anxiety, too tired for connected thought. I had moments of grim exultation and then my heart would sink awfully at the thought of that forecastle at the other end of the dark deck, full of fever-stricken men—some of them dying. By my fault. But never mind. Remorse must wait. I had to steer.

In the small hours the breeze weakened, then failed altogether. About five it returned, gentle enough, enabling us to head for the roadstead. Daybreak found Mr. Burns sitting wedged up with coils of rope on the stern-grating, and from the depths of his overcoat steering the ship with very white bony hands; while Ransome and I rushed along the decks letting go all the sheets and halyards by the run. We dashed next up on to the forecastle head. The perspiration of labour and sheer nervousness simply poured off our heads as we toiled to get the anchors cock-billed. I dared not look at Ransome as we worked side by side. We exchanged curt words; I could hear him panting close to me and I avoided turning my eyes his way for fear of seeing him fall down and expire in the act of putting out his strength—for what? Indeed for some distinct ideal.

The consummate seaman in him was aroused. He needed no directions. He knew what to do. Every effort, every movement was an act of consistent hero-ism. It was not for me to look at a man thus inspired.

At last all was ready, and I heard him say, "Hadn't I better go down and open the compressors now, sir?"

"Yes. Do," I said. And even then I did not glance his way. After a time his voice came up from the main deck:

"When you like, sir. All clear on the windlass here."

I made a sign to Mr. Burns to put the helm down and then I let both anchors go one after another, leaving the ship to take as much cable as she wanted. She took the best part of them both before she brought up. The loose sails coming aback ceased their maddening racket above my head. A perfect stillness reigned in the ship. And while I stood forward feeling a little giddy in that sudden peace, I caught faintly a moan or two and the incoherent mut-terings of the sick in the forecastle.

As we had a signal for medical assistance flying on the mizzen it is a fact that before the ship was fairly at rest three steam-launches from various men-of-war arrived alongside; and at least five naval surgeons clambered on board. They stood in a knot gazing up and down the empty main deck, then looked aloft—where not a man could be seen either.

I went towards them—a solitary figure in a blue and grey striped sleeping suit and a pipe-clayed cork helmet on its head. Their disgust was extreme. They had expected surgical cases. Each one had brought his carving tools with him. But they soon got over their little disappointment. In less than five min-utes one of the steam-launches was rushing shorewards to order a big boat and some hospital people for the removal of the crew. The big steam-pinnace went off to her ship to bring over a few bluejackets to furl my sails for me.

One of the surgeons had remained on board. He came out of the forecastle looking impenetrable, and noticed my inquiring gaze.

"There's nobody dead in there, if that's what you want to know," he said deliberately. Then added in a tone of wonder: "The whole crew!"

"And very bad?"

"And very bad," he repeated. His eyes were roaming all over the ship. "Heavens! What's that?"

"That," I said, glancing aft, "is Mr. Burns, my chief officer."

Mr. Burns with his moribund head nodding on the stalk of his lean neck was a sight for any one to exclaim at. The surgeon asked:

"Is he going to the hospital too?"

"Oh, no," I said jocosely. "Mr. Burns can't go on shore till the mainmast goes. I am very proud of him. He's my only convalescent."

"You look . . ." began the doctor staring at me. But I interrupted him angrily:

"I am not ill."

"No. . . . You look queer."

"Well, you see, I have been seventeen days on deck."

"Seventeen! . . . But you must have slept."

"I suppose I must have. I don't know. But I'm certain that I didn't sleep for the last forty hours."

"Phew! . . . You will be going ashore presently, I suppose?"

"As soon as ever I can. There's no end of business waiting for me there."

The surgeon released my hand, which he had taken while we talked, pulled out his pocket-book, wrote in it rapidly, tore out the page, and offered it to me.

"I strongly advise you to get this prescription made up for yourself ashore. Unless I am much mistaken you will need it this evening."

"What is it then?" I asked with suspicion.

"Sleeping draught," answered the surgeon curtly; and moving with an air of interest towards Mr. Burns he engaged him in conversation.

As I went below to dress to go ashore, Ransome followed me. He begged my pardon; he wished, too, to be sent ashore and paid off.

I looked at him in surprise. He was waiting for my answer with an air of anxiety.

"You don't mean to leave the ship!" I cried out.

"I do really, sir. I want to go and be quiet somewhere. Anywhere. The hospital will do."

"But, Ransome," I said, "I hate the idea of parting with you."

"I must go," he broke in. "I have a right!" He gasped and a look of almost savage determination passed over his face. For an instant he was another being. And I saw under the worth and the comeliness of the man the humble reality of things. Life was a boon to him—this precarious hard life—and he was thoroughly alarmed about himself.

"Of course I shall pay you off if you wish it," I hastened to say. "Only I must ask you to remain on board till this afternoon. I can't leave Mr. Burns absolutely by himself in the ship for hours."

He softened at once and assured me with a smile and in his natural pleasant voice that he understood that very well.

When I returned on deck everything was ready for the removal of the men. It was the last ordeal of that episode which had been maturing and tempering my character—though I did not know it.

It was awful. They passed under my eyes one after another—each of them an embodied reproach of the bitterest kind, till I felt a sort of revolt wake up in me. Poor Frenchy had gone suddenly under. He was carried past me insensible, his comic face horribly flushed and as if swollen, breathing stertorously. He looked more like Mr. Punch than ever; a disgracefully intoxicated Mr. Punch.

The austere Gambril, on the contrary, had improved temporarily. He insisted on walking on his own feet to the rail—of course with assistance on each side of him. But he gave way to a sudden panic at the moment of being swung over the side and began to wail pitifully:

"Don't let them drop me, sir. Don't let them drop me, sir!" While I kept on shouting to him in most soothing accents: "All right, Gambril. They won't! They won't!"

It was no doubt very ridiculous. The bluejackets on our deck were grinning quietly, while even Ransome himself (much to the fore in lending a hand) had to enlarge his wistful smile for a fleeting moment.

I left for the shore in the steam-pinnace, and on looking back beheld Mr. Burns actually standing up by the taffrail, still in his enormous woolly overcoat. The bright sunlight brought out his weirdness amazingly. He looked like a frightful and elaborate scarecrow set up on the poop of a death-stricken ship, to keep the seabirds from the corpses.

Our story had got about already in town and everybody on shore was most kind. The marine office let me off the port dues, and as there happened to be a shipwrecked crew staying in the Home I had no difficulty in obtaining as many men as I wanted. But when I inquired if I could see Captain Ellis for a moment I was told in accents of pity for my ignorance that our deputy-Neptune had retired and gone home on a pension about three weeks after I left the port. So I suppose that my appointment was the last act, outside the daily routine, of his official life.

It is strange how on coming ashore I was struck by the springy step, the lively eyes, the strong vitality of everyone I met. It impressed me enormously. And amongst those I met there was Captain Giles of course. It would have been very extraordinary if I had not met him. A prolonged stroll in the business part of the town was the regular employment of all his mornings when he was ashore.

I caught the glitter of the gold watch-chain across his chest ever so far away. He radiated benevolence.

"What is it I hear?" he queried with a "kind uncle" smile, after shaking hands. "Twenty-one days from Bankok?"

"Is this all you've heard?" I said. "You must come to tiffin with me. I want you to know exactly what you have let me in for."

He hesitated for almost a minute.

"Well—I will," he decided condescendingly at last.

We turned into the hotel. I found to my surprise that I could eat quite a lot. Then over the cleared table-cloth I unfolded to Captain Giles all the story since I took command in all its professional and emotional aspects, while he smoked patiently the big cigar I had given him.

Then he observed sagely:

"You must feel jolly well tired by this time."

"No," I said. "Not tired. But I'll tell you, Captain Giles, how I feel. I feel old. And I must be. All of you on shore look to me just a lot of skittish youngsters that have never known a care in the world."

He didn't smile. He looked insufferably exemplary. He declared: "That will pass. But you do look older—it's a fact."

"Aha!" I said.

"No! No! The truth is that one must not make too much of anything in life, good or bad."

"Live at half-speed," I murmured perversely. "Not everybody can do that."

"You'll be glad enough presently if you can keep going even at that rate," he retorted with his air of conscious virtue. "And there's another thing: a man should stand up to his bad luck, to his mistakes, to his conscience, and all that sort of thing. Why—what else would you have to fight against?"

I kept silent. I don't know what he saw in my face, but he asked abruptly: "Why—you aren't faint-hearted?"

"God only knows, Captain Giles," was my sincere answer.

"That's all right," he said calmly. "You will learn soon how not to be faint-hearted. A man has got to learn everything—and that's what so many of those youngsters don't understand."

"Well I am no longer a youngster."

"No," he conceded. "Are you leaving soon?"

"I am going on board directly," I said. "I shall pick up one of my anchors and heave in to half-cable on the other as soon as my new crew comes on board and I shall be off at daylight to-morrow."

"You will?" grunted Captain Giles approvingly. "That's the way. You'll do."

"What did you expect? That I would want to take a week ashore for a rest?" I said, irritated by his tone. "There's no rest for me till she's out in the Indian Ocean and not much of it even then."

He puffed at the cigar moodily, as if transformed.

"Yes, that's what it amounts to," he said in a musing tone. It was as if a ponderous curtain had rolled up disclosing an unexpected Captain Giles. But it was only for a moment, merely the time to let him add: "Precious little rest in life for anybody. Better not think of it."

We rose, left the hotel, and parted from each other in the street with a warm handshake, just as he began to interest me for the first time in our intercourse.

The first thing I saw when I got back to the ship was Ransome on the quarter-deck sitting quietly on his neatly lashed sea-chest.

I beckoned him to follow me into the saloon where I sat down to write a letter of recommendation for him to a man I knew on shore.

When finished I pushed it across the table. "It may be of some good to you when you leave the hospital."

He took it, put it in his pocket. His eyes were looking away from me— nowhere. His face was anxiously set.

"How are you feeling now?" I asked.

"I don't feel bad now, sir," he answered stiffly. "But I am afraid of its coming on. . . ." The wistful smile came back on his lips for a moment. "I—I am in a blue funk about my heart, sir."

I approached him with extended hand. His eyes, not looking at me, had a strained expression. He was like a man listening for a warning call.

"Won't you shake hands, Ransome?" I said gently.

He exclaimed, flushed up dusky red, gave my hand a hard wrench—and next moment, left alone in the cabin, I listened to him going up the companion stairs cautiously, step by step, in mortal fear of starting into sudden anger our common enemy it was his hard fate to carry consciously within his faithful breast.

part two

Love

Anton Chekhov

About Love

For breakfast next day delicious little patties, crayfish and mutton croquettes were served, and while we were eating Nikanor the cook came up to ask what the guests would like for dinner. He was a man of medium height, with a puffy face and small eyes; he was clean-shaven, and it looked as though his mustache had not been shaven off but plucked out.

According to Alyohin, the beautiful Pelageya was in love with this cook. As he drank and had a violent temper, she did not want to marry him, but was willing to live with him just so. But he was very devout, and his religious convictions did not allow him to live "just so"; he insisted that she marry him, and didn't want it otherwise, and when he was drunk he used to swear at her and even beat her. Whenever he was drunk she would hide upstairs and sob, and on such occasions Alyohin and the servants stayed in the house to defend her if necessary.

The conversation turned to love.

"How love is born," said Alyohin, "why Pelageya hasn't fallen in love with somebody more like herself both inwardly and outwardly, and why she fell in love with Nikanor, that mug—we all call him the Mug—to what extent personal happiness counts in love—all that is uncertain; and one can argue about it as one pleases. So far only one incontestable truth has been stated about love: 'This is a great mystery'; everything else that has been written or said about love is not a solution, but only a statement of questions that have remained unanswered. The explanation that would fit one case does not apply to a dozen others, and the very best thing, to my mind, would be to explain

ABOUT LOVE From *The Portable Chekhov,* edited by Avrahm Yarmolinsky. Copyright 1947 by The Viking Press, Inc. Reprinted by permission of The Viking Press, Inc. Written in 1898.

every case separately without attempting to generalize. Each case should be individualized, as the doctors say."

"Perfectly true," Burkin assented.

"We Russians who are cultivated have a weakness for these questions that remain unanswered. Love is usually poeticized, embellished with roses, night-ingales; but we Russians embellish our loves with these fatal questions, and choose the least interesting of them, at that. In Moscow, when I was a student, there was a girl with whom I lived, a charming creature, and every time I held her in my arms she was thinking about what I would allow her a month for housekeeping and about the price of beef. Similarly, when we are in love, we never stop asking ourselves whether it is honorable or dishonorable, sensible or stupid, what this love will lead to, and so on. If that is a good thing or not I don't know, but that it is a hindrance and a source of dissatisfaction and irritation, of that I am certain."

It looked as though he wanted to tell a story. People who lead a lonely existence always have something on their minds that they are eager to talk about. In town bachelors visit baths and restaurants in order to have a chance to talk, and sometimes tell very interesting stories to bath attendants and waiters; in the country they usually unbosom themselves to their guests. At the moment we could see a gray sky from the windows and trees drenched with rain; in such weather we could go nowhere and there was nothing for us to do but to tell and listen to stories.

"I have been living at Sofyino and been farming for a long time," Alyohin began, "ever since I graduated from the University. My education did not fit me for rough work and temperamentally I am a bookish fellow, but when I came here the estate was heavily mortgaged, and as my father had gone into debt partly because he had spent a great deal on my education, I decided not to leave the place but to work till I had paid off the debt. I made up my mind to this and set to work, not, I must confess, without some repugnance. The land here does not yield much, and if you are not to farm at a loss you must employ serf labor or hired help, which comes to almost the same thing, or work it like a peasant—that is, you must work in the fields yourself with your family. There is no middle way. But in those days I did not go into such niceties. I did not leave an inch of earth unturned; I got together all the peasants, men and women, from the neighboring villages; the work hummed. I myself plowed and sowed and reaped, and found it awfully tedious, and frowned with disgust, like a village cat driven by hunger to eat cucumbers in the kitchen garden. My body ached, and I slept on my feet.

"At first it seemed to me that I could easily reconcile this life of toil with civilized living; to achieve that, I thought, all that was necessary was to secure a certain external order. I established myself upstairs here in the best rooms, and had them serve me coffee and liqueurs after lunch and dinner, and every night I read *The Messenger of Europe* in bed. But one day our priest, Father Ivan, came and drink up all my liqueurs at one sitting, and the *The Messenger of Europe* went to the priest's daughters, because in summer, especially at hay-making time, I couldn't drag myself to bed at all, but fell asleep on a sledge in the shed or somewhere in a shack in the woods, and how could I think of reading? Little by little I moved downstairs, began to eat in the servants' kitchen, and nothing is left of my former luxury but the people who were in father's service and whom it would be painful to discharge.

"Before I had been here many years I was elected honorary justice of the peace. Now and then I had to go to town and take part in the assizes of the peace and the sessions of the circuit court, and this diverted me. When you live here for two or three months without seeing a soul, especially in winter, you begin at last to pine for a black coat. And at the circuit court there were black coats and uniforms and frock coats, too, all worn by lawyers, educated men; there were always people to talk to. After sleeping on the sledge and dining in the kitchen, to sit in an armchair wearing clean linen, in light boots, with the chain of office around one's neck—that was such luxury!

"I would be warmly received in the town. I made friends readily. And of all my friendships the most intimate and, to tell the truth, the most agreeable to me was my acquaintance with Luganovich, the assistant president of the circuit court. You both know him: an extremely charming man. This was just after the celebrated arson case; the preliminary investigation had lasted two days and we were worn out. Luganovich looked at me and said:

" 'You know what? Come and dine with me.'

"This was unexpected, as I knew Luganovich very slightly, only officially, and I had never been to his house. I went to my hotel room for a minute to change and then went off to dinner. And here came my opportunity to meet Anna Alexeyevna, Luganovich's wife. She was then still a very young woman, not more than twenty-two, and her first baby had been born just six months before. It is all a thing of the past; and now I should find it hard to deter-mine what was so exceptional about her, what it was about her that I liked so much; but at the time, at dinner, it was all perfectly clear to me. I saw a young woman, beautiful, kind, intelligent, fascinating, such a woman as I had never met before; and at once I sensed in her a being near to me and already fa-miliar, as though I had seen that face, those friendly, intelligent eyes long ago, in my childhood, in the album which lay on my mother's chest of drawers.

"In the arson case the defendants were four Jews who were charged with collusion, and in my opinion they were quite innocent. At dinner I was very much agitated and out of sorts, and I don't recall what I said, but Anna Alexeyevna kept shaking her head, and saying to her husband,

" 'Dmitry, how can this be?'

"Luganovich is one of those good-natured, simple-minded people who firmly adhere to the belief that once a man is indicted in court he is guilty, and that one should not express doubt as to the correctness of a verdict except with all legal formalities on paper, but never at dinner and in private con-versation.

" 'You and I didn't commit arson,' he said gently, 'and you see we are not on trial and not in prison.'

"Both husband and wife tried to make me eat and drink as much as possible. From some details, from the way they made the coffee together, for instance, and the way they understood each other without completing their phrases, I gathered that they lived in peace and harmony, and that they were glad of a guest. After dinner they played a duet on the piano; then it got dark, and I drove home.

"That was at the beginning of spring. I spent the whole summer at Sofyino without a break, and I had no time even to think of the town, but the memory of the willowy, fair-haired woman remained in my mind all those months; I did not think of her, but it was as though her shadow were lying lightly on my soul.

"In the late autumn a benefit performance was given in the town. I entered the governor's box (I had been invited there in the intermission); and there I saw Anna Alexeyevna sitting beside the governor's wife; and again there was the same irresistible, striking impression of beauty and lovely, caressing eyes, and again the same feeling of nearness. We sat side by side, then went out into the foyer.

" 'You've grown thinner,' she said; 'have you been ill?'

" 'Yes, I had rheumatism in my shoulder, and in rainy weather I sleep badly.'

" 'You look listless. In spring, when you came to dinner, you seemed younger, livelier. You were animated, and talked a great deal then; you were interesting, and I must confess I was a little carried away. For some reason I often thought of you during the summer, and this evening when I was getting ready to go to the theater it occurred to me that I might see you.'

"And she laughed.

" 'But you look listless tonight,' she repeated; 'it makes you seem older.'

"The next day I lunched at the Luganoviches'. After lunch they drove out to their summer villa, to make arrangements to close it up for the winter, and I went along. I went back to the town with them, and at midnight we had tea together in quiet domesticity, while the fire glowed, and the young mother kept going to see if her little girl were asleep. And after that, every time I went to the town I never failed to visit the Luganoviches. They grew used to me and I grew used to them. As a rule I went in unannounced, as though I were one of the family.

" 'Who is there?' would be heard from a faraway room, in the drawling voice that seemed to me so lovely.

" 'It is Pavel Konstantinovich,' the maid or the nurse would answer.

"Anna Alexeyevna would come out to me with an anxious air and would invariably ask, 'Why haven't we seen you for so long? Is anything wrong?'

"Her gaze, the elegant, exquisite hand she gave me, her simple dress, the way she did her hair, her voice, her gait, always produced the same impression on me of something new and extraordinary, and very significant. We would talk together for hours, there would be long silences, while we were each thinking our own thoughts, or she would play to me for hours on the piano. If I found no one in, I stayed and waited, chatted with the nurse, played with the child, or lay on the couch in the study, and read a newspaper; and when Anna Alexeyevna came back I met her in the hall, took all her parcels from her, and for some reason I carried those parcels every time with as much love, as much solemnity, as if I were a boy.

" 'The old woman had it easy,' the proverb runs, 'so she bought a pig.' The Luganoviches had it easy, so they made friends with me. If I was long in coming to the town, I must be ill, or something must have happened to me, and both of them would be very anxious. They were distressed that I, an educated man with a knowledge of languages, instead of devoting myself to scholarship or literary work, should live in the country, rush around like a squirrel in a cage, work hard and yet always be penniless. They imagined that I was unhappy, and that I only talked, laughed, and ate to conceal my sufferings, and even at cheerful moments when I was quite at ease I was aware of their searching eyes fixed upon me. They were particularly touching when I was really in trouble, when I was being hard pressed by some creditor and was unable to meet a payment on time. The two of them, husband and wife, would whisper together at the window; then he would come over to me and say with a grave face:

" 'If you are in need of money at the moment, Pavel Konstantinovich, my wife and I beg you not to stand on ceremony, but borrow from us.'

"And in his agitation his ears would turn red. Or again, after whispering in the same way at the window, he would come up to me, his ears red, and say, 'My wife and I earnestly beg you to accept this present from us.'

"And he would hand me studs, a cigarette case, or a lamp, and I would send them fowls, butter, and flowers from the farm. Both of them, by the way, were very well off. In the early days I often borrowed money, and was not very choosy about it—borrowed wherever I could—but nothing in the world would have induced me to borrow from the Luganoviches. But why mention the matter?

"I was unhappy. At home, in the fields, in the shed, I kept thinking of her. I tried to understand the mystery of a beautiful, intelligent young woman marrying someone so uninteresting, almost an old man (her husband was over forty), and having children by him; I tried to fathom the mystery of this dull, kindly, simple-hearted man, who reasoned with such tiresome good sense, who at evening parties and balls kept near the more substantial people, looking listless and superfluous, with a submissive, apathetic expression, as though he had been brought there for sale, who yet believed in his right to be happy, to have children by her; and I kept trying to understand why she had met just him first and not me, and why such a terrible mistake need have happened in our lives.

"And every time I came to the town I saw from her eyes that she had been expecting me, and she would tell me herself that she had had a peculiar feeling all that day and had guessed that I would come. We would talk a long time, and then we would be silent, yet we did not confess our love to each other, but timidly and jealously concealed it. We were afraid of everything that would reveal our secret to ourselves. I loved her tenderly, deeply, but I reflected and kept asking myself what our love could lead to if we did not have the strength to fight against it. It seemed incredible to me that my gentle, sad love could all at once rudely break up the even course of the life of her husband, her children, and the whole household in which I was so loved and trusted. Would it be honorable? She would follow me, but where? Where could I take her? It would have been different if I had led a beautiful, interesting life—if I had been fighting for the liberation of my country, for instance, or had been a celebrated scholar, an actor, or a painter; but as things were it would mean taking her from one humdrum life to another as humdrum or perhaps more so. And how long would our happiness last? What would happen to her if I fell ill, if I died, or if we simply stopped loving each other?

"And she apparently reasoned the same way. She thought of her husband, her children, and of her mother, who loved her son-in-law like a son. If she yielded to her feeling she would have to lie, or else to tell the truth, and in her position either would have been equally inconvenient and terrible. And she was tormented by the question whether her love would bring me happiness—whether she would not complicate my life, which as it was she believed to be hard enough and full of all sorts of trouble. It seemed to her that she was not young enough for me, that she was not industrious or energetic enough to begin a new life, and she often said to her husband that I ought to marry a girl of intelligence and worth who would be a good housewife and a helpmate—and she would add at once that such a girl was not likely to be found in the whole town.

"Meanwhile the years were passing. Anna Alexeyevna already had two children. Whenever I arrived at the Luganoviches' the servants smiled cordially, the children shouted that Uncle Pavel Konstantinovich had come, and hung on my neck; everyone was happy. They did not understand what was going on within me, and thought that I too was happy. Everyone regarded me as a noble fellow. Both grown-ups and children felt that a noble fellow was walking about the room, and that gave a peculiar charm to their relations with me, as though in my presence their life, too, was purer and more beautiful. Anna Alexeyevna and I used to go to the theater together, always on foot. We used to sit side by side, our shoulders touching; I would take the opera glass from her hands without a word, and feel at that moment that she was close to me, that she was mine, that we could not live without each other. But by some strange misunderstanding, when we came out of the theater we always said good-by and parted like strangers. Goodness knows what people were saying about us in the town already, but there was not a word of truth in it all.

"Latterly Anna Alexeyevna took to going away frequently to stay with her mother or her sister; she began to be moody, she was coming to recognize that her life was without satisfaction, was ruined, and at such times she did not care to see her husband or her children. She was already being treated for nervous prostration.

"We continued to say nothing, and in the presence of strangers she displayed an odd irritation with me; no matter what I said she disagreed with me, and if I had an argument she sided with my opponent. If I dropped something, she would say coldly:

" 'I congratulate you.'

"If I forgot to take the opera glass when we were going to the theater she would say afterwards:

" 'I knew you would forget.'

"Luckily or not, there is nothing in our lives that does not come to an end sooner or later. The time came when we had to part, as Luganovich received an appointment in one of the western provinces. They had to sell their furniture, their horses, their summer villa. When we drove out to the villa and afterwards, as we were going away, looked back to see the garden and the green roof for the last time, everyone was sad, and I realized that the time had come to say good-by not only to the villa. It was arranged that at the end of August we should see Anna Alexeyevna off to the Crimea, where the doctors were sending her, and that a little later Luganovich and the children would set off for the western province.

"A great crowd had collected to see Anna Alexeyevna off. When she had said good-by to her husband and children and there was only a minute left before the third bell, I ran into her compartment to place on the rack a basket that she had almost forgotten, and then I had to say good-by. When our eyes met right there in the compartment our spiritual strength deserted us both, I took her in my arms, she pressed her face to my breast, and tears flowed from her eyes. Kissing her face, her shoulders, her hands wet with tears—oh, how miserable we were!—I confessed my love to her, and with a burning pain in my heart I realized how needless and petty and deceptive was all that had hindered us from loving each other. I realized that when you love you must either, in your reasoning about that love, start from what is higher, more important than happiness or unhappiness, sin or virtue in their usual meaning, or you must not reason at all.

"I kissed her for the last time, pressed her hand, and we parted forever. The train was already moving. I walked into the next compartment—it was empty—and until I reached the next station I sat there crying. Then I walked home to Sofyino. . . ."

While Alyohin was telling his story, the rain stopped and the sun came out. Burkin and Ivan Ivanych went out on the balcony, from which there was a fine view of the garden and the river, which was shining now in the sunshine like a mirror. They admired it, and at the same time they were sorry that this man with the kind, intelligent eyes who had told them his story with such candor should be rushing round and round on this huge estate like a squirrel in a cage instead of devoting himself to some scholarly pursuit or something else which would have made his life pleasanter; and they thought what a sorrowful face Anna Alexeyevna must have had when he said good-by to her in the compartment and kissed her face and shoulders. Both of them had come across her in the town, and Burkin was acquainted with her and thought she was beautiful.

Translated from the Russian
by Avrahm Yarmolinsky

The Tone of Time

I was too pleased with what it struck me that, as an old, old friend, I had done for her, not to go to her that very afternoon with the news. I knew she worked late, as in general I also did; but I sacrificed for her sake a good hour of the February daylight. She was in her studio, as I had believed she would be, where her card ("Mary J. Tredick"—not Mary Jane, but Mary Juliana) was manfully on the door; a little tired, a little old and a good deal spotted, but with her ugly spectacles taken off, as soon as I appeared, to greet me. She kept on, while she scraped her palette and wiped her brushes, the big stained apron that covered her from head to foot and that I have often enough before seen her retain in conditions giving the measure of her renunciation of her desire to dazzle. Every fresh reminder of this brought home to me that she had given up everything but her work, and that there had been in her history some reason. But I was as far from the reason as ever. She had given up too much; this was just why one wanted to lend her a hand. I told her, at any rate, that I had a lovely job for her.

"To copy something I do like?"

Her complaint, I knew, was that people only gave orders, if they gave them at all, for things she did not like. But this wasn't a case of copying—not at all, at least, in the common sense. "It's for a portrait—quite in the air."

"Ah, you do portraits yourself!"

"Yes, and you know how. My trick won't serve for this. What's wanted is a pretty picture."

"Then of whom?"

THE TONE OF TIME   From *The Better Sort* by Henry James. Copyright 1903. Reprinted by permission of Alexander R. James.

"Of nobody. That is of anybody. Anybody you like."

She naturally wondered. "Do you mean I'm myself to choose my sitter?"

"Well, the oddity is that there is to *be* no sitter."

"Whom then is the picture to represent?"

"Why, a handsome, distinguished, agreeable man, of not more than forty, clean-shaven, thoroughly well-dressed, and a perfect gentleman."

She continued to stare. "And I'm to find him myself?"

I laughed at the term she used. "Yes, as you 'find' the canvas, the colours and the frame." After which I immediately explained. "I've just had the 'rummest' visit, the effect of which was to make me think of you. A lady, unknown to me and unintroduced, turned up at my place at three o'clock. She had come straight, she let me know, without preliminaries, on account of one's high reputation—the usual thing—and of her having admired one's work. Of course I instantly saw—I mean I saw it as soon as she named her affair—that she hadn't understood my work at all. What am I good for in the world but just the impression of the given, the presented case? I can do but the face I see."

"And do you think I can do the face I don't?"

"No, but you see so many more. You see them in fancy and memory, and they've come out, for you, from all the museums you've haunted and all the great things you've studied. I *know* you'll be able to see the one my visitor wants and to give it—what's the *crux* of the business—the tone of time."

She turned the question over. "What does she want it for?"

"Just *for* that—for the tone of time. And, except that it's to hang over her chimney, she didn't tell me. I've only my idea that it's to represent, to symbolise, as it were, her husband, who's not alive and who perhaps never was. This is exactly what will give you a free hand."

"With nothing to go by—no photographs or other portraits?"

"Nothing."

"She only proposes to describe him?"

"Not even; she wants the picture itself to do that. Her only condition is that he be a *très-bel homme*."[1]

She had begun at last, a little thoughtfully, to remove her apron. "Is she French?"

"I don't know. I give it up. She calls herself Mrs. Bridgenorth."

Mary wondered. "*Connais pas!*[2] I never heard of her."

"You wouldn't."

"You mean its not her real name?"

I hesitated. "I mean that she's a very downright fact, full of the implication that she'll pay a downright price. It's clear to me that you can ask what you like; and it's therefore a chance that I can't consent to your missing."

[1] *Très-bel homme*. Very handsome man.
[2] *Connais pas!* I don't know her.

My friend gave no sign either way, and I told my story. "She's a woman of fifty, perhaps of more, who has been pretty, and who still presents herself, with her grey hair a good deal powdered, as I judge, to carry it off, extraordinarily well. She was a little frightened and a little free; the latter because of the former. But she did uncommonly well, I thought, considering the oddity of her wish. This oddity she quite admits; she began indeed by insisting on it so in advance that I found myself expecting I didn't know what. She broke at moments into French, which was perfect, but no better than her English, which isn't vulgar; not more at least than that of everybody else. The things people *do* say, and the way they say them, to artists! She wanted immensely, I could see, not to fail of her errand, not to be treated as absurd; and she was extremely grateful to me for meeting her so far as I did. She was beautifully dressed and she came in a brougham."

My listener took it in; then, very quietly, "Is she respectable?" she inquired.

"Ah, there you are!" I laughed; "and how you always pick the point right out, even when one has endeavoured to diffuse a specious glamour! She's extraordinary," I pursued after an instant; "and just what she wants of the picture, I think, is to make her a little less so."

"Who is she, then? What is she?" my companion simply went on.

It threw me straightway back on one of my hobbies. "Ah, my dear, what is so interesting as life? What is, above all, so stupendous as London? There's everything in it, everything in the world, and nothing too amazing not some day to pop out at you. What is a woman, faded, preserved, pretty, powdered, vague, odd, dropping on one without credentials, but with a carriage and very good lace? What is such a person but a person who *may* have had adventures, and have made them, in one way or another pay? They're, however, none of one's business; it's scarcely on the cards that one should ask her. I should like, with Mrs. Bridgenorth, to see a fellow ask! She goes in for propriety, the real thing. If I suspect her of being the creation of her own talents, she has clearly, on the other hand, seen a lot of life. Will you meet her?" I next demanded.

My hostess waited. "No."

"Then you won't try?"

"Need I meet her to try?" And the question made me guess that, so far as she had understood, she began to feel herself a little taken. "It seems strange," she none the less mused, "to attempt to please her on such a basis. To attempt," she presently added, "to please her at all. It's your idea that she's not married?" she, with this, a trifle inconsequentially asked.

"Well," I replied, "I've only had an hour to think of it, but I somehow already see the scene. Not immediately, not the day after, or even perhaps the year after the thing she desires is set up there, but in due process of time and on convenient opportunity, the transfiguration will occur. 'Who is that awfully handsome man?' 'That? Oh, that's an old sketch of my dear dead husband.' Because I told her—insidiously sounding her—that she would want it to look old, and that the tone of time is exactly what you're full of."

"I believe I am," Mary sighed at last.

"Then put on your hat." I had proposed to her on my arrival to come out to tea with me, and it was when left alone in the studio while she went to her room that I began to feel sure of the success of my errand. The vision that had an hour before determined me grew deeper and brighter for her while I moved about and looked at her things. There were more of them there on her hands than one liked to see; but at least they sharpened my confidence, which was pleasant for me in view of that of my visitor, who had accepted without reserve my plea for Miss Tredick. Four or five of her copies of famous portraits—ornaments of great public and private collections—were on the walls, and to see them again together was to feel at ease about my guarantee. The mellow manner of them was what I had had in my mind in saying, to excuse myself to Mrs. Bridgenorth, "Oh, my things, you know, look as if they had been painted tomorrow!" It made no difference that Mary's Vandykes and Gainsboroughs were reproductions and replicas, for I had known her more than once to amuse herself with doing the thing quite, as she called it, off her own bat. She had copied so bravely so many brave things that she had at the end of her brush an extraordinary bag of tricks. She had always replied to me that such things were mere clever humbug, but mere clever humbug was what our client happened to want. The thing was to let her have it— one could trust her for the rest. And at the same time that I mused in this way I observed to myself that there was already something more than, as the phrase is, met the eye in such response as I felt my friend had made. I had touched, without intention, more than one spring; I had set in motion more than one impulse. I found myself indeed quite certain of this after she had come back in her hat and her jacket. She was different—her idea had flowered; and she smiled at me from under her tense veil, while she drew over her firm, narrow hands a pair of fresh gloves, with a light distinctly new. "Please tell your friend that I'm greatly obliged to both of you and that I take the order."

"Good. And to give him all his good looks?"

"It's just to do *that* that I accept. I shall make him supremely beautiful— and supremely base."

"Base?" I just demurred.

"The finest gentleman you'll ever have seen, and the worst friend."

I wondered, as I was startled; but after an instant I laughed for joy. "Ah well, so long as he's not mine! I see we *shall* have him," I said as we went, for truly I had touched a spring. In fact I had touched *the* spring.

It rang, more or less, I was presently to find, all over the place. I went, as I had promised, to report to Mrs. Bridgenorth on my mission, and though she declared herself much gratified at the success of it I could see she a little resented the apparent absence of any desire on Miss Tredick's part for a preliminary conference. "I only thought she might have liked just to see me, and have imagined I might like to see *her*."

But I was full of comfort. "You'll see her when it's finished. You'll see her in time to thank her."

"And to pay her, I suppose," my hostess laughed, with an asperity that was, after all, not excessive. "Will she take very long?"

I thought. "She's so full of it that my impression would be that she'll do it off at a heat."

"She *is* full of it then?" she asked; and on hearing to what tune, though I told her but half, she broke out with admiration. "You artists are the most extraordinary people!" It was almost with a bad conscience that I confessed we indeed were, and while she said that what she meant was that we seemed to understand everything, and I rejoined that this was also what *I* meant, she took me into another room to see the place for the picture—a proceeding of which the effect was singularly to confirm the truth in question. The place for the picture—in her own room, as she called it, a boudoir at the back, overlooking the general garden of the approved modern row and, as she said, only just wanting that touch—proved exactly the place (the space of a large panel in the white woodwork over the mantel) that I had spoken of to my friend. She put it quite candidly, "Don't you see what it will do?" and looked at me, wonderfully, as for a sign that I could sympathetically take from her what she didn't literally say. She said it, poor woman, so very nearly that I had no difficulty whatever. The portrait, tastefully enshrined there, of the finest gentleman one should ever have seen, would do even more for herself than it would do for the room.

I may as well mention at once that my observation of Mrs. Bridgenorth was not in the least of a nature to unseat me from the hobby I have already named. In the light of the impression she made on me life seemed quite as prodigious and London quite as amazing as I had ever contended, and nothing could have been more in the key of that experience than the manner in which everything was vivid between us and nothing expressed. We remained on the surface with the tenacity of shipwrecked persons clinging to a plank. Our plank was our concentrated gaze at Mrs. Bridgenorth's mere present. We allowed her past to exist for us only in the form of the prettiness that she had gallantly rescued from it and to which a few scraps of its identity still adhered. She was amiable, gentle, consistently proper. She gave me more than anything else the sense, simply, of waiting. She was like a house so freshly and successfully "done up" that you were surprised it wasn't occupied. She was waiting for something to happen—for somebody to come. She was waiting, above all, for Mary Tredick's work. She clearly counted that it would help her.

I had foreseen the fact—the picture was produced at a heat; rapidly, directly, at all events, for the sort of thing it proved to be. I left my friend alone at first, left the ferment to work, troubling her with no questions and asking her for no news; two or three weeks passed, and I never went near her. Then at last, one afternoon as the light was failing, I looked in. She immediately knew what I wanted. "Oh yes, I'm doing him."

"Well," I said, "I've respected your intensity, but I *have* felt curious."

I may not perhaps say that she was never so sad as when she laughed, but it's certain that she always laughed when she was sad. When, however, poor dear, for that matter, was she, secretly, not? Her little gasps of mirth were the mark of her worst moments. But why should she have one of these just now? "Oh, I know your curiosity!" she replied to me; and the small chill of her amusement scarcely met it. "He's coming out, but I can't show him to you yet. I must muddle it through in my own way. It has insisted on being, after all, a 'likeness,' " she added. "But nobody will ever know."

"Nobody?"

"Nobody *she* sees."

"Ah, she doesn't, poor thing," I returned, "seem to see anybody!"

"So much the better. I'll risk it." On which I felt I should have to wait, though I had suddenly grown impatient. But I still hung about, and while I did so she explained. "If what I've done is really a portrait, the condition itself prescribed it. If I was to do the most beautiful man in the world I could do but one."

We looked at each other; then I laughed. "It can scarcely be *me!* But you're getting," I asked, "the great thing?"

"The infamy? Oh yes, please God."

It took away my breath a little, and I even for the moment scarce felt at liberty to press. But one could always be cheerful. "What I meant is the tone of time."

"Getting it, my dear man? Didn't I get it long ago? Don't I *show* it—the tone of time?" she suddenly, strangely sighed at me, with something in her face I had never yet seen. "I can't give it to him more than—for all these years—he was to have given it to *me.*"

I scarce knew what smothered passion, what remembered wrong, what mixture of joy and pain my words had accidentally quickened. Such an effect of them could only become, for me, an instant pity, which, however, I brought out but indirectly. "It's the tone," I smiled, "in which you're speaking now."

This served, unfortunately, as something of a check. "I didn't mean to speak now." Then with her eyes on the picture, "I've said everything there. Come back," she added, "in three days. He'll be all right."

He was indeed when at last I saw him. She had produced an extraordinary thing—a thing wonderful, ideal, for the part it was to play. My only reserve, from the first, was that it was too fine for its part, that something much less "sincere" would equally have served Mrs. Bridgenorth's purpose, and that relegation to that lady's "own room"—whatever charm it was to work there—might only mean for it cruel obscurity. The picture is before me now, so that I could describe it if description availed. It represents a man of about five-and-thirty, seen only as to the head and shoulders, but dressed, the observer gathers, in a fashion now almost antique and which was far from contemporaneous with the date of the work. His high, slightly narrow face, which would be perhaps too aquiline but for the beauty of the forehead and the sweetness of the mouth, has a charm that even, after all these years, still stirs my imagination. His type has altogether a distinction that you feel to have been firmly caught and yet not vulgarly emphasised. The eyes are just too near together, but they are, in a wondrous way, both careless and intense, while lip, cheek, and chin, smooth and clear, are admirably drawn. Youth is still, you see, in all his presence, the joy and pride of life, the perfection of a high spirit and the expectation of a great fortune, which he takes for granted with unconscious insolence. Nothing has ever happened to humiliate or disappoint him, and if my fancy doesn't run away with me the whole presentation of him is a guarantee that he will die without having suffered. He is so handsome in short, that you can scarcely say what he means, and so happy that you can scarcely guess what he feels.

It is of course, I hasten to add, an appreciably feminine rendering, light, delicate, vague, imperfectly synthetic—insistent and evasive, above all, in the wrong places; but the composition, none the less, is beautiful and the suggestion infinite. The grandest air of the thing struck me in fact, when first I saw it, as coming from the high artistic impertinence with which it offered itself as painted about 1850. It would have been a rare flower of refinement for that dark day. The "tone"—that of such a past as it pretended to—was there almost to excess, a brown bloom into which the image seemed mysteriously to retreat. The subject of it looks at me now across more years and more knowledge, but what I felt at the moment was that he managed to be at once a triumphant trick and a plausible evocation. He hushed me, I remember, with so many kinds of awe that I shouldn't have dreamt of asking who he was. All I said, after my first incoherences of wonder at my friend's practised skill, was: "And you've arrived at this truth without documents?"

"It depends on what you call documents."

"Without notes, sketches, studies?"

"I destroyed them years ago."

"Then you once had them?"

She just hung fire. "I once had everything."

It told me both more and less than I had asked; enough at all events to make my next question, as I uttered it, sound even to myself a little foolish. "So that it's all memory?"

From where she stood she looked once more at her work; after which she jerked away and, taking several steps, came back to me with something new— whatever it was I had already seen—in her air and answer. "It's all *hate!*" she threw at me, and then went out of the room. It was not till she had gone that I quite understood why. Extremely affected by the impression visibly made on me, she had burst into tears but had wished me not to see them. She left me alone for some time with her wonderful subject, and I again, in her absence, made things out. He was dead—he had been dead for years; the sole humiliation, as I have called it, that he was to know had come to him in that form. The canvas held and cherished him, in any case, as it only holds the dead. She had suffered from him, it came to me, the worst that a woman can suffer, and the wound he had dealt her, though hidden, had never effectually healed. It had bled again while she worked. Yet when she at last reappeared there was but one thing to say. "The beauty, heaven knows, I see. But I don't see what you call the infamy."

She gave him a last look—again she turned away. "Oh, he was like that."

"Well, whatever he was like," I remember replying, "I wonder you can bear to part with him. Isn't it better to let her see the picture first here?"

As to this she doubted. "I don't think I want her to come."

I wondered. "You continue to object so to meet her?"

"What good will it do? It's quite impossible I should alter him for her."

"Oh, she won't want *that!*" I laughed. "She'll adore him as he is."

"Are you quite sure of your idea?"

"That he's to figure as Mr. Bridgenorth? Well, if I hadn't been from the first, my dear lady, I should be now. Fancy, with the chance, her *not* jumping at him! Yes, he'll figure as Mr. Bridgenorth."

"Mr. Bridgenorth!" she echoed, making the sound, with her small, cold laugh, grotesquely poor for him. He might really have been a prince, and I wondered if he hadn't been. She had, at all events, a new notion. "Do you mind my having it taken to your place and letting her come to see it there?" Which—as I immediately embraced her proposal, deferring to her reasons, whatever they were—was what was speedily arranged.

II

The next day therefore I had the picture in charge, and on the following Mrs. Bridgenorth, whom I had notified, arrived. I had placed it, framed and on an easel, well in evidence, and I have never forgotten the look and the cry that, as she became aware of it, leaped into her face and from her lips. It was an extraordinary moment, all the more that it found me quite unprepared—so extraordinary that I scarce knew at first what had happened. By the time I really perceived, moreover, more things had happened than one, so that when I pulled myself together it was to face the situation as a whole. She had recognised on the instant the subject; that came first and was irrepressibly vivid in her. Her recognition had, for the length of a flash, lighted for her the possibility that the stroke had been directed. That came second, and she flushed with it as with a blow in the face. What came third—and it was what was really most wondrous—was the quick instinct of getting both her strange recognition and her blind suspicion well in hand. She couldn't control, however, poor woman, the strong colour in her face and the quick tears in her eyes. She could only glare at the canvas, gasping, grimacing, and try to gain time. Whether in surprise or in resentment she intensely reflected, feeling more than anything else how little she might prudently show; and I was conscious even at the moment that nothing of its kind could have been finer than her effort to swallow her shock in ten seconds.

How many seconds she took I didn't measure; enough, assuredly, for me also to profit. I gained more time than she, and the greatest oddity doubtless was my own private maneuver—the quickest calculation that, acting from a mere confused instinct, I had ever made. If she had known the great gentleman represented there and yet had determined on the spot to carry herself as ignorant, all my loyalty to Mary Tredick came to the surface in a prompt counter-move. What gave me opportunity was the red in her cheek. "Why, you've known him!"

I saw her ask herself for an instant if she mightn't successfully make her startled state pass as the mere glow of pleasure—her natural greeting to her acquisition. She was pathetically, yet at the same time almost comically, divided. Her line was so to cover her tracks that every avowal of a past connection was a danger; but it also concerned her safety to learn, in the light of our astounding coincidence, how far she already stood exposed. She meanwhile begged the question. She smiled through her tears. "He's too magnificent!"

But I gave her, as I say, all too little time. "Who is he? Who *was* he?"

It must have been my look still more than my words that determined her. She wavered but an instant longer, panted, laughed, cried again, and then, dropping into the nearest seat, gave herself up so completely that I was almost ashamed. "Do you think I'd tell you his *name?*" The burden of the backward years—all the effaced and ignored—lived again, almost like an accent unlearned but freshly breaking out at a touch, in the very sound of the words. These perceptions she, however, the next thing showed me, were a game at which two could play. She had to look at me but an instant. "Why, you really *don't* know it!"

I judged best to be frank. "I don't know it."

"Then how does *she?*"

"How do you?" I laughed. "I'm a different matter."

She sat a minute turning things round, staring at the picture. "The likeness, the likeness!" It was almost too much.

"It's so true?"

"Beyond everything."

I considered. "But a resemblance to a known individual—that wasn't what you wanted."

She sprang up at this in eager protest. "Ah, no one else would see it."

I showed again, I fear, my amusement. "No one but you and she?"

"It's her doing *him!*" She was held by her wonder. "Doesn't she, on your honour, know?"

"That his is the very head you would have liked if you had dared? Not a bit. How *should* she? She knows nothing—on my honour."

Mrs. Bridgenorth continued to marvel. "She just painted him for the kind of face—?"

"That corresponds with my description of what you wished? Precisely."

"But *how*—after so long? From memory? As a friend?"

"As a reminiscence—yes. Visual memory, you see, in our uncanny race, is wonderful. As the ideal thing, simply, for your purpose. You *are* then suited?" I, after an instant added.

She had again been gazing, and at this turned her eyes on me; but I saw she couldn't speak, couldn't do more at least than sound, unutterably, "Suited!" so that I was positively not surprised when suddenly—just as Mary had done, the power to produce this effect seeming a property of the model—she burst into tears. I feel no harsher in relating it, however I may appear, than I did at the moment, but it is a fact that while she just wept I literally had a fresh inspiration on behalf of Miss Tredick's interests. I knew exactly, moreover, before my companion had recovered herself, what she would next ask me; and I consciously brought this appeal on in order to have it over. I explained that I had not the least idea of the identity of our artist's sitter, to which she had given me no clue. I had nothing but my impression that she had known him—known him well; and, from whatever material she had worked, the fact of his having also been known to Mrs. Bridgenorth was a coincidence pure and simple. It partook of the nature of prodigy, but such prodigies did occur. My visitor listened with avidity and credulity. She was so far reassured. Then I saw her question come. "Well, if she doesn't dream he was ever anything to me—or what he will be now—I'm going to ask you, as a very particular favour, never to tell her. She will want to know of course exactly how I've been struck. You'll naturally say that I'm delighted, but may I exact from you that you say nothing else?"

There was supplication in her face, but I had to think. "There are conditions I must put to you first, and one of them is also a question, only more frank than yours. Was this mysterious personage—frustrated by death—to have married you?"

She met it bravely. "Certainly, if he had lived."

I was only amused at an artlessness in her "certainly." "Very good. But why do you wish the coincidence—"

"Kept from her?" She knew exactly why. "Because if she suspects it she won't let me have the picture. Therefore," she added with decision, "you must let me pay for it on the spot."

"What do you mean by on the spot?"

"I'll send you a cheque as soon as I get home."

"Oh," I laughed, "let us understand. Why do you consider she won't let you have the picture?"

She made me wait a little for this, but when it came it was perfectly lucid. "Because she'll then see how much more I must want it."

"How much less—wouldn't it be rather, since the bargain was, as the more convenient thing, not for a likeness?"

"Oh," said Mrs. Bridgenorth with impatience, "the likeness will take care of itself. She'll put this and that together." Then she brought out her real apprehension. "She'll be jealous."

"Oh!" I laughed. But I was startled.

"She'll hate me!"

I wondered. "But I don't think she liked him."

"Don't think?" She stared at me, with her echo, over all that might be in it, then seemed to find little enough. "I *say!*"

It was almost comically the old Mrs. Bridgenorth. "But I gather from her that he was bad."

"Then what was *she?*"

I barely hesitated. "What were *you?*"

"That's my own business." And she turned again to the picture. "He was good enough for her to do *that* of him."

I took it in once more. "Artistically speaking, for the way it's done, it's one of the most curious things I've ever seen."

"It's a grand treat!" said poor Mrs. Bridgenorth more simply.

It was, it *is* really; which is exactly what made the case so interesting. "Yet I feel somehow that, as I say, it wasn't done with love."

It was wonderful how she understood. "It was done with rage."

"Then what have you to fear?"

She knew again perfectly. "What happened when he made *me* jealous. So much," she declared, "that if you'll give me your word for silence—"

"Well?"

"Why, I'll double the money."

"Oh," I replied, taking a turn about in the excitement of our concurrence, "that's exactly what—to do a still better stroke for her—it had just come to *me* to propose!"

"It's understood then, on your oath, as a gentleman?" She was so eager that practically this settled it, though I moved to and fro a little while she watched me in suspense. It vibrated all round us that she had gone out to the thing in a stifled flare, that a whole close relation had in the few minutes revived. We know it of the truly amiable person that he will strain a point for another that he wouldn't strain for himself. The stroke to put in for Mary was positively prescribed. The work represented really much more than had been covenanted, and if the purchaser chose so to value it this was her own affair. I decided. "If it's understood also on *your* word."

We were so at one that we shook hands on it. "And when may I send?"

"Well, I shall see her this evening. Say early tomorrow."

"Early tomorrow." And I went with her to her brougham, into which, I remember, as she took leave, she expressed regret that she mightn't then and there have introduced the canvas for removal. I consoled her with remarking that she couldn't have got it in—which was not quite true.

I saw Mary Tredick before dinner, and though I was not quite ideally sure of my present ground with her I instantly brought out my news. "She's so delighted that I felt I must in conscience do something still better for you. She's not to have it on the original terms. I've put up the price."

Mary wondered. "But to what?"

"Well, to four hundred. If you say so, I'll try even for five."

"Oh, she'll never give that."

"I beg your pardon."

"After the agreement?" She looked grave. "I don't like such leaps and bounds."

"But, my dear child, they're yours. You contracted for a decorative trifle, and you've produced a breathing masterpiece."

She thought. "Is that what she calls it?" Then, as having to think too, I hesitated. "What does she know?" she pursued.

"She knows she wants it."

"So much as that?"

At this I had to brace myself a little. "So much that she'll send me the cheque this afternoon, and that you'll have mine by the first post in the morning."

"Before she has even received the picture?"

"Oh, she'll send for it tomorrow." And as I was dining out and had still to dress, my time was up. Mary came with me to the door, where I repeated my assurance. "You shall receive my cheque by the first post." To which I added: "If it's little enough for a lady so much in need to pay for *any* husband, it isn't worth mentioning as the price of such a one as you've given her!"

I was in a hurry, but she held me. "Then you've felt your idea confirmed?"

"My idea?"

"That that's what I *have* given her?"

I suddenly fancied I had perhaps gone too far; but I had kept my cab and was already in it. "Well, put it," I called with excess of humour over the front, "that you've, at any rate, given *him* a wife!"

When on my return from dinner that night I let myself in, my first care, in my dusty studio, was to make light for another look at Mary's subject. I felt the impulse to bid him good night; but, to my astonishment, he was no longer there. His place was a void—he had already disappeared. I saw, however, after my first surprise, what had happened—saw it moreover, frankly, with some relief. As my servants were in bed I could ask no questions, but it was clear that Mrs. Bridgenorth, whose note, containing its cheque, lay on my table, had been after all unable to wait. The note, I found, mentioned nothing but the enclosure; but it had come by hand, and it was her silence that told the tale. Her messenger had been instructed to "act"; he had come with a vehicle, he had transferred to it canvas and frame. The prize was now therefore landed and the incident closed. I didn't altogether, the next morning, know why, but I had slept the better for the sense of these things, and as soon as my attendant came in I asked for details. It was on this that his answer surprised me. "No, sir, there was no man; she came herself. She had only a four-wheeler, but I helped her, and we got it in. It was a squeeze, sir, but she *would* take it."

I wondered. "She had a four-wheeler? and not her servant?"

"No, no, sir. She came, as you may say, single-handed."

"And not even in her brougham, which would have been larger."

My man, with his habit, weighed it. "But *have* she a brougham, sir?"

"Why, the one she was here in yesterday."

Then light broke. "Oh, *that* lady! It wasn't her, sir. It was Miss Tredick."

Light broke, but darkness a little followed it—a darkness that, after breakfast, guided my steps back to my friend. There, in its own first place, I met her creation; but I saw it would be a different thing meeting *her*. She immediately put down on a table, as if she had expected me, the cheque I had sent her overnight. "Yes, I've brought it away. And I can't take the money."

I found myself in despair. "You want to keep him?"

"I don't understand what has happened."

"You just back out?"

"I don't understand," she repeated, "what has happened." But what I had already perceived was, on the contrary, that she very nearly, that she in fact quite remarkably, did understand. It was as if in my zeal I had given away my case, and I felt that my test was coming. She had been thinking all night with intensity, and Mrs. Bridgenorth's generosity, coupled with Mrs. Bridgenorth's promptitude, had kept her awake. Thence, for a woman nervous and critical, imaginations, visions, questions. "Why, in writing me last night, did you take for granted it was *she* who had swooped down? Why," asked Mary Tredick, "should she swoop?"

Well, if I could drive a bargain for Mary, I felt I could *a fortiori*[3] lie for her. "Because it's her way. She does swoop. She's impatient and uncontrolled. And it's affectation for you to pretend," I said with diplomacy, "that you see no reason for her falling in love—"

"Falling in love?" She took me straight up.

"With that gentleman. Certainly. What woman wouldn't? What woman didn't? I really don't see, you know, your right to back out."

"I won't back out," she presently returned, "if you'll answer me a question. Does she know the man represented?" Then as I hung fire: "It has come to me that she must. It would account for so much. For the strange way I feel," she went on, "and for the extraordinary sum you've been able to extract from her."

It was a pity, and I flushed with it, besides wincing at the word she used. But Mrs. Bridgenorth and I, between us, had clearly made the figure too high. "You think that, if she *had* guessed, I would naturally work it to 'extract' more?"

She turned away from me on this and, looking blank in her trouble, moved vaguely about. Then she stopped. "I see him set up there. I hear her say it. What you said she would make him pass for."

I believe I foolishly tried—though only for an instant—to look as if I didn't remember what I had said. "Her husband?"

---

[3] *A fortiori.* For a still stronger reason.

"He wasn't."

The next minute I had risked it. "Was he yours?"

I don't know what I had expected, but I found myself surprised at her mere pacific headshake. "No."

"Then why mayn't he have been—?"

"Another woman's? Because he died, to my absolute knowledge, unmarried." She spoke as quietly. "He had known many women, and there was one in particular with whom he became—and too long remained—ruinously intimate. She tried to make him marry her, and he was near it. Death, however, saved him. But she was the reason—"

"Yes?' I feared again from her a wave of pain, and I went on while she kept it back. "Did you know her?"

"She was one I wouldn't." Then she brought it out. "She was the reason he failed me." Her successful detachment somehow said all, reduced me to a flat, kind "Oh!" that marked my sense of her telling me, against my expectation, more than I knew what to do with. But it was just while I wondered how to turn her confidence that she repeated, in a changed voice, her challenge of a moment before. "Does she know the man represented?"

"I haven't the least idea." And having so acquitted myself I added, with what strikes me now as futility: "She certainly—yesterday—didn't name him."

"Only recognised him?"

"If she did she brilliantly concealed it."

"So that you got nothing from her?"

It was a question that offered me a certain advantage. "I thought you accused me of getting too much."

She gave me a long look, and I now saw everything in her face. "It's very nice—what you're doing for me, and you do it handsomely. It's beautiful—beautiful, and I thank you with all my heart. But I know."

"And what do you know?"

She went about now preparing her usual work. "What he must have been to her."

"You mean she was the person?"

"Well," she said, putting on her old spectacles, "she was one of them."

"And you accept so easily the astounding coincidence—?"

"Of my finding myself, after years, in so extraordinary a relation with her? What do you call easily? I've passed a night of torment."

"But what put it into your head—?"

"That I had so blindly and strangely given him back to her? *You* put it—yesterday."

"And how?"

"I can't tell you. You didn't in the least mean to—on the contrary. But you dropped the seed. The plant, after you had gone," she said with a businesslike pull at her easel, "the plant began to grow. I *saw* them there—in your studio—face to face."

"You were jealous?" I laughed.

She gave me through her glasses another look, and they seemed, from this moment, in their queerness, to have placed her quite on the other side of the gulf of time. She was firm there; she was settled; I couldn't get at her now. "I see she told you I *would* be." I doubtless kept down too little my start at it, and she immediately pursued. "You say I accept the coincidence, which is of course prodigious. But such things happen. Why shouldn't I accept it if you do?"

"*Do* I?" I smiled.

She began her work in silence, but she presently exclaimed: "I'm glad I didn't meet her!"

"I don't yet see why you wouldn't."

"Neither do I. It was an instinct."

"Your instincts"—I tried to be ironic—"are miraculous."

"They *have* to be, to meet such accidents. I must ask you kindly to tell her, when you return her gift, that now I have done the picture I find I must after all keep it for myself."

"Giving no reason?"

She painted away. "She'll know the reason."

Well, by this time I knew it too; I knew so many things that I feared my resistance was weak. If our wonderful client hadn't been his wife in fact, she was not to be helped to become his wife in fiction. I knew almost more than I can say, more at any rate than I could then betray. He had been bound in common mercy to stand by my friend, and he had basely forsaken her. This indeed brought up the obscure, into which I shyly gazed. "Why, even granting your theory, should you grudge her the portrait? It was painted in bitterness."

"Yes. Without that—!"

"It wouldn't have come? Precisely. Is it in bitterness, then, you'll keep it?"

She looked up from her canvas. "In what would *you* keep it?"

It made me jump. "Do you mean I *may?*" Then I had my idea. "I'd give you her price for it!"

Her smile through her glasses was beautiful. "And afterwards make it over to her? You shall have it when I die." With which she came away from her easel, and I saw that I was staying her work and should properly go. So I put out my hand to her. "It took—whatever you will!—to paint it," she said, "but I shall keep it in joy." I could answer nothing now—had to cease to pretend; the thing was in her hands. For a moment we stood there, and I had again the sense, melancholy and final, of her being, as it were, remotely glazed and fixed into what she had done. "He's taken from me, and for all those years he's kept. Then she herself, by a prodigy—!" She lost herself again in the wonder of it.

"Unwittingly gives him back?"

She fairly, for an instant over the marvel, closed her eyes. "Gives him back."

Then it was I saw how he would be kept! But it was the end of my vision. I could only write, ruefully enough, to Mrs. Bridgenorth, whom I never met again, but of whose death—preceding by a couple of years Mary Tredick's—I happened to hear. This is an old man's tale. I have inherited the picture, in the deep beauty of which, however, darkness still lurks. No one, strange to say, has ever recognised the model, but everyone asks his name. I don't even know it.

D. H. Lawrence

The Horse-Dealer's Daughter

"Well, Mabel, and what are you going to do with yourself?" asked Joe, with foolish flippancy. He felt quite safe himself. Without listening for an answer, he turned aside, worked a grain of tobacco to the tip of his tongue, and spat it out. He did not care about anything, since he felt safe himself.

The three brothers and the sister sat round the desolate breakfast table, attempting some sort of desultory consultation. The morning's post had given the final tap to the family fortune, and all was over. The dreary dining-room itself, with its heavy mahogany furniture, looked as if it were waiting to be done away with.

But the consultation amounted to nothing. There was a strange air of ineffectuality about the three men, as they sprawled at table, smoking and reflecting vaguely on their own condition. The girl was alone, a rather short, sullen-looking young woman of twenty-seven. She did not share the same life as her brothers. She would have been good-looking, save for the impassive fixity of her face, "bull-dog," as her brothers called it.

There was a confused tramping of horses' feet outside. The three men all sprawled round in their chairs to watch. Beyond the dark holly-bushes that separated the strip of lawn from the highroad, they could see a cavalcade of shire horses swinging out of their own yard, being taken for exercise. This was the last time. These were the last horses that would go through their hands. The young men watched with critical, callous look. They were all

THE HORSE-DEALER'S DAUGHTER From *The Complete Short Stories of D. H. Lawrence,* Volume II. Copyright 1922 by Thomas B. Seltzer, Inc., renewed 1950 by Frieda Lawrence. Reprinted by permission of The Viking Press, Inc.

frightened at the collapse of their lives, and the sense of disaster in which they were involved left them no inner freedom.

Yet they were three fine, well-set fellows enough. Joe, the eldest, was a man of thirty-three, broad and handsome in a hot, flushed way. His face was red, he twisted his black moustache over a thick finger, his eyes were shallow and restless. He had a sensual way of uncovering his teeth when he laughed, and his bearing was stupid. Now he watched the horses with a glazed look of helplessness in his eyes, a certain stupor of downfall.

The great draught-horses swung past. They were tied head to tail, four of them, and they heaved along to where a lane branched off from the highroad, planting their great hoofs floutingly in the fine black mud, swinging their great rounded haunches sumptuously, and trotting a few sudden steps as they were led into the lane, round the corner. Every movement showed a massive, slumbrous strength, and a stupidity which held them in subjection. The groom at the head looked back, jerking the leading rope. And the cavalcade moved out of sight up the lane, the tail of the last horse, bobbed up tight and stiff, held out taut from the swinging great haunches as they rocked behind the hedges in a motion like sleep.

Joe watched with glazed hopeless eyes. The horses were almost like his own body to him. He felt he was done for now. Luckily he was engaged to a woman as old as himself, and therefore her father, who was steward of a neighbouring estate, would provide him with a job. He would marry and go into harness. His life was over, he would be a subject animal now.

He turned uneasily aside, the retreating steps of the horses echoing in his ears. Then, with foolish restlessness, he reached for the scraps of bacon-rind from the plates, and making a faint whistling sound, flung them to the terrier that lay against the fender. He watched the dog swallow them, and waited till the creature looked into his eyes. Then a faint grin came on his face, and in a high, foolish voice he said:

"You won't get much more bacon, shall you, you little bitch?"

The dog faintly and dismally wagged its tail, then lowered its haunches, circled round, and lay down again.

There was another helpless silence at the table. Joe sprawled uneasily in his seat, not willing to go till the family conclave was dissolved. Fred Henry, the second brother, was erect, clean-limbed, alert. He had watched the passing of the horses with more sang-froid. If he was an animal, like Joe, he was an animal which controls, not one which is controlled. He was master of any horse, and he carried himself with a well-tempered air of mastery. But he was not master of the situations of life. He pushed his coarse brown moustache upwards, off his lip, and glanced irritably at his sister, who sat impassive and inscrutable.

"You'll go and stop with Lucy for a bit, shan't you?" he asked. The girl did not answer.

"I don't see what else you can do," persisted Fred Henry.

"Go as a skivvy," Joe interpolated laconically.

The girl did not move a muscle.

"If I was her, I should go in for training for a nurse," said Malcolm, the youngest of them all. He was the baby of the family, a young man of twenty-two, with a fresh, jaunty *museau*.

But Mabel did not take any notice of him. They had talked at her and round her for so many years, that she hardly heard them at all.

The marble clock on the mantelpiece softly chimed the half-hour, the dog rose uneasily from the hearthrug and looked at the party at the breakfast table. But still they sat on in ineffectual conclave.

"Oh, all right," said Joe suddenly, apropos of nothing. "I'll get a move on."

He pushed back his chair, straddled his knees with a downward jerk, to get them free, in horsey fashion, and went to the fire. Still he did not go out of the room; he was curious to know what the others would do or say. He began to charge his pipe, looking down at the dog and saying, in a high, affected voice:

"Going wi' me? Going wi' me are ter? Tha'rt goin' further than tha counts on just now, dost hear?"

The dog faintly wagged its tail, the man stuck out his jaw and covered his pipe with his hands, and puffed intently, losing himself in the tobacco, looking down all the while at the dog with an absent brown eye. The dog looked up at him in mournful distrust. Joe stood with his knees stuck out, in real horsey fashion.

"Have you had a letter from Lucy?" Fred Henry asked of his sister.

"Last week," came the neutral reply.

"And what does she say?"

There was no answer.

"Does she *ask* you to go and stop there?" persisted Fred Henry.

"She says I can if I like."

"Well, then, you'd better. Tell her you'll come on Monday."

This was received in silence.

"That's what you'll do then, is it?" said Fred Henry, in some exasperation.

But she made no answer. There was a silence of futility and irritation in the room. Malcolm grinned fatuously.

"You'll have to make up your mind between now and next Wednesday," said Joe loudly, "or else find yourself lodgings on the kerbstone."

The face of the young woman darkened, but she sat on immutable.

"Here's Jack Fergusson!" exclaimed Malcolm, who was looking aimlessly out of the window.

"Where?" exclaimed Joe, loudly.

"Just gone past."

"Coming in?"

Malcolm craned his neck to see the gate.

"Yes," he said.

There was a silence. Mabel sat on like one condemned, at the head of the table. Then a whistle was heard from the kitchen. The dog got up and barked sharply. Joe opened the door and shouted:

"Come on."

After a moment a young man entered, He was muffled up in overcoat and a purple woollen scarf, and his tweed cap, which he did not remove, was pulled down on his head. He was of medium height, his face was rather long and pale, his eyes looked tired.

"Hello, Jack! Well, Jack!" exclaimed Malcolm and Joe. Fred Henry merely said, "Jack."

"What's doing?" asked the newcomer, evidently addressing Fred Henry.

"Same. We've got to be out by Wednesday. Got a cold?"

"I have—got it bad, too."

"Why don't you stop in?"

"*Me* stop in? When I can't stand on my legs, perhaps I shall have a chance." The young man spoke huskily. He had a slight Scotch accent.

"It's a knock-out, isn't it," said Joe, boisterously, "if a doctor goes round croaking with a cold. Looks bad for the patients, doesn't it?"

The young doctor looked at him slowly.

"Anything the matter with *you*, then?" he asked sarcastically.

"Not as I know of. Damn your eyes, I hope not. Why?"

"I thought you were very concerned about the patients, wondered if you might be one yourself."

"Damn it, no, I've never been patient to no flaming doctor, and hope I never shall be," returned Joe.

At this point Mabel rose from the table, and they all seemed to become aware of her existence. She began putting the dishes together. The young doctor looked at her, but did not address her. He had not greeted her. She went out of the room with the tray, her face impassive and unchanged.

"When are you off then, all of you?" asked the doctor.

"I'm catching the eleven-forty," replied Malcolm. "Are you goin' down wi' th' trap, Joe?"

"Yes, I've told you I'm going down wi' th' trap, haven't I?"

"We'd better be getting her in then. So long, Jack, if I don't see you before I go," said Malcolm, shaking hands.

He went out, followed by Joe, who seemed to have his tail between his legs.

"Well, this is the devil's own," exclaimed the doctor, when he was left alone with Fred Henry. "Going before Wednesday, are you?"

"That's the orders," replied the other.

"Where, to Northampton?"

"That's it."

"The devil!" exclaimed Fergusson, with quiet chagrin.

And there was silence between the two.

"All settled up, are you?" asked Fergusson.

"About."

There was another pause.

"Well, I shall miss yer, Freddy, boy," said the young doctor.

"And I shall miss thee, Jack," returned the other.

"Miss you like hell," mused the doctor.

Fred Henry turned aside. There was nothing to say. Mabel came in again, to finish clearing the table.

"What are *you* going to do, then, Miss Pervin?" asked Fergusson. "Going to your sister's, are you?"

Mabel looked at him with her steady, dangerous eyes, that always made him uncomfortable, unsettling his superficial ease.

"No," she said.

"Well, what in the name of fortune *are* you going to do? Say what you mean to do," cried Fred Henry, with futile intensity.

But she only averted her head, and continued her work. She folded the white table-cloth, and put on the chenille cloth.

"The sulkiest bitch that ever trod!" muttered her brother.

But she finished her task with perfectly impassive face, the young doctor watching her interestedly all the while. Then she went out.

Fred Henry stared after her, clenching his lips, his blue eyes fixing in sharp antagonism, as he made a grimace of sour exasperation.

"You could bray her into bits, and that's all you'd get out of her," he said in a small, narrowed tone.

The doctor smiled faintly.

"What's she *going* to do, then?" he asked.

"Strike me if *I* know!" returned the other.

There was a pause. Then the doctor stirred.

"I'll be seeing you to-night, shall I?" he said to his friend.

"Ay—where's it to be? Are we going over to Jessdale?"

"I don't know. I've got such a cold on me. I'll come round to the Moon and Stars, anyway."

"Let Lizzie and May miss their night for once, eh?"

"That's it—if I feel as I do now."

"All's one—"

The two young men went through the passage and down to the back door together. The house was large, but it was servantless now, and desolate. At the back was a small bricked house-yard, and beyond that a big square, gravelled fine and red, and having stables on two sides. Sloping, dank, winter-dark fields stretched away on the open sides.

But the stables were empty. Joseph Pervin, the father of the family, had been a man of no education, who had become a fairly large horse dealer. The stables had been full of horses, there was a great turmoil and come-and-go of horses and of dealers and grooms. Then the kitchen was full of servants. But of late things had declined. The old man had married a second time, to retrieve his fortunes. Now he was dead and everything was gone to the dogs, there was nothing but debt and threatening.

For months, Mabel had been servantless in the big house, keeping the home together in penury for her ineffectual brothers. She had kept house for ten years. But previously it was with unstinted means. Then, however brutal and coarse everything was, the sense of money had kept her proud, confident. The men might be foul-mouthed, the women in the kitchen might have bad reputations, her brothers might have illegitimate children. But so long as there was money, the girl felt herself established, and brutally proud, reserved.

No company came to the house, save dealers and coarse men. Mabel had no associates of her own sex, after her sister went away. But she did not mind. She went regularly to church, she attended to her father. And she lived in the memory of her mother, who had died when she was fourteen, and whom she had loved. She had loved her father, too, in a different way, depending upon him, and feeling secure in him, until at the age of fifty-four he married again. And then she had set hard against him. Now he had died and left them all hopelessly in debt.

She had suffered badly during the period of poverty. Nothing, however, could shake the curious sullen, animal pride that dominated each member of the family. Now, for Mabel, the end had come. Still she would not cast about her. She would follow her own way just the same. She would always hold the keys of her own situation. Mindless and persistent, she endured from day to day. Why should she think? Why should she answer anybody? It was enough that this was the end, and there was no way out. She need not pass any more darkly along the main street of the small town, avoiding every eye. She need not demean herself any more, going into the shops and buying the cheapest food. This was at an end. She thought of nobody, not even of herself. Mindless and persistent, she seemed in a sort of ecstasy to be coming nearer to her fulfilment, her own glorification, approaching her dead mother, who was glorified.

In the afternoon she took a little bag, with shears and sponge and a small scrubbing brush, and went out. It was a grey, wintry day, with saddened, dark green fields and an atmosphere blackened by the smoke of foundries not far off. She went quickly, darkly along the causeway, heeding nobody, through the town to the churchyard.

There she always felt secure, as if no one could see her, although as a matter of fact she was exposed to the stare of every one who passed along under the churchyard wall. Nevertheless, once under the shadow of the great looming church, among the graves, she felt immune from the world, reserved within the thick churchyard wall as in another country.

Carefully she clipped the grass from the grave, and arranged the pinky white, small chrysanthemums in the tin cross. When this was done, she took an empty jar from a neighbouring grave, brought water, and carefully, most scrupulously sponged the marble head-stone and the coping-stone.

It gave her sincere satisfaction to do this. She felt in immediate contact with the world of her mother. She took minute pains, went through the park in a state bordering on pure happiness, as if in performing this task she came into a subtle, intimate connection with her mother. For the life she followed here in the world was far less real than the world of death she inherited from her mother.

The doctor's house was just by the church. Fergusson, being a mere hired assistant, was slave to the country-side. As he hurried now to attend to the outpatients in the surgery, glancing across the graveyard with his quick eye, he saw the girl at her task at the grave. She seemed so intent and remote, it was like looking into another world. Some mystical element was touched in him. He slowed down as he walked, watching her as if spell-bound.

She lifted her eyes, feeling him looking. Their eyes met. And each looked away again at once, each feeling, in some way, found out by the other. He lifted his cap and passed on down the road. There remained distinct in his consciousness, like a vision, the memory of her face, lifted from the tombstone in the churchyard, and looking at him with slow, large, portentous eyes. It *was* portentous, her face. It seemed to mesmerize him. There was a heavy power in her eyes which laid hold of his whole being, as if he had drunk some powerful drug. He had been feeling weak and done before. Now the life came back into him, he felt delivered from his own fretted, daily self.

He finished his duties at the surgery as quickly as might be, hastily filling up the bottle of the waiting people with cheap drugs. Then, in perpetual haste, he set off again to visit several cases in another part of his round, before teatime. At all times he preferred to walk if he could, but particularly when he was not well. He fancied the motion restored him.

The afternoon was falling. It was grey, deadened, and wintry, with a slow, moist, heavy coldness sinking in and deadening all the faculties. But why should he think or notice? He hastily climbed the hill and turned across the dark green fields, following the black cinder-track. In the distance, across a shallow dip in the country, the small town was clustered like smouldering ash, a tower, a spire, a heap of low, raw, extinct houses. And on the nearest fringe of the town, sloping into the dip, was Oldmeadow, the Pervins' house. He could see the stables and the outbuildings distinctly, as they lay towards him on the slope. Well, he would not go there many more times! Another resource would be lost to him, another place gone: the only company he cared for in the alien, ugly little town he was losing. Nothing but work, drudgery, constant hastening from dwelling to dwelling among the colliers and the iron-workers. It wore him out, but at the same time he had a craving for it. It was a stimulant to him to be in the homes of the working people, moving as it were through the innermost body of their life. His nerves were excited and gratified. He could come so near, into the very lives of the rough, inarticulate, powerfully emotional men and women. He grumbled, he said he hated the hellish hole. But as a matter of fact it excited him, the contact with the rough, strongly-feeling people was a stimulant applied direct to his nerves.

Below Oldmeadow, in the green, shallow, soddened hollow of fields, lay a square, deep pond. Roving across the landscape, the doctor's quick eye detected a figure in black passing through the gate of the field, down towards the pond. He looked again. It would be Mabel Pervin. His mind suddenly became alive and attentive.

Why was she going down there? He pulled up on the path on the slope above, and stood staring. He could just make sure of the small black figure moving in the hollow of the failing day. He seemed to see her in the midst of such obscurity, that he was like a clairvoyant, seeing rather with the mind's eye than with ordinary sight. Yet he could see her positively enough, whilst he kept his eye attentive. He felt, if he looked away from her, in the thick, ugly falling dusk, he would lose her altogether.

He followed her minutely as she moved, direct and intent, like something transmitted rather than stirring in voluntary activity, straight down the field towards the pond. There she stood on the bank for a moment. She never raised her head. Then she waded slowly into the water.

He stood motionless as the small black figure walked slowly and deliberately towards the centre of the pond, very slowly, gradually moving deeper into the motionless water, and still moving forward as the water got up to her breast. Then he could see her no more in the dusk of the dead afternoon.

"There!" he exclaimed. "Would you believe it?"

And he hastened straight down, running over the wet, soddened fields, pushing through the hedges, down into the depression of callous wintry obscurity. It took him several minutes to come to the pond. He stood on the bank, breathing heavily. He could see nothing. His eyes seemed to penetrate the dead water. Yes, perhaps that was the dark shadow of her black clothing beneath the surface of the water.

He slowly ventured into the pond. The bottom was deep, soft clay, he sank in, and the water clasped dead cold round his legs. As he stirred he could smell the cold, rotten clay that fouled up into the water. It was objectionable in his lungs. Still, repelled and yet not heeding, he moved deeper into the pond. The cold water rose over his thighs, over his loins, upon his abdomen. The lower part of his body was all sunk in the hideous cold element. And the bottom was so deeply soft and uncertain, he was afraid of pitching with his mouth underneath. He could not swim, and was afraid.

He crouched a little, spreading his hands under the water and moving them round, trying to feel for her. The dead cold pond swayed upon his chest. He moved again, a little deeper, and again, with his hands underneath, he felt all around under the water. And he touched her clothing. But it evaded his fingers. He made a desperate effort to grasp it.

And so doing he lost his balance and went under, horribly, suffocating in the foul earthy water, struggling madly for a few moments. At last, after what seemed an eternity, he got his footing, rose again into the air and looked around. He gasped, and knew he was in the world. Then he looked at the water. She had risen near him. He grasped her clothing, and drawing her nearer, turned to take his way to land again.

He went very slowly, carefully, absorbed in the slow progress. He rose higher, climbing out of the pond. The water was now only about his legs; he was thankful, full of relief to be out of the clutches of the pond. He lifted her and staggered on to the bank, out of the horror of wet, grey clay.

He laid her down on the bank. She was quite unconscious and running with water. He made the water come from her mouth, he worked to restore her. He did not have to work very long before he could feel the breathing begin again in her; she was breathing naturally. He worked a little longer. He could feel her live beneath his hands; she was coming back. He wiped her face, wrapped her in his overcoat, looked round into the dim, dark grey world, then lifted her and staggered down the bank and across the fields.

It seemed an unthinkably long way, and his burden so heavy he felt he would never get to the house. But at last he was in the stable-yard, and then in the house-yard. He opened the door and went into the house. In the kitchen he laid her down on the hearthrug, and called. The house was empty. But the fire was burning in the grate.

Then again he kneeled to attend to her. She was breathing regularly, her eyes were wide open and as if conscious, but there seemed something missing in her look. She was conscious in herself, but unconscious of her surroundings.

He ran upstairs, took blankets from a bed, and put them before the fire to warm. Then he removed her saturated, earthy-smelling clothing, rubbed her dry with a towel, and wrapped her naked in the blankets. Then he went into the dining-room, to look for spirits. There was a little whisky. He drank a gulp himself, and put some into her mouth.

The effect was instantaneous. She looked full into his face, as if she had been seeing him for some time, and yet had only just become conscious of him.

"Dr. Fergusson?" she said.

"What?" he answered.

He was divesting himself of his coat, intending to find some dry clothing upstairs. He could not bear the smell of the dead, clayey water, and he was mortally afraid for his own health.

"What did I do?" she asked.

"Walked into the pond," he replied. He had begun to shudder like one sick, and could hardly attend to her. Her eyes remained full on him, he seemed to be going dark in his mind, looking back at her helplessly. The shuddering became quieter in him, his life came back in him, dark and unknowing, but strong again.

"Was I out of my mind?" she asked, while her eyes were fixed on him all the time.

"Maybe, for the moment," he replied. He felt quiet, because his strength had come back. The strange fretful strain had left him.

"Am I out of my mind now?" she asked.

"Are you?" he reflected a moment. "No," he answered truthfully, "I don't see that you are." He turned his face aside. He was afraid now, because he felt dazed, and felt dimly that her power was stronger than his, in this issue. And she continued to look at him fixedly all the time. "Can you tell me where I shall find some dry things to put on?" he asked.

"Did you dive into the pond for me?" she asked.

"No," he answered. "I walked in. But I went in overhead as well."

There was silence for a moment. He hesitated. He very much wanted to go upstairs to get into dry clothing. But there was another desire in him. And she seemed to hold him. His will seemed to have gone to sleep, and left him, standing there slack before her. But he felt warm inside himself. He did not shudder at all, though his clothes were sodden on him.

"Why did you?" she asked.

"Because I didn't want you to do such a foolish thing," he said.

"It wasn't foolish," she said, still gazing at him as she lay on the floor, with a sofa cushion under her head. "It was the right thing to do. *I* knew best, then."

"I'll go and shift these wet things," he said. But still he had not the power to move out of her presence, until she sent him. It was as if she had the life of his body in her hands, and he could not extricate himself. Or perhaps he did not want to.

Suddenly she sat up. Then she became aware of her own immediate condition. She felt the blankets about her, she knew her own limbs. For a moment it seemed as if her reason were going. She looked round, with wild eye, as if seeking something. He stood still with fear. She saw her clothing lying scattered.

"Who undressed me?" she asked, her eyes resting full and inevitable on his face.

"I did," he replied, "to bring you round."

For some moments she sat and gazed at him awfully, her lips parted.

"Do you love me, then?" she asked.

He only stood and stared at her, fascinated. His soul seemed to melt.

She shuffled forward on her knees, and put her arms round him, round his legs, as he stood there, pressing her breasts against his knees and thighs, clutching him with strange, convulsive certainty, pressing his thighs against her, drawing him to her face, her throat, as she looked up at him with flaring, humble eyes of transfiguration, triumphant in first possession.

"You love me," she murmured, in strange transport, yearning and triumphant and confident. "You love me. I know you love me, I know."

And she was passionately kissing his knees, through the wet clothing, passionately and indiscriminately kissing his knees, his legs, as if unaware of everything.

He looked down at the tangled wet hair, the wild, bare, animal shoulders. He was amazed, bewildered, and afraid. He had never thought of loving her. He had never wanted to love her. When he rescued her and restored her, he was a doctor, and she was a patient. He had had no single personal thought of her. Nay, this introduction of the personal element was very distasteful to him, a violation of his professional honour. It was horrible to have her there embracing his knees. It was horrible. He revolted from it, violently. And yet —and yet—he had not the power to break away.

She looked at him again, with the same supplication of powerful love, and that same transcendent, frightening light of triumph. In view of the delicate flame which seemed to come from her face like a light, he was powerless. And yet he had never intended to love her. He had never intended. And something stubborn in him could not give way.

"You love me," she repeated, in a murmur of deep, rhapsodic assurance. "You love me."

Her hands were drawing him, drawing him down to her. He was afraid, even a little horrified. For he had, really, no intention of loving her. Yet her hands were drawing him towards her. He put out his hand quickly to steady himself, and grasped her bare shoulder. A flame seemed to burn the hand that grasped her soft shoulder. He had no intention of loving her: his whole will was against his yielding. It was horrible. And yet wonderful was the touch of her shoulders, beautiful the shining of her face. Was she perhaps mad? He had a horror of yielding to her. Yet something in him ached also.

He had been staring away at the door, away from her. But his hand remained on her shoulder. She had gone suddenly very still. He looked down at her. Her eyes were now wide with fear, with doubt, the light was dying from her face, a shadow of terrible greyness was returning. He could not bear the touch of her eyes' question upon him, and the look of death behind the question.

With an inward groan he gave way, and let his heart yield towards her. A sudden gentle smile came on his face. And her eyes, which never left his face, slowly, slowly filled with tears. He watched the strange water rise in her eyes, like some slow fountain coming up. And his heart seemed to burn and melt away in his breast.

He could not bear to look at her any more. He dropped on his knees and caught her head with his arms and pressed her face against his throat. She was very still. His heart, which seemed to have broken, was burning with a kind of agony in his breast. And he felt her slow, hot tears wetting his throat. But he could not move.

He felt the hot tears wet his neck and the hollows of his neck, and he remained motionless, suspended through one of man's eternities. Only now it had become indispensable to him to have her face pressed close to him; he could never let her go again. He could never let her head go away from the close clutch of his arm. He wanted to remain like that for ever, with his heart hurting him in a pain that was also life to him. Without knowing, he was looking down on her damp, soft brown hair.

Then, as it were suddenly, he smelt the horrid stagnant smell of that water. And at the same moment she drew away from him and looked at him. Her eyes were wistful and unfathomable. He was afraid of them, and he fell to kissing her, not knowing what he was doing. He wanted her eyes not to have that terrible, wistful, unfathomable look.

When she turned her face to him again, a faint delicate flush was glowing, and there was again dawning that terrible shining of joy in her eyes, which really terrified him, and yet which he now wanted to see, because he feared the look of doubt still more.

"You love me?" she said, rather faltering.

"Yes." The word cost him a painful effort. Not because it wasn't true. But because it was too newly true, the *saying* seemed to tear open again his newly-torn heart. And he hardly wanted it to be true, even now.

She lifted her face to him, and he bent forward and kissed her on the mouth, gently, with the one kiss that is an eternal pledge. And as he kissed her his heart strained again in his breast. He never intended to love her. But now it was over. He had crossed over the gulf to her, and all that he had left behind had shrivelled and become void.

After the kiss, her eyes again slowly filled with tears. She sat still, away from him, with her face drooped aside, and her hands folded in her lap. The tears fell very slowly. There was complete silence. He too sat there motionless and silent on the hearthrug. The strange pain of his heart that was broken seemed to consume him. That he should love her? That this was love! That he should be ripped open in this way! Him, a doctor! How they would all jeer if they knew! It was agony to him to think they might know.

In the curious naked pain of the thought he looked again to her. She was sitting there drooped into a muse. He saw a tear fall, and his heart flared hot. He saw for the first time that one of her shoulders was quite uncovered, one arm bare, he could see one of her small breasts; dimly, because it had become almost dark in the room.

"Why are you crying?" he asked, in an altered voice.

She looked up at him, and behind her tears the consciousness of her situation for the first time brought a dark look of shame to her eyes.

"I'm not crying, really," she said, watching him half frightened.

He reached his hand, and softly closed it on her bare arm.

"I love you! I love you!" he said in a soft, low vibrating voice, unlike himself.

She shrank, and dropped her head. The soft, penetrating grip of his hand on her arm distressed her. She looked up at him.

"I want to go," she said. "I want to go and get you some dry things."

"Why?" he said. "I'm all right."

"But I want to go," she said. "And I want you to change your things."

He released her arm, and she wrapped herself in the blanket, looking at him rather frightened. And still she did not rise.

"Kiss me," she said wistfully.

He kissed her, but briefly, half in anger.

Then, after a second, she rose nervously, all mixed up in the blanket. He watched her in her confusion, as she tried to extricate herself and wrap herself up so that she could walk. He watched her relentlessly, as she knew. And as she went, the blanket trailing, and as he saw a glimpse of her feet and her white leg, he tried to remember her as she was when he had wrapped her in the blanket. But then he didn't want to remember, because she had been nothing to him then, and his nature revolted from remembering her as she was when she was nothing to him.

A tumbling, muffled noise from within the dark house startled him. Then he heard her voice:—"There are clothes." He rose and went to the foot of the stairs, and gathered up the garments she had thrown down. Then he came back to the fire, to rub himself down and dress. He grinned at his own appearance when he had finished.

The fire was sinking, so he put on coal. The house was now quite dark, save for the light of a street-lamp that shone in faintly from beyond the holly trees. He lit the gas with matches he found on the mantelpiece. Then he emptied the pockets of his own clothes, and threw all his wet things in a heap into the scullery. After which he gathered up her sodden clothes, gently, and put them in a separate heap on the copper-top in the scullery.

It was six o'clock on the clock. His own watch had stopped. He ought to go back to the surgery. He waited, and still she did not come down. So he went to the foot of the stairs and called:

"I shall have to go."

Almost immediately he heard her coming down. She had on her best dress of black voile, and her hair was tidy, but still damp. She looked at him—and in spite of herself, smiled.

"I don't like you in those clothes," she said.

"Do I look a sight?" he answered.

They were shy of one another.

"I'll make you some tea," she said.

"No, I must go."

"Must you?" And she looked at him again with the wide, strained, doubtful eyes. And again, from the pain of his breast, he knew how he loved her. He went and bent to kiss her, gently, passionately, with his heart's painful kiss.

"And my hair smells so horrible," she murmured in distraction. "And I'm so awful, I'm so awful! Oh, no, I'm too awful." And she broke into bitter, heart-broken sobbing. "You can't want to love me, I'm horrible."

"Don't be silly, don't be silly," he said, trying to comfort her, kissing her, holding her in his arms. "I want you, I want to marry you, we're going to be married, quickly, quickly—tomorrow if I can."

But she only sobbed terribly, and cried:

"I feel awful. I feel awful. I feel I'm horrible to you."

"No, I want you, I want you," was all he answered, blindly, with that terrible intonation which frightened her almost more than her horror lest he should *not* want her.

Babylon Revisited

"And where's Mr. Campbell?" Charlie asked.

"Gone to Switzerland. Mr. Campbell's a pretty sick man, Mr. Wales."

"I'm sorry to hear that. And George Hardt?" Charlie inquired.

"Back in America, gone to work."

"And where is the snow bird?"

"He was in here last week. Anyway, his friend, Mr. Schaeffer, is in Paris."

Two familiar names from the long list of a year and a half ago. Charlie scribbled an address in his notebook and tore out the page.

"If you see Mr. Schaeffer, give him this," he said. "It's my brother-in-law's address. I haven't settled on a hotel yet."

He was not really disappointed to find Paris was so empty. But the stillness in the bar was strange, almost portentous.

It was not an American bar any more—he felt polite in it, and not as if he owned it. It had gone back into France. He had felt the stillness from the moment he got out of the taxi and saw the doorman, usually in a frenzy of activity at this hour, gossiping with a *chasseur* by the servants' entrance.

Passing through the corridor, he heard only a single, bored voice in the once-clamorous women's room. When he turned into the bar he traveled the twenty feet of green carpet with his eyes fixed straight ahead by old habit; and then, with his foot firmly on the rail, he turned and surveyed the room, encountering only a single pair of eyes that fluttered up from a newspaper in the corner. Charlie asked for the head barman, Paul, who in the

latter days of the bull market had come to work in his own custom-built car
—disembarking, however, with due nicety at the nearest corner. But Paul
was at his country house to-day and Alix was giving him his information.

"No, no more. I'm going slow these days."

Alix congratulated him: "Hope you stick to it, Mr. Wales. You were going
pretty strong a couple of years ago."

"I'll stick to it all right," Charlie assured him. "I've stuck to it for over
a year and a half now."

"How do you find conditions in America?"

"I haven't been to America for months. I'm in business in Prague, repre-
senting a couple of concerns there. They don't know about me down there."
He smiled faintly. "Remember the night of George Hardt's bachelor dinner
here? . . . By the way, what's become of Claude Fessenden?"

Alix lowered his voice confidentially: "He's in Paris, but he doesn't come
here any more. Paul doesn't allow it. He ran up a bill of thirty thousand
francs, charging all his drinks and his lunches, and usually his dinner, for
more than a year. And when Paul finally told him he had to pay, he gave
him a bad check."

Alix pressed his lips together and shook his head.

"I don't understand it, such a dandy fellow. Now he's all bloated up—"
He made a plump apple of his hands.

A thin world, resting on a common weakness, shredded away now like
tissue paper. Turning, Charlie saw a group of effeminate young men installing
themselves in a corner.

"Nothing affects them," he thought. "Stocks rise and fall, people loaf or
work, but they go on forever." The place oppressed him. He called for the
dice and shook with Alix for the drink.

"Here for long, Mr. Wales?"

"I'm here for four or five days to see my little girl."

"Oh-h! You have a little girl?"

Outside, the fire-red, gas-blue, ghost-green signs shone smokily through
the tranquil rain. It was late afternoon and the streets were in movement; the
bistros gleamed. At the corner of the Boulevard des Capucines he took a
taxi. The Place de la Concorde moved by in pink majesty; they crossed the
logical Seine, and Charlie felt the sudden provincial quality of the left bank.

"I spoiled this city for myself," he thought. "I didn't realize it, but the
days came along one after another, and then two years were gone, and everything was gone, and I was gone."

He was thirty-five, a handsome man, with the Irish mobility of his face
sobered by a deep wrinkle between his eyes. As he rang his brother-in-law's
bell in the Rue Palatine, the wrinkle deepened till it pulled down his brows;
he felt a cramping sensation in his belly. From behind the maid who opened
the door darted a lovely little girl of nine who shrieked "Daddy!" and flew
up, struggling like a fish, into his arms. She pulled his head around by one
ear and set her cheek against his.

"My old pie," he said.

"Oh, daddy, daddy, daddy, daddy, dads, dads, dads!"

She drew him into the salon, where the family waited, a boy and girl his daughter's age, his sister-in-law and her husband. He greeted Marion with his voice pitched carefully to avoid either feigned enthusiasm or dislike, but her response was more frankly tepid, and she minimized her expression of unshakable distrust by directing her regard toward his child. The two men clasped hands in a friendly way and Lincoln Peters rested his for a moment on Charlie's shoulder.

The room was warm and comfortably American. The three children moved intimately about, playing through the yellow oblongs that led to other rooms; the cheer of six o'clock spoke in the eager smacks of the fire and the sounds of French activity in the kitchen. But Charlie did not relax; his heart sat up rigidly in his body and he drew confidence from his daughter, who from time to time came close to him, holding in her arms the doll he had brought.

"Really extremely well," he declared in answer to Lincoln's question. "There's a lot of business there that isn't moving at all, but we're doing even better than ever. In fact, damn well. I'm bringing my sister over from America next month to keep house for me. In fact, my income is bigger than it was when I had money. You see, the Czechs—"

His boasting was for a specific purpose; but after a moment, seeing a faint restiveness in Lincoln's eye, he changed the subject:

"Those are fine children of yours, well brought up, good manners."

"We think Honoria's a great little girl too."

Marion Peters came back into the little salon. She was a tall woman with worried eyes, who had once possessed a fresh American loveliness. Charlie had never been sensitive to it and was always surprised when people spoke of how pretty she had been. From the first there had been an instinctive antipathy between them.

"Well, how do you find Honoria?" she asked.

"Wonderful. I was astonished how much she's grown in ten months. All the children are looking well."

"We haven't had a doctor for a year. How do you like being back in Paris?"

"It seems very funny to see so few Americans around."

"I'm delighted," Marion said vehemently. "Now at least you can go into a store without their assuming you're a millionaire. We've suffered like everybody, but on the whole it's a good deal pleasanter."

"But it was nice while it lasted," Charlie said. "We were a sort of royalty, almost infallible, with a sort of magic around us. In the bar this afternoon—he stumbled, seeing his mistake—"there wasn't a man I know."

She looked at him keenly. "I should think you'd have had enough of bars."

"I only stayed a minute. I take one drink every afternoon, and no more."

"Don't you want a cocktail before dinner?" Lincoln asked.

"I take only one drink every afternoon, and I've had that."

"I hope you keep to it," said Marion.

Her dislike was evident in the coldness with which she spoke, but Charlie only smiled; he had larger plans. Her very aggressiveness gave him an advantage, and he knew enough to wait. He wanted them to initiate the discussion of what they knew had brought him to Paris.

Honoria was to spend the following afternoon with him. At dinner he couldn't decide whether she was most like him or her mother. Fortunate if she didn't combine the traits of both that had brought them to disaster. A great wave of protectiveness went over him. He thought he knew what to do for her. He believed in character; he wanted to jump back a whole generation and trust in character again as the eternally valuable element. Everything wore out now. Parents expected genius, or at least brilliance, and both the forcing of children and the fear of forcing them, the fear of warping natural abilities, were poor substitutes for that long, careful watchfulness, that checking and balancing and reckoning of accounts, the end of which was that there should be no slipping below a certain level of duty and integrity.

That was what the elders had been unable to teach plausibly since the break between the generations ten or twelve years ago.

He left soon after dinner, but not to go home. He was curious to see Paris by night with clearer and more judicious eyes. He bought a *strapontin* for the Casino and watched Josephine Baker go through her chocolate arabesques.

After an hour he left and strolled toward Montmartre, up the Rue Pigalle into the Place Blanche. The rain had stopped and there were a few people in evening clothes disembarking from taxis in front of cabarets, and *cocottes* prowling singly or in pairs, and many Negroes. He passed a lighted door from which issued music, and stopped with the sense of familiarity; it was Bricktop's, where he had parted with so many hours and so much money. A few doors farther on he found another ancient rendezvous and incautiously put his head inside. Immediately an eager orchestra burst into sound, a pair of professional dancers leaped to their feet and a maître d'hôtel swooped toward him, crying, "Crowd's just arriving, sir!" But he withdrew quickly.

"You have to be damn drunk," he thought.

Zelli's was closed, the bleak and sinister cheap hotels surrounding it were dark; up in the Rue Blanche there was more light and a local, colloquial French crowd. The Poet's Cave had disappeared, but the two great mouths of the Café of Heaven and the Café of Hell still yawned—even devoured, as he watched, the meager contents of a tourist bus—a German, a Japanese, and an American couple who glanced at him with frightened eyes.

So much for the effort and ingenuity of Montmartre. All the catering to vice and waste was on an utterly childish scale, and he suddenly realized the meaning of the word "dissipate"—to dissipate into thin air; to make nothing out of something. In the little hours of the night every move from place to place was an enormous human jump, an increase of paying for the privilege of slower and slower motion.

He remembered thousand-franc notes given to an orchestra for playing a single number, hundred-franc notes tossed to a doorman for calling a cab. But it hadn't been given for nothing.

It had been given, even the most wildly squandered sum, as an offering to destiny that he might not remember the things most worth remembering, the things that now he would always remember—his child taken from his control, his wife escaped to a grave in Vermont.

In the glare of a *brasserie* a woman spoke to him. He bought her some eggs and coffee, and then, eluding her encouraging stare, gave her a twenty-franc note and took a taxi to his hotel.

II

He woke upon a fine fall day—football weather. The depression of yesterday was gone and he liked the people on the streets. At noon he sat opposite Honoria at the Grand Vatel, the only restaurant he could think of not reminiscent of champagne dinners and long luncheons that began at two and ended in a blurred and vague twilight.

"Now, how about vegetables? Oughtn't you to have some vegetables?"

"Well, yes."

"Here's *épinards* and *chou-fleur* and carrots and *haricots*."

"I'd like *choux-fleurs*."

"Wouldn't you like to have two vegetables?"

"I usually only have one at lunch."

The waiter was pretending to be inordinately fond of children. *"Qu'elle est mignonne la petite? Elle parle exactment comme une française."*

"How about dessert? Shall we wait and see?"

The waiter disappeared. Honoria looked at him expectantly.

"What are we going to do?"

"First we're going to that toy store in the Rue St. Honoré and buy you anything you like. And then we're going to the vaudeville at the Empire."

She hesitated. "I like it about the vaudeville, but not the toy store."

"Why not?"

"Well, you brought me this doll." She had it with her. "And I've got lots of things. And we're not rich any more, are we?"

"We never were. But to-day you are to have anything you want."

"All right," she agreed resignedly.

He had always been fond of her, but when there had been her mother and a French nurse he had been inclined to be strict; now he extended himself, reached out for a new tolerance; he must be both parents to her and not shut any of her out of communication.

"I want to get to know you," he said gravely. "First let me introduce myself. My name is Charles J. Wales, of Prague."

"Oh, daddy!" her voice cracked with laughter.

"And who are you, please?" he persisted, and she accepted a rôle immediately: "Honoria Wales, Rue Palatine, Paris."

"Married or single?"

"No, not married. Single."

He indicated the doll. "But I see you have a child, madame."

Unwilling to disinherit it, she took it to her heart and thought quickly: "Yes, I've been married, but I'm not married now. My husband is dead."

He went on quickly, "And the child's name?"

"Simone. That's after my best friend at school."

"I'm very pleased that you're doing so well at school."

"I'm third this month," she boasted. "Elsie"—that was her cousin—"is only about eighteenth, and Richard is about at the bottom."

"You like Richard and Elsie, don't you?"

"Oh, yes. I like Richard quite well and I like her all right."

Cautiously and casually he asked: "And Aunt Marion and Uncle Lincoln —which do you like best?"

"Oh, Uncle Lincoln, I guess."

He was increasingly aware of her presence. As they came in, a murmur of "What an adorable child" followed them, and now the people at the next table bent all their silences upon her, staring as if she were something no more conscious than a flower.

"Why don't I live with you?" she asked suddenly. "Because mamma's dead?"

"You must stay here and learn more French. It would have been hard for daddy to take care of you so well."

"I don't really need much taking care of any more. I do everything for myself."

Going out of the restaurant, a man and a woman unexpectedly hailed him!

"Well, the old Wales!"

"Hello there, Lorraine . . . Dunc."

Sudden ghosts out of the past: Duncan Schaeffer, a friend from college. Lorraine Quarrles, a lovely, pale blond of thirty; one of a crowd who had helped them make months into days in the lavish times of two years ago.

"My husband couldn't come this year," she said, in answer to his question. "We're poor as hell. So he gave me two hundred a month and told me I could do my worst on that. . . . This your little girl?"

"What about sitting down?" Duncan asked.

"Can't do it." He was glad for an excuse. As always, he felt Lorraine's passionate, provocative attraction, but his own rhythm was different now.

"Well, how about dinner?" she asked.

"I'm not free. Give me your address and let me call you."

"Charlie, I believe you're sober," she said judicially. "I honestly believe he's sober, Dunc. Pinch him and see if he's sober."

Charlie indicated Honoria with his head. They both laughed.

"What's your address?" said Duncan skeptically.

He hesitated, unwilling to give the name of his hotel.

"I'm not settled yet. I'd better call you. We're going to see the vaudeville at the Empire."

"There! That's what I want to do," Lorraine said. "I want to see some clowns and acrobats and jugglers. That's just what we'll do, Dunc."

"We've got to do an errand first," said Charlie. "Perhaps we'll see you there."

"All right, you snob. . . . Good-by, beautiful little girl."

"Good-by." Honoria bobbed politely.

Somehow, an unpleasant encounter, Charlie thought. They liked him because he was functioning, because he was serious; they wanted to see him, because he was stronger than they were now, because they wanted to draw a certain sustenance from his strength.

At the Empire, Honoria proudly refused to sit upon her father's folded coat. She was already an individual with a code of her own, and Charlie was more and more absorbed by the desire of putting a little of himself into her before she crystallized utterly. It was hopeless to try to know her in so short a time.

Between the acts they came upon Duncan and Lorraine in the lobby where the band was playing.

"Have a drink?"

"All right, but not up at the bar. We'll take a table."

"The perfect father."

Listening abstractedly to Lorraine, Charlie watched Honoria's eyes leave them all, and he followed them wistfully about the room, wondering what they saw. He met them and she smiled.

"I liked that lemonade," she said.

What had she said? What had he expected? Going home in a taxi afterward, he pulled her over until her head rested against his chest.

"Darling, do you ever think about your mother?"

"Yes, sometimes," she answered vaguely.

"I don't want you to forget her. Have you got a picture of her?"

"Yes, I think so. Anyhow, Aunt Marion has. Why don't you want me to forget her?"

"She loved you very much."

"I loved her too."

They were silent for a moment.

"Daddy, I want to come and live with you," she said suddenly.

His heart leaped; he had wanted it to come like this.

"Aren't you perfectly happy?"

"Yes, but I love you better than anybody. And you love me better than anybody, don't you, now that mummy's dead?"

"Of course I do. But you won't always like me best, honey. You'll grow up and meet somebody your own age and go marry him and forget you ever had a daddy."

"Yes, that's true," she agreed tranquilly.

He didn't go in. He was coming back at nine o'clock and he wanted to keep himself fresh and new for the thing he must say then.

"When you're safe inside, just show yourself in that window."

"All right. Good-by, dads, dads, dads, dads."

He waited in the dark street until she appeared, all warm and glowing, in the window above and kissed her fingers out into the night.

III

They were waiting. Marion sat behind empty coffee cups in a dignified black dinner dress that just faintly suggested mourning. Lincoln was walking up and down with the animation of one who had already been talking. They were as anxious as he was to get into the question. He opened it almost immediately:

"I suppose you know what I want to see you about—why I really came to Paris."

Marion fiddled with the glass grapes on her necklace and frowned.

"I'm awfully anxious to have a home," he continued. "And I'm awfully anxious to have Honoria in it. I appreciate your taking in Honoria for her mother's sake, but things have changed now"—he hesitated and then continued strongly—"changed radically with me, and I want to ask you to reconsider the matter. It would be silly for me to deny that about two years ago I was acting badly—"

Marion looked up at him with hard eyes.

"—but all that's over. As I told you, I haven't had more than a drink a day for over a year, and I take that drink deliberately, so that the idea of alcohol won't get too big in my imagination. You see the idea?"

"No," said Marion succinctly.

"It's a sort of stunt I set myself. It keeps the matter in proportion."

"I get you," said Lincoln. "You don't want to admit it's got any attraction for you."

"Something like that. Sometimes I forget and don't take it. But I try to take it. Anyhow, I couldn't afford to drink in my position. The people I represent are more than satisfied with what I've done, and I'm bringing my sister over from Burlington to keep house for me, and I want awfully to have Honoria too. You know that even when her mother and I weren't getting along well I never let anything that happened touch Honoria. I know she's fond of me and I know I'm able to take care of her and—well, there you are. How do you feel about it?"

He knew that now he would have to take a beating. It would last an hour or two hours, and it would be difficult, but if he modulated his inevitable resentment to the chastened attitude of the reformed sinner, he might win his point in the end. "Keep your temper," he told himself. "You don't want to be justified. You want Honoria."

Lincoln spoke first: "We've been talking it over ever since we got your letter last month. We're happy to have Honoria here. She's a dear little thing, and we're glad to be able to help her, but of course that isn't the question—"

Marion interrupted suddenly. "How long are you going to stay sober, Charlie?" she asked.

"Permanently, I hope."

"How can anybody count on that?"

"You know I never did drink heavily until I gave up business and came over here with nothing to do. Then Helen and I began to run around with—"

"Please leave Helen out of it. I can't bear to hear you talk about her like that."

He stared at her grimly; he had never been certain how fond of each other the sisters were in life.

"My drinking only lasted about a year and a half—from the time we came over until I—collapsed."

"It was time enough."

"It was time enough," he agreed.

"My duty is entirely to Helen," she said. "I try to think what she would have wanted me to do. Frankly, from the night you did that terrible thing you haven't really existed for me. I can't help that. She was my sister."

"Yes."

"When she was dying she asked me to look out for Honoria. If you hadn't been in a sanitarium then, it might have helped matters."

He had no answer.

"I'll never in my life be able to forget the morning when Helen knocked at my door, soaked to the skin and shivering, and said you'd locked her out."

Charlie gripped the sides of the chair. This was more difficult than he expected; he wanted to launch out into a long expostulation and explanation, but he only said: "The night I locked her out—" and she interrupted, "I don't feel up to going over that again."

After a moment's silence Lincoln said: "We're getting off the subject. You want Marion to set aside her legal guardianship and give you Honoria. I think the main point for her is whether she has confidence in you or not."

"I don't blame Marion," Charlie said slowly, "but I think she can have entire confidence in me. I had a good record up to three years ago. Of course, it's within human possibilities I might go wrong any time. But if we wait much longer I'll lose Honoria's childhood and my chance for a home. I'll simply lose her, don't you see?"

"Yes, I see," said Lincoln.

"Why didn't you think of all this before?" Marion asked.

"I suppose I did, from time to time, but Helen and I were getting along badly. When I consented to the guardianship, I was flat on my back in a sanitarium and the market had cleaned me out of every sou. I knew I'd acted badly, and I thought if it would bring any peace to Helen, I'd agree to anything. But now it's different. I'm well, I'm functioning, I'm behaving damn well, so far as—"

"Please don't swear at me," Marion said.

He looked at her, startled. With each remark the force of her dislike became more and more apparent. She had built up all her fear of life into one wall and faced it toward him. This trivial reproof was possibly the result of some trouble with the cook several hours before. Charlie became increasingly alarmed at leaving Honoria in this atmosphere of hostility against himself; sooner or later it would come out, in a word here, a shake of the head there, and some of that distrust would be irrevocably implanted in Honoria. But he pulled his temper down out of his face and shut it up inside him; he had won a point, for Lincoln realized the absurdity of Marion's remark and asked her lightly since when she had objected to the word "damn."

"Another thing," Charlie said: "I'm able to give her certain advantages now. I'm going to take a French governess to Prague with me. I've got a lease on a new apartment—"

He stopped, realizing that he was blundering. They couldn't be expected to accept with equanimity the fact that his income was again twice as large as their own.

"I suppose you can give her more luxuries than we can," said Marion. "When you were throwing away money we were living along watching every ten francs. . . . I suppose you'll start doing it again."

"Oh, no," he said. "I've learned. I worked hard for ten years, you know—until I got lucky in the market, like so many people. Terribly lucky. It didn't seem any use working any more, so I quit. It won't happen again."

There was a long silence. All of them felt their nerves straining, and for the first time in a year Charlie wanted a drink. He was sure now that Lincoln Peters wanted him to have his child.

Marion shuddered suddenly; part of her saw that Charlie's feet were planted on the earth now, and her own maternal feeling recognized the naturalness of his desire; but she had lived for a long time with a prejudice —a prejudice founded on a curious disbelief in her sister's happiness, and which in the shock of one terrible night, had turned to hatred for him. It had all happened at a point in her life where the discouragement of ill-health and adverse circumstances made it necessary for her to believe in tangible villainy and a tangible villain.

"I can't help what I think!" she cried out suddenly. "How much you were responsible for Helen's death, I don't know. It's something you'll have to square with your own conscience."

An electric current of agony surged through him; for a moment he was almost on his feet, an unuttered sound echoing in his throat. He hung on to himself for a moment, another moment.

"Hold on there," said Lincoln uncomfortably. "I never thought you were responsible for that."

"Helen died of heart trouble," Charlie said dully.

"Yes, heart trouble." Marion spoke as if the phrase had another meaning for her.

Then, in the flatness that followed her outburst, she saw him plainly and she knew he had somehow arrived at control over the situation. Glancing at her husband, she found no help from him, and as abruptly as if it were a matter of no importance, she threw up the sponge.

"Do what you like!" she cried, springing up from her chair. "She's your child. I'm not the person to stand in your way. I think if it were my child I'd rather see her—" She managed to check herself. "You two decide it. I can't stand this. I'm sick. I'm going to bed."

She hurried from the room; after a moment Lincoln said:

"This has been a hard day for her. You know how strongly she feels—" His voice was almost apologetic: "When a woman gets an idea in her head."

"Of course."

"It's going to be all right. I think she sees now that you—can provide for the child, and so we can't very well stand in your way or Honoria's way."

"Thank you, Lincoln."

"I'd better go along and see how she is."

"I'm going."

He was still trembling when he reached the street, but a walk down the Rue Bonaparte to the quais set him up, and as he crossed the Seine, dotted with many cold moons, he felt exultant. But back in his room he couldn't sleep. The image of Helen haunted him. Helen whom he had loved so until they had senselessly begun to abuse each other's love and tear it into shreds. On that terrible February night that Marion remembered so vividly, a slow quarrel that had gone on for hours. There was a scene at the Florida, and then he attempted to take her home, and then Helen kissed Ted Wilder at a table, and what she had hysterically said. Charlie's departure and, on his arrival home, his turning the key in the lock in wild anger. How could he know she would arrive an hour later alone, that there would be a snowstorm in which she wandered about in slippers for an hour, too confused to find a taxi? Then the aftermath, her escaping pneumonia by a miracle, and all the attendant horror. They were "reconciled," but that was the beginning of the end, and Marion, who had seen with her own eyes and who imagined it to be one of many scenes from her sister's martyrdom, never forgot.

Going over it again brought Helen nearer, and in the white, soft light that steals upon half sleep near morning he found himself talking to her again. She said that he was perfectly right about Honoria and that she wanted Honoria to be with him. She said she was glad he was being good and doing better. She said a lot of other things—very friendly things—but she was in a swing in a white dress, and swinging faster and faster all the time, so that at the end he could not hear clearly all that she said.

IV

He woke up feeling happy. The door of the world was open again. He made plans, vistas, futures for Honoria and himself, but suddenly he grew sad, remembering all the plans he and Helen had made. She had not planned to die. The present was the thing—work to do and some one to love. But not to love too much, for Charlie had read in D. H. Lawrence about the injury that a father can do to a daughter or a mother to a son by attaching them too closely. Afterward, out in the world, the child would seek in the marriage partner the same blind, unselfish tenderness and, failing in all human probability to find it, develop a grudge against love and life.

It was another bright, crisp day. He called Lincoln Peters at the bank where he worked and asked if he could count on taking Honoria when he left for Prague. Lincoln agreed that there was no reason for delay. One thing—the legal guardianship. Marion wanted to retain that a while longer. She was upset by the whole matter, and it would oil things if she felt that the situation was still in her control for another year. Charlie agreed, wanting only the tangible, visible child.

Then the question of a governess. Charlie sat in a gloomy agency and talked to a buxom Breton peasant whom he knew he couldn't endure. There were others whom he could see to-morrow.

He lunched with Lincoln Peters at the Griffon, trying to keep down his exultation.

"There's nothing quite like your own child," Lincoln said. "But you understand how Marion feels too."

"She's forgotten how hard I worked for seven years there," Charlie said. "She just remembers one night."

"There's another thing." Lincoln hesitated. "While you and Helen were tearing around Europe throwing money away, we were just getting along. I didn't touch any of the prosperity because I never got ahead enough to carry anything but my insurance. I think Marion felt there was some kind of injustice in it—you not even working and getting richer and richer."

"It went just as quick as it came," said Charlie.

"A lot did. And a lot of it stayed in the hands of *chasseurs* and saxophone players and maîtres d'hôtel—well, the big party's over now. I just said that to explain Marion's feeling about those crazy years. If you drop in about six o'clock to-night before Marion's too tired, we'll settle the details on the spot."

Back at his hotel, Charlie took from his pocket a *pneumatique* that Lincoln had given him at luncheon. It had been redirected by Paul from the hotel bar.

> Dear Charlie:
>
> You were so strange when we saw you the other day that I wondered if I did something to offend you. If so, I'm not conscious of it. In fact, I have

thought about you too much for the last year, and it's always been in the back of my mind that I might see you if I came over here. We did have such good times that crazy spring, like the night you and I stole the butcher's tricycle, and the time we tried to call on the president and you had the old derby and the wire cane. Everybody seems so old lately, but I don't feel old a bit. Couldn't we get together sometime to-day for old time's sake? I've got a vile hang-over for the moment, but will be feeling better this afternoon and will look for you about five at the bar.

Always devotedly,
Lorraine.

His first feeling was one of awe that he had actually, in his mature years, stolen a tricycle and pedaled Lorraine all over the Étoile between the small hours and dawn. In retrospect it was a nightmare. Locking out Helen didn't fit in with any other act of his life, but the tricycle incident did—it was one of many. How many weeks or months of dissipation to arrive at that condition of utter irresponsibility?

He tried to picture how Lorraine had appeared to him then—very attractive; so much so that Helen had been jealous. Yesterday, in the restaurant, she had seemed so trite, blurred, worn away. He emphatically did not want to see her, and he was glad no one knew at what hotel he was staying. It was a relief to think of Honoria, to think of Sundays spent with her and of saying good morning to her and of knowing she was there in his house at night, breathing quietly in the darkness.

At five he took a taxi and bought presents for all the Peterses—a piquant cloth doll, a box of Roman soldiers, flowers for Marion, big linen handkerchiefs for Lincoln.

He saw, when he arrived in the apartment, that Marion had accepted the inevitable. She greeted him now as though he were a recalcitrant member of the family, rather than a menacing outsider. Honoria had been told she was going, and Charlie was glad to see that her tact was sufficient to conceal her excessive happiness. Only on his lap did she whisper her delight and the question "When?" before she slipped away.

He and Marion were alone for a minute in the room, and on an impulse he spoke out boldly:

"Family quarrels are bitter things. They don't go according to my rules. They're not like aches or wounds; they're more like splits in the skin that won't heal because there's not enough material. I wish you and I could be on better terms."

"Some things are hard to forget," she answered. "It's a question of confidence. If you behave yourself in the future I won't have any criticism." There was no answer to this, and presently she asked, "When do you propose to take her?"

"As soon as I can get a governess. I hoped the day after tomorrow."

"That's impossible. I've got to get her things in shape. Not before Saturday."

He yielded. Coming back into the room, Lincoln offered him a drink.

"I'll take my daily whisky," he said.

It was warm here, it was a home, people together by the fire. The children felt very safe and important; the mother and father were serious, watchful. They had things to do for the children more important than his visit here. A spoonful of medicine was, after all, more important than the strained relations between Marion and himself. They were not dull people, but they were very much in the grip of life and circumstances, and their gestures as they turned in a cramped space lacked largeness and grace. He wondered if he couldn't do something to get Lincoln out of that rut at the bank.

There was a long peal at the doorbell; the maid crossed the room and went down the corridor. The door opened upon another long ring, and then voices, and the three in the salon looked up expectantly; Richard moved to bring the corridor within his range of vision, and Marion rose. Then the maid came along the corridor, closely followed by the voices, which developed under the light into Duncan Schaeffer and Lorraine Quarrles.

They were gay, they were hilarious, they were roaring with laughter. For a moment Charlie was astounded; then he realized they had got the address he had left at the bar.

"Ah-h-h!" Duncan wagged his finger roguishly at Charlie. "Ah-h-h!"

They both slid down into another cascade of laughter. Anxious and at a loss, Charlie shook hands with them quickly and presented them to Lincoln and Marion. Marion nodded, scarcely speaking. She had drawn back a step toward the fire; her little girl stood beside her, and Marion put an arm about her shoulder.

With growing annoyance at the intrusion, Charlie waited for them to explain themselves. After some concentration Duncan said:

"We came to take you to dinner. Lorraine and I insist that all this shi-shi, cagy business got to stop."

Charlie came closer to them, as if to force them backward down the corridor.

"Sorry, but I can't. Tell me where you'll be and we'll call you in half an hour."

This made no impression. Lorraine sat down suddenly on the side of a chair, and focusing her eyes on Richard, cried, "Oh, what a nice little boy! Come here, little boy." Richard glanced at his mother, but did not move. With a perceptible shrug of her shoulders, Lorraine turned back to Charlie:

"Come on out to dinner. Be yourself, Charlie. Come on."

"How about a little drink?" said Duncan to the room at large.

Lincoln Peters had been somewhat uneasily occupying himself by swinging Honoria from side to side with her feet off the ground.

"I'm sorry, but there isn't a thing in the house," he said. "We just this minute emptied the only bottle."

"All the more reason for coming to dinner," Lorraine assured Charlie.

"I can't," said Charlie, almost sharply. "You two go have dinner and I'll phone you."

"Oh, you will, will you?" Her voice became suddenly unpleasant. "All right, we'll go along. But I remember, when you used to hammer on my door, I used to be enough of a good sport to give you a drink. Come on, Dunc."

Still in slow motion, with blurred, angry faces, with uncertain feet, they retired along the corridor.

"Good night," Charlie said.

"Good night!" responded Lorraine emphatically.

When he went back into the salon Marion had not moved, only now her son was standing in the circle of her other arm. Lincoln was still swinging Honoria back and forth like a pendulum from side to side.

"What an outrage!" Charlie broke out. "What an absolute outrage!"

Neither of them answered. Charlie dropped down into an armchair, picked up his drink, set it down again and said:

"People I haven't seen for two years having the colossal nerve—"

He broke off. Marion had made the sound "Oh!" in one swift, furious breath, turned her body from him with a jerk and left the room.

Lincoln set down Honoria carefully.

"You children go in and start your soup," he said, and when they obeyed, he said to Charlie:

"Marion's not well and she can't stand shocks. That kind of people make her really physically sick."

"I didn't tell them to come here. They wormed this address out of Paul at the bar. They deliberately—"

"Well, it's too bad. It doesn't help matters. Excuse me a minute."

Left alone, Charlie sat tense in his chair. In the next room he could hear the children eating, talking in monosyllables, already oblivious of the scene among their elders. He heard a murmur of conversation from a farther room and then the ticking bell of a phone picked up, and in a panic he moved to the other side of the room and out of earshot.

In a minute Lincoln came back. "Look here, Charlie. I think we'd better call off dinner for to-night. Marion's in bad shape."

"Is she angry with me?"

"Sort of," he said, almost roughly. "She's not strong and—"

"You mean she's changed her mind about Honoria?"

"She's pretty bitter right now. I don't know. You phone me at the bank to-morrow."

"I wish you'd explain to her I never dreamed these people would come here. I'm just as sore as you are."

"I couldn't explain anything to her now."

Charlie got up. He took his coat and hat and started down the corridor.

Then he opened the door of the dining room and said in a strange voice, "Good night, children."

Honoria rose and ran around the table to hug him.

"Good night, sweetheart," he said vaguely, and then trying to make his voice more tender, trying to conciliate something, "Good night, dear children."

V

Charlie went directly to the bar with the furious idea of finding Lorraine and Duncan, but they were not there, and he realized that in any case there was nothing he could do. He had not touched his drink at the Peterses,' and now he ordered a whisky-and-soda. Paul came over to say hello.

"It's a great change," he said sadly. "We do about half the business we did. So many fellows I hear about back in the States lost everything, maybe not in the first crash, but then in the second, and now when everything keeps going down. Your friend George Hardt lost every cent, I hear. Are you back in the States?"

"No, I'm in business in Prague."

"I heard that you lost a lot in the crash."

"I did," and he added grimly, "but I lost everything I wanted in the boom."

"Selling short."

"Something like that."

Again the memory of those days swept over him like a nightmare—the people they had met traveling; then people who couldn't add a row of figures or speak a coherent sentence. The little man Helen had consented to dance with at the ship's party, who had insulted her ten feet from the table; the human mosaic of pearls who sat behind them at the Russian ballet and, when the curtain rose on a scene, remarked to her companion: "Luffly; just luffly. Zomebody ought to baint a bicture of it." Men who locked their wives out in the snow, because the snow of twenty-nine wasn't real snow. If you didn't want it to be snow, you just paid some money.

He went to the phone and called the Peters apartment; Lincoln himself answered.

"I called up because, as you can imagine, this thing is on my mind. Has Marion said anything definite?"

"Marion's sick," Lincoln answered shortly. "I know this thing isn't altogether your fault, but I can't have her go to pieces about this. I'm afraid we'll have to let it slide for six months; I can't take the chance of working her up to this state again."

"I see."

"I'm sorry, Charlie."

He went back to his table. His whisky glass was empty, but he shook his head when Alix looked at it questioningly. There wasn't much he could do now except send Honoria some things; he would send her a lot of things tomorrow. He thought rather angrily that that was just money—he had given so many people money.

"No, no more," he said to another waiter. "What do I owe you?"

He would come back some day; they couldn't make him pay forever. But he wanted his child, and nothing was much good now, beside that fact. He wasn't young any more, with a lot of nice thoughts and dreams to have by himself. He was absolutely sure Helen wouldn't have wanted him to be so alone.

A Country Love Story

An antique sleigh stood in the yard, snow after snow banked up against its eroded runners. Here and there upon the bleached and splintery seat were wisps of horsehair and scraps of the black leather that had once upholstered it. It bore, with all its jovial curves, an air not so much of desuetude as of slowed-down dash, as if weary horses, unable to go another step, had at last stopped here. The sleigh had come with the house. The former owner, a gifted businesswoman from Castine who bought old houses and sold them again with all their pitfalls still intact, had said when she was showing them the place, "A picturesque detail, I think," and, waving it away, had turned to the well, which, with enthusiasm and at considerable length, she said had never gone dry. Actually, May and Daniel had found the detail more distracting than picturesque, so nearly kin was it to outdoor arts and crafts, and when the woman, as they departed in her car, gestured toward it again and said, "Paint that up a bit with something cheery and it will really add no end to your yard," simultaneous shudders coursed them. They had planned to remove the sleigh before they did anything else.

But partly because there were more important things to be done, and partly because they did not know where to put it (a sleigh could not, in the usual sense of the words, be thrown away), and partly because it seemed defiantly a part of the yard, as entitled to be there permanently as the trees, they did nothing about it. Throughout the summer they saw birds briefly pause on its rakish front and saw the fresh rains wash its runners; in the

A COUNTRY LOVE STORY Reprinted with the permission of Farrar, Straus & Giroux, Inc. from *The Collected Stories of Jean Stafford,* copyright © 1950, 1969 by Jean Stafford, first published in the *New Yorker.*

autumn they watched the golden leaves fill the seat and nestle dryly down; and now, with the snow, they watched this new accumulation.

The sleigh was visible from the windows of the big, bright kitchen where they ate all their meals and, sometimes too bemused with country solitude to talk, they gazed out at it, forgetting their food in speculating on its history. It could have been driven cavalierly by the scion of some sea captain's family, or it could have been used soberly to haul the household's Unitarians to church or to take the womenfolk around the countryside on errands of good will. They did not speak of what its office might have been, and the fact of their silence was often nettlesome to May, for she felt they were silent too much of the time; a little morosely, she thought, If something as absurd and as provocative as this at which we look together—and which is, even though we didn't want it, our own property—cannot bring us to talk, what can? But she did not disturb Daniel in his private musings; she held her tongue, and out of the corner of her eye she watched him watch the winter cloak the sleigh, and, as if she were computing a difficult sum in her head, she tried to puzzle out what it was that had stilled tongues that earlier, before Daniel's illness, had found the days too short to communicate all they were eager to say.

It had been Daniel's doctor's idea, not theirs, that had brought them to the solemn hinterland to stay after all the summer gentry had departed in their beach wagons. The Northern sun, the pristine air, the rural walks and soundless nights, said Dr. Tellenbach, perhaps pining for his native Switzerland, would do more for the "Professor's" convalescent lung than all the doctors and clinics in the world. Privately he had added to May that after so long a season in the sanitarium (Daniel had been there a year), where everything was tuned to a low pitch, it would be difficult and it might be shattering for "the boy" (not now the "Professor," although Daniel, nearly fifty, was his wife's senior by twenty years and Dr. Tellenbach's by ten) to go back at once to the excitements and the intrigues of the university, to what, with finicking humor, the Doctor called "the omnium-gatherum of the school master's life." The rigors of a country winter would be as nothing, he insisted, when compared to the strain of feuds and cocktail parties. All professors wanted to write books, didn't they? Surely Daniel, a historian with all the material in the world at his fingertips, must have something up his sleeve that could be the *raison d'être* for this year away? May said she supposed he had, she was not sure. She could hear the reluctance in her voice as she escaped the Doctor's eyes and gazed through his windows at the mountains behind the sanitarium. In the dragging months Daniel had been gone, she had taken solace in imagining the time when they *would* return to just that pandemonium the Doctor so deplored, and because it had been pandemonium on the smallest and most discreet scale, she smiled through her disappointment at the little man's Swiss innocence and explained that they had always lived quietly, seldom dining out or entertaining more than twice a week.

"Twice a week!" He was appalled.

"But I'm afraid," she had protested, "that he would find a second year of inactivity intolerable. He does intend to write a book, but he means to write it in England, and we can't go to England now."

"England!" Dr. Tellenbach threw up his hands. "Good *air* is my recommendation for your husband. Good air and little talk."

She said, "It's talk he needs, I should think, after all this time of communing only with himself except when I came to visit."

He had looked at her with exaggerated patience, and then, courtly but authoritative, he said, "I hope you will not think I importune when I tell you that I am very well acquainted with your husband, and, as his physician, I order this retreat. *He* quite agrees."

Stung to see that there was a greater degree of understanding between Daniel and Dr. Tellenbach than between Daniel and herself, May had objected further, citing an occasion when her husband had put his head in his hands and mourned, "I hear talk of nothing but sputum cups and X-rays. Aren't people interested in the state of the world any more?"

But Dr. Tellenbach had been adamant, and at the end, when she had risen to go, he said, "You are bound to find him changed a little. A long illness removes a thoughtful man from his fellow-beings. It is like living with an exacting mistress who is not content with half a man's attention but must claim it all." She had thought his figure of speech absurd and disdained to ask him what he meant.

Actually, when the time came for them to move into the new house and she found no alterations in her husband but found, on the other hand, much pleasure in their country life, she began to forgive Dr. Tellenbach. In the beginning, it was like a second honeymoon, for they had moved to a part of the North where they had never been and they explored it together, sharing its charming sights and sounds. Moreover, they had never owned a house before but had always lived in city apartments, and though the house they bought was old and derelict, its lines and doors and window lights were beautiful, and they were possessed by it. All through the summer, they reiterated, "To think that we own all of this! That it actually belongs to us!" And they wandered from room to room marveling at their windows, from none of which was it possible to see an ugly sight. They looked to the south upon a river, to the north upon a lake; to the west of them were pine woods where the wind forever sighed, voicing a vain entreaty; and to the east a rich man's long meadow that ran down a hill to his old, magisterial house. It was true, even in those bewitched days, that there were times on the lake, when May was gathering water lilies as Daniel slowly rowed, that she had seen on his face a look of abstraction and she had known that he was worlds away, in his memories, perhaps, of his illness and the sanitarium (of which he would never speak) or in the thought of the book he was going to write as soon, he said, as the winter set in and there was nothing to do but work. Momentarily the look frightened her and she remembered the Doctor's words, but then, immediately herself again in the security of married love, she caught at another water lily and pulled at its long stem. Companionably, they gardened, taking special pride in the nicotiana that sent its nighttime fragrance into their bedroom. Together, and with fascination, they consulted carpenters, plasterers, and chimney sweeps. In the blue evenings they read at ease, hearing no sound but that of the night birds—the loons on the lake and the owls in the tops of trees. When the days began to cool and shorten, a cricket came to bless their house, nightly singing behind the kitchen stove. They got two fat and idle tabby cats, who lay insensible beside the fireplace and only stirred themselves to purr perfunctorily.

Because they had not moved in until July and by that time the workmen of the region were already engaged, most of the major repairs of the house were to be postponed until the spring, and in October, when May and Daniel had done all they could by themselves and Daniel had begun his own work, May suddenly found herself without occupation. Whole days might pass when she did nothing more than cook three meals and walk a little in the autumn mist and pet the cats and wait for Daniel to come down from his upstairs study to talk to her. She began to think with longing of the crowded days in Boston before Daniel was sick, and even in the year past, when he had been away and she had gone to concerts and recitals and had done good deeds for crippled children and had endlessly shopped for presents to lighten the tedium of her husband's unwilling exile. And, longing, she was remorseful, as if by desiring another she betrayed this life, and, remorseful, she hid away in sleep. Sometimes she slept for hours in the daytime, imitating the cats, and when at last she got up, she had to push away the dense sleep as if it were a door.

One day at lunch, she asked Daniel to take a long walk with her that afternoon to a farm where the owner smoked his own sausages.

"You never go outdoors," she said, "and Dr. Tellenbach said you must. Besides, it's a lovely day."

"I can't," he said. "I'd like to, but I can't. I'm busy. You go alone."

Overtaken by a gust of loneliness, she cried, "Oh, Daniel, I have nothing to *do!*"

A moment's silence fell, and then he said, "I'm sorry to put you through this, my dear, but you must surely admit that it's not my fault I got sick."

In her shame, her rapid, overdone apologies, her insistence that nothing mattered in the world except his health and peace of mind, she made everything worse, and at last he said shortly to her, "Stop being a child, May. Let's just leave each other alone."

This outbreak, the very first in their marriage of five years, was the beginning of a series. Hardly a day passed that they did not bicker over something; they might dispute a question of fact, argue a matter of taste, catch each other out in an inaccuracy, and every quarrel ended with Daniel's saying to her,

"Why don't you leave me alone?" Once he said, "I've been sick and now I'm busy and I'm no longer young enough to shift the focus of my mind each time it suits your whim." Afterward, there were always apologies, and then Daniel went back to his study and did not open the door of it again until the next meal. Finally, it seemed to her that love, the very center of their being, was choked off, overgrown, invisible. And silent with hostility or voluble with trivial reproach, they tried to dig it out impulsively and could not—could only maul it in its unkempt grave. Daniel, in his withdrawal from her and from the house, was preoccupied with his research, of which he never spoke except to say that it would bore her, and most of the time, so it appeared to May, he did not worry over what was happening to them. She felt the cold old house somehow enveloping her as if it were their common enemy, maliciously bent on bringing them to disaster. Sunken in faithlessness, they stared, at mealtimes, atrophied within the present hour, at the irrelevant and whimsical sleigh that stood abandoned in the mammoth winter.

May found herself thinking, If we redeemed it and painted it, our house would have something in common with Henry Ford's Wayside Inn. And I might make this very observation to him and he might greet it with disdain and we might once again be able to talk to each other. Perhaps we could talk of Williamsburg and how we disapproved of it. Her mind went toiling on. Williamsburg was part of our honeymoon trip; somewhere our feet were entangled in suckers as we stood kissing under a willow tree. Soon she found that she did not care for this line of thought, nor did she care what his response to it might be. In her imagined conversations with Daniel, she never spoke of the sleigh. To the thin, ill scholar whose scholarship and illness had usurped her place, she had gradually taken a weighty but unviolent dislike.

The discovery of this came, not surprising her, on Christmas Day. The knowledge sank like a plummet, and at the same time she was thinking about the sleigh, connecting it with the smell of the barn on damp days, and she thought perhaps it had been drawn by the very animals who had been stabled there and had pervaded the timbers with their odor. There must have been much life within this house once—but long ago. The earth immediately behind the barn was said by everyone to be extremely rich because of the horses, although there had been none there for over fifty years. Thinking of this soil, which earlier she had eagerly sifted through her fingers, May now realized that she had no wish for the spring to come, no wish to plant a garden, and, branching out at random, she found she had no wish to see the sea again, or children, or favorite pictures, or even her own face on a happy day. For a minute or two, she was almost enraptured in this state of no desire, but then, purged swiftly of her cynicism, she knew it to be false, knew that actually she did have a desire—the desire for a desire. And now she felt that she was stationary in a whirlpool, and at the very moment she conceived the notion a bit of wind brought to the seat of the sleigh the final leaf from the elm tree that stood beside it. It crossed her mind that she might consider the wood of the sleigh in its juxtaposition to the living tree and to the horses, who, although they were long since dead, reminded her of their passionate, sweating, running life every time she went to the barn for firewood.

They sat this morning in the kitchen full of sun, and, speaking not to him but to the sleigh, to icicles, to the dark, motionless pine woods, she said, "I wonder if on a day like this they used to take the pastor home after lunch." Daniel gazed abstractedly at the bright-silver drifts beside the well and said nothing. Presently a wagon went past hauled by two oxen with bells on their yoke. This was the hour they always passed, taking to an unknown destination an aged man in a fur hat and an aged woman in a shawl. May and Daniel listened.

Suddenly, with impromptu anger, Daniel said, "What did you just say?"

"Nothing," she said. And then, after a pause, "It would be lovely at Jamaica Pond today."

He wheeled on her and pounded the table with his fist. "I did not ask for this!" The color rose feverishly to his thin cheeks and his breath was agitated. "You are trying to make me sick again. It was wonderful, wasn't it, for you while I was gone?"

"Oh, no, no! Oh, no, Daniel, it was hell!"

"Then, by the same token, this must be heaven." He smiled, the professor catching out a student in a fallacy.

"Heaven." She said the word bitterly.

"Then why do you stay here?" he cried.

It was a cheap impasse, desolate, true, unfair. She did not answer him. After a while he said, "I almost believe there's something you haven't told me."

She began to cry at once, blubbering across the table at him. "You have said that before. What am I to say? What have I done?"

He looked at her, impervious to her tears, without mercy and yet without contempt. "I don't know. But you've done something."

It was as if she were looking through someone else's scrambled closets and bureau drawers for an object that had not been named to her, but nowhere could she find her gross offense.

Domestically she asked him if he would have more coffee and he peremptorily refused and demanded, "Will you tell me why it is you must badger me? Is it a compulsion? Can't you control it? Are you going mad?"

From that day onward, May felt a certain stirring of life within her solitude, and now and again, looking up from a book to see if the damper on the stove was right, to listen to a rat renovating its house-within-a-house, to watch the belled oxen pass, she nursed her wound, hugged it, repeated his awful words exactly as he had said them, reproduced the way his wasted lips had looked and his bright, farsighted eyes. She could not read for long at any time, nor could she sew. She cared little now for planning changes in her house; she had meant to sand the painted floors to uncover the wood of the wide boards and she had imagined how the long, paneled windows of the drawing room would look when yellow velvet curtains hung there in the spring. Now, schooled by silence and indifference, she was immune to disrepair and to the damage done by the wind and snow, and she looked, as Daniel did, without dislike upon the old and nasty wallpaper and upon the shabby kitchen floor. One day, she knew that the sleigh would stay where it was so long as they stayed there. From every thought, she returned to her deep, bleeding injury. He had asked her if she were going mad.

She repaid him in the dark afternoons while he was closeted away in his study, hardly making a sound save when he added wood to his fire or paced a little, deep in thought. She sat at the kitchen table looking at the sleigh, and she gave Daniel insult for his injury by imagining a lover. She did not imagine his face, but she imagined his clothing, which would be costly and in the best of taste, and his manner, which would be urbane and anticipatory of her least whim, and his clever speech, and his adept courtship that would begin the moment he looked at the sleigh and said, "I must get rid of that for you at once." She might be a widow, she might be divorced, she might be committing adultery. Certainly there was no need to specify in an affair so securely legal. There was no need, that is, up to a point, and then the point came when she took in the fact that she not only believed in this lover but loved him and depended wholly on his companionship. She complained to him of Daniel and he consoled her; she told him stories of her girlhood, when she had gaily gone to parties, squired by boys her own age; she dazzled him sometimes with the wise comments she made on the books she read. It came to be true that if she so much as looked at the sleigh, she was weakened, failing with starvation.

Often, about her daily tasks of cooking food and washing dishes and tending the fires and shopping in the general store of the village, she thought she should watch her step, that it was this sort of thing that *did* make one go mad; for a while, then, she went back to Daniel's question, sharpening its razor edge. But she could not corral her alien thoughts and she trembled as she bought split peas, fearful that the old men loafing by the stove could see the incubus of her sins beside her. She could not avert such thoughts when they rushed upon her sometimes at tea with one of the old religious ladies of the neighborhood, so that, in the middle of a conversation about a deaconess in Bath, she retired from them, seeking her lover, who came, faceless, with his arms outstretched, even as she sat up straight in a Boston rocker, even as she accepted another cup of tea. She lingered over the cake plates and the simple talk, postponing her return to her own house and to Daniel, whom she continually betrayed.

It was not long after she recognized her love that she began to wake up even before the dawn and to be all day quick to everything, observant of all the signs of age and eccentricity in her husband, and she compared him in every particular—to his humiliation, in her eyes—with the man whom now it seemed to her she had always loved at fever pitch.

Once when Daniel, in a rare mood, kissed her, she drew back involuntarily and he said gently, "I wish I knew what you had done, poor dear." He looked as if for written words in her face.

"You said you knew," she said, terrified.

"I do."

"Then why do you wish you knew?" Her baffled voice was high and frantic. "You don't talk sense!"

"I do," he said sedately. "I talk sense always. It is you who are oblique." Her eyes stole like a sneak to the sleigh. "But I wish I knew your motive," he said impartially.

For a minute, she felt that they were two maniacs answering each other questions that had not been asked, never touching the matter at hand because they did not know what the matter was. But in the next moment, when he turned back to her spontaneously and clasped her head between his hands and said, like a tolerant father, "I forgive you, darling, because you don't know how you persecute me. No one knows except the sufferer what this sickness is," she knew again, helplessly, that they were not harmonious even in their aberrations.

These days of winter came and went, and on each of them, after breakfast and as the oxen passed, he accused her of her concealed misdeed. She could no longer truthfully deny that she was guilty, for she was in love, and she heard the subterfuge in her own voice and felt the guilty fever in her veins. Daniel knew it, too, and watched her. When she was alone, she felt her lover's presence protecting her—when she walked past the stiff spiraea, with icy cobwebs hung between its twigs, down to the lake, where the black, unmeasured water was hidden beneath a lid of ice; when she walked, instead, to the salt river to see the tar-paper shacks where the men caught smelt through the ice; when she walked in the dead dusk up the hill from the store, catching her breath the moment she saw the sleigh. But sometimes this splendid being mocked her when, freezing with fear of the consequences of her sin, she ran up the stairs to Daniel's room and burrowed her head in his shoulder and cried, "Come downstairs! I'm lonely, please come down!" But he would never come, and at last, bitterly, calmed by his calmly inquisitive regard, she went back alone and stood at the kitchen window, coyly half hidden behind the curtains.

For months she lived with her daily dishonor, rattled, ashamed, stubbornly clinging to her secret. But she grew more and more afraid when, oftener and oftener, Daniel said, "Why do you lie to me? What does this mood of yours mean?" and she could no longer sleep. In the raw nights, she lay straight beside him as he slept, and she stared at the ceiling, as bright as the snow it reflected, and tried not to think of the sleigh out there under the elm tree but could think only of it and of the man, her lover, who was connected with it somehow. She said to herself, as she listened to his breathing, "If I confessed to Daniel, he would understand that I was lonely and he would comfort me, saying, 'I am here, May. I shall never let you be lonely again.' " At these times, she was so separated from the world, so far removed from his touch and his voice, so solitary, that she would have sued a stranger for companionship. Daniel slept deeply, having no guilt to make him toss. He slept, indeed, so well that he never even heard the ditcher on snowy nights rising with a groan over the hill, flinging the snow from the road and warning of its approach by lights that first flashed red, then blue. As it passed their house, the hurled snow swashed like flames. All night she heard the squirrels adding up their nuts in the walls and heard the spirit of the house creaking and softly clicking upon the stairs and in the attics.

In early spring, when the whippoorwills begged in the cattails and the marsh reeds, and the northern lights patinated the lake and the tidal river, and the stars were large, and the huge vine of Dutchman's-pipe had started to leaf out, May went to bed late. Each night she sat on the back steps waiting, hearing the snuffling of a dog as it hightailed it for home, the single cry of a loon. Night after night, she waited for the advent of her rebirth while upstairs Daniel, who had spoken tolerantly of her vigils, slept, keeping his knowledge of her to himself. "A symptom," he had said, scowling in concentration, as he remarked upon her new habit. "Let it run its course. Perhaps when this is over, you will know the reason why you torture me with these obsessions and will stop. You know, you may really have a slight disorder of the mind. It would be nothing to be ashamed of; you could go to a sanitarium."

One night, looking out the window, she clearly saw her lover sitting in the sleigh. His hand was over his eyes and his chin was covered by a red silk scarf. He wore no hat and his hair was fair. He was tall and his long legs stretched indolently along the floorboard. He was younger than she had imagined him to be and he seemed rather frail, for there was a delicate pallor on his high, intelligent forehead and there was an invalid's languor in his whole attitude. He wore a white blazer and gray flannels and there was a yellow rosebud in his lapel. Young as he was, he did not, even so, seem to belong to her generation; rather, he seemed to be the reincarnation of someone's uncle as he had been fifty years before. May did not move until he vanished, and then, even though she knew now that she was truly bedeviled, the only emotion she had was bashfulness, mingled with doubt; she was not sure, that is, that he loved her.

That night, she slept a while. She lay near to Daniel, who was smiling in the moonlight. She could tell that the sleep she would have tonight would be as heavy as a coma, and she was aware of the moment she was overtaken.

She was in a canoe in a meadow of water lilies and her lover was tranquilly taking the shell off a hard-boiled egg. "How intimate," he said, "to eat an egg with you." She was nervous lest the canoe tip over, but at the same time she was charmed by his wit and by the way he lightly touched her shoulder with the varnished paddle.

"May? May? I love you, May."

"Oh!" enchanted, she heard her voice replying. "Oh, I love you, too!"

"The winter is over, May. You must forgive the hallucinations of a sick man."

She woke to see Daniel's fair, pale head bending toward her. "He is old! He is ill!" she thought, but through her tears, to deceive him one last time, she cried, "Oh, thank God, Daniel!"

He was feeling cold and wakeful and he asked her to make him a cup of tea; before she left the room, he kissed her hands and arms and said, "If I am ever sick again, don't leave me, May."

Downstairs, in the kitchen, cold with shadows and with the obtrusion of dawn, she was belabored by a chill. "What time is it?" she said aloud, although she did not care. She remembered, not for any reason, a day when she and Daniel had stood in the yard last October wondering whether they should cover the chimneys that would not be used and he decided that they should not, but he had said, "I hope no birds get trapped." She had replied, "I thought they all left at about this time for the South," and he had answered, with an unintelligible reproach in his voice, "The starlings stay." And she remembered, again for no reason, a day when, in pride and excitement, she had burst into the house crying, "I saw an ermine. It was terribly poised and let me watch it quite a while." He had said categorically, "There are no ermines here."

She had not protested; she had sighed as she sighed now and turned to the window. The sleigh was livid in this light and no one was in it; nor had anyone been in it for many years. But at that moment the blacksmith's cat came guardedly across the dewy field and climbed into it, as if by careful plan, and curled up on the seat. May prodded the clinkers in the stove and started to the barn for kindling. But she thought of the cold and the damp and the smell of the horses, and she did not go but stood there, holding the poker and leaning upon it as if it were an umbrella. There was no place warm to go. "What time is it?" she whimpered, heartbroken, and moved the poker, stroking the lion foot of the fireless stove.

She knew now that no change would come, and that she would never see her lover again. Confounded utterly, like an orphan in solitary confinement, she went outdoors and got into the sleigh. The blacksmith's imperturbable cat stretched and rearranged his position, and May sat beside him with her hands locked tightly in her lap, rapidly wondering over and over again how she would live the rest of her life.

The Magic Barrel

Not long ago there lived in uptown New York, in a small, almost meager room, though crowded with books, Leo Finkle, a rabbinical student in the Yeshivah University. Finkle, after six years of study, was to be ordained in June and had been advised by an acquaintance that he might find it easier to win himself a congregation if he were married. Since he had no present prospects of marriage, after two tormented days of turning it over in his mind, he called in Pinye Salzman, a marriage broker whose two-line advertisement he had read in the *Forward*.

The matchmaker appeared one night out of the dark fourth-floor hallway of the graystone rooming house where Finkle lived, grasping a black, strapped portfolio that had been worn thin with use. Salzman, who had been long in the business, was of slight but dignified build, wearing an old hat, and an overcoat too short and tight for him. He smelled frankly of fish, which he loved to eat, and although he was missing a few teeth, his presence was not displeasing, because of an amiable manner curiously contrasted with mournful eyes. His voice, his lips, his wisp of beard, his bony fingers were animated, but give him a moment of repose and his mild blue eyes revealed a depth of sadness, a characteristic that put Leo a little at ease although the situation, for him, was inherently tense.

He at once informed Salzman why he had asked him to come, explaining that his home was in Cleveland, and that but for his parents, who had married comparatively late in life, he was alone in the world. He had for six years devoted himself almost entirely to his studies, as a result of which, understandably, he had found himself without time for a social life and the company of young women. Therefore he thought it the better part of trial and error—of embarrassing fumbling—to call in an experienced person to advise him on these matters. He remarked in passing that the function of the marriage broker was ancient and honorable, highly approved in the Jewish community, because it made practical the necessary without hindering joy. Moreover, his own parents had been brought together by a matchmaker. They had made, if not a financially profitable marriage—since neither had possessed any worldly goods to speak of—at least a successful one in the sense of their everlasting devotion to each other. Salzman listened in embarrassed surprise, sensing a sort of apology. Later, however, he experienced a glow of pride in his work, an emotion that had left him years ago, and he heartily approved of Finkle.

The two went to their business. Leo had led Salzman to the only clear place in the room, a table near a window that overlooked the lamp-lit city. He seated himself at the matchmaker's side but facing him, attempting by an act of will to suppress the unpleasant tickle in his throat. Salzman eagerly unstrapped his portfolio and removed a loose rubber band from a thin packet of much-handled cards. As he flipped through them, a gesture and sound that physically hurt Leo, the student pretended not to see and gazed steadfastly out the window. Although it was still February, winter was on its last legs, signs of which he had for the first time in years begun to notice. He now observed the round white moon, moving high in the sky through a cloud menagerie, and watched with half-open mouth as it penetrated a huge hen, and dropped out of her like an egg laying itself. Salzman, though pretending through eyeglasses he had just slipped on, to be engaged in scanning the writing on the cards, stole occasional glances at the young man's distinguished face, noting with pleasure the long, severe scholar's nose, brown eyes heavy with learning, sensitive yet ascetic lips, and a certain, almost hollow quality of the dark cheeks. He gazed around at shelves upon shelves of books and let out a soft, contented sigh.

When Leo's eyes fell upon the cards, he counted six spread out in Salzman's hand.

"So few?" he asked in disappointment.

"You wouldn't believe me how much cards I got in my office," Salzman replied. "The drawers are already filled to the top, so I keep them now in a barrel, but is every girl good for a new rabbi?"

Leo blushed at this, regretting all he had revealed of himself in a curriculum vitae he had sent to Salzman. He had thought it best to acquaint him with his strict standards and specifications, but in having done so, felt he had told the marriage broker more than was absolutely necessary.

He hesitantly inquired, "Do you keep photographs of your clients on file?"

"First comes family, amount of dowry, also what kind promises," Salzman replied, unbuttoning his tight coat and settling himself in the chair. "After comes pictures, rabbi."

"Call me Mr. Finkle. I'm not yet a rabbi."

Salzman said he would, but instead called him doctor, which he changed to rabbi when Leo was not listening too attentively.

Salzman adjusted his horn-rimmed spectacles, gently cleared his throat and read in an eager voice the contents of the top card:

"Sophie P. Twenty-four years. Widow one year. No children. Educated high school and two years college. Father promises eight thousand dollars. Has wonderful wholesale business. Also real estate. On the mother's side comes teachers, also one actor. Well known on Second Avenue."

Leo gazed up in surprise. "Did you say a widow?"

"A widow don't mean spoiled, rabbi. She lived with her husband maybe four months. He was a sick boy she made a mistake to marry him."

"Marrying a widow has never entered my mind."

"This is because you have no experience. A widow, especially if she is young and healthy like this girl, is a wonderful person to marry. She will be thankful to you the rest of her life. Believe me, if I was looking now for a bride, I would marry a widow."

Leo reflected, then shook his head.

Salzman hunched his shoulders in an almost imperceptible gesture of disappointment. He placed the card down on the wooden table and began to read another:

"Lily H. High school teacher. Regular. Not a substitute. Has savings and new Dodge car. Lived in Paris one year. Father is successful dentist thirty-five years. Interested in professional man. Well Americanized family. Wonderful opportunity."

"I knew her personally," said Salzman. "I wish you could see this girl. She is a doll. Also very intelligent. All day you could talk to her about books and theyater and what not. She also knows current events."

"I don't believe you mentioned her age?"

"Her age?" Salzman said, raising his brows. "Her age is thirty-two years."

Leo said after a while, "I'm afraid that seems a little too old."

Salzman let out a laugh. "So how old are you, rabbi?"

"Twenty-seven."

"So what is the difference, tell me, between twenty-seven and thirty-two? My own wife is seven years older than me. So what did I suffer?—Nothing. If Rothschild's a daughter wants to marry you, would you say on account her age, no?"

"Yes," Leo said dryly.

Salzman shook off the no in the yes. "Five years don't mean a thing. I give you my word that when you will live with her for one week you will forget her age. What does it mean five years—that she lived more and knows more than somebody who is younger? On this girl, God bless her, years are not wasted. Each one that it comes makes better the bargain."

"What subject does she teach in high school?"

"Languages. If you heard the way she speaks French, you will think it is music. I am in the business twenty-five years, and I recommend her with my whole heart. Believe me, I know what I'm talking, rabbi."

"What's on the next card?" Leo said abruptly.

Salzman reluctantly turned up the third card:

"Ruth K. Nineteen years. Honor student. Father offers thirteen thousand cash to the right bridegroom. He is a medical doctor. Stomach specialist with marvelous practice. Brother in law owns own garment business. Particular people."

Salzman looked as if he had read his trump card.

"Did you say nineteen?" Leo asked with interest.

"On the dot."

"Is she attractive?" He blushed. "Pretty?"

Salzman kissed his finger tips. "A little doll. On this I give you my word. Let me call the father tonight and you will see what means pretty."

But Leo was troubled. "You're sure she's that young?"

"This I am positive. The father will show you the birth certificate."

"Are you positive there isn't something wrong with her?" Leo insisted.

"Who says there is wrong?"

"I don't understand why an American girl her age should go to a marriage broker."

A smile spread over Salzman's face.

"So for the same reason you went, she comes."

Leo flushed. "I am pressed for time."

Salzman, ᵥrealizing he had been tactless, quickly explained. "The father came, not her. He wants she should have the best, so he looks around himself. When we will locate the right boy he will introduce him and encourage. This makes a better marriage than if a young girl without experience takes for herself. I don't have to tell you this."

"But don't you think this young girl believes in love?" Leo spoke uneasily.

Salzman was about to guffaw but caught himself and said soberly, "Love comes with the right person, not before."

Leo parted dry lips but did not speak. Noticing that Salzman had snatched a glance at the next card, he cleverly asked, "How is her health?"

"Perfect," Salzman said, breathing with difficulty. "Of course, she is a little lame on her right foot from an auto accident that it happened to her when she was twelve years, but nobody notices on account she is so brilliant and also beautiful."

Leo got up heavily and went to the window. He felt curiously bitter and upbraided himself for having called in the marriage broker. Finally, he shook his head.

"Why not?" Salzman persisted, the pitch of his voice rising.

"Because I detest stomach specialists."

"So what do you care what is his business? After you marry her do you need him? Who says he must come every Friday night in your house?"

Ashamed of the way the talk was going, Leo dismissed Salzman, who went home with heavy, melancholy eyes.

Though he had felt only relief at the marriage broker's departure, Leo was in low spirits the next day. He explained it as arising from Salzman's failure to produce a suitable bride for him. He did not care for his type of clientele. But when Leo found himself hesitating whether to seek out another match-maker, one more polished than Pinye, he wondered if it could be—his pro-testations to the contrary, and although he honored his father and mother—that he did not, in essence, care for the matchmaking institution? This thought he quickly put out of mind yet found himself still upset. All day he ran around in the woods—missed an important appointment, forgot to give out his laundry, walked out of a Broadway cafeteria without paying and had to run back with the ticket in his hand; had even not recognized his landlady in the street when she passed with a friend and courteously called out, "A good evening to you, Doctor Finkle." By nightfall, however, he had regained sufficient calm to sink his nose into a book and there found peace from his thoughts.

Almost at once there came a knock on the door. Before Leo could say enter, Salzman, commercial cupid, was standing in the room. His face was gray and meager, his expression hungry, and he looked as if he would expire on his feet. Yet the marriage broker managed, by some trick of the muscles, to display a broad smile.

"So good evening. I am invited?"

Leo nodded, disturbed to see him again, yet unwilling to ask the man to leave.

Beaming still, Salzman laid his portfolio on the table. "Rabbi, I got for you tonight good news."

"I've asked you not to call me rabbi. I'm still a student."

"Your worries are finished. I have for you a first-class bride."

"Leave me in peace concerning this subject." Leo pretended lack of interest.

"The world will dance at your wedding."

"Please, Mr. Salzman, no more."

"But first must come back my strength," Salzman said weakly. He fumbled with the portfolio straps and took out of the leather case an oily paper bag, from which he extracted a hard, seeded roll and a small, smoked white fish. With a quick motion of his hand he stripped the fish out of its skin and began ravenously to chew. "All day in a rush," he muttered.

Leo watched him eat.

"A sliced tomato you have maybe?" Salzman hesitantly inquired.

"No."

The marriage broker shut his eyes and ate. When he had finished he carefully cleaned up the crumbs and rolled up the remains of the fish, in the paper bag. His spectacled eyes roamed the room until he discovered, amid some piles of books, a one-burner gas stove. Lifting his hat he humbly asked, "A glass tea you got, rabbi?"

Conscience-stricken, Leo rose and brewed the tea. He served it with a chunk of lemon and two cubes of lump sugar, delighting Salzman.

After he had drunk his tea, Salzman's strength and good spirits were restored.

"So tell me, rabbi," he said amiably, "you considered some more the three clients I mentioned yesterday?"

"There was no need to consider."

"Why not?"

"None of them suits me."

"What then suits you?"

Leo let it pass because he could give only a confused answer.

Without waiting for a reply, Salzman asked, "You remember this girl I talked to you—the high school teacher?"

"Age thirty-two?"

But, surprisingly, Salzman's face lit in a smile, "Age twenty-nine."

Leo shot him a look. "Reduced from thirty-two?"

"A mistake," Salzman avowed. "I talked today with the dentist. He took me to his safety deposit box and showed me the birth certificate. She was twenty-nine years last August. They made her a party in the mountains where she went for her vacation. When her father spoke to me the first time I forgot to write the age and I told you thirty-two, but now I remember this was a different client, a widow."

"The same one you told me about? I thought she was twenty-four?"

"A different. Am I responsible that the world is filled with widows?"

"No, but I'm not interested in them, nor for that matter, in school teachers."

Salzman pulled his clasped hands to his breast. Looking at the ceiling he devoutly exclaimed, "Yiddishe kinder, what can I say to somebody that he is not interested in high school teachers? So what then you are interested?"

Leo flushed but controlled himself.

"In what else will you be interested," Salzman went on, "if you not interterested in this fine girl that she speaks four languages and has personally in the bank ten thousand dollars? Also her father guarantees further twelve thousand. Also she has a new car, wonderful clothes, talks on all subjects, and she will give you a first-class home and children. How near do we come in our life to paradise?"

"If she's so wonderful, why wasn't she married ten years ago?"

"Why?" said Salzman with a heavy laugh. "—Why? Because she is *partikiler*. This is why. She wants the *best*."

Leo was silent, amused at how he had entangled himself. But Salzman had aroused his interest in Lily H., and he began seriously to consider calling on her. When the marriage broker observed how intently Leo's mind was at work on the facts he had supplied, he felt certain they would soon come to an agreement.

Late Saturday afternoon, conscious of Salzman, Leo Finkle walked with Lily Hirschorn along Riverside Drive. He walked briskly and erectly, wearing with distinction the black fedora he had that morning taken with trepidation out of the dusty hat box on his closet shelf, and the heavy black Saturday coat he had thoroughly whisked clean. Leo also owned a walking stick, a present from a distant relative, but quickly put temptation aside and did not use it. Lily, petite and not unpretty, had on something signifying the approach of spring. She was au courant, animatedly, with all sorts of subjects, and he weighed her words and found her surprisingly sound—score another for Salzman, whom he uneasily sensed to be somewhere around, hiding perhaps high in a tree along the street, flashing the lady signals with a pocket mirror; or perhaps a cloven-hoofed Pan, piping nuptial ditties as he danced his invisible way before them, strewing wild buds on the walk and purple grapes in their path, symbolizing fruit of a union, though there was of course still none.

Lily startled Leo by remarking, "I was thinking of Mr. Salzman, a curious figure, wouldn't you say?"

Not certain what to answer, he nodded.

She bravely went on, blushing, "I for one am grateful for his introducing us. Aren't you?"

He courteously replied, "I am."

"I mean," she said with a little laugh—and it was all in good taste, or at least gave the effect of being not in bad—"do you mind that we came together so?"

He was not displeased with her honesty, recognizing that she meant to set the relationship aright, and understanding that it took a certain amount of experience in life, and courage, to want to do it quite that way. One had to have some sort of past to make that kind of beginning.

He said that he did not mind. Salzman's function was traditional and honorable—valuable for what it might achieve, which, he pointed out, was frequently nothing.

Lily agreed with a sigh. They walked on for a while and she said after a long silence, again with a nervous laugh, "Would you mind if I asked you something a little bit personal? Frankly, I find the subject fascinating." Although Leo shrugged, she went on half embarrassedly, "How was it that you came to your calling? I mean was it a sudden passionate inspiration?"

Leo, after a time, slowly replied, "I was always interested in the Law."

"You saw revealed in it the presence of the Highest?"

He nodded and changed the subject. "I understand that you spent a little time in Paris, Miss Hirschorn?"

"Oh, did Mr. Salzman tell you, Rabbi Finkle?" Leo winced but she went on, "It was ages ago and almost forgotten. I remember I had to return for my sister's wedding."

And Lily would not be put off. "When," she asked in a trembly voice, "did you become enamored of God?"

He stared at her. Then it came to him that she was talking not about Leo Finkle, but of a total stranger, some mystical figure, perhaps even passionate prophet that Salzman had dreamed up for her—no relation to the living or dead. Leo trembled with rage and weakness. The trickster had obviously sold her a bill of goods, just as he had him, who'd expected to become acquainted with a young lady of twenty-nine, only to behold, the moment he laid eyes upon her strained and anxious face, a woman past thirty-five and aging rapidly. Only his self control had kept him this long in her presence.

"I am not," he said gravely, "a talented religious person," and in seeking words to go on, found himself possessed by shame and fear. "I think," he said in a strained manner, "that I came to God not because I loved Him, but because I did not."

This confession he spoke harshly because its unexpectedness shook him.

Lily wilted. Leo saw a profusion of loaves of bread go flying like ducks high over his head, not unlike the winged loaves by which he had counted himself to sleep last night. Mercifully, then, it snowed, which he would not put past Salzman's machinations.

He was infuriated with the marriage broker and swore he would throw him out of the room the minute he reappeared. But Salzman did not come that night, and when Leo's anger had subsided, an unaccountable despair grew in its place. At first he thought this was caused by his disappointment in Lily, but before long it became evident that he had involved himself with Salzman without a true knowledge of his own intent. He gradually realized—with an emptiness that seized him with six hands—that he had called in the broker to find him a bride because he was incapable of doing it himself. This terrifying insight he had derived as a result of his meeting and conversation with Lily Hirschorn. Her probing questions had somehow irritated him into revealing—to himself more than her—the true nature of his relationship to God, and from that it had come upon him, with shocking force, that apart from his parents, he had never loved anyone. Or perhaps it went the other way, that he did not love God so well as he might, because he had not loved man. It seemed to Leo that his whole life stood starkly revealed and he saw himself for the first time as he truly was—unloved and loveless. This bitter but somehow not fully unexpected revelation brought him to a point of panic, controlled only by extraordinary effort. He covered his face with his hands and cried.

The week that followed was the worst of his life. He did not eat and lost weight. His beard darkened and grew ragged. He stopped attending seminars and almost never opened a book. He seriously considering leaving the Yeshivah, although he was deeply troubled at the thought of the loss of all his

years of study—saw them like pages torn from a book, strewn over the city—
and at the devastating effect of this decision upon his parents. But he had
lived without knowledge of himself, and never in the Five Books and all the
Commentaries—mea culpa—had the truth been revealed to him. He did not
know where to turn, and in all this desolating loneliness there was no *to whom,*
although he often thought of Lily but not once could bring himself to go
downstairs and make the call. He became touchy and irritable, especially with
his landlady, who asked him all manner of personal questions; on the other
hand, sensing his own disagreeableness, he waylaid her on the stairs and
apologized abjectly, until mortified, she ran from him. Out of this, however,
he drew the consolation that he was a Jew and that a Jew suffered. But
gradually, as the long and terrible week drew to a close, he regained his composure and some idea of purpose in life: to go on as planned. Although he
was imperfect, the ideal was not. As for his quest of a bride, the thought of
continuing afflicted him with anxiety and heartburn, yet perhaps with this new
knowledge of himself he would be more successful than in the past. Perhaps
love would now come to him and a bride to that love. And for this sanctified
seeking who needed a Salzman?

The marriage broker, a skeleton with haunted eyes, returned that very
night. He looked, withal, the picture of frustrated expectancy—as if he had
steadfastly waited the week at Miss Lily Hirschorn's side for a telephone call
that never came.

Casually coughing, Salzman came immediately to the point: "So how did
you like her?"

Leo's anger rose and he could not refrain from chiding the matchmaker:
"Why did you lie to me, Salzman?"

Salzman's pale face went dead white, the world had snowed on him.

"Did you not state that she was twenty-nine?" Leo insisted.

"I give you my word—"

"She was thirty-five, if a day. *At least* thirty-five."

"Of this don't be too sure. Her father told me—"

"Never mind. The worst of it was that you lied to her."

"How did I lie to her, tell me?"

"You told her things about me that weren't true. You made me out to be
more, consequently less than I am. She had in mind a totally different person,
a sort of semimystical Wonder Rabbi."

"All I said, you was a religious man."

"I can imagine."

Salzman sighed. "This is my weakness that I have," he confessed. "My
wife says to me I shouldn't be a salesman, but when I have two fine people
that they would be wonderful to be married, I am so happy that I talk too
much." He smiled wanly. "This is why Salzman is a poor man."

Leo's anger left him. "Well, Salzman, I'm afraid that's all."

The marriage broker fastened hungry eyes on him.

"You don't want any more a bride?"

" I do," said Leo, "but I have decided to seek her in a different way. I am no longer interested in an arranged marriage. To be frank, I now admit the necessity of premarital love. That is, I want to be in love with the one I marry."

"Love?" said Salzman, astounded. After a moment he remarked, "For us, our love is our life, not for the ladies. In the ghetto they—"

"I know, I know," said Leo. "I've thought of it often. Love, I have said to myself, should be a by-product of living and worship rather than its own end. Yet for myself I find it necessary to establish the level of my need and fulfill it."

Salzman shrugged but answered, "Listen, rabbi, if you want love, this I can find for you also. I have such beautiful clients that you will love them the minute your eyes will see them."

Leo smiled unhappily. "I'm afraid you don't understand."

But Salzman hastily unstrapped his portfolio and withdrew a manila packet from it.

"Pictures," he said, quickly laying the envelope on the table.

Leo called after him to take the pictures away, but as if on the wings of the wind, Salzman had disappeared.

March came. Leo had returned to his regular routine. Although he felt not quite himself yet—lacked energy—he was making plans for a more active social life. Of course it would cost something, but he was an expert in cutting corners; and when there were no corners left he would make circles rounder. All the while Salzman's pictures had lain on the table, gathering dust. Occasionally as Leo sat studying, or enjoying a cup of tea, his eyes fell on the manila envelope, but he never opened it.

The days went by and no social life to speak of developed with a member of the opposite sex—it was difficult, given the circumstances of his situation. One morning Leo toiled up the stairs to his room and stared out the window at the city. Although the day was bright his view of it was dark. For some time he watched the people in the street below hurrying along and then turned with a heavy heart to his little room. On the table was the packet. With a sudden relentless gesture he tore it open. For a half-hour he stood by the table in a state of excitement, examining the photographs of the ladies Salzman had included. Finally, with a deep sigh he put them down. There were six, of varying degrees of attractiveness, but look at them long enough and they all became Lily Hirschorn: all past their prime, all starved behind bright smiles, not a true personality in the lot. Life, despite their frantic yoohooings, had passed them by; they were pictures in a brief case that stank of fish. After a while, however, as Leo attempted to return the photographs into the envelope, he found in it another, a snapshot of the type taken by a machine for a quarter. He gazed at it a moment and let out a cry.

Her face deeply moved him. Why, he could at first not say. It gave him the impression of youth—spring flowers, yet age—a sense of having been used to the bone, wasted; this came from the eyes, which were hauntingly familiar, yet absolutely strange. He had a vivid impression that he had met her before, but try as he might he could not place her although he could almost recall her name, as if he had read it in her own handwriting. No, this couldn't be; he would have remembered her. It was not, he affirmed, that she had an extraordinary beauty—no, though her face was attractive enough; it was that *something* about her moved him. Feature for feature, even some of the ladies of the photographs could do better; but she leaped forth to his heart—had *lived*, or wanted to—more than just wanted, perhaps regretted how she had lived—had somehow deeply suffered it: it could be seen in the depths of those reluctant eyes, and from the way the light enclosed and shone from her, and within her, opening realms of possibility: this was her own. Her he desired. His head ached and eyes narrowed with the intensity of his gazing, then as if an obscure fog had blown up in the mind, he experienced fear of her and was aware that he had received an impression, somehow, of evil. He shuddered, saying softly, it is thus with us all. Leo brewed some tea in a small pot and sat sipping it without sugar, to calm himself. But before he had finished drinking, again with excitement he examined the face and found it good: good for Leo Finkle. Only such a one could understand him and help him seek whatever he was seeking. She might, perhaps, love him. How she had happened to be among the discards in Salzman's barrel he could never guess, but he knew he must urgently go find her.

Leo rushed downstairs, grabbed up the Bronx telephone book, and searched for Salzman's home address. He was not listed, nor was his office. Neither was he in the Manhattan book. But Leo remembered having written down the address on a slip of paper after he had read Salzman's advertisement in the "personals" column of the *Forward.* He ran up to his room and tore through his papers, without luck. It was exasperating. Just when he needed the matchmaker he was nowhere to be found. Fortunately Leo remembered to look in his wallet. There on a card he found his name written and a Bronx address. No phone number was listed, the reason—Leo now recalled—he had originally communicated with Salzman by letter. He got on his coat, put a hat on over his skull cap and hurried to the subway station. All the way to the far end of the Bronx he sat on the edge of his seat. He was more than once tempted to take out the picture and see if the girl's face was as he remembered it, but he refrained, allowing the snapshot to remain in his inside coat pocket, content to have her so close. When the train pulled into the station he was waiting at the door and bolted out. He quickly located the street Salzman had advertised.

The building he sought was less than a block from the subway, but it was not an office building, nor even a loft, nor a store in which one could rent office space. It was a very old tenement house. Leo found Salzman's name in pencil on a soiled tag under the bell and climbed three dark flights to his apartment. When he knocked, the door was opened by a thin, asthmatic, gray-haired woman, in felt slippers.

"Yes?" she said, expecting nothing. She listened without listening. He could have sworn he had seen her, too, before but knew it was an illusion.

"Salzman—does he live here? Pinye Salzman," he said, "the matchmaker?"

She stared at him a long minute. "Of course."

He felt embarrassed. "Is he in?"

"No." Her mouth, though left open, offered nothing more.

"The matter is urgent. Can you tell me where his office is?"

"In the air." She pointed upward.

"You mean he has no office?" Leo asked.

"In his socks."

He peered into the apartment. It was sunless and dingy, one large room divided by a half-open curtain, beyond which he could see a sagging metal bed. The near side of a room was crowded with rickety chairs, old bureaus, a three-legged table, racks of cooking utensils, and all the apparatus of a kitchen. But there was no sign of Salzman or his magic barrel, probably also a figment of the imagination. An odor of frying fish made Leo weak to the knees.

"Where is he?" he insisted. "I've got to see your husband."

At length she answered, "So who knows where he is? Every time he thinks a new thought he runs to a different place. Go home, he will find you."

"Tell him Leo Finkle."

She gave no sign she had heard.

He walked downstairs, depressed.

But Salzman, breathless, stood waiting at his door.

Leo was astounded and overjoyed. "How did you get here before me?"

"I rushed."

"Come inside."

They entered. Leo fixed tea, and a sardine sandwich for Salzman. As they were drinking he reached behind him for the packet of pictures and handed them to the marriage broker.

Salzman put down his glass and said expectantly, "You found somebody you like?"

"Not among these."

The marriage broker turned away.

"Here is the one I want." Leo held forth the snapshot.

Salzman slipped on his glasses and took the picture into his trembling hand. He turned ghastly and let out a groan.

"What's the matter?" cried Leo.

"Excuse me. Was an accident this picture. She isn't for you."

Salzman frantically shoved the manila packet into his portfolio. He thrust the snapshot into his pocket and fled down the stairs.

Leo, after momentary paralysis, gave chase and cornered the marriage broker in the vestibule. The landlady made hysterical outcries but neither of them listened.

"Give me back the picture, Salzman."

"No." The pain in his eyes was terrible.

"Tell me who she is then."

"This I can't tell you. Excuse me."

He made to depart, but Leo, forgetting himself, seized the matchmaker by his tight coat and shook him frenziedly.

"Please," sighed Salzman. *"Please."*

Leo ashamedly let him go. "Tell me who she is," he begged. "It's very important for me to know."

"She is not for you. She is a wild one—wild, without shame. This is not a bride for a rabbi."

"What do you mean wild?"

"Like an animal. Like a dog. For her to be poor was a sin. This is why to me she is dead now."

"In God's name, what do you mean?"

"Her I can't introduce to you," Salzman cried.

"Why are you so excited?"

"Why, he asks," Salzman said, bursting into tears. "This is my baby, my Stella, she should burn in hell."

Leo hurried up to bed and hid under the covers. Under the covers he thought his life through. Although he soon fell asleep he could not sleep her out of his mind. He woke, beating his breast. Though he prayed to be rid of her, his prayers went unanswered. Through days of torment he endlessly struggled not to love her; fearing success, he escaped it. He then concluded to convert her to goodness, himself to God. The idea alternately nauseated and exalted him.

He perhaps did not know that he had come to a final decision until he encountered Salzman in a Broadway cafeteria. He was sitting alone at a rear table, sucking the bony remains of a fish. The marriage broker appeared haggard, and transparent to the point of vanishing.

Salzman looked up at first without recognizing him. Leo had grown a pointed beard and his eyes were weighted with wisdom.

"Salzman," he said, "love has at last come to my heart."

"Who can love from a picture?" mocked the marriage broker.

"It is not impossible."

"If you can love her, then you can love anybody. Let me show you some new clients that they just sent me their photographs. One is a little doll."

"Just her I want," Leo murmured.

"Don't be a fool, doctor. Don't bother with her."

"Put me in touch with her, Salzman," Leo said humbly. "Perhaps I can be of service."

Salzman had stopped eating and Leo understood with emotion that it was now arranged.

Leaving the cafeteria, he was, however, afflicted by a tormenting suspicion that Salzman had planned it all to happen this way.

Leo was informed by letter that she would meet him on a certain corner, and she was there one spring night, waiting under a street lamp. He appeared, carrying a small bouquet of violets and rosebuds. Stella stood by the lamp post, smoking. She wore white with red shoes, which fitted his expectations, although in a troubled moment he had imagined the dress red, and only the shoes white. She waited uneasily and shyly. From afar he saw that her eyes—clearly her father's—were filled with desperate innocence. He pictured, in her, his own redemption. Violins and lit candles revolved in the sky. Leo ran forward with flowers outthrust.

Around the corner, Salzman, leaning against a wall, chanted prayers for the dead.

John Updike

Separating

The day was fair. Brilliant. All that June the weather had mocked the Maples' internal misery with solid sunlight—golden shafts and cascades of green in which their conversations had wormed unseeing, their sad murmuring selves the only stain in Nature. Usually by this time of the year they had acquired tans; but when they met their elder daughter's plane on her return from a year in England they were almost as pale as she, though Judith was too dazzled by the sunny opulent jumble of her native land to notice. They did not spoil her homecoming by telling her immediately. Wait a few days, let her recover from jet lag, had been one of their formulations, in that string of gray dialogues—over coffee, over cocktails, over Cointreau—that had shaped the strategy of their dissolution, while the earth performed its annual stunt of renewal unnoticed beyond their closed windows. Richard had thought to leave at Easter; Joan had insisted they wait until the four children were at last assembled, with all exams passed and ceremonies attended, and the bauble of summer to console them. So he had drudged away, in love, in dread, repairing screens, getting the mowers sharpened, rolling and patching their new tennis court.

The court, clay, had come through its first winter pitted and windswept bare of redcoat. Years ago, the Maples had observed how often, among their friends, divorce followed a dramatic home improvement, as if the marriage

SEPARATING   Reprinted by permission; © 1975 The New Yorker Magazine, Inc.

were making one last twitchy effort to live; their own worst crisis had come amid the plaster dust and exposed plumbing of a kitchen renovation. Yet, a summer ago, as canary-yellow bulldozers gaily churned a grassy, daisy-dotted knoll into a muddy plateau, and a crew of pigtailed young men raked and tamped clay into a plane, this transformation did not strike them as ominous, but festive in its impudence; their marriage could rend the earth for fun. The next spring, waking each day at dawn to a sliding sensation as if the bed were being tipped, Richard found the barren tennis court, its net and tapes still rolled in the barn, an environment congruous with his mood of purposeful desolation, and the crumbling of handfuls of clay into cracks and holes (dogs had frolicked on the court in a thaw; rivulets had evolved trenches) an activity suitably elemental and interminable. In his sealed heart he hoped the day would never come.

Now it was here. A Friday. Judith was reacclimated; all four children were assembled, before jobs and camps and visits again scattered them. Joan thought they should be told one by one. Richard was for making an announcement at the table. She said, "I think just making an announcement is a cop-out. They'll start quarrelling and playing to each other instead of focussing. They're each individuals, you know, not just some corporate obstacle to your freedom."

"O.K., O.K. I agree." Joan's plan was exact. That evening, they were giving Judith a belated welcome-home dinner, of lobster and champagne. Then, the party over, they, the two of them, who nineteen years before would push her in a baby carriage along Tenth Street to Washington Square, were to walk her out of the house, to the bridge across the salt creek, and tell her, swearing her to secrecy. Then Richard Jr., who was going directly from work to a rock concert in Boston, would be told, either late when he returned on the train or early Saturday morning before he went off to his job; he was seventeen and employed as one of a golf-course maintenance crew. Then the two younger children, John and Margaret, could, as the morning wore on, be informed.

"Mopped up, as it were," Richard said.

"Do you have any better plan? That leaves you the rest of Saturday to answer any questions, pack, and make your wonderful departure."

"No," he said, meaning he had no better plan, and agreed to hers, though it had an edge of false order, a plea for control in the semblance of its achievement, like Joan's long chore lists and financial accountings and, in the days when he first knew her, her too copious lecture notes. Her plan turned one hurdle for him into four—four knife-sharp walls, each with a sheer blind drop on the other side.

All spring he had been morbidly conscious of insides and outsides, of barriers and partitions. He and Joan stood as a thin barrier between the children and the truth. Each moment was a partition, with the past on one side and the future on the other, a future containing this unthinkable *now*. Beyond four knifelike walls a new life for him waited vaguely. His skull cupped a secret, a white face, a face both frightened and soothing, both strange and known, that he wanted to shield from tears, which he felt all about him, solid as the sunlight. So haunted, he had become obsessed with battening down the house against his absence, replacing screens and sash cords, hinges and latches—a Houdini making things snug before his escape.

The lock. He had still to replace a lock on one of the doors of the screened porch. The task, like most such, proved more difficult than he had imagined. The old lock, aluminum frozen by corrosion, had been deliberately rendered obsolete by manufacturers. Three hardware stores had nothing that even approximately matched the mortised hole its removal (surprisingly easy) left. Another hole had to be gouged, with bits too small and saws too big, and the old hole fitted with a block of wood—the chisels dull, the saw rusty, his fingers thick with lack of sleep. The sun poured down, beyond the porch, on a world of neglect. The bushes already needed pruning, the windward side of the house was shedding flakes of paint, rain would get in when he was gone, insects, rot, death. His family, all those he would lose, filtered through the edges of his awareness as he struggled with screw holes, splinters, opaque instructions, minutiae of metal.

Judith sat on the porch, a princess returned from exile. She regaled them with stories of fuel shortages, of bomb scares in the Underground, of Pakistani workmen loudly lusting after her as she walked past on her way to dance school. Joan came and went, in and out of the house, calmer than she should have been, praising his struggles with the lock as if this were one more and not the last of their chain of shared chores. The younger of his sons, John, now at fifteen suddenly, unwittingly handsome, for a few minutes held the rickety screen door while his father clumsily hammered and chiseled, each blow a kind of sob in Richard's ears. His younger daughter, having been at a slumber party, slept on the porch hammock through all the noise—heavy and pink, trusting and forsaken. Time, like the sunlight, continued relentlessly; the sunlight slowly slanted. Today was one of the longest days. The lock clicked, worked. He was through. He had a drink; he drank it on the porch, listening to his daughter. "It was so sweet," she was saying, "during the worst of it, how all the butcher's and bakery shops kept open by candlelight. They're all so plucky and cute. From the papers, things sounded so much worse here—people shooting people in gas lines, and everybody freezing."

Richard asked her, "Do you still want to live in England forever?" *Forever:* the concept, now a reality upon him, pressed and scratched at the back of his throat.

"No," Judith confessed, turning her oval face to him, its eyes still childishly far apart, but the lips set as over something succulent and satisfactory. "I was anxious to come home. I'm an American." She was a woman. They had raised her; he and Joan had endured together to raise her, alone of the four. The others had still some raising left in them. Yet it was the thought of telling Judith—the image of her, their first baby, walking between them arm in arm to the bridge—that broke him. The partition between himself and the tears broke. Richard sat down to the celebratory meal with the back of his throat aching; the champagne, the lobster seemed phases of sunshine; he saw them and tasted them through tears. He blinked, swallowed, croakily joked about hay fever. The tears would not stop leaking through; they came not through a hole that could be plugged but through a permeable spot in a membrane, steadily, purely, endlessly, fruitfully. They became, his tears, a shield for himself against these others—their faces, the fact of their assembly, a last time as innocents, at a table where he sat the last time as head. Tears dropped from his nose as he broke the lobster's back; salt flavored his champagne as he sipped it; the raw clench at the back of his throat was delicious. He could not help himself.

His children tried to ignore his tears. Judith, on his right, lit a cigarette, gazed upward in the direction of her too energetic, too sophisticated exhalation; on her other side, John earnestly bent his face to the extraction of the last morsels—legs, tail segments—from the scarlet corpse. Joan, at the opposite end of the table, glanced at him surprised, her reproach displaced by a quick grimace, of forgiveness, or of salute to his superior gift of strategy. Between them, Margaret, no longer called Bean, thirteen and large for her age, gazed from the other side of his pane of tears as if into a shopwindow at something she coveted—at her father, a crystalline heap of splinters and memories. It was not she, however, but John who, in the kitchen, as they cleared the plates and carapaces away, asked Joan the question: *"Why is Daddy crying?"*

Richard heard the question but not the murmured answer. Then he heard Bean cry, "Oh, no-oh!"—the faintly dramatized exclamation of one who had long expected it.

John returned to the table carrying a bowl of salad. He nodded tersely at his father and his lips shaped the conspiratorial words "She told."

"Told what?" Richard asked aloud, insanely.

The boy sat down as if to rebuke his father's distraction with the example of his own good manners and said quietly, "The separation."

Joan and Margaret returned; the child, in Richard's twisted vision, seemed diminished in size, and relieved, relieved to have had the boogeyman at last proved real. He called out to her—the distances at the table had grown immense—"You knew, you always knew," but the clenching at the back of his throat prevented him from making sense of it. From afar he heard Joan talking, levelly, sensibly, reciting what they had prepared: it was a separation for the summer, an experiment. She and Daddy both agreed it would be good for them; they needed space and time to think; they liked each other but did not make each other happy enough, somehow.

Judith, imitating her mother's factual tone, but in her youth off-key, too cool, said, "I think it's silly. You should either live together or get divorced."

Richard's crying, like a wave that has crested and crashed, had become tumultuous; but it was overtopped by another tumult, for John, who had been so reserved, now grew larger and larger at the table. Perhaps his younger sister's being credited with knowing set him off. "Why didn't you *tell* us?" he asked, in a large round voice quite unlike his own. "You should have *told* us you weren't getting along."

Richard was startled into attempting to force words through his tears. "We *do* get along, that's the trouble, so it doesn't show even to us—" "That we do not love each other" was the rest of the sentence; he couldn't finish it.

Joan finished for him, in her style. "And we've always, *especially*, loved our children."

John was not mollified. "What do you care about *us?*" he boomed. "We're just little things you *had*." His sisters' laughing forced a laugh from him, which he turned hard and parodistic: "Ha ha *ha*." Richard and Joan realized simultaneously that the child was drunk, on Judith's homecoming champagne. Feeling bound to keep the center of the stage, John took a cigarette from Judith's pack, poked it into his mouth, let it hang from his lower lip, and squinted like a gangster.

"You're not little things we had," Richard called to him. "You're the whole point. But you're grown. Or almost."

The boy was lighting matches. Instead of holding them to his cigarette (for they had never seen him smoke; being "good" had been his way of setting himself apart), he held them to his mother's face, closer and closer, for her to blow out. Then he lit the whole folder—a hiss and then a torch, held against his mother's face. Prismed by his tears, the flame filled Richard's vision; he didn't know how it was extinguished. He heard Margaret say, "Oh stop showing off," and saw John, in response, break the cigarette in two and put the halves entirely into his mouth and chew, sticking out his tongue to display the shreds to his sister.

Joan talked to him, reasoning—a fountain of reason, unintelligible. "Talked about it for years . . . our children must help us . . . Daddy and I both want . . ." As the boy listened, he carefully wadded a paper napkin into the leaves of his salad, fashioned a ball of paper and lettuce, and popped it into his mouth, looking around the table for the expected laughter. None came. Judith said, "Be mature," and dismissed a plume of smoke.

Richard got up from this stifling table and led the boy outside. Though the house was in twilight, the outdoors still brimmed with light, the long waste light of high summer. Both laughing, he supervised John's spitting out the lettuce and paper and tobacco into the pachysandra. He took him by the hand—a square gritty hand, but for its softness a man's. Yet, it held on. They ran together up into the field, past the tennis court. The raw banking left by the bulldozers was dotted with daisies. Past the court and a flat stretch where they used to play family baseball stood a soft green rise glorious in the sun, each weed and species of grass distinct as illumination on parchment. "I'm sorry, so sorry," Richard cried. "You were the only one who ever tried to help me with all the goddam jobs around this place."

Sobbing, safe within his tears and the champagne, John explained, "It's not just the separation, it's the whole crummy year, I *hate* that school, you can't make any friends, the history teacher's a scud."

They sat on the crest of the rise, shaking and warm from their tears but easier in their voices, and Richard tried to focus on the child's sad year—the weekdays long with homework, the weekends spent in his room with model airplanes, while his parents murmured down below, nursing their separation. How selfish, how blind, Richard thought; his eyes felt scoured. He told his son, "We'll think about getting you transferred. Life's too short to be miserable."

They had said what they could, but did not want the moment to heal, and talked on, about the school, about the tennis court, whether it would ever again be as good as it had been that first summer. They walked to inspect it and pressed a few more tapes more firmly down. A little stiltedly, perhaps trying to make too much of the moment, to prolong it. Richard led the boy to the spot in the field where the view was best, of the metallic blue river, the emerald marsh, the scattered islands velvet with shadow in the low light, the white bits of beach far away. "See," he said. "It goes on being beautiful. It'll be here tomorrow."

"I know," John answered, impatiently. The moment had closed.

Back in the house, the others had opened some white wine, the champagne being drunk, and still sat at the table, the three females, gossiping. Where Joan sat had become the head. She turned, showing him a tearless face, and asked, "All right?"

"We're fine," he said, resenting it, though relieved, that the party went on without him.

In bed she explained, "I couldn't cry I guess because I cried so much all spring. It really wasn't fair. It's your idea, and you made it look as though I was kicking you out."

"I'm sorry," he said. "I couldn't stop. I wanted to but couldn't't."

"You *didn't* want to. You loved it. You were having your way, making a general announcement."

"I love having it over," he admitted. "God, those kids were great. So brave and funny." John, returned to the house, had settled to a model airplane in his room, and kept shouting down to them, "I'm O.K. No sweat." "And the way," Richard went on, cozy in his relief, "they never questioned the reasons we gave. No thought of a third person. Not even Judith."

"That *was* touching," Joan said.

He gave her a hug. "You were great too. Thank you." Guiltily, he realized he did not feel separated.

"You still have Dickie to do," she told him. These words set before him a black mountain in the darkness; its cold breath, its near weight affected his chest. Of the four children Dickie was most nearly his conscience. Joan did not need to add, "That's one piece of your dirty work I won't do for you."

"I know. I'll do it. You go to sleep."

Within minutes, her breathing slowed, became oblivious and deep. It was quarter to midnight. Dickie's train from the concert would come in at one-fourteen. Richard set the alarm for one. He had slept atrociously for weeks. But whenever he closed his lids some glimpse of the last hours scorched them—Judith exhaling toward the ceiling in a kind of aversion, Bean's mute staring, the sunstruck growth of the field where he and John had rested. The mountain before him moved closer, moved within him; he was huge, momentous. The ache at the back of his throat felt stale. His wife slept as if slain beside him. When, exasperated by his hot lids, his crowded heart, he rose from bed and dressed, she awoke enough to turn over. He told her then, "If I could undo it all, I would."

"Where would you begin?" she asked. There was no place. Giving him courage, she was always giving him courage. He put on shoes without socks in the dark. The children were breathing in their rooms, the downstairs was hollow. In their confusion they had left lights burning. He turned off all but one, the kitchen overhead. The car started. He had hoped it wouldn't. He met only moonlight on the road; it seemed a diaphanous companion, flickering in the leaves along the roadside, haunting his rearview mirror like a pursuer, melting under his headlights. The center of town, not quite deserted, was eerie at this hour. A young cop in uniform kept company with a gang of T-shirted kids on the steps of the bank. Across from the railroad station, several bars kept open. Customers, mostly young, passed in and out of the warm night, savoring summer's novelty. Voices shouted from cars as they passed; an immense conversation seemed in progress. Richard parked and in his weariness put his head on the passenger seat, out of the commotion and wheeling lights. It was as when, in the movies, an assassin grimly carries his mission through the jostle of a carnival—except the movies cannot show the precipitous, palpable slope you cling to within. You cannot climb back down; you can only fall. The synthetic fabric of the car seat, warmed by his cheek, confided to him an ancient, distant scene of vanilla.

A train whistle caused him to lift his head. It was on time; he had hoped it would be late. The slender drawgates descended. The bell of approach tingled happily. The great metal body, horizontally fluted, rocked to a stop, and sleepy teen-agers disembarked, his son among them. Dickie did not show surprise that his father was meeting him at this terrible hour. He sauntered to the car with two friends, both taller than he. He said "Hi" to his father and took the passenger's seat with an exhausted promptness that expressed gratitude. The friends got into the back, and Richard was grateful; a few more minutes' postponement would be won by driving them home.

He asked, "How was the concert?"

"Groovy," one boy said from the back seat.

"It bit," the other said.

"It was O.K.," Dickie said, moderate by nature, so reasonable that in his childhood the unreason of the world had given him headaches, stomach aches, nausea. When the second friend had been dropped off at his dark house, the boy blurted, "Dad, my eyes are killing me with hay fever! I'm out there cutting that mothering grass all day!"

"Do we still have those drops?"

"They didn't do any good last summer."

"They might this." Richard swung a U-turn on the empty street. The drive home took a few minutes. The mountain was here, in his throat. "Richard," he said, and felt the boy, slumped and rubbing his eyes, go tense at his tone, "I didn't come to meet you just to make your life easier. I came because your mother and I have some news for you, and you're a hard man to get ahold of these days. It's sad news."

"That's O.K." The reassurance came out soft, but quick, as if released from the tip of a spring.

Richard had feared that his tears would return and choke him, but the boy's manliness set an example, and his voice issued forth steady and dry. "It's sad news, but it needn't be tragic news, at least for you. It should have no practical effect on your life, though it's bound to have an emotional effect. You'll work at your job, and go back to school in September. Your mother and I are really proud of what you're making of your life; we don't want that to change at all."

"Yeah," the boy said lightly, on the intake of his breath, holding himself up. They turned the corner; the church they went to loomed like a gutted fort. The home of the woman Richard hoped to marry stood across the green. Her bedroom light burned.

"Your mother and I," he said, "have decided to separate. For the summer. Nothing legal, no divorce yet. We want to see how it feels. For some years now, we haven't been doing enough for each other, making each other as happy as we should be. Have you sensed that?"

"No," the boy said. It was an honest, unemotional answer: true or false in a quiz.

Glad for the factual basis, Richard pursued, even garrulously, the details. His apartment across town, his utter accessibility, the split vacation arrangements, the advantages to the children, the added mobility and variety of the summer. Dickie listened, absorbing. "Do the others know?"

Richard described how they had been told.

"How did they take it?"

"The girls pretty calmly. John flipped out; he shouted and ate a cigarette

and made a salad out of his napkin and told us how much he hated school."
His brother chuckled. "He did?"

"Yeah. The school issue was more upsetting for him than Mom and me.
He seemed to feel better for having exploded."

"He did?" The repetition was the first sign that he was stunned.

"Yes. Dickie, I want to tell you something. This last hour, waiting for
your train to get in, has been about the worst of my life. I hate this. *Hate* it.
My father would have died before doing it to me." He felt immensely lighter,
saying this. He had dumped the mountain on the boy. They were home.
Moving swiftly as a shadow, Dickie was out of the car, through the bright
kitchen. Richard called after him, "Want a glass of milk or anything?"

"No thanks."

"Want us to call the course tomorrow and say you're too sick to work?"

"No, that's all right." The answer was faint, delivered at the door to his
room; Richard listened for the slam of a tantrum. The door closed normally.
The sound was sickening.

Joan had sunk into that first deep trough of sleep and was slow to awake.
Richard had to repeat, "I told him."

"What did he say?"

"Nothing much. Could you go say good night to him? Please."

She left their room, without putting on a bathrobe. He sluggishly changed
back into his pajamas and walked down the hall. Dickie was already in bed,
Joan was sitting beside him, and the boy's bedside clock radio was murmuring music. When she stood, an inexplicable light—the moon?—outlined her
body through the nightie. Richard sat on the warm place she had indented
on the child's narrow mattress. He asked him, "Do you want the radio on
like that?"

"It always is."

"Doesn't it keep you awake? It would me."

"No."

"Are you sleepy?"

"Yeah."

"Good. Sure you want to get up and go to work? You've had a big night."

"I want to."

Away at school this winter he had learned for the first time that you can
go short of sleep and live. As an infant he had slept with an immobile sweating intensity that had alarmed his babysitters. As the children aged, he became the first to go to bed, earlier for a time than his younger brother and
sister. Even now, he would go slack in the middle of a television show, his
sprawled legs hairy and brown. "O.K. Good boy. Dickie, listen. I love you
so much, I never knew how much until now. No matter how this works
out, I'll always be with you. Really."

Richard bent to kiss an averted face but his son, sinewy, turned and with
wet cheeks embraced him and gave him a kiss, on the lips, passionate as a

woman's. In his father's ear he moaned one word, the crucial, intelligent word: *"Why?"*

Why. It was a whistle of wind in a crack, a knife thrust, a window thrown open on emptiness. The white face was gone, the darkness was featureless. Richard had forgotten why.

Katherine Anne Porter

Pale Horse, Pale Rider

In sleep she knew she was in her bed, but not the bed she had lain down in a
few hours since, and the room was not the same but it was a room she had
known somewhere. Her heart was a stone lying upon her breast outside of her;
her pulses lagged and paused, and she knew that something strange was going
to happen, even as the early morning winds were cool through the lattice, the
streaks of light were dark blue and the whole house was snoring in its sleep.

Now I must get up and go while they are all quiet. Where are my things?
Things have a will of their own in this place and hide where they like. Daylight will strike a sudden blow on the roof startling them all up to their feet;
faces will beam asking, Where are you going, What are you doing, What are
you thinking, How do you feel, Why do you say such things, What do you
mean? No more sleep. Where are my boots and what horse shall I ride?
Fiddler or Graylie or Miss Lucy with the long nose and the wicked eye? How
I have loved this house in the morning before we are all awake and tangled
together like badly cast fishing lines. Too many people have been born here,
and have wept too much here, and have laughed too much, and have been too
angry and outrageous with each other here. Too many have died in this bed
already, there are far too many ancestral bones propped up on the mantel-
pieces, there have been too damned many antimacassars in this house, she said
loudly, and oh, what accumulation of storied dust never allowed to settle in
peace for one moment.

And the stranger? Where is that lank greenish stranger I remember hanging about the place, welcomed by my grandfather, my great-aunt, my five

times removed cousin, my decrepit hound and my silver kitten? Why did they take to him, I wonder? And where are they now? Yet I saw him pass the window in the evening. What else besides them did I have in the world? Nothing. Nothing is mine, I have only nothing but it is enough, it is beautiful and it is all mine. Do I even walk about in my own skin or is it something I have borrowed to spare my modesty? Now what horse shall I borrow for this journey I do not mean to take, Graylie or Miss Lucy or Fiddler who can jump ditches in the dark and knows how to get the bit between his teeth? Early morning is best for me because trees are trees in one stroke, stones are stones set in shades known to be grass, there are no false shapes or surmises, the road is still asleep with the crust of dew unbroken. I'll take Graylie because he is not afraid of bridges.

Come now, Graylie, she said, taking his bridle, we must outrun Death and the Devil. You are no good for it, she told the other horses standing saddled before the stable gate, among them the horse of the stranger, gray also, with tarnished nose and ears. The stranger swung into his saddle beside her, leaned far towards her and regarded her without meaning, the blank still stare of mindless malice that makes no threats and can bide its time. She drew Graylie around sharply, urged him to run. He leaped the low rose hedge and the narrow ditch beyond, and the dust of the lane flew heavily under his beating hoofs. The stranger rode beside her, easily, lightly, his reins loose in his half-closed hand, straight and elegant in dark shabby garments that flapped upon his bones; his pale face smiled in an evil trance, he did not glance at her. Ah, I have seen this fellow before, I know this man if I could place him. He is no stranger to me.

She pulled Graylie up, rose in her stirrups and shouted, I'm not going with you this time—ride on! Without pausing or turning his head the stranger rode on. Graylie's ribs heaved under her, her own ribs rose and fell. Oh, why am I so tired, I must wake up. "But let me get a fine yawn first," she said, opening her eyes and stretching, "a slap of cold water in my face, for I've been talking in my sleep again, I heard myself but what was I saying?"

Slowly, unwillingly, Miranda drew herself up inch by inch out of the pit of sleep, waited in a daze for life to begin again. A single word struck in her mind, a gong of warning, reminding her for the day long what she forgot happily in sleep, and only in sleep. The war, said the gong, and she shook her head. Dangling her feet idly with their slippers hanging, she was reminded of the way all sorts of persons sat upon her desk at the newspaper office. Every day she found someone there, sitting upon her desk instead of the chair provided, dangling his legs, eyes roving, full of his important affairs, waiting to pounce about something or other. "*Why* won't they sit in the chair? Should I put a sign on it, saying. 'For God's sake, sit here'?"

Far from putting up a sign, she did not even frown at her visitors. Usually she did not notice them at all until their determination to be seen was greater than her determination not to see them. Saturday, she thought, lying comfortably in her tub of hot water, will be pay day, as always. Or I hope always.

Her thoughts roved hazily in a continual effort to bring together and unite firmly the disturbing oppositions in her day-to-day existence, where survival, she could see clearly, had become a series of feats of sleight of hand. I owe— let me see, I wish I had pencil and paper—well, suppose I *did* pay five dollars now on a Liberty Bond, I couldn't possibly keep it up. Or maybe. Eighteen dollars a week. So much for rent, so much for food, and I mean to have a few things besides. About five dollars' worth. Will leave me twenty-seven cents. I suppose I can make it. I suppose I should be worried. I am worried. Very well, now I am worried and what next? Twenty-seven cents. That's not so bad. Pure profit, really. Imagine if they should suddenly raise me to twenty I should then have two dollars and twenty-seven cents left over. But they aren't going to raise me to twenty. They are in fact going to throw me out if I don't buy a Liberty Bond. I hardly believe that. I'll ask Bill. (Bill was the city editor.) I wonder if a threat like that isn't a kind of blackmail. I don't believe even a Lusk Committeeman can get away with that.

Yesterday there had been two pairs of legs dangling, on either side of her typewriter, both pairs stuffed thickly into funnels of dark expensive-looking material. She noticed at a distance that one of them was oldish and one was youngish, and they both of them had a stale air of borrowed importance which apparently they had got from the same source. They were both much too well nourished and the younger one wore a square little mustache. Being what they were, no matter what their business was it would be something unpleasant. Miranda had nodded at them, pulled out her chair and without removing her cap or gloves had reached into a pile of letters and sheets from the copy desk as if she had not a moment to spare. They did not move, or take off their hats. At last she had said "Good morning" to them, and asked if they were, perhaps, waiting for her?

The two men slid off the desk, leaving some of her papers rumpled, and the oldish man had inquired why she had not bought a Liberty Bond. Miranda had looked at him then, and got a poor impression. He was a pursy-faced man, gross-mouthed, with little lightless eyes, and Miranda wondered why nearly all of those selected to do the war work at home were of his sort. He might be anything at all, she thought; advance agent for a road show, promoter of a wildcat oil company, a former saloon keeper announcing the opening of a new cabaret, an automobile salesman—any follower of any one of the crafty, haphazard callings. But he was now all Patriot, working for the government. "Look here," he asked her, "do you know there's a war, or don't you?"

Did he expect an answer to that? Be quiet, Miranda told herself, this was bound to happen. Sooner or later it happens. Keep your head. The man wagged his finger at her, "Do you?" he persisted, as if he were prompting an obstinate child.

"Oh, the war," Miranda had echoed on a rising note and she almost smiled at him. It was habitual, automatic, to give that solemn, mystically uplifted grin when you spoke the words or heard them spoken. *"C'est la guerre,"* whether you could pronounce it or not, was even better, and always, always, you shrugged.

"Yeah," said the younger man in a nasty way, "the war." Miranda, startled by the tone, met his eye; his stare was really stony, really viciously cold, the kind of thing you might expect to meet behind a pistol on a deserted corner. This expression gave temporary meaning to a set of features otherwise nondescript, the face of those men who have no business of their own. "We're having a war, and some people are buying Liberty Bonds and others just don't seem to get around to it," he said. "That's what we mean."

Miranda frowned with nervousness, the sharp beginnings of fear. "Are you selling them?" she asked, taking the cover off her typewriter and putting it back again.

"No, we're not selling them," said the older man. "We're just asking you why you haven't bought one." The voice was persuasive and ominous.

Miranda began to explain that she had no money, and did not know where to find any, when the older man interrupted: "That's no excuse, no excuse at all, and you know it, with the Huns overrunning martyred Belgium."

"With our American boys fighting and dying in Belleau Wood," said the younger man, "anybody can raise fifty dollars to help beat the Boche."

Miranda said hastily, "I have eighteen dollars a week and not another cent in the world. I simply cannot buy anything."

"You can pay for it five dollars a week," said the older man (they had stood there cawing back and forth over her head), "like a lot of other people in this office, and a lot of other offices besides are doing."

Miranda, desperately silent, had thought, "Suppose I were not a coward, but said what I really thought? Suppose I said to hell with this filthy war? Suppose I asked that little thug, What's the matter with you, why aren't you rotting in Belleau Wood? I wish you were . . ."

She began to arrange her letters and notes, her fingers refusing to pick up things properly. The older man went on making his little set speech. It was hard, of course. Everybody was suffering, naturally. Everybody had to do his share. But as to that, a Liberty Bond was the safest investment you could make. It was just like having the money in the bank. Of course. The government was back of it and where better could you invest?

"I agree with you about that," said Miranda, "but I haven't any money to invest."

And of course, the man had gone on, it wasn't so much her fifty dollars that was going to make any difference. It was just a pledge of good faith on her part. A pledge of good faith that she was a loyal American doing her duty. And the thing was safe as a church. Why, if he had a million dollars he'd be glad to put every last cent of it in these Bonds. . . . "You can't lose by it," he said, almost benevolently, "and you can lose a lot if you don't. Think it over. You're the only one in this whole newspaper office that hasn't come in. And every firm in this city has come in one hundred per cent. Over at the *Daily Clarion* nobody had to be asked twice."

"They pay better over there," said Miranda. "But next week, if I can. Not now, next week."

"See that you do," said the younger man. "This ain't any laughing matter."

They lolled away, past the Society Editor's desk, past Bill the City Editor's desk, past the long copy desk where old man Gibbons sat all night shouting at intervals, "Jarge! Jarge!" and the copy boy would come flying. "Never say *people* when you mean *persons*," old man Gibbons had instructed Miranda, "and never say *practically*, say *virtually*, and don't for God's sake ever so long as I am at this desk use the barbarism *inasmuch* under any circumstances whatsoever. Now you're educated, you may go." At the head of the stairs her inquisitors had stopped in their fussy pride and vainglory, lighting cigars and wedging their hats more firmly over their eyes.

Miranda turned over in the soothing water, and wished she might fall asleep there, to wake up only when it was time to sleep again. She had a burning slow headache, and noticed it now, remembering she had waked up with it and it had in fact begun the evening before. While she dressed she tried to trace the insidious career of her headache, and it seemed reasonable to suppose it had started with the war. "It's been a headache, all right, but not quite like this." After the Committeemen had left, yesterday, she had gone to the cloakroom and had found Mary Townsend, the Society Editor, quietly hysterical about something. She was perched on the edge of the shabby wicker couch with ridges down the center, knitting on something rose-colored. Now and then she would put down her knitting, seize her head with both hands and rock, saying, "My *God*," in a surprised, inquiring voice. Her column was called Ye Towne Gossyp, so of course everybody called her Towney. Miranda and Towney had a great deal in common, and liked each other. They had both been real reporters once, and had been sent together to "cover" a scandalous elopement, in which no marriage had taken place, after all, and the recaptured girl, her face swollen, had sat with her mother, who was moaning steadily under a mound of blankets. They had both wept painfully and implored the young reporters to suppress the worst of the story. They had suppressed it, and the rival newspaper printed it all the next day. Miranda and Towney had then taken their punishment together, and had been degraded publicly to routine female jobs, one to the theaters, the other to society. They had this in common, that neither of them could see what else they could possibly have done, and they knew they were considered fools by the rest of the staff—nice girls, but fools. At sight of Miranda, Towney had broken out in a rage. "I can't do it. I'll never be able to raise the money, I told them, I can't, I can't, but they wouldn't listen."

Miranda said, "I knew I wasn't the only person in this office who couldn't raise five dollars. I told them I couldn't, too, and I can't."

"My *God*," said Towney, in the same voice, "they told me I'd lose my job—"

"I'm going to ask Bill," Miranda said; "I don't believe Bill would do that."

"It's not up to Bill," said Towney. "He'd have to if they got after him. Do you suppose they could put us in jail?"

"I don't know," said Miranda. "If they do, we won't be lonesome." She sat down beside Towney and held her own head. "What kind of soldier are you knitting that for? It's a sprightly color, it ought to cheer him up."

"Like hell," said Towney, her needles going again. "I'm making this for myself. That's that."

"Well," said Miranda, "we won't be lonesome and we'll catch up on our sleep." She washed her face and put on fresh make-up. Taking clean gray gloves out of her pocket she went out to join a group of young women fresh from the country club dances, the morning bridge, the charity bazaar, the Red Cross workrooms, who were wallowing in good works. They gave tea dances and raised money, and with the money they bought quantities of sweets, fruit, cigarettes, and magazines for the men in the cantonment hospitals. With this loot they were now setting out, a gay procession of high-powered cars and brightly tinted faces to cheer the brave boys who already, you might very well say, had fallen in defense of their country. It must be frightfully hard on them, the dears, to be floored like this when they're all crazy to get overseas and into the trenches as quickly as possible. Yes, and some of them are the cutest things you ever saw, I didn't know there were so many good-looking men in this country, good heavens, I said, where do they come from? Well, my dear, you may ask yourself that question, who knows where they did come from? You're quite right, the way I feel about it is this, we must do everything we can to make them contented, but I draw the line at talking to them. I told the chaperons at those dances for enlisted men, I'll dance with them, every dumbbell who asks me, but I will NOT talk to them, I said, even if there is a war. So I danced hundreds of miles without opening my mouth except to say, Please keep your knees to yourself. I'm glad we gave those dances up. Yes, and the men stopped coming, anyway. But listen, I've heard that a great many of the enlisted men come from very good families; I'm not good at catching names, and those I did catch I'd never heard before, so I don't know . . . but it seems to me if they were from good families, you'd know it, wouldn't you? I mean, if a man is well bred he doesn't step on your feet, does he? At least not that. I used to have a pair of sandals ruined at every one of those dances. Well, I think any kind of social life is in very poor taste just now, I think we should all put on our Red Cross head dresses and wear them for the duration of the war—

Miranda, carrying her basket and her flowers, moved in among the young women, who scattered out and rushed upon the ward uttering girlish laughter meant to be refreshingly gay, but there was a grim determined clang in it calculated to freeze the blood. Miserably embarrassed at the idiocy of her errand, she walked rapidly between the long rows of high beds, set foot to foot with a narrow aisle between. The men, a selected presentable lot, sheets drawn up to their chins, not seriously ill, were bored and restless, most of them willing to be amused at anything. They were for the most part pic- turesquely bandaged as to arm or head, and those who were not visibly wounded invariably replied "Rheumatism" if some tactless girl, who had been solemnly warned never to ask this question, still forgot and asked a man what his illness was. The good-natured, eager ones, laughing and calling out from their hard narrow beds, were soon surrounded. Miranda, with her wilting bouquet and her basket of sweets and cigarettes, looking about, caught the unfriendly bitter eye of a young fellow lying on his back, his right leg in a cast and pulley. She stopped at the foot of his bed and continued to look at him, and he looked back with an unchanged, hostile face. Not having any, thank you and be damned to the whole business, his eyes said plainly to her, and will you be so good as to take your trash off my bed? For Miranda had set it down, leaning over to place it where he might be able to reach it if he would. Having set it down, she was incapable of taking it up again, but hurried away, her face burning, down the long aisle and out into the cool October sunshine, where the dreary raw barracks swarmed and worked with an aimless life of scurrying, dun-colored insects; and going around to a window near where he lay, she looked in, spying upon her soldier. He was lying with his eyes closed, his eyebrows in a sad bitter frown. She could not place him at all, she could not imagine where he came from nor what sort of being he might have been "in life," she said to herself. His face was young and the features sharp and plain, the hands were not laborer's hands but not well-cared-for hands either. They were good useful properly shaped hands, lying there on the coverlet. It occurred to her that it would be her luck to find him, instead of a jolly hungry puppy glad of a bite to eat and a little chatter. It is like turning a corner absorbed in your painful thoughts and meeting your state of mind embodied, face to face, she said. "My own feelings about this whole thing, made flesh. Never again will I come here, this is no sort of thing to be doing. This is disgusting," she told herself plainly. "Of course I would pick him out," she thought, getting into the back seat of the car she came in, "serves me right, I know better."

Another girl came out looking very tired and climbed in beside her. After a short silence, the girl said in a puzzled way, "I don't know what good it does, really. Some of them wouldn't take anything at all. I don't like this, do you?"

"I hate it," said Miranda.

"I suppose it's all right, though," said the girl, cautiously.

"Perhaps," said Miranda, turning cautious also.

That was for yesterday. At this point Miranda decided there was no good in thinking of yesterday, except for the hour after midnight she had spent dancing with Adam. He was in her mind so much, she hardly knew when she was thinking about him directly. His image was simply always present in more or less degree, he was sometimes nearer the surface of her thoughts, the pleasantest, the only really pleasant thought she had. She examined her face in the mirror between the windows and decided that her uneasiness was not all imagination. For three days at least she had felt odd and her expression was unfamiliar. She would have to raise that fifty dollars somehow, she supposed, or who knows what can happen? She was hardened to stories of personal disaster, of outrageous accusations and extraordinarily bitter penalties that had grown monstrously out of incidents very little more important than her failure—her refusal—to buy a Bond. No, she did not find herself a pleasing sight, flushed and shiny, and even her hair felt as if it had decided to grow in the other direction. I must do something about this, I can't let Adam see me like this, she told herself, knowing that even now at that moment he was listening for the turn of her door knob, and he would be in the hallway, or on the porch when she came out, as if by sheerest coincidence. The noon sunlight cast cold slanting shadows in the room where, she said, I suppose I live, and this day is beginning badly, but they all do now, for one reason or another. In a drowse, she sprayed perfume on her hair, put on her moleskin cap and jacket, now in their second winter, but still good, still nice to wear, again being glad she had paid a frightening price for them. She had enjoyed them all this time, and in no case would she have had the money now. Maybe she could manage for that Bond. She could not find the lock without leaning to search for it, then stood undecided a moment possessed by the notion that she had forgotten something she would miss seriously later on.

Adam was in the hallway, a step outside his own door; he swung about as if quite startled to see her, and said, "Hello. I don't have to go back to camp today after all—isn't that luck?"

Miranda smiled at him gaily because she was always delighted at the sight of him. He was wearing his new uniform, and he was all olive and tan and tawny, hay colored and sand colored from hair to boots. She half noticed again that he always began by smiling at her; that his smile faded gradually; that his eyes became fixed and thoughtful as if he were reading in a poor light.

They walked out together into the fine fall day, scuffling bright ragged leaves under their feet, turning their faces up to a generous sky really blue and spotless. At the first corner they waited for a funeral to pass, the mourners seated straight and firm as if proud in their sorrow.

"I imagine I'm late," said Miranda, "as usual. What time is it?"

"Nearly half past one," he said, slipping back his sleeve with an exaggerated thrust of his arm upward. The young soldiers were still self-conscious about their wrist watches. Such of them as Miranda knew were boys from southern and southwestern towns, far off the Atlantic seaboard, and they had always believed that only sissies wore wrist watches. "I'll slap you on the wrist watch," one vaudeville comedian would simper to another, and it was always a good joke, never stale.

"I think it's a most sensible way to carry a watch," said Miranda. "You needn't blush."

"I'm nearly used to it," said Adam, who was from Texas. "We've been told time and again how all the he-manly regular army men wear them. It's the horrors of war," he said; "are we downhearted? I'll say we are."

It was the kind of patter going the rounds. "You look it," said Miranda.

He was tall and heavily muscled in the shoulders, narrow in the waist and flanks, and he was infinitely buttoned, strapped, harnessed into a uniform as tough and unyielding in cut as a strait jacket, though the cloth was fine and supple. He had his uniforms made by the best tailor he could find, he confided to Miranda one day when she told him how squish he was looking in his new soldier suit. "Hard enough to make anything of the outfit, anyhow," he told her. "It's the least I can do for my beloved country, not to go around looking like a tramp." He was twenty-four years old and a Second Lieutenant in an Engineers Corps, on leave because his outfit expected to be sent over shortly. "Came in to make my will," he told Miranda, "and get a supply of toothbrushes and razor blades. By what gorgeous luck do you suppose," he asked her, "I happened to pick on your rooming house? How did I know you were there?"

Strolling, keeping step, his stout polished well-made boots setting themselves down firmly beside her thin-soled black suède, they put off as long as they could the end of their moment together, and kept up as well as they could their small talk that flew back and forth over little grooves worn in the thin upper surface of the brain, things you could say and hear clink reassuringly at once without disturbing the radiance which played and darted about the simple and lovely miracle of being two persons named Adam and Miranda, twenty-four years old each, alive and on the earth at the same moment: "Are you in the mood for dancing, Miranda?" and "I'm always in the mood for dancing, Adam!" but there were things in the way, the day that ended with dancing was a long way to go.

He really did look, Miranda thought, like a fine healthy apple this morning. One time or another in their talking, he had boasted that he had never had a pain in his life that he could remember. Instead of being horrified at this monster, she approved his monstrous uniqueness. As for herself, she had had too many pains to mention, so she did not mention them. After working for three years on a morning newspaper she had an illusion of maturity and experience; but it was fatigue merely, she decided, from keeping what she had been brought up to believe were unnatural hours, eating casually at dirty little restaurants, drinking bad coffee all night, and smoking too much. When she said something of her way of living to Adam, he studied her face a few seconds as if he had never seen it before, and said in a forthright way, "Why, it hasn't hurt you a bit, I think you're beautiful," and left her dangling there, wondering if he had thought she wished to be praised. She did wish to be praised, but not at that moment. Adam kept unwholesome hours too, or had in the ten days they had known each other, staying awake until one o'clock to take her out for supper; he smoked also continually, though if she did not stop him he was apt to explain to her exactly what smoking did to the lungs. "But," he said, "does it matter so much if you're going to war, anyway?"

"No," said Miranda, "and it matters even less if you're staying at home knitting socks. Give me a cigarette, will you?" They paused at another corner, under a half-foliaged maple, and hardly glanced at a funeral procession approaching. His eyes were pale tan with orange flecks in them, and his hair was the color of a haystack when you turn the weathered top back to the clear straw beneath. He fished out his cigarette case and snapped his silver lighter at her, snapped it several times in his own face, and they moved on, smoking.

"I can see you knitting socks," he said. "That would be just your speed. You know perfectly well you can't knit."

"I do worse," she said soberly; "I write pieces advising other young women to knit and roll bandages and do without sugar and help win the war."

"Oh, well," said Adam, with the easy masculine morals in such questions, "that's merely your job, that doesn't count."

"I wonder," said Miranda. "How did you manage to get an extension of leave?"

"They just gave it," said Adam, "for no reason. The men are dying like flies out there, anyway. This funny new disease. Simply knocks you into a cocked hat."

"It seems to be a plague," said Miranda, "something out of the Middle Ages. Did you ever see so many funerals, ever?"

"Never did. Well, let's be strong minded and not have any of it. I've got four days more straight from the blue and not a blade of grass must grow under our feet. What about tonight?"

"Same thing," she told him, "but make it about half past one. I've got a special job beside my usual run of the mill."

"What a job you've got," said Adam, "nothing to do but run from one dizzy amusement to another and then write a piece about it."

"Yes, it's too dizzy for words," said Miranda. They stood while a funeral passed, and this time they watched it in silence. Miranda pulled her cap to an angle and winked in the sunlight, her head swimming slowly "like a goldfish," she told Adam, "my head swims. I'm only half awake, I must have some coffee."

They lounged on their elbows over the counter of a drug store. "No more cream for the stay-at-homes," she said, "and only one lump of sugar. I'll have two or none; that's the kind of martyr I'm being. I mean to live on boiled cabbage and wear shoddy from now on and get in good shape for the next round. No war is going to sneak up on me again."

"Oh, there won't be any more wars, don't you read the newspapers?" asked Adam. "We're going to mop 'em up this time, and they're going to stay mopped, and this is going to be all."

"So they told me," said Miranda, tasting her bitter lukewarm brew and making a rueful face. Their smiles approved of each other, they felt they had got the right tone, they were taking the war properly. Above all, thought Miranda, no tooth-gnashing, no hair-tearing, it's noisy and unbecoming and it doesn't get you anywhere.

"Swill," said Adam rudely, pushing back his cup. "Is that all you're having for breakfast?"

"It's more than I want," said Miranda.

"I had buckwheat cakes, with sausage and maple syrup, and two bananas, and two cups of coffee, at eight o'clock, and right now, again, I feel like a famished orphan left in the ashcan. I'm all set," said Adam, "for broiled steak and fried potatoes and—"

"Don't go on with it," said Miranda, "it sounds delirious to me. Do all that after I'm gone." She slipped from the high seat, leaned against it slightly, glanced at her face in her round mirror, rubbed rouge on her lips and decided that she was past praying for.

"There's something terribly wrong," she told Adam. "I feel too rotten. It can't just be the weather, and the war."

"The weather is perfect," said Adam, "and the war is simply too good to be true. But since when? You were all right yesterday."

"I don't know," she said slowly, her voice sounding small and thin. They stopped as always at the open door before the flight of littered steps leading up to the newspaper loft. Miranda listened for a moment to the rattle of typewriters above, the steady rumble of presses below. "I wish we were going to spend the whole afternoon on a park bench," she said, "or drive to the mountains."

"I do too," he said; "let's do that tomorrow."

"Yes, tomorrow, unless something else happens. I'd like to run away," she told him; "let's both."

"Me?" said Adam. "Where I'm going there's no running to speak of. You mostly crawl about on your stomach here and there among the debris. You know, barbed wire and such stuff. It's going to be the kind of thing that happens once in a lifetime." He reflected a moment, and went on, "I don't know a darned thing about it, really, but they make it sound awfully messy. I've heard so much about it I feel as if I had been there and back. It's going to be an anticlimax," he said, "like seeing the pictures of a place so often you can't see it at all when you actually get there. Seems to me I've been in the army all my life."

Six months, he meant. Eternity. He looked so clear and fresh, and he had never had a pain in his life. She had seen them when they had been there and back and they never looked like this again. "Already the returned hero," she said, "and don't I wish you were."

"When I learned the use of the bayonet in my first training camp," said Adam, "I gouged the vitals out of more sandbags and sacks of hay than I could keep track of. They kept bawling at us, 'Get him, get that Boche, stick him before he sticks you'—and we'd go for those sandbags like wildfire, and honestly, sometimes I felt a perfect fool for getting so worked up when I saw the sand trickling out. I used to wake up in the night sometimes feeling silly about it."

"I can imagine," said Miranda. "It's perfect nonsense." They lingered, unwilling to say good-by. After a little pause, Adam, as if keeping up the conversation, asked, "Do you know what the average life expectation of a sapping party is after it hits the job?"

"Something speedy, I suppose."

"Just nine minutes," said Adam; "I read that in your own newspaper not a week ago."

"Make it ten and I'll come along," said Miranda.

"Not another second," said Adam, "exactly nine minutes, take it or leave it."

"Stop bragging," said Miranda. "Who figured that out?"

"A noncombatant," said Adam, "a fellow with rickets."

This seemed very comic, they laughed and leaned towards each other and Miranda heard herself being a little shrill. She wiped the tears from her eyes. "My, it's a funny war," she said; "isn't it? I laugh every time I think about it."

Adam took her hand in both of his and pulled a little at the tips of her gloves and sniffed them. "What nice perfume you have," he said, "and such a lot of it, too. I like a lot of perfume on gloves and hair," he said, sniffing again.

"I've got probably too much," she said. "I can't smell or see or hear today. I must have a fearful cold."

"Don't catch cold," said Adam; "my leave is nearly up and it will be the last, the very last." She moved her fingers in her gloves as he pulled at the fingers and turned her hands as if they were something new and curious and of great value, and she turned shy and quiet. She liked him, she liked him, and there was more than this but it was no good even imagining, because he was not for her nor for any woman, being beyond experience already, committed without any knowledge or act of his own to death. She took back her hands. "Good-by," she said finally, "until tonight."

She ran upstairs and looked back from the top. He was still watching her, and raised his hand without smiling. Miranda hardly ever saw anyone look back after he had said good-by. She could not help turning sometimes for one glimpse more of the person she had been talking with, as if that would save too rude and too sudden a snapping of even the lightest bond. But people hurried away, their faces already changed, fixed, in their straining towards their next stopping place, already absorbed in planning their next act or encounter. Adam was waiting as if he expected her to turn, and under his brows fixed in a strained frown, his eyes were very black.

At her desk she sat without taking off jacket or cap, slitting envelopes and pretending to read the letters. Only Chuck Rouncivale, the sports reporter, and Ye Towne Gossyp were sitting on her desk today, and them she liked having there. She sat on theirs when she pleased. Towney and Chuck were talking and they went on with it.

"They say," said Towney, "that it is really caused by germs brought by a German ship to Boston, a camouflaged ship, naturally, it didn't come in under its own colors. Isn't that ridiculous?"

"Maybe it was a submarine," said Chuck, "sneaking in from the bottom of the sea in the dead of night. Now that sounds better."

"Yes, it does," said Towney; "they always slip up somewhere in these details . . . and they think the germs were sprayed over the city—it started in Boston, you know—and somebody reported seeing a strange, thick, greasy-looking cloud float up out of Boston Harbor and spread slowly all over that end of town. I think it was an old woman who saw it."

"Should have been," said Chuck.

"I read it in a New York newspaper," said Towney; "so it's bound to be true."

Chuck and Miranda laughed so loudly at this that Bill stood up and glared at them. "Towney still reads the newspapers," explained Chuck.

"Well, what's funny about that?" asked Bill, sitting down again and frowning into the clutter before him.

"It was a noncombatant saw that cloud," said Miranda.

"Naturally," said Towney.

"Member of the Lusk Committee, maybe," said Miranda.

"The Angel of Mons," said Chuck, "or a dollar-a-year man."

Miranda wished to stop hearing, and talking, she wished to think for just five minutes of her own about Adam, really to think about him, but there was no time. She had seen him first ten days ago, and since then they had been crossing streets together, darting between trucks and limousines and pushcarts and farm wagons; he had waited for her in doorways and in little restaurants that smelled of stale frying fat; they had eaten and danced to the urgent whine and bray of jazz orchestras, they had sat in dull theaters because Miranda was there to write a piece about the play. Once they had gone to the mountains and, leaving the car, had climbed a stony trail, and had come out on a ledge upon a flat stone, where they sat and watched the lights change on a valley landscape that was, no doubt, Miranda said, quite apocryphal—"We need not believe it, but it is fine poetry," she told him; they had leaned their shoulders together there, and had sat quite still, watching. On two Sundays they had gone to the geological museum, and had pored in shared fascination over bits of meteors, rock formations, fossilized tusks and trees, Indian arrows, grottoes from the silver and gold lodes. "Think of those old miners washing out fortunes in little pans beside the streams," said Adam, "and inside the earth there was this—" and he had told her he liked better those things that took long to make; he loved airplanes too, all sorts of machinery, things carved out of wood or stone. He knew nothing much about them, but he recognized them when he saw them. He had confessed that he simply could not get through a book, any kind of book except textbooks on engineering; reading bored him to crumbs; he regretted now he hadn't brought his roadster, but he hadn't thought he would need a car; he loved driving, he wouldn't expect her to believe how many hundreds of miles he could get over in a day . . . he had showed her snapshots of himself at the wheel of his roadster; of himself sailing a boat, looking very free and windblown, all angles, hauling on the ropes; he would have joined the air force, but his mother had hysterics every time he mentioned it. She didn't seem to realize that dog fighting in the air was a good deal safer than sapping parties on the ground at night. But he hadn't argued, because of course she did not realize about sapping parties. And here he was, stuck, on a plateau a mile high with no water for a boat and his car at home, otherwise they could really have had a good time. Miranda knew he was trying to tell her what kind of person he was when he had his machinery with him. She felt she knew pretty well what kind of person he was, and would have liked to tell him that if he thought he had left himself at home in a boat or an automobile, he was much mistaken. The telephones were ringing, Bill was shouting at somebody who kept saying, "Well, but listen, well, but listen—" but nobody was going to listen, of course, nobody. Old man Gibbons bellowed in despair, "Jarge, Jarge—"

"Just the same," Towney was saying in her most complacent patriotic voice. "Hut Service is a fine idea, and we should all volunteer even if they don't want us." Towney does well at this, thought Miranda, look at her; remembering the rose-colored sweater and the tight rebellious face in the cloakroom. Towney was now all open-faced glory and goodness, willing to sacrifice herself for her country. "After all," said Towney, "I *can* sing and dance well enough for the Little Theater, and I could write their letters for them, and at a pinch I might drive an ambulance. I have driven a Ford for years."

Miranda joined in: "Well, I can sing and dance too, but who's going to do the bed-making and the scrubbing up? Those huts are hard to keep, and it would be a dirty job and we'd be perfectly miserable; and as I've got a hard dirty job and am perfectly miserable, I'm going to stay at home."

"I think the women should keep out of it," said Chuck Rouncivale. "They just add skirts to the horrors of war." Chuck had bad lungs and fretted a good deal about missing the show. "I could have been there and back with a leg off by now; it would have served the old man right. Then he'd either have to buy his own hooch or sober up."

Miranda had seen Chuck on pay day giving the old man money for hooch. He was a good-humored ingratiating old scoundrel, too, that was the worst of him. He slapped his son on the back and beamed upon him with the bleared eye of paternal affection while he took his last nickel.

"It was Florence Nightingale ruined wars," Chuck went on. "What's the idea of petting soldiers and binding up their wounds and soothing their fevered brows? That's not war. Let 'em perish where they fall. That's what they're there for."

"You can talk," said Towney, with a slantwise glint at him.

"What's the idea?" asked Chuck, flushing and hunching his shoulders. "You know I've got this lung, or maybe half of it anyway by now."

"You're much too sensitive," said Towney. "I didn't mean a thing."

Bill had been raging about, chewing his half-smoked cigar, his hair standing up in a brush, his eyes soft and lambent but wild, like a stag's. He would never, thought Miranda, be more than fourteen years old if he lived for a century, which he would not, at the rate he was going. He behaved exactly like city editors in the moving pictures, even to the chewed cigar. Had he formed his style on the films, or had scenario writers seized once for all on the type Bill in its inarguable purity? Bill was shouting to Chuck: *"And if he comes back here take him up the alley and saw his head off by hand!"*

Chuck said, "He'll be back, don't worry." Bill said mildly, already off on another track, "Well, saw him off." Towney went to her own desk, but Chuck sat waiting amiably to be taken to the new vaudeville show. Miranda, with two tickets, always invited one of the reporters to go with her on Monday. Chuck was lavishly hardboiled and professional in his sports writing, but he had told Miranda that he didn't give a damn about sports, really; the job kept him out in the open, and paid him enough to buy the old man's hooch. He preferred shows and didn't see why women always had the job.

"Who does Bill want sawed today?" asked Miranda.

"That hoofer you panned in this morning's," said Chuck. "He was up here bright and early asking for the guy that writes up the show business. He said he was going to take the goof who wrote that piece up the alley and bop him in the nose. He said . . ."

"I hope he's gone," said Miranda; "I do hope he had to catch a train."

Chuck stood up and arranged his maroon-colored turtle-necked sweater, glanced down at the peasoup tweed plus fours and the hobnailed tan boots which he hoped would help to disguise the fact that he had a bad lung and didn't care for sports, and said, "He's long gone by now, don't worry. Let's get going; you're late as usual."

Miranda, facing about, almost stepped on the toes of a little drab man in a derby hat. He might have been a pretty fellow once, but now his mouth drooped where he had lost his side teeth, and his sad red-rimmed eyes had given up coquetry. A thin brown wave of hair was combed out with brilliantine and curled against the rim of the derby. He didn't move his feet, but stood planted with a kind of inert resistance, and asked Miranda: "Are you the so-called dramatic critic on this hick newspaper?"

"I'm afraid I am," said Miranda.

"Well," said the little man, "I'm just asking for one minute of your valuable time." His underlip shot out, he began with shaking hands to fish about in his waistcoat pocket. "I just hate to let you get away with it, that's all." He riffled through a collection of shabby newspaper clippings. "Just give these the once-over, will you? And then let me ask you if you think I'm gonna stand for being knocked by a tanktown critic," he said, in a toneless voice; "look here, here's Buffalo, Chicago, Saint Looey, Philadelphia, Frisco, besides New York. Here's the best publications in the business, *Variety,* the *Billboard,* they all broke down and admitted that Danny Dickerson knows his stuff. So you don't think so, hey? That's all I wanta ask you."

"No, I don't," said Miranda, as bluntly as she could, "and I can't stop to talk about it."

The little man leaned nearer, his voice shook as if he had been nervous for a long time. "Look here, what was there you didn't like about me? Tell me that."

Miranda said, "You shouldn't pay any attention at all. What does it matter what I think?"

"I don't care what you think, it ain't that," said the little man, "but these thing get round and booking agencies back East don't know how it is out here. We get panned in the sticks and they think it's the same as getting panned in Chicago, see? They don't know the difference. They don't know that the more high class an act is the more the hick critics pan it. But I've been called the best in the business by the best in the business and I wanta know what you think is wrong with me."

Chuck said, "Come on, Miranda, curtain's going up." Miranda handed the little man his clippings, they were mostly ten years old, and tried to edge past him. He stepped before her again and said without much conviction, "If you was a man I'd knock your block off." Chuck got up at that and lounged over, taking his hands out of his pockets, and said, "Now you've done your song and dance you'd better get out. Get the hell out now before I throw you downstairs."

The little man pulled at the top of his tie, a small blue tie with red polka dots, slightly frayed at the knot. He pulled it straight and repeated as if he had rehearsed it, "Come out in the alley." The tears filled his thickened red lids. Chuck said, "Ah, shut up," and followed Miranda, who was running towards the stairs. He overtook her on the sidewalk. "I left him sniveling and shuffling his publicity trying to find the joker," said Chuck, "the poor old heel."

Miranda said, "There's too much of everything in this world just now. I'd like to sit down here on the curb, Chuck, and die, and never again see —I wish I could lose my memory and forget my own name . . . I wish—"

Chuck said, "Toughen up, Miranda. This is no time to cave in. Forget that fellow. For every hundred people in show business, there are ninety-nine like him. But you don't manage right, anyway. You bring it on yourself. All you have to do is play up the headliners, and you needn't even mention the also-rans. Try to keep in mind that Rypinsky has got show business cornered in this town; please Rypinsky and you'll please the advertising department, please them and you'll get a raise. Hand-in-glove, my poor dumb child, will you never learn?"

"I seem to keep learning all the wrong things," said Miranda, hopelessly.

"You do for a fact," Chuck told her cheerfully. "You are as good at it as I ever saw. Now do you feel better?"

"This is a rotten show you've invited me to," said Chuck. "Now what are you going to do about it? If I were writing it up, I'd—"

"Do write it up," said Miranda. "You write it up this time. I'm getting ready to leave, anyway, but don't tell anybody yet."

"You mean it? All my life," said Chuck, "I've yearned to be a so-called dramatic critic on a hick newspaper, and this is positively my first chance."

"Better take it," Miranda told him. "It may be your last." She thought, This is the beginning of the end of something. Something terrible is going to happen to me. I shan't need bread and butter where I'm going. I'll will it to Chuck, he has a venerable father to buy hooch for. I hope they let him have it. Oh, Adam, I hope I see you once more before I go under with whatever is the matter with me. "I wish the war were over," she said to Chuck, as if they had been talking about that. "I wish it were over and I wish it had never begun."

Chuck had got out his pad and pencil and was already writing his review. What she had said seemed safe enough but how would he take it? "I don't care how it started or when it ends," said Chuck, scribbling away, "I'm not going to be there."

All the rejected men talked like that, thought Miranda. War was the one thing they wanted, now they couldn't have it. Maybe they wanted badly to go, some of them. All of them had a sidelong eye for the women they talked with about it, a guarded resentment which said, "Don't pin a white feather on me, you bloodthirsty female. I've offered my meat to the crows and they won't have it." The worst thing about war for the stay-at-homes is there isn't anyone to talk to any more. The Lusk Committee will get you if you don't watch out. Bread will win the war. Work will win, sugar will win, peach pits will win the war. Nonsense. *Not* nonsense, I tell you, there's some kind of valuable high explosive to be got out of peach pits. So all the happy housewives hurry during the canning season to lay their baskets of peach pits on the altar of their country. It keeps them busy and makes them feel useful, and all these women running wild with the men away are dangerous, if they aren't given something to keep their little minds out of mischief. So rows of young girls, the intact cradles of the future, with their pure serious faces framed becomingly in Red Cross wimples, roll cock-eyed bandages that will never reach a base hospital, and knit sweaters that will never warm a manly chest, their minds dwelling lovingly on all the blood and mud and the next dance at the Acanthus Club for the officers of the flying corps. Keeping still and quiet will win the war.

"I'm simply not going to be there," said Chuck, absorbed in his review.

No, Adam will be there, thought Miranda. She slipped down in the chair and leaned her head against the dusty plush, closed her eyes and faced for one instant that was a lifetime the certain, the overwhelming and awful knowledge that there was nothing at all ahead for Adam and for her. Nothing. She opened her eyes and held hands together palms up, gazing at them and trying to understand oblivion.

"Now look at this," said Chuck, for the lights had come on and the audience was rustling and talking again. "I've got it all done, even before the headliner comes on. It's old Stella Mayhew, and she's always good, she's been good for forty years, and she's going to sing 'O the blues ain't nothin' but the easy-going heart disease.' That's all you need to know about her. Now just glance over this. Would you be willing to sign it?"

Miranda took the pages and stared at them conscientiously, turning them over, she hoped, at the right moment, and gave them back. "Yes, Chuck, yes, I'd sign that. But I won't. We must tell Bill you wrote it, because it's your start, maybe."

"You don't half appreciate it," said Chuck. "You read it too fast. Here, listen to this—" and he began to mutter excitedly. While he was reading she watched his face. It was a pleasant face with some kind of spark of life in it, and a good severity in the modeling of the brow above the nose. For the first time since she had known him she wondered what Chuck was thinking about. He looked preoccupied and unhappy, he wasn't so frivolous as he sounded. The people were crowding into the aisle, bringing out their cigarette cases ready to strike a match the instant they reached the lobby; women with waved hair clutched at their wraps, men stretched their chins to ease them of their stiff collars, and Chuck said, "We might as well go now." Miranda, buttoning her jacket, stepped into the moving crowd, thinking, What did I ever know about them? There must be a great many of them here who think as I do, and we dare not say a word to each other of our desperation, we are speechless animals letting ourselves be destroyed, and why? Does anybody here believe the things we say to each other?

Stretched in unease on the ridge of the wicker couch in the cloakroom, Miranda waited for time to pass and leave Adam with her. Time seemed to proceed with more than usual eccentricity, leaving twilight gaps in her mind for thirty minutes which seemed like a second, and then hard flashes of light that shone clearly on her watch proving that three minutes is an intolerable stretch of waiting, as if she were hanging by her thumbs. At last it was reasonable to imagine Adam stepping out of the house in the early darkness into the blue mist that might soon be rain, he would be on the way, and there was nothing to think about him, after all. There was only the wish to see him and the fear, the present threat, of not seeing him again; for every step they took towards each other seemed perilous, drawing them apart instead of together, as a swimmer in spite of his most determined strokes is yet drawn slowly backward by the tide. "I don't want to love," she would think in spite of herself, "not Adam, there is no time and we are not ready for it and yet this is all we have—"

And there he was on the sidewalk, with his foot on the first step, and Miranda almost ran down to meet him. Adam, holding her hands, asked, "Do you feel well now? Are you hungry? Are you tired? Will you feel like dancing after the show?"

"Yes to everything," said Miranda, "yes, yes. . . ." Her head was like a feather, and she steadied herself on his arm. The mist was still mist that might be rain later, and though the air was sharp and clean in her mouth, it did not, she decided, make breathing any easier. "I hope the show is good, or at least funny," she told him, "but I promise nothing."

It was a long, dreary play, but Adam and Miranda sat very quietly together waiting patiently for it to be over. Adam carefully and seriously pulled off her glove and held her hand as if he were accustomed to holding her hand in theaters. Once they turned and their eyes met, but only once, and the two pairs of eyes were equally steady and noncommittal. A deep tremor set up in Miranda, and she set about resisting herself methodically as if she were closing windows and doors and fastening down curtains against a rising storm. Adam sat watching the monotonous play with a strange shining excitement, his face quite fixed and still.

When the curtain rose for the third act, the third did not take place at once. There was instead disclosed a backdrop almost covered with an American flag improperly and disrespectfully exposed, nailed at each upper corner, gathered in the middle and nailed again, sagging dustily. Before it posed a local dollar-a-year man, now doing his bit as a Liberty Bond salesman. He was an ordinary man past middle life, with a neat little melon buttoned into his trousers and waistcoat, an opinionated tight mouth, a face and figure in which nothing could be read save the inept sensual record of fifty years. But for once in his life he was an important fellow in an impressive situation, and he reveled, rolling his words in an actorish tone.

"Looks like a penguin," said Adam. They moved, smiled at each other, Miranda reclaimed her hand, Adam folded his together and they prepared to wear their way again through the same old moldy speech with the same old dusty backdrop. Miranda tried not to listen, but she heard. These vile Huns—glorious Belleau Wood—our keyword is Sacrifice—Martyred Belgium —give till it hurts—our noble boys Over There—Big Berthas—the death of civilization—the Boche—

"My head aches," whispered Miranda. "Oh, why won't he hush?"

"He won't," whispered Adam. "I'll get you some aspirin."

"In Flanders Field the poppies grow, Between the crosses row on row"— "He's getting into the home stretch," whispered Adam—atrocities, innocent babes hoisted on Boche bayonets—your child and my child—if our children are spared these things, then let us say with all reverence that these dead have not died in vain—the war, the *war*, the WAR to end WAR, war for Democracy, for humanity, a safe world forever and ever—and to prove our faith in Democracy to each other, and to the world, let everybody get together and buy Liberty Bonds and do without sugar and wool socks—was that it? Miranda asked herself, Say that over, I didn't catch the last line. Did you mention Adam? If you didn't I'm not interested. What about Adam, you little pig? And what are we going to sing this time, "Tipperary" or "There's a Long, Long Trail"? Oh, please do let the show go on and get over with. I must write a piece about it before I can go dancing with Adam and we have no time. Coal, iron, gold, international finance, why don't you tell us about them, you little liar?

The audience rose and sang, "There's a Long Long Trail A-winding," their opened mouths black and faces pallid in the reflected footlights; some of the faces grimaced and wept and had shining streaks like snail's tracks on them. Adam and Miranda joined in at the tops of their voices, grinning shamefacedly at each other once or twice.

In the street, they lit their cigarettes and walked slowly as always. "Just another nasty old man who would like to see the young ones killed," said Miranda in a low voice; "the tomcats try to eat the little tom-kittens, you know. They don't fool you really, do they, Adam?"

The young people were talking like that about the business by then. They felt they were seeing pretty clearly through that game. She went on, "I hate these potbellied baldheads, too fat, too old, too cowardly, to go to war themselves, they know they're safe; it's you they are sending instead—"

Adam turned eyes of genuine surprise upon her. "Oh, *that* one," he said. "Now what could the poor sap do if they did take him? It's not his fault," he explained, "he can't do anything but talk." His pride in his youth, his forbearance and tolerance and contempt for that unlucky being breathed out of his very pores as he strolled, straight and relaxed in his strength. "What *could* you expect of him, Miranda?"

She spoke his name often, and he spoke hers rarely. The little shock of pleasure the sound of her name in his mouth gave her stopped her answer. For a moment she hesitated, and began at another point of attack. "Adam," she said, "the worst of war is the fear and suspicion and the awful expression in all the eyes you meet . . . as if they had pulled down the shutters over their minds and their hearts and were peering out at you, ready to leap if you make one gesture or say one word they do not understand instantly. It frightens me; I live in fear too, and no one should have to live in fear. It's the skulking about, and the lying. It's what war does to the mind and the heart, Adam, and you can't separate these two—what it does to them is worse than what it can do to the body."

Adam said soberly, after a moment, "Oh, yes, but suppose one comes back whole? The mind and the heart sometimes get another chance, but if anything happens to the poor old human frame, why, it's just out of luck, that's all."

"Oh, yes," mimicked Miranda. "It's just out of luck, that's all."

"If I didn't go," said Adam, in a matter-of-fact voice, "I couldn't look myself in the face."

So that's all settled. With her fingers flattened on his arm, Miranda was silent, thinking about Adam. No, there was no resentment or revolt in him. Pure, she thought, all the way through, flawless, complete, as the sacrificial lamb must be. The sacrificial lamb strode along casually, accommodating his long pace to hers, keeping her on the inside of the walk in the good American style, helping her across street corners as if she were a cripple—"I hope we don't come to a mud puddle, he'll carry me over it"—giving off whiffs of tobacco smoke, a manly smell of scentless soap, freshly cleaned leather and freshly washed skin, breathing through his nose and carrying his chest easily. He threw back his head and smiled into the sky which still misted, promising rain. "Oh, boy," he said, "what a night. Can't you hurry that review of yours so we can get started?"

He waited for her before a cup of coffee in the restaurant next to the pressroom, nicknamed The Greasy Spoon. When she came down at last, freshly washed and combed and powdered, she saw Adam first, sitting near the dingy big window, face turned to the street, but looking down. It was an extraordinary face, smooth and fine and golden in the shabby light, but now set in a blind melancholy, a look of pained suspense and disillusion. For just one split second she got a glimpse of Adam when he would have been older, the face of the man he would not live to be. He saw her then, rose, and the bright glow was there.

Adam pulled their chairs together at their table; they drank hot tea and listened to the orchestra jazzing "Pack Up Your Troubles."

"In an old kit bag, and smoil, smoil, smoil," shouted half a dozen boys under the draft age, gathered around a table near the orchestra. They yelled incoherently, laughed in great hysterical bursts of something that appeared to be merriment, and passed around under the tablecloth flat bottles containing a clear liquid—for in this western city founded and built by roaring drunken miners, no one was allowed to take his alcohol openly—splashed it into their tumblers of ginger ale, and went on singing, "It's a Long Way to Tipperary." When the tune changed to "Madelon," Adam said, "Let's dance." It was a tawdry little place, crowded and hot and full of smoke, but there was nothing better. The music was gay; and life is completely crazy anyway, thought Miranda, so what does it matter? This is what we have, Adam and I, this is all we're going to get, this is the way it is with us. She wanted to say, "Adam, come out of your dream and listen to me. I have pains in my chest and my head and my heart and they're real. I am in pain all over, and you are in such danger as I can't bear to think about, and why can we not save each other?" When her hand tightened on his shoulder his arm tightened about her waist instantly, and stayed there, holding firmly. They said nothing but smiled continually at each other, odd changing smiles as though they had found a new language. Miranda, her face near Adam's shoulder, noticed a dark young pair sitting at a corner table, each with an arm around the waist of the other, their heads together, their eyes staring at the same thing, whatever it was, that hovered in space before them. Her right hand lay on the table, his hand over it, and her face was a blur with weeping. Now and then he raised her hand and kissed it, and set it down and held it, and her eyes would fill again. They were not shameless, they had merely forgotten where they were, or they had no other place to go, perhaps. They said not a word, and the small pantomime repeated itself, like a melancholy short film running monotonously over and over again. Miranda envied them. She envied that girl. At least she can weep if that helps, and he does not even have to ask, What is the matter? Tell me. They had cups of coffee before them, and after a long while—Miranda and Adam had danced and sat down again twice—when the coffee was quite cold, they drank it suddenly, then embraced as before, without a word and scarcely a glance at each other. Something was done and settled between them, at least; it was enviable, enviable, that they could sit quietly together and have the same expression on their faces while they looked into the hell they shared, no matter what kind of hell, it was theirs, they were together.

At the table nearest Adam and Miranda a young woman was leaning on her elbow, telling her young man a story. "And I don't like him because he's too fresh. He kept on asking me to take a drink and I kept telling him, I don't drink and he said, Now look here, I want a drink the worst way and I think it's mean of you not to drink with me, I can't sit up here and drink by myself, he said. I told him, You're not by yourself in the first place; I like that, I said, and if you want a drink go ahead and have it, I told him, why drag *me* in? So he called the waiter and ordered ginger ale and two glasses and I drank straight ginger ale like I always do but he poured a shot of hooch in his. He was awfully proud of that hooch, said he made it himself out of potatoes. Nice homemade likker, warm from the pipe, he told me, three drops of this and your ginger ale will taste like Mumm's Extry. But I said, No, and I mean no, can't you get that through your bean? He took another drink and said, Ah, come on, honey, don't be so stubborn, this'll make your shimmy shake. So I just got tired of the argument, and I said, I don't need to drink, to shake my shimmy, I can strut my stuff on tea, I said. Well, why don't you then, he wanted to know, and I just told him—"

She knew she had been asleep for a long time when all at once without even a warning footstep or creak of the door hinge, Adam was in the room turning on the light, and she knew it was he, though at first she was blinded and turned her head away. He came over at once and sat on the side of the bed and began to talk as if he were going on with something they had been talking about before. He crumpled a square of paper and tossed it in the fireplace.

"You didn't get my note," he said. "I left it under the door. I was called back suddenly to camp for a lot of inoculations. They kept me longer than I expected, I was late. I called the office and they told me you were not coming in today. I called Miss Hobbe here and she said you were in bed and couldn't come to the telephone. Did she give you my message?"

"No," said Miranda drowsily, "but I think I have been asleep all day. Oh, I do remember. There was a doctor here. Bill sent him. I was at the telephone once, for Bill told me he would send an ambulance and have me taken to the hospital. The doctor tapped my chest and left a prescription and said he would be back, but he hasn't come."

"Where is it, the prescription?" asked Adam.

"I don't know. He left it, though, I saw him."

Adam moved about searching the tables and the mantelpiece. "Here it is," he said. "I'll be back in a few minutes. I must look for an all-night drug store. It's after one o'clock. Good-by."

Good-by, good-by. Miranda watched the door where he had disappeared for quite a while, then closed her eyes, and thought, When I am not here I cannot remember anything about this room where I have lived for nearly a year, except that the curtains are too thin and there was never any way of shutting out the morning light. Miss Hobbe had promised heavier curtains, but they had never appeared. When Miranda in her dressing gown had been at the telephone that morning, Miss Hobbe had passed through, carrying a tray. She was a little red-haired nervously friendly creature, and her manner said all too plainly that the place was not paying and she was on the ragged edge.

"My dear *child*," she said sharply, with a glance at Miranda's attire, "what is the matter?"

Miranda, with the receiver to her ear, said, "Influenza, I think."

"*Horrors*," said Miss Hobbe, in a whisper, and tray wavered in her hands. "Go back to bed at once . . . go at *once!*"

"I must talk to Bill first," Miranda had told her, and Miss Hobbe had hurried on and had not returned. Bill had shouted directions at her, promising everything, doctor, nurse, ambulance, hospital, her check every week as usual, everything, but she was to get back to bed and stay there. She dropped into bed, thinking that Bill was the only person she had ever seen who actually tore his own hair when he was excited enough . . . I suppose I should ask to be sent home, she thought, it's a respectable old custom to inflict your death on the family if you can manage it. No, I'll stay here, this is my business, but not in this room, I hope . . . I wish I were in the cold mountains in the snow, that's what I should like best; and all about her rose the measured ranges of the Rockies wearing their perpetual snow, their majestic blue laurels of cloud, chilling her to the bone with their sharp breath. Oh, no, I must have warmth—and her memory turned and roved after another place she had known first and loved best, that now she could see only in drifting fragments of palm and cedar, dark shadows and a sky that warmed without dazzling, as this strange sky had dazzled without warming her; there was the long slow wavering of gray moss in the drowsy oak shade, the spacious hovering of buzzards overhead, the smell of crushed water herbs along a bank, and without warning a broad tranquil river into which flowed all the rivers she had known. The walls shelved away in one deliberate silent movement on either side, and a tall sailing ship was moored near by, with a gangplank weathered to blackness touching the foot of her bed. Back of the ship was jungle, and even as it appeared before her, she knew it was all she had ever read or had been told or felt or thought about jungles; a writhing terribly alive and secret place of death, creeping with tangles of spotted serpents, rainbow-colored birds with malign eyes, leopards with humanly wise faces and extravagantly crested lions; screaming long-armed monkeys tumbling among broad fleshy leaves that glowed with sulphur-colored light and exuded the ichor of death, and rotting trunks of unfamiliar trees sprawled in crawling slime. Without surprise, watching from her pillow, she saw herself run swiftly down this gangplank to the slanting deck, and standing there, she leaned on the rail and waved gaily to herself in bed, and the slender ship spread its wings and sailed away into the jungle. The air trembled with the shattering scream and the hoarse bellow of voices all crying together, rolling and colliding above her like ragged stormclouds, and the words became two words only rising and falling and clamoring about her head. Danger, danger, danger, the voices said, and War, war, war. There was her door half open, Adam standing with his hand on the knob, and Miss Hobbe with her face all out of shape with terror was crying shrilly, "I tell you, they must come for her *now,* or I'll put her on the sidewalk . . . I tell you, this is a plague, a plague, my God, and I've got a houseful of people to think about!"

Adam said, "I know that. They'll come for her tomorrow morning."

"Tomorrow morning, my God, they'd better come now!"

"They can't get an ambulance," said Adam, "and there aren't any beds. And we can't find a doctor or a nurse. They're all busy. That's all there is to it. You stay out of the room, and I'll look after her."

"Yes, you'll look after her, I can see that," said Miss Hobbe, in a particularly unpleasant tone.

"Yes, that's what I said," answered Adam, drily, "and you keep out."

He closed the door carefully. He was carrying an assortment of misshapen packages, and his face was astonishingly impassive.

"Did you hear that?" he asked, leaning over and speaking very quietly.

"Most of it," said Miranda, "it's a nice prospect, isn't it?"

"I've got your medicine," said Adam, "and you're to begin with it this minute. She can't put you out."

"So it's really as bad as that," said Miranda.

"It's as bad as anything can be," said Adam, "all the theaters and nearly all the shops and restaurants are closed, and the streets have been full of funerals all day and ambulances all night—"

"But not one for me," said Miranda, feeling hilarious and lightheaded. She sat up and beat her pillow into shape and reached for her robe. "I'm glad you're here, I've been having a nightmare. Give me a cigarette, will you, and light one for yourself and open all the windows and sit near one of them. You're running a risk," she told him, "don't you know that? Why do you do it?"

"Never mind," said Adam, "take your medicine," and offered her two large cherry-colored pills. She swallowed them promptly and instantly vomited them up. "*Do* excuse me," she said, beginning to laugh. "I'm so sorry." Adam without a word and with a very concerned expression washed her face with a wet towel, gave her some cracked ice from one of the packages, and firmly offered her two more pills. "That's what they always did at home," she explained to him, "and it worked." Crushed with humiliation, she put her hands over her face and laughed again, painfully.

"There are two more kinds yet," said Adam, pulling her hands from her face and lifting her chin. "You've hardly begun. And I've got other things, like orange juice and ice cream—they told me to feed you ice cream—and coffee in a thermos bottle, and a thermometer. You have to work through the whole lot so you'd better take it easy."

"This time last night we were dancing," said Miranda, and drank something from a spoon. Her eyes followed him about the room, as he did things for her with an absent-minded face, like a man alone; now and again he would come back, and slipping his hand under her head, would hold a cup or a tumbler to her mouth, and she drank, and followed him with her eyes again, without a clear notion of what was happening.

"Adam," she said, "I've just thought of something. Maybe they forgot St. Luke's Hospital. Call the sisters there and ask them not to be so selfish with their silly old rooms. Tell them I only want a very small dark ugly one for three days, or less. Do try them, Adam."

He believed, apparently, that she was still more or less in her right mind, for she heard him at the telephone explaining in his deliberate voice. He was back again almost at once, saying, "This seems to be my day for getting mixed up with peevish old maids. The sister said that even if they had a room you couldn't have it without doctor's orders. But they didn't have one, anyway. She was pretty sour about it."

"Well," said Miranda in a thick voice, "I think that's abominably rude and mean, don't you?" She sat up with a wide gesture of both arms, and began to retch again, violently.

"Hold it, as you were," called Adam, fetching the basin. He held her head, washed her face and hands with ice water, put her head straight on the pillow, and went over and looked out of the window. "Well," he said at last, sitting beside her again, "they haven't got a room. They haven't got a bed. They haven't even got a baby crib, the way she talked. So I think that's straight enough, and we may as well dig in."

"Isn't the ambulance coming?"

"Tomorrow, maybe."

He took off his tunic and hung it on the back of a chair. Kneeling before the fireplace, he began carefully to set kindling sticks in the shape of an Indian tepee, with a little paper in the center for them to lean upon. He lighted this and placed other sticks upon them, and larger bits of wood. When they were going nicely he added still heavier wood, and coal a few lumps at a time, until there was a good blaze, and a fire that would not need rekindling. He rose and dusted his hands together, the fire illuminated him from the back and his hair shone.

"Adam," said Miranda, "I think you're very beautiful." He laughed out at this, and shook his head at her. "What a hell of a word," he said, "for me." "It was the first that occurred to me," she said, drawing up on her elbow to catch the warmth of the blaze. "That's a good job, that fire."

He sat on the bed again, dragging up a chair and putting his feet on the rungs. They smiled at each other for the first time since he had come in that night. "How do you feel now?" he asked.

"Better, much better," she told him, "Let's talk. Let's tell each other what we meant to do."

"You tell me first," said Adam. "I want to know about you."

"You'd get the notion I had a very sad life," she said, "and perhaps it was, but I'd be glad enough to have it now. If I could have it back, it would be easy to be happy about almost anything at all. That's not true, but that's the way I feel now." After a pause, she said, "There's nothing to tell, after all, if it ends now, for all this time I was getting ready for something that was going to happen later, when the time came. So now it's nothing much."

"But it must have been worth having until now, wasn't it?" he asked seriously as if it were something important to know.

"Not if this is all," she repeated obstinately.

"Weren't you ever—happy?" asked Adam, and he was plainly afraid of the word; he was shy of it as he was of the word *love,* he seemed never to have spoken it before, and was uncertain of its sound or meaning.

"I don't know," she said, "I just lived and never thought about it. I remember things I liked, though, and things I hoped for."

"I was going to be an electrical engineer," said Adam. He stopped short. "And I shall finish up when I get back," he added, after a moment.

"Don't you love being alive?" asked Miranda. "Don't you love weather and the colors at different times of the day, and all the sounds and noises like children screaming in the next lot, and automobile horns and little bands playing in the street and the smell of food cooking?"

"I love to swim, too," said Adam.

"So do I," said Miranda; "we never did swim together."

"Do you remember any prayers?" she asked him suddenly. "Did you ever learn anything at Sunday School?"

"Not much," confessed Adam without contrition. "Well, the Lord's Prayer."

"Yes, and there's Hail Mary," she said, "and the really useful one beginning, I confess to Almighty God and to blessed Mary ever virgin and to the holy Apostles Peter and Paul—"

"Catholic," he commented.

"Prayers just the same, you big Methodist. I'll bet you *are* a Methodist."

"No, Presbyterian."

"Well, what others do you remember?"

"Now I lay me down to sleep—" said Adam.

"Yes, that one, and Blessed Jesus meek and mild—you see that my religious education wasn't neglected either. I even know a prayer beginning O Apollo. Want to hear it?"

"No," said Adam, "you're making fun."

"I'm not," said Miranda, "I'm trying to keep from going to sleep. I'm afraid to go to sleep, I may not wake up. Don't let me go to sleep, Adam. Do you know Matthew, Mark, Luke and John? Bless the bed I lie upon?"

"If I should die before I wake, I pray the Lord my soul to take. Is that it?" asked Adam. "It doesn't sound right, somehow."

"Light me a cigarette, please, and move over and sit near the window. We keep forgetting about fresh air. You must have it." He lighted the cigarette and held it to her lips. She took it between her fingers and dropped it under the edge of her pillow. He found it and crushed it out in the saucer under the water tumbler. Her head swam in darkness for an instant, cleared, and she sat up in panic, throwing off the covers and breaking into a sweat. Adam leaped up with an alarmed face, and almost at once was holding a cup of hot coffee to her mouth.

"You must have some too," she told him, quiet again, and they sat huddled together on the edge of the bed, drinking coffee in silence.

Adam said, "You must lie down again. You're awake now."

"Let's sing," said Miranda. "I know an old spiritual, I can remember some of the words." She spoke in a natural voice. "I'm fine now." She began in a hoarse whisper, " 'Pale horse, pale rider, done taken my lover away . . .' Do you know that song?"

"Yes," said Adam, "I heard Negroes in Texas sing it, in an oil field."

"I heard them sing it in a cotton field," she said; "it's a good song."

They sang that line together. "But I can't remember what comes next," said Adam.

" 'Pale horse, pale rider,' " said Miranda, "(We really need a good banjo) 'done taken my lover away—' " Her voice cleared and she said, "But we ought to get on with it. What's the next line?"

"There's a lot more to it than that," said Adam, "about forty verses, the rider done taken away mammy, pappy, brother, sister, the whole family besides the lover—"

"But not the singer, not yet," said Miranda. "Death always leaves one singer to mourn. 'Death,' " she sang, " 'oh, leave one singer to mourn—' "

" 'Pale horse, pale rider,' " chanted Adam, coming in on the beat, " 'done taken my lover away!' (I think we're good, I think we ought to get up an act—)"

"Go in Hut Service," said Miranda, "entertain the poor defenseless heroes Over There."

"We'll play banjos," said Adam; "I always wanted to play the banjo."

Miranda sighed, and lay back on the pillow and thought, I must give up, I can't hold out any longer. There was only that pain, only that room, and only Adam. There were no longer any multiple planes of living, no tough filaments of memory and hope pulling taut backwards and forwards holding her upright between them. There was only this one moment and it was a dream of time, and Adam's face, very near hers, eyes still and intent, was a shadow, and there was to be nothing more. . . .

"Adam," she said out of the heavy soft darkness that drew her down, down, "I love you, and I was hoping you would say that to me, too."

He lay down beside her with his arm under her shoulder, and pressed his smooth face against hers, his mouth moved towards her mouth and stopped. "Can you hear what I am saying? . . . What do you think I have been trying to tell you all this time?"

She turned towards him, the cloud cleared and she saw his face for an instant. He pulled the covers about her and held her, and said, "Go to sleep, darling, darling, if you will go to sleep now for one hour I will wake you up and bring you hot coffee and tomorrow we will find somebody to help. I love you, go to sleep—"

Almost with no warning at all, she floated into the darkness, holding his hand, in sleep that was not sleep but clear evening light in a small green wood, an angry dangerous wood full of inhuman concealed voices singing sharply like the whine of arrows and she saw Adam transfixed by a flight of these singing arrows that struck him in the heart and passed shrilly cutting their path through the leaves. Adam fell straight back before her eyes, and rose again unwounded and alive; another flight of arrows loosed from the invisible bow struck him again and he fell, and yet he was there before her untouched in a perpetual death and resurrection. She threw herself before him, angrily and selfishly she interposed between him and the track of the arrow, crying, No, no, like a child cheated in a game, It's my turn now, why must you always be the one to die? and the arrows struck her cleanly through the heart and through his body and he lay dead, and she still lived, and the wood whistled and sang and shouted, every branch and leaf and blade of grass had its own terrible accusing voice. She ran then, and Adam caught her in the middle of the room, running, and said, "Darling, I must have been asleep too. What happened, you screamed terribly?"

After he had helped her to settle again, she sat with her knees drawn up under her chin, resting her head on her folded arms and began carefully searching for her words because it was important to explain clearly. "It was a very odd sort of dream, I don't know why it could have frightened me. There was something about an old-fashioned valentine. There were two hearts carved on a tree, pierced by the same arrow—you know, Adam—"

"Yes, I know, honey," he said in the gentlest sort of way, and sat kissing her on the cheek and forehead with a kind of accustomedness, as if he had been kissing her for years, "one of those lace paper things."

"Yes, and yet they were alive, and were us, you understand—this doesn't seem to be quite the way it was, but it was something like that. It was in a wood—"

"Yes," said Adam. He got up and put on his tunic and gathered up the thermos bottle. "I'm going back to that little stand and get us some ice cream and hot coffee," he told her, "and I'll be back in five minutes, and you keep quiet. Good-by for five minutes," he said, holding her chin in the palm of his hand and trying to catch her eye, "and you be very quiet."

"Good-by," she said. "I'm awake again." But she was not, and the two alert young internes from the County hospital who had arrived, after frantic urgings from the noisy city editor of the Blue Mountain *News,* to carry her away in a police ambulance, decided that they had better go down and get the stretcher. Their voices roused her, she sat up, got out of bed at once and stood glancing about brightly. "Why, you're all right," said the darker and stouter of the two young men, both extremely fit and competent-looking in their white clothes, each with a flower in his buttonhole. "I'll just carry you." He unfolded a white blanket and wrapped it around her. She gathered up the folds and asked, "But where is Adam?" taking hold of the doctor's arm. He laid a hand on her drenched forehead, shook his head, and gave her a shrewd look. "Adam?"

"Yes," Miranda told him, lowering her voice confidentially, "he was here and now he is gone."

"Oh, he'll be back," the interne told her easily, "he's just gone round the block to get cigarettes. Don't worry about Adam. He's the least of your troubles."

"Will he know where to find me?" she asked, still holding back.

"We'll leave him a note," said the interne. "Come now, it's time we got out of here."

He lifted and swung her up to his shoulder. "I feel very badly," she told him; "I don't know why."

"I'll bet you do," said he, stepping out carefully, the other doctor going before them, and feeling for the first step of the stairs. "Put your arms around my neck," he instructed her. "It won't do you any harm and it's a great help to me."

"What's your name?" Miranda asked as the other doctor opened the front door and they stepped out into the frosty sweet air.

"Hildesheim," he said, in the tone of one humoring a child.

"Well, Dr. Hildesheim, aren't we in a pretty mess?"

"We certainly are," said Dr. Hildesheim.

The second young interne, still quite fresh and dapper in his white coat, though his carnation was withering at the edges, was leaning over listening to her breathing through a stethoscope, whistling thinly, "There's a Long,

Long Trail—" From time to time he tapped her ribs smartly with two fingers, whistling. Miranda observed him for a few moments until she fixed his bright busy hazel eye not four inches from hers. "I'm not unconscious," she explained, "I know what I want to say." Then to her horror she heard herself babbling nonsense, knowing it was nonsense though she could not hear what she was saying. The flicker of attention in the eye near her vanished, the second interne went on tapping and listening, hissing softly under his breath.

"I wish you'd stop whistling," she said clearly. The sound stopped. "It's a beastly tune," she added. Anything, anything at all to keep her small hold on the life of human beings, a clear line of communication, no matter what, between her and the receding world. "Please let me see Dr. Hildesheim," she said, "I have something important to say to him. I must say it now." The second interne vanished. He did not walk away, he fled into the air without a sound, and Dr. Hildesheim's face appeared in his stead.

"Dr. Hildesheim, I want to ask you about Adam."

"That young man? He's been here, and left you a note, and has gone again," said Dr. Hildesheim, "and he'll be back tomorrow and the day after." His tone was altogether too merry and flippant.

"I don't believe you," said Miranda, bitterly, closing her lips and eyes and hoping she might not weep.

"Miss Tanner," called the doctor, "have you got that note?"

Miss Tanner appeared beside her, handed her an unsealed envelope, took it back, unfolded the note and gave it to her.

"I can't see it," said Miranda, after a pained search of the page full of hasty scratches in black ink.

"Here, I'll read it," said Miss Tanner. "It says, 'They came and took you while I was away and now they will not let me see you. Maybe tomorrow they will, with my love, Adam,' " read Miss Tanner in a firm dry voice, pronouncing the words distinctly. "Now, do you see?" she asked soothingly.

Miranda, hearing the words one by one, forgot them one by one. "Oh, read it again, what does it say?" she called out over the silence that pressed upon her, reaching towards the dancing words that just escaped as she almost touched them. "That will do," said Dr. Hildesheim, calmly authoritarian. "Where is that bed?"

"There is no bed yet," said Miss Tanner, as if she said, We are short of oranges. Dr. Hildesheim said, "Well, we'll manage something," and Miss Tanner drew the narrow trestle with bright crossed metal supports and small rubbery wheels into a deep jut of the corridor, out of the way of the swift white figures darting about, whirling and skimming like water flies all in silence. The white walls rose sheer as cliffs, a dozen frosted moons followed each other in perfect self-possession down a white lane and dropped mutely one by one into a snowy abyss.

What is this whiteness and silence but the absence of pain? Miranda lay lifting the nap of her white blanket softly between eased fingers, watching a dance of tall deliberate shadows moving behind a wide screen of sheets spread upon a frame. It was there, near her, on her side of the wall where she could see it clearly and enjoy it, and it was so beautiful she had no curiosity as to its meaning. Two dark figures nodded, bent, curtsied to each other, retreated and bowed again, lifted long arms and spread great hands against the white shadow of the screen; then with a single round movement, the sheets were folded back, disclosing two speechless men in white, standing, and another speechless man in white, lying on the bare springs of a white iron bed. The man on the springs was swathed smoothly from head to foot in white, with folded bands across the face, and a large stiff bow like merry rabbit ears dangled at the crown of his head.

The two living men lifted a mattress standing hunched against the wall, spread it tenderly and exactly over the dead man. Wordless and white they vanished down the corridor, pushing the wheeled bed before them. It had been an entrancing and leisurely spectacle, but now it was over. A pallid white fog rose in their wake insinuatingly and floated before Miranda's eyes, a fog in which was concealed all terror and all weariness, all the wrung faces and twisted backs and broken feet of abused, outraged living things, all the shapes of their confused pain and their estranged hearts; the fog might part at any moment and loose the horde of human torments. She put up her hands and said, Not yet, not yet, but it was too late. The fog parted and two executioners, white clad, moved towards her pushing between them with marvelously deft and practiced hands the misshapen figure of an old man in filthy rags whose scanty beard waggled under his opened mouth as he bowed his back and braced his feet to resist and delay the fate they had prepared for him. In a high weeping voice he was trying to explain to them that the crime of which he was accused did not merit the punishment he was about to receive; and except for this whining cry there was silence as they advanced. The soiled cracked bowls of the old man's hands were held before him beseechingly as a beggar's as he said, "Before God I am not guilty," but they held his arms and drew him onward, passed, and were gone.

The road to death is a long march beset with all evils, and the heart fails little by little at each new terror, the bones rebel at each step, the mind sets up its own bitter resistance and to what end? The barriers sink one by one, and no covering of the eyes shuts out the landscape of disaster, nor the sight of crimes committed there. Across the field came Dr. Hildesheim, his face a skull beneath his German helmet, carrying a naked infant writhing on the point of his bayonet, and a huge stone pot marked Poison in Gothic letters. He stopped before the well that Miranda remembered in a pasture on her father's farm, a well once dry but now bubbling with living water, and into its pure depths he threw the child and the poison, and the violated water sank back soundlessly into the earth. Miranda, screaming, ran with her arms above her head; her voice echoed and came back to her like a wolf's howl. Hildesheim is a Boche, a spy, a Hun, kill him, kill him before he kills you. . . . She woke howling, she heard the foul words accusing Dr. Hildesheim tumbling from her mouth; opened her eyes and knew she was in a bed in a small white room, with Dr. Hildesheim sitting beside her, two firm fingers on her pulse. His hair was brushed sleekly and his buttonhole flower was fresh. Stars gleamed through the window, and Dr. Hildesheim seemed to be gazing at them with no particular expression, his stethoscope dangling around his neck. Miss Tanner stood at the foot of the bed writing something on a chart.

"Hello," said Dr. Hildesheim, "at least you take it out in shouting. You don't try to get out of bed and go running around." Miranda held her eyes open with a terrible effort, saw his rather heavy, patient face clearly even as her mind tottered and slithered again, broke from its foundation and spun like a cast wheel in a ditch. "I didn't mean it, I never believed it, Dr. Hildesheim, you mustn't remember it—" and was gone again, not being able to wait for an answer.

The wrong she had done followed her and haunted her dream: this wrong took vague shapes of horror she could not recognize or name, though her heart cringed at sight of them. Her mind, split in two, acknowledged and denied what she saw in the one instant, for across an abyss of complaining darkness her reasoning coherent self watched the strange frenzy of the other coldly, reluctant to admit the truth of its visions, its tenacious remorses and despairs.

"I know those are your hands," she told Miss Tanner, "I know it, but to me they are white tarantulas, don't touch me."

"Shut your eyes," said Miss Tanner.

"Oh, no," said Miranda, "for then I see worse things," but her eyes closed in spite of her will, and the midnight of her internal torment closed about her.

Oblivion, thought Miranda, her mind feeling among her memories of words she had been taught to describe the unseen, the unknowable, is a whirlpool of gray water turning upon itself for all eternity . . . eternity is perhaps more than the distance to the farthest star. She lay on a narrow ledge over a pit that she knew to be bottomless, though she could not comprehend it; the ledge was her childhood dream of danger, and she strained back against a reassuring wall of granite at her shoulders, staring into the pit, thinking. There it is, there it is at last, it is very simple; and soft carefully shaped words like oblivion and eternity are curtains hung before nothing at all. I shall not know when it happens, I shall not feel or remember, why can't I consent now, I am lost, there is no hope for me. Look, she told herself, there it is, that is death and there is nothing to fear. But she could not consent, still shrinking stiffly against the granite wall that was her childhood dream of safety, breathing slowly for fear of squandering breath, saying desperately, Look, don't be afraid, it is nothing, it is only eternity.

Granite walls, whirlpools, stars are things. None of them is death, nor the image of it. Death is death, said Miranda, and for the dead it has no attributes. Silenced she sank easily through deeps under deeps of darkness until she lay like a stone at the farthest bottom of life, knowing herself to be blind, deaf, speechless, no longer aware of the members of her own body, entirely withdrawn from all human concerns, yet alive with a peculiar lucidity and coherence; all notions of the mind, the reasonable inquiries of doubt, all ties of blood and the desires of the heart, dissolved and fell away from her, and there remained of her only a minute fiercely burning particle of being that knew itself alone, that relied upon nothing beyond itself for its strength; not susceptible to any appeal or inducement, being itself composed entirely of one single motive, the stubborn will to live. This fiery motionless particle set itself unaided to resist destruction, to survive and to be in its own madness of being, motiveless and planless beyond that one essential end. Trust me, the hard unwinking angry point of light said. Trust me. I stay.

At once it grew, flattened, thinned to a fine radiance, spread like a great fan and curved out into a rainbow through which Miranda, enchanted, altogether believing, looked upon a deep clear landscape of sea and sand, of soft meadow and sky, freshly washed and glistening with transparencies of blue. Why, of course, of course, said Miranda, without surprise but with serene rapture as if some promise made to her had been kept long after she had ceased to hope for it. She rose from her narrow ledge and ran lightly through the tall portals of the great bow that arched in its splendor over the burning blue of the sea and the cool green of the meadow on either hand.

The small waves rolled in and over unhurriedly, lapped upon the sand in silence and retreated; the grasses flurried before a breeze that made no sound. Moving towards her leisurely as clouds through the shimmering air came a great company of human beings, and Miranda saw in an amazement of joy that they were all the living she had known. Their faces were transfigured, each in its own beauty, beyond what she remembered of them, their eyes were clear and untroubled as good weather, and they cast no shadows. They were pure identities and she knew them every one without calling their names or remembering what relation she bore to them. They surrounded her smoothly on silent feet, then turned their entranced faces again towards the sea, and she moved among them easily as a wave among waves. The drifting circle widened, separated, and each figure was alone but not solitary; Miranda, alone too, questioning nothing, desiring nothing, in the quietude of her ecstasy, stayed where she was, eyes fixed on the overwhelming deep sky where it was always morning.

Lying at ease, arms under her head, in the prodigal warmth which flowed evenly from sea and sky and meadow, within touch but not touching the serenely smiling familiar beings about her, Miranda felt without warning a vague tremor of apprehension, some small flick of distrust in her joy; a thin frost touched the edges of this confident tranquillity; something, somebody, was missing, she had lost something, she had left something valuable in another country, oh, what could it be? There are no trees, no trees here, she said in fright, I have left something unfinished. A thought struggled at the back of her mind, came clearly as a voice in her ear. Where are the dead? We have forgotten the dead, oh, the dead, where are they? At once as if a curtain had fallen, the bright landscape faded, she was alone in a strange stony place of bitter cold, picking her way along a steep path of slippery snow, calling out, Oh, I must go back! But in what direction? Pain returned, a terrible compelling pain running through her veins like heavy fire, the stench of corruption filled her nostrils, the sweetish sickening smell of rotting flesh and pus;

she opened her eyes and saw pale light through a coarse white cloth over her face, knew that the smell of death was in her own body, and struggled to lift her hand. The cloth was drawn away; she saw Miss Tanner filling a hypodermic needle in her methodical expert way, and heard Dr. Heidesheim saying, "I think that will do the trick. Try another." Miss Tanner plucked firmly at Miranda's arm near the shoulder, and the unbelievable current of agony ran burning through her veins again. She struggled to cry out, saying, Let me go, let me go; but heard only incoherent sounds of animal suffering. She saw doctor and nurse glance at each other with the glance of initiates at a mystery, nodding in silence, their eyes alive with knowledgeable pride. They looked briefly at their handiwork and hurried away.

Bells screamed all off key, wrangling together as they collided in mid air, horns and whistles mingled shrilly with cries of human distress; sulphur colored light exploded through the black window pane and flashed away in darkness. Miranda waking from a dreamless sleep asked without expecting an answer, "What is happening?" for there was a bustle of voices and footsteps in the corridor, and a sharpness in the air; the far clamor went on, a furious exasperated shrieking like a mob in revolt.

The light came on, and Miss Tanner said in a furry voice, "Hear that? They're celebrating. It's the Armistice. The war is over, my dear." Her hands trembled. She rattled a spoon in a cup, stopped to listen, held the cup out to Miranda. From the ward for old bedridden women down the hall floated a ragged chorus of cracked voices singing, "My country, 'tis of thee . . ."

Sweet land . . . oh, terrible land of this bitter world where the sound of rejoicing was a clamor of pain, where ragged tuneless old women, sitting up waiting for their evening bowl of cocoa, were singing, "Sweet land of Liberty—"

"Oh, say, can you see?" their hopeless voices were asking next, the hammer strokes of metal tongues drowning them out. "The war is over," said Miss Tanner, her underlip held firmly, her eyes blurred. Miranda said, "Please open the window, please, I smell death in here."

Now if real daylight such as I remember having seen in this world would only come again, but it is always twilight or just before morning, a promise of day that is never kept. What has become of the sun? That was the longest and loneliest night and yet it will not end and let the day come. Shall I ever see light again?

Sitting in a long chair, near a window, it was in itself a melancholy wonder to see the colorless sunlight slanting on the snow, under a sky drained of its blue. "Can this be my face?" Miranda asked her mirror. "Are these my own hands?" she asked Miss Tanner, holding them up to show the yellow tint like melted wax glimmering between the closed fingers. The body is a curious monster, no place to live in, how could anyone feel at home there? Is it possible I can ever accustom myself to this place? she asked herself. The human faces around her seemed dulled and tired, with no radiance of skin and eyes as Miranda remembered radiance; the once white walls of her room were now a soiled gray. Breathing slowly, falling asleep and waking again, feeling the splash of water on her flesh, taking food, talking in bare phrases with Dr. Hildesheim and Miss Tanner, Miranda looked about her with the covertly hostile eyes of an alien who does not like the country in which he finds himself, does not understand the language nor wish to learn it, does not mean to live there and yet is helpless, unable to leave it at his will.

"It is morning," Miss Tanner would say, with a sigh, for she had grown old and weary once for all in the past month, "morning again, my dear," showing Miranda the same monotonous landscape of dulled evergreens and leaden snow. She would rustle about in her starched skirts, her face bravely powdered, her spirit unbreakable as good steel, saying, "Look, my dear, what a heavenly morning, like a crystal," for she had an affection for the salvaged creature before her, the silent ungrateful human being whom she, Cornelia Tanner, a nurse who knew her business, had snatched back from death with her own hands. "Nursing is nine-tenths, just the same," Miss Tanner would tell the other nurses; "keep that in mind." Even the sunshine was Miss Tanner's own prescription for the further recovery of Miranda, this patient the doctors had given up for lost, and who yet sat here, visible proof of Miss Tanner's theory. She said, "Look at the sunshine, now," as she might be saying, "I ordered this for you, my dear, do sit up and take it."

"It's beautiful," Miranda would answer, even turning her head to look, thanking Miss Tanner for her goodness, most of all her goodness about the weather, "beautiful, I always loved it." And I might love it again if I saw it, she thought, but truth was, she could not see it. There was no light, there might never be light again, compared as it must always be with the light she had seen beside the blue sea that lay so tranquilly along the shore of her paradise. That was a child's dream of the heavenly meadow, the vision of repose that comes to a tired body in sleep, she thought, but I have seen it when I did not know it was a dream. Closing her eyes she would rest for a moment remembering that bliss which had repaid all the pain of the journey to reach it; opening them again she saw with a new anguish the dull world to which she was condemned, where the light seemed filmed over with cobwebs, all the bright surfaces corroded, the sharp planes melted and formless, all objects and beings meaningless, ah, dead and withered things that believed themselves alive!

At night, after the long effort of lying in her chair, in her extremity of grief for what she had so briefly won, she folded her painful body together and wept silently, shamelessly, in pity for herself and her lost rapture. There was no escape. Dr. Hildesheim, Miss Tanner, the nurses in the diet kitchen, the chemist, the surgeon, the precise machine of the hospital, the whole humane conviction and custom of society, conspired to pull her inseparable rack of bones and wasted flesh to its feet, to put in order her disordered mind, and to set her once more safely in the road that would lead her again to death.

Chuck Rouncivale and Mary Townsend came to see her, bringing her a bundle of letters they had guarded for her. They brought a basket of delicate small hothouse flowers, lilies of the valley with sweet peas and feathery fern, and above these blossoms their faces were merry and haggard.

Mary said, "You *have* had a tussle, haven't you?" and Chuck said, "Well, you made it back, didn't you?" Then after an uneasy pause, they told her that everybody was waiting to see her again at her desk. "They've put me back on sports already, Miranda," said Chuck. For ten minutes Miranda smiled and told them how gay and what a pleasant surprise it was to find herself alive. For it will not do to betray the conspiracy and tamper with the courage of the living; there is nothing better than to be alive, everyone has agreed on that; it is past argument, and who attempts to deny it is justly outlawed. "I'll be back in no time at all," she said; "this is almost over."

Her letters lay in a heap in her lap and beside her chair. Now and then she turned one over to read the inscription, recognized this handwriting or that, examined the blotted stamps and the postmarks, and let them drop again. For two or three days they lay upon the table beside her, and she continued to shrink from them. "They will all be telling me again how good it is to be alive, they will say again they love me, they are glad I am living too, and what can I answer to that?" and her hardened, indifferent heart shuddered in despair at itself, because before it had been tender and capable of love.

Dr. Hildesheim said, "What, all these letters not opened yet?" and Miss Tanner said, "Read your letters, my dear, I'll open them for you." Standing beside the bed, she slit them cleanly with a paper knife. Miranda, cornered, picked and chose until she found a thin one in an unfamiliar handwriting. "Oh, no, now," said Miss Tanner, "take them as they come. Here, I'll hand them to you." She sat down, prepared to be helpful to the end.

What a victory, what triumph, what happiness to be alive, sang the letters in a chorus. The names were signed with flourishes like the circles in air of bugle notes, and they were the names of those she had loved best; some of those she had known well and pleasantly; and a few who meant nothing to her, then or now. The thin letter in the unfamiliar handwriting was from a strange man at the camp where Adam had been, telling her that Adam had died of influenza in the camp hospital. Adam had asked him, in case anything happened, to be sure to let her know.

If anything happened. To be sure to let her know. If anything happened. "Your friend, Adam Barclay," wrote the strange man. It had happened—she looked at the date—more than a month ago.

"I've been here a long time, haven't I?" she asked Miss Tanner, who was folding letters and putting them back in their proper envelopes.

"Oh, quite a while," said Miss Tanner, "but you'll be ready to go soon now. But you must be careful of yourself and not overdo, and you should come back now and then and let us look at you, because sometimes the aftereffects are very—"

Miranda, sitting up before the mirror, wrote carefully: "One lipstick, medium, one ounce flask Bois d'Hiver perfume, one pair of gray suède gaunt-lets without straps, two pairs gray sheer stockings without clocks—"

Towney, reading after her, said, "Everything without something so that it will be almost impossible to get?"

"Try it, though," said Miranda, "they're nicer without. One walking stick of silvery wood with a silver knob."

"That's going to be expensive," warned Towney. "Walking is hardly worth it."

"You're right," said Miranda, and wrote in the margin, "a nice one to match my other things. Ask Chuck to look for this, Mary. Good looking and not too heavy." Lazarus, come forth. Not unless you bring me my top hat and stick. Stay where you are then, you snob. Not at all. I'm coming forth. "A jar of cold cream," wrote Miranda, "a box of apricot powder—and, Mary, I don't need eye shadow, do I?" She glanced at her face in the mirror and away again. "Still, no one need pity this corpse if we look properly to the art of the thing."

Mary Townsend said, "You won't recognize yourself in a week."

"Do you suppose, Mary," asked Miranda, "I could have my old room back again?"

"That should be easy," said Mary. "We stored away all your things there with Miss Hobbe." Miranda wondered again at the time and trouble the living took to be helpful to the dead. But not quite dead now, she reassured herself, one foot in either world now; soon I shall cross back and be at home again. The light will seem real and I shall be glad when I hear that someone I know has escaped from death. I shall visit the escaped ones and help them dress and tell them how lucky they are, and how lucky I am still to have them. Mary will be back soon with my gloves and my walking stick, I must go now, I must begin saying good-by to Miss Tanner and Dr. Hildesheim. Adam, she said, now you need not die again, but still I wish you were here; I wish you had come back, what do you think I came back for, Adam, to be deceived like this?

At once he was there beside her, invisible but urgently present, a ghost but more alive than she was, the last intolerable cheat of her heart; for knowing it was false she still clung to the lie, the unpardonable lie of her bitter desire. She said, "I love you," and stood up trembling, trying by the mere act of her will to bring him to sight before her. If I could call you up from the grave I would, she said, if I could see your ghost I would say, I believe . . . "I be-lieve," she said aloud. "Oh, let me see you once more." The room was silent, empty, the shade was gone from it, struck away by the sudden violence of her rising and speaking aloud. She came to herself as if out of sleep. Oh, no, that is not the way, I must never do that, she warned herself. Miss Tanner said, "Your taxicab is waiting, my dear," and there was Mary. Ready to go.

No more war, no more plague, only the dazed silence that follows the ceas-ing of the heavy guns; noiseless houses with the shades drawn, empty streets, the dead cold light of tomorrow. Now there would be time for everything.

part three

Outsiders

Leo Tolstoy

The Three Hermits

An Old Legend Current in the Vólga District

> *And in praying use not vain repetitions, as the Gentiles do: for they think that they shall be heard for their much speaking. Be not therefore like unto them: for your Father knoweth what things ye have need of, before ye ask Him.*
>
> MATTHEW 6:7–8

A bishop was sailing from Archangel to the Solovétsk Monastery, and on the same vessel were a number of pilgrims on their way to visit the shrines at that place. The voyage was a smooth one, the wind favourable and the weather fair. The pilgrims lay on deck, eating, or sat in groups talking to one another. The Bishop, too, came on deck, and as he was pacing up and down he noticed a group of men standing near the prow and listening to a fisherman, who was pointing to the sea and telling them something. The Bishop stopped, and looked in the direction in which the man was pointing. He could see nothing, however, but the sea glistening in the sunshine. He drew nearer to listen, but when the man saw him, he took off his cap and was silent. The rest of the people also took off their caps and bowed.

"Do not let me disturb you, friends," said the Bishop. "I came to hear what this good man was saying."

"The fisherman was telling us about the hermits," replied one, a tradesman, rather bolder than the rest.

"What hermits?" asked the Bishop, going to the side of the vessel and seating himself on a box. "Tell me about them. I should like to hear. What were you pointing at?"

"Why, that little island you can just see over there," answered the man,

THE THREE HERMITS From *Twenty-Three Tales* by Leo Tolstoy, translated by Louise and Aylmer Maude and published by Oxford University Press. Written in 1886.

pointing to a spot ahead and a little to the right. "That is the island where the hermits live for the salvation of their souls."

"Where is the island?" asked the Bishop. "I see nothing."

"There, in the distance, if you will please look along my hand. Do you see that little cloud? Below it, and a bit to the left, there is just a faint streak. That is the island."

The Bishop looked carefully, but his unaccustomed eyes could make out nothing but the water shimmering in the sun.

"I cannot see it," he said. "But who are the hermits that live there?"

"They are holy men," answered the fisherman. "I had long heard tell of them, but never chanced to see them myself till the year before last."

And the fisherman related how once, when he was out fishing, he had been stranded at night upon that island, not knowing where he was. In the morning, as he wandered about the island, he came across an earth hut, and met an old man standing near it. Presently two others came out, and after having fed him and dried his things, they helped him mend his boat.

"And what are they like?" asked the Bishop.

"One is a small man and his back is bent. He wears a priest's cassock and is very old; he must be more than a hundred, I should say. He is so old that the white of his beard is taking a greenish tinge, but he is always smiling, and his face is as bright as an angel's from heaven. The second is taller, but he also is very old. He wears a tattered peasant coat. His beard is broad, and of a yellowish grey colour. He is a strong man. Before I had time to help him, he turned my boat over as if it were only a pail. He too is kindly and cheerful. The third is tall, and has a beard as white as snow and reaching to his knees. He is stern, with overhanging eyebrows; and he wears nothing but a piece of matting tied round his waist."

"And did they speak to you?" asked the Bishop.

"For the most part they did everything in silence, and spoke but little even to one another. One of them would just give a glance, and the others would understand him. I asked the tallest whether they had lived there long. He frowned, and muttered something as if he were angry; but the oldest one took his hand and smiled, and then the tall one was quiet. The oldest one only said: 'Have mercy upon us,' and smiled."

While the fisherman was talking, the ship had drawn nearer to the island.

"There, now you can see it plainly, if your Lordship will please to look," said the tradesman, pointing with his hand.

The Bishop looked, and now he really saw a dark streak—which was the island. Having looked at it a while, he left the prow of the vessel, and going to the stern, asked the helmsman:

"What island is that?"

"That one," replied the man, "has no name. There are many such in this sea."

"Is it true that there are hermits who live there for the salvation of their souls?"

"So it is said, Your Lordship, but I don't know if it's true. Fishermen say they have seen them; but of course they may only be spinning yarns."

"I should like to land on the island and see these men," said the Bishop. "How could I manage it?"

"The ship cannot get close to the island," replied the helmsman, "but you might be rowed there in a boat. You had better speak to the captain."

The captain was sent for and came.

"I should like to see these hermits," said the Bishop. "Could I not be rowed ashore?"

The captain tried to dissuade him.

"Of course it could be done," said he, "but we should lose much time. And if I might venture to say so to your Lordship, the old men are not worth your pains. I have heard say that they are foolish old fellows, who understand nothing, and never speak a word, any more than the fish in the sea."

"I wish to see them," said the Bishop, "and I will pay you for your trouble and loss of time. Please let me have a boat."

There was no help for it; so the order was given. The sailors trimmed the sails, the steersman put up the helm, and the ship's course was set for the island. A chair was placed at the prow for the Bishop, and he sat there, looking ahead. The passengers all collected at the prow, and gazed at the island. Those who had the sharpest eyes could presently make out the rocks on it, and then a mud hut was seen. At last one man saw the hermits themselves. The captain brought a telescope and, after looking through it, handed it to the Bishop.

"It's right enough. There are three men standing on the shore. There, a little to the right of that big rock."

The Bishop took the telescope, got it into position, and he saw the three men: a tall one, a shorter one, and one very small and bent, standing on the shore and holding each other by the hand.

The captain turned to the Bishop.

"The vessel can get no nearer in than this, your Lordship. If you wish to go ashore, we must ask you to go in the boat, while we anchor here."

The cable was quickly let out; the anchor cast, and the sails furled. There was a jerk, and the vessel shook. Then, a boat having been lowered, the oarsmen jumped in, and the Bishop descended the ladder and took his seat. The men pulled at their oars and the boat moved rapidly towards the island. When they came within a stone's throw, they saw three old men: a tall one with only a piece of matting tied round his waist, a shorter one in a tattered peasant coat, and a very old one bent with age and wearing an old cassock— all three standing hand in hand.

The oarsmen pulled in to the shore, and held on with the boathook while the Bishop got out.

The old men bowed to him, and he gave them his blessing, at which they bowed still lower. Then the Bishop began to speak to them.

"I have heard," he said, "that you, godly men, live here saving your own

souls and praying to our Lord Christ for your fellow men. I, an unworthy
servant of Christ, am called, by God's mercy, to keep and teach His flock. I
wished to see you, servants of God, and to do what I can to teach you, also."

The old men looked at each other, smiling, but remained silent.

"Tell me," said the Bishop, "what you are doing to save your souls, and
how you serve God on this island."

The second hermit sighed, and looked at the oldest, the very ancient one.
The latter smiled, and said:

"We do not know how to serve God. We only serve and support ourselves,
servant of God."

"But how do you pray to God?" asked the Bishop.

"We pray in this way," replied the hermit. " 'Three are ye, three are we,
have mercy upon us.' "

And when the old man said this, all three raised their eyes to heaven, and
repeated:

"Three are ye, three are we, have mercy upon us!"

The Bishop smiled.

"You have evidently heard something about the Holy Trinity," said he.
"But you do not pray aright. You have won my affection, godly men. I see
you wish to please the Lord, but you do not know how to serve Him. That
is not the way to pray; but listen to me, and I will teach you. I will teach
you, not a way of my own, but the way in which God in the Holy Scriptures
has commanded all men to pray to Him."

And the Bishop began explaining to the hermits how God had revealed
Himself to men; telling them of God the Father, and God the Son, and God
the Holy Ghost.

"God the Son came down on earth," said he, "to save men, and this is
how He taught us all to pray. Listen, and repeat after me: 'Our Father.' "

And the first old man repeated after him, "Our Father," and the second
said, "Our Father," and the third said, "Our Father."

"Which art in heaven," continued the Bishop.

The first hermit repeated, "Which art in heaven," but the second blundered
over the words, and the tall hermit could not say them properly. His hair had
grown over his mouth so that he could not speak plainly. The very old hermit,
having no teeth, also mumbled indistinctly.

The Bishop repeated the words again, and the old men repeated them
after him. The Bishop sat down on a stone, and the old men stood before
him, watching his mouth, and repeating the words as he uttered them. And
all day long the Bishop laboured, saying a word twenty, thirty, a hundred
times over, and the old men repeated it after him. They blundered, and he
corrected them, and made them begin again.

The Bishop did not leave off till he had taught them the whole of the
Lord's Prayer so that they could not only repeat it after him, but could say
it by themselves. The middle one was the first to know it, and to repeat the

whole of it alone. The Bishop made him say it again and again, and at last the others could say it too.

It was getting dark and the moon was appearing over the water, before the Bishop rose to return to the vessel. When he took leave of the old men they all bowed down to the ground before him. He raised them, and kissed each of them, telling them to pray as he had taught them. Then he got into the boat and returned to the ship.

And as he sat in the boat and was rowed to the ship he could hear the three voices of the hermits loudly repeating the Lord's Prayer. As the boat drew near the vessel their voices could no longer be heard, but they could still be seen in the moonlight, standing as he had left them on the shore, the shortest in the middle, the tallest on the right, the middle one on the left. As soon as the Bishop had reached the vessel and got on board, the anchor was weighed and the sails unfurled. The wind filled them and the ship sailed away, and the Bishop took a seat in the stern and watched the island they had left. For a time he could still see the hermits, but presently they disappeared from sight, though the island was still visible. At last it too vanished, and only the sea was to be seen, rippling in the moonlight.

The pilgrims lay down to sleep, and all was quiet on deck. The Bishop did not wish to sleep, but sat alone at the stern, gazing at the sea where the island was no longer visible, and thinking of the good old men. He thought how pleased they had been to learn the Lord's Prayer; and he thanked God for having sent him to teach and help such godly men.

So the Bishop sat, thinking, and gazing at the sea where the island had disappeared. And the moonlight flickered before his eyes, sparkling, now here, now there, upon the waves. Suddenly he saw something white and shining, on the bright path which the moon cast across the sea. Was it a seagull, or the little gleaming sail of some small boat? The Bishop fixed his eyes on it, wondering.

"It must be a boat sailing after us," thought he, "but it is overtaking us very rapidly. It was far, far away a minute ago, but now it is much nearer. It cannot be a boat, for I can see no sail; but whatever it may be, it is following us and catching us up."

And he could not make out what it was. Not a boat, nor a bird, nor a fish! It was too large for a man, and besides a man could not be out there in the midst of the sea. The Bishop rose, and said to the helmsman:

"Look there, what is that, my friend? What is it?" the Bishop repeated, though he could now see plainly what it was—the three hermits running upon the water, all gleaming white, their grey beards shining, and approaching the ship as quickly as though it were not moving.

The steersman looked, and let go the helm in terror.

"Oh Lord! The hermits are running after us on the water as though it were dry land!"

The passengers, hearing him, jumped up and crowded to the stern. They saw the hermits coming along hand in hand, and the two outer ones beckoning the ship to stop. All three were gliding along upon the water without moving their feet. Before the ship could be stopped, the hermits had reached it, and raising their heads, all three as with one voice, began to say:

"We have forgotten your teaching, servant of God. As long as we kept repeating it we remembered, but when we stopped saying it for a time, a word dropped out, and now it has all gone to pieces. We can remember nothing of it. Teach us again."

The Bishop crossed himself, and leaning over the ship's side, said:

"Your own prayer will reach the Lord, men of God. It is not for me to teach you. Pray for us sinners."

And the Bishop bowed low before the old men; and they turned and went back across the sea. And a light shone until daybreak on the spot where they were lost to sight.

Translated from the Russian
by Louise and Aylmer Maude

Sherwood Anderson

Hands

Upon the half-decayed veranda of a small frame house that stood near the edge of a ravine near the town of Winesburg, Ohio, a fat little old man walked nervously up and down. Across a long field that has been seeded for clover but that had produced only a dense crop of yellow mustard weeds, he could see the public highway along which went a wagon filled with berry pickers returning from the fields. The berry pickers, youths and maidens, laughed and shouted boisterously. A boy clad in a blue shirt leaped from the wagon and attempted to drag after him one of the maidens who screamed and protested shrilly. The feet of the boy in the road kicked up a cloud of dust that floated across the face of the departing sun. Over the long field came a thin girlish voice. "Oh, you Wing Biddlebaum, comb your hair, it's falling into your eyes," commanded the voice to the man, who was bald and whose nervous little hands fiddled about the bare white forehead as though arranging a mass of tangled locks.

Wing Biddlebaum, forever frightened and beset by a ghostly band of doubts, did not think of himself as in any way a part of the life of the town where he had lived for twenty years. Among all the people of Winesburg but one had come close to him. With George Willard, son of Tom Willard, the proprietor of the new Willard House, he had formed something like a friendship. George Willard was the reporter on the *Winesburg Eagle* and sometimes in the evenings he walked out along the highway to Wing Biddlebaum's house. Now as the old man walked up and down on the ve-

HANDS From *Winesburg, Ohio* by Sherwood Anderson. Copyright 1919 by B. W. Huebsch, Inc., renewed 1947 by Eleanor Copenhaver Anderson. Reprinted by permission of The Viking Press, Inc.

randa, his hands moving nervously about, he was hoping that George Willard would come and spend the evening with him. After the wagon containing the berry pickers had passed, he went across the field through the tall mustard weeds and climbing a rail fence peered anxiously along the road to the town. For a moment he stood thus, rubbing his hands together and looking up and down the road, and then, fear overcoming him, ran back to walk again upon the porch on his own house.

In the presence of George Willard, Wing Biddlebaum, who for twenty years had been the town mystery, lost something of his timidity, and his shadowy personality, submerged in a sea of doubts, came forth to look at the world. With the young reporter at his side, he ventured in the light of day into Main Street or strode up and down on the rickety front porch of his own house, talking excitedly. The voice that had been low and trembling became shrill and loud. The bent figure straightened. With a kind of wriggle, like a fish returned to the brook by the fisherman, Biddlebaum the silent began to talk, striving to put into words the ideas that had been accumulated by his mind during long years of silence.

Wing Biddlebaum talked much with his hands. The slender expressive fingers, forever active, forever striving to conceal themselves in his pockets or behind his back, came forth and became the piston rods of his machinery of expression.

The story of Wing Biddlebaum is a story of hands. Their restless activity, like unto the beating of the wings of an imprisoned bird, had given him his name. Some obscure poet of the town had thought of it. The hands alarmed their owner. He wanted to keep them hidden away and looked with amazement at the quiet inexpressive hands of other men who worked beside him in the fields, or passed, driving sleepy teams on country roads.

When he talked to George Willard, Wing Biddlebaum closed his fists and beat with them upon a table or on the walls of his house. The action made him more comfortable. If the desire to talk came to him when the two were walking in the fields, he sought out a stump or the top board of a fence and with his hands pounding busily talked with renewed ease.

The story of Wing Biddlebaum's hands is worth a book in itself. Sympathetically set forth it would tap many strange, beautiful qualities in obscure men. It is a job for a poet. In Winesburg the hands had attracted attention merely because of their activity. With them Wing Biddlebaum had picked as high as a hundred and forty quarts of strawberries in a day. They became his distinguishing feature, the source of his fame. Also they made more grotesque an already grotesque and elusive individuality. Winesburg was proud of the hands of Wing Biddlebaum in the same spirit in which it was proud of Banker White's new stone house and Wesley Moyer's bay stallion, Tony Tip, that had won the two-fifteen trot at the fall races in Cleveland.

As for George Willard, he had many times wanted to ask about the hands. At times an almost overwhelming curiosity had taken hold of him. He felt that there must be a reason for their strange activity and their inclination to keep hidden away and only a growing respect for Wing Biddlebaum kept him from blurting out the questions that were often in his mind.

Once he had been on the point of asking. The two were walking in the fields on a summer afternoon and had stopped to sit upon a grassy bank. All afternoon Wing Biddlebaum had talked as one inspired. By a fence he had stopped and beating like a giant woodpecker upon the top board had shouted at George Willard, condemning his tendency to be too much influenced by the people about him. "You are destroying yourself," he cried. "You have the inclination to be alone and to dream and you are afraid of dreams. You want to be like others in town here. You hear them talk and you try to imitate them."

On the grassy bank Wing Biddlebaum had tried again to drive his point home. His voice became soft and reminiscent, and with a sigh of contentment he launched into a long rambling talk, speaking as one lost in a dream.

Out of the dream Wing Biddlebaum made a picture for George Willard. In the picture men lived again in a kind of pastoral golden age. Across a green open country came clean-limbed young men, some afoot, some mounted upon horses. In crowds the young men came to gather about the feet of an old man who sat beneath a tree in a tiny garden and who talked to them.

Wing Biddlebaum became wholly inspired. For once he forgot the hands. Slowly they stole forth and lay upon George Willard's shoulders. Something new and bold came into the voice that talked. "You must try to forget all you have learned," said the old man. "You must begin to dream. From this time on you must shut your ears to the roaring of the voices."

Pausing in his speech, Wing Biddlebaum looked long and earnestly at George Willard. His eyes glowed. Again he raised the hands to caress the boy and then a look of horror swept over his face.

With a convulsive movement of his body, Wing Biddlebaum sprang to his feet and thrust his hands deep into his trousers pockets. Tears came to his eyes. "I must be getting along home. I can talk no more with you," he said nervously.

Without looking back, the old man had hurried down the hillside and across a meadow, leaving George Willard perplexed and frightened upon the grassy slope. With a shiver of dread the boy arose and went along the road toward town. "I'll not ask him about his hands," he thought, touched by the memory of the terror he had seen in the man's eyes. "There's something wrong, but I don't want to know what it is. His hands have something to do with his fear of me and of everyone."

And George Willard was right. Let us look briefly into the story of the hands. Perhaps our talking of them will arouse the poet who will tell the hidden wonder story of the influence for which the hands were but fluttering pennants of promise.

In his youth Wing Biddlebaum had been a school teacher in a town in

Pennsylvania. He was not then known as Wing Biddlebaum, but went by the less euphonic name of Adolph Myers. As Adolph Myers he was much loved by the boys of his school.

Adolph Myers was meant by nature to be a teacher of youth. He was one of those rare, little-understood men who rule by a power so gentle that it passes as a lovable weakness. In their feeling for the boys under their charge such men are not unlike the finer sort of women in their love of men.

And yet that is but crudely stated. It needs the poet there. With the boys of his school, Adolph Myers had walked in the evening or had sat talking until dusk upon the schoolhouse steps lost in a kind of dream. Here and there went his hands, caressing the shoulders of the boys, playing about the tousled heads. As he talked his voice became soft and musical. There was a caress in that also. In a way the voice and the hands, the stroking of the shoulders and the touching of the hair was a part of the schoolmaster's effort to carry a dream into the young minds. By the caress that was in his fingers he expressed himself. He was one of those men in whom the force that creates life is diffused, not centralized. Under the caress of his hands doubt and disbelief went out of the minds of the boys and they began also to dream.

And then the tragedy. A half-witted boy of the school became enamored of the young master. In his bed at night he imagined unspeakable things and in the morning went forth to tell his dreams as facts. Strange, hideous accusations fell from his loose-hung lips. Through the Pennsylvania town went a shiver. Hidden, shadowy doubts that had been in men's minds concerning Adolph Myers were galvanized into beliefs.

The tragedy did not linger. Trembling lads were jerked out of bed and questioned. "He put his arms about me," said one. "His fingers were always playing in my hair," said another.

One afternoon a man of the town, Henry Bradford, who kept a saloon, came to the schoolhouse door. Calling Adoph Myers into the school yard he began to beat him with his fists. As his hard knuckles beat down into the frightened face of the schoolmaster, his wrath became more and more terrible. Screaming with dismay, the children ran here and there like disturbed insects. "I'll teach you to put your hands on my boy, you beast," roared the saloon keeper, who, tired of beating the master, had begun to kick him about the yard.

Adolph Myers was driven from the Pennsylvania town in the night. With lanterns in their hands a dozen men came to the door of the house where he lived alone and commanded that he dress and come forth. It was raining and one of the men had a rope in his hands. They had intended to hang the schoolmaster, but something in his figure, so small, white, and pitiful, touched their hearts and they let him escape. As he ran away into the darkness they repented of their weakness and ran after him, swearing and throwing sticks and great balls of soft mud at the figure that screamed and ran faster and faster into the darkness.

For twenty years Adolph Myers had lived alone in Winesburg. He was but forty but looked sixty-five. The name of Biddlebaum he got from a box of goods seen at a freight station as he hurried through an eastern Ohio town. He had an aunt in Winesburg, a black-toothed old woman who raised chickens, and with her he lived until she died. He had been ill for a year after the experience in Pennsylvania, and after his recovery worked as a day laborer in the fields, going timidly about and striving to conceal his hands. Although he did not understand what had happened he felt that the hands must be to blame. Again and again the fathers of the boys had talked of the hands. "Keep your hands to yourself," the saloon keeper had roared, dancing with fury in the schoolhouse yard.

Upon the veranda of his house by the ravine, Wing Biddlebaum continued to walk up and down until the sun had disappeared and the road beyond the field was lost in the grey shadows. Going into his house he cut slices of bread and spread honey upon them. When the rumble of the evening train that took away the express cars loaded with the day's harvest of berries had passed and restored the silence of the summer night, he went again to walk upon the veranda. In the darkness he could not see the hands and they became quiet. Although he still hungered for the presence of the boy, who was the medium through which he expressed his love of man, the hunger became again a part of his loneliness and his waiting. Lighting a lamp, Wing Biddlebaum washed the few dishes soiled by his simple meal and, setting up a folding cot by the screen door that led to the porch, prepared to undress for the night. A few stray white bread crumbs lay on the cleanly washed floor by the table; putting the lamp upon a low stool he began to pick up the crumbs, carrying them to his mouth one by one with unbelievable rapidity. In the dense blotch of light beneath the table, the kneeling figure looked like a priest engaged in some service of his church. The nervous expressive fingers, flashing in and out of the light, might well have been mistaken for the fingers of the devotee going swiftly through decade after decade of his rosary.

Doris Lessing

The Second Hut

Before that season and his wife's illness, he had thought things could get no worse: until then, poverty had meant not to deviate further than snapping point from what he had been brought up to think of as a normal life.

Being a farmer (he had come to it late in life, in his forties) was the first test he had faced as an individual. Before he had always been supported, invisibly perhaps, but none the less strongly, by what his family expected of him. He had been a regular soldier, not an unsuccessful one, but his success had been at the cost of a continual straining against his own inclinations; and he did not know himself what his inclinations were. Something stubbornly unconforming kept him apart from his fellow officers. It was an inward difference: he did not think of himself as a soldier. Even in his appearance, square, close-bitten, disciplined, there had been a hint of softness, or of strain, showing itself in his smile, which was too quick, like the smile of a deaf person afraid of showing incomprehension, and in the anxious look of his eyes. After he left the army he quickly slackened into an almost slovenly carelessness of dress and carriage. Now, in his farm clothes there was nothing left to suggest the soldier. With a loose, stained felt hat on the back of his head, khaki shorts a little too long and too wide, sleeves flapping over spare brown arms, his wispy moustache hiding a strained, set mouth, Major Carruthers looked what he was, a gentleman farmer going to seed.

The house had that brave, worn appearance of those struggling to keep up appearances. It was a four-roomed shack, its red roof dulling to streaky brown. It was the sort of house an apprentice farmer builds as a temporary shelter till he can afford better. Inside, good but battered furniture stood over worn places in the rugs; the piano was out of tune and the notes stuck; the silver tea things from the big narrow house in England where his brother (a lawyer) now lived were used as ornaments, and inside were bits of paper, accounts, rubber rings, old corks.

The room where his wife lay, in a greenish sun-lanced gloom, was a place of seedy misery. The doctor said it was her heart; and Major Carruthers knew this was true: she had broken down through heart-break over the conditions they lived in. She did not want to get better. The harsh light from outside was shut out with dark blinds, and she turned her face to the wall and lay there, hour after hour, inert and uncomplaining, in a stoicism of defeat nothing could penetrate. Even the children hardly moved her. It was as if she had said to herself: "If I cannot have what I wanted for them, then I wash my hands of life."

Sometimes Major Carruthers thought of her as she had been, and was filled with uneasy wonder and with guilt. That pleasant conventional pretty English girl had been bred to make a perfect wife for the professional soldier she had imagined him to be, but chance had wrenched her on to this isolated African farm, into a life which she submitted herself to, as if it had nothing to do with her. For the first few years she had faced the struggle humorously, courageously: it was a sprightly attitude towards life, almost flirtatious, as a woman flirts lightly with a man who means nothing to her. As the house grew shabby, and the furniture, and her clothes could not be replaced; when she looked into the mirror and saw her drying, untidy hair and roughening face, she would give a quick high laugh and say, "Dear me, the things one comes to!" She was facing this poverty as she would have faced, in England, poverty of a narrowing, but socially accepted kind. What she could not face was a different kind of fear; and Major Carruthers understood that too well, for it was now his own fear.

The two children were pale, fine-drawn creatures, almost transparent-looking in their thin nervous fairness, with the defensive and wary manners of the young who have been brought up to expect a better way of life than they enjoy. Their anxious solicitude wore on Major Carruthers' already over-sensitised nerves. Children had no right to feel the aching pity, which showed on their faces whenever they looked at him. They were too polite, too careful, too scrupulous. When they went into their mother's room she grieved sorrow-fully over them, and they submitted patiently to her emotion. All those weeks of the school holidays after she was taken ill, they moved about the farm like two strained and anxious ghosts, and whenever he saw them his sense of guilt throbbed like a wound. He was glad they were going back to school soon, for then—so he thought—it would be easier to manage. It was an intolerable strain, running the farm and coming back to the neglected house and the problems of food and clothing, and a sick wife who would not get better until he could offer her hope.

But when they had gone back, he found that after all, things were not much easier. He slept little, for his wife needed attention in the night; and he became afraid for his own health, worrying over what he ate and wore. He learnt to treat himself as if his health was not what he was, what made him, but something apart, a commodity like efficiency, which could be estimated in terms of money at the end of a season. His health stood between them and complete ruin; and soon there were medicine bottles beside his bed as well as beside his wife's.

One day, while he was carefully measuring out tonics for himself in the bedroom, he glanced up and saw his wife's small reddened eyes staring incredulously but ironically at him over the bedclothes. "What are you doing?" she asked.

"I need a tonic," he explained awkwardly, afraid to worry her by explanations.

She laughed, for the first time in weeks; then the slack tears began welling under the lids, and she turned to the wall again.

He understood that some vision of himself had been destroyed, finally, for her. Now she was left with an ageing, rather fussy gentleman, carefully measuring medicine after meals. But he did not blame her; he never had blamed her; not even though he knew her illness was a failure of will. He patted her cheek uncomfortably, and said: "It wouldn't do for me to get run down, would it?" Then he adjusted the curtains over the windows to shut out a streak of dancing light that threatened to fall over her face, set a glass nearer to her hand, and went out to arrange for her tray of slops to be carried in.

Then he took, in one swift, painful movement, as if he were leaping over an obstacle, the decision he had known for weeks he must take sooner or later. With a straightening of his shoulders, an echo from his soldier past, he took on the strain of an extra burden: he must get an assistant, whether he liked it or not.

So much did he shrink from any self-exposure, that he did not even consider advertising. He sent a note by native bearer to his neighbour, a few miles off, asking that it should be spread abroad that he was wanting help. He knew he would not have to wait long. It was 1931, in the middle of a slump, and there was unemployment, which was a rare thing for this new, sparsely populated country.

He wrote the following to his two sons at boarding-school:

> I expect you will be surprised to hear I'm getting another man on the place. Things are getting a bit too much, and as I plan to plant a bigger acreage of maize this year, I thought it would need two of us. Your mother is better this week, on the whole, so I think things are looking up. She is

looking forward to your next holidays, and asks me to say she will write soon. Between you and me, I don't think she's up to writing at the moment. It will soon be getting cold, I think, so if you need any clothes, let me know, and I'll see what I can do . . .

A week later, he sat on the little verandah, towards evening, smoking, when he saw a man coming through the trees on a bicycle. He watched him closely, already trying to form an estimate of his character by the tests he had used all his life; the width between the eyes, the shape of the skull, the way the legs were set on to the body. Although he had been taken in a dozen times, his belief in these methods never wavered. He was an easy prey for any trickster, lending money he never saw again, taken in by professional adventurers who (it seemed to him, measuring others by his own decency and the quick warmth he felt towards people) were the essence of gentlemen. He used to say that being a gentleman was a question of instinct: one could not mistake a gentleman.

As the visitor stepped off his bicycle and wheeled it to the verandah, Major Carruthers saw he was young, thirty perhaps, sturdily built, with enormous strength in the thick arms and shoulders. His skin was burnt a healthy orange-brown colour. His close hair, smooth as the fur of an animal, reflected no light. His obtuse, generous features were set in a round face, and the eyes were pale grey, nearly colourless.

Major Carruthers instinctively dropped his standards of value as he looked, for this man was an Afrikaner, and thus came into an outside category. It was not that he disliked him for it, although his father had been killed in the Boer War, but he had never had anything to do with the Afrikaans people before, and his knowledge of them was hearsay, from Englishmen who had the old prejudice. But he liked the look of the man: he liked the honest and straightforward face.

As for Van Heerden, he immediately recognised his traditional enemy, and his inherited dislike was strong. For a moment he appeared obstinate and wary. But they needed each other too badly to nurse old hatreds, and Van Heerden sat down when he was asked, though awkwardly, suppressing reluctance, and began drawing patterns in the dust with a piece of straw he had held between his lips.

Major Carruthers did not need to wonder about the man's circumstances: his quick acceptance of what were poor terms spoke of a long search for work.

He said scrupulously: "I know the salary is low and the living quarters are bad, even for a single man. I've had a patch of bad luck, and I can't afford more. I'll quite understand if you refuse."

"What are the living quarters?" asked Van Heerden. His was the rough voice of the uneducated Afrikaner: because he was uncertain where the accent should fall in each sentence, his speech had a wavering, halting sound, though his look and manner were direct enough.

Major Carruthers pointed ahead of them. Before the house the bush sloped gently down to the fields. "At the foot of the hill there's a hut I've been using as a storehouse. It's quite well-built. You can put up a place for a kitchen."

Van Heerden rose. "Can I see it?"

They set off. It was not far away. The thatched hut stood in uncleared bush. Grass grew to the walls and reached up to meet the slanting thatch. Trees mingled their branches overhead. It was round, built of poles and mud and with a stamped dung floor. Inside there was a stale musty smell because of the ants and beetles that had been at the sacks of grain. The one window was boarded over, and it was quite dark. In the confusing shafts of light from the door, a thick sheet of felted spider web showed itself, like a curtain halving the interior, as full of small flies and insects as a butcherbird's cache. The spider crouched, vast and glittering, shaking gently, glaring at them with small red eyes, from the centre of the web. Van Heerden did what Major Carruthers would have died rather than do: he tore the web across with his bare hands, crushed the spider between his fingers, and brushed them lightly against the walls to free them from the clinging silky strands and the sticky mush of insect-body.

"It will do fine," he announced.

He would not accept the invitation to a meal, thus making it clear this was merely a business arrangement. But he asked, politely (hating that he had to beg a favour), for a month's salary in advance. Then he set off on his bicycle to the store, ten miles off, to buy what he needed for his living.

Major Carruthers went back to his sick wife with a burdened feeling, caused by his being responsible for another human being having to suffer such conditions. He could not have the man in the house: the idea came into his head and was quickly dismissed. They had nothing in common, they would make each other uncomfortable—that was how he put it to himself. Besides, there wasn't really any room. Underneath, Major Carruthers knew that if his new assistant had been an Englishman, with the same upbringing, he would have found a corner in his house and a welcome as a friend. Major Carruthers threw off these thoughts: he had enough to worry him without taking on another man's problems.

A person who had always hated the business of organisation, which meant dividing responsibility with others, he found it hard to arrange with Van Heerden how the work was to be done. But as the Dutchman was good with cattle, Major Carruthers handed over all the stock on the farm to his care, thus relieving his mind of its most nagging care, for he was useless with beasts, and knew it. So they began, each knowing exactly where they stood. Van Heerden would make laconic reports at the end of each week, in the manner of an expert foreman reporting to a boss ignorant of technicalities— and Major Carruthers accepted this attitude, for he liked to respect people, and it was easy to respect Van Heerden's inspired instinct for animals.

For a few weeks Major Carruthers was almost happy. The fear of having to apply for another loan to his brother—worse, asking for the passage money to England and a job, thus justifying his family's belief in him as a failure, was pushed away; for while taking on a manager did not in itself improve things, it was an action, a decision, and there was nothing that he found more dismaying than decisions. The thought of his family in England, and particularly his elder brother, pricked him into slow burning passions of resentment. His brother's letters galled him so that he had grown to hate mail-days. They were crisp, affectionate letters, without condescension, but about money, bank-drafts, and insurance policies. Major Carruthers did not see life like that. He had not written to his brother for over a year. His wife, when she was well, wrote once a week, in the spirit of one propitiating fate.

Even she seemed cheered by the manager's coming; she sensed her husband's irrational lightness of spirit that short time. She stirred herself to ask about the farm; and he began to see that her interest in living would revive quickly if her sort of life came within reach again.

But some two months after Van Heerden's coming, Major Carruthers was walking along the farm road towards his lands, when he was astonished to see, disappearing into the bushes, a small flaxen-haired boy. He called, but the child froze as an animal freezes, flattening himself against the foliage. At last, since he could get no reply, Major Carruthers approached the child, who dissolved backwards through the trees, and followed him up the path to the hut. He was very angry, for he knew what he would see.

He had not been to the hut since he handed it over to Van Heerden. Now there was a clearing, and amongst the stumps of trees and the flattened grass, were half a dozen children, each as tow-headed as the first, with that bleached sapless look common to white children in the tropics who have been subjected to too much sun.

A lean-to had been built against the hut. It was merely a roof of beaten petrol tins, patched together like cloth with wire and nails and supported on two unpeeled sticks. There, holding a cooking pot over an open fire that was dangerously close to the thatch, stood a vast slatternly woman. She reminded him of a sow among her litter, as she lifted her head, the children crowding about her, and stared at him suspiciously from pale and white-lashed eyes.

"Where is your husband?" he demanded.

She did not answer. Her suspicion deepened into a glare of hate: clearly she knew no English.

Striding furiously to the door of the hut, he saw that it was crowded with two enormous native-style beds: strips of hide stretched over wooden poles embedded in the mud of the floor. What was left of the space was heaped with the stained and broken belongings of the family. Major Carruthers strode off in search of Van Heerden. His anger was now mingled with the shamed discomfort of trying to imagine what it must be to live in such squalor.

Fear rose high in him. For a few moments he inhabited the landscape of his dreams, a grey country full of sucking menace, where he suffered what he would not allow himself to think of while awake: the grim poverty that could overtake him if his luck did not turn, and if he refused to submit to his brother and return to England.

Walking through the fields, where the maize was now waving over his head, pale gold with a froth of white, the sharp dead leaves scything crisply against the wind, he could see nothing but that black foetid hut and the pathetic futureless children. That was the lowest he could bring his own children to! He felt moorless, helpless, afraid: his sweat ran cold on him. And he did not hesitate in his mind; driven by fear and anger, he told himself to be hard; he was searching in his mind for the words with which he would dismiss the Dutchman who had brought his worst nightmares to life, on his own farm, in glaring daylight, where they were inescapable.

He found him with a screaming rearing young ox that was being broken to the plough, handling it with his sure understanding of animals. At a cautious distance stood the natives who were assisting; but Van Heerden, fearless and purposeful, was fighting the beast at close range. He saw Major Carruthers, let go the plunging horn he held, and the ox shot away backwards, roaring with anger, into the crowd of natives, who gathered loosely about it with sticks and stones to prevent it running away altogether.

Van Heerden stood still, wiping the sweat off his face, still grinning with the satisfaction of the fight, waiting for his employer to speak.

"Van Heerden," said Major Carruthers, without preliminaries, "why didn't you tell me you had a family?"

As he spoke the Dutchman's face changed, first flushing into guilt, then setting hard and stubborn. "Because I've been out of work for a year, and I knew you would not take me if I told you."

The two men faced each other, Major Carruthers tall, flyaway, shambling, bent with responsibility; Van Heerden stiff and defiant. The natives remained about the ox, to prevent its escape—for them this was a brief intermission in the real work of the farm—and their shouts mingled with the incessant bellowing. It was a hot day; Van Heerden wiped the sweat from his eyes with the back of his hand.

"You can't keep a wife and all those children here—how many children?" "Nine."

Major Carruthers thought of his own two, and his perpetual dull ache of worry over them; and his heart became grieved for Van Heerden. Two children, with all the trouble over everything they ate and wore and thought, and what would become of them, were too great a burden; how did this man, with nine, manage to look so young?

"How old are you?" he asked abruptly, in a different tone.

"Thirty-four," said Van Heerden, suspiciously, unable to understand the direction Major Carruthers followed.

The only marks on his face were sun-creases; it was impossible to think of him as the father of nine children and the husband of that terrible broken-down woman. As Major Carruthers gazed at him, he became conscious of the strained lines on his own face, and tried to loosen himself, because he took so badly what this man bore so well.

"You can't keep a wife and children in such conditions."

"We were living in a tent in the bush on mealie meal and what I shot for nine months, and that was through the wet season," said Van Heerden drily.

Major Carruthers knew he was beaten. "You've put me in a false position, Van Heerden," he said angrily. "You know I can't afford to give you more money. I don't know where I'm going to find my own children's school fees, as it is. I told you the position when you came. I can't afford to keep a man with such a family."

"Nobody can afford to have me either," said Van Heerden sullenly.

"How can I have you living on my place in such a fashion? Nine children! They should be at school. Didn't you know there is a law to make them go to school! Hasn't anybody been to see you about them?"

"They haven't got me yet. They won't get me unless someone tells them."

Against this challenge, which was also an unwilling appeal, Major Carruthers remained silent, until he said brusquely: "Remember, I'm not responsible." And he walked off, with all the appearance of anger.

Van Heerden looked after him, his face puzzled. He did not know whether or not he had been dismissed. After a few moments he moistened his dry lips with his tongue, wiped his hand again over his eyes and turned back to the ox. Looking over his shoulder from the edge of the field, Major Carruthers could see his wiry, stocky figure leaping and bending about the ox whose bellowing made the whole farm ring with anger.

Major Carruthers decided, once and for all, to put the family out of his mind. But they haunted him; he even dreamed of them; and he could not determine whether it was his own or the Dutchman's children who filled his sleep with fear.

It was a very busy time of the year. Harassed, like all his fellow-farmers, by labour difficulties, apportioning out the farm tasks was a daily problem. All day his mind churned slowly over the necessities: this fencing was urgent, that field must be reaped at once. Yet, in spite of this, he decided it was his plain duty to build a second hut beside the first. It would do no more than take the edge off the discomfort of that miserable family, but he knew he could not rest until it was built.

Just as he had made up his mind and was wondering how the thing could be managed, the boss-boy came to him, saying that unless the Dutchman went, he and his friends would leave the farm.

"Why?" asked Major Carruthers, knowing what the answer would be. Van Heerden was a hard worker, and the cattle were improving week by week under his care, but he could not handle natives. He shouted at them, lost his temper, treated them like dogs. There was continual friction.

"Dutchmen are no good," said the boss-boy simply, voicing the hatred of the black man for that section of the white people he considers his most brutal oppressors.

Now, Major Carruthers was proud that at a time when most farmers were forced to buy labour from the contractors, he was able to attract sufficient voluntary labour to run his farm. He was a good employer, proud of his reputation for fair dealing. Many of his natives had been with him for years, taking a few months off occasionally for a rest in their kraals, but always returning to him. His neighbours were complaining of the sullen attitude of their labourers: so far Major Carruthers had kept this side of that form of passive resistance which could ruin a farmer. It was walking on a knife-edge, but his simple human relationship with his workers was his greatest asset as a farmer, and he knew it.

He stood and thought, while his boss-boy, who had been on this farm twelve years, waited for a reply. A great deal was at stake. For a moment Major Carruthers thought of dismissing the Dutchman; he realized he could not bring himself to do it: what would happen to all those children? He decided on a course which was repugnant to him. He was going to appeal to his employee's pity.

"I have always treated you square?" he asked. "I've always helped you when you were in trouble?"

The boss-boy immediately and warmly assented.

"You know that my wife is ill, and that I'm having a lot of trouble just now? I don't want the Dutchman to go, just now when the work is so heavy. I'll speak to him, and if there is any more trouble with the men, then come to me and I'll deal with it myself."

It was a glittering blue day, with a chill edge on the air that stirred Major Carruthers' thin blood as he stood, looking in appeal into the sullen face of the native. All at once, feeling the fresh air wash along his cheeks, watching the leaves shake with a ripple of gold on the trees down the slope, he felt superior to his difficulties, and able to face anything. "Come," he said, with his rare, diffident smile. "After all these years, when we have been working together for so long, surely you can do this for me. It won't be for very long."

He watched the man's face soften in response to his own; and wondered at the unconscious use of the last phrase, for there was no reason, on the face of things, why the situation should not continue as it was for a very long time.

They began laughing together; and separated cheerfully; the African shaking his head ruefully over the magnitude of the sacrifice asked of him, thus making the incident into a joke; and he dived off into the bush to explain the position to his fellow-workers.

Repressing a strong desire to go after him, to spend the lovely fresh day walking for pleasure, Major Carruthers went into his wife's bedroom, inexplicably confident and walking like a young man.

She lay as always, face to the wall, her protruding shoulders visible beneath the cheap pink bed-jacket he had bought for her illness. She seemed neither better nor worse. But as she turned her head, his buoyancy infected her a little; perhaps, too, she was conscious of the exhilarating day outside her gloomy curtains.

What kind of a miraculous release was she waiting for? he wondered, as he delicately adjusted her sheets and pillows and laid his hand gently on her head. Over the bony cage of the skull, the skin was papery and blueish. What was she thinking? He had a vision of her brain as a small frightened animal pulsating under his fingers.

With her eyes still closed, she asked in her querulous thin voice: "Why don't you write to George?"

Involuntarily his fingers contracted on her hair, causing her to start and to open her reproachful, red-rimmed eyes. He waited for her usual appeal: the children, my health, our future. But she sighed and remained silent, still loyal to the man she had imagined she was marrying; and he could feel her thinking: *the lunatic stiff pride of men.*

Understanding that for her it was merely a question of waiting for his defeat, as her deliverance, he withdrew his hand, in dislike of her, saying: "Things are not as bad as that yet." The cheerfulness of his voice was genuine, holding still the courage and hope instilled into him by the bright day outside.

"Why, what has happened?" she asked swiftly, her voice suddenly strong, looking at him in hope.

"Nothing," he said; and the depression settled down over him again. Indeed, nothing had happened; and his confidence was a trick of the nerves. Soberly he left the bedroom, thinking: I must get that well built; and when that is done, I must do the drains, and then . . . He was thinking, too, that all these things must wait for the second hut.

Oddly, the comparatively small problem of that hut occupied his mind during the next few days. A slow and careful man, he set milestones for himself and overtook them one by one.

Since Christmas the labourers had been working a seven-day week, in order to keep ahead in the race against the weeds. They resented it, of course, but that was the custom. Now that the maize was grown, they expected work to slack off, they expected their Sundays to be restored to them. To ask even half a dozen of them to sacrifice their weekly holiday for the sake of the hated Dutchman might precipitate a crisis. Major Carruthers took his time, stalking his opportunity like a hunter, until one evening he was talking with his boss-boy as man to man, about farm problems; but when he broached the subject of a hut, Major Carruthers saw that it would be as he feared: the man at once turned stiff and unhelpful. Suddenly impatient, he said: "It must be done next Sunday. Six men could finish it in a day, if they worked hard."

The black man's glance became veiled and hostile. Responding to the authority in the voice he replied simply: "Yes, baas." He was accepting the order from above, and refusing responsibility: his cooperation was switched off; he had become a machine for transmitting orders. Nothing exasperated Major Carruthers more than when this happened. He said sternly: "I'm not having any nonsense. If that hut isn't built, there'll be trouble."

"Yes, baas," said the boss-boy again. He walked away, stopped some natives who were coming off the fields with their hoes over their shoulders, and transmitted the order in a neutral voice. Major Carruthers saw them glance at him in fierce antagonism; then they turned away their heads, and walked off in a group, towards their compound.

It would be all right, he thought, in disproportionate relief. It would be difficult to say exactly what it was he feared, for the question of the hut had loomed so huge in his mind that he was beginning to feel an almost super-stitious foreboding. Driven downwards through failure after failure, fate was becoming real to him as a cold malignant force; the careful balancing of unfriendly probabilities that underlay all his planning had developed in him an acute sensitivity to the future; and he had learned to respect his dreams and omens. Now he wondered at the strength of his desire to see that hut built, and whatever danger it represented behind him.

He went to the clearing to find Van Heerden and tell him what had been planned. He found him sitting on a candlebox in the doorway of the hut, playing good-humouredly with his children, as if they had been puppies, tumbling them over, snapping his fingers in their faces, and laughing outright with boyish exuberance when one little boy squared up his fists at him in a moment of temper against this casual, almost contemptuous treatment of them. Major Carruthers heard that boyish laugh with amazement; he looked blankly at the young Dutchman, and then from him to his wife, who was standing, as usual, over a petrol tin that balanced on the small fire. A smell of meat and pumpkin filled the clearing. The woman seemed to Major Carruthers less a human being than the expression of an elemental, irrepressi-ble force: he saw her, in her vast sagging fleshiness, with her slow stupid face, her instinctive responses to her children, whether for affection or tem-per, as the symbol of fecundity, a strong, irresistible heave of matter. She frightened him. He turned his eyes from her and explained to Van Heerden that a second hut would be built here, beside the existing one.

Van Heerden was pleased. He softened into quick confiding friendship. He looked doubtfully behind him at the small hut that sheltered eleven human beings, and said that it was really not easy to live in such a small space with so many children. He glanced at the children, cuffing them affectionately as he spoke, smiling like a boy. He was proud of his family, of his own capacity for making children: Major Carruthers could see that. Almost, he smiled; then he glanced through the doorway at the grey squalor of the interior and hurried off, resolutely preventing himself from dwelling on the repulsive facts that such close-packed living implied.

The next Saturday evening he and Van Heerden paced the clearing with tape measure and spirit level, determining the area of the new hut. It was to be a large one. Already the sheaves of thatching grass had been stacked ready for next day, shining brassily in the evening sun; and the thorn poles for the walls lay about the clearing, stripped of bark, the smooth inner wood showing white as kernels.

Major Carruthers was waiting for the natives to come up from the compound for the building before daybreak that Sunday. He was there even before the family woke, afraid that without his presence something might go wrong. He feared the Dutchman's temper because of the labourers' sulky mood.

He leaned against a tree, watching the bush come awake, while the sky flooded slowly with light, and the birds sang about him. The hut was, for a long time, silent and dark. A sack hung crookedly over the door, and he could glimpse huddled shapes within. It seemed to him horrible, a stinking kennel shrinking ashamedly to the ground away from the wide hall of fresh blue sky. Then a child came out, and another; soon they were spilling out of the doorway, in their little rags of dresses, or hitching khaki pants up over the bony jut of a hip. They smiled shyly at him, offering him friendship. Then came the woman, moving sideways to ease herself through the narrow door-frame—she was so huge it was almost a fit. She lumbered slowly, thick and stupid with sleep, over to the cold fire, raising her arms in a yawn, so that wisps of dull yellow hair fell over her shoulders and her dark slack dress lifted in creases under her neck. Then she saw Major Carruthers and smiled at him. For the first time he saw her as a human being and not as something fatally ugly. There was something shy, yet frank, in that smile; so that he could imagine the strong, laughing adolescent girl, with the frank, inviting, healthy sensuality of the young Dutchwoman—so she had been when she married Van Heerden. She stooped painfully to stir up the ashes, and soon the fire spurted up under the leaning patch of tin roof. For a while Van Heerden did not appear; neither did the natives who were supposed to be here a long while since; Major Carruthers continued to lean against a tree, smiling at the children, who nevertheless kept their distance from him, unable to play naturally because of his presence there, smiling at Mrs. Van Heerden who was throwing handfuls of mealie meal into a petrol tin of boiling water, to make native-style porridge.

It was just on eight o'clock, after two hours of impatient waiting, that the labourers filed up the bushy incline, with the axes and picks over their shoulders, avoiding his eyes. He pressed down his anger: after all it was Sunday, and they had had no day off for weeks; he could not blame them.

They began by digging the circular trench that would hold the wall poles. As their picks rang out on the pebbly ground, Van Heerden came out of the hut, pushing aside the dangling sack with one hand and pulling up his trousers with the other, yawning broadly, then smiling at Major Carruthers apologetically. "I've had my sleep out," he said; he seemed to think his employer might be angry.

Major Carruthers stood close over the workers, wanting it to be understood by them and by Van Heerden that he was responsible. He was too conscious of their resentment, and knew that they would scamp the work if possible. If the hut was to be completed as planned, he would need all his tact and good-humour. He stood there patiently all morning, watching the thin sparks flash up as the picks swung into the flinty earth. Van Heerden lingered nearby, unwilling to be thus publicly superseded in the responsibility for his own dwelling in the eyes of the natives.

When they flung their picks and went to fetch the poles, they did so with a side glance at Major Carruthers, challenging him to say the trench was not deep enough. He called them back, laughingly, saying: "Are you digging for a dog-kennel then, and not a hut for a man?" One smiled unwillingly in response; the others sulked. Perfunctorily they deepened the trench to the very minimum that Major Carruthers was likely to pass. By noon, the poles were leaning drunkenly in place and the natives were stripping the binding from beneath the bark of nearby trees. Long fleshy strips of fibre, rose-coloured and apricot and yellow, lay tangled over the grass, and the wounded trees showed startling red gashes around the clearing. Swiftly the poles were laced together with this natural rope, so that when the frame was complete it showed up against green trees and sky like a slender gleaming white cage, interwoven lightly with rosy-yellow. Two natives climbed on top to bind the roof poles into their conical shape, while the others stamped a slushy mound of sand and earth to form plaster for the walls. Soon they stopped—the rest could wait until after the midday break.

Worn out by the strain of keeping the balance between the fiery Dutchman and the resentful workers, Major Carruthers went off home to eat. He had one and a half hour's break. He finished his meal in ten minutes, longing to be able to sleep for once till he woke naturally. His wife was dozing, so he lay down on the other bed and at once dropped off to sleep himself. When he woke it was long after the time he had set himself. It was after three. He rose in a panic and strode to the clearing, in the grip of one of his premonitions.

There stood the Dutchman, in a flaring temper, shouting at the natives who lounged in front of him, laughing openly. They had only just returned to work. As Major Carruthers approached, he saw Van Heerden using his open palms in a series of quick swinging slaps against their faces, knocking them sideways against each other: it was as if he were cuffing his own children in a fit of anger. Major Carruthers broke into a run, erupting into the group before anything else could happen. Van Heerden fell back on seeing him. He was beef-red with fury. The natives were bunched together, on the point of throwing down their tools and walking off the job.

"Get back to work," snapped Major Carruthers to the men: and to Van Heerden: "I'm dealing with this." His eyes were an appeal to recognise the need for tact, but Van Heerden stood squarely there in front of him, on planted legs, breathing heavily. "But Major Carruthers . . ." he began, implying that as a white man, his employer not there, it was right that he should take the command. "Do as I say," said Major Carruthers. Van Heerden, with a deadly look at his opponents, swung on his heel and marched off into the hut. The slapping swing of the grain-bag was as if a door had been slammed. Major Carruthers turned to the natives. "Get on," he ordered briefly, in a calm decisive voice. There was a moment of uncertainty. Then they picked up their tools and went to work.

Some laced the framework of the roof; others slapped the mud on to the walls. This business of plastering was usually a festival, with laughter and raillery, for there were gaps between the poles, and a handful of mud could fly through a space into the face of a man standing behind: the thing could become a game, like children playing snowballs. Today there was no pretence at good-humour. When the sun went down the men picked up their tools and filed off into the bush without a glance at Major Carruthers. The work had not prospered. The grass was laid untidily over the roof-frame, still uncut and reaching to the ground in long swatches. The first layer of mud had been unevenly flung on. It would be a shabby building.

"His own fault," thought Major Carruthers, sending his slow, tired blue glance to the hut where the Dutchman was still cherishing the seeds of wounded pride. Next day, when Major Carruthers was in another part of the farm, the Dutchman got his own back in a fine flaming scene with the plough-boys: they came to complain to the boss-boy, but not to Major Carruthers. This made him uneasy. All that week he waited for fresh complaints about the Dutchman's behaviour. So much was he keyed up, waiting for the scene between himself and a grudging boss-boy, that when nothing happened his apprehensions deepened into a deep foreboding.

The building was finished the following Sunday. The floors were stamped hard with new dung, the thatch trimmed, and the walls grained smooth. Another two weeks must elapse before the family could move in, for the place smelled of damp. They were weeks of worry for Major Carruthers. It was unnatural for the Africans to remain passive and sullen under the Dutchman's handling of them, and especially when they knew he was on their side. There was something he did not like in the way they would not meet his eyes and in the over-polite attitude of the boss-boy.

The beautiful clear weather that he usually loved so much, May weather, sharpened by cold, and crisp under deep clear skies, pungent with gusts of wind from the dying leaves and grasses of the veld, was spoilt for him this year: something was going to happen.

When the family eventually moved in, Major Carruthers became discouraged because the building of the hut had represented such trouble and worry, while now things seemed hardly better than before: what was the use of two small round huts for a family of eleven? But Van Heerden was very pleased, and expressed his gratitude in a way that moved Major Carruthers deeply: unable to show feeling himself, he was grateful when others did, so relieving him of the burden of his shyness. There was a ceremonial atmosphere on the evening when one of the great sagging beds was wrenched out of the floor of the first hut and its legs plastered down newly into the second hut.

That very same night he was awakened towards dawn by voices calling to him from outside his window. He started up, knowing that whatever he had dreaded was here, glad that the tension was over. Outside the back door stood his boss-boy, holding a hurricane lamp which momentarily blinded Major Carruthers.

"The hut is on fire."

Blinking his eyes, he turned to look. Away in the darkness flames were lapping over the trees, outlining branches so that as a gust of wind lifted them patterns of black leaves showed clear and fine against the flowing red light of the fire. The veld was illuminated with a fitful plunging glare. The two men ran off into the bush down the rough road, towards the blaze.

The clearing was lit up, as bright as morning, when they arrived. On the roof of the first hut squatted Van Heerden, lifting tins of water from a line of natives below, working from the water-butt, soaking the thatch to prevent it catching the flames from the second hut that was only a few yards off. That was a roaring pillar of fire. Its frail skeleton was still erect, but twisting and writhing incandescently within its envelope of flame, and it collapsed slowly as he came up, subsiding in a crash of sparks.

"The children," gasped Major Carruthers to Mrs. Van Heerden, who was watching the blaze fatalistically from where she sat on a scattered bundle of bedding, the tears soaking down her face, her arms tight round a swathed child.

As she spoke she opened the clothes to display the smallest infant. A swathe of burning grass from the roof had fallen across its head and shoulders. He sickened as he looked, for there was nothing but raw charred flesh. But it was alive: the limbs still twitched a little.

"I'll get the car and we'll take it in to the doctor."

He ran out of the clearing and fetched the car. As he tore down the slope back again he saw he was still in his pyjamas, and when he gained the clearing for the second time, Van Heerden was climbing down the roof, which dripped water as if there had been a storm. He bent over the burnt child.

"Too late," he said.

"But it's still alive."

Van Heerden almost shrugged; he appeared dazed. He continually turned his head to survey the glowing heap that had so recently sheltered his children. He licked his lips with a quick unconscious movement, because of their burning dryness. His face was grimed with smoke and inflamed from the great heat, so that his young eyes showed startlingly clear against the black skin.

"Get into the car," said Major Carruthers to the woman. She automatically moved towards the car, without looking at her husband, who said: "But it's too late, man."

Major Carruthers knew the child would die, but his protest against the waste and futility of the burning expressed itself in this way: that everything must be done to save this life, even against hope. He started the car and slid off down the hill. Before they had gone half a mile he felt his shoulder plucked from behind, and, turning, saw the child was now dead. He reversed the car into the dark bush off the road, and drove back to the clearing. Now the woman had begun wailing, a soft monotonous, almost automatic sound that kept him tight in his seat, waiting for the next cry.

The fire was now a dark heap, fanning softly to a glowing red as the wind passed over it. The children were standing in a half-circle, gazing fascinated at it. Van Heerden stood near them, laying his hands gently, restlessly, on their heads and shoulders, reassuring himself of their existence there, in the flesh and living, beside him.

Mrs. Van Heerden got clumsily out of the car, still wailing, and disappeared into the hut, clutching the bundled dead child.

Feeling out of place among that bereaved family, Major Carruthers went up to his house, where he drank cup after cup of tea, holding himself tight and controlled, conscious of over-strained nerves.

Then he stooped into his wife's room, which seemed small and dark and airless. The cave of a sick animal, he thought, in disgust; then, ashamed of himself, he returned out of doors, where the sky was filling with light. He sent a message for the boss-boy, and waited for him in a condition of tensed anger.

When the man came Major Carruthers asked immediately: "Why did that hut burn?"

The boss-boy looked at him straight and said: "How should I know?" Then, after a pause, with guileful innocence: "It was the fault of the kitchen, too close to the thatch."

Major Carruthers glared at him, trying to wear down the straight gaze with his own accusing eyes.

"That hut must be rebuilt at once. It must be rebuilt today."

The boss-boy seemed to say that it was a matter of indifference to him whether it was rebuilt or not. "I'll go and tell the others," he said, moving off.

"Stop," barked Major Carruthers. Then he paused, frightened, not so much at his rage, but his humiliation and guilt. He had foreseen it! He had foreseen it all! And yet, that thatch could so easily have caught alight from the small incautious fire that sent up sparks all day so close to it.

Almost, he burst out in wild reproaches. Then he pulled himself together and said: "Get away from me." What was the use? He knew perfectly well that one of the Africans whom Van Heerden had kicked or slapped or shouted at had fired that hut; no one could ever prove it.

He stood quite still, watching his boss-boy move off, tugging at the long wisps of his moustache in frustrated anger.

And what would happen now?

He ordered breakfast, drank a cup of tea, and spoilt a piece of toast. Then he glanced in again at his wife, who would sleep for a couple of hours yet.

Again tugging fretfully at his moustache, Major Carruthers set off for the clearing.

Everything was just as it had been, though the pile of black débris looked low and shabby now that morning had come and heightened the wild colour of sky and bush. The children were playing nearby, their hands and faces black, their rags of clothing black—everything seemed patched and smudged with black, and on one side the trees hung withered and grimy and the soil was hot underfoot.

Van Heerden leaned against the framework of the first hut. He looked subdued and tired, but otherwise normal. He greeted Major Carruthers, and did not move.

"How is your wife?" asked Major Carruthers. He could hear a moaning sound from inside the hut.

"She's doing well."

Major Carruthers imagined her weeping over the dead child; and said: "I'll take your baby into town for you and arrange for the funeral."

Van Heerden said: "I've buried her already." He jerked his thumb at the bush behind them.

"Didn't you register its birth?"

Van Heerden shook his head. His gaze challenged Major Carruthers as if to say: Who's to know if no one tells them? Major Carruthers could not speak: he was held in silence by the thought of that charred little body, huddled into a packing-case or wrapped in a piece of cloth, thrust into the ground, at the mercy of wild animals or of white ants.

"Well, one comes and another goes," said Van Heerden at last, slowly, reaching out for philosophy as a comfort, while his eyes filled with rough tears.

Major Carruthers stared: he could not understand. At last the meaning of the words came into him, and he heard the moaning from the hut with a new understanding.

The idea had never entered his head; it had been a complete failure of the imagination. If nine children, why not ten? Why not fifteen, for that matter, or twenty? Of course there would be more children.

"It was the shock," said Van Heerden. "It should be next month."

Major Carruthers leaned back against the wall of the hut and took out a cigarette clumsily. He felt weak. He felt as if Van Heerden had struck him, smiling. This was an absurd and unjust feeling, but for a moment he hated Van Heerden for standing there and saying: this grey country of poverty that you fear so much, will take on a different look when you actually enter it. You will cease to exist; there is no energy left, when one is wrestling naked, with life, for your kind of fine feelings and scruples and regrets.

"We hope it will be a boy," volunteered Van Heerden, with a tentative friendliness, as if he thought it might be considered a familiarity to offer his private notions to Major Carruthers. "We have five boys and four girls— three girls," he corrected himself, his face contracting.

Major Carruthers asked stiffly: "Will she be all right?"

"I do it," said Van Heerden. "The last was born in the middle of the night, when it was raining. That was when we were in the tent. It's nothing to her," he added, with pride. He was listening, as he spoke, to the slow moaning from inside. "I'd better be getting in to her," he said, knocking out his pipe against the mud of the walls. Nodding to Major Carruthers, he lifted the sack and disappeared.

After a while Major Carruthers gathered himself together and forced himself to walk erect across the clearing under the curious gaze of the children. His mind was fixed and numb, but he walked as if moving to a destination. When he reached the house, he at once pulled paper and pen towards him and wrote, and each slow difficult word was a nail in the coffin of his pride as a man.

Some minutes later he went in to his wife. She was awake, turned on her side, watching the door for the relief of his coming. "I've written for a job at home," he said simply, laying his hand on her thin dry wrist, and feeling the slow pulse beat up suddenly against his palm.

He watched curiously as her face crumpled and the tears of thankfulness and release ran slowly down her cheeks and soaked the pillow.

Isaac Bashevis Singer

Gimpel the Fool

I

I am Gimpel the fool. I don't think myself a fool. On the contrary. But that's what folks call me. They gave me the name while I was still in school. I had seven names in all: imbecile, donkey, flax-head, dope, glump, ninny, and fool. The last name stuck. What did my foolishness consist of? I was easy to take in. They said, "Gimpel, you know the rabbi's wife has been brought to childbed?" So I skipped school. Well, it turned out to be a lie. How was I supposed to know? She hadn't had a big belly. But I never looked at her belly. Was that really so foolish? The gang laughed and hee-hawed, stomped and danced and chanted a good-night prayer. And instead of the raisins they give when a woman's lying in, they stuffed my hand full of goat turds. I was no weakling. If I slapped someone he'd see all the way to Cracow. But I'm really not a slugger by nature. I think to myself, Let it pass. So they take advantage of me.

I was coming home from school and heard a dog barking. I'm not afraid of dogs, but of course I never want to start up with them. One of them may be mad, and if he bites there's not a Tartar in the world who can help you. So I made tracks. Then I looked around and saw the whole market place wild with laughter. It was no dog at all but Wolf-Leib the thief. How was I supposed to know it was he? It sounded like a howling bitch.

When the pranksters and leg-pullers found that I was easy to fool, every one of them tried his luck with me. "Gimpel, the Czar is coming to Frampol;

GIMPEL THE FOOL From *A Treasury of Yiddish Stories* edited by Irving Howe and Eliezer Greenberg. Copyright 1953 by Isaac Bashevis Singer. Reprinted by permission of The Viking Press, Inc.

Gimpel, the moon fell down in Turbeen; Gimpel, little Hodel Furpiece found a treasure behind the bathhouse." And I like a *golem* believed everyone. In the first place, everything is possible, as it is written in the Wisdom of the Fathers, I've forgotten just how. Second, I had to believe when the whole town came down on me! If I ever dared to say, "Ah, you're kidding!" there was trouble. People got angry. "What do you mean! You want to call everyone a liar?" What was I to do? I believed them, and I hope at least that did them some good.

I was an orphan. My grandfather who brought me up was already bent toward the grave. So they turned me over to a baker, and what a time they gave me there! Every woman or girl who came to bake a pan of cookies or dry a batch of noodles had to fool me at least once. "Gimpel, there's a fair in heaven; Gimpel, the rabbi gave birth to a calf in the seventh month; Gimpel, a cow flew over the roof and laid brass eggs." A student from the yeshiva came once to buy a roll, and he said, "You, Gimpel, while you stand here scraping with your baker's shovel the Messiah has come. The dead have arisen." "What do you mean?" I said. "I heard no one blowing the ram's horn!" He said, "Are you deaf?" And all began to cry, "We heard it, we heard!" Then in came Reitze the candle-dipper and called out in her hoarse voice, "Gimpel, your father and mother have stood up from the grave. They're looking for you."

To tell the truth, I knew very well that nothing of the sort had happened, but all the same, as folks were talking, I threw on my wool vest and went out. Maybe something had happened. What did I stand to lose by looking? Well, what a cat music went up! And then I took a vow to believe nothing more. But that was no go either. They confused me so that I didn't know the big end from the small.

I went to the rabbi to get some advice. He said, "It is written, better to be a fool all your days than for one hour to be evil. You are not a fool. They are the fools. For he who causes his neighbor to feel shame loses Paradise himself." Nevertheless the rabbi's daughter took me in. As I left the rabbinical court she said, "Have you kissed the wall yet?" I said, "No; what for?" She answered, "It's a law; you've got to do it after every visit." Well, there didn't seem to be any harm in it. And she burst out laughing. It was a fine trick. She put one over on me, all right.

I wanted to go off to another town, but then everyone got busy matchmaking, and they were after me so they nearly tore my coat tails off. They talked at me and talked until I got water on the ear. She was no chaste maiden, but they told me she was virgin pure. She had a limp, and they said it was deliberate, from coyness. She had a bastard, and they told me the child was her little brother. I cried, "You're wasting your time. I'll never marry that whore." But they said indignantly, "What a way to talk! Aren't you ashamed of yourself? We can take you to the rabbi and have you fined for giving her a bad name." I saw then that I wouldn't escape them so easily and I thought, They're set on making me their butt. But when you're married the husband's the master, and if that's all right with her it's agreeable to me too. Besides, you can't pass through life unscathed, nor expect to.

I went to her clay house, which was built on the sand, and the whole gang, hollering and chorusing, came after me. They acted like bearbaiters. When we came to the well they stopped all the same. They were afraid to start anything with Elka. Her mouth would open as if it were on a hinge, and she had a fierce tongue. I entered the house. Lines were strung from wall to wall and clothes were drying. Barefoot she stood by the tub, doing the wash. She was dressed in a worn hand-me-down gown of plush. She had her hair put up in braids and pinned across her head. It took my breath away, almost, the reek of it all.

Evidently she knew who I was. She took a look at me and said, "Look who's here! He's come, the drip. Grab a seat."

I told her all; I denied nothing. "Tell me the truth," I said, "are you really a virgin, and is that mischievous Yechiel actually your little brother? Don't be deceitful with me, for I'm an orphan."

"I'm an orphan myself," she answered, "and whoever tries to twist you up, may the end of his nose take a twist. But don't let them think they can take advantage of me. I want a dowry of fifty guilders, and let them take up a collection besides. Otherwise they can kiss my you-know-what." She was very plainspoken. I said, "It's the bride and not the groom who gives a dowry." Then she said, "Don't bargain with me. Either a flat 'yes' or a flat 'no'—go back where you came from."

I thought, No bread will ever be baked from *this* dough. But ours is not a poor town. They consented to everything and proceeded with the wedding. It so happened that there was a dysentery epidemic at the time. The ceremony was held at the cemetery gates, near the little corpse-washing hut. The fellows got drunk. While the marriage contract was being drawn up I heard the most pious high rabbi ask, "Is the bride a widow or a divorced woman?" And the sexton's wife answered for her, "Both a widow and divorced." It was a black moment for me. But what was I to do, run away from under the marriage canopy?

There was singing and dancing. An old granny danced opposite me, hugging a braided white *chalah*. The master of revels made a "God 'a mercy" in memory of the bride's parents. The schoolboys threw burrs, as on *Tishe b'Av* fast day. There were a lot of gifts after the sermon: a noodle board, a kneading trough, a bucket, brooms, ladles, household articles galore. Then I took a look and saw two strapping young men carrying a crib. "What do we need this for?" I asked. So they said, "Don't rack your brains about it. It's all right, it'll come in handy." I realized I was going to be rooked. Take it another way though, what did I stand to lose? I reflected, I'll see what comes of it. A whole town can't go altogether crazy.

II

At night I came where my wife lay, but she wouldn't let me in. "Say, look here, is this what they married us for?" I said. And she said, "My monthly has come." "But yesterday they took you to the ritual bath, and that's afterward, isn't it supposed to be?" "Today isn't yesterday," said she, "and yesterday's not today. You can beat it if you don't like it." In short, I waited.

Not four months later she was in childbed. The townsfolk hid their laughter with their knuckles. But what could I do? She suffered intolerable pains and clawed at the walls. "Gimpel," she cried, "I'm going. Forgive me!" The house filled with women. They were boiling pans of water. The screams rose to the welkin.

The thing to do was to go to the House of Prayer to repeat Psalms, and that was what I did.

The townsfolk liked that, all right. I stood in a corner saying Psalms and prayers, and they shook their heads at me. "Pray, pray!" they told me. "Prayer never made any woman pregnant." One of the congregation put a straw to my mouth and said, "Hay for the cows." There was something to that too, by God!

She gave birth to a boy. Friday at the synagogue the sexton stood up before the Ark, pounded on the reading table, and announced, "The wealthy Reb Gimpel invites the congregation to a feast in honor of the birth of a son." The whole House of Prayer rang with laughter. My face was flaming. But there was nothing I could do. After all, I *was* the one responsible for the circumcision honors and rituals.

Half the town came running. You couldn't wedge another soul in. Women brought peppered chick-peas, and there was a keg of beer from the tavern. I ate and drank as much as anyone, and they all congratulated me. Then there was a circumcision, and I named the boy after my father, may he rest in peace. When all were gone and I was left with my wife alone, she thrust her head through the bed-curtain and called me to her.

"Gimpel," said she, "why are you silent? Has your ship gone and sunk?"

"What shall I say?" I answered. "A fine thing you've done to me! If my mother had known of it she'd have died a second time."

She said, "Are you crazy, or what?"

"How can you make such a fool," I said, "of one who should be the lord and master?"

"What's the matter with you?" she said. "What have you taken it into your head to imagine?"

I saw that I must speak bluntly and openly. "Do you think this is the way to use an orphan?" I said. "You have borne a bastard."

She answered, "Drive this foolishness out of your head. The child is yours."

"How can he be mine?" I argued. "He was born seventeen weeks after the wedding."

She told me then that he was premature. I said, "Isn't he a little too premature?" She said she had had a grandmother who carried just as short a time and she resembled this grandmother of hers as one drop of water does another. She swore to it with such oaths that you would have believed a peasant at the fair if he had used them. To tell the plain truth, I didn't believe her; but when I talked it over next day with the schoolmaster he told me that the very same thing had happened to Adam and Eve. Two they went up to bed, and four they descended.

"There isn't a woman in the world who is not the granddaughter of Eve," he said.

That was how it was—they argued me dumb. But then, who really knows how such things are?

I began to forget my sorrow. I loved the child madly, and he loved me too. As soon as he saw me he'd wave his little hands and want me to pick him up, and when he was colicky I was the only one who could pacify him. I bought him a little bone teething ring and a little gilded cap. He was forever catching the evil eye from someone, and then I had to run to get one of those abracadabras for him that would get him out of it. I worked like an ox. You know how expenses go up when there's an infant in the house. I don't want to lie about it; I didn't dislike Elka either, for that matter. She swore at me and cursed, and I couldn't get enough of her. What strength she had! One of her looks could rob you of the power of speech. And her orations! Pitch and sulphur, that's what they were full of, and yet somehow also full of charm. I adored her every word. She gave me bloody wounds though.

In the evening I brought her a white loaf as well as a dark one, and also poppyseed rolls I baked myself. I thieved because of her and swiped everything I could lay hands on, macaroons, raisins, almonds, cakes. I hope I may be forgiven for stealing from the Saturday pots the women left to warm in the baker's oven. I would take out scraps of meat, a chunk of pudding, a chicken leg or head, a piece of tripe, whatever I could nip quickly. She ate and became fat and handsome.

I had to sleep away from home all during the week, at the bakery. On Friday nights when I got home she always made an excuse of some sort. Either she had heartburn, or a stitch in the side, or hiccups, or headaches. You know what women's excuses are. I had a bitter time of it. It was rough. To add to it, this little brother of hers, the bastard, was growing bigger. He'd put lumps on me, and when I wanted to hit back she'd open her mouth and curse so powerfully I saw a green haze floating before my eyes. Ten times a day she threatened to divorce me. Another man in my place would have taken French leave and disappeared. But I'm the type that bears it and says nothing. What's one to do? Shoulders are from God, and burdens too.

One night there was a calamity in the bakery; the oven burst, and we almost had a fire. There was nothing to do but go home, so I went home. Let me, I thought, also taste the joy of sleeping in bed in midweek. I didn't want to wake the sleeping mite and tiptoed into the house. Coming in, it seemed to me that I heard not the snoring of one but, as it were, a double snore, one a thin enough snore and the other like the snoring of a slaughtered ox. Oh, I didn't like that! I didn't like it at all. I went up to the bed, and things suddenly turned black. Next to Elka lay a man's form. Another in my place would have made an uproar, and enough noise to rouse the whole town, but the thought occurred to me that I might wake the child. A little thing like that—why frighten a little swallow like that, I thought. All right then, I went back to the bakery and stretched out on a sack of flour, and till morning I never shut an eye. I shivered as if I had had malaria. "Enough of being a donkey," I said to myself. "Gimpel isn't going to be a sucker all his life. There's a limit even to the foolishness of a fool like Gimpel."

In the morning I went to the rabbi to get advice, and it made a great commotion in the town. They sent the beadle for Elka right away. She came, carrying the child. And what do you think she did? She denied it, denied everything, bone and stone! "He's out of his head," she said. "I know nothing of dreams or divinations." They yelled at her, warned her, hammered on the table, but she stuck to her guns: it was a false accusation, she said.

The butchers and the horse-traders took her part. One of the lads from the slaughterhouse came by and said to me, "We've got our eye on you, you're a marked man." Meanwhile the child started to bear down and soiled itself. In the rabbinical court there was an Ark of the Covenant, and they couldn't allow that, so they sent Elka away.

I said to the rabbi, "What shall I do?"

"You must divorce her at once," said he.

"And what if she refuses?" I asked.

He said, "You must serve the divorce, that's all you'll have to do."

I said, "Well, all right, Rabbi. Let me think about it."

"There's nothing to think about," said he. "You mustn't remain under the same roof with her."

"And if I want to see the child?" I asked.

"Let her go, the harlot," said he, "and her brood of bastards with her."

The verdict he gave was that I mustn't even cross her threshold—never again, as long as I should live.

During the day it didn't bother me so much. I thought, It was bound to happen, the abscess had to burst. But at night when I stretched out upon the sacks I felt it all very bitterly. A longing took me, for her and for the child. I wanted to be angry, but that's my misfortune exactly, I don't have it in me to be really angry. In the first place—this was how my thoughts went—there's bound to be a slip sometimes. You can't live without errors. Probably that lad who was with her led her on and gave her presents and what not, and women are often long on hair and short on sense, and so he got around her. And then since she denies it so, maybe I was only seeing things? Hallucinations do happen. You see a figure or a mannikin or something, but when you come up closer it's nothing, there's not a thing there. And if that's so, I'm doing her an injustice. And when I got so far in my thoughts I started to weep. I sobbed so that I wet the flour where I lay. In the morning I went to the rabbi and told him that I had made a mistake. The rabbi wrote on with his quill, and he said that if that were so he would have to reconsider the whole case. Until he had finished I wasn't to go near my wife, but I might send her bread and money by messenger.

III

Nine months passed before all the rabbis could come to an agreement. Letters went back and forth. I hadn't realized that there could be so much erudition about a matter like this.

Meantime Elka gave birth to still another child, a girl this time. On the Sabbath I went to the synagogue and invoked a blessing on her. They called me up to the Torah, and I named the child for my mother-in-law, may she rest in peace. The louts and loudmouths of the town who came into the bakery gave me a going over. All Frampol refreshed its spirits because of my trouble and grief. However, I resolved that I would always believe what I was told. What's the good of *not* believing? Today it's your wife you don't believe; tomorrow it's God Himself you won't take stock in.

By an apprentice who was her neighbor I sent her daily a corn or a wheat loaf, or a piece of pastry, rolls or bagels, or, when I got the chance, a slab of pudding, a slice of honeycake, or wedding strudel—whatever came my way. The apprentice was a goodhearted lad, and more than once he added something on his own. He had formerly annoyed me a lot, plucking my nose and digging me in the ribs, but when he started to be a visitor to my house he became kind and friendly. "Hey, you, Gimpel," he said to me, "you have a very decent little wife and two fine kids. You don't deserve them."

"But the things people say about her," I said.

"Well, they have long tongues," he said, "and nothing to do with them but babble. Ignore it as you ignore the cold of last winter."

One day the rabbi sent for me and said, "Are you certain, Gimpel, that you were wrong about your wife?"

I said, "I'm certain."

"Why, but look here! You yourself saw it."

"It must have been a shadow," I said.

"The shadow of what?"

"Just of one of the beams, I think."

"You can go home then. You owe thanks to the Yanover rabbi. He found an obscure reference in Maimonides that favored you."

I seized the rabbi's hand and kissed it.

I wanted to run home immediately. It's no small thing to be separated for so long a time from wife and child. Then I reflected, I'd better go back to work now, and go home in the evening. I said nothing to anyone, although as far as my heart was concerned it was like one of the Holy Days. The women teased and twitted me as they did every day, but my thought was, Go on, with your loose talk. The truth is out, like the oil upon the water. Maimonides says it's right, and therefore it is right!

At night, when I had covered the dough to let it rise, I took my share of bread and a little sack of flour and started homeward. The moon was full and the stars were glistening, something to terrify the soul. I hurried onward, and before me darted a long shadow. It was winter, and a fresh snow had fallen. I had a mind to sing, but it was growing late and I didn't want to wake the householders. Then I felt like whistling, but remembered that you don't whistle at night because it brings the demons out. So I was silent and walked as fast as I could.

Dogs in the Christian yards barked at me when I passed, but I thought, Bark your teeth out! What are you but mere dogs? Whereas I am a man, the husband of a fine wife, the father of promising children.

As I approached the house my heart started to pound as though it were the heart of a criminal. I felt no fear, but my heart went thump! thump! Well, no drawing back. I quietly lifted the latch and went in. Elka was asleep. I looked at the infant's cradle. The shutter was closed, but the moon forced its way through the cracks. I saw the newborn child's face and loved it as soon as I saw it—immediately—each tiny bone.

Then I came nearer to the bed. And what did I see but the apprentice lying there beside Elka. The moon went out all at once, It was utterly black, and I trembled. My teeth chattered. The bread fell from my hands and my wife waked and said, "Who is that, ah?"

I muttered, "It's me."

"Gimpel?" she asked. "How come you're here? I thought it was forbidden."

"The rabbi said," I answered and shook as with a fever.

"Listen to me, Gimpel," she said, "go out to the shed and see if the goat's all right. It seems she's been sick." I have forgotten to say that we had a goat. When I heard she was unwell I went into the yard. The nannygoat was a good little creature. I had a nearly human feeling for her.

With hesitant steps I went up to the shed and opened the door. The goat stood there on her four feet. I felt her everywhere, drew her by the horns, examined her udders, and found nothing wrong. She had probably eaten too much bark. "Good night, little goat," I said. "Keep well." And the little beast answered with a "Maa" as though to thank me for the good will.

I went back. The apprentice had vanished.

"Where," I asked, "is the lad?"

"What lad?" my wife answered.

"What do you mean?" I said. "The apprentice. You were sleeping with him."

"The things I have dreamed this night and the night before," she said, "may they come true and lay you low, body and soul! An evil spirit has taken root in you and dazzles your sight." She screamed out, "You hateful creature! You moon calf! You spook! You uncouth mane! Get out, or I'll scream all Frampol out of bed!"

Before I could move, her brother sprang out from behind the oven and struck me a blow on the back of the head. I thought he had broken my neck. I felt that something about me was deeply wrong, and I said, "Don't make a scandal. All that's needed now is that people should accuse me of raising spooks and *dybbuks*." For that was what she had meant. "No one will touch bread of my baking."

In short, I somehow calmed her.

"Well," she said, "that's enough. Lie down, and be shattered by wheels."

Next morning I called the apprentice aside. "Listen here, brother!" I said. And so on and so forth. "What do you say?" He stared at me as though I had dropped from the roof or something.

"I swear," he said, "you'd better go to an herb doctor or some healer. I'm afraid you have a screw loose, but I'll hush it up for you." And that's how the thing stood.

To make a long story short, I lived twenty years with my wife. She bore me six children, four daughters and two sons. All kinds of things happened, but I neither saw nor heard. I believed, and that's all. The rabbi recently said to me, "Belief in itself is beneficial. It is written that a good man lives by his faith."

Suddenly my wife took sick. It began with a trifle, a little growth upon the breast. But she evidently was not destined to live long; she had no years. I spent a fortune on her. I have forgotten to say that by this time I had a bakery of my own and in Frampol was considered to be something of a rich man. Daily the healer came, and every witch doctor in the neighborhood was brought. They decided to use leeches, and after that to try cupping. They even called a doctor from Lublin, but it was too late. Before she died she called me to her bed and said, "Forgive me, Gimpel."

I said, "What is there to forgive? You have been a good and faithful wife."

"Woe, Gimpel!" she said. "It was ugly how I deceived you all these years. I want to go clean to my Maker, and so I have to tell you that the children are not yours."

If I had been clouted on the head with a piece of wood it couldn't have bewildered me more.

"Whose are they?" I asked.

"I don't know," she said, "there were a lot. . . . But they're not yours." And as she spoke she tossed her head to the side, her eyes turned glassy, and it was all up with Elka. On her whitened lips there remained a smile.

I imagined that, dead as she was, she was saying, "I deceived Gimpel. That was the meaning of my brief life."

IV

One night, when the period of mourning was done, as I lay dreaming on the flour sacks, there came the Spirit of Evil himself and said to me, "Gimpel, why do you sleep?"

I said, "What should I be doing? Eating *kreplach*?"

"The whole world deceives you," he said, "and you ought to deceive the world in your turn."

"How can I deceive all the world?" I asked him.

He answered, "You might accumulate a bucket of urine every day and at night pour it into the dough. Let the sages of Frampol eat filth."

"What about judgment in the world to come?" I said.

"There is no world to come," he said. "They've sold you a bill of goods and talked you into believing you carried a cat in your belly. What nonsense!"

"Well then," I said, "and is there a God?"

He answered, "There is no God either."

"What," I said, "*is* there, then?"

"A thick mire."

He stood before my eyes with a goatish beard and horns, long-toothed, and with a tail. Hearing such words, I wanted to snatch him by the tail, but I tumbled from the flour sacks and nearly broke a rib. Then it happened that I had to answer the call of nature, and, passing, I saw the risen dough, which seemed to say to me, "Do it!" In brief, I let myself be persuaded.

At dawn the apprentice came. We kneaded the bread, scattered caraway seeds on it, and set it to bake. Then the apprentice went away, and I was left sitting in the little trench by the oven, on a pile of rags. Well, Gimpel, I thought, you've revenged yourself on them for all the shame they've put on you. Outside the frost glittered, but it was warm beside the oven. The flames heated my face. I bent my head and fell into a doze.

I saw in a dream, at once, Elka in her shroud. She called to me, "What have you done, Gimpel?"

I said to her, "It's all your fault," and started to cry.

"You fool!" she said. "You fool! Because I was false is everything false too? I never deceived anyone but myself. I'm paying for it all, Gimpel. They spare you nothing here."

I looked at her face. It was black. I was startled and waked, and remained sitting dumb. I sensed that everything hung in the balance. A false step now and I'd lose Eternal Life. But God gave me His help. I seized the long shovel and took out the loaves, carried them into the yard, and started to dig a hole in the frozen earth.

My apprentice came back as I was doing it. "What are you doing, boss?" he said, and grew pale as a corpse.

"I know what I'm doing," I said, and I buried it all before his very eyes.

Then I went home, took my hoard from its hiding place, and divided it among the children. "I saw your mother tonight," I said. "She's turning black, poor thing."

They were so astounded they couldn't speak a word.

"Be well," I said, "and forget that such a one as Gimpel ever existed." I put on my short coat, a pair of boots, took the bag that held my prayer shawl in one hand, my stick in the other, and kissed the *mezzuzah*. When people saw me in the street they were greatly surprised.

"Where are you going?" they said.

I answered, "Into the world." And so I departed from Frampol.

I wandered over the land, and good people did not neglect me. After many years I became old and white; I heard a great deal, many lies and falsehoods, but the longer I lived the more I understood that there were really no lies. Whatever doesn't really happen is dreamed at night. It happens to one if it doesn't happen to another, tomorrow if not today, or a century hence if not next year. What difference can it make? Often I heard tales of which I said, "Now this is a thing that cannot happen." But before a year had elapsed I heard that it actually had come to pass somewhere.

Going from place to place, eating at strange tables, it often happens that I spin yarns—improbable things that could never have happened—about devils, magicians, windmills, and the like. The children run after me, calling, "Grandfather, tell us a story." Sometimes they ask for particular stories, and I try to please them. A fat young boy once said to me, "Grandfather, it's the same story you told us before." The little rogue, he was right.

So it is with dreams too. It is many years since I left Frampol, but as soon as I shut my eyes I am there again. And whom do you think I see? Elka. She is standing by the washtub, as at our first encounter, but her face is shining and her eyes are as radiant as the eyes of a saint, and she speaks outlandish words to me, strange things. When I wake I have forgotten it all. But while the dream lasts I am comforted. She answers all my queries, and what comes out is that all is right. I weep and implore, "Let me be with you." And she consoles me and tells me to be patient. The time is nearer than it is far. Sometimes she strokes and kisses me and weeps upon my face. When I awaken I feel her lips and taste the salt of her tears.

No doubt the world is entirely an imaginary world, but it is only once removed from the true world. At the door of the hovel where I lie, there stands the plank on which the dead are taken away. The gravedigger Jew has his spade ready. The grave waits and the worms are hungry; the shrouds are prepared—I carry them in my beggar's sack. Another *shnorrer* is waiting to inherit my bed of straw. When the time comes I will go joyfully. Whatever may be there, it will be real, without complication, without ridicule, without deception. God be praised: there even Gimpel cannot be deceived.

Translated from the Yiddish
by Saul Bellow

Albert Camus

The Guest

The schoolmaster was watching the two men climb toward him. One was on horseback, the other on foot. They had not yet tackled the abrupt rise leading to the schoolhouse built on the hillside. They were toiling onward, making slow progress in the snow, among the stones, on the vast expanse of the high, deserted plateau. From time to time the horse stumbled. Without hearing anything yet, he could see the breath issuing from the horse's nostrils. One of the men, at least, knew the region. They were following the trail although it had disappeared days ago under a layer of dirty white snow. The schoolmaster calculated that it would take them half an hour to get onto the hill. It was cold; he went back into the school to get a sweater.

He crossed the empty, frigid classroom. On the blackboard the four rivers of France, drawn with four different colored chalks, had been flowing toward their estuaries for the past three days. Snow had suddenly fallen in mid-October after eight months of drought without the transition of rain, and the twenty pupils, more or less, who lived in the villages scattered over the plateau had stopped coming. With fair weather they would return. Daru now heated only the single room that was his lodging, adjoining the classroom and giving also onto the plateau to the east. Like the class windows, his window looked to the south too. On that side the school was a few kilometers from the point where the plateau began to slope toward the south. In clear weather could be seen the purple mass of the mountain range where the gap opened onto the desert.

THE GUEST From *Exile and the Kingdom,* by Albert Camus, translated by Justin O'Brien. Copyright © 1957, 1958 by Alfred A. Knopf, Inc. Reprinted by permission of Alfred A. Knopf, Inc.

343

Somewhat warmed, Daru returned to the window from which he had first seen the two men. They were no longer visible. Hence they must have tackled the rise. The sky was not so dark, for the snow had stopped falling during the night. The morning had opened with a dirty light which had scarcely become brighter as the ceiling of clouds lifted. At two in the afternoon it seemed as if the day were merely beginning. But still this was better than those three days when the thick snow was falling amidst unbroken darkness with little gusts of wind that rattled the double door of the classroom. Then Daru had spent long hours in his room, leaving it only to go to the shed and feed the chickens or get some coal. Fortunately the delivery truck from Tadjid, the nearest village to the north, had brought his supplies two days before the blizzard. It would return in forty-eight hours.

Besides, he had enough to resist a siege, for the little room was cluttered with bags of wheat that the administration left as a stock to distribute to those of his pupils whose families had suffered from the drought. Actually they had all been victims because they were all poor. Every day Daru would distribute a ration to the children. They had missed it, he knew, during these bad days. Possibly one of the fathers or big brothers would come this afternoon and he could supply them with grain. It was just a matter of carrying them over to the next harvest. Now shiploads of wheat were arriving from France and the worst was over. But it would be hard to forget that poverty, that army of ragged ghosts wandering in the sunlight, the plateaus burned to a cinder month after month, the earth shriveled up little by little, literally scorched, every stone bursting into dust under one's foot. The sheep had died then by thousands and even a few men, here and there, sometimes without anyone's knowing.

In contrast with such poverty, he who lived almost like a monk in his remote schoolhouse, nonetheless satisfied with the little he had and with the rough life, had felt like a lord with his whitewashed walls, his narrow couch, his unpainted shelves, his well, and his weekly provision of water and food. And suddenly this snow, without warning, without the foretaste of rain. This is the way the region was, cruel to live in, even without men—who didn't help matters either. But Daru had been born here. Everywhere else, he felt exiled.

He stepped out onto the terrace in front of the schoolhouse. The two men were now halfway up the slope. He recognized the horseman as Balducci, the old gendarme he had known for a long time. Balducci was holding on the end of a rope an Arab who was walking behind him with hands bound and head lowered. The gendarme waved a greeting to which Daru did not reply, lost as he was in contemplation of the Arab dressed in a faded blue jellaba, his feet in sandals but covered with socks of heavy raw wool, his head surmounted by a narrow, short *chèche*. They were approaching. Balducci was holding back his horse in order not to hurt the Arab, and the group was advancing slowly.

Within earshot, Balducci shouted: "One hour to do the three kilometers from El Ameur!" Daru did not answer. Short and square in his thick sweater, he watched them climb. Not once had the Arab raised his head. "Hello," said Daru when they got up onto the terrace. "Come in and warm up." Balducci painfully got down from his horse without letting go the rope. From under his bristling mustache he smiled at the schoolmaster. His little dark eyes, deep-set under a tanned forehead, and his mouth surrounded with wrinkles made him look attentive and studious. Daru took the bridle, led the horse to the shed, and came back to the two men, who were now waiting for him in the school. He led them into his room. "I am going to heat up the classroom," he said. "We'll be more comfortable there." When he entered the room again, Balducci was on the couch. He had undone the rope tying him to the Arab, who had squatted near the stove. His hands still bound, the *chèche* pushed back on his head, he was looking toward the window. At first Daru noticed only his huge lips, fat, smooth, almost Negroid; yet his nose was straight, his eyes were dark and full of fever. The *chèche* revealed an obstinate forehead and, under the weathered skin now rather discolored by the cold, the whole face had a restless and rebellious look that struck Daru when the Arab, turning his face toward him, looked him straight in the eyes. "Go into the other room," said the schoolmaster, "and I'll make you some mint tea." "Thanks," Balducci said. "What a chore! How I long for retirement." And addressing his prisoner in Arabic: "Come on, you." The Arab got up and, slowly, holding his bound wrists in front of him, went into the classroom.

With the tea, Daru brought a chair. But Balducci was already enthroned on the nearest pupil's desk and the Arab had squatted against the teacher's platform facing the stove, which stood between the desk and the window. When he held out the glass of tea to the prisoner, Daru hesitated at the sight of his bound hands. "He might perhaps be untied." "Sure," said Balducci. "That was for the trip." He started to get to his feet. But Daru, setting the glass on the floor, had knelt beside the Arab. Without saying anything, the Arab watched him with his feverish eyes. Once his hands were free, he rubbed his swollen wrists against each other, took the glass of tea, and sucked up the burning liquid in swift little sips.

"Good," said Daru. "And where are you headed?"

Balducci withdrew his mustache from the tea. "Here, son."

"Odd pupils! And you're spending the night?"

"No. I'm going back to El Ameur. And you will deliver this fellow to Tinguit. He is expected at police headquarters."

Balducci was looking at Daru with a friendly little smile.

"What's the story?" asked the schoolmaster. "Are you pulling my leg?"

"No, son. Those are the orders."

"The orders? "I'm not . . ." Daru hesitated, not wanting to hurt the old Corsican. "I mean, that's not my job."

"What! What's the meaning of that? In wartime people do all kinds of jobs."

"Then I'll wait for the declaration of war!"

Balducci nodded.

"O.K. But the orders exist and they concern you too. Things are brewing, it appears. There is talk of a forthcoming revolt. We are mobilized, in a way."

Daru still had his obstinate look.

"Listen, son," Balducci said. "I like you and you must understand. There's only a dozen of us at El Ameur to patrol throughout the whole territory of a small department and I must get back in a hurry. I was told to hand this guy over to you and return without delay. He couldn't be kept there. His village was beginning to stir; they wanted to take him back. You must take him to Tinguit tomorrow before the day is over. Twenty kilometers shouldn't faze a husky fellow like you. After that, all will be over. You'll come back to your pupils and your comfortable life."

Behind the wall the horse could be heard snorting and pawing the earth. Daru was looking out the window. Decidedly, the weather was clearing and the light was increasing over the snowy plateau. When all the snow was melted, the sun would take over again and once more would burn the fields of stone. For days, still, the unchanging sky would shed its dry light on the solitary expanse where nothing had any connection with man.

"After all," he said, turning around toward Balducci, "what did he do?" And, before the gendarme had opened his mouth, he asked: "Does he speak French?"

"No, not a word. We had been looking for him for a month, but they were hiding him. He killed his cousin."

"Is he against us?"

"I don't think so. But you can never be sure."

"Why did he kill?"

"A family squabble, I think. One owed the other grain, it seems. It's not at all clear. In short, he killed his cousin with a billhook. You know, like a sheep, *kreezk!*"

Balducci made the gesture of drawing a blade across his throat and the Arab, his attention attracted, watched him with a sort of anxiety. Daru felt a sudden wrath against the man, against all men with their rotten spite, their tireless hates, their blood lust.

But the kettle was singing on the stove. He served Balducci more tea, hesitated, then served the Arab again, who, a second time, drank avidly. His raised arms made the jellaba fall open and the schoolmaster saw his thin, muscular chest.

"Thanks, kid," Balducci said. "And now, I'm off."

He got up and went toward the Arab, taking a small rope from his pocket.

"What are you doing?" Daru asked dryly.

Balducci, disconcerted, showed him the rope.

"Don't bother."

The old gendarme hesitated. "It's up to you. Of course, you are armed?"

"I have my shotgun."

"Where?"

"In the trunk."

"You ought to have it near your bed."

"Why? I have nothing to fear."

"You're crazy, son. If there's an uprising, no one is safe, we're all in the same boat."

"I'll defend myself. I'll have time to see them coming."

Balducci began to laugh, then suddenly the mustache covered the white teeth.

"You'll have time? O.K. That's just what I was saying. You have always been a little cracked. That's why I like you, my son was like that."

At the same time he took out his revolver and put it on the desk.

"Keep it; I don't need two weapons from here to El Ameur."

The revolver shone against the black paint of the table. When the gendarme turned toward him, the schoolmaster caught the smell of leather and horseflesh.

"Listen, Balducci," Daru said suddenly, "every bit of this disgusts me, and first of all your fellow here. But I won't hand him over. Fight, yes, if I have to. But not that."

The old gendarme stood in front of him and looked at him severely.

"You're being a fool," he said slowly. "I don't like it either. You don't get used to putting a rope on a man even after years of it, and you're even ashamed—yes, ashamed. But you can't let them have their way."

"I won't hand him over," Daru said again.

"It's an order, son, and I repeat it."

"That's right. Repeat to them what I've said to you: I won't hand him over."

Balducci made a visible effort to reflect. He looked at the Arab and at Daru. At last he decided.

"No, I won't tell them anything. If you want to drop us, go ahead; I'll not denounce you. I have an order to deliver the prisoner and I'm doing so. And now you'll just sign this paper for me."

"There's no need. I'll not deny that you left him with me."

"Don't be mean with me. I know you'll tell the truth. You're from here-abouts and you are a man. But you must sign, that's the rule."

Daru opened his drawer, took out a little square bottle of purple ink, the red wooden penholder with the "sergeant-major" pen he used for making models of penmanship, and signed. The gendarme carefully folded the paper and put it into his wallet. Then he moved toward the door.

"I'll see you off," Daru said.

"No," said Balducci. "There's no use being polite. You insulted me."

He looked at the Arab, motionless in the same spot, sniffed peevishly, and turned away toward the door. "Good-by, son," he said. The door shut behind him. Balducci appeared suddenly outside the window and then disappeared. His footsteps were muffled by the snow. The horse stirred on the other side of the wall and several chickens fluttered in fright. A moment later Balducci reappeared outside the window leading the horse by the bridle. He walked toward the little rise without turning around and disappeared from sight with the horse following him. A big stone could be heard bouncing down. Daru walked back toward the prisoner, who, without stirring, never took his eyes off him. "Wait," the schoolmaster said in Arabic and went toward the bedroom. As he was going through the door, he had a second thought, went to the desk, took the revolver, and stuck it in his pocket. Then, without looking back, he went into his room.

For some time he lay on his couch watching the sky gradually close over, listening to the silence. It was this silence that had seemed painful to him during the first days here, after the war. He had requested a post in the little town at the base of the foothills separating the upper plateaus from the desert. There, rocky walls, green and black to the north, pink and lavender to the south, marked the frontier of eternal summer. He had been named to a post farther north, on the plateau itself. In the beginning, the solitude and the silence had been hard for him on these wastelands peopled only by stones. Occasionally, furrows suggested cultivation, but they had been dug to uncover a certain kind of stone good for building. The only plowing here was to harvest rocks. Elsewhere a thin layer of soil accumulated in the hollows would be scraped out to enrich paltry village gardens. This is the way it was: bare rock covered three quarters of the region. Towns sprang up, flourished, then disappeared; men came by, loved one another or fought bitterly, then died. No one in this desert, neither he nor his guest, mattered. And yet, outside this desert neither of them, Daru knew, could have really lived.

When he got up, no noise came from the classroom. He was amazed at the unmixed joy he derived from the mere thought that the Arab might have fled and that he would be alone with no decision to make. But the prisoner was there. He had merely stretched out between the stove and the desk. With eyes open, he was staring at the ceiling. In that position, his thick lips were particularly noticeable, giving him a pouting look. "Come," said Daru. The Arab got up and followed him. In the bedroom, the schoolmaster pointed to a chair near the table under the window. The Arab sat down without taking his eyes off Daru.

"Are you hungry?"

"Yes," the prisoner said.

Daru set the table for two. He took flour and oil, shaped a cake in a frying-pan, and lighted the little stove that functioned on bottled gas. While the cake was cooking, he went out to the shed to get cheese, eggs, dates, and condensed milk. When the cake was done he set it on the window sill to cool, heated some condensed milk diluted with water, and beat up the eggs into an omelette. In one of his motions he knocked against the revolver stuck in his right pocket. He set the bowl down, went into the classroom, and put the revolver in his desk drawer. When he came back to the room, night was falling. He put on the light and served the Arab. "Eat," he said. The Arab took a piece of the cake, lifted it eagerly to his mouth, and stopped short.

"And you?" he asked.

"After you. I'll eat too."

The thick lips opened slightly. The Arab hesitated, then bit into the cake determinedly.

The meal over, the Arab looked at the schoolmaster. "Are you the judge?"

"No, I'm simply keeping you until tomorrow."

"Why do you eat with me?"

"I'm hungry."

The Arab fell silent. Daru got up and went out. He brought back a folding bed from the shed, set it up between the table and the stove, perpendicular to his own bed. From a large suitcase which, upright in a corner, served as a shelf for papers, he took two blankets and arranged them on the camp bed. Then he stopped, felt useless, and sat down on his bed. There was nothing more to do or to get ready. He had to look at this man. He looked at him, therefore, trying to imagine his face bursting with rage. He couldn't do so. He could see nothing but the dark yet shining eyes and the animal mouth.

"Why did you kill him?" he asked in a voice whose hostile tone surprised him.

The Arab looked away.

"He ran away. I ran after him."

He raised his eyes to Daru again and they were full of a sort of woeful interrogation. "Now what will they do to me?"

"Are you afraid?"

He stiffened, turning his eyes away.

"Are you sorry?"

The Arab stared at him openmouthed. Obviously he did not understand. Daru's annoyance was growing. At the same time he felt awkward and self-conscious with his big body wedged between the two beds.

"Lie down there," he said impatiently. "That's your bed."

The Arab didn't move. He called to Daru:

"Tell me!"

The schoolmaster looked at him.

"Is the gendarme coming back tomorrow?"

"I don't know."

"Are you coming with us?"

"I don't know. Why?"

The prisoner got up and stretched out on top of the blankets, his feet toward the window. The light from the electric bulb shone straight into his eyes and he closed them at once.

"Why?" Daru repeated, standing beside the bed.

The Arab opened his eyes under the blinding light and looked at him, trying not to blink.

"Come with us," he said.

In the middle of the night, Daru was still not asleep. He had gone to bed after undressing completely; he generally slept naked. But when he suddenly realized that he had nothing on, he hesitated. He felt vulnerable and the temptation came to him to put his clothes back on. Then he shrugged his shoulders; after all, he wasn't a child and, if need be, he could break his adversary in two. From his bed he could observe him, lying on his back, still motionless with his eyes closed under the harsh light. When Daru turned out the light, the darkness seemed to coagulate all of a sudden. Little by little, the night came back to life in the window where the starless sky was stirring gently. The schoolmaster soon made out the body lying at his feet. The Arab still did not move, but his eyes seemed open. A faint wind was prowling around the schoolhouse. Perhaps it would drive away the clouds and the sun would reappear.

During the night the wind increased. The hens fluttered a little and then were silent. The Arab turned over on his side with his back to Daru, who thought he heard him moan. Then he listened for his guest's breathing, become heavier and more regular. He listened to that breath so close to him and mused without being able to go to sleep. In this room where he had been sleeping alone for a year, this presence bothered him. But it bothered him also by imposing on him a sort of brotherhood he knew well but refused to accept in the present circumstances. Men who share the same rooms, soldiers or prisoners, develop a strange alliance as if, having cast off their armor with their clothing, they fraternized every evening, over and above their differences, in the ancient community of dream and fatigue. But Daru shook himself; he didn't like such musings, and it was essential to sleep.

A little later, however, when the Arab stirred slightly, the schoolmaster was still not asleep. When the prisoner made a second move, he stiffened, on the alert. The Arab was lifting himself slowly on his arms with almost the motion of a sleepwalker. Seated upright in bed, he waited motionless without turning his head toward Daru, as if he were listening attentively. Daru did not stir; it had just occurred to him that the revolver was still in the drawer of his desk. It was better to act at once. Yet he continued to observe the prisoner, who, with the same slithery motion, put his feet on the ground, waited again, then began to stand up slowly. Daru was about to call out to him when the Arab began to walk, in a quite natural but extraordinarily silent way. He was heading toward the door at the end of the room that opened into the shed. He lifted the latch with precaution and went out, pushing the door behind him but without shutting it. Daru had not stirred. "He is running away," he merely thought. "Good riddance!" Yet he listened attentively. The hens were not fluttering; the guest must be on the plateau. A faint sound of water reached him, and he didn't know what it was until the Arab again stood framed in the doorway, closed the door carefully, and came back to bed without a sound. Then Daru turned his back on him and fell asleep. Still later he seemed, from the depths of his sleep, to hear furtive steps around the schoolhouse. "I'm dreaming! I'm dreaming!" he repeated to himself. And he went on sleeping.

When he awoke, the sky was clear; the loose window let in a cold, pure air. The Arab was asleep, hunched up under the blankets now, his mouth open, utterly relaxed. But when Daru shook him, he started dreadfully, staring at Daru with wild eyes as if he had never seen him and such a frightened expression that the schoolmaster stepped back. "Don't be afraid.

It's me. You must eat." The Arab nodded his head and said yes. Calm had returned to his face, but his expression was vacant and listless.

The coffee was ready. They drank it seated together on the folding bed as they munched their pieces of the cake. Then Daru led the Arab under the shed and showed him the faucet where he washed. He went back into the room, folded the blankets and the bed, made his own bed and put the room in order. Then he went through the classroom and out onto the terrace. The sun was already rising in the blue sky; a soft, bright light was bathing the deserted plateau. On the ridge the snow was melting in spots. The stones were about to reappear. Crouched on the edge of the plateau, the schoolmaster looked at the deserted expanse. He thought of Balducci. He had hurt him, for he had sent him off in a way as if he didn't want to be associated with him. He could still hear the gendarme's farewell and, without knowing why, he felt strangely empty and vulnerable. At that moment, from the other side of the school-house, the prisoner coughed. Daru listened to him almost despite himself and then, furious, threw a pebble that whistled through the air before sinking into the snow. That man's stupid crime revolted him, but to hand him over was contrary to honor. Merely thinking of it made him smart with humili-ation. And he cursed at one and the same time his own people who had sent him this Arab and the Arab too who had dared to kill and not managed to get away. Daru got up, walked in a circle on the terrace, waited motionless, and then went back into the schoolhouse.

The Arab, leaning over the cement floor of the shed, was washing his teeth with two fingers. Daru looked at him and said: "Come." He went back into the room ahead of the prisoner. He slipped a hunting-jacket on over his sweater and put on walking-shoes. Standing, he waited until the Arab had put on his *chèche* and sandals. They went into the classroom and the schoolmaster pointed to the exit, saying: "Go ahead." The fellow didn't budge. "I'm com-ing," said Daru. The Arab went out. Daru went back into the room and made a package of pieces of rusk, dates, and sugar. In the classroom, before going out, he hesitated a second in front of his desk, then crossed the threshold and locked the door. "That's the way," he said. He started toward the east, fol-lowed by the prisoner. But, a short distance from the schoolhouse, he thought he heard a slight sound behind them. He retraced his steps and examined the surroundings of the house; there was no one there. The Arab watched him without seeming to understand. "Come on," said Daru.

They walked for an hour and rested beside a sharp peak of limestone. The snow was melting faster and faster and the sun was drinking up the puddles at once, rapidly cleaning the plateau, which gradually dried and vibrated like the air itself. When they resumed walking, the ground rang under their feet. From time to time a bird rent the space in front of them with a joyful cry. Daru breathed in deeply the fresh morning light. He felt a sort of rapture before the vast familiar expanse, now almost entirely yellow under its dome of blue sky. They walked an hour more, descending toward the south. They reached a level height made up of crumbly rocks. From there on, the plateau sloped down, eastward, toward a low plain where there were a few spindly trees and, to the south, toward outcroppings of rock that gave the landscape a chaotic look.

Daru surveyed the two directions. There was nothing but the sky on the horizon. Not a man could be seen. He turned toward the Arab, who was looking at him blankly. Daru held out the package to him. "Take it," he said. "There are dates, bread, and sugar. You can hold out for two days. Here are a thousand francs too." The Arab took the package and the money but kept his full hands at chest level as if he didn't know what to do with what was being given him. "Now look," the schoolmaster said as he pointed in the direction of the east, "there's the way to Tinguit. You have a two-hour walk. At Tinguit you'll find the administration and the police. They are expecting you." The Arab looked toward the east, still holding the package and the money against his chest. Daru took his elbow and turned him rather roughly toward the south. At the foot of the height on which they stood could be seen a faint path. "That's the trail across the plateau. In a day's walk from here you'll find pasturelands and the first nomads. They'll take you in and shelter you according to their law." The Arab had now turned toward Daru and a sort of panic was visible in his expression. "Listen," he said. Daru shook his head: "No, be quiet. Now I'm leaving you." He turned his back on him, took two long steps in the direction of the school, looked hesitantly at the motionless Arab, and started off again. For a few minutes he heard nothing but his own step resounding on the cold ground and did not turn his head. A moment later, however, he turned around. The Arab was still there on the edge of the hill, his arms hanging now, and he was looking at the schoolmaster. Daru felt something rise in his throat. But he swore with impatience, waved vaguely, and started off again. He had already gone some distance when he again stopped and looked. There was no longer anyone on the hill.

Daru hesitated. The sun was now rather high in the sky and was beginning to beat down on his head. The schoolmaster retraced his steps, at first somewhat uncertainly, then with decision. When he reached the little hill, he was bathed in sweat. He climbed it as fast as he could and stopped, out of breath, at the top. The rock-fields to the south stood out sharply against the blue sky, but on the plain to the east a steamy heat was already rising. And in that slight haze, Daru, with heavy heart, made out the Arab walking slowly on the road to prison.

A little later, standing before the window of the classroom, the schoolmaster was watching the clear light bathing the whole surface of the plateau, but he hardly saw it. Behind him on the blackboard, among the winding French rivers, sprawled the clumsily chalked-up words he had just read: "You handed over our brother. You will pay for this." Daru looked at the sky, the plateau, and, beyond, the invisible lands stretching all the way to the sea. In this vast landscape he had loved so much, he was alone.

Translated from the French
by Justin O'Brien

Gabriel García Márquez

The Last Voyage
of the Ghost Ship

Now they're going to see who I am, he said to himself in his strong new man's voice, many years after he had first seen the huge ocean liner without lights and without any sound which passed by the village one night like a great uninhabited palace, longer than the whole village and much taller than the steeple of the church, and it sailed by in the darkness toward the colonial city on the other side of the bay that had been fortified against buccaneers, with its old slave port and the rotating light, whose gloomy beams transfigured the village into a lunar encampment of glowing houses and streets of volcanic deserts every fifteen seconds, and even though at that time he'd been a boy without a man's strong voice but with his mother's permission to stay very late on the beach to listen to the wind's night harps, he could still remember, as if still seeing it, how the liner would disappear when the light of the beacon struck its side and how it would reappear when the light had passed, so that it was an intermittent ship sailing along, appearing and disappearing, toward the mouth of the bay, groping its way like a sleep-walker for the buoys that marked the harbor channel until something must have gone wrong with the compass needle, because it headed toward the shoals, ran aground, broke up, and sank without a single sound, even though a collision against the reefs like that should have produced a crash of metal and the explosion of engines that would have frozen with fright the soundest-sleeping dragons in the prehistoric jungle that began with the

THE LAST VOYAGE OF THE GHOST SHIP   From *Leaf Storm and Other Stories* by Gabriel García Márquez. Copyright © 1972 by Harper & Row, Publishers, Inc. By permission of the publishers.

last streets of the village and ended on the other side of the world, so that he himself thought it was a dream, especially the next day, when he saw the radiant fishbowl of the bay, the disorder of colors of the Negro shacks on the hills above the harbor, the schooners of the smugglers from the Guianas loading their cargoes of innocent parrots whose craws were full of diamonds, he thought, I fell asleep counting the stars and I dreamed about that huge ship, of course, he was so convinced that he didn't tell anyone nor did he remember the vision again until the same night on the following March when he was looking for the flash of dolphins in the sea and what he found was the illusory line, gloomy, intermittent, with the same mistaken direction as the first time, except that then he was so sure he was awake that he ran to tell his mother and she spent three weeks moaning with disappointment, because your brain's rotting away from doing so many things backward, sleeping during the day and going out at night like a criminal, and since she had to go to the city around that time to get something comfortable where she could sit and think about her dead husband, because the rockers on her chair had worn out after eleven years of widowhood, she took advantage of the occasion and had the boatman go near the shoals so that her son could see what he really saw in the glass of the sea, the lovemaking of manta rays in a springtime of sponges, pink snappers and blue corvinas diving into the other wells of softer waters that were there among the waters, and even the wandering hairs of victims of drowning in some colonial shipwreck, no trace of sunken liners or anything like it, and yet he was so pigheaded that his mother promised to watch with him the next March, absolutely, not knowing that the only thing absolute in her future now was an easy chair from the days of Sir Francis Drake which she had bought at an auction in a Turk's store, in which she sat down to rest that same night, sighing, oh, my poor Olofernos, if you could only see how nice it is to think about you on this velvet lining and this brocade from the casket of a queen, but the more she brought back the memory of her dead husband, the more the blood in her heart bubbled up and turned to chocolate, as if instead of sitting down she were running, soaked from chills and fevers and her breathing full of earth, until he returned at dawn and found her dead in the easy chair, still warm, but half rotted away as after a snakebite, the same as happened afterward to four other women before the murderous chair was thrown into the sea, far away where it wouldn't bring evil to anyone, because it had been used so much over the centuries that its faculty for giving rest had been used up, and so he had to grow accustomed to his miserable routine of an orphan who was pointed out by everyone as the son of the widow who had brought the throne of misfortune into the village, living not so much from public charity as from fish he stole out of the boats, while his voice was becoming a roar, and not remembering his visions of past times anymore until another night in March when he chanced to look seaward and suddenly, good Lord, there it is, the huge asbestos whale, the behemoth beast, come see it, he shouted madly, come see it, raising such an uproar of dogs' barking and women's panic that even the oldest men remembered the frights of their great-grandfathers and crawled under their beds, thinking that William Dampier had come back, but those who ran into the street didn't make the effort to see the unlikely apparatus which at that instant was lost again in the east and raised up in its annual disaster, but they covered him with blows and left him so twisted that it was then he said to himself, drooling with rage, now they're going to see who I am, but he took care not to share his determination with anyone, but spent the whole year with the fixed idea, now they're going to see who I am, waiting for it to be the eve of the apparition once more in order to do what he did, which was steal a boat, cross the bay, and spend the evening waiting for his great moment in the inlets of the slave port, in the human brine of the Caribbean, but so absorbed in his adventure that he didn't stop as he always did in front of the Hindu shops to look at the ivory mandarins carved from the whole tusk of an elephant, nor did he make fun of the Dutch Negroes in their orthopedic velocipedes, nor was he frightened as at other times of the copper-skinned Malayans, who had gone around the world enthralled by the chimera of a secret tavern where they sold roast filets of Brazilian women, because he wasn't aware of anything until night came over him with all the weight of the stars and the jungle exhaled a sweet fragrance of gardenias and rotten salamanders, and there he was, rowing in the stolen boat toward the mouth of the bay, with the lantern out so as not to alert the customs police, idealized every fifteen seconds by the green wing flap of the beacon and turned human once more by the darkness, knowing that he was getting close to the buoys that marked the harbor channel, not only because its oppressive glow was getting more intense, but because the breathing of the water was becoming sad, and he rowed like that, so wrapped up in himself, that he didn't know where the fearful shark's breath that suddenly reached him came from or why the night became dense, as if the stars had suddenly died, and it was because the liner was there, with all of its inconceivable size, Lord, bigger than any other big thing in the world and darker than any other dark thing on land or sea, three hundred thousand tons of shark smell passing so close to the boat that he could see the seams of the steel precipice, without a single light in the infinite portholes, without a sigh from the engines, without a soul, and carrying its own circle of silence with it, its own dead air, its halted time, its errant sea in which a whole world of drowned animals floated, and suddenly it all disappeared with the flash of the beacon and for an instant it was the diaphanous Caribbean once more, the March night, the everyday air of the pelicans, so he stayed alone among the buoys, not knowing what to do, asking himself, startled, if perhaps he wasn't dreaming while he was awake, not just now but the other times too, but no sooner had he asked himself than a breath of mystery snuffed out the buoys, from the first to the last, so that when the light of the beacon passed by the liner appeared again and now its compasses were out of order, perhaps not even knowing what part of the ocean sea it was in, groping for the invisible channel but actually heading for the shoals, until he got the overwhelming revelation that that misfortune of the buoys was the last key to the enchantment and he lighted the lantern in the boat, a tiny red light that had no reason to alarm anyone in the watchtowers but which would be like a guiding sun for the pilot, because, thanks to it, the liner corrected its course and passed into the main gate of the channel in a maneuver of lucky resurrection, and then all the lights went on at the same time so that the boilers wheezed again, the stars were fixed in their places, and the animal corpses went to the bottom, and there was a clatter of plates and a fragrance of laurel sauce in the kitchens, and one could hear the pulsing of the orchestra on the moon decks and the throbbing of the arteries of high-sea lovers in the shadows of the staterooms, but he still carried so much leftover rage in him that he would not let himself be confused by emotion or be frightened by the miracle, but said to himself with more decision than ever, now they're going to see who I am, the cowards, now they're going to see, and instead of turning aside so that the colossal machine would not charge into him, he began to row in front of it, because now they really are going to see who I am, and he continued guiding the ship with the lantern until he was so sure of its obedience that he made it change course from the direction of the docks once more, took it out of the invisible channel, and led it by the halter as if it were a sea lamb toward the lights of the sleeping village, a living ship, invulnerable to the torches of the beacon, that no longer made it invisible but made it aluminum every fifteen seconds, and the crosses of the church, the misery of the houses, the illusion began to stand out, and still the ocean liner followed behind him, following his will inside of it, the captain asleep on his heart side, the fighting bulls in the snow of their pantries, the solitary patient in the infirmary, the orphan water of its cisterns, the unredeemed pilot who must have mistaken the cliffs for the docks, because at that instant the great roar of the whistle burst forth, once, and he was soaked with the downpour of steam that fell on him, again, and the boat belonging to someone else was on the point of capsizing, and again, but it was too late, because there were the shells of the shoreline, the stones of the street, the doors of the disbelievers, the whole village illuminated by the lights of the fearsome liner itself, and he barely had time to get out of the way to make room for the cataclysm, shouting in the midst of the confusion, there it is, you cowards, a second before the huge steel cask shattered the ground and one could hear the neat destruction of ninety thousand five hundred champagne glasses breaking, one after the other, from stem to stern, and then the light came out and it was no longer a March dawn but the noon of a radiant Wednesday, and he was able to give himself the pleasure of watching the disbelievers as with open mouths they contemplated the largest ocean liner in this world and the other aground in the front of the church, whiter than anything, twenty time taller than the steeple and some ninety-seven times longer than the village with its name engraved in iron letters, *Halàlcsillag,* and the ancient and languid waters of the sea of death dripping down its sides.

Translated from the Spanish
by Gregory Rabassa

"I Always Wanted You to Admire My Fasting"; or, Looking at Kafka

"I always wanted you to admire my fasting," said the hunger artist. "We do admire it," said the overseer, affably. "But you shouldn't admire it," said the hunger artist. "Well then we don't admire it," said the overseer, "but why shouldn't we admire it?" "Because I have to fast, I can't help it," said the hunger artist. "What a fellow you are," said the overseer, "and why can't you help it?" "Because," said the hunger artist, lifting his head a little and speaking, with his lips pursed, as if for a kiss, right into the overseer's ear, so that no syllable might be lost, "because I couldn't find the food I liked. If I had found it, believe me, I should have made no fuss and stuffed myself like you or anyone else." These were his last words, but in his dimming eyes remained the firm though no longer proud persuasion that he was still continuing to fast.

—"A Hunger Artist," Franz Kafka

1

I am looking, as I write of Kafka, at the photograph taken of him at the age of forty (my age)—it is 1924, as sweet and hopeful a year as he may ever have known as a man, and the year of his death. His face is sharp and skeletal, a burrower's face: pronounced cheekbones made even more conspicuous by the absence of sideburns; the ears shaped and angled on his

head like angel wings, an intense, creaturely gaze of startled composure—
enormous fears, enormous control; a black towel of Levantine hair pulled
close around the skull the only sensuous feature; there is a familiar Jewish
flare in the bridge of the nose, the nose itself is long and weighted slightly
at the tip—the nose of half the Jewish boys who were my friends in high
school. Skulls chiseled like this one were shoveled by the thousands from
the ovens; had he lived, his would have been among them, along with the
skulls of his three younger sisters. Of course it is no more horrifying to
think of Franz Kafka in Auschwitz than to think of anyone in Auschwitz—
to paraphrase Tolstoy, it is just horrifying in its own way. But he died too
soon for the holocaust. Had he lived, perhaps he would have escaped with
his good friend and great advocate Max Brod, who eventually found refuge
in Palestine, a citizen of Israel until his death there in 1970. But *Kafka*
escaping? It seems unlikely for one so fascinated by entrapment and careers
that culminate in anguished death. Still, there is Karl Rossman, his American
greenhorn. Having imagined Karl's escape to America and his mixed luck
here, could not Kafka have found a way to execute an escape for himself?
The New School for Social Research in New York becoming *his* Great
Nature Theater of Oklahoma? Or perhaps through the influence of Thomas
Mann, a position in the German department at Princeton . . . But then had
Kafka lived it is not at all certain that the books of his which Mann celebrated from *his* refuge in New Jersey would ever have been published;
eventually Kafka might either have destroyed those manuscripts that he
had once bid Max Brod to dispose of at his death, or, at the least, continued
to keep them his secret. The Jewish refugee arriving in America in 1938
would not then have been Mann's "religious humorist," but a frail and
bookish fifty-five-year-old bachelor, formerly a lawyer for a government
insurance firm in Prague, retired on a pension in Berlin at the time of Hitler's
rise to power—an author, yes, but of a few eccentric stories, mostly about
animals, stories no one in America had ever heard of and only a handful
in Europe had read; a homeless K., but without K.'s willfulness and purpose,
a homeless Karl, but without Karl's youthful spirit and resilience; just a Jew
lucky enough to have escaped with his life, in his possession a suitcase containing some clothes, some family photos, some Prague mementos, and the
manuscripts, still unpublished and in pieces, of *Amerika, The Trial, The
Castle,* and (stranger things happen) three more fragmented novels, no less
remarkable than the bizarre masterworks that he keeps to himself out of
Oedipal timidity, perfectionist madness, and insatiable longings for solitude
and spiritual purity.

July, 1923: Eleven months before he will die in a Vienna sanatorium, Kafka
somehow finds the resolve to leave Prague and his father's home for good.
Never before has he even remotely succeeded in living apart, independent of
his mother, his sisters and his father, nor has he been a writer other than in
those few hours when he is not working in the legal department of the

Workers' Accident Insurance Office in Prague; since taking his law degree at the university, he has been by all reports the most dutiful and scrupulous of employees, though he finds the work tedious and enervating. But in June of 1923—having some months earlier been pensioned from his job because of his illness—he meets a young Jewish girl of nineteen at a seaside resort in Germany. Dora Dymant, an employee at the vacation camp of the Jewish People's Home of Berlin has left her Orthodox Polish family to make a life of her own (at half Kafka's age); she and Kafka—who has just turned forty—fall in love . . . Kafka has by now been engaged to two somewhat more conventional Jewish girls—twice to one of them—hectic, anguished engagements wrecked largely by his fears. "I am mentally incapable of marrying," he writes his father in the forty-five page letter he gave to his mother to deliver, ". . . the moment I make up my mind to marry I can no longer sleep, my head burns day and night, life can no longer be called life." He explains why. "Marrying is barred to me," he tells his father, "because it is your domain. Sometimes I imagine the map of the world spread out and you stretched diagonally across it. And I feel as if I could consider living in only those regions that either are not covered by you or are not within your reach. And in keeping with the conception I have of your magnitude, these are not many and not very comforting regions—and marriage is not among them." The letter explaining what is wrong between this father and this son is dated November, 1919; the mother thought it best not even to deliver it, perhaps for lack of courage, probably, like the son, for lack of hope.

During the following two years Kafka attempts to wage an affair with Milena Jesenská-Pollak, an intense young woman of twenty-four who has translated a few of his stories into Czech and is most unhappily married in Vienna; his affair with Milena, conducted feverishly, but by and large through the mails, is even more demoralizing to Kafka than the fearsome engagements to the nice Jewish girls. They aroused only the paterfamilias longings that he dared not indulge, longings inhibited by his exaggerated awe of his father—"spellbound," says Brod, "in the family circle—and the hypnotic spell of his own solitude; but the Czech Milena, impetuous, frenetic, indifferent to conventional restraints, a woman of appetite and anger, arouses more elemental yearnings and more elemental fears. According to a Prague critic, Rio Preisner, Milena was "psychopathic"; according to Margaret Buber-Neumann, who lived two years beside her in the German concentration camp where Milena died following a kidney operation in 1944, she was powerfully sane, extraordinarily human and courageous. Milena's obituary for Kafka was the only one of consequence to appear in the Prague press; the prose is strong, so are the claims she makes for Kafka's accomplishment. She is still only in her twenties, the dead man is hardly known as a writer beyond his small circle of friends—yet Milena writes, "His knowledge of the world was exceptional and deep, and he was a deep and exceptional world in himself . . . [He had] a delicacy of feeling bordering on the miraculous and a mental clarity that was terrifyingly uncompromising, and in turn he loaded on to his illness the whole burden of his mental fear of life . . . . He wrote the most important books in recent German literature." One can imagine this vibrant young woman stretched diagonally across the bed, as awesome to Kafka as his own father spread out across the map of the world. His letters to her are disjointed, unlike anything else of his in print; the word fear, frequently emphasized, appears on page after page. "We are both married, you in Vienna, I to my Fear in Prague." He yearns to lay his head upon her breast; he calls her "Mother Milena"; during at least one of their two brief rendezvous, he is hopelessly impotent. At last he has to tell her to leave him be, an edict that Milena honors though it leaves her hollow with grief. "Do not write," Kafka tells her, "and let us not see each other; I ask you only to quietly fulfill this request of mine; only on those conditions is survival possible for me; everything else continues the process of destruction."

Then in the early summer of 1923, during a visit to his sister who is vacationing with her children by the Baltic Sea, he finds young Dora Dymant, and within a month Franz Kafka has gone off to live with her in two rooms in a suburb of Berlin, out of reach at last of the "claws" of Prague and home. How can it be? How can he, in his illness, have accomplished so swiftly and decisively the leave-taking that was so beyond him in his healthiest days? The impassioned letter-writer who could equivocate interminably about which train to catch to Vienna to meet with Milena (if he should meet with her for the weekend at all); the bourgeois suitor in the high collar, who, during his drawn-out agony of an engagement with the proper Fräulein Bauer, secretly draws up a memorandum for himself, countering the arguments "for" marriage with the arguments "against"; the poet of the ungraspable and the unresolved, whose belief in the immovable barrier separating the wish from its realization is at the heart of his excruciating visions of defeat, the Kafka whose fictions refute every easy, touching, humanish daydream of salvation and justice and fulfillment with densely imagined counter-dreams that mock all solutions and escapes—this Kafka, escapes! Overnight! K. penetrates the Castle walls—Joseph K. evades his indictment—"a breaking away from it altogether, a mode of living completely outside the jurisdiction of the court." Yes, the possibility of which Joseph K. has just a glimmering in the Cathedral, but can neither fathom nor effectuate—"not . . . some influential manipulation of the case, but . . . a circumvention of it"—Kafka realizes in the last year of his life.

Was it Dora Dymant or was it death that pointed the new way? Perhaps it could not have been one without the other. We know that the "illusory emptiness" at which K. gazed upon first entering the village and looking up through the mist and the darkness to the Castle was no more vast and incomprehensible than was the idea of himself as husband and father to the young Kafka; but now it seems the prospect of a Dora forever, of a wife, home, and children everlasting, is no longer the terrifying, bewildering prospect it would once have been, for now "everlasting" is undoubtedly not much more than a matter of months. Yes, the dying Kafka is determined to marry, and writes to Dora's Orthodox father for his daughter's hand. But the imminent death that has resolved all contradictions and uncertainties in Kafka is the very obstacle placed in his path by the young girl's father. The request of Franz Kafka, a dying man, to bind to him in his invalidism Dora Dymant, a healthy young girl, is—denied!

If there is not one father standing in Kafka's way, there is another—and, to be sure, another beyond him. Dora's father, writes Max Brod in his biography of Kafka, "set off with [Kafka's] letter to consult the man he honored most, whose authority counted more than anything else for him, the 'Gerer Rebbe.' The rabbi read the letter, put it to one side, and said nothing more than the single syllable. 'No.' " *No.* Klamm himself could have been no more abrupt—or any more removed from the petitioner. *No.* In its harsh finality, as telling and inescapable as the curselike threat delivered by his father to Georg Bendemann, that thwarted fiancé: "Just take your bride on your arm and try getting in my way. I'll sweep her from your very side, you don't know how!" *No.* Thou shalt not have, say the fathers, and Kafka agrees that he shall not. The habit of obedience and renunciation; also his own distaste for the diseased and reverence for strength, appetite, and health. " 'Well, clear this out now!' said the overseer, and they buried the hunger artist, straw and all. Into the cage they put a young panther. Even the most insensitive felt it refreshing to see this wild creature leaping around the cage that had so long been dreary. The panther was all right. The food he liked was brought him without hesitation by the attendants; he seemed not even to miss his freedom; his noble body, furnished almost to the bursting point with all that it needed, seemed to carry freedom around with it too; somewhere in his jaws it seemed to lurk; and the joy of life streamed with such ardent passion from his throat that for the onlookers it was not easy to stand the shock of it. But they braced themselves, crowded around the cage, and did not want ever to move away." So no is no; he knew as much himself. A healthy young girl of nineteen cannot, *should* not, be given in matrimony to a sickly man twice her age, who spits up blood ("I sentence you," cries Georg Bendemann's father, "to death by drowning!") and shakes in his bed with fevers and chills. What sort of un-Kafka-like dream had Kafka been dreaming?

And those nine months spent with Dora have still other "Kafkaesque" elements: a fierce winter in quarters inadequately heated; the inflation that makes a pittance of his own meager pension, and sends into the streets of Berlin the hungry and needy whose sufferings, says Dora, turn Kafka "ash-gray"; and his tubercular lungs, flesh transformed and punished. Dora cares as devotedly and tenderly for the diseased writer as does Gregor Samsa's sister for her brother, the bug. Gregor's sister plays the violin so beautifully that Gregor "felt as if the way were opening before him to the unknown nourishment he craved"; he dreams, in his condition, of sending his gifted sister to the Conservatory! Dora's music is Hebrew, which she reads aloud to Kafka, and with such skill that, according to Brod, "Franz recognized her dramatic talent; on his advice and under his direction she later educated herself in the art . . ."

Only Kafka is hardly vermin to Dora Dymant, *or to himself.* Away from Prague and his father's home, Kafka, in his fortieth year, seems at last to have been delivered from the self-loathing, the self-doubt, and those guilt-ridden impulses to dependence and self-effacement that had nearly driven him mad throughout his twenties and thirties; all at once he seems to have shed the pervasive sense of hopeless despair that informs the great punitive fantasies of *The Trial,* "The Penal Colony," and "The Metamorphosis." Years earlier, in Prague, he had directed Max Brod to destroy all his papers, including three unpublished novels, upon his death; now, in Berlin, when Brod introduces him to a German publisher interested in his work, Kafka consents to the publication of a volume of four stories, and consents, says Brod, "without much need of long arguments to persuade him." With Dora to help, he diligently resumes his study of Hebrew; despite his illness and the harsh winter, he travels to the Berlin Academy for Jewish Studies to attend a series of lectures on the Talmud—a very different Kafka from the estranged melancholic who once wrote in his diary, "What have I in common with the Jews? I have hardly anything in common with myself and should stand very quietly in a corner, content that I can breathe." And to further mark the change, there is ease and happiness with a woman: with this young and adoring companion, he is playful, he is pedagogical, and one would guess, in light of his illness (*and* his happiness), he is chaste. If not a husband (such as he had striven to be to the conventional Fräulein Bauer), if not a lover (as he struggled hopelessly to be with Milena), he would seem to have become something no less miraculous in his scheme of things: a father, a kind of father to this sisterly, mothering daughter. *As Franz Kafka awoke one morning from uneasy dreams he found himself transformed in his bed into a father, a writer, and a Jew.*

"I have completed the construction of my burrow," begins the long, exquisite, and tedious story that he wrote that winter in Berlin, "and it seems to be successful. . . . Just the place where, according to my calculations, the Castle Keep should be, the soil was very loose and sandy and had literally to be hammered and pounded into a firm state to serve as a wall for the beautifully vaulted chamber. But for such tasks the only tool I possess is my forehead. So I had to run with my forehead thousands and thousands of times, for whole days and nights, against the ground, and I was glad when the blood came, for that was proof that the walls were beginning to harden; in that way, as everybody must admit, I richly paid for my Castle Keep." "The Burrow" is the story of an animal with a keen sense of peril whose life is organized around the principle of defense, and whose deepest longings are for security and serenity; with teeth and claws—*and* forehead—the burrower constructs an elaborate and ingeniously intricate system of underground chambers and corridors that are designed to afford it some peace of mind; however, while this burrow does succeed in reducing the sense of danger from without, its maintenance and protection are equally fraught with anxiety: "these anxieties are different from ordinary ones, prouder, richer in content, often long repressed, but in their destructive effects they are perhaps much the same as the anxieties that existence in the outer world gives rise to." The story (whose ending is lost) terminates with the burrower fixated upon distant subterranean noises that cause it "to assume the existence of a great beast," itself burrowing in the direction of the Castle Keep.

Another grim tale of entrapment, and of obsession so absolute that no distinction is possible between character and predicament. Yet this fiction imagined in the last "happy" months of his life is touched with a spirit of personal reconciliation and sardonic self-acceptance, with a tolerance for one's own brand of madness, that is not apparent in "The Metamorphosis"; the piercing masochistic irony of the early animal story—as of "The Judgment" and *The Trial*—has given way here to a critique of the self and its preoccupations that, though bordering on mockery, no longer seeks to resolve itself in images of the uttermost humiliation and defeat . . . But there is more here than a metaphor for the insanely defended ego, whose striving for invulnerability produces a defensive system that must in its turn become the object of perpetual concern—there is also a very unromantic and hard-headed fable about how and why art is made, a portrait of the artist in all his ingenuity, anxiety, isolation, dissatisfaction, relentlessness, obsessiveness, secretiveness, paranoia, and self-addiction, a portrait of the magical thinker at the end of his tether, Kafka's Prospero . . . It is an infinitely suggestive story, this story of life in a hole. For, finally, remember the proximity of Dora Dymant during the months that Kafka was at work on "The Burrow" in the two underheated rooms that was their illicit home. Certainly a dreamer like Kafka need never have entered the young girl's body for her tender presence to kindle in him a fantasy of a hidden orifice that promises "satisfied desire," "achieved ambition," and "profound slumber," but that once penetrated and in one's possession, arouses the most terrifying and heartbreaking fears of retribution and loss. "For the rest I try to unriddle the beast's plans. Is it on its wanderings, or is it working on its own burrow? If it is on its wanderings then perhaps an understanding with it might be possible. If it should really break through to the burrow I shall give it some of my stores and it will go on its way again. It will go on its way again, a fine story! Lying in my heap of earth I can naturally dream of all sorts of things, even of an understanding with the beast, though I know well enough that no such thing can happen, and that at the instant when we see each other, more, at the moment when we merely guess at each other's presence, we shall blindly bare our claws and teeth . . ."

He died of tuberculosis of the lungs and the larynx a month short of his forty-first birthday, June 3, 1924. Dora, inconsolable, whispers for days afterward, "My love, my love, my good one . . ."

2

1942. I am nine; my Hebrew school teacher, Dr. Kafka, is fifty-nine. To the little boys who must attend his "four to five" class each afternoon, he is known—in part because of his remote and melancholy foreignness, but largely because we vent on him our resentment at having to learn an ancient calligraphy at the very hour we should be out screaming our heads off on the ballfield—he is known as Dr. Kishka. Named, I confess, by me. His sour breath, spiced with intestinal juices by five in the afternoon, makes the Yiddish word for "insides" particularly telling, I think. Cruel, yes, but in truth I would have cut out my tongue had I ever imagined the name would become legend. A coddled child, I do not yet think of myself as persuasive, nor, quite yet, as a literary force in the world. My jokes don't hurt, how could they, I'm so adorable. And if you don't believe me, just ask my family and the teachers in school. Already at nine, one foot in Harvard, the other in amuse my friends Schlossman and Ratner on the dark walk home from Hebrew school with an imitation of Kishka, his precise and finicky professorial manner, his German accent, his cough, his gloom. "Doctor *Kishka!*" cries Schlossman, and hurls himself savagely against the newsstand that belongs to the candy store owner whom Schlossman drives just a little crazier each night. the Catskills. Little Borscht Belt comic that I am outside the classroom, I "Doctor Franz—Doctor Franz—Doctor Franz—*Kishka;*" screams Ratner, and my chubby little friend who lives upstairs from me on nothing but chocolate milk and Mallomars does not stop laughing until, as is his wont (his mother has asked me "to keep an eye on him" for just this reason), he wets his pants. Schlossman takes the occasion of Ratner's humiliation to pull the little boy's paper out of his notebook and wave it in the air—it is the assignment Dr. Kafka has just returned to us, graded; we were told to make up an alphabet of our own, out of straight lines and curved lines and dots. "That is all an alphabet is," he had explained. "That is all Hebrew is. That is all English is. Straight lines and curved lines and dots." Ratner's alphabet, for which he received a C, looks like twenty-six skulls strung in a row. I received my A for a curlicued alphabet inspired largely (as Dr. Kafka would seem to have surmised from his comment at the top of the page) by the number eight. Schlossman received an F for forgetting even to do it—and a lot he seems to care, too. He is content—he is *overjoyed*—with things as they are. Just waving a piece of paper in the air, and screaming, *"Kishka! Kishka!"* makes him deliriously happy. We should all be so lucky.

At home, alone in the glow of my goose-necked "desk" lamp (plugged after dinner into an outlet in the kitchen, my study) the vision of our refugee teacher, sticklike in a fraying three-piece blue suit, is no longer very funny—particularly after the entire beginner's Hebrew class, of which I am the most studious member, takes the name "Kishka" to its heart. My guilt awakens redemptive fantasies of heroism. I have them often about "the Jews in Europe." I must save him. If not me, who? The demonic Schlossman? The babyish Ratner? And if not now, when? For I have learned in the ensuing weeks that Dr. Kafka lives in "a room" in the house of an elderly Jewish lady on the shabby lower stretch of Avon Avenue, where the trolley still runs, and the poorest of Newark's Negroes shuffle meekly up and down the street, for all they seem to know still back in Mississippi. A *room*. And *there!* My family's apartment is no palace, but it is ours at least, so long as we pay the thirty-eight-fifty a month in rent; and though our neighbors are not rich, they refuse to be poor and they refuse to be meek. Tears of shame and sorrow in my eyes, I rush into the living room to tell my parents what I have heard (though not that I heard it during a quick game of "aces up" played a minute before class against the synagogue's rear wall—worse, played directly beneath a stained glass window embossed with the names of the dead): "My Hebrew teacher lives in a *room*."

My parents go much further than I could imagine anybody going in the real world. Invite him to dinner, my mother says. *Here?* Of course here—Friday night; I'm sure he can stand a home-cooked meal and a little pleasant company. Meanwhile my father gets on the phone to call my Aunt Rhoda, who lives with my grandmother and tends her and her potted plants in the apartment house at the corner of our street. For nearly two decades now my father has been introducing my mother's forty-year-old "baby" sister to the Jewish bachelors and widowers of New Jersey. No luck so far. Aunt Rhoda, an "interior decorator" in the dry goods department of "The Big Bear," a mammoth merchandise and produce market in industrial Elizabeth, wears falsies (this information by way of my older brother) and sheer frilly blouses, and family lore has it that she spends hours in the bathroom every day applying powders and sweeping her stiffish hair up into a dramatic pile on her head; but despite all this dash and display, she is, in my father's words, "still afraid of the facts of life." He, however, is undaunted, and administers therapy regularly and gratis: "Let 'em squeeze ya, Rhoda—it *feels* good!" I am his flesh and blood, I can reconcile myself to such scandalous talk in our kitchen—*but what will Dr. Kafka think?* Oh, but it's too late to do anything now. The massive machinery of matchmaking has been set in motion by my undiscourageable father, and the smooth engines of my proud homemaking mother's hospitality are already purring away. To throw my body into the works in an attempt to bring it all to a halt—well, I might as well try to bring down the New Jersey Bell Telephone Company by leaving our receiver off the hook. Only Dr. Kafka can save me now. But to my muttered invitation, he replies, with a formal bow that turns me scarlet—who has ever seen a person do such a thing outside of a movie house?—he replies that he would be *honored* to be my family's dinner guest. "My aunt," I rush to tell him, "will be there too." It appears that I have just said something mildly humorous; odd to see Dr. Kafka smile. Sighing, he says, "I will be delighted to meet her." Meet her? He's supposed to *marry* her. How do I warn him? And how do I warn Aunt Rhoda (a very great admirer of me and my marks) about his sour breath, his roomer's pallor, his Old World ways, so at odds with her up-to-dateness? My face feels as if it will ignite of its own—and spark the fire that will engulf the synagogue, Torah and all—when I see Dr. Kafka scrawl our address in his notebook, and beneath it, some words *in German*. "Good night, Dr. Kafka!" "Good night, and thank you, thank you." I turn to run, I go, but not fast enough: out on the street I hear Schlossman— that fiend!—announcing to my classmates who are punching one another under the lamplight down from the synagogue steps (where a card game is also in progress, organized by the Bar Mitzvah boys): "Roth invited Kishka to his *house!* To *eat!*"

Does my father do a job on Kafka! Does he make a sales pitch for familial bliss! What it means to a man to have two fine boys and a wonderful wife! Can Dr. Kafka imagine what that's like? The thrill? The satisfaction? The pride? He tells our visitor of the network of relatives on his mother's side that are joined in a "family association" of over two hundred and fifty people located in seven states, including the state of Washington! Yes, relatives even in the Far West: here are their photographs, Dr. Kafka; this is a beautiful book we published entirely on our own for five dollars a copy, pictures of every member of the family, including infants, and a family history by "Uncle" Lichtblau, the eighty-five-year-old patriarch of the clan. This is our family newsletter that is published twice a year and distributed nationwide to all the relatives. This, in the frame, is the menu from the banquet of the family association, held last year in a ballroom of the "Y" in Newark, in honor of my father's mother on her seventy-fifth birthday. My mother, Dr. Kafka learns, has served *six consecutive years* as the secretary-treasurer of the family association. My father has served a two-year term as president, as have each of his three brothers. We now have fourteen boys in the family in uniform. Philip writes a letter on V-mail stationery to five of his cousins in the Army every single month. "Religiously," my mother puts in, smoothing my hair. "I firmly believe," says my father, "that the family is the cornerstone of everything." Dr. Kafka, who has listened with close attention to my father's *spiel,* handling the various documents that have been passed to him with great delicacy and poring over them with a kind of rapt absorption that reminds me of myself over the watermarks of my stamps, now for the first time expresses himself on the subject of family; softly he says, "I agree," and inspects again the pages of our family book. "Alone," says my father, in conclusion, "alone, Dr. Kafka, is a stone." Dr. Kafka, setting the book gently upon my mother's gleaming coffee table, allows with a nod how that is so. My mother's fingers are now turning in the curls behind my ears; not that I even know it at the time, or that she does. Being stroked is my life; stroking me, my father, and my brother is hers.

My brother goes off to a Boy Scout "council" meeting, but only after my father has him stand in his neckerchief before Dr. Kafka and describe to him the skills he has mastered to earn each of his badges. I am invited to bring my stamp album into the living room and show Dr. Kafka my set of triangular stamps from Zanzibar. "Zanzibar!" says my father rapturously, as though I, not even ten, have already been there and back. My father accompanies Dr. Kafka and myself into the "sun parlor," where my tropical fish swim in the aerated, heated, and hygienic paradise I have made for them with my weekly allowance and my Hanukah *gelt*. I am encouraged to tell Dr. Kafka what I know about the temperament of the angelfish, the function of the catfish, and the family life of the black molly. I know quite a bit. "All on his own he does that," my father says to Kafka. "He gives me a lecture on one of those fish, it's seventh heaven, Dr. Kafka." "I can imagine," Kafka replies.

Back in the living room my Aunt Rhoda suddenly launches into a rather recondite monologue on "scotch plaids," designed, it would appear, only for the edification of my mother. At least she looks fixedly at my mother while she delivers it. I have not yet seen her look directly at Dr. Kafka; she did not even turn his way at dinner when he asked how many employees there were at "The Big Bear." "How would I know?" she replies, and continues conversing with my mother, something about a grocer or a butcher who would take care of her "under the counter" if she could find him nylons for his wife. It never occurs to me that she will not look at Dr. Kafka because she is shy—nobody that dolled up could, in my estimation, be shy—I can only think that she is outraged. *It's his breath. It's his accent. It's his age.* I'm wrong—it turns out to be what Aunt Rhoda calls his "superiority complex." "Sitting there, sneering at us like that," says my aunt, somewhat superior now herself. "Sneering?" repeats my father, incredulous. "Sneering and laughing, yes!" says Aunt Rhoda. My mother shrugs: *"I* didn't think he was laughing." "Oh, don't worry, by himself there he was having a very good time—*at our expense*. I know the European-type man. Underneath they think they're all lords of the manor," Rhoda says. "You know something, Rhoda?" says my father, tilting his head and pointing a finger, "I think you fell in love." "With *him?* Are you *crazy?"* "He's too quiet for Rhoda," my mother says, "I think maybe he's a little bit of a wallflower. Rhoda is a lively person, she needs lively people around her." "Wallflower? He's not a wallflower! He's a gentleman that's all. And he's lonely," my father say assertively, glaring at my mother for coming in over his head like this *against* Kafka. My Aunt Rhoda is forty years old—it is not exactly a shipment of brand-new goods that he is trying to move. "He's a gentleman, he's an educated man, and I'll tell you something, he'd give his eye teeth to have a nice home and a wife." "Well," says my Aunt Rhoda, "let him find one then, if he's so educated. Somebody who's his equal, who he doesn't have to look down his nose at with his big sad refugee eyes!" "Yep, she's in love," my father announces, squeezing Rhoda's knee in triumph. "With him?" she cries, jumping to her feet, taffeta crackling around her like a bonfire. "With *Kafka?*" she snorts, "I wouldn't give an old man like him the time of day!"

Dr. Kafka calls and takes my Aunt Rhoda to a movie. I am astonished, both that he calls and that she goes; it seems there is more desperation in life than I have come across yet in my fish tank. Dr. Kafka takes my Aunt Rhoda to a play performed at the "Y." Dr. Kafka eats Sunday dinner with my grandmother and my Aunt Rhoda, and at the end of the afternoon, accepts with that formal bow of his the Mason jar of barley soup that my grandmother presses him to carry back to his room with him on the No. 8 bus. Apparently he was very taken with my grandmother's jungle of potted plants—and she, as a result, with him. Together they spoke in Yiddish about gardening. One Wednesday morning, only an hour after the store has opened for the day, Dr. Kafka shows up at the dry goods department of "The Big Bear"; he tells Aunt Rhoda that he just wanted to see where she worked. That night he writes in his diary, "With the customers she is forthright and cheery, and so managerial about 'taste' that when I hear her explain to a chubby young bride why green and blue do not 'go,' I am myself ready to believe that Nature is in error and R. is correct."

One night, at ten, Dr. Kafka and Aunt Rhoda come by unexpectedly, and a small impromptu party is held in the kitchen—coffee and cake, even a thimbleful of whiskey all around, to celebrate the resumption of Aunt Rhoda's career on the stage. I have only heard tell of my aunt's theatrical ambitions. My brother says that when I was small she used to come to entertain the two of us on Sundays with her puppets—she was at that time employed by the W.P.A. to travel around New Jersey and put on puppet shows in schools and even in churches; Aunt Rhoda did all the voices, male and female, and with the help of another young girl, manipulated the manikins on their strings. Simultaneously she had been a member of the "Newark Collective Theater," a troupe organized primarily to go around to strike groups to perform *Waiting for Lefty;* everybody in Newark (as I understood it) had had high hopes that Rhoda Pilchik would go on to Broadway—everybody except my grandmother. To me this period of history is as difficult to believe in as the era of the lake-dwellers that I am studying in school; of course, people say it was once so, so I believe them, but nonetheless it is hard to grant such stories the status of the real, given the life I see around me.

Yet my father, a very avid realist, is in the kitchen, *schnapps* glass in hand, toasting Aunt Rhoda's success. She has been awarded one of the starring roles in the Russian masterpiece, *The Three Sisters,* to be performed six weeks hence by the amateur group at the Newark "Y." Everything, announces Aunt Rhoda, everything she owes to Franz, and his encouragement. One conversation—"One!" she cries gaily—and Dr. Kafka had apparently talked my grandmother out of her lifelong belief that actors are not serious human beings. And what an actor *he* is, in his own right, says Aunt Rhoda. How he had opened her eyes to the meaning of things, by reading her the famous Chekhov play—yes, read it to her from the opening line to the final curtain, all the parts, and actually left her in tears. Here Aunt Rhoda says, "Listen, listen—this is the first line of the play—it's the key to everything. Listen—I just think about what it was like that night Pop passed away, how I thought and thought what would happen, what would we all do—and, and, listen—"

"We're listening," laughs my father.

Pause; she must have walked to the center of the kitchen linoleum. She says, sounding a little surprised, " 'It's just a year ago today that father died.' "

"Shhh," warns my mother, "you'll give the little one nightmares."

I am not alone in finding my aunt "a changed person" during the ensuing weeks of rehearsal. My mother says this is just what she was like as a little girl. "Red cheeks, always those hot, red cheeks—and everything exciting, even taking a bath." "She'll calm down, don't worry," says my father, "and then he'll pop the question." "Knock on wood," says my mother. "Come on," says my father, "he knows what side his bread is buttered on—he sets foot in this house, he sees what a family is all about, and believe me, he's licking his chops. Just look at him when he sits in that club chair. This is his dream come true." "Rhoda says that in Berlin, before Hitler, he had a young girlfriend, years and years it went on, and then she left him. For somebody else. She got tired of waiting." "Don't worry," says my father, "when the time comes I'll give him a little nudge. He ain't going to live forever, either, and he knows it."

Then one weekend, as a respite from the "strain" of nightly rehearsals—which Dr. Kafka regularly visits, watching in his hat and coat from a seat at the back of the auditorium until it is time to accompany Aunt Rhoda home—they take a trip to Atlantic City. Ever since he arrived on these shores Dr. Kafka has wanted to see the famous boardwalk and the horse that dives from the high board. But in Atlantic City something happens that I am not allowed to know about; any discussion of the subject conducted in my presence is in Yiddish. Dr. Kafka sends Aunt Rhoda four letters in three days. She comes to us for dinner and sits till midnight crying in our kitchen; she calls the "Y" on our phone to tell them (weeping) that her mother is still ill and she cannot come to rehearsal again—she may even have to drop out of the play—no, she can't, she can't, her mother is too ill, she herself is too upset! Good-bye! Then back to the kitchen table to cry; she wears no pink powder and no red lipstick, and her stiff brown hair, down, is thick and spiky as a new broom.

My brother and I listen from our bedroom, through the door that silently he has pushed ajar.

"Have you ever?" says Aunt Rhoda, weeping. "Have you *ever?*"

"Poor soul," says my mother.

"*Who?*" I whisper to my brother. "Aunt Rhoda or—"

"Shhhh!" he says, "Shut *up!*"

In the kitchen my father grunts. "Hmm. Hmm." I hear him getting up and walking around and sitting down again—and then grunting. I am listening so hard that I can hear the letters being folded and unfolded, stuck back into their envelopes and then removed to be puzzled over one more time.

"Well?" demands Aunt Rhoda. "*Well?*"

"Well what?" answers my father.

"Well what do you want to say now?"

"He's *meshugeh*," admits my father. "Something is wrong with him all right."

"But," sobs Aunt Rhoda, "no one would believe me when *I* said it!"

"Rhody, Rhody," croons my mother in that voice I know from those times that I have had to have stitches taken, or when I awaken in tears, somehow on the floor beside my bed. "Rhody, don't be hysterical, darling. It's over, kitten, it's all over."

I reach across to my brother's "twin" bed and tug on the blanket. I don't think I've ever been so confused in my life, not even by death. The speed of things! Everything good undone in a moment! By what? "*What?*" I whisper. "*What is it?*"

My brother, the Boy Scout, smiles leeringly and with a fierce hiss that is no answer and enough answer, addresses my bewilderment: "Sex!"

Years later, a junior at college, I receive an envelope from home containing Dr. Kafka's obituary, clipped from the *Jewish News,* the tabloid of Jewish affairs that is mailed each week to the homes of the Jews of Essex County. It is summer, the semester is over, but I have stayed on at school, alone in my room in the town, trying to write short stories; I am fed by a young English professor and his wife in exchange for babysitting; I tell the sympathetic couple, who are also loaning me the money for my rent, why it is I can't go home. My tearful fights with my father are all I can talk about at their dinner table. "Keep him away from me!" I scream at my mother. "But, darling," she asks me, "what is going on? What is this all about?"—the very same question with which I used to plague my older brother, asked of me now out of the same bewilderment and innocence. "He *loves* you," she explains. But that, of all things, seems to me to be precisely what is blocking my way. Others are crushed by paternal criticism—I find myself oppressed by his high opinion of me! Can it possibly be true (and can I possibly admit) that I am coming to hate him for loving me so? praising me so? But that makes no sense—the ingratitude! the stupidity! the contrariness! Being loved is so obviously a blessing, *the* blessing, praise such a rare bequest; only listen late at night to my closest friends on the literary magazine and in the drama society—they tell horror stories of family life to rival *The Way of All Flesh,* they return shell-shocked from vacations, drift back to school as though from the wars. What they would give to be in my golden slippers! "What's going on?" my mother begs me to tell her; but how can I, when I can neither fully believe that this is happening to us, nor that I am the one who is making it happen. That they, who together cleared all obstructions from my path, should seem now to be my final obstruction! No wonder my rage must filter through a child's tears of shame, confusion, and loss. All that we have constructed together over the course of two century-long decades, and look how I must bring it down—in the name of this tyrannical need that I call my "independence"! Born, I am told, with the umbilical cord around my neck, it seems I will always come close to strangulation trying to deliver myself from my past into my future. . . . My mother, keeping the lines of communication open, sends a note to me at school: "We miss you"—and encloses the very brief obituary notice. Across the margin at the bottom of the clipping, she has written (in the same hand that she wrote notes to my teachers and signed my report cards, in the very same handwriting that once eased my way in the world), "Remember poor Kafka, Aunt Rhoda's beau?"

"Dr. Franz Kafka," the notice reads, "a Hebrew teacher at the Talmud Torah of the Schley Street Synagogue from 1939 to 1948, died on June 3 in the Deborah Tuberculosis Sanitorium in Browns Mills, New Jersey. Dr. Kafka had been a patient there since 1950. He was 70 years old. Dr. Kafka was born in Prague, Czechoslovakia, and was a refugee from the Nazis. He leaves no survivors."

He also leaves no books: no *Trial*, no *Castle*, no "Diaries." The dead man's papers are claimed by no one, and disappear—all except those four *"meshugeneh"* letters that are, to this day as far as I know, still somewhere in amongst the memorabilia accumulated in her dresser drawers by my spinster aunt, along with a collection of Broadway "Playbills," sales citations from "The Big Bear," and transatlantic steamship stickers.

Thus all trace of Dr. Kafka disappears. Destiny being destiny, how could it be otherwise? Does the Land Surveyor reach the Castle? Does K. escape the judgment of the Court, or Georg Bendemann the judgment of his father? " 'Well, clear this out now!' said the overseer, and they buried the hunger artist, straw and all." No, it simply is not in the cards for Kafka ever to become *the* Kafka—why, that would be stranger even than a man turning into an insect. No one would believe it, Kafka least of all.

Franz Kafka

The Metamorphosis

I

As Gregor Samsa awoke one morning from uneasy dreams he found himself transformed in his bed into a gigantic insect. He was lying on his hard, as it were armor-plated, back and when he lifted his head a little he could see his dome-like brown belly divided into stiff arched segments on top of which the bed quilt could hardly keep in position and was about to slide off completely. His numerous legs, which were pitifully thin compared to the rest of his bulk, waved helplessly before his eyes.

What has happened to me? he thought. It was no dream. His room, a regular human bedroom, only rather too small, lay quiet between the four familiar walls. Above the table on which a collection of cloth samples was unpacked and spread out—Samsa was a commercial traveler—hung the picture which he had recently cut out of an illustrated magazine and put into a pretty gilt frame. It showed a lady, with a fur cap on and a fur stole, sitting upright and holding out to the spectator a huge fur muff into which the whole of her forearm had vanished!

Gregor's eyes turned next to the window, and the overcast sky—one could hear rain drops beating on the window gutter—made him quite melancholy. What about sleeping a little longer and forgetting all this nonsense, he thought, but it could not be done, for he was accustomed to sleep on his right side and in his present condition he could not turn himself over. However violently he forced himself towards his right side he always rolled on to his

THE METAMORPHOSIS   Reprinted by permission of Schocken Books, Inc. from *The Penal Colony* by Franz Kafka. Copyright © 1948 by Schocken Books, Inc.

back again. He tried it at least a hundred times, shutting his eyes to keep from seeing his struggling legs, and only desisted when he began to feel in his side a faint dull ache he had never experienced before.

Oh God, he thought, what an exhausting job I've picked on! Traveling about day in, day out. It's much more irritating work than doing the actual business in the office, and on top of that there's the trouble of constant traveling, of worrying about train connections, the bed and irregular meals, casual acquaintances that are always new and never become intimate friends. The devil take it all! He felt a slight itching up on his belly; slowly pushed himself on his back nearer to the top of the bed so that he could lift his head more easily; identified the itching place which was surrounded by many small white spots the nature of which he could not understand and made to touch it with a leg, but drew the leg back immediately, for the contact made a cold shiver run through him.

He slid down again into his former position. This getting up early, he thought, makes one quite stupid. A man needs his sleep. Other commercials live like harem women. For instance, when I come back to the hotel of a morning to write up the orders I've got, these others are only sitting down to breakfast. Let me just try that with my chief; I'd be sacked on the spot. Anyhow, that might be quite a good thing for me, who can tell? If I didn't have to hold my hand because of my parents I'd have given notice long ago, I'd have gone to the chief and told him exactly what I think of him. That would knock him endways from his desk! It's a queer way of doing, too, this sitting on high at a desk and talking down to employees, especially when they have to come quite near because the chief is hard of hearing. Well, there's still hope; once I've saved enough money to pay back my parents' debts to him— that should take another five or six years—I'll do it without fail. I'll cut myself completely loose then. For the moment, though, I'd better get up, since my train goes at five.

He looked at the alarm clock ticking on the chest. Heavenly Father! he thought. It was half-past six o'clock and the hands were quietly moving on, it was even past the half-hour, it was getting on toward a quarter of seven. Had the alarm clock not gone off? From the bed one could see it had been properly set for four o'clock; of course it must have gone off. Yes, but was it possible to sleep quietly through that ear-splitting noise? Well, he had not slept quietly, but apparently all the more soundly for that. But what was he to do now? The next train went at seven o'clock; to catch that he would need to hurry like mad and his samples weren't even packed up, and he himself wasn't feeling particularly fresh and active. And even if he did catch the train he wouldn't avoid a row with the chief, since the firm's porter would have been waiting for the five o'clock train and would have long since reported his failure to turn up. The porter was a creature of the chief's, spineless and stupid. Well, supposing he were to say he was sick? But that would be most unpleasant and would look suspicious, since during his five years' employment he had not been ill once. The chief himself would be sure to come with the sick-insurance doctor, would reproach his parents with the son's laziness and would cut all excuses short by referring to the insurance doctor, who of course regarded all mankind as perfectly healthy malingerers. And would he be so far wrong on this occasion? Gregor really felt quite well, apart from a drowsiness that was utterly superfluous after such a long sleep, and he was even unusually hungry.

As all this was running through his mind at top speed without his being able to decide to leave his bed—the alarm clock had just struck a quarter to seven—there came a cautious tap at the door behind the head of his bed. "Gregor," said a voice—it was his mother's—"it's a quarter to seven. Hadn't you a train to catch?" That gentle voice! Gregor had a shock as he heard his own voice answering hers, unmistakably his own voice, it was true, but with a persistent horrible twittering squeak behind it like an undertone, that left the words in their clear shape only for the first moment and then rose up reverberating round them to destroy their sense, so that one could not be sure one had heard them rightly. Gregor wanted to answer at length and explain everything, but in the circumstances he confined himself to saying: "Yes, yes, thank you, Mother, I'm getting up now." The wooden door between them must have kept the change in his voice from being noticeable outside, for his mother contented herself with this statement and shuffled away. Yet this brief exchange of words had made the other members of the family aware that Gregor was still in the house, as they had not expected, and at one of the side doors his father was already knocking, gently, yet with his fist. "Gregor, Gregor," he called, "what's the matter with you?" And after a little while he called again in a deeper voice: "Gregor! Gregor!" At the other side door his sister was saying in a low, plaintive tone: "Gregor? Aren't you well? Are you needing anything?" He answered them both at once: "I'm just ready," and did his best to make his voice sound as normal as possible by enunciating the words very clearly and leaving long pauses between them. So his father went back to his breakfast, but his sister whispered: "Gregor, open the door, do." However, he was not thinking of opening the door, and felt thankful for the prudent habit he had acquired in traveling of locking all doors during the night, even at home.

His immediate intention was to get up quietly without being disturbed, to put on his clothes and above all eat his breakfast, and only then to consider what else was to be done, since in bed, he was well aware, his meditations would come to no sensible conclusion. He remembered that often enough in bed he had felt small aches and pains, probably caused by awkward postures, which had proved purely imaginary once he got up, and he looked forward eagerly to seeing this morning's delusions gradually fall away. That the change in his voice was nothing but the precursor of a severe chill, a standing ailment of commercial travelers, he had not the least possible doubt.

To get rid of the quilt was quite easy; he had only to inflate himself a little and it fell off by itself. But the next move was difficult, especially because he was so uncommonly broad. He would have needed arms and hands to hoist himself up; instead he had only the numerous little legs which never stopped waving in all directions and which he could not control in the least. When he tried to bend one of them it was the first to stretch itself straight; and did he succeed at last in making it do what he wanted, all the other legs meanwhile waved the more wildly in a high degree of unpleasant agitation. "But what's the use of lying idle in bed," said Gregor to himself.

He thought that he might get out of bed with the lower part of his body first, but this lower part, which he had not yet seen and of which he could form no clear conception, proved too difficult to move; it shifted so slowly; and when finally, almost wild with annoyance, he gathered his forces together and thrust out recklessly, he had miscalculated the direction and bumped heavily against the lower end of the bed, and the stinging pain he felt informed him that precisely this lower part of his body was at the moment probably the most sensitive.

So he tried to get the top part of himself out first, and cautiously moved his head towards the edge of the bed. That proved easy enough, and despite its breadth and mass the bulk of his body at last slowly followed the movement of his head. Still, when he finally got his head free over the edge of the bed he felt too scared to go on advancing, for after all if he let himself fall in this way it would take a miracle to keep his head from being injured. And at all costs he must not lose consciousness now, precisely now; he would rather stay in bed.

But when after a repetition of the same efforts he lay in his former position again, sighing, and watched his little legs struggling against each other more wildly than ever, if that were possible, and saw no way of bringing any order into this arbitrary confusion, he told himself again that it was impossible to stay in bed and that the most sensible course was to risk everything for the smallest hope of getting away from it. At the same time he did not forget meanwhile to remind himself that cool reflection, the coolest possible, was much better than desperate resolves. In such moments he focused his eyes as sharply as possible on the window, but, unfortunately, the prospect of the morning fog, which muffled even the other side of the narrow street, brought him little encouragement and comfort. "Seven o'clock already," he said to himself when the alarm clock chimed again, "seven o'clock already and still such a thick fog." And for a little while he lay quiet, breathing lightly, as if perhaps expecting such complete repose to restore all things to their real and normal condition.

But then he said to himself: "Before it strikes a quarter past seven I must be quite out of this bed, without fail. Anyhow, by that time someone will have come from the office to ask for me, since it opens before seven." And he set himself to rocking his whole body at once in a regular rhythm, with the idea of swinging it out of the bed. If he tipped himself out in that way he could keep his head from injury by lifting it at an acute angle when he fell. His back seemed to be hard and was not likely to suffer from a fall on the carpet. His biggest worry was the loud crash he would not be able to help making, which would probably cause anxiety, if not terror, behind all the doors. Still, he must take the risk.

When he was already half out of the bed—the new method was more a game than an effort, for he needed only to hitch himself across by rocking to and fro—it struck him how simple it would be if he could get help. Two strong people—he thought of his father and the servant girl—would be amply sufficient; they would only have to thrust their arms under his convex back, lever him out of the bed, bend down with their burden and then be patient enough to let him turn himself right over on the floor, where it was to be hoped his legs would then find their proper function. Well, ignoring the fact that the doors were all locked, ought he really to call for help? In spite of his misery he could not suppress a smile at the very idea of it.

He had got so far that he could barely keep his equilibrium when he rocked himself strongly, and he would have to nerve himself very soon for the final decision since in five minutes' time it would be a quarter past seven—when the front door bell rang. "That's someone from the office," he said to himself, and grew almost rigid, while his little legs only jigged about all the faster. For a moment everything stayed quiet. "They're not going to open the door," said Gregor to himself, catching at some kind of irrational hope. But then of course the servant girl went as usual to the door with her heavy tread and opened it. Gregor needed only to hear the first good morning of the visitor to know immediately who it was—the chief clerk himself. What a fate, to be condemned to work for a firm where the smallest omission at once gave rise to the gravest suspicion! Were all employees in a body nothing but scoundrels, was there not among them one single loyal devoted man who, had he wasted only an hour or so of the firm's time in the morning, was so tormented by conscience as to be driven out of his mind and actually incapable of leaving his bed? Wouldn't it really have been sufficient to send an apprentice to inquire—if any inquiry were necessary at all—did the chief clerk himself have to come and thus indicate to the entire family, an innocent family, that this suspicious circumstance could be investigated by no one less versed in affairs than himself? And more through the agitation caused by these reflections than through any act of will Gregor swung himself out of bed with all his strength. There was a loud thump, but it was not really a crash. His fall was broken to some extent by the carpet, his back, too, was less stiff than he thought, and so there was merely a dull thud, not so very startling. Only he had not lifted his head carefully enough and had hit it; he turned it and rubbed it on the carpet in pain and irritation.

"That was something falling down in there," said the chief clerk in the next room to the left. Gregor tried to suppose to himself that something like what had happened to him today might some day happen to the chief clerk; one really could not deny that it was possible. But as if in brusque reply to this supposition the chief clerk took a couple of firm steps in the next-door room and his patent leather boots creaked. From the right-hand room his sister was whispering to inform him of the situation: "Gregor, the chief clerk's here." "I know," muttered Gregor to himself; but he didn't dare to make his voice loud enough for his sister to hear it.

"Gregor," said his father now from the left-hand room, "the chief clerk has come and wants to know why you didn't catch the early train. We don't know what to say to him. Besides, he wants to talk to you in person. So open the door, please. He will be good enough to excuse the untidiness of your room." "Good morning, Mr. Samsa," the chief clerk was calling amiably meanwhile. "He's not well," said his mother to the visitor, while his father was still speaking through the door, "he's not well, sir, believe me. What else would make him miss a train! The boy thinks about nothing but his work. It makes me almost cross the way he never goes out in the evenings; he's been here the last eight days and has stayed at home every single evening. He just sits there quietly at the table reading a newspaper or looking through railway timetables. The only amusement he gets is doing fretwork. For instance, he spent two or three evenings cutting out a little picture frame; you would be surprised to see how pretty it is; it's hanging in his room; you'll see it in a minute when Gregor opens the door. I must say I'm glad you've come, sir; we should never have got him to unlock the door by ourselves; he's so obstinate; and I'm sure he's unwell, though he wouldn't have it to be so this morning." "I'm just coming," said Gregor slowly and carefully, not moving an inch for fear of losing one word of the conversation. "I can't think of any other explanation, madam," said the chief clerk, "I hope it's nothing serious. Although on the other hand I must say that we men of business—fortunately or unfortunately—very often simply have to ignore any slight indisposition, since business must be attended to." "Well, can the chief clerk come in now?" asked Gregor's father impatiently, again knocking on the door. "No," said Gregor. In the left-hand room a painful silence followed this refusal, in the right-hand room his sister began to sob.

Why didn't his sister join the others? She was probably newly out of bed and hadn't even begun to put on her clothes yet. Well, why was she crying? Because he wouldn't get up and let the chief clerk in, because he was in danger of losing his job, and because the chief would begin dunning his parents again for the old debts? Surely these were things one didn't need to worry about for the present. Gregor was still at home and not in the least thinking of deserting the family. At the moment, true, he was lying on the carpet and no one who knew the condition he was in could seriously expect him to admit the chief clerk. But for such a small discourtesy, which could plausibly be explained away somehow later on, Gregor could hardly be dismissed on the spot. And it seemed to Gregor that it would be much more sensible to leave him in peace for the present than to trouble him with tears and entreaties. Still, of course, their uncertainty bewildered them all and excused their behavior.

"Mr. Samsa," the chief clerk called now in a louder voice, "what's the matter with you? Here you are, barricading yourself in your room, giving only 'yes' and 'no' for answers, causing your parents a lot of unnecessary trouble and neglecting—I mention this only in passing—neglecting your business duties in an incredible fashion. I am speaking here in the name of your parents and of your chief, and I beg you quite seriously to give me an immediate and precise explanation. You amaze me, you amaze me. I thought you were a quiet, dependable person, and now all at once you seem bent on making a disgraceful exhibition of yourself. The chief did hint to me early this morning a possible explanation for your disappearance—with reference to the cash payments that were entrusted to you recently—but I almost pledged my solemn word of honor that this could not be so. But now that I see how incredibly obstinate you are, I no longer have the slightest desire to take your part at all. And your position in the firm is not so unassailable. I came with the intention of telling you all this in private, but since you are wasting my time so needlessly I don't see why your parents shouldn't hear it too. For some time past your work has been most unsatisfactory; this is not the season of the year for a business boom, of course, we admit that, but a season of the year for doing no business at all, that does not exist, Mr. Samsa, must not exist."

"But, sir," cried Gregor, beside himself and in his agitation forgetting everything else, "I'm just going to open the door this very minute. A slight illness, an attack of giddiness, has kept me from getting up. I'm still lying in bed. But I feel all right again. I'm getting out of bed now. Just give me a moment or two longer! I'm not quite so well as I thought. But I'm all right, really. How a thing like that can suddenly strike one down! Only last night I was quite well, my parents can tell you, or rather I did have a slight presentiment. I must have showed some sign of it. Why didn't I report it at the office! But one always thinks that an indisposition can be got over without staying in the house. Oh sir, do spare my parents! All that you're reproaching me with now has no foundation; no one has ever said a word to me about it. Perhaps you haven't looked at the last orders I sent in. Anyhow, I can still catch the eight o'clock train, I'm much the better for my few hours' rest. Don't let me detain you here, sir; I'll be attending to business very soon, and do be good enough to tell the chief so and to make my excuses to him!"

And while all this was tumbling out pell-mell and Gregor hardly knew what he was saying, he had reached the chest quite easily, perhaps because of the practice he had had in bed, and was now trying to lever himself upright by means of it. He meant actually to open the door, actually to show himself and speak to the chief clerk; he was eager to find out what the others, after all their insistence, would say at the sight of him. If they were horrified then the responsibility was no longer his and he could stay quiet. But if they took it calmly, then he had no reason either to be upset, and could really get to the station for the eight o'clock train if he hurried. At first he slipped down a few times from the polished surface of the chest, but at length with a last heave he stood upright; he paid no more attention to the pains in the lower part of his body, however they smarted. Then he let himself fall against the back of a near-by chair, and clung with his little legs to the edges of it. That brought him into control of himself again and he stopped speaking, for now he could listen to what the chief clerk was saying.

"Did you understand a word of it?" the chief clerk was asking; "surely he can't be trying to make fools of us?" "Oh dear," cried his mother, in tears, "perhaps he's terribly ill and we're tormenting him. Grete! Grete!" she called out then. "Yes Mother?" called his sister from the other side. They were calling to each other across Gregor's room. "You must go this minute for the doctor. Gregor is ill. Go for the doctor, quick. Did you hear how he was speaking?" "That was no human voice," said the chief clerk in a voice noticeably low beside the shrillness of the mother's. "Anna! Anna!" his father was calling through the hall to the kitchen, clapping his hands, "get a locksmith at once!" And the two girls were already running through the hall with a swish of skirts—how could his sister have got dressed so quickly?—and were tearing the front door open. There was no sound of its closing again; they had evidently left it open, as one does in houses where some great misfortune has happened.

But Gregor was now much calmer. The words he uttered were no longer understandable, apparently, although they seemed clear enough to him, even clearer than before, perhaps because his ear had grown accustomed to the sound of them. Yet at any rate people now believed that something was wrong with him, and were ready to help him. The positive certainty with which these first measures had been taken comforted him. He felt himself drawn once more into the human circle and hoped for great and remarkable results from both the doctor and the locksmith, without really distinguishing precisely between them. To make his voice as clear as possible for the decisive conversation that was now imminent he coughed a little, as quietly as he could, of course, since this noise too might not sound like a human cough for all he was able to judge. In the next room meanwhile there was complete silence. Perhaps his parents were sitting at the table with the chief clerk, whispering, perhaps they were all leaning against the door and listening.

Slowly Gregor pushed the chair towards the door, then let go of it, caught hold of the door for support—the soles at the end of his little legs were somewhat sticky—and rested against it for a moment after his efforts. Then he set himself to turning the key in the lock with his mouth. It seemed, unhappily, that he hadn't really any teeth—what could he grip the key with? —but on the other hand his jaws were certainly very strong; with their help he did manage to set the key in motion, heedless of the fact that he was undoubtedly damaging them somewhere, since a brown fluid issued from his mouth, flowed over the key and dripped on the floor. "Just listen to that," said the chief clerk next door; "he's turning the key." That was a great encouragement to Gregor; but they should all have shouted encouragement to him, his father and mother too: "Go on, Gregor," they should have called out, "keep going, hold on to that key!" And in the belief that they were all following his efforts intently, he clenched his jaws recklessly on the key with all the force at his command. As the turning of the key progressed he circled round the lock, holding on now only with his mouth, pushing on the key, as required, or pulling it down again with all the weight of his body. The louder click of the finally yielding lock literally quickened Gregor. With a deep breath of relief he said to himself: "So I didn't need the locksmith," and laid his head on the handle to open the door wide.

Since he had to pull the door towards him, he was still invisible when it was really wide open. He had to edge himself slowly round the near half of the double door, and to do it very carefully if he was not to fall plump upon his back just on the threshold. He was still carrying out this difficult manoeuvre, with no time to observe anything else, when he heard the chief clerk utter a loud "Oh!"—it sounded like a gust of wind—and now he could see the man, standing as he was nearest to the door, clapping one hand before his open mouth and slowly backing away as if driven by some invisible steady pressure. His mother—in spite of the chief clerk's being there her hair was still undone and sticking up in all directions—first clasped her hands and looked at his father, then took two steps towards Gregor and fell on the floor among her outspread skirts, her face quite hidden on her breast. His father knotted his fist with a fierce expression on his face as if he meant to knock Gregor back into his room, then looked uncertainly round the living room, covered his eyes with his hands and wept till his great chest heaved.

Gregor did not go now into the living room, but leaned against the inside of the firmly shut wing of the door, so that only half his body was visible and his head above it bending sideways to look at the others. The light had meanwhile strengthened; on the other side of the street one could see clearly a section of the endlessly long dark gray building opposite—it was a hospital —abruptly punctuated by its row of regular windows; the rain was still falling, but only in large singly discernible and literally singly splashing drops. The breakfast dishes were set out on the table lavishly, for breakfast was the most important meal of the day to Gregor's father, who lingered it out for hours over various newspapers. Right opposite Gregor on the wall hung a photograph of himself on military service, as a lieutenant, hand on sword, a carefree smile on his face, inviting one to respect his uniform and military bearing. The door leading to the hall was open, and one could see that the front door stood open too, showing the landing beyond and the beginning of the stairs going down.

"Well," said Gregor, knowing perfectly that he was the only one who had retained any composure, "I'll put my clothes on at once, pack up my samples and start off. Will you only let me go? You see, sir, I'm not obstinate, and I'm willing to work; traveling is a hard life, but I couldn't live without it. Where are you going, sir? To the office? Yes? Will you give a true account of all this? One can be temporarily incapacitated, but that's just the moment for remembering former services and bearing in mind that later on, when the incapacity has been got over, one will certainly work with all the more industry and concentration. I'm loyally bound to serve the chief, you know that very well. Besides, I have to provide for my parents and my sister. I'm in great difficulties, but I'll get out of them again. Don't make things any worse for me than they are. Stand up for me in the firm. Travelers are not popular there, I know. People think they earn sacks of money and just have a good time. A prejudice there's no particular reason for revising. But you, sir, have a more comprehensive view of affairs than the rest of the staff, yes, let me tell you in confidence, a more comprehensive view than the chief himself, who, being the owner, lets his judgment easily be swayed against one of his employees. And you know very well that the traveler, who is never seen in the office almost the whole year round, can so easily fall a victim to gossip and ill luck and unfounded complaints, which he mostly knows nothing about, except when he comes back exhausted from his rounds, and only then suffers in person from their evil consequences, which he can no longer trace back to the original causes. Sir, sir, don't go away without a word to me to show that you think me in the right at least to some extent!"

But at Gregor's very first words the chief clerk had already backed away and only stared at him with parted lips over one twitching shoulder. And while Gregor was speaking he did not stand still one moment but stole away towards the door, without taking his eyes off Gregor, yet only an inch at a time, as if obeying some secret injunction to leave the room. He was already at the hall, and the suddenness with which he took his last step out of the living room would have made one believe he had burned the sole of his foot. Once in the hall he stretched his right arm before him towards the staircase, as if some supernatural power were waiting there to deliver him.

Gregor perceived that the chief clerk must on no account be allowed to go away in this frame of mind if his position in the firm were not to be endangered to the utmost. His parents did not understand this so well; they had convinced themselves in the course of years that Gregor was settled for life in this firm, and besides they were so occupied with their immediate troubles that all foresight had forsaken them. Yet Gregor had this foresight. The chief clerk must be detained, soothed, persuaded and finally won over; the whole future of Gregor and his family depended on it! If only his sister had been there! She was intelligent; she had begun to cry while Gregor was still lying quietly on his back. And no doubt the chief clerk, so partial to ladies, would have been guided by her; she would have shut the door of the flat and in the hall talked him out of his horror. But she was not there, and Gregor would have to handle the situation himself. And without remembering that he was still unaware what powers of movement he possessed, without even remembering that his words in all possibility, indeed in all likelihood, would again be unintelligible, he let go the wing of the door, pushed himself through the opening, started to walk towards the chief clerk, who was already ridiculously clinging with both hands to the railing on the landing; but immediately, as he was feeling for a support, he fell down with a little cry upon all his numerous legs. Hardly was he down when he experienced for the first time this morning a sense of physical comfort; his legs had firm ground under them; they were completely obedient, as he noted with joy; they even strove to carry him forward in whatever direction he chose; and he was inclined to believe that a final relief from all his sufferings was at hand. But in the same moment as he found himself on the floor, rocking with suppressed eagerness to move, not far from his mother, indeed just in front of her, she, who had seemed so completely crushed, sprang all at once to her feet, her arms and fingers outspread, cried: "Help, for God's sake, help!" bent her head down as if to see Gregor better, yet on the contrary kept backing senselessly away; had quite forgotten that the laden table stood behind her; sat upon it hastily, as if in absence of mind, when she bumped into it; and seemed altogether unaware that the big coffee pot beside her was upset and pouring coffee in a flood over the carpet.

"Mother, Mother," said Gregor in a low voice, and looked up at her. The chief clerk, for the moment, had quite slipped from his mind; instead, he could not resist snapping his jaws together at the sight of the streaming coffee. That made his mother scream again, she fled from the table and fell into the arms of his father, who hastened to catch her. But Gregor had now no time to spare for his parents; the chief clerk was already on the stairs; with his chin on the banisters he was taking one last backward look. Gregor made a spring, to be as sure as possible of overtaking him; the chief clerk must have divined his intention, for he leaped down several steps and vanished; he was still yelling "Ugh!" and it echoed through the whole staircase.

Unfortunately, the flight of the chief clerk seemed completely to upset Gregor's father, who had remained relatively calm until now, for instead of running after the man himself, or at least not hindering Gregor in his pursuit, he seized in his right hand the walking stick which the chief clerk had left behind on a chair, together with a hat and greatcoat, snatched in his left hand a large newspaper from the table and began stamping his feet and flourishing the stick and the newspaper to drive Gregor back into his room. No entreaty of Gregor's availed, indeed no entreaty was even understood, however humbly he bent his head his father only stamped on the floor the more loudly. Behind his father his mother had torn open a window, despite the cold weather, and was leaning far out of it with her face in her hands. A strong draught set in from the street to the staircase, the window curtains blew in, the newspapers on the table fluttered, stray pages whisked over the floor. Pitilessly Gregor's father drove him back, hissing and crying "Shoo!" like a savage. But Gregor was quite unpracticed in walking backwards, it really was a slow business. If he only had a chance to turn round he could get back to his room at once, but he was afraid of exasperating his father by the slowness of such a rotation and at any moment the stick in his father's hand might hit him a fatal blow on the back or on the head. In the end, however, nothing else was left for him to do since to his horror he observed that in moving backwards he could not even control the direction he took; and so, keeping an anxious eye on his father all the time over his shoulder, he began to turn round as quickly as he could, which was in reality very slowly. Perhaps his father noted his good intentions, for he did not interfere except every now and then to help him in the manoeuvre from a distance with the point of the stick. If only he would have stopped making that unbearable hissing noise! It made Gregor quite lose his head. He had turned almost completely round when the hissing noise so distracted him that he even turned a little the wrong way again. But when at last his head was fortunately right in front of the doorway, it appeared that his body was too broad simply to get through the opening. His father, of course, in his present mood was far from thinking of such a thing as opening the other half of the door, to let Gregor have enough space. He had merely the fixed idea of driving Gregor back into his room as quickly as possible. He would never have suffered Gregor to make the circumstantial preparations for standing up on end and perhaps slipping his way through the door. Maybe he was now making more noise than ever to urge Gregor forward, as if no obstacle impeded him; to Gregor, anyhow, the noise in his rear sounded no longer like the voice of one single father; this was really no joke, and Gregor thrust himself—come what might—into the doorway. One side of his body rose up, he was tilted at an angle in the doorway, his flank was quite bruised, horrid blotches stained the white door, soon he was stuck fast and, left to himself, could not have moved at all, his legs on one side fluttered trembling in the air, those on the other were crushed painfully to the floor—when from behind his father gave him a strong push which was literally a deliverance and he flew far into the room, bleeding freely. The door was slammed behind him with the stick, and then at last there was silence.

II

Not until it was twilight did Gregor awake out of a deep sleep, more like a swoon than a sleep. He would certainly have waked up of his own accord not much later, for he felt himself sufficiently rested and well-slept, but it seemed to him as if a fleeting step and a cautious shutting of the door leading into the hall had aroused him. The electric lights in the street cast a pale sheen here and there on the ceiling and the upper surfaces of the furniture, but down below, where he lay, it was dark. Slowly, awkwardly trying out his feelers, which he now first learned to appreciate, he pushed his way to the door to see what had been happening there. His left side felt like one single long, unpleasantly tense scar, and he had actually to limp on his two rows of legs. One little leg, moreover, had been severely damaged in the course of that morning's events—it was almost a miracle that only one had been damaged—and trailed uselessly behind him.

He had reached the door before he discovered what had really drawn him to it: the smell of food. For there stood a basin filled with fresh milk in which floated little sops of white bread. He could almost have laughed with joy, since he was now still hungrier than in the morning, and he dipped his head almost over the eyes straight into the milk. But soon in disappointment he withdrew it again; not only did he find it difficult to feed because of his tender left side—and he could only feed with the palpitating collaboration of his whole body—he did not like the milk either, although milk had been his favorite drink and that was certainly why his sister had set it there for him, indeed it was almost with repulsion that he turned away from the basin and crawled back to the middle of the room.

He could see through the crack of the door that the gas was turned on in the living room, but while usually at this time his father made a habit of reading the afternoon newspaper in a loud voice to his mother and occasionally to his sister as well, not a sound was now to be heard. Well, perhaps his father had recently given up this habit of reading aloud, which his sister had mentioned so often in conversation and in her letters. But there was the same silence all around, although the flat was certainly not empty of occupants. "What a quiet life our family has been leading," said Gregor to himself, and as he sat there motionless staring into the darkness he felt great pride in the fact that he had been able to provide such a life for his parents and sister in such a fine flat. But what if all the quiet, the comfort, the contentment were now to end in horror? To keep himself from being lost in such thoughts Gregor took refuge in movement and crawled up and down the room.

Once during the long evening one of the side doors was opened a little and quickly shut again, later the other side door too; someone had apparently wanted to come in and then thought better of it. Gregor now stationed himself immediately before the living room door, determined to persuade any hesitating visitor to come in or at least to discover who it might be; but the door was not opened again and he waited in vain. In the early morning, when the doors were locked, they had all wanted to come in, now that he had opened one door and the other had apparently been opened during the day, no one came in and even the keys were on the other side of the doors.

It was late at night before the gas went out in the living room, and Gregor could easily tell that his parents and his sister had all stayed awake until then, for he could clearly hear the three of them stealing away on tiptoe. No one was likely to visit him, not until the morning, that was certain; so he had plenty of time to meditate at his leisure on how he was to arrange his life afresh. But the lofty, empty room in which he had to lie flat on the floor filled him with an apprehension he could not account for, since it had been his very own room for the past five years—and with a half-unconscious action, not without a slight feeling of shame, he scuttled under the sofa, where he felt comfortable at once, although his back was a little cramped and he could not lift his head up, and his only regret was that his body was too broad to get the whole of it under the sofa.

He stayed there all night, spending the time partly in a light slumber, from which his hunger kept waking him up with a start, and partly in worrying and sketching vague hopes, which all led to the same conclusion, that he must lie low for the present and, by exercising patience and the utmost consideration, help the family to bear the inconvenience he was bound to cause them in his present condition.

Very early in the morning, it was still almost night, Gregor had the chance to test the strength of his new resolutions, for his sister, nearly fully dressed, opened the door from the hall and peered in. She did not see him at once, yet when she caught sight of him under the sofa—well, he had to be somewhere, he couldn't have flown away, could he?—she was so startled that without being able to help it she slammed the door shut again. But as if regretting her behavior she opened the door again immediately and came in on tiptoe, as if she were visiting an invalid or even a stranger. Gregor had pushed his head forward to the very edge of the sofa and watched her. Would she notice that he had left the milk standing, and not for lack of hunger, and would she bring in some other kind of food more to his taste? If she did not do it of her own accord, he would rather starve than draw her attention to the fact, although he felt a wild impulse to dart out from under the sofa, throw himself at her feet and beg her for something to eat. But his sister at once noticed, with surprise, that the basin was still full, except for a little milk that had been spilt all around it, she lifted it immediately, not with her bare hands, true, but with a cloth and carried it away. Gregor was wildly curious to know what she would bring instead, and made various speculations about it. Yet what she actually did next, in the goodness of her heart, he could never have guessed at. To find out what he liked she brought him a whole selection of food, all set out on an old newspaper. There were old, half-decayed vegetables, bones from last night's supper covered with a white sauce that had thickened; some raisins and almonds; a piece of cheese that Gregor would have called uneatable two days ago; a dry roll of bread, a buttered roll, and a roll both buttered and salted. Besides all that, she set down again the same basin, into which she had poured some water, and which was apparently to be reserved for his exclusive use. And with fine tact, knowing that Gregor would not eat in her presence, she withdrew quickly and even turned the key, to let him understand that he could take his ease as much as he liked. Gregor's legs all whizzed towards the food. His wounds must have healed completely, moreover, for he felt no disability, which amazed him and made him reflect how more than a month ago he had cut one finger a little with a knife and had still suffered pain from the wound only the day before yesterday. Am I less sensitive now? he thought, and sucked greedily at the cheese, which above all the other edibles attracted him at once and strongly. One after another and with tears of satisfaction in his eyes he quickly devoured the cheese, the vegetables and the sauce; the fresh food, on the other hand, had no charms for him, he could not even stand the smell of it and actually dragged away to some little distance the things he could eat. He had long finished his meal and was only lying lazily on the same spot when his sister turned the key slowly as a sign for him to retreat. That roused him at once, although he was nearly asleep, and he hurried under the sofa again. But it took considerable self-control for him to stay under the sofa, even for the short time his sister was in the room, since the large meal had swollen his body somewhat and he was so cramped he could hardly breathe. Slight attacks of breathlessness afflicted him and his eyes were starting a little out of his head as he watched his unsuspecting sister sweeping together with a broom not only the remains of what he had eaten but even the things he had not touched, as if these were now of no use to anyone, and hastily shoveling it all into a bucket, which she covered with a wooden lid and carried away. Hardly had she turned her back when Gregor came from under the sofa and stretched and puffed himself out.

In this manner Gregor was fed, once in the early morning while his parents and the servant girl were still asleep, and a second time after they had all had their midday dinner, for then his parents took a short nap and the servant girl could be sent out on some errand or other by his sister. Not that they would have wanted him to starve, of course, but perhaps they could not have borne to know more about his feeding than from hearsay, perhaps too his sister wanted to spare them such little anxieties wherever possible, since they had quite enough to bear as it was.

Under what pretext the doctor and the locksmith had been got rid of on that first morning Gregor could not discover, for since what he said was not understood by the others it never struck any of them, not even his sister, that he could understand what they said, and so whenever his sister came into his room he had to content himself with hearing her utter only a sigh now and then and an occasional appeal to the saints. Later on, when she had got a little used to the situation—of course she could never get completely used to it—she sometimes threw out a remark which was kindly meant or could be so interpreted. "Well, he liked his dinner today," she would say when Gregor had made a good clearance of his food; and when he had not eaten, which gradually happened more and more often, she would say almost sadly: "Everything's been left standing again."

But although Gregor could get no news directly, he overheard a lot from the neighboring rooms, and as soon as voices were audible, he would run to the door of the room concerned and press his whole body against it. In the first few days especially there was no conversation that did not refer to him somehow, even if only indirectly. For two whole days there were family consultations at every mealtime about what should be done; but also between meals the same subject was discussed, for there were always at least two members of the family at home, since no one wanted to be alone in the flat and to leave it quite empty was unthinkable. And on the very first of these days the household cook—it was not quite clear what and how much she knew of the situation—went down on her knees to his mother and begged leave to go, and when she departed, a quarter of an hour later, gave thanks for her dismissal with tears in her eyes as if for the greatest benefit that could have been conferred on her, and without any prompting swore a solemn oath that she would never say a single word to anyone about what had happened.

Now Gregor's sister had to cook too, helping her mother; true, the cooking did not amount to much, for they ate scarcely anything. Gregor was always hearing one of the family vainly urging another to eat and getting no answer but: "Thanks, I've had all I want," or something similar. Perhaps they drank nothing either. Time and again his sister kept asking his father if he wouldn't like some beer and offered kindly to go and fetch it herself, and when he made no answer suggested that she could ask the concierge to fetch it, so that he need feel no sense of obligation, but then a round "No" came from his father and no more was said about it.

In the course of that very first day Gregor's father explained the family's financial position and prospects to both his mother and his sister. Now and then he rose from the table to get some voucher or memorandum out of the small safe he had rescued from the collapse of his business five years earlier. One could hear him opening the complicated lock and rustling papers out and shutting it again. This statement made by his father was the first cheerful information Gregor had heard since his imprisonment. He had been of the opinion that nothing at all was left over from his father's business, at least his father had never said anything to the contrary, and of course he had not asked him directly. At that time Gregor's sole desire was to do his utmost to help the family to forget as soon as possible the catastrophe which had overwhelmed the business and thrown them all into a state of complete despair. And so he had set to work with unusual ardor and almost overnight had become a commercial traveler instead of a little clerk, with of course much greater chances of earning money, and his success was immediately translated into good round coin which he could lay on the table for his amazed and happy family. These had been fine times, and they had never recurred, at least not with the same sense of glory, although later on Gregor had earned so much money that he was able to meet the expenses of the whole household and did so. They had simply got used to it, both the family and Gregor; the money was gratefully accepted and gladly given, but there was no special uprush of warm feeling. With his sister alone had he remained intimate, and it was a secret plan of his that she, who loved music, unlike himself, and could play movingly on the violin, should be sent next year to study at the Conservatorium, despite the great expense that would entail, which must be made up in some other way. During his brief visits home the Conservatorium was often mentioned in the talks he had with his sister, but always merely as a beautiful dream which could never come true, and his parents discouraged even these innocent references to it; yet Gregor had made up his mind firmly about it and meant to announce the fact with due solemnity on Christmas Day.

Such were the thoughts, completely futile in his present condition, that went through his head as he stood clinging upright to the door and listening. Sometimes out of sheer weariness he had to give up listening and let his head fall negligently against the door, but he always had to pull himself together again at once, for even the slight sound his head made was audible next door and brought all conversation to a stop. "What can he be doing now?" his father would say after a while, obviously turning towards the door, and only then would the interrupted conversation gradually be set going again.

Gregor was now informed as amply as he could wish—for his father tended to repeat himself in his explanations, partly because it was a long time since he had handled such matters and partly because his mother could not always grasp things at once—that a certain amount of investments, a very small amount it was true, had survived the wreck of their fortunes and had even increased a little because the dividends had not been touched meanwhile. And besides that, the money Gregor brought home every month—he had kept only a few dollars for himself—had never been quite used up and now amounted to a small capital sum. Behind the door Gregor nodded his head eagerly, rejoiced at this evidence of unexpected thrift and foresight. True, he could really have paid off some more of his father's debts to the chief with his extra money, and so brought much nearer the day on which he could quit his job, but doubtless it was better the way his father had arranged it.

Yet this capital was by no means sufficient to let the family live on the interest of it; for one year, perhaps, or at the most two, they could live on the principal, that was all. It was simply a sum that ought not to be touched and should be kept for a rainy day; money for living expenses would have to be earned. Now his father was still hale enough but an old man, and he had done no work for the past five years and could not be expected to do much; during these five years, the first years of leisure in his laborious though unsuccessful life, he had grown rather fat and become sluggish. And Gregor's old mother, how was she to earn a living with her asthma, which troubled her even when she walked through the flat and kept her lying on a sofa every other day panting for breath beside an open window? And was his sister to earn her bread, she who was still a child of seventeen and whose life hitherto had been so pleasant, consisting as it did in dressing herself nicely, sleeping long, helping in the housekeeping, going out to a few modest entertainments and above all playing the violin? At first whenever the need for earning money was mentioned Gregor let go his hold on the door and threw himself down on the cool leather sofa beside it, he felt so hot with shame and grief.

Often he just lay there the long nights through without sleeping at all, scrabbling for hours on the leather. Or he nerved himself to the great effort of pushing an armchair to the window, then crawled up over the window sill and, braced against the chair, leaned against the window panes, obviously in some recollection of the sense of freedom that looking out of a window always used to give him. For in reality day by day things that were even a little way off were growing dimmer to his sight; the hospital across the street, which he used to execrate for being all too often before his eyes, was now quite beyond his range of vision, and if he had not known that he lived in Charlotte Street, a quiet street but still a city street, he might have believed that his window gave on a desert waste where gray sky and gray land blended indistinguishably into each other. His quick-witted sister only needed to observe twice that the armchair stood by the window; after that whenever she had tidied the room she always pushed the chair back to the same place at the window and even left the inner casements open.

If he could have spoken to her and thanked her for all she had to do for him, he could have borne her ministrations better; as it was, they oppressed him. She certainly tried to make as light as possible of whatever was disagreeable in her task, and as time went on she succeeded, of course, more and more, but time brought more enlightenment to Gregor too. The very way she came in distressed him. Hardly was she in the room when she rushed to the window, without even taking time to shut the door, careful as she was usually to shield the sight of Gregor's room from the others, and as if she were almost suffocating tore the casements open with hasty fingers, standing then in the open draught for a while even in the bitterest cold and drawing deep breaths. This noisy scurry of hers upset Gregor twice a day; he would crouch trembling under the sofa all the time, knowing quite well that she would certainly have spared him such a disturbance had she found it at all possible to stay in his presence without opening the window.

On one occasion, about a month after Gregor's metamorphosis, when there was surely no reason for her to be still startled at his appearance, she came a little earlier than usual and found him gazing out of the window, quite motionless, and thus well placed to look like a bogey. Gregor would not have been surprised had she not come in at all, for she could not immediately open the window while he was there, but not only did she retreat, she jumped back as if in alarm and banged the door shut; a stranger might well have thought that he had been lying in wait for her there meaning to bite her. Of course he hid himself under the sofa at once, but he had to wait until midday before she came again, and she seemed more ill at ease than usual. This made him realize how repulsive the sight of him still was to her, and that it was bound to go on being repulsive, and what an effort it must cost her not to run away even from the sight of the small portion of his body that stuck out from under the sofa. In order to spare her that, therefore, one day he carried a sheet on his back to the sofa—it cost him four hours' labor—and arranged it there in such a way as to hide him completely, so that even if she were to bend down she could not see him. Had she considered the sheet unnecessary, she would certainly have stripped it off the sofa again, for it was clear enough that this curtaining and confining of himself was not likely to conduce to Gregor's comfort, but she left it where it was, and Gregor even fancied that he caught a thankful glance from her eye when he lifted the sheet carefully a very little with his head to see how she was taking the new arrangement.

For the first fortnight his parents could not bring themselves to the point of entering his room, and he often heard them expressing their appreciation of his sister's activities, whereas formerly they had frequently scolded her for being as they thought a somewhat useless daughter. But now, both of them often waited outside the door, his father and his mother, while his sister tidied his room, and as soon as she came out she had to tell them exactly how things were in the room, what Gregor had eaten, how he had conducted himself this time and whether there was not perhaps some slight improvement in his condition. His mother, moreover, began relatively soon to want to visit him, but his father and sister dissuaded her at first with arguments which Gregor listened to very attentively and altogether approved. Later, however, she had to be held back by main force, and when she cried out: "Do let me in to Gregor, he is my unfortunate son! Can't you understand that I must go to him?" Gregor thought that it might be well to have her come in, not every day, of course, but perhaps once a week; she understood things, after all, much better than his sister, who was only a child despite the efforts she was making and had perhaps taken on so difficult a task merely out of childish thoughtlessness.

Gregor's desire to see his mother was soon fulfilled. During the daytime he did not want to show himself at the window, out of consideration for his parents, but he could not crawl very far around the few square yards of floor space he had, nor could he bear lying quietly at rest all during the night, while he was fast losing any interest he had ever taken in food, so that for mere recreation he had formed the habit of crawling crisscross over the walls and ceiling. He especially enjoyed hanging suspended from the ceiling; it was much better than lying on the floor; one could breathe more freely; one's body swung and rocked lightly; and in the almost blissful absorption induced by this suspension it could happen to his own surprise that he let go and fell plump on the floor. Yet he now had his body much better under control than formerly, and even such a big fall did him no harm. His sister at once remarked the new distraction Gregor had found for himself—he left traces behind him of the sticky stuff on his soles wherever he crawled—and she got the idea in her head of giving him as wide a field as possible to crawl in and of removing the pieces of furniture that hindered him, above all the chest of drawers and the writing desk. But that was more than she could manage all by herself; she did not dare ask her father to help her; and as for the servant girl, a young creature of sixteen who had had the courage to stay on after the cook's departure, she could not be asked to help, for she had begged as an especial favor that she might keep the kitchen door locked and open it only on a definite summons; so there was nothing left but to apply to her mother at an hour when her father was out. And the old lady did come, with exclamations of joyful eagerness, which, however, died away at the door of Gregor's room. Gregor's sister, of course, went in first, to see that everything was in order before letting his mother enter. In great haste Gregor pulled the sheet lower and rucked it more in folds so that it really looked as if it had been thrown accidentally over the sofa. And this time he did not peer out from under it; he renounced the pleasure of seeing his mother on this occasion and was only glad that she had come at all. "Come in, he's out of sight," said his sister, obviously leading her mother in by the hand. Gregor could now hear the two women struggling to shift the heavy old chest from its place, and his sister claiming the greater part of the labor for herself, without listening to the admonitions of her mother who feared she might overstrain herself. It took a long time. After at least a quarter of an hour's tugging his mother objected that the chest had better be left where it was, for in the first place it was too heavy and could never be got out before his father came home, and standing in the middle of the room like that it would only hamper Gregor's movements, while in the second place it was not at all certain that removing the furniture would be doing a service to Gregor. She was inclined to think to the contrary; the sight of the naked walls made her own heart heavy, and why shouldn't Gregor have the same feeling, considering that he had been used to his furniture for so long and might feel forlorn without it. "And doesn't it look," she concluded in a low voice—in fact she had been almost whispering all the time as if to avoid letting Gregor, whose exact whereabouts she did not know, hear even the tones of her voice, for she was convinced that he could not understand her words—"doesn't it look as if we were showing him, by taking away his furniture, that we have given up hope of his ever getting better and are just leaving him coldly to himself? I think it would be best to keep his room exactly as it has always been, so that when he comes back to us he will find everything unchanged and be able all the more easily to forget what has happened in between."

On hearing these words from his mother Gregor realized that the lack of all direct human speech for the past two months together with the monotony of family life must have confused his mind, otherwise he could not account for the fact that he had quite earnestly looked forward to having his room emptied of furnishing. Did he really want his warm room, so comfortably fitted with old family furniture, to be turned into a naked den in which he would certainly be able to crawl unhampered in all directions but at the price of shedding simultaneously all recollection of his human background? He had indeed been so near the brink of forgetfulness that only the voice of his mother, which he had not heard for so long, had drawn him back from it. Nothing should be taken out of his room; everything must stay as it was; he could not dispense with the good influence of the furniture on his state of mind; and even if the furniture did hamper him in his senseless crawling round and round, that was no drawback but a great advantage.

Unfortunately his sister was of the contrary opinion; she had grown accustomed, and not without reason, to consider herself an expert in Gregor's affairs as against her parents, and so her mother's advice was now enough to make her determined on the removal not only of the chest and the writing desk, which had been her first intention, but of all the furniture except the indispensable sofa. This determination was not, of course, merely the outcome of childish recalcitrance and of the self-confidence she had recently developed so unexpectedly and at such cost; she had in fact perceived that Gregor needed a lot of space to crawl about in, while on the other hand he never used the furniture at all, so far as could be seen. Another factor might have been also the enthusiastic temperament of an adolescent girl, which seeks to indulge itself on every opportunity and which now tempted Grete to exaggerate the horror of her brother's circumstances in order that she might do all the more for him. In a room where Gregor lorded it all alone over empty walls no one save herself was likely ever to set foot.

And so she was not to be moved from her resolve by her mother, who seemed moreover to be ill at ease in Gregor's room and therefore unsure of herself, was soon reduced to silence and helped her daughter as best she could to push the chest outside. Now, Gregor could do without the chest, if need be, but the writing desk he must retain. As soon as the two women had got the chest out of his room, groaning as they pushed it, Gregor stuck his head out from under the sofa to see how he might intervene as kindly and cautiously as possible. But as bad luck would have it, his mother was the first to return, leaving Grete clasping the chest in the room next door where she was trying to shift it all by herself, without of course moving it from the spot. His mother however was not accustomed to the sight of him, it might sicken her and so in alarm Gregor backed quickly to the other end of the sofa, yet could not prevent the sheet from swaying a little in front. That was enough to put her on the alert. She paused, stood still for a moment and then went back to Grete.

Although Gregor kept reassuring himself that nothing out of the way was happening, but only a few bits of furniture were being changed round, he soon had to admit that all this trotting to and fro of the two women, their little ejaculations and the scraping of furniture along the floor affected him like a vast disturbance coming from all sides at once, and however much he tucked in his head and legs and cowered to the very floor he was bound to confess that he would not be able to stand it for long. They were clearing his room out; taking away everything he loved; the chest in which he kept his fret saw and other tools was already dragged off; they were now loosening the writing desk which had almost sunk into the floor, the desk at which he had done all his homework when he was at the commercial academy, at the grammar school before that, and, yes, even at the primary school—he had no more time to waste in weighing the good intentions of the two women, whose existence he had by now almost forgotten, for they were so exhausted that they were laboring in silence and nothing could be heard but the heavy scuffling of their feet.

And so he rushed out—the women were just leaning against the writing desk in the next room to give themselves a breather—and four times changed his direction, since he really did not know what to rescue first, then on the wall opposite, which was already otherwise cleared, he was struck by the picture of the lady muffled in so much fur and quickly crawled up to it and pressed himself to the glass, which was a good surface to hold on to and comforted his hot belly. This picture at least, which was entirely hidden beneath him, was going to be removed by nobody. He turned his head towards the door of the living room so as to observe the women when they came back.

They had not allowed themselves much of a rest and were already coming; Grete had twined her arm round her mother and was almost supporting her. "Well, what shall we take now?" said Grete, looking round. Her eyes met Gregor's from the wall. She kept her composure, presumably because of her mother, bent her head down to her mother, to keep her from looking up, and said, although in a fluttering, unpremeditated voice: "Come, hadn't we better go back to the living room for a moment?" Her intentions were clear enough to Gregor, she wanted to bestow her mother in safety and then chase him down from the wall. Well, just let her try it! He clung to his picture and would not give it up. He would rather fly in Grete's face.

But Grete's words had succeeded in disquieting her mother, who took a step to one side, caught sight of the huge brown mass on the flowered wallpaper, and before she was really conscious that what she saw was Gregor screamed in a loud, hoarse voice: "Oh God, oh God!" fell with outspread arms over the sofa as if giving up and did not move. "Gregor!" cried his sister, shaking her fist and glaring at him. This was the first time she had directly addressed him since his metamorphosis. She ran into the next room for some aromatic essence with which to rouse her mother from her fainting fit. Gregor wanted to help too—there was still time to rescue the picture—but he was stuck fast to the glass and had to tear himself loose; he then ran after his sister into the next room as if he could advise her, as he used to do; but then had to stand helplessly behind her; she meanwhile searched among various small bottles and when she turned round started in alarm at the sight of him; one bottle fell on the floor and broke; a splinter of glass cut Gregor's face and some kind of corrosive medicine splashed him; without pausing a moment longer Grete gathered up all the bottles she could carry and ran to her mother with them; she banged the door shut with her foot. Gregor was now cut off from his mother, who was perhaps nearly dying because of him; he dared not open the door for fear of frightening away his sister, who had to stay with her mother; there was nothing he could do but wait; and harassed by self-reproach and worry he began now to crawl to and fro, over everything, walls, furniture and ceiling, and finally in his despair, when the whole room seemed to be reeling round him, fell down on to the middle of the big table.

A little while elapsed, Gregor was still lying there feebly and all around was quiet, perhaps that was a good omen. Then the doorbell rang. The servant girl was of course locked in her kitchen, and Grete would have to open the door. It was his father. "What's been happening?" were his first words; Grete's face must have told him everything. Grete answered in a muffled voice, apparently hiding her head on his breast: "Mother has been fainting, but she's better now. Gregor's broken loose." "Just what I expected," said his father, "just what I've been telling you, but you women would never listen." It was clear to Gregor that his father had taken the worst interpretation of Grete's all too brief statement and was assuming that Gregor had been guilty of some violent act. Therefore Gregor must now try to propitiate his father, since he had neither time nor means for an explanation. And so he fled to the door of his own room and crouched against it, to let his father see as soon as he came in from the hall that his son had the good intention of getting back into his room immediately and that it was not necessary to drive him there, but that if only the door were opened he would disappear at once.

Yet his father was not in the mood to perceive such fine distinctions. "Ah!" he cried as soon as he appeared, in a tone which sounded at once angry and exultant. Gregor drew his head back from the door and lifted it to look at his father. Truly, this was not the father he had imagined to himself; admittedly he had been too absorbed of late in his new recreation of crawling over the ceiling to take the same interest as before in what was happening elsewhere in the flat, and he ought really to be prepared for some changes. And yet, and yet, could that be his father? The man who used to lie wearily sunk in bed whenever Gregor set out on a business journey; who welcomed him back of an evening lying in a long chair in a dressing gown; who could not really rise to his feet but only lifted his arms in greeting, and on the rare occasions when he did go out with his family, on one or two Sundays a year and on high holidays, walked between Gregor and his mother, who were slow walkers anyhow, even more slowly than they did, muffled in his old greatcoat, shuffling laboriously forward with the help of his crook-handled stick which he set down most cautiously at every step and, whenever he wanted to say anything, nearly always came to a full stop and gathered his escort around him? Now he was standing there in fine shape, dressed in a smart blue uniform with gold buttons, such as bank messengers wear; his strong double chin bulged over the stiff high collar of his jacket; from under his bushy eyebrows his black eyes darted fresh and penetrating glances; his onetime tangled white hair had been combed flat on either side of a shining and carefully exact parting. He pitched his cap, which bore a gold monogram, probably the badge of some bank, in a wide sweep across the whole room on to a sofa and with the tail-ends of his jacket thrown back, his hands in his trouser pockets, advanced with a grim visage towards Gregor. Likely enough he did not himself know what he meant to do; at any rate he lifted his feet uncommonly high, and Gregor was dumbfounded at the enormous size of his shoe soles. But Gregor could not risk standing up to him, aware as he had been from the very first day of his new life that his father believed only the severest measures suitable for dealing with him. And so he ran before his father, stopping when he stopped and scuttling forward again when his father made any kind of move. In this way they circled the room several times without anything decisive happening; indeed the whole operation did not even look like a pursuit because it was carried out so slowly. And so Gregor did not leave the floor, for he feared that his father might take as a piece of peculiar wickedness any excursion of his over the walls or the ceiling. All the same, he could not stay this course much longer, for while his father took one step he had to carry out a whole series of movements. He was already beginning to feel breathless, just as in his former life his lungs had not been very dependable. As he was staggering along, trying to concentrate his energy on running, hardly keeping his eyes open; in his dazed state never even thinking of any other escape than simply going forward; and having almost forgotten that the walls were free to him, which in this room were well provided with finely carved pieces of furniture full of knobs and crevices—suddenly something lightly flung landed close behind him and rolled before him. It was an apple; a second apple followed immediately; Gregor came to a stop in alarm; there was no point in running on, for his father was determined to bombard him. He had filled his pockets with fruit from the dish on the sideboard and was now shying apple after apple, without taking particularly good aim for the moment. The small red apples rolled about the floor as if magnetized and cannoned into each other. An apple thrown without much force grazed Gregor's back and glanced off harmlessly. But another following immediately landed right on his back and sank in; Gregor wanted to drag himself forward, as if this startling, incredible pain could be left behind him; but he felt as if nailed to the spot and flattened himself out in a complete derangement of all his senses. With his last conscious look he saw the door of his room being torn open and his mother rushing out ahead of his screaming sister, in her underbodice, for her daughter had loosened her clothing to let her breathe more freely and recover from her swoon, he saw his mother rushing towards his father, leaving one after another behind her on the floor her loosened petticoats, stumbling over her petticoats straight to his father and embracing him, in complete union with him—but here Gregor's sight began to fail—with her hands clasped round his father's neck as she begged for her son's life.

III

The serious injury done to Gregor, which disabled him for more than a month—the apple went on sticking in his body as a visible reminder, since no one ventured to remove it—seemed to have made even his father recollect that Gregor was a member of the family, despite his present unfortunate and repulsive shape, and ought not to be treated as an enemy, that, on the contrary, family duty required the suppression of disgust and the exercise of patience, nothing but patience.

And although his injury had impaired, probably for ever, his power of movement, and for the time being it took him long, long minutes to creep across his room like an old invalid—there was no question now of crawling up the wall—yet in his own opinion he was sufficiently compensated for this worsening of his condition by the fact that towards evening the living-room door, which he used to watch intently for an hour or two beforehand, was always thrown open, so that lying in the darkness of his room, invisible to the family, he could see them all at the lamp-lit table and listen to their talk, by general consent as it were, very different from his earlier eavesdropping.

True, their intercourse lacked the lively character of former times, which he had always called to mind with a certain wistfulness in the small hotel bedrooms where he had been wont to throw himself down, tired out, on damp bedding. They were now mostly very silent. Soon after supper his father would fall asleep in his armchair; his mother and sister would admonish each other to be silent; his mother, bending low over the lamp, stitched at fine sewing for an underwear firm; his sister, who had taken a job as a sales-girl, was learning shorthand and French in the evenings on the chance of bettering herself. Sometimes his father woke up, and as if quite unaware that he had been sleeping said to his mother: "What a lot of sewing you're doing today!" and at once fell asleep again, while the two women exchanged a tired smile.

With a kind of mulishness his father persisted in keeping his uniform on even in the house; his dressing gown hung uselessly on its peg and he slept fully dressed where he sat, as if he were ready for service at any moment and even here only at the beck and call of his superior. As a result, his uniform, which was not brand-new to start with, began to look dirty, despite all the loving care of the mother and sister to keep it clean, and Gregor often spent whole evenings gazing at the many greasy spots on the garment, gleam-ing with gold buttons always in a high state of polish, in which the old man sat sleeping in extreme discomfort and yet quite peacefully.

As soon as the clock struck ten his mother tried to rouse his father with gentle words and to persuade him after that to get into bed, for sitting there he could not have a proper sleep and that was what he needed most, since he had to go on duty at six. But with the mulishness that had obsessed him since he became a bank messenger he always insisted on staying longer at the table, although he regularly fell asleep again and in the end only with the greatest trouble could be got out of his armchair and into his bed. How-ever insistently Gregor's mother and sister kept urging him with gentle reminders, he would go on slowly shaking his head for a quarter of an hour, keeping his eyes shut, and refuse to get to his feet. The mother plucked at his sleeve, whispering endearments in his ear, the sister left her lessons to come to her mother's help, but Gregor's father was not to be caught. He would only sink down deeper in his chair. Not until the two women hoisted him up by the armpits did he open his eyes and look at them both, one after the other, usually with the remark: "This is a life. This is the peace and quiet of my old age." And leaning on the two of them he would heave himself up, with difficulty, as if he were a great burden to himself, suffer them to lead him as far as the door and then wave them off and go on alone, while the mother abandoned her needlework and the sister her pen in order to run after him and help him farther.

Who could find time, in this overworked and tired-out family, to bother about Gregor more than was absolutely needful? The household was reduced more and more; the servant girl was turned off; a gigantic bony charwoman with white hair flying round her head came in morning and evening to do the rough work; everything else was done by Gregor's mother, as well as great piles of sewing. Even various family ornaments, which his mother and sister used to wear with pride at parties and celebrations, had to be sold, as Gregor discovered of an evening from hearing them all discuss the prices obtained. But what they lamented most was the fact that they could not leave the flat which was much too big for their present circumstances, because they could not think of any way to shift Gregor. Yet Gregor saw well enough that consideration for him was not the main difficulty preventing the removal, for they could have easily shifted him in some suitable box with a few air holes in it; what really kept them from moving into another flat was rather their own complete hopelessness and the belief that they had been singled out for a misfortune such as had never happened to any of their relations or acquaintances. They fulfilled to the uttermost all that the world demands of poor people, the father fetched breakfast for the small clerks in the bank, the mother devoted her energy to making underwear for strangers, the sister trotted to and fro behind the counter at the behest of customers, but more than this they had not the strength to do. And the wound in Gregor's back began to nag at him afresh when his mother and sister, after getting his father into bed, came back again, left their work lying, drew close to each other and sat cheek by cheek; when his mother, pointing towards his room, said: "Shut that door now, Grete," and he was left again in darkness, while next door the women mingled their tears or perhaps sat dry-eyed staring at the table.

Gregor hardly slept at all by night or by day. He was often haunted by the idea that next time the door opened he would take the family's affairs in hand again just as he used to do; once more, after this long interval, there appeared in his thoughts the figures of the chief and the chief clerk, the commercial travelers and the apprentices, the porter who was so dull-witted, two or three friends in other firms, a chambermaid in one of the rural hotels, a sweet and fleeting memory, a cashier in a milliner's shop, whom he had wooed earnestly but too slowly—they all appeared, together with strangers or people he had quite forgotten, but instead of helping him and his family they were one and all unapproachable and he was glad when they vanished. At other times he would not be in the mood to bother about his family, he was only filled with rage at the way they were neglecting him, and although he had no clear idea of what he might care to eat he would make plans for getting into the larder to take the food that was after all his due, even if he were not hungry. His sister no longer took thought to bring him what might especially please him, but in the morning and at noon before she went to business hurriedly pushed into his room with her foot any food that was available, and in the evening cleared it out again with one sweep of the broom, heedless of whether it had been merely tasted, or—as most frequently happened—left untouched. The cleaning of his room, which she now did always in the evenings, could not have been more hastily done. Streaks of dirt stretched along the walls, here and there lay balls of dust and filth. At first Gregor used to station himself in some particularly filthy corner when his sister arrived, in order to reproach her with it, so to speak. But he could have sat there for weeks without getting her to make any improvement; she could see the dirt as well as he did, but she had simply made up her mind to leave it alone. And yet, with a touchiness that was new to her, which seemed anyhow to have infected the whole family, she jealously guarded her claim to be the sole caretaker of Gregor's room. His mother once subjected his room to a thorough cleaning, which was achieved only by means of several buckets of water—all this dampness of course upset Gregor too and he lay wide-spread, sulky and motionless on the sofa—but she was well punished for it. Hardly had his sister noticed the changed aspect of his room that evening than she rushed in high dudgeon into the living room and, despite the imploringly raised hands of her mother, burst into a storm of weeping, while her parents—her father had of course been startled out of his chair—looked on at first in helpless amazement; then they too began to go into action; the father reproached the mother on his right for not having left the cleaning of Gregor's room to his sister; shrieked at the sister on his left that never again was she to be allowed to clean Gregor's room; while the mother tried to pull the father into his bedroom, since he was beyond himself with agitation; the sister, shaken with sobs, then beat upon the table with her small fists; and Gregor hissed loudly with rage because not one of them thought of shutting the door to spare him such a spectacle and so much noise.

Still, even if the sister, exhausted by her daily work, had grown tired of looking after Gregor as she did formerly, there was no need for his mother's intervention or for Gregor's being neglected at all. The charwoman was there. This old widow, whose strong bony frame had enabled her to survive the worst a long life could offer, by no means recoiled from Gregor. Without being in the least curious she had once by chance opened the door of his room and at the sight of Gregor, who, taken by surprise, began to rush to and fro although no one was chasing him, merely stood there with her arms folded. From that time she never failed to open his door a little for a moment, morning and evening, to have a look at him. At first she even used to call him to her, with words which apparently she took to be friendly, such as: "Come along, then, you old dung beetle!" or "Look at the old dung beetle, then!" To such allocutions Gregor made no answer, but stayed motionless where he was, as if the door had never been opened. Instead of being allowed to disturb him so senselessly whenever the whim took her, she should rather have been ordered to clean out his room daily, that charwoman! Once, early in the morning—heavy rain was lashing on the windowpanes, perhaps a sign that spring was on the way—Gregor was so exasperated when she began addressing him again that he ran at her, as if to attack her, although slowly and feebly enough. But the charwoman instead of showing fright merely lifted high a chair that happened to be beside the door, and as she stood there with her mouth wide open it was clear that she meant to shut it only when she brought the chair down on Gregor's back. "So you're not coming any nearer?" she asked, as Gregor turned away again, and quietly put the chair back into the corner.

Gregor was now eating hardly anything. Only when he happened to pass the food laid out for him did he take a bit of something in his mouth as a pastime, kept it there for an hour at a time and usually spat it out again. At first he thought it was chagrin over the state of his room that prevented him from eating, yet he soon got used to the various changes in his room. It had become a habit in the family to push into his room things there was no room for elsewhere, and there were plenty of these now, since one of the rooms had been let to three lodgers. These serious gentlemen—all three of them with full beards, as Gregor once observed through a crack in the door—had a passion for order, not only in their own room but, since they were now members of the household, in all its arrangements, especially in the kitchen. Superfluous, not to say dirty, objects they could not bear. Besides, they had brought with them most of the furnishings they needed. For this reason many things could be dispensed with that it was no use trying to sell but that should not be thrown away either. All of them found their way into Gregor's room. The ash can likewise and the kitchen garbage can. Anything that was not needed for the moment was simply flung into Gregor's room by the charwoman, who did everything in a hurry; fortunately Gregor usually saw only the object, whatever it was, and the hand that held it. Perhaps she intended to take the things away again as time and opportunity offered, or to collect them until she could throw them all out in a heap, but in fact they just lay wherever she happened to throw them, except when Gregor pushed his way through the junk heap and shifted it somewhat, at first out of necessity, because he had not room enough to crawl, but later with increasing enjoyment, although after such excursions, being sad and weary to death, he would lie motionless for hours. And since the lodgers often ate their supper at home in the common living room, the living-room door stayed shut many an evening, yet Gregor reconciled himself quite easily to the shutting of the door, for often enough on evenings when it was opened he had disregarded it entirely and lain in the darkest corner of his room, quite unnoticed by the family. But on one occasion the charwoman left the door open a little and it stayed ajar even when the lodgers came in for supper and the lamp was lit. They set themselves at the top end of the table where formerly Gregor and his father and mother had eaten their meals, unfolded their napkins and took knife and fork in hand. At once his mother appeared in the other doorway with a dish of meat and close behind her his sister with a dish of potatoes piled high. The food steamed with a thick vapor. The lodgers bent over the food set before them as if to scrutinize it before eating, in fact the man in the middle, who seemed to pass for an authority with the other two, cut a piece of meat as it lay on the dish, obviously to discover if it were tender or should be sent back to the kitchen. He showed satisfaction, and Gregor's mother and sister, who had been watching anxiously, breathed freely and began to smile.

The family itself took its meals in the kitchen. None the less, Gregor's father came into the living room before going into the kitchen and with one prolonged bow, cap in hand, made a round of the table. The lodgers all stood up and murmured something in their beards. When they were alone again they ate their food in almost complete silence. It seemed remarkable to Gregor that among the various noises coming from the table he could always distinguish the sound of their masticating teeth, as if this were a sign to Gregor that one needed teeth in order to eat, and that with toothless jaws even of the finest make one could do nothing. "I'm hungry enough," said Gregor sadly to himself, "but not for that kind of food. How these lodgers are stuffing themselves, and here am I dying of starvation!"

On that very evening—during the whole of his time there Gregor could not remember ever having heard the violin—the sound of violin-playing came from the kitchen. The lodgers had already finished their supper, the one in the middle had brought out a newspaper and given the other two a page apiece, and now they were leaning back at ease reading and smoking. When the violin began to play they pricked up their ears, got to their feet, and went on tiptoe to the hall door where they stood huddled together. Their movements must have been heard in the kitchen, for Gregor's father called out: "Is the violin-playing disturbing you, gentlemen? It can be stopped at once." "On the contrary," said the middle lodger, "could not Fräulein Samsa come and play in this room, beside us, where it is much more convenient and comfortable?" "Oh certainly," cried Gregor's father, as if he were the violin-player. The lodgers came back into the living room and waited. Presently Gregor's father arrived with the music stand, his mother carrying the music and his sister with the violin. His sister quietly made everything ready to start playing; his parents, who had never let rooms before and so had an exaggerated idea of the courtesy due to lodgers, did not venture to sit down on their own chairs; his father leaned against the door, the right hand thrust between two buttons of his livery coat, which was formally buttoned up; but his mother was offered a chair by one of the lodgers and, since she left the chair just where he had happened to put it, sat down in a corner to one side.

Gregor's sister began to play; the father and mother, from either side, intently watched the movements of her hands. Gregor, attracted by the playing, ventured to move forward a little until his head was actually inside the living room. He felt hardly any surprise at his growing lack of consideration for the others; there had been a time when he prided himself on being considerate. And yet just on this occasion he had more reason than ever to hide himself, since owing to the amount of dust which lay thick in his room and rose into the air at the slightest movement, he too was covered with dust; fluff and hair and remnants of food trailed with him, caught on his back and along his sides; his indifference to everything was much too great for him to turn on his back and scrape himself clean on the carpet, as once he had done several times a day. And in spite of his condition, no shame deterred him from advancing a little over the spotless floor of the living room.

To be sure, no one was aware of him. The family was entirely absorbed in the violin-playing; the lodgers, however, who first of all had stationed themselves, hands in pockets, much too close behind the music stand so that they could all have read the music, which must have bothered his sister, had soon retreated to the window, half-whispering with downbent heads, and stayed there while his father turned an anxious eye on them. Indeed, they were making it more than obvious that they had been disappointed in their expectation of hearing good or enjoyable violin-playing, that they had had more than enough of the performance and only out of courtesy suffered a continued disturbance of their peace. From the way they all kept blowing the smoke of their cigars high in the air through nose and mouth one could divine their irritation. And yet Gregor's sister was playing so beautifully. Her face leaned sideways, intently and sadly her eyes followed the notes of music. Gregor crawled a little farther forward and lowered his head to the ground so that it might be possible for his eyes to meet hers. Was he an animal, that music had such an effect upon him? He felt as if the way were opening before him to the unknown nourishment he craved. He was determined to push forward till he reached his sister, to pull at her skirt and so let her know that she was to come into his room with her violin, for no one here appreciated her playing as he would appreciate it. He would never let her out of his room, at least, not so long as he lived; his frightful appearance would become, for the first time, useful to him; he would watch all the doors of his room at once and spit at intruders; but his sister should need no constraint, she should stay with him of her own free will; she should sit beside him on the sofa, bend down her ear to him and hear him confide that he had had the firm intention of sending her to the Conservatorium, and that, but for his mishap, last Christmas—surely Christmas was long past?—he would have announced it to everybody without allowing a single objection. After this confession his sister would be so touched that she would burst into tears, and Gregor would then raise himself to her shoulder and kiss her on the neck, which, now that she went to business, she kept free of any ribbon or collar.

"Mr. Samsa!" cried the middle lodger, to Gregor's father, and pointed, without wasting any more words, at Gregor, now working himself slowly forwards. The violin fell silent, the middle lodger first smiled to his friends with a shake of the head and then looked at Gregor again. Instead of driving Gregor out, his father seemed to think it more needful to begin by soothing down the lodgers, although they were not at all agitated and apparently found Gregor more entertaining than the violin-playing. He hurried towards them and, spreading out his arms, tried to urge them back into their own room and at the same time to block their view of Gregor. They now began to be really a little angry, one could not tell whether because of the old man's behavior or because it had just dawned on them that all unwittingly they had such a neighbor as Gregor next door. They demanded explanations of his father, they waved their arms like him, tugged uneasily at their beards, and only with reluctance backed towards their room. Meanwhile Gregor's sister, who stood there as if lost when her playing was so abruptly broken off, came to life again, pulled herself together all at once after standing for a while holding violin and bow in nervelessly hanging hands and staring at her music, pushed her violin into the lap of her mother, who was still sitting in her chair fighting asthmatically for breath, and ran into the lodgers' room to which they were now being shepherded by her father rather more quickly than before. One could see the pillows and blankets on the beds flying under her accustomed fingers and being laid in order. Before the lodgers had actually reached their room she had finished making the beds and slipped out.

The old man seemed once more to be so possessed by his mulish self-assertiveness that he was forgetting all the respect he should show to his lodgers. He kept driving them on and driving them on until in the very door of the bedroom the middle lodger stamped his foot loudly on the floor and so brought him to a halt. "I beg to announce," said the lodger, lifting one hand and looking also at Gregor's mother and sister, "that because of the disgusting conditions prevailing in this household and family"—here he spat on the floor with emphatic brevity—"I give you notice on the spot. Naturally I won't pay you a penny for the days I have lived here, on the contrary I shall consider bringing an action for damages against you, based on claims—believe me— that will be easily susceptible of proof." He ceased and stared straight in front of him, as if he expected something. In fact his two friends at once rushed into the breach with these words: "And we too give notice on the spot." On that he seized the door-handle and shut the door with a slam.

Gregor's father, groping with his hands, staggered forward and fell into his chair; it looked as if he were stretching himself there for his ordinary evening nap, but the marked jerkings of his head, which was as if uncontrollable, showed that he was far from asleep. Gregor had simply stayed quietly all the time on the spot where the lodgers had espied him. Disappointment at the failure of his plan, perhaps also the weakness arising from extreme hunger, made it impossible for him to move. He feared, with a fair degree of certainty, that at any moment the general tension would discharge itself in a combined attack upon him, and he lay waiting. He did not react even to the noise made by the violin as it fell off his mother's lap from under her trembling fingers and gave out a resonant note.

"My dear parents," said his sister, slapping her hand on the table by way of introduction, "things can't go on like this. Perhaps you don't realize that, but I do. I won't utter my brother's name in the presence of this creature, and so all I say is: we must try to get rid of it. We've tried to look after it and to put up with it as far as is humanly possible, and I don't think anyone could reproach us in the slightest."

"She is more than right," said Gregor's father to himself. His mother, who was still choking for lack of breath, began to cough hollowly into her hand with a wild look in her eyes.

His sister rushed over to her and held her forehead. His father's thoughts seemed to have lost their vagueness at Grete's words, he sat more upright, fingering his service cap that lay among the plates still lying on the table from the lodgers' supper, and from time to time looked at the still form of Gregor.

"We must try to get rid of it," his sister now said explicitly to her father, since her mother was coughing too much to hear a word, "it will be the death of both of you, I can see that coming. When one has to work as hard as we do, all of us, one can't stand this continual torment at home on top of it. At least I can't stand it any longer." And she burst into such a passion of sobbing that her tears dropped on her mother's face, where she wiped them off mechanically.

"My dear," said the old man sympathetically, and with evident understanding, "but what can we do?"

Gregor's sister merely shrugged her shoulders to indicate the feeling of helplessness that had now overmastered her during her weeping fit, in contrast to her former confidence.

"If he could understand us," said her father, half questioningly; Grete, still sobbing, vehemently waved a hand to show how unthinkable that was.

"If he could understand us," repeated the old man, shutting his eyes to consider his daughter's conviction that understanding was impossible, "then perhaps we might come to some agreement with him. But as it is—"

"He must go," cried Gregor's sister, "that's the only solution, Father. You must just try to get rid of the idea that this is Gregor. The fact that we've believed it for so long is the root of all our trouble. But how can it be Gregor? If this were Gregor, he would have realized long ago that human beings can't live with such a creature, and he'd have gone away on his own accord. Then we wouldn't have any brother, but we'd be able to go on living and keep his memory in honor. As it is, this creature persecutes us, drives away our lodgers, obviously wants the whole apartment to himself and would have us all sleep in the gutter. Just look, Father," she shrieked all at once, "he's at it again!" And in an access of panic that was quite incomprehensible to Gregor she even quitted her mother, literally thrusting the chair from her as if she would rather sacrifice her mother than stay so near to Gregor, and rushed behind her father, who also rose up, being simply upset by her agitation, and half-spread his arms out as if to protect her.

Yet Gregor had not the slightest intention of frightening anyone, far less his sister. He had only begun to turn round in order to crawl back to his room, but it was certainly a startling operation to watch, since because of his disabled condition he could not execute the difficult turning movements except by lifting his head and then bracing it against the floor over and over again. He paused and looked round. His good intentions seemed to have been recognized; the alarm had only been momentary. Now they were all watching him in melancholy silence. His mother lay in her chair, her legs stiffly out-stretched and pressed together, her eyes almost closing for sheer weariness; his father and his sister were sitting beside each other, his sister's arm around the old man's neck.

Perhaps I can go on turning round now, thought Gregor, and began his labors again. He could not stop himself from panting with the effort, and had to pause now and then to take breath. Nor did anyone harass him, he was left entirely to himself. When he had completed the turn-round he began at once to crawl straight back. He was amazed at the distance separating him from his room and could not understand how in his weak state he had managed to accomplish the same journey so recently, almost without remarking it. Intent on crawling as fast as possible, he barely noticed that not a single word, not an ejaculation from his family, interfered with his progress. Only when he was already in the doorway did he turn his head round, not completely, for his neck muscles were getting stiff, but enough to see that nothing had changed behind him except that his sister had risen to her feet. His last glance fell on his mother, who was not quite overcome by sleep.

Hardly was he well inside his room when the door was hastily pushed shut, bolted and locked. The sudden noise in his rear startled him so much that his little legs gave beneath him. It was his sister who had shown such haste. She had been standing ready waiting and had made a light spring forward, Gregor had not even heard her coming, and she cried "At last!" to her parents as she turned the key in the lock.

"And what now?" said Gregor to himself, looking round in the darkness. Soon he made the discovery that he was now unable to stir a limb. This did not surprise him, rather it seemed unnatural that he should ever actually have been able to move on these feeble little legs. Otherwise he felt relatively comfortable. True, his whole body was aching, but it seemed that the pain was gradually growing less and would finally pass away. The rotting apple in his back and the inflamed area around it, all covered with soft dust, already hardly troubled him. He thought of his family with tenderness and love. The decision that he must disappear was one that he held to even more strongly than his sister, if that were possible. In this state of vacant and peaceful meditation he remained until the tower clock struck three in the morning. The first broadening of light in the world outside the window entered his consciousness once more. Then his head sank to the floor of its own accord and from his nostrils came the last faint flicker of his breath.

When the charwoman arrived early in the morning—what between her strength and her impatience she slammed all the doors so loudly, never mind how often she had been begged not to do so, that no one in the whole apart-ment could enjoy any quiet sleep after her arrival—she noticed nothing un-usual as she took her customary peep into Gregor's room. She thought he was lying motionless on purpose, pretending to be in the sulks; she credited him with every kind of intelligence. Since she happened to have the long-handled broom in her hand she tried to tickle him up with it from the doorway. When that too produced no reaction she felt provoked and poked at him a little harder, and only when she had pushed him along the floor without meeting any resistance was her attention aroused. It did not take her long to establish the truth of the matter, and her eyes widened, she let out a whistle, yet did not waste much time over it but tore open the door of the Samsas' bedroom and yelled into the darkness at the top of her voice: "Just look at this, it's dead; it's lying here dead and done for!"

Mr. and Mrs. Samsa started up in their double bed and before they realized the nature of the charwoman's announcement had some difficulty in overcoming the shock of it. But then they got out of bed quickly, one on either side, Mr. Samsa throwing a blanket over his shoulders, Mrs. Samsa in nothing but her nightgown; in this array they entered Gregor's room. Meanwhile the door of the living room opened, too, where Grete had been sleeping since the advent of the lodgers; she was completely dressed as if she had not been to bed, which seemed to be confirmed also by the paleness of her face. "Dead?" said Mrs. Samsa, looking questioningly at the charwoman, although she could have investigated for herself, and the fact was obvious enough without investigation. "I should say so," said the charwoman, proving her words by pushing Gregor's corpse a long way to one side with her broomstick. Mrs. Samsa made a movement as if to stop her, but checked it. "Well," said Mr. Samsa, "now thanks be to God." He crossed himself, and the three women followed his example. Grete, whose eyes never left the corpse, said: "Just see how thin he was. It's such a long time since he's eaten anything. The food came out again just as it went in." Indeed, Gregor's body was completely flat and dry, as could only now be seen when it was no longer supported by the legs and nothing prevented one from looking closely at it.

"Come in beside us, Grete, for a little while," said Mrs. Samsa with a tremulous smile, and Grete, not without looking back at the corpse, followed her parents into their bedroom. The charwoman shut the door and opened the window wide. Although it was so early in the morning a certain softness was perceptible in the fresh air. After all, it was already the end of March.

The three lodgers emerged from their room and were surprised to see no breakfast; they had been forgotten. "Where's our breakfast?" said the middle lodger peevishly to the charwoman. But she put her finger to her lips and hastily, without a word, indicated by gestures that they should go into Gregor's room. They did so and stood, their hands in the pockets of their somewhat shabby coats, around Gregor's corpse in the room where it was now fully light.

At that the door of the Samsas' bedroom opened and Mr. Samsa appeared in his uniform, his wife on one arm, his daughter on the other. They all looked a little as if they had been crying; from time to time Grete hid her face on her father's arm.

"Leave my house at once!" said Mr. Samsa, and pointed to the door without disengaging himself from the women. "What do you mean by that?" said the middle lodger, taken somewhat aback, with a feeble smile. The two others put their hands behind them and kept rubbing them together, as if in gleeful expectation of a fine set-to in which they were bound to come off the winners. "I mean just what I say," answered Mr. Samsa, and advanced in a straight line with his two companions towards the lodger. He stood his ground at first quietly, looking at the floor as if his thoughts were taking a new pattern in his head. "Then let us go, by all means," he said, and looked up at Mr. Samsa as if in a sudden access of humility he were expecting some renewed sanction for this decision. Mr. Samsa merely nodded briefly once or twice with meaning eyes. Upon that the lodger really did go with long strides into the hall, his two friends had been listening and had quite stopped rubbing their hands for some moments and now went scuttling after him as if afraid that Mr. Samsa might get into the hall before them and cut them off from their leader. In the hall they all three took their hats from the rack, their sticks from the umbrella stand, bowed in silence and quitted the apartment. With a suspiciousness which proved quite unfounded Mr. Samsa and the two women followed them out to the landing; leaning over the banister they watched the three figures slowly but surely going down the long stairs, vanishing from sight at a certain turn of the staircase on every floor and coming into view again after a moment or so; the more they dwindled, the more the Samsa family's interest in them dwindled, and when a butcher's boy met them and passed them on the stairs coming up proudly with a tray on his head, Mr. Samsa and the two women soon left the landing and as if a burden had been lifted from them went back into their apartment.

They decided to spend this day in resting and going for a stroll; they had not only deserved such a respite from work, but absolutely needed it. And so they sat down at the table and wrote three notes of excuse, Mr. Samsa to his board of management, Mrs. Samsa to her employer and Grete to the head of her firm. While they were writing, the charwoman came in to say that she was going now, since her morning's work was finished. At first they only nodded without looking up, but as she kept hovering there they eyed her irritably. "Well?" said Mr. Samsa. The charwoman stood grinning in the doorway as if she had good news to impart to the family but meant not to say a word unless properly questioned. The small ostrich feather standing upright on her hat, which had annoyed Mr. Samsa ever since she was engaged, was waving gaily in all directions. "Well, what is it then?" asked Mrs. Samsa, who obtained more respect from the charwoman than the others. "Oh," said the charwoman, giggling so amiably that she could not at once continue, "just this, you don't need to bother about how to get rid of the thing next door. It's been seen to already." Mrs. Samsa and Grete bent over their letters again, as if preoccupied; Mr. Samsa, who perceived that she was eager to begin describing it all in detail, stopped her with a decisive hand. But since she was not allowed to tell her story, she remembered the great hurry she was in, being obviously deeply huffed: "Bye, everybody," she said, whirling off violently, and departed with a frightful slamming of doors.

"She'll be given notice tonight," said Mr. Samsa, but neither from his wife nor his daughter did he get any answer, for the charwoman seemed to have shattered again the composure they had barely achieved. They rose, went to the window and stayed there, clasping each other tight. Mr. Samsa turned in his chair to look at them and quietly observed them for a little. Then he called out: "Come along, now, do. Let bygones be bygones. And you might have some consideration for me." The two of them complied at once, hastened to him, caressed him and quickly finished their letters.

Then they all three left the apartment together, which was more than they had done for months, and went by tram into the open country outside the town. The tram, in which they were the only passengers, was filled with warm sunshine. Leaning comfortably back in their seats they canvassed their prospects for the future, and it appeared on closer inspection that these were not at all bad, for the jobs they had got, which so far they had never really discussed with each other, were all three admirable and likely to lead to better things later on. The greatest immediate improvement in their condition would of course arise from moving to another house; they wanted to take a smaller and cheaper but also better situated and more easily run apartment than the one they had, which Gregor had selected. While they were thus conversing, it struck both Mr. and Mrs. Samsa, almost at the same moment, as they became aware of their daughter's increasing vivacity, that in spite of all the sorrow of recent times, which had made her cheeks pale, she had bloomed into a pretty girl with a good figure. They grew quieter and half unconsciously exchanged glances of complete agreement, having come to the conclusion that it would soon be time to find a good husband for her. And it was like a confirmation of their new dreams and excellent intentions that at the end of their journey their daughter sprang to her feet first and stretched her young body.

Translated from the German
by Willa and Edwin Muir

Questions for study and writing

My Kinsman, Major Molineux

1. All works of fiction include a mixture of individualizing, or particular, elements and generalizing, or typical, ones, but the mixture varies with each writer—even with each work—according to the author's instincts and intentions. Hawthorne is widely known for the symbolic, even allegorical, character of his work and for his relatively limited interest in concrete, realistic detail. In what specific ways does "My Kinsman, Major Molineux" support this view of Hawthorne? Are there passages that suggest a commitment to providing a credibly realistic sense of character and of place? What is the function of the opening paragraph in relation to this matter of realistic detail? Why does Hawthorne name so few of his characters and instead speak of "the stranger," "the gentleman," "the old man," "the innkeeper," and so forth? What is the ultimate effect of these and similar techniques of generalization?

2. "My Kinsman, Major Molineux" takes place at night. Why is it important to Hawthorne's theme that this be so?

3. What is Robin's habitual mode of speech? Does he tend to make statements or to ask questions? How does his mode of speech help us understand the theme of the story?

4. Why does Hawthorne emphasize Robin's country background? Why does he emphasize his youthfulness? With the exception of the saucy-eyed woman who nearly entices Robin into her dwelling, the people he encounters in the story are older than he. How is this relevant to the meaning of the story? Do the woman and these older men share a quality Robin lacks? If so, what quality?

5. How do Robin's encounters with the residents resemble one another? Does his continuing failure to reach his goal have a discernible effect on him? In what ways do the appearance and atmosphere of the city alter as Robin's search continues? How is this change connected with the alteration in Robin's own attitude? Cite passages that illustrate the progression in Robin's attitude toward himself and his quest.

6. Like the other stories in Part One, "My Kinsman, Major Molineux" deals with thwarted expectations. What specific expectation of Robin's is upset in the story? How would you generalize, or extend, the meaning of the specific discovery Robin makes at the end of the story?

7. It becomes clear to the reader fairly early that Robin misunderstands what is happening to him. Cite passages in which Robin's explanation of events seems inadequate or misguided. How would you account for the fact that Robin holds the reader's sympathy despite his mistakes and miscalculations? What is the attitude of "the gentleman" who remains with Robin at the end? Is his attitude similar to that of the reader?

An Encounter

1. *Plot* is the sequence of events or actions in a story. In successful fiction, this pattern of events or actions contributes fundamentally to the story's meaning, and also resembles—or is reflected in—the plot of smaller episodes within the story. Describe as accurately as possible the plot of "An Encounter." What does this sequence of actions signify? Compare this total sequence with a single episode (for example, the opening account of Joe Dillon's career, the boys' visit to the quays and the three-masted ship, or the brief adventure at the Smoothing Iron where the two boys arrange a siege). In what ways does the pattern of these smaller units of action resemble the larger plot enacted by the story as a whole?

2. "An Encounter" is told by a first-person narrator who is the protagonist, or central figure, in the story. Does the narrator's style—his sentence structure, his vocabulary, his general tone of voice—suggest that the events of the story occurred in the recent or the distant past? Find passages that support your conclusion. What is the significance of this conclusion in terms of the total meaning of the story?

3. The strange old man whom the boys meet at the end of the day appears to be a sexual deviate. Some readers have suggested that Joyce's difficulties with prudish publishers may have contributed to his delicate treatment of the old man. Is this explanation adequate? Can you find evidence in the story for a more satisfying explanation for the oblique presentation of the old man's perversion?

4. Why does the narrator think it important to tell us that the old man had green eyes? At what point does he make this discovery? Is there another, larger discovery implicit in this one?

5. Serious readers expect fiction to present characters who are believable. This does not mean that strange, even impossible events have no place in good fiction. But it does mean that serious writers must create characters whose behavior is consistent with what we are told or can infer about their inner natures; it also means that we must be given characters whose actions at one moment will be congruent with their behavior at all other moments. Consider the protagonist and his friend, Mahony, according to this standard. Is the narrator's paralysis in the encounter with the old man consistent with his character as it is presented to us earlier in the Indian games? In school? During this day of adventure itself? Is Mahony's easy, unselfconscious escape from the old man consistent with *his* character as it has been revealed to us earlier? How can we explain the fact that it is the narrator who plans the outing? Which boy is more vulnerable to the shocks of experience? Why should this be so? Which boy is more decisive and self-possessed in the face of the unexpected? Which is more intelligent? What discovery about himself does the narrator articulate in the final paragraph?

The Story of My Dovecot

1. "The Story of My Dovecot" is one of the most powerful fictional accounts ever written about prejudice and political oppression. Yet the story contains no passage that moralizes about prejudice or explicitly decries injustice. What is the effect of Babel's refusal to speak about general principles of justice? How is his intention served by his focusing on the fragmented, private experiences of a young boy? How do we know what Babel's attitude is?

2. Babel is deeply committed to evoking the atmosphere of a particular place and time. Cite passages that aim especially at such realistic rendering. How does the narrator's tone of voice contribute to our sense of the story's authenticity? What does this tone of voice seem to assume about the world? Compare Babel's realistic treatment of his setting with Hawthorne's descriptions of the New England town that is the setting for "My Kinsman, Major Molineux." Why is it important to Babel's story that the reader have a sense of the concrete, individual reality of the ghetto?

3. Why is admission to the first class so important to the boy? To his family? To the whole Jewish community of his city? How do the boy's parents react to the news of his success? Do their very different reactions stem from similar causes?

4. The boy in this story is initiated into the real world in a particularly brutal and terrifying way. How would you define the full meaning of that initiation? Why are we told that when the boy falls to the ground after being struck he is wearing his new overcoat? What is implied by

the fact that the boy sees a Russian peasant smashing the residence of Khariton Efrussi, the wealthy Jewish corn-dealer who had bribed school officials to advance his son instead of the narrator? What is the connection between the outbreak of anti-Semitic violence, which concludes the story, and the history of the narrator's family, which is given on page 37? How is the brutal killing of the boy's pigeon related to the meaning of the story?

5. What precisely are the guests at the "pauper's ball" celebrating? What is implied concerning the fulfillment of their hopes when we are told that the narrator's mother "just couldn't imagine how women managed with Russian husbands"? What comment on those hopes is made by the anti-Semitic riot at the end? What is the significance of the boy's sense during the pogrom that one of the rioters is shouting in "some unknown, non-Russian language"?

The Killers

1. This famous and characteristic Hemingway story aims at an effect of radical purity and austerity. How does Hemingway's reliance on dialogue contribute to this effect? Do the characters' ways of talking distinguish them from one another? How does Hemingway's use of italics deepen, or complicate, the dialogue. What do you make of the simple but crucial fact that dialogue comprises so large a proportion of the whole story?

2. Examine one or two descriptive passages in "The Killers." How much information does Hemingway provide in such passages? How concrete, or particularizing, are his descriptions of characters and objects? Are there any passages that supply details concerning the feelings or thoughts of the characters? What are the chief qualities of the syntax and diction in these passages? On the basis of your answers to these questions, speculate about Hemingway's notions concerning the powers and limits of language and art.

3. The events in "The Killers" take place during a little more than two hours. This compression is characteristic of many short stories, though not of all. What does "The Killers" gain from such a concentrated, limited action? How is the compression of the plot related to other techniques of restraint, or limitation, in the story?

4. What expectations about the plot and characters are encouraged by the story's title? In what ways do the actual events in the story thwart or undermine such expectations? At a critical point in the story one of the killers is likened to "a photographer arranging for a group picture"; later, both killers, in "their tight overcoats and derby hats" are said to resemble "a vaudeville team." What is the significance of such ironic disjunctions between who these men are and what they look like? Analyze other moments in the story—for instance, Nick's encounter with Ole

Andreson or his strange conversation with the landlady—that are similarly concerned with the difference between the outward appearance of
things and their "real" significance.

5. Why does Nick decide to leave town at the end of the story? Why does
    George encourage him to do so? Can we conceive that George himself,
    or Sam, might feel free to make a similar choice? Why or why not? How
    does Ole Andreson's behavior affect Nick? What does Ole's passivity
    "teach" him? Can you cite passages from the conclusion of the story that
    indicate that Nick's understanding of life has altered? Could he himself
    articulate this change? Is there evidence to suggest that Nick is reluctant
    to acknowledge consciously what his recent experiences signify?

Battle Royal

1. Why is the protagonist so troubled by his memory of his grandfather's
    deathbed confession? What does the confession from this "quiet old man
    who had never made any trouble" suggest about the protagonist's hopes
    and ambitions as a young man?

2. The brutal smoker where the narrator is initiated into the realities of
    prejudice dramatizes several kinds of indignity and degradation. How
    does the smoker degrade the blonde dancer? The black adolescents who
    participate in the battle royal? How is the indignity they suffer a com-
    mentary on the audience? What is the significance of the fact that the
    audience is composed of "bankers, lawyers, fire chiefs, teachers, mer-
    chants"? Do the actions and appearances of these men suggest that they,
    too, are degraded victims? In what sense? By what forces and inner needs
    are they victimized? Which passages explicitly measure the degradation
    of the audience?

3. Although primarily about racial prejudice, "Battle Royal" is also about
    ambition. How can we account for the fact that the protagonist clings
    to his hope of delivering his speech even when his audience is watching
    him in the battle royal and even after his unspeakably degrading expe-
    rience with the electrified carpet? What is the subject of the narrator's
    graduation speech? Why does it find such favor with the white com-
    munity? What does the story as a whole imply about the value of humility
    as a way of achievement for blacks?

4. While the dancer and the nine boxers are performing only for money,
    the protagonist is competing for the audience's approval. Point to pas-
    sages in the story which clarify this distinction. What does this difference
    between the protagonist and the other performers suggest about the
    meaning of the protagonist's experience? Who, finally, bears the primary
    responsibility for the protagonist's humiliation? Is his humiliation deeper,
    more disturbing, than that of the other performers? Why?

5. Although set in radically different cultures, "Battle Royal" and "The

Story of My Dovecot" are profoundly similar stories. What techniques of style and organization do these stories share? In what ways do the events in each story resemble one another? What role does violence play in each story? In what ways do the Jewish community in Babel's story and the black community in Ellison's resemble one another? What qualities do the protagonists share? What truths about prejudice are suggested by these shared qualities?

Good Country People

1. The tone of this elusive and powerful story is a special blend of bleakness and of bizarre, grim comedy. Which details of plot and character contribute particularly to the story's dark humor? How does O'Connor's use of dialogue affect the tone of her story? Try to define the comedy and the significance of the following passage:

   "Okay," he almost whined, "but do you love me or don'tcher?"
   "Yes," she said and added, "in a sense. But I must tell you something. There mustn't be anything dishonest between us." She lifted his head and looked him in the eye. "I am thirty years old," she said. "I have a number of degrees."

2. Why does Joy change her name? What larger rejection is implied in her repudiation of the name she was born with?
3. None of the characters in "Good Country People" is especially attractive or sympathetic. What is the author's attitude toward these characters? What attitude or response does the story elicit from the reader? Are we to feel simply superior to these limited, crippled people? If this response seems inadequate, what response would be more appropriate and justified?
4. What is Hulga's attitude toward her mother? Toward Mrs. Freeman and her daughters? Toward the Bible salesman? What physical and psychological needs help to explain those attitudes? Is Hulga's condescension toward other people a trait she shares with others in the story? What similarities exist between her attitude toward the salesman and her mother's attitude toward Mrs. Freeman?
5. Hulga's experience in the hayloft is clearly a kind of violation. What is the connection between the violation she suffers and actual sexual violation? What is the significance of the salesman's failure or refusal to take her sexually? How does her treatment of the salesman help to account for his final cruelty to her? What notions about herself and her sense of the world are undermined by the salesman's duplicity? What is suggested at the end of the story by the loss of her artificial leg and her glasses?
6. How would you account for the religious overtones in "Good Country People"? For the fact that Hulga's betrayer sells Bibles? For her remarks

about salvation (p. 75)? For the fact that her final view of the salesman is one in which he appears to be "struggling successfully" to walk across water? In what sense might the salesman's treatment of Hulga be said to lead her to a kind of salvation?

Lost in the Funhouse

1. "Lost in the Funhouse" is deeply concerned with the act of storytelling itself, with the verbal, grammatical, and even the typographical, conventions that readers and authors usually take for granted. How many such conventions are explicitly discussed in the first four paragraphs of the story? What is the effect on the reader of these open references to the way stories are made and understood? Is the "reality" of Ambrose and his family's trip to Ocean City compromised by these references? What is the balance, or proportion, in these opening paragraphs—and in the story as a whole—of material concerned with Ambrose's experience as opposed to material concerned with the problems of telling a story? How are these separate matters related to each other? Does their linkage grow clearer as the story continues? What specific passages explicitly join Ambrose's story to the narrator's obsession with the problems of fiction making? Why does the narrator repeatedly complain that he is making no progress in his storytelling? What have these confessions to do with Ambrose's fantasized experiences in the funhouse?

2. The tone of this story is disturbingly unsteady, or changeable, a mingling of many different "voices" or ways of talking and writing. Try to identify several of these voices precisely. What kind of book, for example, sounds like this: "Description of physical appearance and mannerisms is one of several standard methods of characterization used by writers of fiction" (p. 81)? Or like this: ". . . he moved and spoke with *deliberate calm* and *adult gravity*" (p. 80)? Or like this: "What relevance does the war have to the story?" (p. 96)?

3. What *is* the war's relevance to the story?

4. Much has been made in recent criticism of the way in which literary tradition can be a burden for modern writers, an affliction or imprisonment for them rather than a nourishing legacy. Barth himself has written a famous essay, "The Literature of Exhaustion," which articulates this notion with special vehemence. In what respects does "Lost in the Funhouse" confirm and dramatize this view of the modern writer? James Joyce is mentioned twice in this story. Why do these references have special significance in the context of "Lost in the Funhouse?" Can you suggest some resemblances between Joyce's "An Encounter" and this story? Is Ambrose's ambivalent relationship with his brother Peter equivalent in any way to the narrator's relationship with Mahony in "An Encounter"? Are the narrators of the two stories like one another?

5. Sexual awakening is a powerful secondary theme in "Lost in the Funhouse." How is this theme illuminated by the portrait of Uncle Karl? By the relations between Ambrose's mother and Uncle Karl? The three adults in the story interact in ways that resemble the behavior of Ambrose, Peter, and Magda. What is the significance of these parallels? Why doesn't Magda go swimming? The narrator disarmingly observes that "the diving would make a suitable literary symbol" and then proceeds to describe the diving in inescapably symbolic ways. What are the sexual connotations of that description?

6. What is the meaning of the title of this story?

The Shadow-Line

1. The first section of *The Shadow-Line*, in which the narrator nearly loses his chance for a command because of the petty machinations of the steward at the Officers' Home, is for some readers less effective than the rest of the novella. Can you suggest any reasons for the seemingly slow pace of this opening chapter? How is the narrator's confusion and boredom in his conversation with Captain Giles related to the narrator's state of mind? How does the narrator's almost stubborn blindness to Captain Giles's helpful suggestions relate to his later experiences aboard ship? In this first chapter the narrator gives up his job aboard another ship without fully understanding his own motives, then fails to understand what is going on around him at the Sailor's Home, and finally hesitates before setting out to try for the command. How are these events reenacted later in the story? What is the steward's motive for trying to get the command for Hamilton? Does the narrator's failure to recognize the possibility of this deceit have a counterpart in his experience aboard ship?

2. *The Shadow-Line* is a classic story of initiation in which experience tests and finally alters a young man's understanding of himself and of the world. But it is also a subtle critique of an assumption basic to many initiation stories—that in single moments of decisive revelation, men lose their illusions and come to see themselves and the world with new maturity. Considering the story as a whole, how is the young captain altered by his experience? What does he learn about himself, about his need for other men, in the course of his first command? Does the protagonist's attitude seem to be based on the idea that difficulties can be solved decisively, in single instants of total success? How do the events of the story conform to that attitude? What repeatedly happens to the young captain's judgments concerning the men around him? What repeatedly happens to his recurring expectation of escape from difficulties?

3. Conrad originally planned to call this short novel *First Command*. Why do you think he altered the title? Which title seems more effective in

extending the implications of the story beyond its particular time and place? What is the shadow-line? How is the title related to the theme of growth? How are we to interpret the final interview between the young captain and Giles? In that scene there is a moment in which the younger man becomes irritated with Giles. How is that irritation related to his response to Giles in the first chapter? What does this irritation imply concerning the narrator's new-found maturity?

4. In several respects *The Shadow-Line* resembles the traditional adventure story. It is usual in such stories for young heroes to be tested by the natural world and by their confrontation with older, more experienced men. These older men are frequently maimed or marked in some exotic way, as the pirate Long John Silver in Robert Louis Stevenson's *Treasure Island* is marked by his peg leg. Which characters in Conrad's story seem closest to the Long John Silver model? What are the major similarities and differences between Conrad's treatment and the conventional treatment of such characters? In conventional adventure the hero almost always emerges with his courage and manhood unequivocally triumphant. How does Conrad's hero fit this pattern? In conventional adventure there is unremitting emphasis on external events, relatively little concern with psychological analysis. How would you describe the balance between external and internal hazards in this novella?

5. Why is the former captain a particularly crucial figure in the young man's education? Why do the dead captain's failures seem especially reprehensible—even treasonable—to the narrator? How does his reluctance to confront the example of the dead captain help to account for his attitude toward Burns? What assumption about the tradition of the sea does the dead captain's example undermine? How do the actions of Ransome, of the sick crew, even of Burns, provide a counterweight to the former captain's treason?

6. What is the relationship between Ransome and the young captain? Why at the end of the story does the narrator describe Ransome's weak heart as "our common enemy"?

7. Why is a voyage aboard a ship an especially appropriate form for a story of initiation? How could one extend the meaning of Conrad's story beyond the confines of the ship and its crew? What is Conrad saying about human community and human survival? What is he saying about the ideal of self-reliance? Consider especially Ransome and the young captain. What does Conrad seem to be saying about how and why people come to recognize and to accept their responsibilities to others? Do they usually come to this recognition easily or willingly, or are they forced, half-unwilling and unaware, into such responsibility? Cite particular passages and episodes which support your answer. How does Conrad's notion of what makes individuals act well contrast with what we might call the heroic ideal? Which view of the world and of human nature do you find more credible and persuasive? Why?

part two: Love

About Love

1. The second paragraph of "About Love" is a brief account of a violent love affair between two servants, the cook Nikanor and "the beautiful Pelageya." Is it significant that Alyohin—who later tells his own love story—is the source of this anecdote? How does this anecdote of consummated but troubled love contrast with Alyohin's own story?

2. Alyohin's first-person narrative of his relationship with Anna Luganovich is the core of "About Love." But his story is enclosed by an account of the occasion and of the setting in which his narrative occurs. How does this "framing technique"—which utilizes a point of view different from the primary narrator's and also reminds the reader that Alyohin's love story took place in the distant past—affect our understanding of Alyohin and his story?

3. An atmosphere of inertia is established in the opening paragraphs of "About Love." Cite some specific details which help to create this atmosphere. Is this air of indecisive leisure suggested again at the end of the story? What is the connection between this atmosphere and Alyohin's behavior with the woman he loves, and the outcome of their relationship?

4. Alyohin remarks that the Luganoviches "were distressed that I, an educated man with a knowledge of languages, instead of devoting myself to scholarship or literary work, should live in the country [and] rush around like a squirrel in a cage . . ." This judgment is echoed in the final paragraph of the story. What is the significance of this repetition and, particularly, of the reference to Alyohin as "a squirrel in a cage"? Is the emphasis on meaningless, empty activity relevant to Aloyhin's love story? To other characters in his story? To his listeners?

5. Explaining his decision not to run off with Anna Luganovich, Alyohin says, "It would have been different if I had led a beautiful, interesting life—if I had been fighting for the liberation of my country, for instance, or had been a celebrated scholar, an actor, or a painter; but as things were it would mean taking her from one humdrum life to another as humdrum or perhaps more so" (p. 180). Is this a convincing explanation for Alyohin's inertia? Why do you think Chekhov chose to write about this "ordinary" man instead of a hero or scholar or actor like those Alyohin mentions? Does Chekhov imply anything about Alyohin's assumption that "celebrated" people lead more decisive and fulfilled lives than the rest of us?

The Tone of Time

1. Disappointed love is perhaps the most overt theme of "The Tone of Time." How does the description of Mary Tredick in the first paragraph of the story establish this theme? Why does the narrator say that her card has been affixed "manfully" on the door to her studio? Why does she habitually wear "ugly spectacles" and a "big stained apron that covered her from head to foot"? What aspects of herself have been suppressed along with what the narrator calls "her desire to dazzle"? What assumptions about love, about its power and consequences in human affairs, are implied in these early passages and in the story as a whole?

2. Describe the highly unlikely coincidence on which this story depends. Do the characters themselves acknowledge that it is unlikely? Cite passages to support your answer. From one perspective, such contrivances as the central coincidence in "The Tone of Time" might be said to distort, or even to falsify, experience by conferring upon events a dramatic and psychological significance that is rarely visible in the muddled incoherence of the "real" world. On the basis of this story, and especially on the basis of what it tells us about passion and memory, how might such strategies of contrivance and manipulation be justified? Consider the narrator's judgment of his friend's remarkable painting, which he calls "at once a triumphant trick and a plausible evocation." In what ways is this view of art applicable to James's story itself?

3. Why does the narrator refuse Mrs. Bridgenorth's commission to do the portrait? Why does he propose that his friend Mary Tredick do the work instead? What kind of insight into his own work, into his own imaginative capacities as a painter, is suggested by his comment that he can paint only "the impression of the given, the presented case," that "I can do but the face I see"? Cite passages elsewhere in the story that indicate that the narrator's attentiveness to what is "presented" to his eye is itself an imaginative gift. Consider, for example, his description of the finished portrait on pages 188–89. What is the narrator able to "see" in the picture? What specific visual "facts" does he cite to support his impression of the man in the picture? What kind of observer would be capable of such interpretations.

4. Why does Mrs. Bridgenorth want the portrait she commissions? How does the narrator know or discover her reasons for wanting it? Why does Mary Tredick refuse to give it to her in the end?

5. In the final moments of the story, standing with Mary Tredick before her portrait of her dead lover, the narrator perceives her as "remotely glazed and fixed into what she had done." The last phrase—"what she had done"—refers specifically to her having painted the picture, but there are wider implications in those simple words. What are they? Why is the painterly term *glazed* applied here to the maker of the picture? In what senses, and for how long, has Mary Tredick been "fixed" by and to the man in her picture? What assumptions about art—about the

energies that engender art, about the labor and sacrifice demanded by art and celebrated in it—are inherent in that final scene and in the story as a whole?

6. The narrator says that his first meeting with Mrs. Bridgenorth had been defined by "the manner in which everything was vivid between us and nothing expressed." How well does this description fit the other conversations and relationships dramatized in the story? Cite one or two examples. During that first conversation, the narrator says, he and Mrs. Bridgenorth "remained on the surface with the tenacity of shipwrecked persons clinging to a plank." What valuation of the inner life and of the emotional forces at work in the ordinary world is implicit in this extravagant metaphor? Cite other passages wherein James's language tries to render and to judge the "prodigious" and "amazing" lives of his characters.

The Horse-Dealer's Daughter

1. "The Horse-Dealer's Daughter" is a highly symbolic story. To say this is merely to say that Lawrence charges ordinary events and objects with meanings and implications not ordinarily associated with them, but with meanings and implications that grow naturally out of, and are consistent with, the objects' realistic function and appearance. Thus, to try to suggest that the massive draught horses in the story are symbols of delicate, Cupid-like love would be nonsense. But to associate the horses with elemental, powerful life energies would make sense, for the real physical appearance of the horses as Lawrence describes them is consistent with, even encourages, this symbolic extension of their natures.

   The brackish pond in which Mabel tries to drown herself has major symbolic overtones. What are these overtones? How does Lawrence's emphasis on the pond's smell, its earthy, clayey dankness, its darkness, help to create the pond's symbolic meaning?

   The return from the pond and the powerful erotic scene by the fire which follows are also symbolic. What larger meanings are suggested by Mabel's nakedness, by the fact that by the end of the scene both the doctor and Mabel have divested themselves of their old clothing and put on new clothes?

2. The strange, charged atmosphere of this story has misled some readers into thinking that the doctor's and Mabel's behavior is inexplicable in realistic terms. Can you find evidence in the story that might explain why the doctor is so powerfully attracted to Mabel? Is there an implicit explanation for Mabel's behavior—for her sullen deadness at first, her attempted suicide, her reawakened vitality after her rescue—in the information Lawrence supplies concerning Mabel's relations with her mother and her father?

3. Lawrence tells this story from the viewpoint of an omniscient narrator

who can move at will into the minds of any of his characters and who has access to thoughts and feelings the characters themselves are not aware of. Compare this point of view with the *first-person* strategy used by Ellison in "Battle Royal" and with the *limited omniscience* of Fitzgerald's narrator in "Babylon Revisited." What advantages does Lawrence's method have for his story? What would be altered or lost had Lawrence chosen a different method of narration?

4. Lawrence's story depends for its effect in part on a distinctive style. Describe the chief qualities of this style and cite specific literary techniques, such as repetition, that help to create Lawrence's special tone.

5. Although the girl and the doctor are the central characters, Lawrence begins by focusing attention on Mabel's brothers, their house, the landscape, the general atmosphere, and he postpones the doctor's entrance for some time. What purpose is served by this strategy? How does Lawrence make his transitions from the mind of one character to that of another?

6. Although it concerns love, "The Horse-Dealer's Daughter" is hardly a conventional love story. What sort of love is the story about? How does it differ from the familiar boy-meets-girl story one might find in a popular magazine? Finally, does "The Horse-Dealer's Daughter" have some qualities in common with such conventional romantic stories?

Babylon Revisited

1. How does Fitzgerald's title, an allusion to the Bible, contribute to our understanding of the story? In what sense does the Biblical Babylon resemble Paris of the 1920s? Why is the title not simply "Babylon"?

2. Describe the point of view from which this story is told. What does Fitzgerald gain by confining himself to what the protagonist sees and thinks? How does this method—sometimes called the method of *limited omniscience*—differ from first-person narrative? What qualities would "Babylon Revisited" lose if Fitzgerald had allowed Charles Wales to tell his own story?

3. One crucial measure of a fiction writer is the ability to dramatize deep and complex motives, rather than to explain them abstractly. Consider this passage from "Babylon Revisited"

> "Really extremely well," he declared in answer to Lincoln's question. "There's a lot of business there that isn't moving at all, but we're doing even better than ever. In fact, damn well. I'm bringing my sister over from America next month to keep house for me. In fact, my income is bigger than it was when I had money. You see, the Czechs—"
> His boasting was for a specific purpose; but after a moment, seeing a faint restiveness in Lincoln's eye, he changed the subject. . . . (p. 214.)

What "specific purpose" is Charles Wales's boasting intended to serve? Why does he so abruptly change the subject? Find other passages in which small details yield similar insights into the characters.

4. What sort of man is Charles Wales? Why is he not more resentful of his sister-in-law's attitude toward him? Despite his past weaknesses and failures and despite his humiliation in his dealings with the Peterses, Wales possesses a stature, a human dignity, to which most readers respond. How would you account for this stature?

5. Fitzgerald's psychological penetration is evident in this story, even in his handling of secondary characters. From the evidence Fitzgerald provides, can you understand what motivates the behavior of Marion Peters? Of her husband? Of Lorraine Quarrles? Why is Marion so unpleasant to Wales? What role does her husband play in regard to her antagonism toward Wales? Why does Lincoln Peters not intervene more forcefully to help Wales? In the tense, complex scenes between Wales and the Peterses, what hidden resentments and jealousies are present? Do we have reason to suspect that Marion Peters may harbor resentments against her husband?

6. From one perspective "Babylon Revisited" might be said to have a surprise ending. Just as Wales is about to succeed in getting his daughter back, "two ghosts from the past" enter to destroy his hopes. Is this turn of events artificial, a piece of easy manipulation, or is it a believable and necessary conclusion? More importantly, is the last-minute loss of his daughter a simple piece of bad luck for Wales, or does it signify something much larger? Why doesn't Wales react to this dashing of his hopes with outrage and resentment?

A Country Love Story

1. The antique sleigh that is described at length in the opening paragraphs of "A Country Love Story" becomes a richly symbolic object before the story is over. Trace the many references to the sleigh as the story proceeds. What have the sleigh's age, its unpainted exterior, its immobility, to do with its symbolic meaning? How do these repeated references begin to transform the sleigh from a simple physical object into a suggestive emblem for May's sense of isolation and estrangement? With what does May associate the sleigh? Why does May's imaginary lover begin their courtship with the promise to get rid of the sleigh at once? Why is it appropriate that May signals her final surrender at the end of the story by getting into the sleigh? What is she surrendering by this action?

2. "A Country Love Story" traces the deterioration of a marriage. Describe carefully the particular stages through which this breakdown occurs. How does May's interview with Dr. Tellenbach prepare us for the estrangement that follows? What causes this deterioration? Is either May or

Daniel responsible for it? In what sense? What have their respective ages to do with the breakdown of their relationship? What role does Daniel's sickness play in their growing estrangement?

3. At which stage in her relationship with Daniel does May begin to imagine her lover? What accusation explains in part why she invents the lover? How does May account for her imaginary lover's appearance? Can you suggest other explanations of which May is not conscious?

4. What causes May's relationship with her invented lover to deepen as the story continues? Why does she at first refrain from imagining his face? As her need for him grows more intense, does the lover become more clearly recognizable? At what point does this imaginary figure's physical appearance emerge most clearly? Why? In her final dream, why does May envision herself and her lover "in a canoe in a meadow of water lilies"? After her dream and her conversation with Daniel, why does May realize she will never see her lover again?

5. Why is the setting of the story important to what happens to May and Daniel? How do seasonal changes affect them? If the coming of winter plays a role in their estrangement, what does this imply concerning human relationships and one's ability to control the course of one's life?

The Magic Barrel

1. "The Magic Barrel" begins almost like a fairy tale, with a good deal of expository material presented quickly and unselfconsciously in the opening paragraph. Does the story as a whole retain affinities with the traditional fairy tale or fable? Does Malamud's style—his choice of words, his sentence structure, his imagery, the tone of his narrator's voice—contribute to the fable-like atmosphere? Does the plot have fable-like qualities?

2. Like all first-rate comedy, "The Magic Barrel" uses comic techniques for an ultimately serious purpose. Study the dialogue between Finkle and Salzman on pages 241–44, and try to define why these scenes are funny and also why they are believable.

3. Salzman himself is a richly comic figure. Is there a connection between his comic aspect and his human qualities? The story repeatedly hints that Salzman somehow really does possess magical powers. Cite passages that suggest this. Considering the change that occurs in Finkle, could it be said that Salzman's "commercial cupid" magic in fact succeeds?

4. In the third paragraph Finkle speaks of the "ancient and honorable" function of the marriage broker. Whom is he really addressing in this speech? Why does he find it necessary to discuss this subject at all?

5. The women in "The Magic Barrel" seem unattractive. How can you explain Finkle's attraction to Stella? How are his nature and personality altered after seeing her picture? Finkle's choice of Stella is clearly irrational and highly romantic. What then is the story saying about human,

living energies and irrational choices? What is it saying about love and passion?

Separating

1. Updike has been writing short stories about the Maples for more than ten years. One of these earlier stories, called "Twin Beds in Rome," begins with this strong paragraph:

    > The Maples had talked and thought about separation so long it seemed it would never come. For their conversations, increasingly ambivalent and ruthless as accusation, retraction, blow and caress alternated and cancelled, had the final effect of knitting them ever tighter together in a painful, helpless, degrading intimacy. And their love-making, like a perversely healthy child whose growth defies every deficiency of nutrition, continued; when their tongues at last fell silent, their bodies collapsed together as two mute armies might gratefully mingle, released from the absurd hostilities decreed by two mad kings. Bleeding, mangled, reverently laid in its tomb a dozen times, their marriage could not die. Burning to leave one another, they left, out of marital habit, together. They took a trip to Rome.

    Does the passage, describing an earlier phase in this modern American marriage, seem congruent with the impression given of Richard and Joan in "Separating"? In the later story, what has replaced their rancorous sensual intimacy? Which passages in "Separating" hint at the nature of their physical relations in this final phase of their marriage?
    The passage quoted above contains two elaborate similes intended to describe the love-making of Richard and Joan. Updike's style in the later story remains as markedly figurative but perhaps less self-consciously so. How might one account for this difference, for the (relative) austerity of Updike's figurative language in "Separating"? Compare one of the similes quoted above with the description of Richard's feelings as he waits in his car for his son's train: "It was as when, in the movies, an assassin grimly carries his mission through the jostle of a carnival— except the movies cannot show the precipitous, palpable slope you cling to within. You cannot climb back down; you can only fall." Which simile seems more effective? Which is visually and intellectually clearer? Which is more psychologically revealing?
2. Why does Richard want to announce the separation at a family gathering? Why does Joan insist that he speak to each of the children individually? Are the reasons she gives the only ones? Although Richard agrees to do as Joan asks, his helpless weeping during their meal undermines her plan. Is Joan right when she later accuses him of consciously

having got his own way after all? Does Updike offer a moral judgment on either Richard or Joan? Does the story offer any evidence that might help the reader to fix the blame for the separation, or that might explain its causes? There is one cryptic sentence referring to "the woman Richard hoped to marry." Why isn't she named? How do you account for the fact that Richard never thinks of this woman, nor of his future life, during the entire course of this important day?

3. Joan shrewdly accuses Richard of having enjoyed his weeping. Can you find passages in the story that suggest that Richard's complex responses to all the experiences of this day of separation include feelings of pleasure? Why is Richard so preoccupied early in the story with the condition of his house and grounds and with the details of his husbandly chores? How does Updike link Richard's work on the screen door with his general obsession with "insides and outsides," "barriers and partitions"?

4. Describe in some detail the different ways in which the children react to the news that their parents plan to separate. How do the ages and sexes of each child help to explain why they react as they do? Why do the boys seem more deeply disturbed or unsettled by the news than the girls? How does the fact that the story is told from Richard's point of view bear on your answer?

5. Though serious and even melancholy, "Separating" is also a strangely comic story. Analyze some openly comic moments in the story, such as Richard's weeping as he eats his lobster and drinks his champagne or John's clownish behavior with the cigarette. Does Richard's interview with John on the tennis court, or his final poignant scene with Dickie, have comic undertones that link these moments to others that are more overtly funny? Cite some passages to support your answer.

6. Neither the adults in this story nor the children seem to know how to react or to speak to one another, partly because none of them have had prior experience with the emotions they are feeling; yet they seem to stumble into moments of intense closeness and generosity. What does this imply about the kind of marriage the Maples must have had? About the kind of people they are? Why has Richard, at the end of the story, entirely forgotten the reasons for the separation? Does this mean the separation will not go forward as planned? On the basis of all the evidence available, speculate concerning the likelihood of a reconciliation between Richard and Joan.

Pale Horse, Pale Rider

1. *Pale Horse, Pale Rider* opens with an extended dream. What is the specific import of this dream? Is the plot of the dream related to the larger plot of the story as a whole?

    Reread this opening sequence after you have finished the story. Does the dream make more sense, seem more explicable, on second reading? Does Porter provide evidence later in the story that explains why Miranda has this dream? Do her public circumstances help explain it? Her personal relationships? Her physical state?

2. This short novel contains a number of other dreams. Do these passages share certain themes? Do they rely on similar stylistic devices? Is there a change or progression in tone and meaning as these visions continue? Compare Porter's treatment of dreams with the dream at the conclusion of Ellison's story in Part One or with Gimpel's encounter with the devil in Singer's story in Part Three.

3. In her delirium after she reaches the hospital, Miranda endures a sequence of fantastic visions. What relationship exists between these visions and the hospital setting in which they occur? Do "real" events trigger some of Miranda's fantasies? Can the reader understand what is actually occurring in the hospital as these incidents are transformed by Miranda's fevered sight? Is this blurring of the real and the imagined, of actuality and nightmare, a quality one might claim for earlier parts of the story as well? If so, what are the implications of this fact?

4. Like Fitzgerald in "Babylon Revisited," Porter uses the point of view of limited omniscience to tell her story. But the tone of *Pale Horse, Pale Rider* is sharply different from the tone of Fitzgerald's story, and our sense of time and of the characters' progress through time is radically different in the two works. How do you account for these differences? In particular, how do you explain the fevered expansion and contraction of time in *Pale Horse, Pale Rider?* What effect does the limited third-person point of view have on the overall organization of Porter's story?

5. Although *Pale Horse, Pale Rider* focuses closely on Miranda's psychological state, it also forcefully dramatizes public conditions in America during the First World War. According to the story, how does the war affect society? What pressures does the war bring to bear on civilians? How does it affect public and private relationships? How does Miranda's increasing delirium reflect the situation or atmosphere of the world at large?

6. Miranda is unsympathetic to seemingly patriotic chores that the society around her insists upon, and on occasion her lack of sympathy shades into active resentment. Choose an instance of this resentment and explain the reasons for Miranda's attitude. Is her response partly selfish? How much of it is grounded in virtues she may possess? What are these virtues?

7. Adam and Miranda know each other for a very short time and are permitted few moments of intimacy. What experience is their most intimate and uninterrupted? How are they parted? Does the fact that their relationship is so vulnerable to destructive pressures beyond their control help us understand the value of their love? Is that value greater or less for being so precarious?

8. Miranda and Adam are unlike one another in important respects. Which passages in the story clarify their differences? What attracts them to each other? Is there evidence to suggest that the qualities in Adam that Miranda finds attractive are qualities that might be more common during a time of peace?

9. What does the plot of *Pale Horse, Pale Rider* imply about the power of love? What is the significance of the fact that Adam dies not of wounds received on the battlefield but of a disease he probably contracted when caring for Miranda?

10. A moving love story, *Pale Horse, Pale Rider* is also a story about death. Miranda suggests that "what war does to the mind and heart . . . is worse than what it can do to the body" (p. 282). Does Adam agree? With whom does the story as a whole persuade us to agree? With whom might Miranda herself agree after her ordeal in the hospital?

During that ordeal, from her arrival at the hospital until her recovery, Miranda rarely thinks of Adam. Do you find this strange? Does it imply that her love for him is superficial, weak? Or is there another explanation, implicit in the vivid descriptions of Miranda's descent to the very edge of death?

part three: Outsiders

The Three Hermits

1. Of the stories in this collection, "The Three Hermits" probably comes closest to being a pure fable in which concrete, realistic elements have minimal importance. What tone is established by this absence of concrete detail, by the fact that no character in Tolstoy's story has a name, by the spare, simple dialogue? How does the plot contribute to this tone?

2. Describe the point of view from which the story is told. How does the point of view contribute to the story? What would be the result if the bishop had told the story in his own voice?

3. Although one must be cautious when discussing the style of a translation, can you make some safe observations concerning the style of "The Three Hermits"? What is the effect of the repetition of the word *and* in the last paragraph? Are there other passages that create a similar effect? Which ones?

4. It is often said that in first-rate fiction there is an intimate, inescapable connection between form and content, between the way a story is told and what the story means. Can you see such a connection in "The Three Hermits"? What is the theme, or meaning, of the story? Is that meaning reflected in the story's style, its plot, its dialogue?

5. How does the Biblical quotation that introduces the story contribute to our understanding of the theme? Why does Tolstoy feel it important to tell us at the start that his story is "an old legend"? What status does this information impart to the story? What expectations are established in the reader by this information?

Hands

1. What is the effect of the narrator's repeated confessions that his story is really "a job for a poet"? Cite other elements in "Hands"—details of style or the overall organization of the story, for example—that give an impression of roughness or suggest that the narrator is not a professional writer. Do you see these qualities as defects? Can you suggest ways in which the apparent awkwardness in the plot and style of "Hands" might be regarded as a strength, as a central source of the story's power?
2. Of what crime is Wing Biddlebaum accused during his career as a teacher? What does this event imply about the people who accuse him? On the evidence provided by Wing's experience in Pennsylvania and by the kind of place Winesburg, Ohio, seems to be, what does Anderson seem to be saying about life in rural America? "Hands" was published in 1919. Do you think the story's picture of small-town life remains true today? Why?
3. What qualities make Wing Biddlebaum an outsider? Are some of these qualities admirable ones? Is there evidence that his inability to understand his own nature is part of the reason for his loneliness? Why is Wing afraid of himself?
4. Anderson's blunt use of figurative language is an important part of his technique. How is our understanding of Wing's character and situation enhanced by the comparison of his restless hands to "the beating of the wings of an imprisoned bird"? What is the relevance of the explicitly religious comparisons in the final paragraph?
5. It is easy to see that Wing's situation is a sad and lonely one, but harder to specify why. Why does his empty life seem important? Why is he deserving of sympathy? Why is his denial of a part of himself saddening? How might one generalize about the human loss and waste that Wing's story dramatizes? Does Wing's story have any relevance for individuals whose circumstances are wholly different? Specify.

The Second Hut

1. Describing the protagonist in the opening paragraphs of "The Second Hut," Lessing attends more thoroughly to his moral and psychological

qualities than to his outward appearance, and even those sentences describing Major Carruthers' clothing and physique aim in part to suggest interior rather than exterior qualities. Compare this description with that of the Afrikaner Van Heerden on page 317. What does the difference between these passages tell us about the central themes of the story? Is the focus on Major Carruthers' inner experience and perceptions maintained through the whole story? Cite passages to support your answer.

2. What is Major Carruthers' attitude toward his children? Why is he pleased when they return to boarding school after the holidays? What aspects of his character are revealed in the letter he writes to his children on pages 316–17? What are his feelings toward his wife? Lessing writes that Major Carruthers does not blame his wife "even though he knew her illness was a failure of will." What is there to blame her for? How does Lessing's treatment of Van Heerden's wife help to explain the nature and cause of Mrs. Carruthers' sickness? What is Van Heerden's attitude toward *his* wife and children?

3. Why does Major Carruthers become so angry when he learns about Van Heerden's family? Why does he decide to build the second hut for them even though he knows "it would do no more than take the edge off the discomfort of that miserable family"? How does the building of the hut represent a "danger" to him?

4. Describe as precisely as possible the differences between Major Carruthers' attitude toward the native workers and that of Van Heerden, citing passages to support your conclusions. How does the story "explain" those differences? Is Van Heerden's brutal indifference to the natives seen as a moral failing? Why or why not? What social and historical realities are implicit in the complex relations between Van Heerden and the blacks? Between Van Heerden and Carruthers? Between Carruthers and the native boss-boy?

5. Why is it significant that Van Heerden has a gift for working with cattle, while his employer is "useless with beasts"? In what ways are the conditions of Van Heerden's life related to this gift? How does the imagery used to describe Van Heerden's wife and children clarify the significance of his intimate knowingness with animals?

6. By the end of the story, Major Carruthers has come to see himself as an outsider in "this grey country of poverty" and to see that the black workers and Van Heerden are at home there. What specific events in the story's violent conclusion force Major Carruthers into this recognition? Why do these events—as opposed, say, to financial reversals or crop failure—have such terrible significance for Carruthers? What sort of person would be so decisively affected by events having so little material consequence for his own life?

7. Major Carruthers' decision to return to England is a great personal disaster for him, the end of "his pride as a man." How is the reader expected

to judge this failure? What unacknowledged but perhaps crucial assumptions about human life is Major Carruthers protecting when he gives up his farm? In what respects does the story indicate that such assumptions are themselves a luxury available only to those who belong to privileged societies?

Gimpel the Fool

1. "Gimpel the Fool" has been translated by one of America's best writers and is a model of successful translation. Considering the special tone of Gimpel's voice as it is established in the opening paragraphs, can you suggest why the story requires a translator of unusual talents? What combination of skills and knowledge seems necessary for a translator of a story such as this?

2. How would you characterize Gimpel's way of speaking? What connection is there between his speaking voice—his diction, his syntax, his reliance on proverbs—and his reputation as a simpleton? What moral qualities are inherent in the tone in which he discusses his mistreatment?

3. According to two distinguished critics, " 'Gimpel the Fool' begins as comedy but soon rises to a deep sadness and tragic statement." Do you concur in this judgment? Cite passages in the text that support your answer. Can you find evidence that shows that comic elements, however muted, are retained even in the story's darkest episodes? Consider the dream encounter between the devil and Gimpel on page 341. How does Singer's use of dialogue contribute to the scene? Reread the first four paragraphs of the story. Does this beginning prepare us for the tonal changes that occur in the story as a whole? Specify.

4. Gimpel has often been described as a *sainted fool,* a literary type especially popular in Yiddish literature but present also in writers as different as Cervantes and Dostoevsky. On the basis of this story, what might this term mean? How does such a character, morally pure but also naive and even clownish, allow a writer to comment on a world in which such characters do not really exist? How is Gimpel's character a judgment on the world that misuses him?

5. The humor in "Gimpel the Fool" has a special character, the result essentially of its roots in the Jewish literary traditions and culture of eastern Europe. What are some of the distinguishing qualities of this humor? What role do disappointment, poverty, loss, play in such humor? Is it the humor of a people accustomed to affluence and political power or to poverty and political oppression? Find passages in the story which support your conclusion. Compare the comedy in "Gimpel the Fool" with that in a story such as Flannery O'Connor's "Good Country People"; what kind of situation, what sort of experience, supply the materials of comedy for each writer? Can you speculate about the regional and cultural pressures that might help to account for their differences?

The Guest

1. The first three paragraphs of "The Guest" devote special attention to details of landscape and climate. What does this carefully rendered setting tell us about the schoolmaster and his circumstances? How does the outward condition of Daru's life reflect his psychological and moral condition?
2. "The Guest" is heavy with the menace of violence, yet the actions in the story are simple, even ordinary ones like walking, eating, and sleeping. What does this tell us about the principal concerns of the story? Why is it particularly significant that Daru shares his sleeping quarters and food with his Arab prisoner?
3. All the stories in this section deal with characters who place themselves or are forced outside of their societies. Daru, an Algerian-born Frenchman, feels himself an exile in any other place, yet finds himself at the end to be entirely alone even in his homeland. What causes his isolation? From whom is he isolated? Is there any way in which Daru could resolve the conflict of loyalties with which he is confronted? What are the conflicting claims the world makes upon him?
4. What is Daru's attitude toward the Arab when Balducci, the French policeman, brings him to the schoolhouse? What is Daru's attitude toward firearms? How do these responses help to dramatize the schoolmaster's character?
5. Although "The Guest" explicitly concerns the political crisis in French-controlled Algeria after the Second World War, it is clearly more interested in a larger matter—the necessity of moral choice. How does Daru's troubled parting with Balducci help to clarify his moral dilemma? How does his treatment of the Arab help to do so? Why do you think Camus chose to make the Arab's crime nonpolitical? Why does Daru give the Arab a choice between imprisonment and freedom? Why does the Arab choose prison instead of life with a nomadic tribe that would shelter him "according to their law"? What is the result of Daru's humane, agonized refusal to choose between the Algerian Arabs and the French?

The Last Voyage of the Ghost Ship

1. "The Last Voyage of the Ghost Ship" is written in the modernist style commonly called *stream of consciousness*. On the basis of this story, what are some of the chief features of this kind of writing? What interests or themes are especially appropriate to this kind of writing? What subjects or experiences would resist treatment in this style?
2. The story begins with the phrase *Now they're going to see who I am* and at crucial intervals repeats these words as if they were a refrain. How does this repetition help to organize the story? The opening lines assume that until "now" the speaker (or thinker) has been misjudged or mis-

understood. Cite some passages from later in the story that help to clarify the speaker's reasons for feeling this way. Who are "they" in that repeated phrase? In what tones, with what emotional inflection, must we imagine that recurring phrase to be spoken or thought?

3. There is no plot here in the usual sense, but the story does trace a chronology of sorts involving the protagonist's passage from a time of weakness as "a boy without a man's strong voice" to a time in which his strength and power are asserted "in his strong new man's voice." How are the protagonist's encounters with the ghost ship linked to this movement toward mature strength? Why does no one else, not even the protagonist's mother, know of the ship's existence? What do you think is the meaning of the boy's newly discovered ability near the end of the story to control the ship's movements? What is the protagonist asserting when he brings "the largest ocean liner in this world and the other" into his village?

4. All through "The Last Voyage of the Ghost Ship" there is a blurring of distinctions between what is real and what is imagined, or fantasized. Cite some passages other than those describing the ghost ship where this merging of reality and fantasy occurs. How does Márquez handle concrete, visual details in such passages? What is signified by the story's refusal to distinguish between outer and inner experience? How is this refusal related to the protagonist's journey toward a grand triumph in which his private "vision" of the ghost ship is magnificently and violently forced upon the attention of "the disbelievers"?

5. Considering the boy's isolation and the mistreatment he suffers, and considering also the "leftover rage" that fortifies him toward the end of the story, what do you think Márquez might say about the origins and motives of his own writing? About the relations between writers and readers? How do you think Márquez would define the word *reality*?

"I Always Wanted You to Admire My Fasting"; or, Looking at Kafka

1. Many of the stories in this collection strain against traditional categories or expectations, but none so decisively as this eccentric, complex piece, which is less a story than a joining of literary and biographical speculation with autobiography. Roth speaks in the first person throughout and claims in part two to be recalling his own real experiences. How does this claim to personal and historical actuality affect the reader? If Roth had given a fictional name to his family in part two, in what ways would the reader's attitude toward the text have been altered? It should be helpful in considering this problem of what some critics have called *the fictional contract* to compare "Looking at Kafka" with stories in this collection, such as those by Joyce or Conrad or Updike or Kafka himself, that have a partly autobiographical tone but that nonetheless insist on their status as invented fictions.

2. Although it presents itself to the reader as nonfiction, "Looking at Kafka" makes use of many devices that are far more common to stories than to essays. Cite some passages, even some specific strategies of style, in which Roth might be said to aim for the same effects as writers of fiction. Consider, for one example, his treatment of character in part two. How are Aunt Rhoda, Dr. Kafka, and Roth's parents presented to us? What sorts of details are provided to give them an air of actuality? What is Roth's authority for presenting or remembering such details? Are there some passages wherein Roth may be discovered to be openly imagining what is told to us? Roth tells us that Dr. Kafka wrote about Aunt Rhoda in his diary and even quotes what he purportedly recorded there. But where is the evidence that Dr. Kafka even kept a diary, much less that Roth has had access to it? Analyze the prose style and moral tone of that brief diary entry. Does it sound plausible to you? What sort of man would have written in this way?

3. How are the dominant themes of the first part of "Looking at Kafka" repeated or reenacted in the second part? Can you detect differences in Roth's tone between the two parts of the piece? Does his writing become more or less colloquial, more or less comic, in the second part? Cite passages to support your answers. If you detect a shift in tone, speculate concerning some of the reasons for it.

4. Which Kafka, the writer or the old immigrant Hebrew teacher, comes across as more mysterious, more baffling, more difficult for Roth to analyze and to conjecture about? Why?

5. Consider the theme of fatherhood in "Looking at Kafka." The writer, Roth tells us, was paralyzed by his father's authority but perhaps miraculously escaped his domination briefly in the months before his death. Given Roth's description of the unfinished story "The Burrow," does this comforting interpretation seem plausible? Roth offers a partially optimistic interpretation of that story, but how well do its details—which Roth describes with brilliant accuracy and subtlety—conform to his interpretation? How does the example of the writer's Oedipal neurosis as dramatized in part one color Roth's descriptions of his own Jewish family in part two? In the context of this earlier tale of a son's entrapment by a dominant father, how do you read Roth's comic account of his own father's hymn to family life?

   Roth's own fiction has many crucial affinities with Kafka's writing and is full of submerged and overt allusions to the older (and greater) writer's *oeuvre*. If we recognize that writers are frequently more preoccupied with their literary ancestors than with their actual ones, how might this complicate further our sense of what Roth is up to in "Looking at Kafka"? A genuine and illuminating act of filial piety on the part of the younger writer, the piece is still in certain respects an attempt to "explain" and thus in a way to dominate the ancestor. How conscious is Roth of this dimension of his story? Can you cite some passages where this consciousness of his filial relations to Kafka is openly acknowledged?

The Metamorphosis

1. The first sentence of *Metamorphosis* is one of the most startling in all modern literature, and one of the most famous. On the basis of what follows, and particularly of what we learn concerning Gregor's place in life, his work as a traveling salesman, his sense of his own worth, what might have been the general content of his "uneasy dreams"? How does Kafka's reference to these dreams help us to understand the significance of Gregor's transformation?

2. This translation captures with fair accuracy the tone of the German original. How would you characterize the story's tone? In what ways does this tone contrast with the literal events of the story? What is the effect of this contrast? One critic has written of the "severe rationality" of Kafka's method. Does this phrase seem appropriate, especially in terms of the story's style? What part does the device of understatement play in creating Kafka's tone?

3. Consider the following sentence from the second part of the novella:

   > He stayed there [under the sofa] all night, spending the time partly in a light slumber, from which his hunger kept waking him up with a start, and partly in worrying and sketching vague hopes, which all led to the same conclusion, that he must lie low for the present and, by exercising patience and the utmost consideration, help the family to bear the inconvenience he was bound to cause them in his present condition (pp. 385–86).

   How is this response related to Gregor's first reaction to his metamorphosis, when he labors to get off the bed, to turn himself over, and to dress and catch his train? What does his desire to "help the family to bear the inconvenience he was bound to cause them" reveal about his character? About why he is an insect? About his awareness or lack of awareness concerning the reality of his condition? About his fear of confronting the enormity of what has happened to him? Are the virtues of patience and consideration relevant to his situation? In what sort of world, for what sort of difficulty, would they be relevant?

4. In the most literal sense, *The Metamorphosis* is not a believable story because men do not turn into insects. Why would an author write a story that could never be literally true? Are there aspects of reality, of human experience and human need, that Kafka's method can illuminate and that cannot be approached by more narrowly realistic fiction? Which aspects? Considering the term "real" in a broader sense, would you say *The Metamorphosis* is an unrealistic story? Why?

5. Like *The Metamorphosis*, Tolstoy's "The Three Hermits" depends on an event beyond realism. Compare the purposes and methods of Tolstoy with those of Kafka. Why does Tolstoy's miracle occur at the very end

of his story, while Kafka's nightmare-transformation occurs in the first sentence? Longer and far more complex psychologically than "The Three Hermits," *The Metamorphosis,* too, has fablelike elements. In what sense is Kafka's short novel a kind of fable? Which fable, Tolstoy's or Kafka's, seems more characteristic of the modern world? Discuss.

6. How do Gregor's mother, father, and sister react to his transformation? Do their attitudes differ significantly? In what degree is Gregor aware of these differences? How does this awareness affect the development of the story in the episode of the violin playing? How do the boarders react to Gregor? Can you account for the difference between the reactions of his family and of others who learn of Gregor's existence?

7. *The Metamorphosis* falls into three parts, each having as a climax an attempt by Gregor to escape from his room. Analyze the novella in terms of these climaxes. Does each part of the story have a particular rhythm or pattern of development? Is that pattern repeated in the other parts? With what differences? What larger meaning is implicit in Gregor's thwarted attempts to return to his family? In his ability to hear and understand but not be understood?

8. The morning after Gregor's death Mr. Samsa chases the boarders from his house with great authority and force. Why is he now able to act so decisively? What is implied by the description of the two boarders "scuttling" after their fellow "as if afraid that Mr. Samsa might get into the hall before them and cut them off from their leader"?

9. Reread the final paragraph of the story. Some readers consider this the most terrifying episode in the whole story. Suggest some reasons for this reaction. What does this ending add to the story? What does the emphasis on the family's apparent ability to forget entirely about Gregor and his suffering suggest about experience? What is the significance of the last line, in which Gregor's sister springs to her feet and stretches "her young body"?